"AWESOME, PROFOUNDLY MOVING ...
this exceptional thriller stands on its own as one
of the most knowing and powerful explorations
of serial killers and those who hunt them."
—*Kirkus Reviews*

"SUPERIOR ... new and scary details about how
the feds catch serial murderers." —*Glamour*

"Van Arman, who has actually helped develop
techniques used by federal agencies to catch
recreational or serial killers, provides a rare and
powerful look into the realm of human monsters
and the sure knowledge that they are real."
—*Library Journal*

"Chilling ... from a master of suspense."
—*Mystery News*

JUST KILLING TIME

DEREK VAN ARMAN

AN ONYX BOOK

ONYX
Published by the Penguin Group
Penguin Books USA Inc., 375 Hudson Street, New York, New York 10014, U.S.A.
Penguin Books Ltd, 27 Wrights Lane, London W8 5TZ, England
Penguin Books Australia Ltd, Ringwood, Victoria, Australia
Penguin Books Canada Ltd, 10 Alcorn Avenue, Toronto, Ontario, Canada M4V 3B2
Penguin Books (N.Z.) Ltd, 182–190 Wairau Road, Auckland 10, New Zealand

Penguin Books Ltd, Registered Offices:
Harmondsworth, Middlesex, England

Published by ONYX, an imprint of New American Library, a division of Penguin
Books USA Inc. Previously appeared in a Dutton edition.

First Onyx Printing, August, 1993
10 9 8 7 6 5 4 3 2 1

Acknowledgments
"In My Room," words amd music by Brian Wilson & Gary Usher. Copyright ©
1964 Irving Music, Inc. (BMI). All rights reserved. International copyright secured.

 REGISTERED TRADEMARK—MARCA REGISTRADA

Printed in the United States of America

BOOKS ARE AVAILABLE AT QUANTITY DISCOUNTS WHEN USED TO PROMOTE PRODUCTS OR
SERVICES. FOR INFORMATION PLEASE WRITE TO PREMIUM MARKETING DIVISION, PENGUIN
BOOKS USA, INC., 375 HUDSON STREET, NEW YORK, NEW YORK 10014.

for Susan

JUST KILLING TIME

PROLOGUE:
SECRET PLACES

The kid on the red Schwinn raced slightly ahead of the three-legged dog, down a dark and wooded hill, then back up into sunlight. Their competing shadows slid over the residential street like two eerie kites, moving slowly against the trees, faster against the sidewalk. Just past Ridgefield Lane and River Road, a main intersection, Elmer Winfield Janson stood on his pedals, whistled sharply, then burst into a power drive, zapping over a sidewalk, a grassy strip, and crashing between a hedgerow. He emerged onto an empty parking lot and leaned his bike into full, lazy circles, aiming his tires at weeds, the small green aliens he imagined were sprouting a full-scale invasion from below.

The blacktop was fractured with weeds jutting through, easy targets for the deep rubber teeth of a dirt bike. For the first time all day he felt free, swerving in expanding arcs until each tire spun with earthen plugs that flew from the wheels as his speed increased. The circles tightened: tires and weeds, weeds and tires, dog after boy, boy after dog, their pace quickening like a giant top; spinning and spinning, faster and faster until the universe whirled from focus and a drunken throbbing battered at Elmer's brain.

"Wow!" The boy breathed hard, hitting his brakes while climbing dizzily from his bike. "There's nothing in the living world like mashing aliens!" He gave a proud smile, standing on a flat of oozing green.

In the graying light Elmer's fine reddish hair took on the color of smoked salmon, matching a mask of freckles that seemed to tighten across the bridge of his nose. His eyes were a sparkling green, just darker than mint, and they always seemed fixed to some distant point within himself. Standing to his full height of four-foot-four he was able to stroke the shepherd's thick mane without bending.

Because Elmer Janson was small, the carrot-top and freckles made him look more like seven, but he was ten years and nine months old, and he kept track of details like that, just as he knew, or thought he knew, every inch of the parking lot to which he laid claim. A heavy mist fell through the air, the kind that leaves a waxy frost on everything when it freezes, and the boy could feel the wet chill on the dog's fluffy coat. "Come on, Tripod," he said, as in the dim afternoon sun he took a last furtive look over his shoulder and started toward the condemned structure at the end of the parking lot.

The building was old and sad and sick. A low-slung fifties-style warehouse with plywood-boarded windows and crumbling concrete blocks, it had been a twenty-six-lane bowling alley with a pool hall and gaming room. Front, facing the roadway and sandwiched between two paste blue panels, was a section of smooth pink aluminum big as a billboard that had once advertised "BOWL PATRIOTS" in tall white letters. The color scheme had been red, white, and blue, suggesting a recreational duty to bowl, but the white characters had been torn off long ago, leaving dark red splotches. Walking at the base of the huge wall, the boy crossed to the rear of the structure, hesitating only a moment near the back of the alley, where the blacktop narrowed with forward-looking signs.

Keep Out! No Trespassing!

He threaded his body first, then his bike, through a tight gap between a galvanized-steel fencepost and concrete corner, then walked his bike down under a dripping overhang that blocked the sun. Elmer paused, waiting for his eyes to adjust, testing the spongy pavement with his feet. Most of the blacktop had broken free of the structure, eroding into a trench, and he started along a length of dingy canyon, some four hundred feet of wet and troubled darkness. An occasional crack nipped a toe, a wad of concrete belted an arch, as the boy and dog steadily worked their way toward the small fenced area at the end of this tunnel.

To Elmer this was a secret place, and from the halfway point he could just see a distant patch of sunlight reflecting against sloping blacktop. He knew this had once been a parking lot and was now just a dump, but in his mind it looked more like the surface of a bright, weird planet left to the ravages of time. More important, the dump was filled with curious things and was impossible for adults to reach without a twelve-foot climb over a chain-link fence. As he walked, he tried to imagine the scene in the alley's heyday, packed with '57 Chevys and Thunderbirds and huge Ford Galaxies. In his mind each car was red, because he had such a picture in a calendar at home. And even though it was now late March, because of that one picture, Elmer's bedroom was stuck on July everlasting.

"Nothing better in the free world than July," he said, smiling an easy summer-vacation smile. School was almost over, that was the important thing, and he waved his bike, dodging broken bottles and debris, a pile of wet boards with nails stabbing through, then car parts, including a broken battery and an oozing oil filter. He stopped and stared at a rainwater puddle, at the oily brown skin floating on top, and his eye was caught by something. A dead thing, bloated and half-buried in the inky well.

"Tripod, sit!" he demanded to the curious straw-colored dog. The boy leaned his bike against a wall and instantly searched out a length of spiked board. He started to rake.

The water rippled as the skin broke, releasing a smell like sweet rotting cheese. The freckles across his nose tightened as he snagged something. And although it was dark, Elmer could clearly discern the head, or what he thought was the head, badly swollen from shape, more like a spongy fist of fur than a head, with eyes the color of spit on asphalt. Elmer poked at it, studying each feature: a greasy snout, cuplike ears, and toothy incisors like yellow needles. A tremble came over him like a chilled and unclean wind.

"Someone walked on my grave," he whispered, pushing a beefy rat back into the water, as he felt an oily splash and a trickle run down his face.

It was cold, he noticed for the first time. The sun was dropping. It was getting colder.

At Bowl America there were two spots behind the alley where the weeds sprouted taller than the others. One outcropping was a tangled swirl of growth that rose into an isolated fountain of grass. The other was a squat patch of plum-headed aliens that looked different from the rest, which were green or yellow. Elmer knew that ordinary plants came and went with the seasons, while these always stayed the same. They didn't bloom. They didn't die either.

They grew just past the "NO DUMPING" sign, next to a discarded V-8 engine block, and inside the fenced lot. As he pushed his bike out from the trench and up a slope, he could see Tripod's broomlike tail swinging full force, hindquarters extended, his entire body heaving as he dug with his one front foot.

During the winter the twosome had made a dozen such trips, only to find the blacktop frozen. Grinning, Elmer leaned his bike against the engine, then stretched catlike, watching with intense concentration. The dog had broken through and down into the clay below.

"Today's the day!" Elmer beamed, crouching alongside Tripod, examining the torn pavement while breathing in the rich, earthy scent. Winter was behind them now, he reasoned, and the ground would be forced to surrender. Pressing hard with both hands, straining against the asphalt until each finger went white, Elmer kept pushing until the soggy pavement moved. The dog was manic, clawing at the ground in a lathered frenzy.

Finally standing up, the boy removed a magazine from inside his sweatshirt and began to read.

"It is best to hunt while the ground is still wet, especially after a flood," his voice stirring. "Look for any indentation where treasure may have settled. Study plant growth. Previous disturbances result in noticeable changes in vegetation. Adjust the metal detector to low yield." He smiled proudly, for he had accomplished that part months ago. Since it had rained for three full days—not a drizzle, but drops that had pounded at the cracks—the instructions had been followed to perfection. The blacktop was clearly sinking in sections— some small as a cup, some large as a tub—and he thought it no coincidence that the purple aliens grew where the pavement sagged most. Respectfully he rolled the magazine beneath the dry safety of his sweatshirt.

To Elmer Janson the written guide was a legacy of sorts, one of several that his father had left when he died, all neatly stored with a metal detector beneath the basement stairs. In them Elmer had found a world of excitement: stories of treasure and exploration, caches looted by Confederate spies, Indian caves dripping with jewels, lost gold, ancient pottery, and all of it free for the taking. Until his discovery Elmer had only heard about history in school, but seeing the treasures and having a metal detector was real—like the difference between being told about germs and getting the flu.

It didn't matter one bit that all of his previous efforts had produced only tin cans, car parts, rusted nails, and a trunk full of bottle tops. There was something spirited and curious and lonely trapped inside this one little boy that pushed at him, that pressed him onward when others would have quit.

Tripod barked, and they began to dig.

An hour passed quickly and they were caked with mud, red like stewed tomatoes but thick as half-dried concrete. All the plum-colored aliens were gone, ripped from the ground, and a small, dark pit four feet across surrounded them.

With each scrabbling stroke Tripod's rear quarters pressed high into the air, looking for all the world like a honey-colored bear fishing a water hole. The dog growled, low and hypnotic, his maniacal rocking unabated. Deeper and deeper, down into the red crater he scraped, his broomlike tail smacking the tarry surface. Elmer felt a trickle of despair as the last vestiges of daylight began to close around them. Black clouds had formed. The smell of winter had returned to the air.

"Nothing ever goes off as you plan," he spat, and a tide of loneliness washed through him. He had waited six months for the thaw, and he felt sad to the bone. He had wanted so badly to believe, to find something, anything, it didn't have to be a real treasure. His lower lip had started to quiver when the world rushed into focus and something caught his eye.

A speck, a promise, a joy.

A fleck of metal sticking out from the earthen wall and trapping light, burning and burning like a diamond through the red beginnings of time.

Elmer's jaw dropped, his breath whooshing out of him. A nervous fluttering swirled from his stomach to chest, filling him with joy. This was no bottle cap. He dropped into the pit, scratching feverishly at the object with his fingernails, trying to grab it before it could disappear. It was cold and wet and slippery, a flat sliver poking up sideways through the dirt.

The boy tugged, the clay wall gave a rooted moan. Then, holding tight with both thumbs and digging in with his heels, he pulled again. Small cracks snaked outward in the red dirt, and his green eyes glistened with excitement. The shape was distinct. He could see it clearly now.

"A coin!" he exclaimed, and a sharp wind snapped the word away.

Elmer knew in that first glance—this thing was old. Ancient as a curse. Older than time.

He worked quickly, wrapping his shirttails around each thumb, fastening a tight grip, and pulling with all his might. The red dirt fizzed and gave up its prize, then ripping free in one hot instant, like a stubborn tooth being pulled from tissue and bone. The boy tumbled into a backward sprawl.

"Yeah," Elmer whispered, his breath visible in small clouds.

An encrusted medallion gleamed in his outstretched hand, dangling what appeared to be a length of wire: slimy, black, and rotting. Nervously he worked the coin's surface with his thumbs, rubbing off clay until words began to shine through. He squinted, holding the object to his nose.

"The Union . . . Must . . . and Shall Be Preserved," he read slowly.

"Oh, yeah!"

The three-legged dog had never stopped digging.

In tandem they dug a trench sideways into the clay wall. Then, working on all fours, Elmer quickly nudged past and slipped his hand farther into the wet darkness, down into the hollow. Just inside, just beyond his grasp, he felt a round thing—round like a ball. The cold slickness of its surface excited him, the smooth hardness intoxicated his senses. He pushed farther, his mask of freckles tightening with determination as he strained to work his face into the cramped opening.

"Tripod," he screamed, "we really have found treasure!" Elmer could just see the curving bottom of a container poking up like an inverted soup bowl, and he worked, widening the tunnel, pondering the delight and strangeness of it all. It looked like a bowl, but it had thin wooden legs poking out that made it resemble a small satellite with weird antennae. He dismissed that thought. "It could have belonged to a slave, it could be African!" he puffed, recalling historical accounts. "Slaves couldn't have valuables, they buried them. Maybe it belonged to a Confederate spy!" The possibilities blew quickly through his mind as he grabbed the longest stick and pulled. The ground gave way and the object tilted toward him. There was a muted thud as a wooden leg snapped loose, and Elmer toppled back into the dirt.

He held it in his hand. It was black and looked like an old

chopstick. The boy quickly folded this inside his shirt, reaching back, grabbing another. The object turned, then settled, the stick holding fast. He pressed his face to the wall. Now he could see each of the feet clearly, jutting up from the red dirt like a giant pincushion, and his hand slipped back like a mole through darkness. Elmer caressed and stroked when he felt the jackpot. "A handle!" he shouted. "It's got a handle!"

White-faced with determination, the boy reached across the centuries, grabbing hold, his entire right arm plunged into the hollow. He pulled. Chunks of red clay spilled loose. Straining with his right shoulder and placing his full weight against the wall, he pulled again. Endless. Tiring. Resolute.

The earth groaned. Red clay poured from the hollow, flowed over his belt and shoes; the wall began to crumble. The hollow became a cave as the wall fell. He was dragging the object closer toward his belly when his thumb punched a hole, a slick edge slicing one knuckle. It was thin, brittle, and sharp as porcelain, and although Elmer winced at the pain, he would not let go. It was coming free. The dirt fizzed.

With a deep, sodden moan the wall surrendered to the will that was Elmer Janson. Even as the image slowly registered in the boy's mind, his flesh began to ripple. His muscles went tight, loosened, and went tight again. Blood flowed from his fingertips and he shook the prize loose, letting it fall away from his body. Tripod growled from a distance.

It was death.

The boy had found death and it had landed with a thud, pinning itself to the wet ground, grinning back at him with human teeth—grinning like so many thousand pictures of death.

Death as an entity. Pictorial death. A grin that could stop a clock, but begged for something more, something living; and while Elmer told his feet to run, they would not obey.

"Tripod!" the boy tried to cry, but fear had snatched his breath, making him pull back even as the dog leaned forward.

The skull was small and pink, stained from years at rest with the sap of red clay leaching through. Up from the pit, bony sockets glistened and stared, the nose forming a dark, lopsided triangle. The teeth sparkled with Elmer's blood, the mouth hanging agape, torn open, leaving one good hinge.

"The bowl's handle," he said, feeling his lips move. But it was the grin that paralyzed him, sneering with ivory, offering silence as an explosion in his head. Laughing at him. Laughing.

Blood banged through the chambers of the boy's heart. He knew he should leave and take Tripod home. But Elmer Janson looked hard at the world, and once he did, he refused to look away.

ViCAT

The only thing necessary for the triumph of evil is for good men to do nothing.
—Edmund Burke, 1751

They sleep not, except they have done mischief; And their sleep is taken away, unless they cause some to fall.
For they eat the bread of wickedness, And drink the wine of violence.
—Proverbs 4:16–17

Talk of the devil and he will appear . . .
—Erasmus: Adagia XVII, 1500

1

The house was a red brick colonial, a sedate residence located in an affluent suburb of Washington, D.C. On the front lawn leaves were neatly raked, cherry trees were beginning to flower, hedges were squared and freshly groomed. From the back, similar dwellings ran in rows nine deep, with sweeping lawns hidden by wooden fencing and ivy-covered walls.

Late on the evening of March 31, the house was locked tight. In an upstairs bedroom Diana Clayton was sitting at her dressing table planning months in advance, turning pages in her desk calendar and preparing lists: groceries, school, work, meetings, vacation, and then sleep. *Kim's 8th B-Day* she wrote across the first page of June while glancing at the family portrait on her desk and into the face of her younger child. Kimberly Ann Clayton was a deceptively fragile, beautiful little girl, and her impish smirk seemed to come alive in the silver frame as Diana positioned the picture closer to her calendar.

The resemblance between them was striking. Bright azure eyes and lightly freckled skin, with streaming blond hair that looked equally good unkempt or combed. They shared a sly but natural turn to the mouth, a sensual turn that could have been a pout but was not.

Behind Kimberly in the picture, and a full head taller, stood Leslie, three years older, more confident, less shy. She looked more like their father, Mark Clayton, and the woman gave a wistful smile, sitting motionless for a moment while studying the image. Leslie had been only six when her father died, and since that time she had come to resemble him in manner as well as looks. She was a sensitive little girl, and that single characteristic was even more like her husband than the child's brown hair, now beginning to darken into a fine chestnut. And the penetrating hazel eyes. "The best of him," Diana whispered with a warm sigh.

Diana took a sip of hot herbal tea and returned to her note-book, her eyes flicking from month to month, week to week, then day to day. Across the entire face of June she scribed the words *Nags Head.* The decisive reference was to a North Car-olina barrier island where the Claytons traditionally vaca-tioned, and she was planning a special trip for Kimberly's birthday.

Diana smiled in contemplation, holding the pen against her cheek. As it had been with her late husband, the beach was the children's first love, she thought. First, that is, after Tofu, a large cream-colored Angora rabbit with buttery ears that re-sembled huge velvet slippers. She shook her head absently. *Tofu to Vet* she dashed into the square for June 2, and then considered Leslie's pronouncement that Tofu would die of loneliness if left alone for a month. The children wanted to take their pet to the beach. A rabbit to the shore?

"Silly," Diana whispered, tapping the page with her pen, a ridge of concern forming across her brow. The children felt they would be abandoning Tofu, and that was not a matter to be taken lightly. *Absence Makes Hearts Grow Fonder!* This she entered cryptically at the top of the page, carefully reserv-ing time on the morning of April 4 for a motherly chat, when it occurred to Diana that her daughters fawned over Tofu's ev-ery need like little mothers themselves. And that thought made her entire body sag with age.

Fatigue was returning now. There was a stinging to her eyes and a stiffness in her muscles that would not go away. With a sudden yawn she arched her back, glancing over at the brass clock on her bureau: 11:45. Her streaming blond hair shimmered as it flowed over the blue silk of her nightgown, and she removed a dark comb from her head. She was closing her eyes when a strange chill suddenly swelled in her body. She curled one fist. Diana gave a quick shiver.

"Funny," she thought, sitting taller at her desk, letting her cup slide from her hands. "Catching cold?"

She rubbed her forehead, feeling tiny hairs prickle as her heart fluttered with a strange sensation. It was like a sour breath had entered her body and was gone in an instant, one heartbeat off, and nothing more.

A shiver. A doubt. A mournful feeling.

In that same second Diana Clayton inhaled, shaking her head, glancing down the hallway to where her children were sleeping. She listened for a moment while releasing her breath, but there was only the safe, familiar silence.

"Flu season," she whispered, jotting a note to add vitamin C to the breakfast menu, and the natural curve to her mouth became a pout.

A minute later she was kneeling in the master bathroom, drawing back a flowered curtain and adjusting the water to a tepid flow. A pool began to form, lending ghostly life to an inflatable pillow that had been lying limp in one corner of the bathtub. She removed a peach-colored towel from beneath the sink and wrapped this around her head like a large bandanna, tying a loose knot at the nape of her neck.

In the thickening steam her pores were beginning to tingle and open, and she cracked the bathroom window. Then, dropping the silken robe off her shoulders, she studied herself for a moment in the mirror. Although Diana was concerned with pending age, and saw an older image of herself in the reflection, she was a handsome woman, with a dancer's long legs and a body blessed with ample curves.

She breathed deeply to clear her sinuses as she dimmed the harsh lights. The water rippled as she climbed in, the warmth taking her like a glove—so relaxing, so quiet, she could hear cicadas outside her window. As she settled back, propping her head against the pillow, her thoughts returned to the shore.

She closed her eyes. She remembered the wild ponies as they ended their yearly migration, racing down the beach as the tide rolled in. And Mark, still half-asleep, chasing off in his pajamas and carrying a child in each arm.

"I don't have time to be sick," she whispered.

Diana Clayton dreamed of wild ponies.

Moving soundlessly while waiting for the bedroom lights to go out, a stranger strolled through the living room. A dark, seamless Dacron body sock covered him, rising into a hood that enveloped the head. The tight fabric masked his throat, chin, and ears, leaving a pale oval face seemingly floating in air.

The mouth protruded, with thin lips that looked sliced from veal. And the nose, unusually faint, was cocked with self-importance. Around each eye the skin was darkened with pitch, and his expression seemed more lifeless than cruel.

He stopped to admire this image in the mirror above Diana

Clayton's baby grand, just killing time, playing with his reflection.

He lifted his upper lip, contorting his face with a grimace
that was meant as a smile, and there was a flash from white
even rows. The mask was pulled tightly across his cheeks,
pinching his ears as he tugged it into place, enthralled with
the feeling of being invisible, dressed for blending with
shadow. With this disguise he knew he could have been anyone, man or woman, beast or angel; a schoolteacher, a salesman, a cop.

But he was not. And with a gloved hand he caressed the
white notes, sweeping back and forth with fingertip strokes,
entertaining himself with the image of smashing the keyboard. Sudden. Merciless. Terrible alternating blows, pounding and pounding, slow and methodical, building a tempo
while calling for Diana; increasing the beat, then demanding
each child by name.

The hardwood of the piano gleamed with the lemon smells
of furniture polish, and his breathing went deep as he fingered
the metronome next to the clock. It was 11:40. He knew the
children were sleeping, and that delighted him.

And he knew about their empty little lives, boring as salt,
regular as a plasma drip.

The heat snapped on.

A whir of circulating air washed over him, and he smelled
apples carry on the current. His eyes closed with a questioning wonderment, for there was a hidden scent, something
deeper, more pungent than fruit or furniture wax. And his
mind and his body wandered as he left the piano behind,
moving leisurely through the house, stepping into the kitchen,
following his nose.

A hard smell. Sharp as wetted wood, yet bitter; and he
stood at the floating island near a breakfast nook, sipping at
the air. He opened blackened lids, closed them again, and
rolled through his memory; every nerve coming alive in the
puzzlement created by the odd smell, when he heard a faint
rapping.

Once, twice, again, coming from the far end of the kitchen.
"A fraying duct," was his first thought. He moved closer.
The heat died with a snap. Black canvas boots advanced
across the linoleum shine, easing closer, stopping at the double sink, where pans were carefully set on a dish towel for
drying. He stood and listened. A brooding *drip, drip, drip*

from the sink. And he strained to place the unusual scent
against a faint sound, his mind working fast and methodically.

Faraway he could hear the distant bray of tires on pavement. The wind licking a leafy branch. The mulling drone of
a jet leaving Washington International Airport. And a rapping,
almost sickly, like a whisper against glass, he thought.

Thin lips curled with amusement, not a smile but forming
a slash across his face. And he moved forward, stopping to
listen, then leaning over the end of the kitchen counter to peer
down into darkness, down through the odorous bite of wet cedar chips.

"Well, well," he hissed with excitement. From between
long, buttery ears a small being awoke and blinked up at him,
narcotic with sleep, the soft nose pulsating for a familiar
scent.

"I should have known," he said in a barely audible voice as
he placed his tongue behind his front teeth, producing a wet
and pleasing noise. He squatted, pressing his face within
inches of the cage.

Tofu, the Angora rabbit, could not sense danger, for she
had never known anything in life but the gentle touch of a
child's wet kiss—thousands upon thousands of warm, wet
kisses. The animal gave a gentle hop forward, raising a velvet
nose into the air.

Ever so slowly, dark and confident gloves lifted the small
door while the rabbit's eyes blinked, soothed by human
breath. Gently he stroked the furry head with three fingers,
the long ears bobbing, folding against cedar chips with each
downward stroke.

"And who are you?" he intoned at the lop eared fluff, placing his hands beneath each leg, lifting the creature smoothly.

Against the warmth of his body Tofu nuzzled a cheek, the
sleepy eyes winking in metered time to each admiring stroke,
the soft nose pulsing against Dacron.

Upstairs, Diana Clayton felt a sudden chill that was gone in
an instant. Instinctively she glanced down the hallway to
where her children were sleeping, then stopped working for
the night.

"Flu season," she had whispered.

"I don't have time to be sick," she had said.

He heard the tub filling.

He saw shadows against the stairway die as Diana dimmed
the lights in her bathroom.

He felt the chambers of Tofu's heart pounding like a watch wound to destruction, nearly bursting with terror as he blew a foul stream across her face for a second time. The powerful rear legs kicked against his chest in a wild plea for survival.

Using the buttery fold of skin around Tofu's neck, he fashioned a garrote with surgical skill and began strangling the animal with its own flesh. He watched the paws flip aimlessly, the torso writhing, dancing through air.

Relaxing his hold, he then pinched the skin taut, leading the animal across the countertop, down into the sink.

The once-trusting eyes teared, dilating into black pools as shock shut down the biological acceptance of pain. And Tofu gave an involuntary thrust, a spasm, her bladder releasing a short but steady stream.

Grabbing both front legs, he gave a sharp and merciless pull. For a second the body shook violently, followed by a predatory stillness that trapped time. Formless and pure. And a darkness that could almost be touched.

Intimate. Arousing.

There was a chill to the night air.

As he closed the front door behind him, he pulled his collar against the wind. It was a quiet, sleeping suburb that greeted him. And he felt curiously alive as his blood pounded through the dark chambers of his heart, ratcheting into every muscle and fiber and nerve, fueling him with an almost unbearable delight.

No dogs came barking. No cars were turning. No signs of a suburb in terror.

Down and across the lawn he started, ever confident, ever at ease. He could see the mute sputterings from a television casting its glow—men like moths clinging to a bulb, he thought, empty lives flapping mindlessly.

And he knew all their names. Counting by house, row upon row, he could recite their most personal concerns. One couple had a village idiot for a son. Another a spaniel with indigestion. One woman had been raped while young. Another was about to retire.

As he strolled, kicking through a small pile of leaves, he felt like a king, as if this were his village, as if these were his subjects.

He pulled back into shadow as headlights approached, filtering through a soft wooded lot, but they came and went like a hollow beam in a dreamscape. Against his cheeks he could taste the perfume of Diana Clayton's bath oil, this tickling his throat as he strolled out into the street.

He stopped briefly, glancing back over his shoulder. The house was now dark, save for a light burning in a second story bedroom window, and he saw her there, dressed and readied for school.

"Yes!" he exhaled forcefully, closing his eyes. "Yes, yes, yes!"

Kimberly Clayton was staring down at him, watching his every move as he vanished into the night.

2

A man in a battered gray raincoat strolled through a cold mist and crossed the intersection at Thirty-seventh and Park. As he walked, he was talking to himself, quiet mutterings that no one else could hear or understand.

"Tofu," he murmured, as if addressing an old friend.

His dove-gray eyes appeared red and swollen, while his hands ached with the slight tremor of arthritis as he removed his coat. Walking quickly, he made a casual effort of dusting lint and ash from a dark gray suit. As he joined a parade entering the lobby of the Sheraton hotel, he checked his watch. He was late. It was 4:06 P.M., April 9, and at the age of fifty-six he stood parked like a hydrant, a solidly built man of slightly less than average height who was wondering how many more hours his stamina would endure, how long until he could return to the work that littered his desk.

His name was John F. Scott. And as he turned through the lobby for the hotel meeting rooms, he felt empty and unfit, as if he had abandoned the most desperate and forlorn of victims, and after willing them to life, was letting them die again and again. With each death the grief was real. The grief his own.

From the corner of his eye he spotted a small sign that read "WELCOME CAP FELLOWSHIP" in red on white, with a little arrow leading through a spotless corridor. He followed twists and turns until he stood before a set of towering double doors.

He ran his fingers through a mane of graying blond hair that curled in every direction, buttoned his collar with one hand, then began pulling at the knot of a silk Dior tie. While inching the door open, he took a deep breath before walking out into a small sea of younger faces.

There were about a hundred men and women dressed in civilian clothes and listening attentively to a woman of about fifty who was standing at the podium of a small stage. ". . . so as our profile of this offender shows, Dennis Statler was in many ways like the series killer Theodore Bundy, with some rather subtle differences. In terms of their behaviors, they were the same types of individuals, but did they have the same motives for killing, and what were those?" she asked with a nod, watching as the man approached.

He smiled in return, for he had noticed the fatigue in her voice and knew she had been playing for time. The woman was a fellow instructor, from the federal behavioral-research laboratory in Quantico, Virginia, and the hall was filled with police officers attending a special training course called CAP, the National Criminal Apprehension Program. The program was conducted once a year by the United States government for police forces nationwide, and included instruction by experts from a dozen federal agencies.

"Ladies and gentlemen," she said with a bite, "both men abducted and sexually molested their victims, both men preferred killing with a blunt instrument, and both discarded human remains in a shallow grave. Were their motives the same? In what other way were they alike?"

Scott raised his hand as he walked onto the stage. "Bundy was a lawyer," he said quietly, speaking directly to the men and women in the soft chairs. "Statler was an accountant. Rather than motive, it is important to note that both were professional men who made their lives in quiet residential neighborhoods. And while Bundy was engaged to be wed, Statler was already married and had two children."

Scott reached into his coat pocket and produced a fistful of notes, forcing his mind into paths of logic. "Sorry I'm late, Dorothy," he said as the woman was collecting her papers off the lectern. With a smile he turned back to the students as the woman leaned up into the microphone.

"Our guest speaker has arrived," she said, and a short burst of laughter filled the hall as Scott removed notecards from inside his jacket and placed them on the lectern.

"The important point about these two killers is not that they shared similar behaviors while stalking prey or even during the kill. No," Scott said with a sharp conviction, holding up one hand while establishing eye contact with several students. He paused, scanning the crowd with precision. "The important thing is their camouflage, the manner in which they were able to evade police investigators. During the next six weeks you will be learning from the leading experts on repeat violent crime, and if you come away with nothing else, please learn this. Most serial killers have very little to do with the myths that are taking form around them. Most do not live in a kind of unemployed isolation, off in some distant wood or asylum. They are your neighbors. Just like Bundy, Statler, Gacey, Williams, Merrin, and a cast of hundreds, they are the people you meet at the PTA or Little League. They ride the bus with you, your children play with their children, they may even break bread with you at family gatherings."

A hushed murmur filled the hall, and Scott gave a knowing nod. "First, as you may have guessed, I am Jack Scott, director of the federal law-enforcement program known as ViCAT, the Violent Criminal Apprehension Team. Our job is in our title. I will be speaking with you from time to time throughout your course work, so if there is no disagreement, let's start with a few numbers that spell out the specific threat to the civilian population and domestic security of our country."

He waited a moment, then read from a card. "In 1985 there were 14,516 murders in America classified as *without motive*—that is, homicide at the hands of a total stranger, someone who has nothing to gain but murder in and of itself. Now, from this group of killings, only sixteen suspects have been captured. Nine have been convicted, and since I'm sure no one here tonight believes nine men could accomplish so much in so short a time, let's cut through to the chase. Also, that number does not include an additional five thousand bodies that simply turn up each year in the category of *Unidentified,* persons who only appear to be murder victims, so let the record show we're being conservative tonight."

Scott eyed the crowd of young police officers. They were silent and attentive, having been hand-selected by police chiefs to represent their home states. "The question remains," he continued, "what type of human animal takes another life without motive, and why, and what does the incidence mean? First," he said clearly, "so-called motiveless murder is usually committed by a person from one of two classifications. The first has a major psychological abnormality, a type of mental illness. I'm sure everyone has seen the movie classic *Psycho*. This was based on a real case, so think of this as representative of the first group.

"The second, and by hundreds to one the larger population, is classified as *Recreational killers,* and they represent your Ted Bundys. Unlike the psychos of America, they are considered to be quite sane and mentally fit. So who are they? Why do they kill?"

The crowd was silent, and Scott paused long enough to let the analytical framework sink in, combing through graying-blond hair with his fingers, brushing curls off his brow. "Recreational killers, also known as Rakes, are invariably male, while their victims are overwhelmingly women and children, and sometimes women and children together." As he blinked, mental images tore at Scott, and he fought back with a verbal detachment. "Their killings are usually intraracial—that is, whites killing whites, blacks killing blacks, and so forth. As our population grows exponentially, so do the numbers of recreational killers, and just at a time when the judicial system is impotent to effectively deal with the mounting threat. We at ViCAT need your help, the help of an educated police force. But first, in addition to the scale of the problem, we must have some basic understanding of why this killing population is so different from the rest of us." Scott paused, scanning the crowd and maintaining eye contact for emphasis.

"By employing computerized artificial intelligence, we have produced a statistic that sounds an alarm for every man, woman, and child in America, and it translates in the following manner. If you are a middle-or upper-middle-class family of four, the chances are thirty-seven percent that you will meet a serial killer in your lifetime, and the chances are one hundred to one it will be from our second group."

Scott gave a nod as a hand rose from the crowd.

"Why now?" asked a thin, neatly dressed man in his mid-thirties. "That number seems quite high, so why all of a sudden?"

Scott nodded thoughtfully. "Well, it wasn't really sudden, although it might appear that way. The population size has just grown until we have now reached a kind of critical threshold. In today's world we just have more of everything—serial killers are no exception. They have always been with us, and their numbers grow as the population blooms." Scott paused again, recognizing a large man in a brown vest who was standing at the back of the room.

"Sorry to interrupt, sir, I'm Sergeant Howard Means, California Highway Patrol. Is the critical difference between these two groups of killers a question of insanity?"

Scott smiled. "Illness and insanity are legal terms, and although we would consider their actions to be quite sick by all human standards, recreational killers are *not* sick, according to current thought. Bundy wasn't sick, and I knew him well. He was, in lay terms, *Lacking* or suffering a *Deficit*." Notepads were suddenly popping open, and Scott held off for a moment.

"Most true serial killers," he continued, "are as sane as you or I, yet they treat other people without regard for human suffering. What's more, they are in full control of their actions. They know what they are doing when they kill—indeed, many are cunning predators. The critical difference between them and seemingly normal people is that these killers are born without the ability to feel emotion."

A hand rose in the front row. "Sir, Kevin Mullin, Boston PD. Isn't it true that all humans have feeling, just to varying degrees, and that many of these killers could have been victims of severe child abuse that numbed them somehow?"

Scott returned a sly but understanding smile. "Officer Mullin you said?"

"Yes, sir."

"Thank you for hitting the target on the first shot. I'm drafting you for an experiment."

"Sorry?"

Scott carefully assessed the young man, making sure the audience knew he was doing just that. "Officer, would you humor an old man and cover your eyes for just one moment? We will be giving you a quick test."

Kevin Mullin quickly glanced about the room, preparing himself in case his powers of observation were to be called into question, and then covered his eyes.

"Thank you," Scott offered. "Now, today I am wearing a gray suit. I want you to describe this for me—not the suit but the color."

"Well," Mullin sighed, hesitating, "that's a tough one. Gray would be like a blue but not as bright . . . it's really not much of a color. Damn," he said, shaking his head. "Sorry, I don't know how to describe gray except by comparing it to other things of a similar color."

"Fair enough," Scott offered. "You must compare the color of my suit to other things that you have experienced, so this little experiment is over. Now, what is color to a man who has always been blind?"

The officer looked pensive as a murmur started to swell in the room.

"Anyone can step in at any time and field this question for Officer Mullin," Scott offered, concerned he was embarrassing the man. But there was only silence as Scott's eye fell back on the policeman before him. "Want to take a shot?" he asked quietly.

"Well," Mullin offered, "a person born blind would never really be able to fully understand color—it would always be just a concept. You would have to have lost sight to understand it."

"This is quite true. Now, let's take it one step further. Ladies and gentlemen, would someone please explain to me the feelings of the following sensations?" With that Scott held up one hand, slowing counting on his fingers. "Joy, sorrow, anger, fear, and hate. Actually, there are six basic emotions, but I have intentionally omitted love from our list so that we can avoid a battle between the sexes."

A small wave of laughter bloomed and died.

"These, then, are the six basic emotions. All the rest are subsets or variations of these. Now, let's say I don't know how any of them feel," Scott said with intensity in his voice. "I was born emotionally blind. So please, isn't there anyone who can help me?"

A noisy wave rolled through the hall as a smaller man stood excitedly, waving his arms halfway through the center section. "Detective D'Angelo, sir, NYPD. In order to explain either color or emotions, you would first have to experience them."

Scott nodded. "That is very true, and what, Detective, do emotions do for us? How do they serve us?"

"Well," he chuckled, rolling his eyes, "emotions give men and women something to share."

Scott interrupted a humorous chatter with a forceful dismissive wave of his hand. "He's right, let's give him a chance, please. What else, Officer D'Angelo? What other part do emotions play in our lives?"

"Everything, I think. Emotions are the reason we enjoy things, and they also keep us in line. I mean, emotions serve as a system of checks and balances on our behavior."

"This is true, and without them what would we have? Certainly no highs and lows in our lives, no joy or sorrow or love. Without them, every stimulus on planet earth plays to the intellect alone, and although I can't ask you to fully comprehend this just yet, I would ask you to grasp this concept." Scott paused and began to pace, his hands clasped behind his back.

"Without feelings, everything becomes meaningless except on a purely intellectual basis. Issues and events and characters, life's comedy and drama, are all meaningless. Without emotions, nothing matters, anything becomes possible. Recreational killers are born without emotion—we label them Devoids, in fact—and if you would like to explain feelings to them, I would suggest you practice by describing color to the blind."

Instantly the hall broke into noisy whispering, and Scott paced to the edge of the stage. "Our studies now indicate that people like these, devoid of emotion, constitute the largest and most dangerous population threatening civilian life. As is the case with Ted Bundy, most have had above-average child-rearing, but as adults they kill women and children with the mercy you might afford a cockroach."

Scott glanced at his watch. "As individuals these killers tend to be quiet socially, their physical appearance is usually neat, and they may be pillars of the community. They function well within society, and can share experiences with others with a rather critical exception. Since they are born nearly devoid of emotion, they must constantly measure their behavior by studying others. For instance, if they see us laugh or cry in a theater, they know they must follow suit, or over time they will face detection. They parrot our emotional displays, and here lies a key for spotting them, which we will delve into at our next meeting. As food for thought, I will tell you that they do recognize this inability to feel, which potentially sets them apart from others."

He began collecting his notes as an excited debate began filling the hall. "It has been a pleasure to meet you, and I wish you well throughout the course. Get your pens at the ready, and write down the following research question. I would like an explanation next time we meet."

The audience went silent.

"Auschwitz," Scott stated coldly. "No place in history ever attracted so many Devoids in a single wrinkle of time."

After a few moments, a young woman offered in confusion, "But that's not a question."

"Yes, it is." Scott nodded bleakly as he left the room. "And Dachau. Treblinka. Bergen-Belsen. Buchenwald . . ."

Scott walked through a downpour, climbing into his car at Park and Thirty-seventh, where his engine caught on the first hit. He pulled into the street, heading south toward the World Trade Center, the mulling of tires on wet pavement producing a monotonous and hypnotic effect. Scott let his thoughts drift with the traffic, his mind unable to concentrate further.

He knew the neighborhood well. Operating on automatic, he slowed at the awning of Enrico's Fine Italian, the windshield wipers slapping at sheets of rain. Once, long ago, little David had worked there as a waiter, he remembered, and Jack Scott smiled darkly.

"I knew you were the one. I knew you could talk to Sam," he blurted before he started to cry.

David Berkowitz believed what he told Scott, that he was a "Divine Messenger." And Scott had taken all the pieces of his sorry life and put them together. That he was the killer of at least thirteen young women was not a question. What remained a mystery was why. Little David would not tell.

One August evening in 1977, after hours of mindless discussion, Scott faced the one-way mirror of the interrogation room, about to signal release, when he winced at the reflection. It was there, in the mirror.

"D-O-G?"

Scott choked on his drink, turning on the demented young man, having solved his motivational riddle, an anagram that sent him off into the night to kill. In frustration Scott had scribbled case elements in large block letters on a legal pad, while for days Berkowitz had babbled about the beagle in the backyard that barked, keeping him awake—the nights he took human life.

"The dog told you, didn't he, David?" Scott asked with mercy in his voice. "The dog told you!"

"Yes, oh yes." Berkowitz was excited and relieved. "I knew you would understand . . . I knew you were the one . . .

I knew . . ." And he broke into a fit of tears, reaching to hold the agent, love the messenger who would carry on his burden for him.

Sick, tormented bastard. In his lonely, twisted world, David killed because the dog woke him at night and told him. The beagle named Sam asked David to kill, and he obeyed. For David was his son. David needed love. Because D-O-G spelled backward is G-O-D.

The Son of Sam could not tell right from wrong, and barely left from right. Mentally ill, a true psycho untouched by reality, incapable of understanding the world into which he was born. Compared to what ViCAT faced daily, David was almost shy, an excitable boy who lacked direction.

He was not the devil incarnate, cult leader, conspirator, and deathmaster portrayed by tabloid hucksters.

David Berkowitz was a sick, sick man.

But he was *not* a recreational killer.

3

7:38 P.M. WORLD TRADE CENTER

With a sharp snap, a flood of light covered a desktop littered with photographs, while a hand was adjusting a glaring beam. It was a tired hand with the small liver spots of encroaching age.

"The moment of death is not as arousing, not as important to you as just being in control—that's what you're after," Scott said aloud, entering a notation on a yellow legal pad. He shook his head, propping his elbows against the desk, his body sagged slightly forward.

"The ability to decide life or death, the process," he repeated, rubbing his palm against his forehead. "The whole time you were after the goddamn process?"

Scott felt as if he had been looking through a kaleidoscope, turning it aimlessly for hours, staring at fragments and meaningless patterns, then had by accident turned it just right and had the bright bits form a realistic image. He made another notation, lifting a photograph from a seemingly endless series. Beneath the focused beam he studied this image for a moment, then flipped through a sequence of close-ups, every detail magnified and preserved.

There was a bowl of apples, and again he recalled the smell of fresh fruit. His own daughter had once kept a rabbit, and he stared at the horrible form of Tofu, bound in a blue ski parka, lying dead on the kitchen table.

Scott swallowed hard. Suddenly he felt uncomfortable in his clothes and tugged at the collar of his white shirt, then removed a cuff link from each sleeve, dropping these into a shirt pocket. Fatigue was returning, and he drained the last of a cold cup of coffee. Standing behind his desk, he cracked the blinds of his fifteenth-floor window, hoping for a ray of sunshine. He looked out onto the Manhattan skyline, but the world to John F. Scott had gone dark.

That morning, in a Washington suburb some three hundred miles to the south, Diana Clayton had been buried. She had been dead for nine days, except in his mind. The mind of Scott, commander of the elite and little-known investigative division of the United States National Security Agency, Vi-CAT. And he wondered how many more hours his stamina would endure as he returned to his chair.

"I am the killer," he said, closing his eyes. "His skin is my body."

Impossibly soft.

He imagined laying Tofu's body out across the kitchen floor by pulling and caressing each ear, tucking her inside of Kimberly Clayton's jacket. He started examining that photo, tacking it gently against a wall of decorative cork, using a clear plastic stickpin.

Drawing upon emotion, creativity, and training, he imagined positioning the bunny's face up through the hooded parka and slowly zipping the jacket closed. "What moved inside of you?" he wondered in a flat voice, working his hands as if tying long ears into a hideous knot. "Like wrapping gifts, but a package for whom, for what purpose, for what occasion?" Scott evoked the sweet smell of apples from his memory, as he began leisurely stuffing the hard fruit into each sleeve, arranging them just so and adding a fullness and bulk to the carcass.

The parka had hung in the kitchen closet near the back door, and he checked the distance to the cage against a blueprint: nine feet. Estimating twelve feet from the window, with, at best, streetlights to work by. "Now," he said, checking a computer-generated time-series chart against a stop-watch, "the bathwater being turned off now."

He tried to evoke that sensory experience, the absence of sound, the termination of water flowing through pipes as a safe little house returned to sleepy stillness. Soundless as thought, he began moving quietly for the staircase, the waiting over, toward Diana and her children, moving room by room through a photographic sequence. He followed champagne carpeting, starting with a wide-angle view of the stairs, a hallway landing, and a dimly lit bedroom entrance. The door opened wide. He pinned this photograph at the center, and then like building spokes on a wheel, placed two more pictures on either side, each detailing the hallway's interior.

The master bedroom came next, and he gently affixed a photo, center, above the rest. Her bedroom looked untouched, unmolested. Dark gray business suit still on a hanger just outside the closet door, pressed and cleaned. An ecru blouse, ruffled at the collar, folded and placed on a chair. Shoes beneath. Light brown pocketbook resting on the carpet next to a maroon briefcase, both closed, the briefcase leaning against her dresser. The room was tidy in a feminine sort of way; there was no doubt that Diana Clayton had planned on living.

He examined an enlarged snapshot taken from the family room. She was standing at the water's edge in a red-and-silver one-piece bathing suit. Nags Head perhaps, and Scott's eyes worked quickly, soaking the image like a sponge: muscular legs, flat stomach, ample cleavage, short brown hair with blond highlights. He checked his notes. Married in 1972 at age twenty-five, her first child born 1977. The years had been kind, he thought. Either maturity or motherhood brought out a refined woman that had been more girlish before. A good-looking woman, not a beauty but unusual.

His fingers flicked from file to file.

A third photo, Diana Clayton's nude body, eyes open, staring up from her bathtub. Her right hand extending, palm down, toward the sink—toward her children. Her chest thrust up, her spine arched, not even relaxed in death. Scott cleared phlegm from his throat and swallowed. Four scratch marks. Blond hair caked in the darkness of congealed blood that had spread into a horrible pool. This picture he studied a moment longer, then placed it on top of the center column. He made a notation, fumbling for a cigarette in his top desk drawer.

"Keep it clinical," a voice inside him warned. "Slow it down."

Stink of sulfur, a few puffs, stale smoke filled his lungs. The harsh burning threw off other, more choking sensations and he pressed the button on a desk tape recorder. "Although victim was found in tub, victim's body cleared water by two to three feet for several seconds, resulting in bloodstains on carpet." She had been held down for a brief duration. "Scratches and bruise on left quadrant, upper chest, and neck suggest assailant is left-handed or ambidextrous," he continued. "Extension of right arm, fingers spread, evidence of reflexive shock." He rechecked the autopsy report.

"Cause of death: cardiopulmonary arrest from cranial bullet trauma." A single lethal blow from a .22-caliber truncated hollow-point bullet, which entered her mouth through the upper lip, splitting teeth, then exited the rear lateral cranial posterior, or the back of her head. Scott closed his eyes and swallowed hard. Like most policemen, he knew that the idea of a bullet to the head being always fatal and instantaneous was a media myth.

"What went through her mind? What did she perceive was happening?" he wondered aloud. "She couldn't even move." Scott was breathing heavily now, pulse quickened, his thoughts beginning to blur. The coroner estimated that although she was paralyzed at the instant of bullet entry, it had taken her between three and five minutes to die. And the killer had waited. The killer did not want to use a second shot.

"The process." He swallowed, a quiet rage stirring Commander Scott to his feet, the black bile rising in his throat. Suddenly his right foot tore into the side of a gray metal trashcan. The object hurtled across the office, clattering as it spun.

"What did you do to her those last few minutes, you evil bastard?"

He stood fixed, blood throbbing at his temples, his gray eyes burning sharp and without mercy.

He closed his eyes.

In the bedroom, standing, I am the killer.

She relaxes in a warm bath, so she does not see my approach up the stairs and into her bedroom. Soundless, I push the bathroom door wide on its hinges, and Diana's horror begins with a sudden cool draft.

"Who's there?" She is startled, peering through the doorway into the bedroom, feeling the unexplained chill on her wet skin.

I do not answer, Scott reasons. I wait so the victim does not scream. By now she is thinking the foundations have settled, popping the hinges, or the heat has come on, pushing against the door. She is seeking a justification in her mind while I know her disorientation will last just long enough.

I walk in, talking. "Let us be calm about this," I say very coolly. "I'm lost, is this the Smith household? Do I have the right address?"

A nightmare bursts, explodes in her head, the blood pounding so hard, so fast, she cannot hear, she cannot think. Operating on instinct, she starts to rise while trying to focus—when a forceful hand strikes her neck and chest.

Godless reality.

She is trying to comprehend, to see, but the room moves frame by frame in anguished slow motion.

"Oh, God!" she prays instantly. "Who are you?" As she tries to stand, the hand strikes, knocking her downward, grabbing her by the hair and preventing her fall.

"Does he know about the children? Kimberly, Leslie?" Thought number one.

"Is he lost? Does he want money? My children! God, no!"

With all her worth Diana fights to stand, but the slick surface of the tub works against her feet. Scott turns to the wall, thinking, "I am between her, the door, her babies." Pushing her back, beating her down with both fists.

"I only want you," I say comfortingly. *The process.* I understand what she is protecting; I know the hope she is clinging to.

She nods her head without making a sound as Scott returns to his chair.

Behind my back I steady the gun in my fist, coming out now, quickly with a dull *pop;* a silenced gunshot splits through her teeth. Her body jerks back in a cough of blood, her hands fight as her body freezes.

I remove my gloves. Five minutes pass.

She dies there.

* * *

Footsteps.

Mercifully, Scott, thought, there are footsteps approaching. A door opened and a familiar voice said, "Talk to me, Jack, do you need anything?"

Scott tried to break loose from the death throes of Diana Clayton, his thoughts failing as thoughts, failing as words. The voice became a hand, and then a mug, which became the smells of freshly brewed coffee beneath the commander's nose. As it tugged at his senses, with a warming reality he leaned forward, his hand groping like a small animal, feeling its way across the desk. He was lifting a cup that seemed made of lead.

The hot liquid splashed back through his throat, mixing with bile, and he swallowed hard. His light gray eyes were red and swollen as he glanced up quickly at the figure who stood beside him, then quickly away, fumbling through his drawers.

"In the ashtray," the voice corrected, and Scott saw a crooked white spire already rising from his desk.

"Sorry," he said before drawing in a long pull of hot gases, filling his lungs. He sat back in his chair. "What was the question?" he asked distantly.

"Nothing pressing." Matthew W. Brennon was smiling at him.

Special Agent Brennon was a tall man in his late thirties, dressed in a dark blue vest with red tie. He was now examining the photographic matrix on the wall as Scott pumped down more coffee and finished off a stale Marlboro.

"With what we're facing, I don't know why the death of a rabbit gets to me so badly, but it does," Brennon confessed, looking away from that series of photos, then peering at Diana Clayton's body. No answer came back, so he turned, establishing eye contact with Scott.

"Tofu," the commander said quietly by way of agreement, releasing a frustrated sigh, removing his glasses, and rubbing a fist into each eye. "I really appreciate the coffee," he said, taking another sip. "You have no idea."

Brennon turned his back to the matrix and leaned forward, both hands on Scott's desk. "You've been at it for three hours. Want to toss it around?"

Scott shrugged. "Tofu was a member of the family, otherwise the bastard wouldn't have cared enough to give the bunny a slap. Killing as an end in itself doesn't do it for him. What he craves is domination, absolute control, that's key."

Scott stood, stretching his back, and with a neatly manicured thumb he smudged away the term *Lepus angorus* from the white margin of an eight-by-ten glossy. He then inserted the rabbit's proper name with a black grease pen and sat down again.

"Did you come to rescue me or did I miss an appointment?"

Matthew Brennon handed him a fist of pink message slips. "Captain Drury has been calling constantly. He attended the Clayton funeral and wants to talk to you. He said he's willing to put the entire Maryland state police on this case if you so order, so I told him you'd be in touch."

"Thanks," Scott sighed. "Anything else?"

"A woman called from the National Neighborhood Watch crime-prevention program, she's writing a nasty letter to the Department of Justice. I told her that was the wrong branch of government. Her comments are on the note."

Scott shook his head.

"And that covers immediate demands." Brennon picked a file off the desk and placed it beneath his arm.

"Matt, have you walked through the path reports on the Clayton case?" he asked, pushing the spring-loaded beam of his desk lamp higher against the wall matrix while opening Diana Clayton's appointment calendar.

"Twice, the second time was to review your notations."

Scott nodded. "Do you recall if they found any traces of infection, bacterial or viral?"

"Negative. They were all in super health. Why?"

"Playing a hunch, but it could change the course of investigation, which I had planned on reviewing only for procedural advice as a favor, then kicking back to the Maryland state police."

"Here we go." Brennon smiled. "Give it to me, Jack, make it a good one." As senior field agent, Brennon knew that in order for a homicide to become a ViCAT investigation, the crime either had to classify as serial or be an atrocity committed by a total stranger, what was referred to as motiveless homicide. These were two types of assault local enforcement had little chance of solving without help.

"Until now we've been operating on the assumption that Diana knew her killer and that the attack was motivated by anger or revenge of some type," Scott stated in a flat voice, "and that, of course, would have kept this one out of our formal purview."

Brennon leaned against the desk. "It's a nasty event, Jack, but I haven't seen any evidence to the contrary."

"Take a look," he said, ignoring the comment, pointing to the notation *Vit. C* on Diana Clayton's calendar. Each page was carefully sealed with a pliable acrylic for protection, and Scott had circled the marking with a red grease pen. Brennon did not respond, but stood fast, a pensive look framed by neatly trimmed black hair, his hazel eyes reflecting confusion.

"Dammit!" Scott spat impatiently. "She felt him coming and mistook that for the flu . . ." His voice sagged abruptly.

"Woman's intuition," Brennon sighed. "We've seen it before, but I don't know, Jack. What you're suggesting is that this notation reflects an instinctual error and that somehow— and God knows you'll come up with it—this will change the scope of our involvement."

Scott tapped the appointment pad with his pen, then pushed out from his desk and started to pace. "I don't recall her stomach contents or blood chemistry, except that she was clean, but we were looking for pollutants, drugs or poison, not vitamins."

Not prepared to argue, Brennon leaned over, placing an index finger on the notation. "You're right, Jack. If she had been taking vitamins, it would have shown in the path report and I'd remember."

"And if she knew this man, if this killer was known to her, do you think she would have reacted to his presence so viscerally? No, she thought she was catching the flu, and I also believe she was taking a hot bath to cure the chills. Diana Clayton felt him with her maternal gut, just like hearing a time bomb tick, only she miscued. Why else would her last request be a reminder to take vitamins, unless she erred on instinct, unless her body warned her, unless she knew but could not interpret her feelings, unless . . . ?" His voice trailed off sharply, his nostrils flared with disgust.

Brennon stood fast. It was starting to make sense. From a microanalysis of her handwriting—such elements as decreasing downward pressure, the loosening of curves and swirls, the amount of perspiration on a page, the incomplete closure of circles and loops—ViCAT technicians had scored each of Diana Clayton's notations in a time series based on the combined effects of fatigue on penmanship. *Vit. C* was her last entry in life.

"She did *not* know him," Scott concluded as he paced, his hands behind his back. "The killer was a total stranger, unfamiliar to the family, and for that reason alone, she felt him." He crossed the room, grabbed the gray metal trashcan, and set it back on end.

"This killer wants us to believe he knew her, but he did not. The Claytons were selected and stalked. And, I might add, that process does not appear to have been random."

Brennon's brow pinched. He knew that less than one percent of all motiveless homicides were ever solved, and Scott was moving toward having the Clayton case reclassified. More to the point, under Executive Order 14595, signed into law by President Jimmy Carter, under the National Security Act, ViCAT could take authority over the investigation.

Scott sat back down. "Let's key on a criminal profile where single mothers have been attacked by strangers," he said, trying to make the request sound like an offering instead of a direct order. "Forget other similarities—wounds, weapons, body positions, sexual contact, and the like. Start from scratch, maybe the computer will give something back this time."

Brennon was jotting into a black notebook.

"There's something familiar here, Matt, I can taste it. Right now I'm betting this man will match against one of our known offenders who has just graduated into the big time. The computer robbed us last time. Let's hit a home run."

Brennon shook his head, thinking of their endlessly mounting caseload. "What priority?" he asked with a sense of dread.

"According to the forensic pattern left at the scene, our offender even doubled back to rough up the pile on the carpet where he had stepped, erasing footprints. He has a working knowledge of police science, and that, my friend, bothers me a great deal. Let's go First Priority."

Brennon released a troubled sigh. "Okay, Jack. Kick the gray intercom if you need me," he offered as Scott began to focus the beam on his desk, lifting a silver frame into the light. It was wrapped in clear plastic and sealed with tape.

"Don't forget your dinner party tonight. I promised to push you out of here about now," Brennon cautioned on his way through the door. "And get some sleep, you look like a parlor corpse."

Scott ignored the comment. Once again Kimberly Clayton's impish grin was melting his heart, and even as he heard the footsteps vanish and the door close quietly, Scott felt his mind beginning to crawl.

"An almost perfect-looking little girl," he said, plunging back into a dark well of cruelty. He hesitated only a moment, taking a deep breath from his own childhood and then a long step forward in time.

According to Captain Maxwell Drury of the Maryland state police, a neighbor named Martha Cory had first stumbled onto the crime scene. According to the report, she had been walking her dog by the house when she saw Kimberly and her sister staring out from a bedroom window.

Martha had waved; the children did not move.

Martha had rung the doorbell; there was no answer.

She had been staring into the lifeless eyes of the Clayton girls, dressed and positioned like store mannequins in the bedroom where they had been sleeping.

4

Down the hall on the fifteenth floor of the World Trade Center, Matthew Brennon returned to the Mix Master, a mainframe computer capable of grinding through a population of close to three million known offenders and prior cases, keying in on related information, then spitting back data in microbursts.

Is Weapon Correct As Listed? A message popped onto a green video display terminal as Brennon returned to instructing a recent graduate from the Federal Law Enforcement Training Academy. Daniel Flores was twenty-six and had been first in his graduating class, specifically requesting assignment to ViCAT in New York. It was his career ambition to work alongside Commander Scott, training on state-of-the-art equipment and studying with America's elite manhunters. Files in hand, Brennon stooped over the keypad as Flores sat in mute attention, staring at the sign over the door through which Brennon had just appeared.

We are the last defense.
We are the last detail.
Sentries at the door of hell,
Who can't afford to fail.
—N. Dobbs—

It was heady stuff to the recent graduate, and Brennon waited patiently before clearing his throat.

"Who is Dobbs?" Flores asked.

"Who *was* Dobbs," Brennon corrected. "The first ViCAT commander, he's been dead a long while." Agent Flores smiled up at the lean agent, who stood six-foot-two, his dark black hair contrasting a face grown pale from working too many nights. Matt Brennon was a soft-spoken thirty-nine, trim with a conviction to stay that way.

"Now, look at the prompt on the screen, the program is challenging you. It is questioning if you entered the data on the murder weapon correctly. Why would it do that?"

Flores looked blank.

"Artificial intelligence does not give leeway for user error. It works on strict probability, and the weapon in this case, a firearm, doesn't make sense with what the system already knows about home intruders, specifically home intruders who kill," Brennon explained. "These types of killings typically are beatings, strangulations, stabbings—anything rather than shootings. The computer thinks a gun is too impersonal a choice for this type of killer."

"So it was expecting a device that required touching, physical contact?"

"Exactly. Now, look at the second question: the computer is asking if the weapon was found at the site, so it's trying to classify the man's personality."

"As a potential repeat offender?"

"Not yet, but it will lead to that. If the killer used whatever weapon was available—a kitchen knife or a lamp cord—that points to a more *disorganized* personality. If the killer brought his own weapon, which is the case here, it points to a stalker, someone who is cunning. If the stalker brought a gun," he shrugged, "who knows what it will come back with? Enter 'twenty-two-caliber pistol,' " he said, " 'brought to scene by the killer.' "

"Do we have evidence for that?" Flores asked correctly.

Brennon reached into the file and handed him a black-and-white enlargement produced by a high-voltage electron microscope (HVEM). The photo looked like the surface of a weird planet exploding. "All of the bullets were twenty-two-caliber, something called a hornet, mass-produced, easy to purchase. Muzzle velocity estimated at sixteen hundred feet per second. No shell casings, and they only recovered bullet fragments like this one from Diana Clayton's tongue, and she did not own a gun."

Agent Flores' hands trembled slightly as he typed the salient data into a form on the screen. He pressed the *enter* button. The screen went blank and delivered another prompt.

Entry Forced // Type of Entry? the computer asked.

"The program is comparing the degree of sophistication of implements and tools used by the killer, looking for burglar equipment. This is the same logic we applied, but in a pure mathematical form. The program assigns skill levels based on the coding of different tools. Unfortunately, we have nothing to feed it, so type in *Unknown*," he said, pulling a sheet from the file. "No sign of forced entry. In fact, no sign of entry at all. You should also note that the locks in the house are registered and were installed by a bonded company, who claims no other keys were issued except those found with the bodies."

It took a few moments, but Flores typed, beginning to understand the sophistication of the case and the computer. The screen swallowed data, went blank, and another prompt appeared:

Other Material Evidence Outstanding?

Brennon was at the ready. "Two strands of Dacron taken from between rear feet of family pet." He paused. "Make that Tofu," he said. "Identify the pet as Tofu."

Flores stared up at him. "Sick bastard," he spat, "the rabbit was kicking its heart out and—"

". . . she caught the killer's clothing with her rear claws, giving us better data." Brennon completed the statement in a positive way, placing another HVEM photo on the desk. The Dacron fibers were rendered porous as Swiss cheese and shaped like alien wasps. Agent Flores typed the data in slowly.

"There were also a dozen strands of nylon rope taken from the children's room, checked under HVEM. There are about twenty-five possible U.S. manufacturers, more abroad. You can buy it anywhere—boat supply, hardware stores, sporting goods." The graduate punched it in, the screen swallowed.

Offender's Blood Type//DNA Code? came a prompt.

Brennon released a sigh, pulling a series of stills and reports from the file. "Body evidence negligible," he said. "Saliva shows AB positive, but the FBI techies don't have enough for DNA decoding. Not even one eyebrow hair. He must have used tape for those or was completely shaven, although Jack thinks he was covered by a Dacron hood."

Agent Flores' chin was against his chest. "Then she was raped," he concluded.

"No," Brennon answered, his face worked into a cold mask. "Enter that we have no fingerprints, no footprints, no latents."

Flores stood, his face and neck flushed with blood. He was a human fireplug, five-foot-seven, with wild hazel eyes and thick lips that looked parched. "Matt, are we going to get this guy?" he asked with a sudden sadness.

Brennon stretched like a cat and then pointed at the sign over the exit door. "Like the man said." He smiled. "Take a break and I'll get us some coffee."

Daniel Flores had already spent the better part of a week reviewing the top ViCAT cases, every type of violent crime the human mind could fathom, and in horridly graphic detail, investigations ranging from multiple rape and child molesting to mass murder and serial killings. Through the use of the Mix Master computer he had already met more human monsters than most cops meet in a lifetime, and he continued to enter data, or what the program saw as a lack of data.

The computer prompt returned, and Flores' eyes flared with horror.

(1) Evidence Negligible for Severity of Crime.

(2) Expert Preforensic Evaluation by Suspect.

(3) Police or Law-Enforcement Officer Probable Suspect.

Daniel Flores pushed away from his seat in a horrified dash to find his training officer.

5

He was a dog of unknown years, for he had been found fully grown along River Road in Bethesda, Maryland, near the posh neighborhood of Kenwood Forest.

Elmer Janson had discovered him after hearing a whine come from a ravine while riding his bike home from school. The boy had pulled the wounded animal to safety, then, using his jacket as a litter, dragged the dog several miles to the Glen Echo fire station. A paramedic applied a tourniquet to a badly mangled left front leg, stabilized the dog's vital signs, and sent for a vet. That was two years ago, according to a newspaper article, and rush-hour commuters never noticed the child fighting his way along the road, pulling with all his might to save a dying dog.

"Give me a break," spat the hard-looking man in a tan Crown Victoria, and a gob flew from the window, landing on the 7-Eleven parking lot. "A little kid dragging a fully grown shepherd down the road and no one noticed?"

He stuffed the newspaper clipping back into the forward pocket of his sweatshirt while speaking to a dirty windshield and sipping at a Styrofoam cup. River Road was already gridlocked, and he figured that the more likely scenario was that hundreds of motorists had seen the child's act of mercy but that no one cared. That would be more typical of Bethesda, he thought, drivers who routinely cursed like cheated whores, making obscene gestures at the slightest provocation. And he remembered a lawyer who had slammed into the side of a school bus while leaking verbiage over his car phone, then later filed suit against the school district, citing the color yellow as a nonreflective road hazard. That was the suburban city he knew.

He eyed a pair of women in a red BMW who had pulled into the parking lot and were now swishing toward the door. The larger of the two seemed to have postnasal drip and was pulling at her front lip while tickling her gums with an index finger; classic signs of cocaine abuse. Dirty blond, dark blue designer threads, about five-eight, 155 pounds, slight scar on chin, Rolex-type watch, red fingernails. He let them pass, studying his reflection in the rearview mirror and grabbing a beaten pack of Marlboros from the dash.

His name was Frank Rivers. At thirty-eight his once-all-American appearance was fading fast into the worn flesh of middle age, producing a severe-looking man. His chin appeared hard and chiseled, the pleasing boyish eyes now seemed menacing, a piercing blue, almost deadly. His hair was thick, the heavy yellow of ripened corn with a thinning patch at the crown of his head that revealed a troubling scar that snaked outward like a pale worm. He licked a palm and batted the hair backward with both hands.

"Dispatch, this is One-Echo-Twenty," he stated quietly, holding a radio mike in his palm and thumbing the indent button impatiently.

"Go ahead, Echo-Twenty . . ."

"Wants and warrants"—he glanced at the plates—"Victor-Alpha-King 5-2-5, Maryland," he instructed, "BMW convertible 1987."

"Roger, Echo-Twenty." The radio went silent as Rivers returned to studying a folder marked *Jane Doe,* the case of an unidentified female, human remains found at County Plat 178, better known as River Bowl. He counted backward.

The remains had been exhumed last Tuesday, the case closed on Thursday. In two days the county medical examiner had identified the bones that Elmer Janson had unearthed as belonging to a girl who had died of unknown causes somewhere before the turn of the century, and that was all that was known. As of today, Friday, April 8, Rivers knew that the county authorities would be filing the bones away in some drawer, to be forgotten until another generation was cleaning through the M.E.'s warehouse. He returned to studying the news clipping, a story on Elmer's adventurous activities and those of his family. The article had appeared in the *Tempo* section of the major Washington paper the day after the boy's discovery, and Rivers gave it a good scan.

Elmer Janson's father was described as a jet-setter who preferred traveling through Europe to raising a child, and *Tempo* staffers pulled the stops to back that theory. "A real gambler," stated one source, "very hard-core." In addition, the boy's mother was an extra-special juicy item.

"She's a party girl, she doesn't care about that child," stated a neighbor who asked not to be identified. "It's all a

charade, a marriage of convenience. It's no wonder that boy is digging up graves. He should be placed in a home...."
Rivers dropped *Tempo* onto the seat and picked up a police report, then checked the news feature against the facts.

Elmer's mother had seen the grave and then called the Montgomery County police, who had notified the state, who had referred it to the M.E., who in turn had declared it all a worthless issue. Routinely, the case was being dismissed, and although Rivers had objected to his captain, he had been ordered to stay clear, on the claim that further investigation would burn precious man-hours.

Rivers shook his head. If the body had been interred one hundred years ago, how come Elmer Janson suddenly connected, finding the site, then digging it up? He checked for some type of dating on the bones—radiocarbon, isotopic tracing—but there was only a work order. The tests had not been completed. Since the county had failed to bring in a forensics crew to excavate in the first place, how were they to know this boy didn't find the body somewhere else and was just now disposing of it? And more important, why no one seemed to care about this dead child, no matter when she died, was even more of a mystery. While disturbing questions raced through his mind, Rivers started to grow angry at the insufferably weak detective work. Incompetence leapt from the official-looking pages.

"Dispatch to Echo-Twenty," a girlish voice said over the speaker, breaking his concentration just as the two women were leaving the store, heading for their car.

"One-Echo-Twenty, go ahead." Rivers spat, and his shiny gob sparkled from the pavement.

"Registration, BMW, Dr. Alan R. Munstein, no wants, no warrants," the dispatcher replied. Rivers' shoulders sagged as he watched the upper-class users pulling away. His jaw ticked. He felt like kicking them into the next world.

"Requests, Echo-Twenty?" the female voice asked.

Rivers hesitated. "Negative," he stated. "One-Echo-Twenty clear." He studied their faces as they glided past, edging toward a Montgomery County police patrol car, then stopping to flirt with that driver for a moment. They were higher than kites, giggling at each other like two schoolgirls.

The uniformed car pulled through the 7-Eleven lot, parked, and a large officer with a belted gut waved in a jaunty salute as he walked by. Halfheartedly Rivers returned the gesture, noticing with disgust that the patrolman's ample midsection was stained with tomato sauce.

"Get them carbos, Lardass," he said under his breath, waiting for the officer to pass. He started his engine and edged out from the parking lot. Placing a fireball on his dash, he pulled into traffic.

He checked his watch: 4:50. School had been out for an hour. He powered up his window and leaned into his siren as civilians cursed his approach.

Frank Rivers circled the block before making a final turn into the shopping center across the street from the abandoned bowling alley. As he stepped into the chill of late-afternoon shadows, he tightened the laces on each running shoe and discreetly studied the angle of the sun. It was a savory time for boys after school, he remembered, too early to think past dinner into homework, yet late enough to kill the pressures of new math, or whatever they called it these days. And if anyone understands little boys like Elmer Janson, that's me, he thought proudly. No boy with any spirit in him would be shut in on an early-spring day like this.

He quickly studied the layout of the building before deciding on his approach, around the back of a Mobil gas station. From the rise in the pavement he could look down into a caged clearing beyond a "NO DUMPING" sign into a trashed lot with fountains of weeds. He could just discern the figure of a young boy with light reddish hair sitting on a junked engine block, scratching the ground in lazy circles with a stick while stroking a large blond dog. Rivers gave a low whistle, then waited for the wind to carry it along. He nodded to himself as the dog raised a massive head.

The man trotted directly toward the building in a half jog, not slow, not fast, just sure and steady. From a distance the boy watched how easily he moved over busted concrete, glass, and litter—with a catlike certainty, a quiet power, almost deadly in purpose. As he came closer, Elmer saw the sharp blue eyes under a brow that was fixed in alertness, and he felt his heart beginning to race. The stranger was moving swiftly upon them, the eyes endlessly searching from side to side, taking it all in, missing nothing.

As the policeman jogged through a short ravine, skipping puddles of oil and battery acid, the boy stood suddenly, his heart racing, staring at the dark and foreboding figure that glided toward them. There was a laziness to his movement that suggested danger, an easiness of stride that suggested tension.

It was the tension of a pending trap, and even as the boy turned and started to run with fright, the man scaled the fenced compound with one powerful leap, landing lightly on his toes and blocking his escape.

Elmer Janson caught his own footing and tumbled backward as his dog growled through a quivering muzzle.

Rivers was standing to his full height inside the dump, instinctively keeping his hands where the shepherd could see them, palms outward, steady by his side. He leaned back against the fence and smiled, showing white even rows.

"That sure is a fine-looking animal," he said quietly, and his voice caused the fur on the dog's back to stiffen and ridge. Rivers watched intently as the boy applied a soothing stroke against the dog's fur, righting himself against the engine block at his back, then dusting himself off.

"I once had a bay retriever, but I don't think as smart as this one," Rivers continued, taking a step closer. "I'll bet he let you know I was coming even before I made up my mind."

The dog moved forward a foot in perfect balance, 100 pounds of menacing exposed fangs. "Easy, boy," the child whispered, stroking the dog's back while staring up at the stranger. "Sit," he said, and the dog obeyed.

Rivers waited. He had intentionally rushed the child, and the boy's heart was clearly thumping, his breath falling in short bursts. "Who are you?" the boy cried suddenly.

The stranger nodded thoughtfully at the question. "Well," he said slowly, "who do you think I am, Elmer, friend or foe?"

The mint-green eyes grew wide at the mention of his own name, and the boy began backing up onto the engine block.

Rivers smiled. "What are you thinking?" he asked, taking on a relaxed posture and pulling a smoke from inside his sweatshirt. He lit up with a flick of his thumb.

"I sure hope you're a cop!" the boy rattled, and his voice broke.

Frank Rivers felt a tickle. He smiled warmly. "You knocked it down on the first try, Rooster. I am a cop," he confirmed. And the boy quickly slipped his rump off the engine and stood, looking up at the tall policeman.

Rivers pushed his posture straight for effect. Although he

stood six-foot-one in socks, he regarded this as only slightly better than average.

"You don't look like a cop," the boy said cautiously. "The others I talked to were wearing suits and ties"—he glanced down at soiled cross-trainers with double knots in the laces—"and dress shoes." He then pointed at the red globe and anchor on Rivers' hooded gray sweatshirt. "You're a marine," he concluded worriedly.

Rivers studied the boy's eyes: they burned with the fires of intelligence. The child looked at him cautiously and then pulled himself back up onto the rusting block, with the big dog standing between them.

"I was a marine, Elmer," he said through a puff of smoke. "I'm a Maryland state police detective and I want to talk."

"And how do I know that?" he asked nervously. "You didn't make an appointment . . ."

Rivers exhaled a puff of smoke. "I'll show you my badge," he offered, "and my I.D."

"Do you carry a gun?" the kid asked, cutting right to the heart of the matter. He was now eyeballing the man's hip, looking for a bulge as the dog crept forward by inches.

Of course, Rivers thought, by this time he's seen so many badges he could care less. "Gun, badge, handcuffs, the complete kit," Rivers offered. "When I turn around, you can take a look, but don't get grabby. You move on me, and that dog of yours will eat my stones, do we have a deal?"

"Deal," the boy said, smiling for the first time.

Rivers turned, exposing his right side and lifting his sweatshirt to reveal a large automatic with ivory grips in a tan high-ride holster. It was no pedestrian police shooter. Alongside, two stuffed clip carriers were loaded with .45 hollowpoints, dark and deadly, and a set of Smith & Wesson cuffs in a leather pouch. When he turned back, the freckled face was smiling at him. Even the three-legged dog was thumping his tail. Rivers grinned. "Boys and dogs, weapons and secrets," he thought. "At least some things in this neurosis factory haven't changed."

"Can I see your badge?" Elmer asked shyly. He knew a good thing when he controlled it.

"No way, deal's over," Rivers said. "You've been staring at county tin, that should be good enough."

"They're a bunch of Twinkies. I wanna see *your* badge."

"Twinkies?" Rivers asked.

"Sugar and air." The boy smiled.

The detective chuckled: this child was old beyond his years. "You said you didn't care if you saw my badge. Your only interest is in fireworks."

"That was then."

"And this is now?" And he laughed, remembering those days when minutes crawled like snails. "No deal, Mr. Janson, I've got work to do." He started to walk away. Without losing a beat, the boy came following after, matching his stride as the dog ran ahead.

"Hey, there, please wait a minute, I got another deal for you . . ." he said, and his voice contained a certain loneliness. Rivers stopped abruptly, meeting Elmer's green eyes in a head-on blaze. "You let me look at your badge and I let you pet Tripod. He's smart, I've trained him to do tricks . . ."

Rivers stifled a laugh. "Is that his name, Tripod? That's a terrific name. Why, he looks like a Belgian shepherd."

"He's part wolf," the kid noted, upping the stakes.

"No shit?"

"No shit."

Then Rivers said, "Okay, you introduce me to Tripod and I'll let you have this for a while, but don't take off on me." He pulled a black leather case from inside the hand warmer on his sweatshirt and flipped it open. A seven-pointed star produced a brilliant yellow flash. "Deal?" he asked, offering the case.

"Wow," the boy said excitedly, grabbing the badge, then pulling the dog by the mane. "Tripod, this is . . ." He looked at the I.D. "Detective Sergeant Francis Dale Rivers, Maryland State Police, Bureau of Violent Crime . . ." His voice went shaky, trailing off.

"Frank to my friends," the cop said quietly.

The boy exhaled, staring at the gleaming star. "Right," he swallowed, "I'm Elmer Janson." He extended his hand, which Rivers shook with firm precision. "And this—" the boy tugged on the collar, pushing with one hip—"this is Tripod."

The shepherd sat up on hindquarters, exposing a white stomach. "He wants to shake hands," the boy suggested.

The policeman held his hand palm down under the dog's muzzle, then, bending at the knees, shook a furry right paw. "Well, you're a good old boy," he said. "Did you meet Rooster in that ravine I read about?" His fingers were scratching through the thick fur, and Rivers could tell that this dog was groomed often. Tripod was swinging his tail, kicking up a small dust devil.

The boy gave the badge a long admiring inspection, then dropped it into a deep pocket.

Elmer Janson, dog at his side, turned down the sidewalk and over a small grassy common with the detective following after, heading up a concrete walk toward the front stoop of the Jansons' compact town house. It was an expensive unit, free-standing with its own small yard and iron gate, and Rivers watched carefully as the boy removed a pocketknife from his pants pocket, then held up a key which dangled from a single ring; Tripod's tail slapped against his jeans as they hurriedly mounted the steps.

"Frank?" Elmer asked shyly, inserting the key into the door. While he had been insistent that Detective Rivers meet his mother, he now seemed uncomfortable with his own request.

"What's the trouble?" he asked thoughtfully, standing next to the steps where he could look directly into the boy's eyes. Elmer was nervously working his hands into fists.

"I just remembered I forgot my bike."

Rivers nodded. "After we speak with your mother, I'll walk back with you."

The child turned to the door and began reaching tentatively when he stopped again. "Frank," he suddenly sighed, "my mom asks a lot of questions . . ."

"I understand," Rivers said thoughtfully, considering his dilemma. "And she will ask you where you left your bike, and the bowling alley is off-limits?"

The boy nodded.

"Elmer," Rivers sighed, taking a step forward. "That's none of my business, but just this once, if she asks, I will refer the question back to you."

"Thanks," he said sincerely, turning back to grab his key, which suddenly veered away from his reach as the door swung wide and a woman appeared.

The dog stood in greeting, wagging his heavy tail with intensity. "Hi, Mom!" Elmer blushed quickly, dropping his hand as she swiftly glanced down at the stranger.

"Hello," she offered without expression, moving forward and reaching down for her child. She placed a gentle hand on his shoulder as Rivers' pulse immediately began to quicken.

Wrapped in a pink apron, covered with flour and crumbs, a truly beautiful woman stood before him: slim and curvy, her shiny blond hair tied on top of her head in a strange little ponytail. Rivers was sure his breath made an annoying sound as it left his body, and he swallowed against the fluttering he felt inside.

"Hello, Mrs. Janson," he said, unable to divert his eyes. Finally he remembered his mission and quickly patted through his pockets for a lump of identification. Elmer was already handing this to his mother.

"Mom," he announced proudly, "this is Frank, he's a state trooper."

She smiled only slightly, holding the badge in her right hand, scanning the particulars, then comparing the photo to the stranger before them. Her green eyes were like large sparkling pools dancing over Rivers, with a voice that was equally fluid.

"Has Elmer been playing at the bowling alley?" she asked with concern. Rivers chuckled quietly to himself, watching as she leaned down, handing back his credentials as his hands were just ending their search.

"Pleased to meet you, Mrs. Janson," he said, extending a hand in greeting, which she shook lightly, and he felt her cautious smile like a small tickle against his ribs.

"Jessica," she nodded at him.

"Mom," Elmer interjected, "can Frank stay for dinner?"

Rivers smiled. "I just stopped by to ask a few questions," he explained. "I thought we'd better check with you first."

At this Elmer cocked his head.

"You do know," she sighed, "that we've already spoken to the county detectives at some length?"

"I understand, Mrs. Janson, and I won't push. I used to live nearby, so I was just curious." He glanced down: the boy could barely hold still, his feet nearly vibrating as he tried to maintain his position. "He's quite a handful. It's good that he has a dog like Tripod."

Jessica was stroking the boy's fine hair, her green eyes filled with pride as she looked directly at the tall policeman. "Do you have any children?" she asked quietly.

Rivers shook his head. "No, ma'am, I'm not married."

"For the past several months Elmer's been an explorer, and before that it was stunt man," she explained. "He doesn't mean any harm."

"Oh, I know that, Mrs. Janson." Rivers smiled warmly. "I feel honored just to have met him."

She nodded.

"If it's all right, I'll walk with Elmer while he retrieves his bike, ask a few questions, and then I'll be on my way. I apologize for any intrusion." And Rivers felt her eyes covering him, seeing him clearly for the first time, summing him up. And he wondered what she saw, suddenly wishing that he had dressed better, when he realized he had been holding his breath. The pent-up air seeped from his lungs.

"You're welcome to stay," she offered, taking Elmer's hand as his excited voice filled in from behind.

"Thanks, Mom!" He grinned and snapped into motion, heading across the small porch for Rivers. "Hey, Frank," he offered with excitement, "we're having homemade pie for dessert . . ."

It was almost seven o'clock by the time he walked Elmer home, the boy pressing him again to stay for dinner. The detective could see the disappointment in his eyes when he declined the invitation.

"Some other time," he said, Elmer leading him by the hand, showing him the remains of a burned-out '64 GTO that had gone to rust since the old alley's heyday, when people drove muscle cars.

"And they'd bowl until the lanes closed, and drag-race all night," Elmer suggested.

The detective received the full tour, inspecting the pit where the bones were found, stomping on weeds that had sprouted through broken asphalt, examining every inch of the boy's hideaway. On the way home, Elmer, dog at his side, asked if he could keep the gold star. "Don't they give you extras?" he asked.

"No, a detective only has one badge and it's real gold, very valuable."

"Can we trade?"

"No deals on this subject."

But the kid came up with his best offer. "I have a coin that's real, real old," he said proudly. "This coin goes back to the Civil War, only one of its kind. I worked real hard for it."

"Then you should keep it, save it for a rainy day when you need to trade for something better."

Without warning the boy stopped, laying his bike on its

side, then turned to the buff-colored canine. "Tripod, sit!" he demanded. The dog obeyed, and Elmer unbuckled his leather collar and removed it. "Look here, Frank." He held the collar by one dog tag. "See this coin, I gave it to Tripod, says right on it: *The Union Must and Shall Be Preserved*!"

Rivers was fascinated. The coin was the size of a quarter. On one side there was a small house entwined by a serpent, with the word "BEWARE" at the bottom. It specified no denomination. He wondered where it had come from, what it was doing on the dog's collar. It really must have value. Did Elmer's parents know about it? Something smelled.

"It belonged to a slave," the small historian stated, "so it's worth a fortune. Let's trade!"

"I'm sure it is," Rivers said thoughtfully. "Where did it come from?"

"Between us?"

"Sure."

"And no one else?"

The detective sensed something amiss: the child was avoiding eye contact. He had been too eager, and was now reluctant. "Elmer, tell me where the coin came from. If there's a problem, I'll be able to help."

The evaluation of trust was not a slight matter, so as they walked the block toward the town houses known as Ridgewell Hamlet, Elmer mulled over the tall policeman in jogging clothes, the stories Frank had told him about Bethesda when he was a kid, especially about the bank robber whose car broke down and hitched a ride from him, and about River Road before the offices and shopping centers. This stranger had spent time with them, had trusted him with his only badge, and it wasn't a matte shield like the others. Frank Rivers was a real cop. And Tripod liked him. After all, the dog was the best judge.

"Promise you won't tell?" Elmer finally asked.

"I promise that if you ever need a partner, you can count on me."

The boy was anxious, dragging his feet, then he stopped and blurted, "I lied to those county cops." Just coming straight out with the truth. "And they asked for it," he added shyly.

"You did?" Rivers asked, crouching down, placing his elbows against his knees, and looking the child straight in the eye. "You lied about what, Elmer? Did you find the coin in the grave?"

He nodded. "They asked my mother if I found anything else and then she asked me, and that's ... secondhand ... like a rumor or something, like I wasn't even there. And I was told not to take part in rumors ... and so I said no. And that's it."

Rivers observed that there was an odd logic to his thinking. "All right," he probed, "that's what, exactly?"

"The coin!" Elmer stressed, a worried look crossing his face. Rivers noticed his green eyes had gone to glass, and tears were just under the surface. "That's what I lied about," he said solemnly. "The coin was chained to the body, only I didn't know that at the time. I really didn't. I told them Tripod found the bones. I have a metal detector, and—"

"You're not in any trouble, Elmer, no one's going to blame you for anything," Rivers cautioned. "I think I understand. You were working with your metal detector and this coin set it off?"

"Yes, sir," said Elmer, "and then I dug and it was right there, only it was attached to a chain, so I pulled it loose. Then, while I was cleaning it off"—his voice trembled—"Tripod started barking and that's when I found ..."

"The bones?"

The boy nodded.

"And don't you think you should tell me what else you found?"

The boy shook his head. "Some weird sticks is all, they were right on top, poking up next to the coin. I think slaves used them for trading."

Rivers was concentrating on a puzzle that was getting deeper and deeper. The boy was guilty of something, but what? "Elmer," he said, "why are you so sure these sticks and the coin belonged to slaves?"

The child squirmed. Then he took a deep breath and rubbed the back of his neck. He pinched his ear. Then he said, "The date on the coin is 1863 and this used to be the South, only rebels around here, and slaves. The rebs buried a slave there. I was grave-robbing."

Grave-robbing at a bowling alley? Rivers shook his head. The poor kid actually believed he had committed some crime. "Elmer," he said, "it's impossible to guess where that body came from, but you weren't grave-robbing, you were exploring, there's no law against that. Tell me about the sticks, how many are there?" he probed, finding a Marlboro and lighting it with a battered Zippo.

"Ten, but two are busted up," he explained. "Some were stuck real hard down in the dirt, and I had to get pliers to pull them out."

Rivers reflected on a passing reference in the county report to postmortem boring of the skull that was unexplained. "Sure would like to borrow your collection, if that's okay with you."

"Are me and Tripod going to get into trouble?"

"No trouble at all. In fact, I'll be back to see you in a few days."

"Great." A smile returned to his face. "Why do you want them?" he asked with an uncertain voice.

The tall policeman said, "Just fishing for a bigger catch. Ever been fishing?"

The boy shook his head.

Rivers tousled his red hair while leaning over to scratch Tripod's chest. "Then ask your folks if I can take you on a fishing trip."

Elmer beamed as he ran up the street for his house, the three-legged dog shadowing his every move, and Rivers watched them vanish up the sidewalk.

The thought of a dead child overlooked these many years and discarded beneath the once-busy parking lot didn't make sense. Over the past thirty years every square inch of Bethesda had been dug up at least once in the process of laying foundations for urban sprawl, and as far as he remembered, the bowling alley was no exception. No matter how he ran the equation—an archaeological site that had been missed by earth-movers, a Civil War child buried in the mists, a quickly fashioned grave for an ancient murder victim—the idea left a foul taste. And as Elmer had shown him, the site was shallow, nowhere near the six-foot depth required by health laws in the 1800's.

The duo was back before Rivers had finished his cigarette, and Elmer Janson was handing over a brown paper bag flecked with dried clay. "This is all I got," the boy puffed, catching his wind. "My mother says I have to come in . . . she has to talk to you again before we go fishing . . . can you stay for dinner? Please? Why won't you stay for dinner, Frank?"

"Some other time," he said, and heard the breath leave the boy's body as his lower lip began to quiver.

"What's wrong?" he asked quietly as Elmer turned to walk away.

"You believe all those lies about us," he stated sadly, and Rivers overtook his retreat with a single giant stride.

"Are you talking about that *Tempo* article?"

The boy gave a silent nod.

"That's just Washington talking to itself, don't take it seriously," Rivers offered, but still the boy's eyes were moist and questioning.

"Then why do they say things to hurt people, why do they print rumors?"

It was not the question that made Rivers pause, but the child's innocent voice poking at his heart. He thought, "Because they need fuel to burn, Elmer, food for their dirty engine. You don't want to understand their itch, how they cackle through the breakfast obituaries, how their thirst for human suffering is never quenched." He looked down at the child and stroked his hair.

"They hurt because they don't know any better," Frank Rivers said quickly, and he was gone, just a shadow among shadows in the day that was dying around them.

6

7:45 P.M. ROCKVILLE, MARYLAND

If it was noticed at all, then the Maryland state police substation on Rockville Pike had once been considered by civilians to be a desolate outpost at the edge of the world. The low-slung brick building was located on a tiny hill in the rolling countryside, far from the famed Washington Beltway with its growing suburban blight.

It had been a quiet little place until 1976, when vandals carted away the station's only Coke machine. In retrospect that act was a harbinger, sounding a big-city death knell for the highway-patrol ambience of the place. By 1980 the population had exploded, bringing the Maryland/District line over thirty miles to the substation's front door, and things changed, seemingly overnight.

Walls were torn down, additions were made, parking lots were paved, ceilings were raised, and decorators were hired to finish off the station's interior. Because of the strategic location to the sprawling cities of Bethesda, Rockville, Gaithersburg, and Wheaton, Substation 4 became headquarters for the Maryland state police, a regular police department no different from any other citified nerve center for trouble. Frank Rivers braced himself as he pushed through modern glass doors to face an insulting throng of humanity.

It was a plush and neatly appointed lobby for a police station, with wall-to-wall carpet, sofas and coffee tables, and idyllic landscapes of the countryside that had been plowed under. He entered to the competing sounds of dime-bag pushers, prostitutes clutching their credit-card presses, illegal aliens, thieves and pickpockets, speeders and drunks—every type of *Mook* imaginable after a routine day in the 'burbs. With bickering voices they were demanding their rights to a speedy process, demanding action from a detached bureaucracy incapable of quick solutions. Above the din was the familiar bark of uniformed Sergeant Sven Tompkins, a burly desk officer who handled complaints strictly according to number.

"Wait your turn!" Tompkins pointed a fat finger as a middle-aged man in a tailored suit approached. Rivers recognized him as an uninsured motorist. In places like Sub 4, Bethesda's true personality popped to the surface very quickly, and it was mostly unpleasant.

"Number thirty-one." Tompkins waved a ticket at the air and a family rushed forward, emptying two couches. Mother and father with five juveniles, all neatly dressed, parting around Frank Rivers like noisy ants around a tree. It had taken him the better part of an hour to drive twelve miles from Elmer Janson's house, so being curbed one more time didn't faze him. With a long reach he grabbed a fist of messages from the desk and raised his eyebrows at the weary sergeant.

"Check the can," the burly officer said, and Rivers moved forward with a nod, dodging civilians, stepping around toys and tots, through a double door and into a hallway leading toward the back of the building. He stopped at the men's room to relieve himself, and was standing at a urinal, giving a shake to help the flow, when he heard a strange moan drift up from the end of the blue stalls. He recognized the sound, which resembled a small animal's dying gasp.

"You okay, buddy?" Rivers asked with a smile.

"Goddamned gut," came a voice from a far booth as Rivers heard the telltale sounds of a Maalox bottle being popped and the pillow-sized pills being crunched by greedy molars.

"How ya feeling, Captain?" he asked calmly as he flushed. "It's Frank Rivers."

"Oh, hello, Frank. How'd the interviews go? Anything solid we can hook into?" Captain Maxwell Drury, head of the Maryland state police, had a voice that sounded like gravel being churned by a blender.

"You there, Frank?" he growled.

"Max, I've been looking into your Jane Doe, and you've got real problems," Rivers stated cautiously. "It's possible we've hit on a—"

"Oh, God, Frank!" he groaned, thumping the stall with a flat palm. "Is that what you've been doing?" Drury exclaimed. "Jane Doe isn't a case, it's an archaeological site. You've been away from your unit since two o'clock, and I told you to recheck sources on the Claytons. You were supposed to be in coat and tie talking to their neighbors. Why," he moaned from the can, "oh, why can't you follow instructions?"

Rivers leaned against the sinks, lighting a cigarette while waiting for the old man to finish. He shrugged in the awkward silence. "Listen, Max, the kid who found the bones was holding out. I need the complete path report, it's not in the files—"

"No! We've got real problems," Drury cut him off. "Frank, forget that shit. Please, I'm begging you ... I'm dying in here. Why do you torment me? The Clayton killing is heating up in the press and I've been dodging calls all day. God save us, wait till you see the news tonight, the maggots are having a field day with this. The funeral was a media circus ..." The captain popped another tablet and bit down.

"Max, I think this little Jane was tortured. I recovered implements," Rivers stated flatly.

"What?" Drury sucked air while chewing. "All right, Frank, what's this about?"

"The M.E. had a passing reference to cranial punctures in the report, only he said it was caused by worms or some sort like that, postmortem, long after death. I need to examine the skull."

"Oh no you don't, Frank!" the voice boomed, echoing. "That bag of bones is small enough to fit in one hand. Forget it, she's been dead a hundred years, can you hear me? We don't have time. It's all very unpleasant, but it would prove nothing."

Rivers heard the toilet flush and turned toward the mirrors, checking his smile. Captain Drury appeared, his face ashen and drawn. He was a small but neatly dressed man, balding on top with a crew-cut fringe that was going gray. His marine-green uniform was hand-tailored and heavily gilded with stars on the epaulets. He shot Rivers a hot glance in the mirror as he stooped, adjusting the flow of tap water.

"You've got two detectives on the Claytons, Max, what's a few moments of my time? Besides, a carbon test was ordered on this, and hasn't come back."

Drury shook his head despairingly. "Let's say she was murdered. That means the killer lived a full life and died in his sleep—fifty years ago, Frank!" Drury reestablished eye contact with Rivers, who was fidgeting with a paper bag. "If I didn't know better, I'd say you're trying to throw the investigation off. This is very counterproductive."

The detective pulled a handful of towels from a white dispenser and handed them to Drury. The captain soaked one and then patted his face, neck, and the top of his head. In the meantime Rivers quickly removed one of Elmer Janson's dowels from a bag, examining it for a second time.

There were ten of them, all identical, like chopsticks. They were four-sided and thick at one end, then tapering down into tips sharp as ice picks, even after being buried in wet clay for so many years. He balanced it across his finger, and gravity pulled it downward at the point, or what he guessed was the point.

"They look like small spikes, Captain," he said slowly, trying to gain Drury's attention. "We saw something similar in sixty-eight. Used in conjunction with wet rope, it's real effective for obtaining information. I remember a guy we found from the Third Platoon, he was still talking when—"

The captain glared at him. "Korea was nasty too, Frank," he muttered. "I'm putting you on narcotics first thing tomorrow. I'm really quite angry about this."

"Max," Rivers said cautiously, "who's your agency pal who's reviewing the Claytons?"

"Frank, why are you pushing me?" He turned to the detective. "I've got serious problems."

"Just kick it into the system and let's see what falls out."

Drury cringed sharply, staring at him, then rubbing an aching belly with one hand.

"Have you seen these bones?" Rivers asked, shadowing him out the door, just one step behind, down the hall, and into his private office. Drury sighed, shaking his head, returning to his swivel chair just as a secretary came forward and handed him a form. He quickly scanned a narcotics search warrant while reflecting on Frank Rivers. Drury knew his subordinate's game: attrition. The bastard enjoyed wearing other people out.

"Yes I have, Frank," he said calmly. "I've seen the bones and there's nothing there, you're pissing into my ear." At which point he signed his name across the wrong line. "Dammit!" he spat, staring at the form, then handing it to a tall female officer in state greens.

"I'm sorry," he said, "can you white it out?" The woman smiled weakly, carrying the warrant out through the doors as Drury eyed Rivers' sheepish grin.

"That's it, Frank, one more chance. You canvass the Clayton neighborhood first thing tomorrow."

"Tell him, please."

"Tell who?"

"Tell your friend. I heard from dispatch that ViCAT's involved, it's no big secret. Didn't you train with these graybeards?"

"One graybeard, Frank, may you live so long."

"Tell him, Captain, I've got a bad feeling about this—"

"Sweet Jesus, tell him what, Frank?" Drury jumped to his feet and started pacing angrily behind his desk. "Tell him that I can't control my troops? I've got a bad feeling too, right here"—he slapped his belly—"a feeling that this sickoid will kill again, and if not here, then somewhere else. So what do you want me to tell him, that I'm really quite upset with you?"

Rivers looked Drury hard in the eye. "Max, I don't know what I've got, but I sure as hell got something," he pleaded. "Tell him that the generations may ring true, like father, like son, like grandson, like great-grandson . . . Hell, Captain, I don't know what to say, or I'd say it. Just tell him us Smokeys don't believe in coincidence—that we got one very bizarre murder on our hands less than a mile from where the Claytons were killed."

"Yes, Frank," Drury said with dripping sarcasm. Turning

back to his desk, he sifted through the pink message slips that had mounted there, dealing some into the trashcan.

"Can you afford not to?"

Drury ignored him.

"And what if you're wrong, Max?" he pushed, his voice filled with a quiet but troubled rejection.

Captain Drury thought it over for about as long as it took Frank Rivers to leave the room.

7

6:10 P.M. SARASOTA, FLORIDA

"What a bitch," hissed Gregory Corless, a soft, obese man of about fifty, as he walked from Bakker's Diner on Interstate 41. It was still a balmy seventy-two degrees, about average for early April. The index finger of his right hand kept disappearing into cheeks that were naturally puffy and red as he picked Irish stew from between his front teeth. "Did you hear what she said when I asked for a toothpick?"

"No, Greg, I didn't," answered Seymour Blatt, a thorn of a man with a thin neck and large larynx that resembled a rock stuck in a rubber pipe.

"Buy a toothbrush," Corless snarled. "The bitch told me to buy a fucking toothbrush."

"I stiffed her," Blatt returned as they crossed the parking lot.

"You can't get stiff."

Corless sneered as Blatt instantly blushed at the insult. "I tipped her five percent, she's a one-dollar whore."

"Well, what she needs," Corless paused, "is a good beating and a hard fuck." The duo stopped alongside a white Dodge van as Corless fumbled in pastel blue pants that were too tight for his heavy build. Producing keys, he then slid the bay loading door open. He retrieved a dark blue sports jacket with shiny gold buttons that was hanging on a hook.

"Should I drive?" Blatt asked.

"You read the map," Corless hissed, putting on his jacket. "Let's get clean."

And together, like a drill team, they swept through the cab, tossing out wrappers and empty cups and old newspapers that they had gathered along their journey. Seymour Blatt was checking under the driver's seat when his hand touched one of Greg's trophies, and he remembered the taunting voice that Corless had used on him all day.

"Better rip this up before we throw it out," he said, the lump in his throat bobbing as he talked. Gregory Corless glanced up from the carpet at the picture of a girl, naked except for a collar and leash. His fat face froze into a mask of hate.

"I'll kill you," Corless said in a relaxed voice. "I'll kill you until you beg me to die!"

Without a word Seymour Blatt placed the picture back where he had found it, under Greg's custom seat, and not in the box with the others in the back of the van. He was too scared of Corless to question anything he said. With a gun or a knife or a club in his hand, fat Corless was the most frightening man he had ever seen, a natural Santa Claus with a passion for hate and violence. If there was one thing he knew about his partner, it was that Gregory Corless never threatened something he was not prepared to deliver.

"Just kidding," Blatt sniffed.

"Check on her," Corless ordered as he moved behind the wheel and fastened his seat belt.

Blatt pulled back the curtain between the seats and slapped the form wrapped in an old blanket behind where his partner sat. There was a whimper and some movement.

"She's okay," Blatt offered, turning back, then opening the Rand McNally. The fat man was staring at him in contempt.

"Last chance," he stated tonelessly.

But Blatt did not respond, he just stared out the window at the people eating in the wayside diner. He had done a lot of that on his previous expedition with Fat Corless, stare at other people. And he wanted to say right to his face for all the abuse he had taken that day: "You aren't what I look at, Corless. You're just an obese and ugly fat man." But instead he remembered Greg's courage to make real what to others remained fantasy. His strongest suit.

"I spoke with Maxine before we left." Blatt's smile showed frail grayish teeth that looked small for his mouth. "She said Donald has been accepted to Yale—"

"Ah, sweet Maxine, my wife, my dream," Corless interrupted with a song as he started the engine and pulled away. "All she cares about is having one of our children graduate from Yale. She never even considers the cost, twenty thousand a year, did you know that? And this time next year I'll have all three kids in college at the same time. Where does it go?"

"Money?"

"The time, you idiot." He shook his round head, covered with a cheap black wig.

"Goes fast, Greg, they're still babies in my mind."

"And I was going to buy a Beechcraft jet when I retired. Just think of the possibilities . . ." His voice trailed off. "I don't see that coming for a long, long time now."

"You'll do it," Blatt assured in a perky voice. "You're the envy of the flight club."

"You're right," he quickly agreed, "but it's just not the same as owning your own plane—a nice one, that is."

"You'll find a way."

And the three riders moved forward in silence, up a ramp and back onto the interstate, heading south toward the Florida Keys.

During dinner they had avoided rush hour.

They were making good time.

8

9:05 P.M. LONG ISLAND, NEW YORK

Scott coasted slowly through a neighborhood in Greenlawn letting his headlights soak a few lawns as he looked for signs of spring, for signs of renewal. Things were going green in the yard across the street, flowers blooming next door. But Jack Scott's perennials merely pitted flowers against squirrels, resulting in a mangled, multicolored row that led to his front door.

The rain had ended. He parked his blue Chrysler in the driveway, removed a heavy black briefcase from the trunk, and walked, tamping with an angry right toe while moving slowly up the path, cursing at each half-eaten crocus bulb. "Nasty little bastards." He sneered, kicking wet earth into a hole.

The house was the oldest in the area, a two-story Victorian, and it had been home to the Scotts for three decades. Linda, his wife of thirty-six years, had left the portico light on for him, and he opened the door to an emptiness that seemed to buzz from hidden recesses. In years past Scott had arrived to a mad concert of televisions blasting at record players competing with telephones, and the pounding of feet against stairs, rolling after him with the turmoil of adolescence: anxious questions and despairing tears, every triumph and failure, the fabric of a family. Their lives were melded with the old house, and to Jack Scott that silence was deafening.

With his right hand he entered a sequenced code on a soft button pad, disarming the alarm system, and he thumbed through the mail on an antique library table. A few bills specifically for him, and a postcard. He studied this for a moment, staring at a moonscape with mountains and cacti, then a signature. "Jody's in the desert," he said sarcastically, dropping the card back into a decorative silver bowl. "Who the hell is Jody?"

He popped the briefcase open, tucked a file beneath his arm, and headed toward the kitchen, where he dropped his wet shoes by the rear door. A note was posted on the almond-colored refrigerator with a shell magnet—the cooler served as both feeding station and information center.

"Dinner," it said. "Heat chops for three mins. on medium, apple sauce in white bowl, make some rice." He grabbed the message and continued to read while digging through an assortment of bottles and containers.

"You forgot Bill and Judy's party," it went on, and Scott winced, lifting a plate covered with plastic wrap, two thick lamb chops cooked many hours before. He searched deeper for mint jelly.

"Matt Brennon has called you twice, eat first." Scott didn't bother to heat the food, but laid it out cold on the table. Removing his jacket with one hand, he then peeled off a shoulder holster and slung the blue steel and gun leather across the back of his chair. He spooned apple sauce into his mouth, filling both cheeks, letting the coolness slide down his throat.

"And Jody," the note explained, "is the behavior analyst you consulted with on the Meade case two years ago, he's semiretired to Arizona. He's fifteen years younger than you are, John."

Scott shook his head. Linda knew him better than he knew himself. He began spooning green jelly over the chops, slicing the cold meat into slivers that in his mind simply tasted like home. Slicing more, slurping sauces, fueling a worn and tired body that had all but forgotten about food, when the phone rang. He picked it up on the fourth ring.

"Commander Scott," he stated firmly, walking the phone from countertop to table.

"Have you eaten, Jack?" asked Agent Brennon.

"What's up?"

"A couple of wrinkles you should know about. We've re-run the crime-scene data through the Mix Master ..." He paused, wondering if the news could wait until morning.

"Yes," Scott interrupted, lifting a spoon of applesauce. "And it said to start looking for a police officer."

"You knew that?" Brennon startled.

"No," Scott answered flatly, "one never really does know. It's just logical, the killer has made a study of police science. What better way to enjoy the pleasures of slaughter than learning to work with a skilled impunity? Did you push the program?"

"Until I thought it would implode, Jack. The computer comes back negative every time. This jerk doesn't even hint at any of our known offenders, so I think you should help me with postmortem behavior, what he did after the killings, so I can build a profile. Tomorrow, I mean, maybe we'll get a hit against some other behavior."

"It's a waste of time," Scott assured him. "I already ran the positions in which the bodies were found, looking for similar criminal behaviors in the existing population. It came back empty, and that's all we have left to run. Every move this bastard takes is aimed at erasing evidence. He kills the way an artist paints: conception, imagination, technique, method, organization. I've broken down each step, every move, and behaviorally we've got a cop."

"Bastard," Brennon mumbled.

"I'll give you an example of what's left—that is, if you're looking at the reconstruction," Scott offered.

"Sure," Brennon responded, sitting up at Scott's desk, staring at the display of horrid photographs mounting up and across on each other.

Scott breathed deeply. "Take it from the beginning, which is crime-scene forensics, farthest left. It only gets worse from there."

Brennon agreed, looking at a picture of the living room,

champagne-colored carpeting, a baby grand piano, plush sofas.

"You knew our offender doubled back to rough up the carpet where he had stepped, erasing footprints, compromising any accurate estimation of body weight and height determination. Who but a professional would have that kind of critical knowledge of our best technology?"

"I programmed all of that in."

"Yes, Matt, I'm sure you did, but I intentionally withheld how he accomplished this task, hoping we'd get a match from a more general approach, and I tried not to bias your interpretation. Count nine photos from the left, moving through the kitchen toward the back door, what do you see? There's an enlargement."

Brennon's eyes flicked from room to room, Tofu's body lying on the table, an empty cage, a kitchen door where Kimberly's parka had hung, and something blurred, something fuzzy. The last shot was an enlargement of a vacuum cleaner on the back of the kitchen door, strung on a hook next to Leslie Clayton's green ski jacket.

"Jesus," Brennon exclaimed. "That fucker knew how to . . ."

"He really took his time, Matt. That's Diana Clayton's Hoover upright, which she kept in a broom closet on the other side of the room. He kept track of the areas where he had walked, and on his way back out used the vacuum. He took the dirt bag with him. That's rather telling, in two ways. Not only does he know about microforensics, he knew enough about Diana to trust her vacuum cleaner, which was in perfect working order, otherwise he'd have brought his own."

"God save us, Jack." Brennon swallowed. "Is there anything we could have missed, an additional motive perhaps?"

"He left two twenties and a five in the master bedroom, along with a flawless one-carat diamond ring, he could care less. Did you read the field interviews from Captain Drury?"

"Sure did," he sighed. "They're detailed, Drury's got some good people. There were no other keys to the house outstanding, including neighbors. The locks are first-rate, registered, installed by a bonded company, and the serial numbers checked against a technician, who happened to be a female locksmith, married, four children. The Claytons had no known male companions. And no one saw or heard anything. A quiet neighborhood."

"It's grim," said Scott, "a hand dealt by the devil. It reminds me of one of my first cases, when police science was still in its infancy, a serial sex killer who subscribed to the *FBI Law Enforcement Journal* through a public library. This is not a good feeling for me . . ." His voice started to drift.

"I don't remember hearing about that . . . Holy Jesus!" Brennon said suddenly, having wandered some distance from the wall and taken in the whole photographic collage for the first time. "You've formed a cross, Jack."

"What?"

"You've laid out a cross on the wall, a crucifix."

Scott pulled back from his subconscious, finding a smile in his voice. "That's because I haven't finished yet, smart guy," he said. "I have two more sequences left."

But Scott didn't really; he was finished. On the wall he had left empty patches reserved for Kimberly and Leslie Clayton—he couldn't force himself to post those graven images. If their short lives had meant anything, it was that other children and other families would be safe from this obscene destruction.

"How long have you known Captain Drury?" Brennon asked.

"Why?"

"He's called several times, but keeps saying not to disturb you, and that smacks of a long-term relationship. Just keeping my wits sharp."

"Very good, Matthew," Scott responded. "Maxwell Drury and I went through the Federal Law Enforcement Training Academy together about thirty-six years ago. I better call him, poor sorry bastard. Running a police agency in the Washington area is akin to managing an insane asylum under a full moon. His whole jurisdiction swarms with the most important people on earth—just ask them."

"He's grasping for straws."

"So are we."

"But his last call was about an archaeological find, the guy is desperate. They're pushing at the envelope, he admitted as much."

"I'll call him. What about archaeology?"

"He said a site was uncovered beneath a parking lot that's near the Clayton house. Civil War it looks like, he said you should know."

"I should. I told Drury I wanted information on anything

that seemed out of the ordinary, especially in the immediate area. What else do we have?"

"He said the bones date back to the mid-1860's."

"What bones?" Scott barked. "You didn't say anything about bones."

"That's what an archaeological site is, Jack. Relax, it doesn't relate."

"And how do we know that? An important person tell us?"

Brennon sighed and reached into his hip pocket for a black-cased notebook. He started flipping pages. "Skeletal remains of a child were discovered by a boy sweeping with a metal detector behind a condemned structure. The boy thought he was digging for treasure when he hooked a jawbone. His mother called the county, who called the local police, who called—"

"Metal detectors don't register bone, Matt. What exactly did this kid find?"

"Hell, I don't know, Jack. This all took place last month. The kid found the site, his mother called the county, and a set of human remains were picked up by the medical examiner's office. One of Drury's detectives also found a Civil War coin."

Scott had lost interest in the story, except for the sloppy field procedure, which was unlike Drury. He was by-the-book, a real detail man. "Why wasn't the coin recovered with the remains?"

"Sorry, Jack, I don't know." He glanced back at his notes. "On the day the bones were reported, March 25, the county medical examiner performed the usual routine. A small female, one century worth of dead."

"You're not answering my question, Matthew."

"Right," he sighed. "I'm not sure I can. The coin was just recovered today, looks like pure enterprise work. After the case was closed, a state detective read the field report and went to see the boy. Drury didn't know what he was up to, so technically this detective wasn't assigned. I guess the guy was just curious, I understand he grew up in the area."

"Go on," Scott said, holding the phone to his ear, searching through the refrigerator for dessert.

"Here it is, Jack, *Archaeology*. I just found the definition under garbage from the past, relics, forgotten monuments—the study of ancient life and boring cultures, lost civilizations." His voice became flush with cheer. "Ah, yes, come away with Indiana Scott to those golden years of yesterday. Send now to ViCAT Old World Video and you will also receive—"

"You're a very funny guy, Matt." Scott found what looked like a slice of leftover cheesecake, which he placed on the table.

"So how was your meeting?" Brennon poked, changing the subject. "That fulfills our service requirements for the quarter."

"They were very attentive," Scott said, smiling, digging into strawberry cheesecake, and flushing down a bite with a glass of milk. "Tell me about the coin, Matthew."

Brennon looked at his notes. "Not much to tell," he said. "According to Drury it was made during the Civil War. There wasn't any other metal found, no belt buckles or buttons, just a few inches' worth of silver from a necklace."

"And the boy's discovery of this coin resulted in recovery of the bones?"

"Right."

"Where are they on the autopsy, how far along?" Scott was focusing on the last sweet mouthful.

"Jack," Brennon laughed, "they don't do autopsies on fossils. Neither do we, so I thanked Drury for the information and got off the line. They also uncovered some utensils made from a black wood . . ."

Scott froze as an image suddenly tore through his mind, a horrid and painful image vanquished for years. He felt his body go stiff.

". . . and that's it, Jack. But I think you should talk to Drury."

Scott closed his eyes and swallowed at the pounding behind his temples.

"Jack?" Brennon asked.

"Was it sharp?" he asked flatly. "This utensil, was it sharp?"

Brennon sensed alarm. "I can't say," he said, confused. "What gives?"

"What do they look like?" Scott's tone and blood pressure climbed, his knuckles were turning white against the phone, and he changed hands.

"What are you asking me, Jack?"

"The wooden utensils, what do they look like?"

"There's just one, a shaft or fork or something, I don't

know. I think Drury said it looked like a chopstick, a black chopstick."

Scott winced, then cleared his throat. "Chopsticks," he stated flatly.

"Right, that's all he said."

"It couldn't be . . ." Scott's breath fell loose as he pressed his ear into the phone. "Were they fire-hardened? Blackened from fire?" His voice rose sharply.

Matt Brennon took a step backward.

"Talk to me," Scott pressed, now angry. "The stick, there was only one? Are you sure? Was this crime-analysis team comprehensive? They didn't cover everything, they didn't take this seriously, did they?" His face was flushed with blood, and a tide of rage pulsed through arms, legs, torso.

Brennon swallowed hard. "They didn't send in a team, Jack. Like I told you, first a few guys from the M.E.'s office, that was last month, and today some detective followed through. What is this? Do you want me to get further information on the stick?"

"No," Scott said, suddenly quiet and resolute. "Who was this detective, the one you said enterprised in the field?"

"I don't know."

"Track him down, I want his complete state and federal records on my desk in an hour. Have them faxed from Washington, and don't trip his wire. I want to know this man, where he lives, how he lives, his home phone, everything. Don't forget tax data, school records, and military service. And call Drury immediately, talk only to him. I want stats of this stick, we'll handle the interpretation. Get copies of the coin too, and this is very important," he said slowly, "I don't want those human remains touched any further, understand? If they have a photographic sequence of the unearthing, let's get that."

"Yes sir," Brennon snapped. "Is this in some way related to Diana Clayton and her children? Is this detective a suspect?"

But Scott didn't hear the questions. "I'll be there as soon as I can," he said, blind to the outside world, operating on instinct as he hung up the phone. In his mind he was seeing faces, once forgotten, and their words were soft and kind.

"She's not coming back," the voice repeated.

Scott ignored the comment, lighting another cigarette. "Nothing to do for her now, nothing left to do for her family," was his thought. "No words of comfort, no assurance of police protection, no psychological counseling. Nothing." And he was filled with despair, just another fool strapped in a watch and counting the minutes, waiting for her to die.

Mary Beth Dodson was sixteen years old. A machine was breathing for her now, and once again Scott could hear the pistons of the artificial lung plunging, driving air into her broken rib cage. He stood at his kitchen window and remembered with a terrible clarity—the girl's pale and beaten face, the movement of the hands batting at the air as if chasing away deadly insects—just as he knew he would remember it during every weak and insufferable turn of his life. Remember. How Mary Beth's eyes had stayed open, stretched with terror but unable to see. From the waiting room outside came the sobbing from parents and siblings.

Scott turned away from the bed to the hospital window as they began strapping her down, and he watched a mad parade filing past: doctors, nurses, technicians, and visitors. Some were smiling, greeting each other, walking arm in arm, unaware of the horror he was living with. As he walked from the room his eyes briefly met those of Mary Beth's father, his steely silence sharper than any words of blame. Scott hesitated a moment, then pushed himself toward the end of the hospital corridor. Dr. Chet Sanders, director of internal medicine, found him a moment later.

"Jack," he called softly, a towering man with tan wrinkled skin. Sanders stood attentively in a blue surgical gown, patting blood from his shirt sleeves, removing a gauze mask.

"There's still hope," Scott answered, refusing to make eye contact. Mary Beth Dodson was the only victim to have survived an attack by a sadistic killer who had stalked the suburbs of New England for several years.

"She's too badly beaten, Jack. The meninges," he explained, "the protective membranes enveloping the brain and spinal cord, have been punctured, and she was shaken so hard that her brain literally bounced within the skull case. It's swelling too rapidly. The next stage will be multiple organ failure."

Scott's gray-blue eyes flashed with violence. "There's still hope," he stated again through clenched teeth.

Dr. Sanders laid a gentle hand on his shoulder. "If we could control the swelling, she'd have a chance, but I'm afraid that's beyond control. For all practical purposes she was dead when you came through the door. I'm sorry."

The young woman had been missing for ten days when Commander Nicholas Dobbs and Special Agent Scott had narrowed their search to within a single neighborhood. She was found in the closet of an abandoned building.

"You look tired, Jack, you've lost weight. There's nothing you can do here . . ." Sanders was saying. "If she did survive, she would have severe brain damage. That's not a life. You've done all you can. It's better this way—"

"Yes, better . . ." Scott interrupted, his voice mechanical, lighting a cigarette end-to-end from another one. He rubbed his eyes with fingertips yellowed from nicotine.

"Jack, I've been treating patients for thirty years, some that have been ripped apart like this one. Take some advice . . ."

Scott breathed deeply.

"Heal thyself," said the doctor.

Scott turned, his eyes burning. "What are you saying to me?"

"How old are you, Jack?" The words bubbled back from beyond time.

"Twenty-seven."

The aged medical practitioner leaned his tall frame from the waist, until Scott felt his breath against his face. "Take some advice from an old man," he whispered. "You must learn to detach yourself clinically, or you will not survive your work."

Scott looked up into eyes that were pools of pained wisdom. "Inside"—Dr. Sanders thumped Scott's chest—"you must learn to walk away or you will lose your humanity. All that protects us is our training, our jobs, and we must remember them at every instant without exception."

Scott rubbed the back of his neck, for suddenly he felt very cold.

"The moment you stop thinking like a cop," Sanders continued, "or I stop thinking like a doctor, we lose the ability to practice effectively. And that is the worst failing of all, I believe. If we faced this brutality like normal men, we would lose ourselves to our own caring, to our own pain."

Scott studied the horror behind Dr. Sanders' quiet demeanor, etched in the lines on his face.

"But I did fail, and now this bastard will be going after a

seventeen-year-old, any seventeen-year-old. What are my chances now?"

Chet Sanders pulled the cigarette from between Scott's fingers and snuffed it into a standing ashtray. "Jack," he promised, "you will get him, and you'll do so with a system that's designed to fail—" Suddenly Scott's statement brought him up short.

"Why seventeen?" he asked incredulously.

Scott paced, hate erasing the humanity from his face. It was a younger man with blue-gray eyes and thick blond hair who was talking now—the older man at his kitchen window could see himself clearly.

"He's playing a sadistic game, and I think he's playing it for me," Scott said quietly. "Mary Beth Dodson was the last victim, she's sixteen," Scott explained. "Genie Katz was fifteen. Lora Baker, fourteen. Linda Carr, thirteen. We haven't found the others. Our man is working his way up chronologically, claiming a victim for every year, like a trophy. Seventeen would be next."

Dr. Sanders rubbed both hands into his eyes, letting air seep slowly from his mouth as Scott smiled weakly. "Chet, what else do we have?" he asked nervously, lighting another cigarette.

Dr. Sanders reached into his coat pocket. "The patient has a punctured lung, low"—he pointed to his own sixth rib— "and that tear seems to extend down to the third lobe of the liver, which is very deep. We removed this during surgery," he said, holding up a wooden dowel sealed in plastic and handing it to Scott.

"What is it?"

"A clue, Jack, I really have no idea."

"And this was stuck in her lung?"

"Lung and liver. It took a great deal of force to drive it there."

Scott winced. "Then the trauma was caused by stabbing?"

"Possibly, but I don't think so—at least not with a hand motion. The wound was too clean and without surface bruising."

Scott slipped it into a pocket as Sanders pointed at his cigarette. "I just received a paper from Sweden that suggests a relationship between that and cancer," he said. And Scott remembered as the harsh smoke drilled his lungs, throwing off other, more burning sensations.

Mary Beth Dodson died that evening, September 5, 1960.

Dr. Chet Sanders was felled by a heart attack in 1963 at the age of fifty-two.

And Jack Scott felt the haunt of time in the arthritic ache across his knuckles. He left the house an old man with his familiar ghosts, driving into a night that could not have been more alone.

9

10:12 P.M. NEW YORK CITY

Under Matthew Brennon's watchful eye, Agent Flores advanced from his usual place at the periphery and took up the command position in the cutout center of an enormous circular desk. The surface had been recently padded and given a fresh coat of battleship gray, but the desk itself was a relic, pirated from an old evening daily. This position was known as the slot. It was the hot seat, the heart of ViCAT, and Daniel Richard Flores had been months in standby, working the outer rim with his training officer and waiting.

Eventually every ViCAT agent served here, surrounded by green computer screens. There were eight of them, representing each region of the country, divided by two. Just above the slot, near eye level and suspended from the ceiling, was imaging equipment, fax machines, and an array of recording equipment. In many ways taking up the position was like sitting at the control board of a missile silo, and emotionally it was a lot more dangerous. An hour never passed without a direct challenge with potentially horrid consequences.

"If you can't answer a question or if you don't know the correct response from computer templates, just have them stand by," Brennon instructed. "It's always better to wait than to give a wrong response. If it's an emergency request, if the information is critical, one of us will always be here. Always check the duty sheet when you come in so you'll know who's available."

"How about Commander Scott?" Flores asked. "When is it proper to call on him?"

Brennon raised an eyebrow and smiled. "Believe me," he said, "you'll know because your gut will tell you. His home is line one on the redial." He pointed to a keypad, then continued to collect forms and dossiers pouring in from a dozen different agencies that were answering a blanket ViCAT request. The outer rim was starting to take on the appearance of an embassy shredding room during enemy assault. There were papers everywhere, which Flores was methodically checking off from a shopping list of demands.

"Six years' worth of tax returns from eighty-two through eighty-seven," Brennon said, shuffling a stack. "And four motions to postpone payment." He held up one sheet and chuckled. "Where does Jack find them?" he laughed. "Look at this." He pushed the paper across the rim to the slot. "This guy declared a losing season for the Washington Redskins as grounds for a tax hardship and ended up paying a six-hundred-dollar fine."

"That's an expensive sense of humor," Flores agreed.

The pieces of Frank Rivers' life were being assembled into a composite that started with his first public record, an application for a Social Security number, lacking a date, bearing his father's signature. From the Defense Intelligence Agency came a demanding form requiring an official justification for his records—bureaucrats buggering bureaucrats, Brennon thought, and he put that aside in a special pile. Surprisingly, the CIA admitted having a file, and fired off a quick fax of Rivers' Marine Corps discharge, which Brennon thought a bit odd, for there was no record of direct employment. JRS, a check assurance company, complied with a complete financial history, most of it average for a cop, but claiming bad paper for a fifty-dollar Chinese dinner. A bell chimed a gentle alert through the chamber, not unlike a doorbell, and Brennon walked around the rim as Flores put on his headset with microphone.

"It's Duncan Powell in Florida," Brennon explained, recognizing a series of alpha numbers scrolling across screen number two, the United States southern region. All that was required for accessing ViCAT was an ongoing case with a previously assigned code, and the recruit punched his authorization onto the pad. A hard disk whirred as green characters began filling the video void. Brennon pressed an intercom button.

"Duncan," he said tonelessly, "we are receiving your file now."

"Reporting Case 117," a deep voice responded. "We believe we have a sixth victim."

Brennon pointed a finger at the younger agent, who was waiting at the keyboard. Tape had begun rolling the instant the phone line was opened. For the past month Daniel Flores had studied the coordination of Multi Agency Investigative Teams, or MAITs, as they were known; using high-tech equipment and analysis that was made available nonstop to agents in the field. Calls were constantly being received, updating or requesting information, seeking emergency advice on the behavior patterns of violent repeat offenders. As was the case with Duncan Powell, the state contact was usually the local chief of police, although that varied depending on jurisdiction.

"I'd like to introduce Daniel Flores, who is handling the slot tonight," Brennon offered. "This is Captain Duncan Powell of the Florida state police . . ."

The two men quickly exchanged greetings as Matthew Brennon walked back to the rim and began assembling stacks of paper. Flores spun in the slot just in time to see Brennon leave the chamber.

The detached voice of a stranger boomed through his ears: "Victim discovered four-eight, twenty hundred hours, description as follows." As he spoke, a photographic transmission hovered overhead like a black wing, sharpening into a focused image. Flores saw a young girl who had been beaten into disfigurement.

"We believe her attacker is repeat offender Case 117. Our postmortem investigation has just begun, but the victim has the same unusual odor emanating from the oral cavity. We would like assessment for your possible interdiction into this case."

Powell described the victim as four-foot-two, with short brown hair, hazel eyes, and a light complexion, although Flores knew they would never have been able to tell from the body. He guessed they were operating from a missing-persons list and had obtained a potential match from more obvious physical characteristics.

"Probable name, Lisa Darlynne Caymann, DOB 7-1-81. Reported missing 3-27, Clearwater, Florida. Parents' address, 1606 McDowell, subdivision Silver Shores. Salient details as follows . . ."

Agent Flores had retrieved a computerized registration of

missing persons that had been compiled for the five-county Florida area, and had found the name. He punched in a code and read quickly. Lisa Caymann had been abducted in the daytime from her backyard, where she had been using a swing set. Parents and relatives had been cleared as potential suspects. Her mother, Denise, had gone into the house to answer the phone. When she returned, her child was gone. Flores bit a lower lip and waited for a hard copy of Lisa Caymann's portrait to materialize.

"Location and general position of victim as found?" Flores asked, his voice trembling.

"Spread-eagle," Captain Powell responded flatly. "Facedown in an open ravine off a back road near Route 41."

Flores had one thirty-six-inch computer screen filled with a detailed chart of the Florida gulf coast. "Yes, sir," he said, "help me find it."

"Hit Sarasota and move south until you see the off ramp marked Hillside Cemetery. If you reach the town of Saint Luke's, you've gone too far."

Flores moved a green cursor across the map, then back up, highlighting the general area off the Florida interstate, just as Jack Scott appeared at his back. Scott's necktie was missing, but he was still dressed in a white shirt with a gray sports jacket. He looked distressed, his eyes red and tired. Above the slot, a photo prompt emitted three short beeps, and Flores pulled a photograph from the image pan. Scott watched the agent compare the third-grade picture of Lisa Caymann with the battered image at the rim. He stood silently, looking every bit like the stalwart federal commander, skimming details that were pouring from a laser printer.

"Agent Flores?" Captain Powell asked suddenly, and Scott saw a physical jolt hit the newcomer as the voice filled his ears. The murder photograph was truly sickening.

"Yes, sir," Flores stammered.

Scott quietly reached into the slot and switched the call back to audio intercom, placing a warm hand on Flores' back while pulling a chair against the outside metal rim. "How are you, Duncan, Jack Scott here," he said. "Can you tell us about the position of the body, please?"

"Spread, facedown, no clothing or personal material items recovered. One blanket, the site is a gravel—"

"One step at a time, Duncan," he said, nodding at Agent Flores, who seemed intent but relieved. "You found no clothing, so you're saying the body was completely exposed to the elements?"

"She was partially covered with a blanket, Jack. We're sending that for lab—"

"Give us a photograph of the body as found, please, with the covering. While you're doing that, tell me about the disposal site."

"Very close to a paved access road off 41, complete gravel, no hope for shoe prints. The road shows no recent tread marks."

"Easily seen from where?"

"From nowhere at night, not much traffic and too far from the interstate. The body was spotted by a young woman who swerved to avoid a jacklighted deer. Do you want—"

"Duncan, did the body look articulated, as if it had been carefully positioned? Were the arms and legs fully extended?"

"No, it was sort of haphazard."

"And the blanket looked like what, tossed on or carefully draped?"

"I'm not sure, Jack, a bit ruffled maybe. We're transmitting the film now, you'll have it any second."

Scott looked at Flores, who could not mask the rage burning inside him. "Duncan," Scott said, "I missed the beginning. Was her mouth cleaned of any fouling?"

"It looks so, Jack. I explained that to Agent Flores, we think it's the same medicinal odor. Her teeth were absent of the expected tartar, which is also in keeping with—"

"Cause of death strangulation?"

"Affirmative."

"It's him," Scott sighed. Agent Flores lifted a Wirephoto from the pan above his head and quickly handed it across the rim. Scott studied this for a moment, looking beyond the readily apparent for small details, micro-behaviors, seemingly insignificant clues that the ordinary policeman could easily miss.

"Duncan," he said, "stand by one." And Scott turned his attention back to the man at the slot.

"Agent Flores," he cautioned, "right now minutes don't count for anything. This child is already dead, so take your time. Develop some feeling for this tragedy, tell me what you see." He placed the photograph in front of Flores' chest. "Start with the history."

Flores nodded and cleared his thoughts. "Yes, sir," he said.

"Case 117 involves a series killing through the Gulf States, two victims in Mobile, three in Florida, Lisa Caymann would be victim number six. Although there's some evidence of oral rape, no traces of semen have been found. Teeth have been excised from some victims. Cause of death is the same in each case: strangulation from behind, with slight variations." Scott nodded approval as Flores turned his attention to the print, studying it closely. Against the gray-peppered landscape of a gravel pit there was a form covered with a dark green blanket. A pale arm protruded. One leg was exposed.

"What can you tell me?" Scott pressed. "And take your time, that's all we've got right now."

Flores knew that the chances were excellent he was looking at the work of a recreational killer, savage and emotionless. But he knew something was amiss as he recalled Scott's profiling seminars. His mind engaged. A man who clothes or covers a victim usually has a small degree of guilt or shame for his act; covering the body is his way of saying "I feel bad." Also, if the body were placed where it could easily be found, that would point to a killer of some feeling who wants his victim to have a decent burial and not be left exposed. If there's any remorse, however slight, micro-behaviors hint at the story. And as Flores was taught, a killer with a hint of emotion is a killer who can be caught.

"Captain Powell," Flores asked directly, "would you consider the spot where the body was found as a hiding place?"

"It's a remote location," the deep voice answered, "and the body was lying at the bottom of a wide ditch, so some effort was made to conceal, though not well. Does that help?"

"Yes, sir, stand by one, please."

Flores turned to Scott. "It doesn't compute. If the disposal site was remote, then that suggests hiding the victim, and that behavior points to a ruthless man without emotion. Yet the use of a blanket to cover her suggests our killer does feel some guilt. We have two conflicting behaviors."

Scott smiled. "Why the blanket?" he asked. "If this man feels shame, why doesn't he simply allow the victim to get dressed?"

Flores thought for a moment, but drew a blank.

Scott rephrased the question. "Why leave a perfectly good blanket behind, covering a body that, as you pointed out, was already hidden in the ravine?"

Flores shook his head. "He feels guilt?"

"Yes, he does," Scott agreed, "but then why didn't he place the body where it would be easily found? If he uses the blanket to protect her from the elements, wouldn't he also want her to have a quick and decent burial?"

"I don't know," Flores sighed.

Scott gave him a knowing look. "We are dealing with two people," he concluded.

Flores' eyes went wide.

"Understand this, Daniel"—it was the first time he had ever used his subordinate's first name—"you are dealing in a brutally violent world where coincidence doesn't count. There's no such thing, so get coincidence out of your mind."

Flores nodded.

"Coincidence is a luxury used by civilians to explain things away. We do just the opposite."

"Yes, sir," Flores agreed.

"Now, you were right about the conflicting behaviors of hiding the body without remorse and then covering the body with a sense of shame, but you didn't allow for the phone call."

Flores smacked a palm against his brow.

"If memory serves, Lisa was playing in the backyard when her mother went for the phone?"

"Two people," Flores said feeling foolish, and anger flamed in his soft hazel eyes. "They were stalking this one particular child."

Scott hit the speaker switch. "Sorry for the delay, Duncan. Have you contacted the parents yet?"

"Negative, we're waiting for dentals. Also a news reporter picked up our radio call, so I'll have to go soon."

"Mrs. Caymann was in her backyard when the phone rang, and she left the child for only a few minutes. Talk to her again, find out everything you can about the voice before they're informed further. We believe the person who called is the one who covered the body with the blanket. Was that a man or a woman?"

"It was a man's voice. Do you really think it's connected?"

"Yes," Scott assured him. "They just slipped up. We have conflicting behaviors that indicate we should be concentrating on a team, at least two men. In their early fifties, maybe late forties." There was a pause on the line.

"We didn't find footprints . . ." Powell was questioning.

"The other victims were alive for three days at best, and their bodies were hard to find, if I recall."

"Affirmative," Powell said.

"Duncan, for whatever reason, they held this child longer. They knew her. And although the actual killer would have still been content to just toss her in a ditch, as an afterthought somebody else covered her up. It's that second man that feels something, ashamed, maybe a sense of loss, it's hard to say. His partner is the more dominant personality. The second man is the type who gets annoyed if he sees a wrinkled shirt."

"You're an amazing man, Jack. How did you reach that conclusion?"

Scott looked at Agent Flores, whose eyes reflected admiration. "Strangulation smacks of a disorganized personality," he stated, "not the type of individual who has tidy personal habits, and that's bothered me. Each victim had her mouth washed, depriving us of any hope of retrieving fluids for DNA decoding. A very organized person. I'm betting the man who made the telephone call to set up the mother, and who later draped the body, is also in charge of this oral hygiene. He is doing the bidding of the dominant male who understands how good our technology is."

"Are they faggots?" Powell asked.

"Who ever knows, Duncan? Sex isn't what this is about. Sex is a secondary act to the excitement of abducting, then killing. One is a recreational killer, and his boyfriend is probably a psychopathic voyeur who enjoys watching other people being dominated, which takes the place of sexual activity."

"I've got to put them away, Jack, I need assistance," Powell demanded.

"I understand, Duncan, but this is the first break we've gotten. I've got nine agents in the field and I can't afford more at the moment. I'm putting Agent Flores in charge of this case, and as usual, I'll be available at all times."

Flores' face flushed and seemed to go blank.

"Duncan," Scott said, "in the meantime you should be concentrating on a late-model station wagon or van. One suspect should be relatively thin and neat, the other overweight, possibly obese, that's just a guess."

"Based on what?"

"Opposites attract. The emotional partner has a health and cleanliness fetish, so I'm sure he watches every calorie. And you might suggest to your detectives that they keep a close watch for signs that would be emotionally disarming."

"I don't follow."

"These characters are cunning, mocking of authority, treating parents with an unusual degree of contempt. They'd get a real charge from throwing suspicion off, so look for anything that would retard normal doubt if they were spotted with a child, a bumper sticker like 'HAVE YOU HUGGED YOUR KID TODAY?'—you know the type."

"I know the type," Powell said grimly.

Jack Scott turned the slot back over to Daniel Flores, who managed alone well into the night with Commander Scott's instructions echoing in his mind: "This is your case. You will assign the file name. You are now the desk officer in charge."

Scott left the rim for his office, where he monitored the twenty-three other ongoing cases that came through the slot before midnight.

Scott aimed a cone of light at his desk, staring down at the photographic image of human bones nestled into a shallow grave. Without looking away he patted through the inside pockets of his coat, removing a crumpled pack of cigarettes, and quickly lit up.

The remains were undoubtedly those of a child. The skull was small and the hands underdeveloped, coming apart at the cartilaginous digits. The rib cage was brittle and broken in several places. The teeth had begun falling from the jaw, and some lay in the dirt surrounded by rotted cloth. He was looking at the products of decay and time.

According to Captain Maxwell Drury, the site had been found by a boy named Elmer Janson, who roamed the neighborhood with a three-legged dog. They had snagged a human jaw while digging for treasure, and if all of that wasn't strange enough, no one seemed to care. Not Captain Drury, not the medical examiner, not the county homicide bureau. Some cop by the name of Frank Rivers had mysteriously tracked the kid down—a cop who knew how to press Maxwell Drury's buttons.

But why? With the scant evidence facing him, Scott contemplated the coincidence, feeling as if he were drowning inside, slowly coming apart into tired pieces.

The bones looked a century old. The image of the coin bore the date 1863. Rather than concentrating, though, he found himself listening to the constant hum of imaging equipment, drilling away at life from the ViCAT slot and producing victims by the score. Scott had decades of experience with the kind of horrid detail that buzzing sound produced, day and night, without stop, a manic buzzing that reminded him of the electric chair. And his mind skipped off-track as he found himself visualizing the way the buzzing volts had hit Theodore Bundy, his brain pan smoking while his body curled into a human snail. And the eyes: even at their last they burned with that cold, strange light that no man of conscience could hope to comprehend. Then Scott remembered all of the killers with that icy inhuman stare—of charges dismissed for lack of evidence, of courtroom theatrics with high-priced lawyers, of lame judges and politicians handing pardons to men who slaughtered women and children for recreation.

He walked across his office, shutting his door to distractions, then lifted the two enlargements from his desk. An ancient coin. *The Union Must and Shall Be Preserved.* His mind fogged.

If given time, he knew they would eventually be able to track the artifact with precision, back to its very maker. Civil War relics were a well-documented element of Americana, and he made a note to have a filing removed for radiocarbon testing to determine age. But if he was right, time was a luxury he had lost long ago.

Antique coin or not, this grave had been dug by a predatory animal who stalked his victims in a pitiless game, man against child, killer against mother. He felt blood pulsing behind both ears. Bile rose in his throat and he flushed it down with freshly brewed coffee. He set out to tackle the abandoned site, prepared to manipulate facts if necessary in order to build a case for official involvement. A *justification.* He hated the word, though he placed the photos of the coin under the heading *Case Similarities* and began working on a yellow pad.

The Clayton girls had been found adorned with jewelry, Latin-style gold crosses; the killer had not been interested. Scott theorized that this coin was also a child's keepsake worn around the neck, a charm of some type, for it had been drilled to accommodate a chain—three inches of the rotted silver had been recovered. On either side of the hole there were block letters in near-perfect position. On one side "JO," and on the other, "IN." "JOIN." But join what? Did the keep-sake even belong to a child of this century?

"Jane Doe," he sighed, picking up the photograph of frail bones, "you deserve better." He dug into a mountain of paper, retrieving a color glossy of Elmer Janson's stick. Scott did not want to look at this picture, and as he held it in his hand, his mind and his body and his soul warned him off.

"Jennifer?" he asked quietly, returning to the first image, and his voice sounded like a man who had lost his way. "That's always been a favorite of mine." He retrieved the medical examiner's report and reviewed the laboratory exam-ination. "Small female, height and weight impossible to deter-mine. Skull plates and dental evolution provide age distribution estimate, ten to fifteen years of maturation. Date, time, cause of death unknown." From the photograph Scott knew it would be an almost impossible job to determine much more, though he pulled the phone closer to his desk, fumbling through a gray Rolodex wheel for a number. Only when he dialed did he think to look at his watch.

It was 11:33 P.M., Friday, April 8. A brief twelve hours had passed since he had received the Clayton files. The phone was answered on the fourth ring.

"I need someone I trust to tell me about this child, about her life," Scott said urgently, bypassing hellos and shared ex-periences.

The voice laughed, the amusement deep and resonant. Scott had reached Dr. Charles McQuade at home, the first time they had spoken in almost a year and their conversation, as usual, started somewhere in the middle.

"Of course you do, Scotty," he said calmly. "If this wasn't a problem, you wouldn't call. So why don't I take a look?"

And that's all there was to it. McQuade, a hulking bear in a white gown, was a frightening, authoritative man who clipped small talk and enormous tasks like so many blades of grass. And Scott knew what "taking a look" meant to the spe-cialist.

Dr. Charles Rand McQuade was the unsung champion of the laboratory war against missing persons. His formal title was chief medical examiner for the Armed Forces Institute of Pathology in Washington, D.C. He first had become promi-nent in the late sixties for identifying plane-crash victims burned beyond recognition, and then for producing faces based on mere bone fragments.

"They tell me she could be from the Civil War period, but I don't think so," Scott continued. He was about to go on when the bone doctor interrupted:

"Do you have a case, Jack? Under what authority is the work assigned?"

Scott released a troubled sigh. There was no case. There was no authority. The job he was requesting could cost an easy sixty thousand federal tax dollars, and for those law-enforcement agencies not in the mainstream, budgets were so tight, audits of every department now fell on the quarter. Scott was asking a giant favor. He related the story as well as he knew it.

"There, there, Scotty!" McQuade boomed. "I'm always prepared to move on your verbal authorization, so let's get started."

"I don't have a shred of evidence," he cautioned weakly, "if you want to postpone."

"Hell, trust your instincts, Jack, that's what you always say. Have them send the child along, we'll see what we can do. You sound tired, go home, get some sleep. I'll call the moment I have something."

McQuade hung up the phone, leaving Scott flush with guilt, like he was taking advantage of an old friendship. But with McQuade's assistance, he felt suddenly satisfied that the world would again know this destroyed child. Within hours the director would be applying calipers, rulers, X rays, magnifying glasses, sketchpads, and clay to bring her face back from the grave. Scott had marveled many times at the man's hulking artistry.

Long tedious hours without food or sleep came first, with McQuade endlessly stooped over a chrome operating table. He would start with a determination of the victim's age and sex. Then, combined with thickness of bone, he would calculate depth of muscle and facial tissue. Any missing fragments would be cast from plaster and added, filling in voids. From that he would judge and reproduce the victim's facial planes, building and molding realism with artist's clay. Few details would escape him.

Though soft tissue like ear shape and eyelids cannot be inferred from bone, McQuade had calculated rules of flesh based on anatomical averages. The mouth, as wide as the front eight teeth. If the teeth were missing, aligned with the centers of the eye sockets and widest points of the chin.

The nose, roughly two times the length of the nasal spine; the
ears, about as long as the nose. As a final touch, glass eyes
of a neutral color would be positioned.

It made no difference what condition the remains were in,
or how many there were. Computers and mathematical models would be employed if necessary.

McQuade, the pacifist and former war protester, had produced entire faces from skull fragments, identifying remains
returned in cardboard boxes from Hanoi. And even though he
trusted Scott's instincts absolutely, for Jack Scott, doubt fes-
tered like an open sore.

10

As far as Matthew Brennon was concerned, there was only
one reason to live in New York. Availability. Night or day you
could find anything you wanted in Manhattan, the city that
never closed. He had double-parked in front of the Central
Records Building, a massive marble expanse with skylights,
and once inside he felt like a weak duckling trapped in a
stone shell. From the main rotunda, with sixteen pillars supporting a giant dome, there were twice as many hallways with
doors peeling off to unknown places. At 11:12 P.M. all rooms
were locked shut, except for the stone bell jar where he stood
waiting in line to view a display.

On two sides of the echo chamber, uniformed guards studied each visitor who came in, then went back to scanning the
crowd. Brennon guessed both were former NYPD, in their
late fifties or early sixties, carefully avoiding eye contact with
each other. A two-man ring of protection. A large black officer with peppery white hair had nodded when he came
through, and every few minutes he would turn, alert to potential trouble.

Brennon knew that locked behind the doors they were
guarding were chambers for every pursuit—from the map
center, which preserved original charts of New York City and
almost every other major eastern municipality, to specific
reading rooms for specialized subjects, art through zoology.
Each was connected to the central library and rotunda by a

labyrinthine maze, and while Brennon was pondering this, he took a place in line, studying the firm calves of the woman in front of him. She could be a dancer, he thought idly, the legs were long and tight and well-toned. There were better things to do late on a Friday night, he thought, than visiting a collection called "Prizes of the Civil War." He smiled absently as the line edged forward.

Soon he was standing before the first display case, a glass enclosure with some nine feet worth of Civil War canteens, belt buckles, daggers, hats, and accoutrements from Dixie, none of which he found interesting. He hopped in line to the next, a glass-encased flag with bullet holes, the Stars and Bars of the Confederacy. Oh, for joy, he thought, a worm-eaten battle flag, where's the good stuff?

He glanced around for an authority figure, the stooge responsible for a lifeless, noninterpretive display of relics that no one could touch. Near the far end of the exhibit he found his mark, a dumpling of an old dandy with a white fringe of hair and a blue blazer with a patch. Under the sentinel's watchful eyes, Brennon edged forward, and the man seemed ruffled by his approach.

Brennon stood over six feet tall and was lean, while the dandy stood about five-foot-two and plump as a neutered house cat. "Hello, are you Dr. Robert Perry?" he asked.

"Yes, I am," said the man, gazing upward and twisting the right end of a handlebar mustache. "And who are you, may I inquire?"

"Special Agent Matthew Brennon, sir. I spoke with you on the phone about an hour ago." He produced a badge, then shoved it back into his coat pocket.

"Yes, Mr. Brennon, as I told you, I don't like phones—no use for them what-so-ever."

"Yes, sir, that's why I'm here." He produced two eight-by-ten photographs from inside his jacket and stripped the rubber band from the roll. "I was wondering what you could tell us about this coin," he said, handing over the package.

Dr. Perry tied his face in a knot. "I thought you were going to bring the coin with you. Can't tell much from a picture," he puffed.

"Yes, sir, we don't have the coin in our possession at this time, so I'm afraid the photo will have to do. Would you try, please?"

"Oh, all right, young man, but I would rather have the ac-

tual coin." He seemed annoyed as he balanced a set of Civil
War-period spectacles, the wire kind, across a button nose.

Brennon thought himself mad, for he could have waited until Monday and pushed the lab in Washington, but it all
seemed urgent the way Scott was behaving.

"Well, sir, what do you think?" he asked, but only after Dr.
Perry had a sufficiently long time to appraise the grainy photos.

"Very interesting, would you like to donate it?"

"I'm sorry, no. We just want to know what it is. The coin
doesn't seem to have any denominational markings. Is it
real?"

"Oh, it's very real, and fairly rare. But it's not a coin." He
took another look, studying the enlargements closely.

"Then what is it?" Brennon felt like he was pulling teeth.

"Hold your breeches!" the dandy snapped back, pushing
the photos out across the top of a glass case. "We'll start with
the obverse, which is the order in which you handed me the
documents." Dr. Perry pulled a chrome telescoping pointer
from inside his club jacket and extended the device into a
long rod. Then, reappraising his stature in relation to the table, he adjusted it back to two feet.

Brennon stifled a laugh at the pudgy curator who stood one
foot away and waist-high at the glass counter. All of this to
look at some pictures?

"The bust of the bearded gentleman," Dr. Perry continued
with authority, pointing with the red-tipped silver rod, "is Major General Andrew Jackson."

Brennon doubted this was important, but he produced a pad
and jotted notes, a psychological signal that the listener was
intensely interested, the opinion valued enough for the record.
Dr. Perry noticed this and paused so that Brennon could catch
up, the downside risk of the technique. "And this phrase here,
'The Union Must and Shall Be Preserved,' is a modified
quote from Jackson's famous speech on states' rights and
constitutional theory, which he gave, let me think . . . in 1830,
which of course was several years yet before the war. You can
quote me."

Brennon was looking at his reflection in the glass case. He
didn't think he had such a dumb face.

"The stars at the bottom represent the Union states, of
course."

"Of course."

Dr. Perry turned to the other photo and laid it over the first. "This," he said with a pause, "is the reverse."

Right, thought Brennon, heads and tails. He was staring down at a shack entwined by a snake.

"The key here is the serpent, which is symbolic of a Confederate sympathizer, hence the warning 'BEWARE' in capitals underneath." The red tip flicked from top to bottom.

"I don't follow you, sir," Brennon said.

"Look at the token, son! Look at the token!"

The red tip was suddenly rapping the counter as Brennon stared down in disbelief. "Sir," he said cautiously, "why do you call it a token?"

Perry sighed with displeasure. "Because that's what it is," he said incredulously. "It is *not* a coin, or any type of currency, but a patriotic token made of copper. These enlargements ruin the aesthetics of the work—the actual token is slightly smaller than a quarter, but much, much thinner."

Brennon took a note. "And what were these tokens used for, how many were there?"

At these questions Perry's eyes flared. "You did come to waste precious time, didn't you!" And his face twitched like a squirrel with a nut. Brennon stepped back, thinking quickly.

"Oh, no, sir, everyone said you were the best man to seek advice from, so I came directly to you. I don't wish to waste your time."

Perry breathed deeply. "Then why didn't you bother to look at our display of tokens? We worked very hard to collect them—they are quite precious."

"Yes, sir, the display. I was just saving it, hoping you would show me personally. It would mean a great deal to me, er, us," Brennon lied, having no idea where it was.

Suddenly Perry waved him aside, lifting the photographs from the case. Beneath a waxy glass glare was a bronze plaque:

"PATRIOTIC TOKENS AND MEDALS FROM THE SOUTH"

Three tokens like the one in the photographs shone in the light, and Brennon felt dumb as the day he was born. "Aren't they handsome?" he exclaimed.

"Well, then," said the curator, sounding relieved by this display of affection. "You understand that before and during the war, many states in the South were divided. Some leaned toward the Union, others not."

"Oh, yes," said Brennon, really starting to get interested.

"All the way from Kentucky and Tennessee, up through North Carolina, Virginia, West Virginia, and Maryland, there operated what we call the Underground Railroad, an elaborate network for rescuing and freeing slaves."

"Yes, sir."

"It was a frightfully dangerous business. A man couldn't trust his neighbor and sometimes even his own brother. During the effort to bring the slaves north to freedom, where they could fight for the federal forces, the single largest threat to the operation was Confederate spies. They were everywhere. Confederates, you know, had an elaborate network of spies."

"Oh, yes, sir, that much I knew, but the way you tell it, one feels transported back." Although Brennon said this, he really felt like he was stroking a house cat.

"Yes, of course one does. Now"—Perry was rapping at the glass—"with the exception of clandestine meetings, the workers of the Underground Railroad communicated mostly during normal social activities, such as shopping, banking transactions, dances, fund-raisers, and the like. Now, since merchants and shoppers couldn't openly discuss their feelings or activities for fear of retribution, these little tokens were a way of communicating. Do you understand?"

"I think I do. Go on."

"Now, let's go back a moment. I shall become the proprietor of a cotton or tobacco auction house, and you are not only a grower but we are both operators of the Underground Railroad."

Brennon nodded. He noticed that the black guard had taken several steps closer and was also listening.

"Now, let's suppose I have reason to believe that a merchant who has come to town is really a rebel spy. How can I warn you without exposing both of us to arrest or kidnapping or execution?" The little man's eyes danced in the light as he looked up through wire spectacles at the tall investigator. "Hmm? What shall we do?" he urged, rapping the counter with his red-tipped wand.

"Well, secret meetings are hard to arrange and wouldn't be practical—"

"Correct!" snapped the curator, whipping his pointer through the air.

"So I would stop by to see you, say, in the middle of town surrounded by people, and you would pass me a token?"

"Not quite, that could kill us both. But if you came and

sold me some cotton or tobacco, or asked for a small advance, I would have to hand you change and I would drop this token in among the coinage—and nobody's the wiser!" He lifted the reverse photo to the center of the counter.

With his pointer again, he went on, "It means just what it says: Beware, there's a rebel spy, a Confederate snake, nearby, do not work the railroad. Pass the word—we are in danger!"

"That's amazing. That's what this photograph is?"

"Yes, son, that's what it is. A patriotic signal token used to secure the Underground Railroad, a way of talking without being heard. And you, of course, would pass the token to someone else."

Brennon had been writing furiously, thinking about the relationship of the token to the human remains found by an abandoned building in the middle of a modern city. "And what about the house being entangled by the serpent?"

"Well," Perry explained, "that's symbolic of what they called a safe house, a hiding spot for slaves and federal troops escaped from prisoner-of-war camps."

Brennon chuckled, truly amazed. "I wonder if that's where the CIA came up with that term."

"That, I assure you, I wouldn't know," Perry huffed. "I have no interest in modern politics, none what-so-ever."

"Then it's no house in particular?"

"No, I don't think so, but it's possible, depending upon where it was minted. Tokens were produced at the California mint, and a few were made at Harpers Ferry in West Virginia. Let's take another look." The bespectacled man bent over the glass, comparing the photograph to tokens in the collection.

"Look here at this one." He tapped the glass with the red-tip. "Notice at the top it says 'White's Ferry'? That's the name of a town, and a token was specially made to alert the community there. So that coin, which is cruder in detail than specimens made in California, was produced at Harpers Ferry. The ones from the West Coast are without names, except for the tiny *S* trademark of the San Francisco mint, which can only be seen with a jeweler's loupe."

"Dr. Perry, in the photograph there is a name at the top with a chain hole through it. The word looks like 'join'—what do you think?"

"I noticed that, a tragic defiling of a historical record. No, it does not say 'join,' " he said, studying the photograph. "It must be the name of a town once held in high esteem by the federal forces at Harpers Ferry. A great tragedy. The token was most likely hand-drilled, separating the letters 'JO' from 'IN.' Several other letters, and hence the meaning, were punched out by the drill. A tragic loss, but I would be willing to acquire the token. This one I would let the public hold, provide them a chance to touch the past. The others, of course, can only be handled with gloves, and rarely then."

Brennon smiled. "I'm afraid the token belongs to another party. Do you know of any town on the railroad with a name that comes close to the word 'join' in configuration?"

"No, sorry, I don't. But in addition to our collection of tokens, we do have many of the original maps and heirlooms from the Underground Railroad system. Let's take a look."

The stubby curator walked around the display case, passing the Confederate flag and protected gun racks, then stood facing a series of hand-drawn charts encased behind heavy glass. "These are Confederate," he said, and the red probe crossed and ticked against the glass faces, again and again, stopping, ticking, moving onward, then stopping.

Finally he turned and said, "I'm sorry, but there is no logical choice. There is one town, Cabin John, but that doesn't seem close." For the first time the curator noticed that only he, Matt Brennon, and two guards were left. "Young man, may I suggest we continue tomorrow? As arranged by the building engineer, we should be closing. You do realize our extended hours only last one more night, after which 'Treasures' will be moving to New Haven for three months, and then Philadelphia?"

"No, sir, I didn't realize," Brennon said. "You've been very kind. One more question?"

"Yes, one only," he twitched.

"Where can I obtain copies of these charts of the Freedom Railway? I would like to—"

"You cannot," Dr. Perry said indignantly. "There are none, which is why we have a priceless exhibit. I would be pleased to provide you with a list of illustrated books on the subject, and while they're inaccurate in many ways—scale and detail—they should do for amateur purposes."

"Could I have a technician come and take a photograph of the maps?" Brennon suggested.

"My Lord, no!" Perry shouted. "That's out of the question! These are fragile, light-sensitive parchments, they will never be attacked by flash or daylight. And, I might add, many have tried to produce renderings, which is why the history books are rife with inaccuracy. You are welcome to visit the collection anytime you like." He was now leading Brennon by the arm, walking past the guard, into the rotunda.

"Of course," Brennon said as he shook hands and headed out into darkness.

The crushing sound of a heavy iron door bolted behind him as he took one step, a century forward.

11

11:15 P.M. POTOMAC, MARYLAND

"Full name?"

"Debra Ralson Patterson."

"Her nickname is Dee?"

"Dee."

"And you said she was going to the store for a few items?"

"Milk," Jonathan Patterson said, shaking his head with anger and a quiet resentment. He was Debra's father. Debra had driven to the store and not returned. Not even her car had been found. That was twenty-seven hours ago.

"God damn you!" he said suddenly, his voice rising. "We've been over and over this . . ." Jon Patterson was a meek-looking, short man with a gaunt, pale face. He was usually very reserved and friendly, and he felt himself coming out of character. He hadn't cursed with anger since his college days.

"For the report, sir. We are filing a formal missing-persons report, and we need accurate data and documentation that's verified."

"What is it with you people?" Patterson was on his feet. "You must have her driving permit, and she's been gone since eight o'clock last night. You have pictures of her. She's never run away before, dammit! She's never even been late—"

"I understand that, Mr. Patterson," stated Sergeant Tyler Conroy of the Montgomery County police, looking for all the world like a manicured diplomat in a starched tan uniform. His jet-black hair was combed thickly back over his head, and he carried an expensive leather briefcase instead of the standard clipboard or duty book. "It's a difficult situation, a painful process to go through, and we're doing all we can. The county code states we have to wait a minimum of seventy-two hours, so we are pushing the rules a bit."

"Pushing the rules?" Patterson mocked coldly. "We're talking about my daughter's life. I'm not interested in your lousy bureaucracy!" He sat back down on his living-room sofa, nervously scratching a buff-colored cocker spaniel.

"Yes, sir," Conroy said, "and her birth date is July 3, 1971?"

"Yes," he said, shaking his head tiredly.

"And what was she wearing when she left the house?"

"I don't remember. Like I told you before, I didn't see her. I was in the den working on taxes, and she called out she was going to the store for some milk. Would her birth certificate help?"

"And what did she say?"

"She said . . ." He bolted to his feet again, his face twitching with a slow anger that was unlike Jon Patterson. "She said she was going to the goddamned store!"

"Please don't make this any harder, Mr. Patterson. Did she say which one?"

"No. No, she didn't."

"And you said Mrs. Patterson is currently in Stratford, Connecticut. Is she the natural mother?"

"Visiting her parents, I told you that . . . of course she's the mother. I've only been married once and I only have one child. Let me get Dee's birth certificate."

"Do you know of any reason that Dee might have been upset? Was there anything going on in her life that may have—?"

"What are you getting at?" Patterson asked sternly.

"Any problems we should know about?"

"What?" Patterson barked. "What kind of problems? She's a perfectly happy, well-adjusted child—even her grades are good!"

The sergeant cleared his throat. "Mr. Patterson," he said slowly, "why is your wife in Connecticut with her parents?"

"That's none of your fucking business," he said, staring the officer directly in the eye. "Now, you listen to me," he charged, "your job is to find my little girl. You have a photograph of her car, you have three current pictures of her, you know all that I do, and now you have even met her dog!" The spaniel was upset and clawing at Patterson's trousers. "Now, why are you wasting time talking to me?" He moved the well-groomed policeman toward the front door.

Sergeant Conroy read back through his list, closing his briefcase. "Is there some reason for your wife being out of town that might have upset Dee?" he asked again just as the telephone rang.

Jonathan Patterson shook his head. "Just one moment," he said, picking up an extension in the foyer. He had a brief conversation with his back to Conroy, who was waiting at the front door.

"That was Beth Meyers," he told the sergeant. Conroy's face remained blank. "My daughter's best friend. You know, Beth Meyers, the other little girl from Montessori School with straight A's and a bright beautiful future." His tone dripped acid.

The sergeant did not respond directly. "Mr. Patterson," he said slowly, "are you and your wife—?"

"And Beth Meyers says," he interrupted, "that she hasn't heard from the police, that no one has even checked with her! And further, she says that this isn't like Dee. No, Sergeant Conroy," he hissed, "not at all like our girl unless someone has detained her while I worked on my taxes to pay your damned salary!"

"Are you and Mrs. Patterson—?"

"The only reason I'll tell you is that this county police force is my only hope, and I don't want you wasting any more time."

Sergeant Conroy backed out the front door.

"You see, Sergeant, my wife's mother is having a hysterectomy, nothing immediately life-threatening unless you're a woman. In the meantime my little girl is out there"—he pointed with a shaky hand—"and she did not run away from home!"

"Yes, sir," Conroy said, "and if we want to verify this with the mother?"

"Then you find her maiden name and use the phone book like anyone else. In fact, I think I'll let my fingers do the walking right now and find the best way to sue this miserable county. Now, stop wasting time and find Debra. Please. I beg you . . ."

From habit, Jonathan Patterson closed the door softly. In his mind he slammed it shut, but fear had stolen his anger.

And he sat sobbing in the darkness, wondering who he could call for help, who he could turn to. Who did other men turn to?

Jon Patterson had no answer, so he cursed at his ignorance. Twenty years of being a tax consultant had not prepared him for the events transpiring on the nights of April 7 and 8. He had called the FBI, who referred him again to the county police, back into the hands of Sergeant Tyler Conroy. And time was wasting. Without a ransom note, there would be no FBI involvement. Precious time wasting away. Minutes becoming hours becoming days.

His child was missing. That's all that mattered. And even a very cordial man like Jonathan knew in his gut the bestial things that other men were capable of, sick men with nothing in life worth losing. The thought made him shake physically.

For a moment he considered retribution, but there was no one to fight. Besides, he had never even shot a gun, much less owned one, so he considered lawyers, which brought him back to the beginning. A lawyer required an opponent. There was no one to fight. Then the family doctor popped into his mind, but there wasn't an illness. "You're not thinking clearly," he mumbled.

Finally he decided to call a private detective. He ripped open the Yellow Pages and stared down at the listings. How did one make such a critical decision, by the size of the ad? Despair was setting in, and he picked up the phone and dialed a familiar number instead.

It was answered before the first ring had ended.

Alice Patterson, his wife of twenty-two years, had been waiting with the phone clutched in a trembling hand.

12

11:21 P.M. ViCAT

Chasing shadows.

Scott's dream was vague, as he was following the sounds of running water down through a dimly lit hallway. There were human cries. There was an empty house where he was arriving too late, again and again, the sounds vanishing, only to be replaced by the bray of pistons sucking air through an artificial lung.

Dr. Chet Sanders was there. And Commander Nicholas Dobbs. And the clutching hands and anguished words of Elizabeth Dodson, Mary Beth's mother. "Catch him . . . please get him . . . get him for me . . ."

Just as he was about to respond, the man behind his desk heard a distant chiming in his memory, thin as a dreamscape, like a doorbell, or a faraway church, or the hazed recollection of a clock ringing. It came again and again, and he lifted his head, staring at the phone and connecting his thoughts with the outside world. Before he could identify himself, Scott recognized Maxwell Drury's voice.

"Sorry, Jack," the captain offered, "I asked to be put through."

"Yes," he stammered, "yes, Max."

"Jack, will you tell me what the devil is going on? I've had tag teams filling your demands all night, and then a courier from the Armed Forces Institute showed up to transfer bones from an archaeological site, and under your authority. Do we have—?"

"Max," Scott cut him off, his eyes glassy, "it's good to hear your voice, but I'm afraid I have nothing for you, I'm just playing a hunch." He poured cold water from a thermos bottle into a glass and took a sip. "Unless you have something better," he added, wetting his fingers and rubbing the cool water into the corners of each eye.

"No, heavens no, Jack. It's just that Matt Brennon made it sound urgent. What's going on up there? Is there anything I can do?"

Scott turned in his chair, lifting a file, forcing his mind into logical paths. "Let's start with Francis Dale Rivers," he said, his right hand searching out a cigarette. "Tell me about him, is he trustworthy?"

There was a heavy sigh, followed by a pause on the line. "Personally I like Frank," Drury finally offered, "but he's a misanthrope, he really hates people. A very antisocial type of guy."

"Be specific, Max, back up your claim."

"Rivers has gone through more partners than anyone I've ever known. He's a one-man team, a walking attitude. Let me put one of my other detectives on this for you."

"Not what I'm after. Where'd he come from?"

"Residence or career?"

"Both."

"Well, he was born and raised in Maryland, has a few political connections too," Drury said thoughtfully. "Served in the Marines, plus I think a free-lance stint with Langley or one of your agencies. I heard he turned down an offer as a career spook, and that sure wouldn't have been with the diplomatic corps."

"Who recruited him?"

"One of my team, Roland Russell, cancer hit him five years back."

Scott turned to a list of commendations attached to Rivers' state police folder. "According to your personnel file, he's received two awards by the Council of Governments as Outstanding Detective of the Year, two years in a row." Scott read on, "He's made more arrests resulting in convictions than any other cop in the tri-state area."

"All true," Drury confirmed. "Detective of the Year and then Rivers fails to show up at a black-tie reception to collect his award. The following Monday he told me the bluefish were running that weekend."

"Were they?"

"Oh, shit, Jack!" Drury cried. "You should have seen me sitting with the governor, acting like I knew what the hell was coming down, and with the local press waiting outside to take photos. 'Oh, it's an emergency, your Honor, hush-hush police business . . .' "

"Did he buy it?"

"No, the governor demanded I write a memo detailing Rivers' activities, why he didn't show. But when I asked Frank to play along—like a sudden break in a case—he looked me right in the eye and said, 'I'm a cop, not a politician. Tell them anything you want to, Captain.' I'll never forget that, Jack. The governor of the state, tell him anything?"

"So what did you say?"

"That Rivers was deep-cover. Every time I eat seafood I think of him and the governor. 'The fish are jumping'? It was not pleasant, Jack. The man has a real problem with authority figures. Fortunately, the governor has the attention span of a poodle, and this year they're giving the award to a young officer who will show up for the ceremony."

"Then it worked out fine," Scott murmured, reading the

personnel file, which had its weaknesses. "When are the awards, Max? It doesn't say."

"First week in May, same time every year, why?"

"Curious."

"It doesn't matter. Like I told you, Jack, he doesn't have an attitude problem, Frank has an attitude that produces problems. He's made lieutenant three times."

Scott noticed: a professional sergeant, first in the Marines, then in the state police. His DD214 listed three tours in Southeast Asia, a Silver Star, Bronze Star, Presidential Unit Citation, and two Purple Hearts. Activities between 1969 and 1972 were still marked *Restricted,* which meant he had had the misfortune of working with military intelligence, an oxymoron if there ever was one. Scott made a note to sequester the government files coded for his civilian activities prior to becoming a policeman.

"Max, Detective Rivers worked patrol his first three years. How did he make out in uniform?"

"Make out?" Drury cried. "The last incident before I put him in plain clothes, he was clocked at one-thirty by a Delaware unit as he was fouling up the state lines chasing after two fugitives. Frank kept running jurisdictions on me. I got a call in the middle of the night, and the man wasn't even on duty. If the driver hadn't been kind enough to eat a bridge abutment, Rivers would have chased them all the way to Canada. Shit, I took a lot of heat for that one too. Jack, what are you asking me?"

"That's not in the file. Those suspects were wanted for what?"

"Hell, I don't remember, we let Delaware take the collar. Armed robbery and I think a rape or murder was involved somewhere—sorry, I can't recall details, just the political fireball that hit when our state had to file the chase report and make the identification for two bodies stuck in Delaware. Rivers had been investigating the case without authority, breaking every written procedure. It was a mess."

"Sounds like it," Scott soothed, "so why did you keep him?"

"Like I said, I really do like Frank. He's a big dog that's not housebroken. I keep hoping he'll change, but I have serious doubts. The chopper pilot who picked up those materials at his house tonight reported that Rivers was all teeth, like a Cheshire cat."

"Sounds like he has some growing up to do."

"My point exactly. So why him, Jack? What does he have that you want so badly?"

"Just playing a hunch."

"It's your call," Drury agreed, "but I've got a couple of real up-and-coming young detectives, detail men, team workers. Think about it. And just in case you need anything, let me give you my beeper number."

"I have it. Good talking to you, Max," Scott said as he terminated the call with a thumb. And he stood, cranking the window open to let the cool air flow through.

Outside, voices and boom boxes and car horns echoed skyward from the street. And he recalled Mary Beth Dodson in her hospital bed, how her hands and arms, weak as a kitten, were flailing at the air to fight off unseen blows. He returned to the Clayton family and Jennifer Doe.

All that connected them was physical proximity on a map. Plus the personnel files of a recalcitrant state police officer who disliked authority. Scott stared down at the folders on his desk, then set out to organize documents into units marked *Physical Evidence, Personal Histories,* and *Case Similarities.* He knew it would take the better part of three hours to collect his thoughts and impose order, and he sat stretching backward in his chair until his spine cracked.

"So what pushes you, Mr. Rivers?" he asked flatly, draining the water from his glass. "What devil do you fight alone this evening?"

The errant fisherman held a secret only Scott knew existed. Through the shallows of night slid the coldest animal of all.

13

11:25 SENECA, MARYLAND

The cramped forty-foot space was not just a room but a small block house with a red shingle roof. It smelled damp as a root cellar, even though the floor was a carpeted slab of concrete. There was only one door, only one window. It had been meant to be a three-car garage for a mansion, but that was never built, and the little white house sat turning gray like a bad tooth lost in a sweeping field of weeds and eroding red clay.

The cramped interior was decorated in Early American honky-tonk. There was a sagging couch badly in need of repair, and over this hung a nude on black velvet with breasts like purple footballs, blowing a kiss from a face which resembled a football player in drag. The picture was covered with personal autographs. On top of a small beaten curio cabinet stood a haphazard row of award trophies, the gold and silver chipped and covered with dust. There were baseball batters and little dog handlers, fly-casters, sailboats, and marksmen, the latter pointing bent rifles aimlessly under aged icons like James Dean, Marlon Brando, Clint Eastwood.

In the center of the room there was a movie poster of a surfer from *Endless Summer,* and a dartboard with open window doors. On the opposite wall, surrounding the door, hung a series of flags, a Rising Sun from Japan, a Vietcong battle star, a battalion group insignia with a Pink Panther clutching the numeral one and dancing merrily through a field of red.

The television was on, a thirty-six-inch color high-tech wonder that filled the space with light, belting out a quiz show in stereo, competing against the sound of a ham radio hooked to cheap bass-heavy speakers. The local police channel was being monitored, and a man was rolling over on a twin mattress in the far corner.

"M-P-R 280," the speaker popped loudly. "Name, Debra Ralson Patterson, age sixteen, missing four-seven . . ."

The man on the bed felt that it was getting hot. And suddenly he leapt into air with a heavy thrust of his legs, just as a cigar ash burned down through his white T-shirt.

"God damn!" he cried, smacking at his stomach with both hands as the microwave oven screamed on timer. He dabbed his stomach with a wet napkin while grabbing a fifties-style microphone from the shelf next to the bed.

"Repeat your date and data, missing-persons report," he hissed. There was a pause.

"This is County-One, M-P-R number 280, state your authorization . . ." a woman's voice demanded back.

"Ahhh," he sighed, feeling the hot sting subside, checking the bedspread for smoldering ash. He had fallen asleep in the middle of his favorite game show.

"Rivers," he said flatly, "State Sergeant Detective 140, radio car One-Echo-Twenty." He pulled off his shirt, dropped it onto the floor, then went for the scalded milk in the micro-wave. He grabbed a bag of chocolate-chip cookies and returned to the bed. As he waited for a response, he increased the volume of his TV show with a remote.

". . . and in the sports category, for an additional five hundred points. In 1916 Washington State University played Brown University in what famous event?"

Rivers shook his head at the idiotic music, breaking a handful of cookies into his mug. "The Rose Bowl, you bimbos, Washington fourteen to zipper."

"I'm sorry, contestants, that would be the first Rose Bowl. Washington won that game, fourteen to zero. Grant, it's your turn at the board . . ."

Rivers was still half-asleep, his eyes were slits, his blond hair a matted mess. "Let's try technology, Mike," the contestant chirped, "we're a technology-minded family . . ."

"Look out, Japan," said Rivers.

"For one hundred points, in 1915 this man developed the farm tractor. Who was—?"

"Henry Ford," said Frank.

"Gee, that's more of an agriculture question, Mike. I'd like to trade in my option before the clock." He moved toward the board.

"In two for one, and Grant is betting his option, which might take him out of the game . . ."

"I'm going to take the hill, Mike. Let's stay with technology!"

"Yeah," said Rivers, "his strong suit."

"In 1915 Dr. Thomas A. Watson received a telephone call from this famous man of the time—"

"Al Bell," said Rivers, "everybody knows that."

The crowd was on its feet. "Zapp-pp! I'm sorry, Grant, would you like to take a shot?"

"Ah, 1915, that would be President Wilson who called?"

"Dipshit."

"That was Alexander Graham Bell calling from New York, the first transcontinental telephone call. Tough break."

"Yeah, tough break," Rivers chuckled as the radio sputtered and came alive.

"County to Echo-Twenty," the cheap speakers buzzed, and Rivers turned down the set with his remote.

"This is One-Echo-Twenty, go ahead," he said, draining the last from his cup, then grabbing his duty book. He pressed the button on a blue Papermate and scribbled a star to get some ink flowing.

"M-P-R 280," she said without tone. "Caucasian, brown hair, green eyes, five-foot-six, weight 110, DOB 7-3-71. Name, Patterson, Debra Ralson. Last seen intersection River Road and Falls, green 1988 Mustang convertible. Maryland tags Victor-Easy-Zulu 9-1-8. Registration Jonathan T. Patterson. Relationship, father."

Rivers waited. "That's it?" he asked.

"Echo-Twenty, please follow police radio procedure," the woman ordered.

"One-Echo-Twenty . . . County-One." Frank swallowed his spit, sneering into the microphone. "Why wasn't state police notified?"

"Echo-Twenty," the woman intoned, "procedural guidelines permit notification of state authority on 4-9-88, within forty-eight hours, contact case officer Sergeant Tyler Conroy."

Rivers smiled. "Not in your lifetime," he said as he switched off the radio, placing the microphone back on the shelf. From a pile on the floor he lifted the Maryland telephone book and flipped through P, finding the address with an index finger. He considered the hour and calculated the basics.

Rivers had been off duty for six hours. He was fed. He was rested. He was bored. He dialed the phone while toying with one of Elmer Janson's wooden sticks, glancing at a passage from an old red-back encyclopedia opened to the naval-history section.

Marlin Spike. It was illustrated. *n. a pointed iron instrument for separating the strands of a rope during splicing or marling.*

"Hello . . . hello . . ." The man had a distressed but somehow pleasing voice.

"Is this Jonathan T. Patterson?"

"Oh, my God, no!" a terrified voice cried with confusion.

"Relax," Rivers said calmly, "if this is Mr. Patterson, then I'm a friend."

There was a lengthy pause. "Yes. Yes, it is . . ." the voice said shakily.

Phone in hand, Frank Rivers began to pace in tight circles, giving Patterson time to gain his senses. "I'm a cop, Mr. Patterson," he said slowly. "I'd be glad to give you my badge number."

"No, no, that won't be necessary. Do you know about Debra? Have you heard anything about my little girl?"

Rivers felt a pang in his chest, and he breathed hard. "I'm really not related to the case, sir. My name is Frank Rivers, I'm a state police detective, and I just heard the missing-persons report come over the radio. I just thought I'd call. I grew up a few miles from your place."

"I've heard from no one—God, this is awful, can you help us?" Patterson blurted with desperation. "We don't know what else to do. Debra's a good child, a responsible girl . . ."

"I'm sure she is, Mr. Patterson, really."

"This is not like her. Debra wasn't raised like this . . ."

Rivers' brow knotted with concern. "Why are you so defensive, sir? I haven't said anything negative. Is there a reason I wouldn't think she's a good kid?"

"You said you're a state trooper?"

"Sure," Rivers smiled, "a real trooper. Mr. Patterson, can you answer that question? Why are you defending her character? Is there something I should know?"

There was a silence on the phone, and Rivers thought he heard the man sob. "They think she ran away from us. . . . They think she left home because of us, my wife and me."

Rivers looked at his watch. "Did she, Mr. Patterson?" he asked coldly.

"No!" he fired back instantly. "No, I swear, something is seriously wrong. Help us, please. Debra would have called if she could . . ."

Rivers sat on the edge of the bed and relit his cigar. "Have you spoken with her friends? Is Debra an only child?"

"Yes," said Patterson, "yes to both questions. Her friends have not seen her. Can you help us?"

Rivers clipped a gun and holster into his pants, stuffing his wallet, badge, cigarettes, knife, and watch into a slate-gray windbreaker. He laid this across the bed, strapping a small automatic pistol to his inside left calf, putting down the phone to unfold a clean sweatshirt from a footlocker, which he then pulled on. He propped the phone back under his chin and was tying his running shoes when he heard Jon Patterson cry out:

"Mr. Reever? Mr. Reever?" his shaky voice asked.

"Yes, sir, I'm right here. It's Frank Rivers, and no need to apologize for the name. Look, Mr. Patterson," he paused, "I'll be there as soon as I can, but it's an informal visit, if that's okay."

"Anything," the distressed father sighed.

"Good. That's real good, Mr. Patterson, because if you want to find your daughter, you've got to understand what you're up against. You are dealing with bureaucrats and politicians. That's what police agencies are all about, and this county is particularly bad. I'm a state man, so I've really got to watch myself."

"I understand," he said weakly, his voice becoming more sober. "Anything you want . . ."

But what Frank Rivers really wanted was to live in a world where life wasn't considered so cheap, there for the taking. Druggies killed innocent people in a crossfire, then referred to them laughingly as mushrooms, as in, "I made a mushroom today, think I'll buy me a Porsche." In open court, group rapists called their victims strays. Pornographers called smut "literature." Hit men referred to their prey as leftovers. And sexual killers called stalking their victims wilding or trolling. Life was as cheap in America as it had ever been in Vietnam, and any fool who told you different never saw the Nam. Or never saw American justice defending the little people.

On the Maryland side of the river, the three most prestigious neighborhoods had always been Chevy Chase, Kenwood, and Potomac Village, slices of real estate that started at more than a half-million dollars a throw. While a teenager, Frank Rivers had dated girls from all of these areas, the daughters of lawyers and government executives, retailers and corporate men. He came flying down River Road in his tan Crown Victoria, slowing only a moment to study the lights that were burning in Karn Foster's window; a third-story room in a massive stone mansion with marble pillars and rolling front acres.

His head turned slowly as he remembered a pink canopy bed with the image of a fragrant girl drifting through his mind, every soft, sensual curve and caress that was Karn. And he wanted to relive the sins of that room as they were then: carefree, young, and reckless. Rivers winced at how things had soured since then. The house had exchanged hands three times that he knew of. And Karn had an unhappy marriage of nearly twenty years and lived in California with her four children. The Crown Vicky rolled silently through the intersection of River and Falls Road to Tara, where he turned right, studying the sweeping front lawns and arched entryways. Only one house on the small cul-de-sac had lights still burning, and he swung into the tiled circular driveway, checking the address, then looking at his reflection in the rearview. On any good night, the drive to Jonathan Patterson's house in Potomac was forty-five minutes. With siren and fireball, Rivers had arrived in twenty.

As the sound of the engine died, he rubbed his front teeth with an index finger, then dug at the corner of each eye. He licked one palm, patting yellow curls back over the crown of his head, then grabbed his clipboard as a man appeared at the front door.

He studied Patterson's approach. He was small and frail, balding on top, and dressed in rumpled but expensive gray slacks. He wore a thick, braided white sweater, and suspenders hung down from his waist to his knees, swinging as he trotted forward. Before Rivers had closed his car door, the man was on him.

"Thank God! Thank you ... thank you for coming," he gushed, extending a shaky hand through the gray light.

"Pleased to meet you, Mr. Patterson, I was—"

"We've got to get started, where do we begin?" he sputtered frantically, and Rivers heard dogs start up barking a block away.

"Well, can we begin by taking it inside?" he suggested calmly.

"Yes, I'm sorry, oh yes, oh yes," he repeated, biting his lower lip, then scurrying up the pathway. He swung the already open door wide, and they walked in.

From the hallway Rivers could see into the family room. There was a phone surrounded by the symptoms of waiting: dirty glasses, plates of half-eaten food, notepads, personal telephone book, and business clothes that had been discarded by the wearer where he camped. Jonathan Patterson led him into the living room, as plush a domestic dream as any man could envision, a room larger than Frank Rivers' entire house. The detective stood waiting for instructions, facing a marble coffee table.

The sofas and chairs were arranged in a semicircle, an expensive green velvet on thick beige carpeting with an Oriental rug positioned in the room's center. Above a jet-black Baldwin baby grand hung an oil of a gorgeous brunette in a lacy low-cut gown. Patterson caught the policeman's stare.

"My wife, Alice," he sighed. "She's in Connecticut with

her parents, her mother's quite ill, she'll be flying home first thing tomorrow," he said apologetically.

"A beautiful woman," Rivers said in a genuine tone, looking around the room. He spotted a picture of a girl in a crystal frame on an end table. "May I?" he said, reaching.

"Please." Patterson nodded. "Can I get you a brandy or . . ." He was trying to size up the hard-looking stranger in a hooded black sweatshirt. "Maybe a beer?" he asked nervously.

"No thanks, Mr. Patterson."

"Jon, please call me Jon," he pleaded, and Rivers saw pain edging out across the little man's face.

"This is Debra?" he asked, looking Patterson in the eyes.

"At her confirmation several years back," he said. "She turned sixteen last July."

"Does she have any lovers?"

Patterson looked like he had been slapped. "She's only sixteen."

"Jon . . ." Rivers rose and put his hand gently on the man's shoulder. "Maybe I will have that drink. Do you have any Coke or coffee, anything will do."

Jonathan Patterson smiled dutifully, running on automatic, his mind flipping into the role of host as he started for the kitchen. Rivers held him by the arm, detaining his escape.

"Listen to me, Mr. Patterson," he said slowly, "if we are going to find your daughter, you had better start getting real. She may be your baby, and I understand all of that, but Debra's a sweet-looking kid and they grow up faster these days. If you don't know her boyfriend, you're off to a tougher start." Rivers tried a smile. "I'll bet half the boys in her class are chasing her."

Patterson gave a troubled sigh. "Well," he cleared his throat, "her phone does ring quite a lot."

Rivers nodded as he released his grip. "Think it over. I'm going to poke around."

Patterson wandered off in a trance while Frank Rivers examined the room. There were three telephone lines coming into the home, he jotted them off. He heard a scratching behind a door at the end of the living room and walked over. There was a bark as he released a cocker spaniel. Patterson returned with a tray.

"You locked the little guy up," Rivers stated.

"Some people don't like animals, you just never know."

Rivers was kneeling by the marble table, scratching the little dog on the head. He then sat Indian-style on the rug as Patterson placed drinks in front of them.

"Do you want me to run through what I've told the other officer?" Patterson asked plaintively, sitting down into green velvet.

Rivers grabbed a cold glass of Coke and took several swallows. "No, I'm sure it was pretty routine. Just tell me the last time you saw her, how she was dressed, and where you think she was when she disappeared."

And Patterson complied. They talked for a good ten minutes, then Rivers finally said, "You really don't know her very well, Mr. Patterson. You've chosen to know only the little girl, when the rest of the world is interested in a woman. Does she keep a diary?"

"I don't know," he answered thoughtfully.

"Does she always go by the name Debra?"

"That or Dee, I think."

"And her best friend, Beth Meyers, you can talk to her?"

"Yes, yes, I can."

"And how are you fixed for bucks?" Rivers asked.

"Anything you want!" Patterson responded quickly. "I'm not rich, but we're very comfortable, if you need money—"

"Hold it, sir, that's not what I mean." Rivers stood, corrected him firmly. "You're a taxpayer, I already work for you."

Patterson sighed, his shoulders falling forward. "I'm sorry," he said. "I've never been through anything like this before."

"Most folks haven't. And there's not much in life that prepares you either." Rivers looked him hard in the eye. "Here's the thing, Mr. Patterson," he said cautiously, sitting back down, then leaning forward on the carpet so his chin hung over the coffee table. "The county government is in charge and they're following the seventy-two-hour rule. In other words, until your daughter is missing for that long, they won't put their full weight behind the wheel. And right now the wheel is turning slowly."

Patterson's head swung on a weakened stalk. "Who can I call?" he asked. "How can you get them moving?"

"Well, I can't," Rivers stated honestly, "I'm just another cop. But you sure as hell can, and you can't afford to wait."

"Tell me," Patterson cried out. "Debra could have been abducted, she could have amnesia . . ."

Frank Rivers thought about the myriad times he had heard that amnesia fantasy. In many cases parents held on to the belief decades after the fact. "Mr. Patterson, the radio report said Debra's car is still missing. You have to start there and be prepared to really turn up the heat."

"I don't follow you," he said, leaning forward in his chair and reaching for a pad of paper.

"Right, I'm not making myself clear." Rivers paused to reconsider. "You need three things, Mr. Patterson. A loud voice, a few extra bucks, and as many air taxis as possible—ah, helicopters, that is."

"Of course!" he exclaimed. "To find her car! How can I get them moving?"

"The county has two choppers, the state has four, and there are an additional ten or so in private hands. Use the phone book."

Jon Patterson was on his feet and starting to move.

"You'll have to wait, sir," Rivers said. "I'm precluded from participating because of departmental rules."

"Oh?" Patterson asked incredulously. "You can't use a phone book?"

Rivers smiled broadly, showing white even rows. "That's not quite it, but close. I can't participate in an investigation conducted by a citizen in my presence."

Patterson nodded, beginning to get the picture.

"Look up WMAL radio in the book. They have a contract pilot, Dan the Airman, he reports on gridlock, I don't know his real name."

"Yes, I've heard him."

"Start there, tell him your story, flip him a couple bucks. And wake him up tonight, don't wait until morning. If you can't track him down, find someone else. There are dozens of traffic reporters, just call the stations. You'll find that night workers are usually easier to get information from than the morning crowd. A lot quieter at night, people are more friendly."

Patterson nodded agreement.

"Then look through the book and find a private pilot. Ask for someone experienced in search pattern navigation—it's a specialty, and a former cop or combat pilot is always best. And get some bids. After that, pick your best shot, your gut will tell you. And listen carefully. I'd bet on the guy who's more interested in your story than how much you're gonna pay."

"I appreciate that," he said, nodding.

"In the morning, call each of the local television stations, they all have pilots. Ask for the metro desk and sweet-talk someone. Let them know how you feel about your kid, and that you've got a local radioman and private jockey in the sky. They're going to ask where the cops are, tell them they're too damn busy. Say that and they'll go nuts, Mr. Patterson"—Rivers was smiling—"everyone's going to go nuts!

"The TV and radio folks will fear if they don't roll on this, then they're going to be losing a helluva good story. And the county cops . . ." Rivers chuckled. "Instead of breaking their seventy-two-hour rule of noninvolvement, they'll write a new rule for action and name it after Debra."

Patterson smiled for the first time. "I'm following every bit of this," he said, his hand moving furiously across a legal pad.

"Just remember that you're not looking to place a news story, though, you're looking for Debra's car. Don't lose the focus. That's first, Mr. Patterson. You've got to find Debra's car, and right away . . ." His voice sagged.

"I understand," he said.

"When the county executive hears what you've done, he'll call the police brass, and next thing you know, a case will be opened and then I'll ask for state police involvement and the assignment."

"But I thought there was a case. There isn't a case?" Patterson asked with alarm, his tired eyes blown wide open.

Rivers combed his fingers through his curly yellow hair. "No, sir," he said. "I know this doesn't make sense, but like I told you on the phone, we're dealing with bureaucrats. All we've got right now is a missing-persons report, which means uniformed units will keep an alert eye for a person matching Debra's description. You won't get a case unless it gets worse—evidence of foul play, that kind of stuff—" He saw the horror register on the man's face and backed off quickly.

Jonathan Patterson was living the worst of all dreams, enduring the kind of event that transpired in other people's lives. The Pattersons were a loving couple with one child. They were not heavy drinkers, they did not live near transients. They never even raised their voices at each other, no matter how angry or upset. Rivers saw the man drift off in thought.

"Listen, Mr. Patterson, if you raise enough hell, you could get a case officer by this time tomorrow."

The man's face was twisted with pain, and Rivers didn't know if he had done a good job of explaining himself, or if this father had the courage to follow through. Then Patterson lifted his weary head, locking eyes with the tall policeman, and extended his hand. "Thank you," he said, and that took a great deal of physical strength, he looked like he hadn't slept in two days. "Thank you so very much."

"Sure," said Rivers, "that should get you started. Do you or Mrs. Patterson have any relatives nearby, any male relatives?"

"No, there's just my older brother, and he's retired in Florida. Alice's parents are it from her side of the family."

Rivers studied this answer closely. "Any men come to the house for work, yard help, plumbers, pest control?"

"Joseph Mallery does all of our yard work, but he's an older man, a nice man."

"Could I have his number and schedule anyway?" he asked coldly.

Patterson nodded, leaving the room for the kitchen, and returned with a slip of paper. He found Rivers standing in the hallway by the front door.

"Are you leaving?" he asked, handing him the paper.

"We've both got work to do," he stated, examining the particulars on the sheet. "When's the last time another workman came to your house?" Rivers pushed.

"I don't know," Patterson sighed. "I'd have to ask my wife, she manages that kind of thing."

"Do that," Rivers suggested, "and another thing, Mr. Patterson. Do yourself a favor and toss Debra's room."

"Toss?" he asked.

"Search it. Maybe she has a diary or something else. If we can't find her in a few days, we'll be here to do just that, so give a good look. It will be easier while her mother's away."

Patterson's swollen eyes blinked, brimming with a film of tears. The detective was right: Alice Patterson would regard that as a violation of Debra's privacy. "I'll toss it," he said solemnly.

Rivers smiled, walking out the front door into the cool overcast night. A slight breeze was blowing in from the Potomac, and he could feel the moisture on his face.

"Detective Rivers," Patterson said, following after him and

again extending his hand. "I really don't know how to thank you."

"No sweat, Mr. Patterson." Rivers gave him a firm shake. "But you could do me a small favor in return?"

"Anything, just name it," he offered, "anything at all."

"We never talked—not that I care, I'm just not in the mood to play politics. It slows me down."

"I understand." He smiled gravely. "I have some idea what we're up against."

Rivers raised an eyebrow. "Good luck, sir," he said. "I'll see you again when the system catches up." And he strolled over the tiled drive, making a mental note to check on the family in the morning.

From inside his jacket pocket he removed the color print that Patterson had given to him, and attached it to the top of his clipboard. Debra was like the portrait of her mother, he thought. Her hair was shiny and soft to look at. Her figure was subtle and genuine. And it made Frank Rivers all the more disheartened.

He gunned his engine down River Road and into the familiar darkness.

He felt truly sorry for Debra Patterson.

She was a pretty little thing.

14

At the ViCAT slot, Daniel Richard Flores felt as if he were trying to build a fence around a sandstorm.

He filed a report off screen number three, watching bright columns vanish and the blinking cursor reappear. Phones and computers and imaging equipment hadn't stopped buzzing all night, with a new report about every twenty minutes. The emergency requests flowed from every American region: as far away as Honolulu, as close to home as the Bronx. The police officers reporting had a variety of voices, young and old, male and female, some blistering with hate, others choked with sorrow.

Captain Duncan Powell had wired a positive dental match from a missing-persons sheet—a victim had been identified by medical examiners—and he was now requesting that Scott come to Florida. Flores promised to speak with his commander, and he tried to read Powell's state of mind, but he could not. Powell's voice was deep and hard with a commanding bite.

As he concentrated, the young agent tried to imagine the features accompanying all of these pleading and detached and demanding voices. In his mind he assembled composites from faces he remembered, people who had drifted in and out of his life. That effort made him feel sadly alone, and feeling lonely, Flores knew, could be a danger. The slot was a difficult job, worse at night, and his goal was to survive until morning. In retrospect, Flores thought it unprofessional when his emotions slipped to the surface as he was talking to the sheriff of Tucson, Arizona, who had invited him for a holiday weekend.

He had been sharing the man's frustration, assisting with behavioral keys in a search for a twenty-three-year-old woman abducted from a convenience store. He had been on the phone for exactly 16:22.03 minutes, and their relationship had gotten that close, that fast. A total stranger. Flores couldn't explain it.

A call from Santa Cruz, California, followed, where a boy had been thrown from a speeding car along a dark interstate. The highway patrol remained at the scene.

In Jacksonville, Florida, a young woman had vanished from a department store parking lot while waiting for her husband. The Dade County police were reporting their case as a series, for they had four similar incidents with no survivors.

At 9:10 P.M. in Christy, Texas, witnesses reported seeing two children being forced into a car by men they could not describe. The offenders' vehicle was found abandoned.

At 9:45 P.M. in Fort Wayne, Indiana, a serial rapist announced his retreat from the home of Joyce and Suzanne Williams by throwing a woman's shoe through a neighbor's window. Joyce, age seventeen, had survived, and Flores pushed detectives to make a last-ditch effort to obtain a dying declaration from her that might provide leads.

At 10:12 P.M. in Jackson Creek, Wyoming, eighteen-year-old Bonnie Caputo was found dead, stabbed a total of eighty-one times and dumped in a graveyard—the Jackknife Ghoul had struck again.

Suddenly Jack Scott stood at the rim in the ViCAT situation

room, his gray eyes knowingly tired, his face drawn into intense focus. He listened to Daniel Flores, watching patiently as he completed the Jackson Creek call, and he felt lucky for his young understudy. It was a slow Friday night for a warming April. Only six previously registered ViCAT cases had gone active.

Scott checked the computer printout. There were killings and rapes and abductions, and Flores had even handled one arson, a series crime terrorizing residents of a small Pennsylvania township. Scott handed over a fresh cup of black coffee as Flores dropped his headset onto the battered gray desktop, breathing a sigh of relief. His eyes were clear and bright, and Scott admired the young man's stamina.

"I've been listening," he said. "You're doing very well, Daniel."

Flores spun his chair in a semicircle like he was born to the slot. "Thanks," he responded, taking the cup in his hands and sipping the hot liquid. Scott noticed he did so rather gingerly.

"How do you take your coffee?"

"This is fine, thank you, sir. I'm not much of a coffee drinker, but I guess I'm going to start."

"Any questions so far?" he asked, looking over the edge of his cup.

Flores propped his elbows against the desk while stifling a yawn. "Nothing that's case-specific, but I am worried about Captain Powell, he—"

"Don't," Scott said, holding up a hand. "Duncan Powell is acclimating to his own skin. It's part of the hunt, and his behavior gets rather testy at times. Florida is a tough state: in addition to drugs, there's more series crime than they can deal with. Ever heard about the sticky wheel?"

Flores smiled.

"That's Duncan," he said, "and we will become the grease. Believe me, this is a man who will not take no for an answer. Does anything else come to mind?"

"I do have a question that's not in the literature," Flores said, taking a sip. "I've read the incidence reports, but what do you really think?"

Scott gave a knowing smile. "Well, at any given time, between one and about two hundred active serial killers work the land, maybe more, maybe less, it's very hard to say. There aren't any reliable statistics, but I have always believed that we touch the bare tip of the iceberg. Does that help?"

The young man went silent, considering the number, which seemed quite high to him. "Where the hell do they all come from?" he asked gravely. "I mean, why now? This wasn't happening when I was growing up."

Scott forced a stiff grin onto his face. "I'm afraid it was, Daniel, it's a question of scale. Serial killers have always been a threat to society. Our planet is just more crowded now, so we have more of everything. But those responsible for telling the tale, government officials and writers, have managed to mask the threat in various ways. That's always been the case, though it's getting more difficult for them now."

Flores shook his head in confusion.

"I'll give you an example," Scott offered. "Have you ever heard of Vlad the Impaler?"

"Did I miss a ViCAT case study?" he asked, concerned.

"No, that I would doubt very much." Scott smiled. "Vlad was in his prime around 1465. His real name was Vladimir Basarab, a sadistic serial killer very much like the suspects we track today. He was emotionally devoid and his recreational thrill came from abducting innocent people off the streets of his hometown, then putting them to a painful death. The circumstances surrounding his place in history are rather telling, in terms of human behavior."

"Then I should know of him," Flores agreed.

Scott leaned against the gray rim and took a sip of coffee. "Over many years he was given a dozen names, at one time they called him General Basarab because he controlled the military. The town's population lived in terror, unable to cope with the fact that Vlad could come marching into their homes at any moment, kidnap them at will, and then impale them on a sharpened pole. He liked to watch his victims suffer."

"It does sound familiar," Flores said, searching his memory. "Did they stop him?"

"No," Scott sighed. "They explained him away. And they did it in much the same way society is explaining away the growing population of killers you've asked about. Then, as now, people had great difficulty accepting the concept of a sane human predator who kills for pleasure."

Flores raised an eyebrow. "I don't really follow you, sir."

"Well, instead of facing the harsh reality, they began justifying their inability to stop him, imbuing Basarab with a divine will, attributing superhuman powers for what he did."

Flores finally made the connection. "Count Dracula?" he murmured, leaning back against his chair.

Scott smiled. "The very same, and he did exist, as real as you or I, only there was nothing occult about him. In fact, Basarab had no interest in cannibalism or drinking human blood—that was a writer's invention. Today the same man would be given a sugar coating of mental illness; instead of divine powers, they would make him into a psycho. Such tales make the whole damn thing easier to swallow. But either way it's mythology, nothing more, nothing less."

Flores looked pensive, remembering the count's movie exploits. "But why didn't they tell the real story?"

Scott's grin was genuine as he placed a hand on the young man's shoulder. "You tell me, Daniel, why doesn't our government tell the real story about all the little Draculas we monitor on a daily basis? That's a better question, I think."

A chime overhead filled the chamber, signaling a case alert as green alpha letters began marching across screen seven, the Northwest. Flores quickly put on his headset, then waited, checking the transmitted code against a clipboard, his index finger moving down the pad. "The Home Intruder," he said flatly.

The case was named for a Northwest countryside killer who took residence in the houses of his victims until all their food was eaten or their bodies had started to decompose. He punched in an authorization.

"Sir, do you want me to handle this?" he asked, working the keypad, his eyes intent on the copy that was starting to fill the screen.

There was no answer, so Daniel Flores spun quickly in his seat to repeat the question, preparing to open a phone line with his left hand.

The commander had already gone.

For a long time Scott sat in silence at his desk, one fist curled under his chin, listening to an inner complaint. He fumbled through a drawer for a fresh pack of cigarettes and struck a match. The tiny blue flame came to life, reflecting in his soft gray eyes like a hellish ember.

And Jack Scott felt equally possessed.

Matthew Brennon had returned with a report of his findings, Elmer Janson's coin was a metal token, one century old. The expert's name was Dr. Robert Perry, with credentials that were beyond reproach, and Scott dropped the file back onto his desk. His mind began to wander.

Flores had dubbed the Florida case the Devoid Callers, and Scott thought it fitting for emotionless animals who used a telephone as a distraction to snatch children in one deadly moment. The Cub Scout Killer had left another victim along a California roadside—he had last been active in New Mexico months before. And from the sounds of it, the Home Intruder had found another meal. And there was more. Every hour of every day. By midnight Jack Scott felt the oppressive weight of a lifetime pushing him down, and his cigarette burned to his fingertips, jolting him back to attention. He snuffed it out.

With meticulous effort he started clearing his mind the way he was clearing his desk, reflecting on files only he understood, then walking through rooms in his memory, closing doors while opening others, lifting, sorting, disposing, and examining motive. It was raining outside his window, thick heavy droplets, and he could hear them falling. It was a quiet rain. And Scott craved quiet the way most men crave a vacation. He pulled it over him like a favorite old coat and flopped back in his chair.

He lifted a file and unfolded it across his desk, adjusting the light just so to reduce shadow. He took out an area map of Bethesda, Maryland. He had scanned it once, and now he studied it with care. The modern suburb sat broad with printed legends advertising *Subway Stations* and *Public Parking* and *Future Skating Rink* and *Historic District* and even *New Sculpture;* making promises in every direction like a fat concrete politician. To the north there was endless urban sprawl sprouting titles like Potomac, Cabin John, Rockville, and Wheaton. To the south there was Chevy Chase and then the nation's capital.

Scott turned a page to a statistical breakdown of the Bethesda population that had arrived from the Department of Justice Research. Interpreting as he read, he looked for figures on Ridgewell Hamlet, the Claytons' neighborhood. According to the report, they had lived in a rather small neighborhood for the area, occupying one of sixty-seven homes with a population of two hundred and sixty-eight people. The Hamlet, in turn, sat in an urban ring of sixty square miles with a population nearing two million people—which was about as far as Scott went. All three critical factors associated with a high incidence of serial killings, abductions, and similar types of violent crime were present: a large population, rapid growth, a high number of transients. Diana Clayton was raising her family in a modern killing zone. His anger sparked, Scott lifted a bound report from the local chamber of commerce, which promoted Bethesda as an urban township within easy commute to a city, then flipped the advertisement into the gray can.

That Bethesda was a quiet residential community away from the multitudes was the illusion that allowed the killer to mask himself. The more quiet the neighborhood, the better. The more detached each neighbor, the more effective the camouflage. With her surrounding communities, when it came to population, Bethesda was twice as large as Buffalo, three times the size of New Haven, almost identical to San Diego. Yet who had ever heard of this strange bedroom city?

Scott shook his head, turning his attention to the skeleton found due east of Diana Clayton's home. Checking the address of the condemned building, he then located Elmer Janson's house on the map.

With a red grease pen he circled Ridgewell Hamlet, darkened River Road, then drew a square around Elmer's house. Changing to a blue pen, he colored in the neighborhood where the grave had been found, and using calipers, estimated the distances at 1.3 miles along the same highway. He made a note. The map made the locations impossibly close, a sharp, lopsided triangle covering a specific plot of territory. Even in timely context with the Civil War, it was just too pat for coincidence, and he thought back to his history, when five hundred years ago Vlad the Impaler proved the importance of territorial claim. In behavioral context, feeling at home, knowing the population well, and being comfortable in the workplace was of primary concern to a devoid killer. Selection, stalking, and an adequate study of prey could not be accomplished as quickly in a strange environment. He folded the map, then placed it into a file marked *Case Similarities*.

Scott was standing now, facing his wall with the two-story brick house tacked beneath the detailed shot of Diana Clayton's master bedroom. Breathing deeply, he removed a folder from his briefcase, producing a picture marked *Kimberly's Room*. With a clear stickpin he tacked this enlargement in place, left, next to a wide-angle perspective showing the upstairs hallway.

Kimberly's door was open. The tiny doorway disappeared

into the grain of darkness and he shook another photograph loose. Kimberly's room was pinkish or peach in color, with posters of rock stars on her walls. A close-cropped shot of the bureau came next. The mirror above it had been shattered in the center, cracks snaking outward and meeting the frame. He checked the analysis report on his desk—no pieces missing or fallen out—and he hit the button on his tape recorder. "Notation," he said thoughtfully, "mirror struck by a blunt object, swift, precise blow. Suggests extreme control, perhaps familiarity with tensile resistance of glass. Sample required for test and type manufacture." He checked the files, searching for a report of other broken glass or mirrors in the house. Nothing.

Another photo showing a close-up of the bedding area, a nightstand with picture and lamp still in place. Between the nightstand and bed frame, just next to the child's pink slippers, was a small splash of blood. He pulled another enlargement and turned a page in the crime-scene analysis. Kimberly's type, B-positive, with slight evidence of drainage from sinus mucosa. He had either struck the child here or she had been startled and hit her nose.

Where was Kimberly when the intruder entered? he questioned. Although the county report concluded that the "attacker had found both girls together, asleep in Leslie's bedroom," Scott did not believe it now. He hit the recorder: "Notation, killer did not bring Kimberly back into room, as suggested. Rather, killer woke child in bed, struck child in facial area with small blunt object used on mirror."

He pressed both hands into the small of his back and stretched, then checked the crime scene report. "What did you take?" he muttered, scanning the pages. "If it wasn't a sliver of glass, then what souvenir gave your shallow little heart a knock?"

As was the case with most recreational killers, Scott knew the chances were excellent that this stalker had removed some item from the Claytons' house, a trophy which he could later fondle to increase the intensity of his fantasies. He quickly scanned each photograph, trying to gain a sense of what was missing, as opposed to what could be easily seen. Besides a cruel death, what men like these were after was the production of memories, something to feed on long after the event was over.

Something tangible.

As he searched, his mind skipped through an inventory, the

macabre and twisted collections they had recovered through the years: toys and clothes, photographs and films, ears and teeth, toes and fingers, scalps and bone. Sometimes even the flesh was removed, sexual organs carefully dried with salts for tanning. If nothing else, he thought, the Claytons had escaped that atrocity, and his mind suddenly turned to Captain Duncan Powell. If he had been right, a killer was collecting the teeth of each victim, sparing Lisa Caymann for reasons that were not known, and Scott swallowed hard, glancing at his watch.

He knew the detail his old friend was facing.

Captain Duncan M. Powell of the Florida state police stood at a door, a towering man who seemed larger than life. His troops liked to point out that he looked a lot like John Wayne, kindly yet strong, with a presence that could fill a house.

He had known John F. Scott since the early years, when he and Captain Maxwell Drury had all graduated together from the enforcement academy at Glenco. Along with Joe Taylor, Alan Grafton, and Leslie Vance Doyle, they had been known as the infamous Team Tiger. The manhunters. Their skills placed them tops of the class of 1954, and they were among the few original graybeards who remained in the enforcement establishment and refused retirement.

More than most men, Duncan Powell was a gifted leader who would send no other to do what he felt was his own responsibility. And so it was that he found himself at 1606 McDowell Drive in Clearwater, removing a gold-braided hat and standing with military precision on a dimly lit porch.

Powell had stopped at the rectory of Our Lady of Mercy and asked for the assistance of Father Thomas O'Brian, a small man who was clutching the good book beneath his left arm, standing in the shadow just off to his right.

Since their daughter had been abducted twelve days ago, Duncan Powell had come to know Mr. and Mrs. Phillip Caymann as good and decent people, and of all the details in the world, the captain now faced what he knew as the hardest. He had started to ring the bell as the door cracked open, revealing a pathetic figure of a man, his head bowed with resignation. Duncan could hear a woman sob convulsively from another part of the house.

"I am truly sorry," Captain Powell said, extending a massive right hand. Phillip Caymann took it limply.

"We saw you pulling into the driveway," he cried. "You have news about Lisa?" he asked. He was fighting to maintain his composure when his eyes flared at the sight of the pastor.

"May we come in?" Powell asked kindly.

"I'm sorry, but I don't want her mother to hear. Tell me first please, Duncan, I beg you, I'm begging you. Is it Lisa? Did you find Lisa? Is she dead?"

Captain Powell stood silent at the doorway, watching the terror contort the man's face. Powell released a heavy sigh, giving the man time to steel himself, if that was possible.

"Earlier this evening," he said slowly, "a patrol car found the body of a young girl near the highway—"

Phillip Caymann took a sharp step backward, hitting the door with his back. "Please!" he shouted, feeling his knees grow weak, holding up one hand to silence the senior officer. "Please, her mother will hear . . ."

Then the man began to tremble violently as the reality took hold. The police would not have come without calling first, unless they were sure. The red lights pulsed from the driveway, but there was no siren, no rush suggesting that life was hanging in the balance. Instead the police had brought a priest.

The primeval role of father quickly superseded the braver role of man and protector, as his knees folded beneath him, and Phillip Caymann double-stepped, tripping forward against the captain's barrel chest.

"What kind of animal would do this?" he cried helplessly. "What kind of monster would kill my baby?"

The captain propped him up as Caymann released a horrible scream, a painful, deafening, and terrifying roar that sounded like a lion whose heart was impaled.

And at that tragic moment, as the pastor prayed, Duncan Powell turned his face into the cold night, holding the shattered man together with all his humanity. Only one thought came to mind.

Find Jack Scott.

There were no others.

15

Scott's desktop was nearly empty.

An ashtray and coffee mug remained, which he now moved aside, and with a tired hand he reached for his bottommost drawer, a large wooden file box that had served as his catchall since 1956, the year he had purchased the executive-style tank.

He felt haunted, as if while surveying the contents he were surrounded by ghosts, moving back through the darkest corners of his life. He aimed the hinged cone of light, clearing shadows, then looked down. The pack-rat things of his life stared back up.

On top there was an assortment of newspapers, haphazardly thrown in, each covering various ViCAT cases, and he lifted them out in a pile, dropping them into the trash. A special edition of *Look* surfaced; Scott paused, trying to remember when he had aspired to the theme issue of country living. The date on the cover was 1968. He quickly dropped it into the can. Next came a worn *World Almanac* for the year 1964, which in turn rested on top of a hand calculator that was about the same thickness and weight. He discarded them both. Underneath there was a large manila envelope containing an original poster of *Speech,* one of the Four Freedoms painted by Norman Rockwell, and he set this aside, recalling how he had meant to frame it for the country house.

There was a box of white linen handkerchiefs, which he had forgotten, yellowed from smoke and age, and as he lifted this, a gold-plated lighter fell to the carpet. He smiled. This he did remember; it had been given and broken nineteen years ago, and he held it in his palm. "Congratulations, Dr. Scott," it was inscribed for his graduation. He turned it over. "Love, Linda." He could not throw this away.

Out went a tie clip, a badge, assorted buttons, then a variety of relics stuffed into a cracked and swollen Belvedere cigar box. He was about to toss the box when he stopped.

"Bless this day with a healthy child." The voice of Nicholas Dobbs filled his ears. Scott had purchased the cigars in

1959 when his first child was born, and he had opened the box for his commander. The old Irishman was so touched that he raced for the door and returned with peppermint candy for Scott to keep under his bed.

Beneath the box lay an outdated double-edged safety razor, blades long spent before a youthful mirror. Next came a small brown cardboard box marked "COLT," containing a pocket pistol. And finally he reached bottom.

And it was there.

In a mass of lint and litter, flecked with gray ash and covered with dust, was a thick pile of bound reports and case summaries. Most had been kept not as trophies, but as precedent-setting documents advancing techniques of criminal investigation. Others had simply been closed by command when leads ran out and budgets went dry. His heart raced as he reached deeper into the shadows, his mouth went dry and he could not swallow.

And it was there. In the darkness. Waiting for him like an ancient, evil debt.

Scott hesitated, a pack rat staring down, a yellow folder staring back up. He shuddered, awash in adrenaline, his sphincter pulling unpleasantly tight as he recognized his own youthful scrawl on the outside tab. No secretary or assistant back then. He felt an ache, a curse of time racing across the ridge of his knuckles.

With a deep breath he pulled it free, preventing the contents from spilling with his left hand. With a faint trembling he laid it down across his desk. Bile filled his throat and he swallowed.

* ZACHARIAH'S ONE MAN CIRCUS! *
Magic * Clowns * Fortunes * Puppets
For Children of All Ages!
—Zak the Master—

Scott was seeing the advertisement in his mind even before he had opened the file, and his throat burned uncomfortably as he removed the printed flier. He took a sip of cold coffee.

Time had not changed a thing, he thought, adjusting it under the beam. There had been a hundred similar fliers left in boxes on the day they arrested Zak. Scott leaned back, staring into space, remembering a more civilized, less complicated age.

American values were purer then. Or perhaps better defined. Maybe his youth was a factor and he was now distorting the past with the resentment of age. He fixed on the memory of seeing Zachariah's collection emerging from the bathroom floor. In 1989 the contents would appear fairly tame, he thought, but in 1960 all such legal products limited their displays to bikini-clad pinups, and Scott, like most law-enforcement professionals, knew that there was a direct link between porn and violent behavior.

The search of Zachariah's apartment had produced an assortment of depraved pictures and film, including graphic photographs of women and children being sexually debased. Even more damning, the seizure included stacks of police procedural manuals, some with detailed instructions on current investigative techniques.

"Sonofabitch!" he had hissed. "Sonofabitch, Nick, over here!" Scott remembered with an uneasy clarity how he had cursed while pulling up a bathroom tile with a pocketknife. In an instant Nicholas Dobbs was standing over him, his commanding voice providing an edge of caution while six other agents started hacking into the floor and walls.

"By the book, fellas," Dobbs said. "Scotty, mind your procedure . . ." Scott waited for his commander, then removed four tiles with gloved hands while keeping a tight rein on his adrenaline. He placed each element of the collection into individual evidence bags, while Dobbs recorded the event with a box camera.

Scott was looking at one of those pictures now, a record of Zak's shower coming apart in the hands of a younger Jack Scott. Under the harsh white beam he could see a blur where his young hands would have been, shaking then as they were now, disappearing into a carefully constructed hollow beneath the drain.

One by one, elements of the collection came free, manual after manual, book after book, primer after primer, diagrams and photographs and films. Scott leaned back on his haunches, handing a book to Commander Dobbs; he was looking at that photographic sequence now, of a man Daniel Flores' age handing a book to an old and trusted friend.

"Expert Restraint, How to Work Livestock with Rope," Dobbs read aloud.

"I'm going to skin him," Scott spat furiously, remembering

what he had said while reading marginal notations in the killer's workbook. "I'm going to cut his goddamned liver out!"

Immediately Dobbs stepped into the shower, leaning over so that only Scott could hear. "Listen to me," he whispered, biting off each word. "We are going to prosecute this man and he is going to the gas chamber, so as of now we start tempering every comment as if a judge were listening."

"But how can you be sure, Nick?"

Scott listened intently then as he was listening now, but it was an older man, less brave and more alone, who waited for his commander in the patter of rain drifting against the tall windows.

The sound of the rain. Hardly a sound at all.

The One Man Circus.

His full name was Zachariah Leslie Dorani, and between 1957 and 1960 he had advertised to parents throughout New England. During that period, 6 bodies had been recovered, women and children, and though more were reported missing, they were never found. Zak Dorani was a recreational killer, a self-taught master of cruelty, illusion, and deceit.

After that brief conversation with Dobbs, Scott returned to digging through the apartment, removing a plethora of the macabre, including a definitive medical reference on poisons, arsenic to Zyklon-B, and a collection of WWII manuals on silent weaponry. These lay next to classic texts on the mortuary arts, with sections dedicated to embalming and cremation. At the end of a series of pornographic materials, Scott found several self-help books for women, long before the pop publishing craze, and these had been stored alongside *The Complete Encyclopedia of Child Psychology.*

They had never doubted that they had arrested the right man, for the abductions had stopped immediately, September 5, 1960. Mary Beth Dodson had been Zak's last victim. Scott had watched her die. She might have been the only person on earth whose words could have placed Zak onto death row, and without her testimony the case crumbled.

Since the forensic sciences were still in their infancy, case elements had to be presented without the luxury of today's comprehensive crime analysis, and the evidence against Zachariah was circumstantial at best. From bruises and rope fibers found on the victims, it was clear that they had been bound with strips of cord in a skilled manner remarkably similar to that found in the manuals. And death always came from critical punctures of the brain.

Pathologists never did determine what had caused the destructive cranial holes, what kind of offending instrument had been used in killing, for Zak had removed the lethal evidence precisely at death's onset. As Dr. Chet Sanders testified, the reaction of the brain to grievous insult is to swell until the organ bursts, turning to jelly within the tight skull case, destroying wound channels while also killing the victim. Whatever it was, the technique rendered the help of medical professionals worthless. They were never able to make a precise reconstruction of events based on the equivalent of shattered bowls filled with a gelatinous soup.

Using time series analysis, Dobbs and Scott attempted to link Zak to his heinous crimes through a reconstruction of events. All of the dead women and children had shared one thing in common: they had been entertained by the One Man Circus. Two children testified that Zak had offered them free magic in a special place where their futures could be seen, an invitation they wisely declined, in spite of the fact that he was a known friend who had been the featured attraction at their birthday parties.

The defense made it sound very innocent, portraying the killer as a tragic figure missing the companionship of his own family. In 1953 Zak had lost his wife and two children in a freak auto accident, and with the help of his attorney Zachariah explained away every claim, skillfully painting the image of a grieved model husband. In his last year as assistant U.S. attorney, David Satter headed the prosecution.

"Your Honor, the state would like to point out that the accident left the defendant sole beneficiary of a substantial insurance policy, paid for by the defendant—"

"Objection!" Meyer Coleman rose sharply out of his chair, pleading to the jury. "Mr. Dorani is not on trial for a great personal loss, your Honor."

"Sustained," ordered Judge Owen Lymann without hesitation. And so it was that Zak was able to relay an incredible yet convincing tale of coincidence and association, explaining away the materials found in his shower.

"They are all very innocent," he cried, sobbing expressly for the three women of the jury. "They belonged to my wife. She was studying sexual response in hopes of earning a college degree and becoming a counselor in sexual dysfunction."

He wiped his eyes and paused for effect. "She only wanted to help others. . . ."

Coleman introduced the dead woman's college transcripts. She had taken two lower-level courses in human sexuality, and Zak played the crowd with daring and skill, an accomplished actor giving the performance of his life, for his life.

The jury was his stage, and he cried over everything, right up to the point were the state introduced the illustrated guides on livestock. At this his eyes flamed with indignant rage.

"I have never seen them before!" he huffed, crossing arms against his chest, his face flushed with the hurtful suggestion. "I have told you quite honestly, my wife and I did own the literature. They were scientific research, and we hid them so the children would not be exposed. Maybe they belonged to a previous tenant. Why would I lie about books on farming?" And so it went.

After a trial lasting nine months, for lack of conclusive evidence, Zak Dorani was found not guilty on nine related counts of abduction and murder, but guilty as to felony possession of pornographic materials in the third degree, by reason of insanity. Today, Scott reflected, such possession is not even considered worthy of court, but then it was simply unexplainable and revolting, the kind of trash that crawled from human sewers. On that much the jury agreed, recommending the maximum sentence, and Zak was given eight years in the Adjunct Psychiatric Facility at Woodside Prison in New York.

Immediately afterward, Scott fell into a deep depression. He took a leave of absence, returning to complete his degree at Yale University. Dobbs attended his graduation, then assigned the young agent to the new concept of criminal behavioral profiling. They never spoke of Zak the Needle again.

"When we lost this case, why did you promote me?" Scott asked, eyeing the coffee ring on the file, placed there more than thirty years before. Scott had always regretted not asking for an explanation, and Dobbs had taken the answer to his grave over a decade ago.

Like so many others, Commander Nicholas Alan Dobbs had fallen to the agent's curse, the policeman's disease. After retirement, when the grisly images accumulated over a lifetime filled his mind one too many times, refusing to let him go, he placed his gun in his mouth and pulled the trigger. In the end, it was a symbol of his failing, of his humanity, of his caring too much to fail.

For some professionals—teachers, editors, accountants, merchants, even doctors—failure was a part of the job. It made you a member of a humble species. An error apologized for, then forgiven, often adjusted. When Nick Dobbs or Jack Scott failed, innocent mothers died with their children. Bombs were set. Infants and small animals were torn apart. Acid was thrown on unsuspecting tourists. Grandparents mourned before closed caskets. And there was no one to apologize to, not even each other. Commander Dobbs had succumbed to a personal haunt that held him, seduced him, that finally took him once and for all.

From inside a glassine evidence bag Scott removed a honed, tapered spike given to him by Dr. Chet Sanders, excised from the left lung of Mary Beth Dodson. He held it under the light. It was black, hardened over fire, sharp as a needle. He held it tightly in his hand, comparing it with the photograph of Elmer Janson's souvenir.

Rough estimates showed six inches of wood, but from a facsimile, critical detail was hard to discern. The boy's stick was worn, eaten away by years underground. Physically they were not exact analogues, but in his mind it was all the same.

"You will pay," Zak Dorani had announced to Scott as he left the courthouse for the last time, fists manacled to his belt, his legs bound by chain.

Scott closed his lids, straining to recall the killer's voice, but the memory evaded him. All he remembered were the eyes, burning like cold, empty lanterns.

Just then a warmth licked against his wrist, jarring him from thought. His blood was flowing, but Scott didn't feel pain.

He had worked the spike up into his palm.

16

11:58 P.M. WASHINGTON, D.C.

After-hours on a weekend, Georgetown was a scant thirty minutes from Bethesda, Maryland, a straight shot down Wisconsin Avenue through the upper northwest part of the city.

Earlier in the evening he had been struck by an urge, and he felt restless, leaving his residence for a brief interlude, just killing time by cruising the streets. These days his back ached, not excruciating pain but a dull, episodic throbbing that ran along his spine, giving him migraines, and he knew they would pass if he kept distracted. He pulled his car through the alley behind Zephyr's Grill on Wisconsin Avenue, a shabby dive five minutes from Georgetown University.

The bar was a local landmark of sorts, and he had been a regular since the late 1960's. It was centrally located to the city and well-known for serving drinks to minors. As he stepped from his car, he placed one hand against the small of his back, then stretched while releasing a satisfied yawn. The only light in the alley came from a naked bulb hanging over the Zephyr's rear door, the feeble glow too weak to illuminate much detail.

The person standing in this light was a plain and little man who could have been anyone: an insurance salesman, a car dealer, a clerk. He had an oval face with bland features and a receding hairline. What was left of his fine brown hair he parted on the left, combed like an altar boy awaiting inspection.

Earlier in the evening he had been restless. Now the lateness of the hour took him by surprise and he felt tired to the bone, releasing another deep yawn. When he opened the door to the passenger side, the darkness remained, for the car's overhead lamp had been removed. He stared woodenly at the young woman sprawled in the red leather seat. Her breathing was deep and labored.

A silver Mercedes turned from a back street and moved slowly past the alley entrance. Two older women in fur coats glanced his way, then averted their eyes as the man smiled. "My kind of town," he said with a nod, and he knew it well, all the paradoxes and refined illusion that fueled this particular city. To him it was simply a place where he could easily procure human flesh, night or day, made no difference. You could romance it, pay for it, or take it by force. These were strictly personal choices that depended more on whim than on wisdom, for there were few rules in the nation's capital beyond *don't get caught*. By day, a land of monuments. By night, a city that swallowed life.

He reached in and dragged her from the car, then dropped her along the curb like a sack of stones. She moaned up at her assailant through a trance, her blue eyes rolling, her lids streaked with mascara, blinking shut with a heavy narcotic slumber. He pushed her closer against the curb, then knelt and manipulated her legs to remove her shoes.

"We're out of time," he said absently, studying the tree line for headlights, but the woman could not hear. She had not known the cocktail she was drinking had been laced with succinylcholine, a powerful but tasteless muscle relaxant with hypnotic consequences.

It was a quick twenty paces from the alley to the sidewalk on the incline above, and in between there was a covered storm drain on a grassy knoll. He pulled the woman onto the grass, then, leaning over at the waist, removed the iron lid with a simple T-bar he carried in his belt. Placing a penlight between his teeth, he stuck his head through the opening to inspect the pit.

The beam struck concrete walls but failed to reach the bottom, while the corrosive smells of wet iron and stone filled his sinuses. The little man huffed, turning to examine her sprawled body, the disheveled slacks and blouse, the torn stockings over bare feet. Without ceremony he grabbed her beneath the arms, flipped her over, then dragged her, toes up.

Because he was supporting her weight, her stocking feet left no visible mark in the coarse brown grass, and he dropped her again as he fumbled at the small of his back with one hand.

With skilled precision he leaned her shoulders and head backward over the gaping darkness, exposing her pale breasts and releasing a shower of brown hair. Parting lids over helpless eyes flashed in his mind like a glassy blue stain.

"It's been fun," he said, rubbing her neck where it strained. Then, grabbing a fist of hair, he suddenly pulled her face toward his, and in one smooth motion fired a single shot from a silenced pistol.

There was a dull *clank* as the bullet hit the concrete below. *Clank, clank.*

And her body followed through the fatal darkness, falling freely through the air as the world went silent and still around him, the sounds of traffic failing, sirens dying, jets finding a void of quiet above his head, her body landing with a harsh thud.

He closed his eyes tightly, standing there in the dim light, the shadows failing into darkness, the darkness failing into death.

"Yes," he breathed hard, and the moisture from his lungs held like a pale cloud.

"Yes, yes, yes . . ."

He proceeded to flip her shoes into the seamless dark and then covered the drain again. The second and third shots had removed her dental forensics, and he knew time and sewer rodents would accomplish the rest.

He was happy now. He returned to his car.

With one hand on the wheel he coasted through the alley, attentive to traffic rules, slowing carefully for a blinking red light at the intersection of Wisconsin Avenue and Foxhall Road. A war-battered District of Columbia police car appeared, moving in his direction, and he gave a weary nod at a tired blue uniform.

He snapped a cassette into the tape player of his black BMW, and settled back into the red leather seats for his midnight drive toward home. He fancied himself a cultured man, so he listened to tapes like Chopin's nocturnes, which he had discovered resting on a baby grand next to a porcelain ballerina.

"Would you mind if I borrow one of your tapes?" he had asked Diana Clayton on the night of March 31 as he tested her bathwater with an index finger, toying with her mind, her body, and her heart.

"No," he quickly agreed, "ask me nicely and I'll think it over."

17

SENECA, MARYLAND

Well after midnight a telephone was ringing.

A hand hovered in front of a television, moving over a footlocker that served as a coffee table, then lifting Mickey Mouse onto the bed. Francis Dale Rivers was watching what is known to cops throughout the Washington area as *Midnight Mass,* a local news show second to none in doom and shabby production. A commercial was coming up, so he let the phone ring while waiting to see if they previewed his announcement concerning the disappearance of Debra Patterson.

There had been five drug-related slayings, a report on a serial rape in Bethesda, a hit-and-run, two suicides, one bombing, three reported burglaries, and a replay of Reagan's latest law-and-order speech. An average six-hour run. Rivers guessed a story about the Patterson kid had been bumped, even though he had stopped by the station to ask for their assistance.

"Yeah," he answered, crunching an aspirin into Mickey's ear.

"Sergeant, my name is Scott," said the voice. "Commander Jack Scott, I'm with ViCAT in New York."

"So that's your name," Rivers said.

As Scott had requested, Captain Maxwell Drury had dispatched a helicopter to the Rivers house earlier in the evening in order to recover Elmer Janson's evidence. Scott carefully considered the nature of that intrusion, rubbing one hand through his graying hair and choosing his words thoughtfully.

"I'd like to thank you for the materials you sent to my attention," he said. "I'm sorry for the delay, I'm looking forward to your cooperation."

Rivers was immediately fascinated with the voice. It was mellow and urbane with a cultured enunciation, yet there was a hint of anger, like a steel hand in a velvet glove. "My cooperation, Mr. Scott?" he questioned sarcastically. "I didn't know who I was dealing with or if I was even dealing. Drury sent a chopper to my house, and that's about all I know. What's your badge number?"

Scott considered the suspicious tone. "One," he said.

"Just routine," Rivers offered, "always like to know who I'm talking with. That would be badge number one, NSA ViCAT, USA," he repeated.

"That's correct, do you require verification?"

"Negative," Rivers said quickly. "So what winds your clock, Mr. Scott, what can I do for you?"

Scott paused. "Perhaps a great deal or perhaps nothing at all, but I like your style, Frank. Could I ask a few questions?"

"Sure," he baited, leaning back across his bed. "Fire away, but you don't have to stroke me first."

"Am I interrupting anything?"

"No dates, no ball game, a rather slow Friday night. I was just doing a little research and writing up an APB for one Debra Patterson, a local kid about sixteen years old."

"What?" Scott hissed. "A missing child, why wasn't I informed ..."

Rivers listened intently to his tone, he could sense the glove coming off.

". . . I asked to be kept posted on any wrinkle."

"Well, I'm sure I wouldn't know, Mr. Scott, might be you're asking the wrong bureaucrat. But if you want my opinion, this is a real sweet-looking kid, and some *Mook* could be dressing her down right now. It won't be on the wire for another twenty-four hours. Rules, paperwork, the usual crap, you know the drill."

"I know the drill," Scott lamented.

"Her parents are going nuts, and I don't blame them. Why don't you lend a hand? I mean, Badge One and all, it's very impressive."

"All right, Frank," Scott retorted, "I'll see what I can do. So what's your story, what winds your recalcitrant ticker?"

"Mine?" Rivers chuckled. "Chevrolet and apple pie. Sounds like you've been reading my sheets."

"Every word, an interesting profile," he stated flatly.

"Well, nothing special in there, but I really hate being treated like a weak-kneed sister to some old billiard ball, so why don't you tell me what you need? Maybe we can work something out."

"Is Captain Drury the old billiard ball?" Scott smiled.

No response.

"Frank, we've got a serious police apprehension problem, and I need your help. I apologize if we stepped on any toes."

Rivers pulled himself forward on his elbows. "Well, I appreciate that, Scott, 'cause you're Bigfoot. Listen, sure as hell burns, I'd like to help with the Claytons, but do you have assignment authority?"

"At the highest level," he said, "in the interest of national security."

"Yeah, yeah, that's not what I mean, Jack. When you duck, who gets hit by the shit?"

Scott pushed off his desk and settled back in his chair. There was something brutally honest, almost severe, about Frank Rivers. "My people come before my career. I've told that to three presidents."

"Interesting," Rivers responded absently. "Tell me something, are you a shrink? That's been the talk for years, you know, that NSA Enforcement is run by a bunch of shrinks."

"I have a degree in psychology. A shrink has an M.D. and hands out pills, I'm a cop."

"I like that," he chuckled, "how can I help?"

"Let's start with the Claytons. What else do you know about the killings?"

"Just what I hear, plus I conducted a few field interviews—I'll bet they're on your desk right now. I was one of the first at the scene, just about the cruelest case ever. I heard you guys were called when the investigation stalled out. The county was handling it, you know, that was a big mistake."

"Why?"

"They're like McGruff the crime dog, all warm and fuzzy at home, but in the field, forget it. The severity of this case was too important. Did you know Drury only took over as an adviser at the request of the governor and then got stuck with the investigation?"

"I figured as much. Tell me about Elmer Janson, how did you know to track him down?"

"Just curiosity. I read about his finding bones in the local paper, got a copy of the postmortem, and went to see for myself. I also read a report on the territorial imperative of the series killer a few years back, and based on that, Elmer's little discovery bothered me. It's within a mile of the Clayton place, but I guess you knew."

"Yes, I did, and Elmer gave you the evidence?"

"That's affirmative. He's quite a kid. So what do you make of it?"

Scott paused. "What's your theory?" he asked.

"Hell, I don't know, but we got something. Based on the territorial imperative, I was thinking we might have a family of wackos handing down their expertise from generation to generation. Maybe the guy who buried that child is the great-grandfather of the Claytons' killer. How's that for a start?"

"Well, it's definitely murder one," Scott provoked.

"I thought so too, Jack. That child had been tortured, I've seen sticks like that in Southeast Asia. You know, it's interesting, during the Civil War this town was swarming with troops while some sickoid was getting his rocks off hurting little kids. Humanity sucks, I've always believed that."

Scott let the man talk, agreeing when he could, building a foundation for trust. Rivers was a serious man, that much was clear. He also cloaked himself in the demeanor of the common man to shield his insight, but there was no doubt in Scott's mind that the classic dagger was close behind. That unassuming diamond-in-the-rough bit had CIA training stamped all over it.

"Frank," Scott interrupted, mustering a voice of reserved authority.

"Yeah?"

"The grave Elmer found is modern, post-Civil War. Your medical examiner is sleepwalking."

"What?" The voice fell short of a cry. "You better beam up, Scotty, you need mission control."

Scott heard him chuckle. "The body found by Elmer Janson and the Clayton killings are the work of the same man," Scott stated more formally.

"Nope," Rivers spat with contempt, "that's crazy talk."

"Is it?" Scott asked quietly.

Rivers carefully considered the claim. The grave found by Elmer Janson was close to becoming a bag of dust, wasn't it? "Dr. Talbard worked the bones and he's a good M.E., Jack. I've seen better, but I doubt he'd miss something like that."

"Answer me one question," Scott offered calmly, "and if I'm wrong I'll buy you tickets to a ball game."

"That's a deal," Rivers said, lying back down across his bed. "How about the World Seriousness?"

"Frank, you turned in a piece of wood to Max Drury, looked akin to a black chopstick?"

"That's right."

"And you spent some time with this boy who found the grave?"

"I'm a pretty fair detective."

"I have no doubt, so be straight with me, Frank. A great deal depends on this." He was staring at his wall, into Diana Clayton's lifeless eyes.

"I'll be straight," he promised.

Scott took a breath. "There are at least nine more of these sticks, but maybe twelve," Scott stated coldly.

The resulting silence was chilling.

A black bile quickly filled Scott's throat, and he hurriedly swallowed a splash of cold coffee. "Isn't that correct, Frank?" he asked, clearing phlegm from his voice.

"Holy Christ!" Rivers cried. Hopping from his bed, he lifted Elmer's paper bag and shook the contents. Scott waited for the excitement to pass, and Rivers sat nervously on the edge of his bed. "There's no way you could have known that,

I've withheld the evidence . . ." he started to say. Then he caught himself, closing his eyes.

"Yes, you did, Rivers," Scott said coldly, "and you made yourself a suspect in the process. So why did you do it?"

Rivers paused, knowing if Scott wanted to file papers, then his state career was over. Rivers had just started to figure it was time for a change anyway, that the job was growing stale, when Scott spoke up.

"I don't care, Frank, but it's not a good practice. So why did you do it?"

"Just a precaution," he answered slowly. "I don't like having my cases jumped, and down here it's routine, politics all the damn time. But how the hell did you know?"

"I think I've arrested the same killer before, but I'm still waiting for evidence. Between you and me, I'm running on empty except for the help you've supplied."

"But how could that be?" Rivers said. "This is getting weird. That body was almost dust, ancient, and the coin—"

"I do have my doubts," Scott confessed, cutting him off. "I'm guessing it's the same man."

"And he killed the Claytons?"

"Possible."

"God, how long has this guy been killing? What's his name?" His voice was starting to race, and Rivers felt his body charge with adrenaline. "Hey, what did he do to those little girls, Jack?"

"Frank," Scott said cautiously, "would you like to work with me on this case?"

"Sure," Rivers stated. "But what are these sticks about? What a slimy bastard, I'm going to break him apart—"

"No, you are not, Sergeant," Scott ordered. "If you want in, then we have to have some ground rules."

"Anything," he promised aimlessly.

"First, you answer only to me," Scott said, biting off each word. "Second, you do not discuss this case without my authorization. Third, if you cause a problem, it's over—no second chances."

"If that's it, you've got yourself a deal, Commander. Let's get started," he said casually.

Scott contemplated the situation. "I'm going to start processing papers to assign you to us on an interagency request, what we call a Multi Agency Investigative Team.

You'll still carry your state badge with our ID. Now, this is important . . ."

"I'm listening," Rivers said, starting to take notes.

"Call Captain Drury at home—wake him up if necessary, tell him I told you to. Don't discuss the case, just tell him to dispatch two officers to the home of Elmer Janson for surveillance. Men you trust. You pick the officers and tell Drury."

"Oh, God, are they in danger?" Rivers exclaimed. Images of a beautiful young mother and a lonely little boy tore through his mind.

There was only silence.

"You answer me, Scott!"

"No, Frank," he corrected quietly, "you answer to me."

Rivers dropped his head into his hand. "Right," he sighed, staring indignantly at Mickey's puss.

"Is Mrs. Janson still married?" Scott asked. "Is her husband at home?"

Frank bit his lip. "Shit, I don't know, now that you mention it. The local paper said he was in Europe, they invited me to stay for dinner. Jack . . ."

"This is just a precaution, I don't think our man will hit a family again this soon. He'll go after single targets, what we call a quick fix."

"Christ!" Rivers shouted. "Then what about Elmer Janson? The kid's a real player, he—"

"He'd require too much planning for the killer, at least for the time being, but they *would* be a likely target."

"But how would our man know?" Rivers pondered.

"You said you read Elmer's story in the newspaper, and you're not the only subscriber, Frank. There are other case elements as well, so just pick two good men and have Drury assign them. Now, according to your jacket, you've lived near the area most of your life. How long?"

"I'm thirty-eight, my folks moved here when I was in eighth grade, so twenty-four years on and off, why?"

"Does anyone know the local history better than you?"

"Only one person I know of, but there's a local historical society—"

"No," Scott blurted, "stay away from them, that's important. And stay clear of preservationists."

"Why, what's this about?"

"We'll get to that in the morning. I just don't want secondhand history from an egghead dropping nose hairs in books. How long has your friend lived there?"

"Forever, he was born here, Jack. Personally we're very close and he's also my landlord, a fourth-generation Marylander. He lives in Cabin John, that's a town real close by."

Scott opened a file and circled the name on the Bethesda map. "We're going to need his help, so give him a call." Scott knew right away the man was trustworthy. Anyone who could get close to Frank Rivers would have to be, by definition, quiet as a lump.

"Anything," he said.

"Good, I appreciate that, Frank. Now, tell me about Debra Patterson. You said you needed an assist."

Rivers gave Scott the details, as much as he knew. "Last seen in her car headed for the store. I need an air search and I don't have the clout."

"But I'll bet you know a decent pilot?"

"Affirmative. Damn good, three tours in air cavalry. Name's Steve Adare, he's a state boy. Why, he could find a tick in a—"

"Ask Drury to get that man airborne, my orders."

"You're kidding?" Rivers laughed. "Easy as that, order Mad Max to—"

"Be nice about it, Frank. That old billiard ball is a dear friend of mine."

"Affirmative," he said quietly.

"And, Frank," Scott warned, "at all times try to remember that the man we're hunting knows exactly what he's doing. For all practical purposes he's as sane as you or I, and he's real clever."

"Who is he, Jack, what's the fucker's name?"

"Doesn't matter. Like I said, he's smart, changes identities like you or I change socks. But if you can follow orders, we'll get him. Are we on the same wavelength?"

"Yes, sir, but I don't get it," Rivers questioned. "Why didn't someone keep an eye on this bastard? How the hell did he get away?"

Scott closed pale lids over eyes that had grown dark and bloodshot, the eyes of an older man who had brooded long after normal people were asleep.

Frank Rivers understood the silence. "So you pooched the tiger, Jack. Everybody does at some time, forget I asked."

Scott wanted to comply, he wanted to forget, he wanted to

go back in time so forgetting wasn't necessary. "I thought he was dead, Frank, and that's just what he wanted me to think. I'm staring at his obituary right now: Zachariah Leslie Dorani, dead at the age of thirty-three, and that was back in 1966. I should have examined the body before the cremation."

As the call was terminated, Scott placed the obit under *Case Similarities* and reached back into the file marked *Children's Room.*

He felt a shiver. He felt cold to the marrow.

Leslie's bedroom overlooked the front lawn and street, two windows large enough to allow a full blast of morning sun. Scott checked the analysis report. The room and front of the house faced due east.

In another shot, Leslie Clayton sat in a white wicker chair, dressed in a pastel flowered blouse with charcoal-gray slacks, ready for school. A blue denim tote bag rested against the chair. He cross-checked the forensics report.

Although only fibers remained, she had been left tied in the chair for hours after death, until rigor mortis had begun, accounting for her rigid posture. The rope was gone, but from lacerations and bruises it was certain the killer had left the moribund child bound at the neck, arms, and back for over two hours. Her eyelids had been held open until her body stiffened, and Scott felt his eyes tear. He was thankful death had been instantaneous.

He recorded a notation: "Had the killer left the house and returned? When did he place the moribund child in front of the window?"

The cause of death was nearly identical to that of Diana Clayton, a single shot, with the exception of the wound channel. According to the report, the bullet punctured the hard palate inside the oral cavity, exiting the top of the child's cranium. Only trace elements of the slug had been recovered. Notation: "How did killer trap and capture the bullet?"

He placed the photo alongside the last, building out from the left. The third was a wide-angle of the room showing the lifeless bodies of both children, sitting in separate chairs, Leslie at the window, Kimberly positioned just behind at her sister's dressing table, seeming to look out toward the street. She was dressed and appeared to be untying her hair, her arms suspended in death.

Cross-referencing, she had been bound in a similar manner until her body stiffened, and knowing that he would live with this image for he didn't know how long, Scott could not bring himself to study the picture too closely. Words on a page, safer, antiseptic.

Kimberly had not been shot. Cause of death was listed as "sequential multiple organ failure," compound trauma resulting from rapid "acceleration-deceleration movement of the head." When death is not instantaneous, Scott knew, the body reacts to acute shock by shutting down organ functions. The most common cause is a swelling of the brain against the tight skull case, the type of trauma most often seen in automobile-accident victims. The child's brain had literally bounced within the cranium case, causing massive swelling, hemorrhaging, and death. The image did not reflect the face of a little girl.

Gently he tacked each exposure into a godless matrix, and closed his eyes, no longer able to concentrate, so Scott did not notice Daniel Flores standing silently in the doorway. The horror of the wall had reached out and touched the young agent. Flores cleared his throat.

"I'm sorry to disturb you, sir," he said, shifting his gaze toward the tops of his wing tips. Scott didn't respond, but fumbled through his drawers, lighting a match. Harsh smoke, old and stale, burned in his lungs as he leaned back in his chair, back into the night.

"What is it, Daniel?" he asked, rubbing fingers into tired eyes. He glanced at his watch. It was 1:46. The night had ascended into Saturday morning.

"Dr. Charles McQuade wired into system one, and the computer automatically authorized his entry, so I thought it might be important. I tried to keep him on line, but he ended transmission."

The young agent stepped forward, handing Scott a sheet from the laser printer along with a file, which the commander then laid across his desk, seeing nothing but a wasteland of white, characters of ink marching in tight little lines.

"That's the report on Mrs. Janson you requested. Is there anything else I can do?" Flores asked, concerned.

"No, no, thank you, Daniel. What time does your shift end?"

"In an hour, but I'll still be fresh if you need me."

"Has Brennon returned?" Scott asked without looking up.

"No, sir, he just radioed to say he's on his way."

"I want to see him the moment he's back. Tell him it's urgent."

"Yes, sir," Flores said as he closed the door softly behind him.

Tricks of time did not evade Dr. Charles McQuade.

"So what's worse," Scott asked aloud, hesitating at the report. "A child afraid of the dark or a cop afraid of the light?" With a hand that ached with age, he lifted the printout from his desk.

Black female. Time of death: Spring/summer 1958. Age: 12 years. Cause of death: Small, critical punctures of cranium. Material evidence: Rope fibers. Materials postmortem: Traces CaO, calcium oxide, commonly known as lime. Traces of mercuric acid.

Scott nodded thoughtfully. He knew firsthand the caustic effects lime could have, and working in combination, acid would have speeded the decomposition process until the ground was smoking, bubbling in a corrosive brine that would rend flesh from bone, that in turn would dissolve bone back into its organic elements. Angrily he lifted the file marked *Jennifer Doe* and removed a photograph of the burial site during excavation. Examining this closely, he then checked a report from the U.S. Soil and Conservation Service.

"Maryland substrate," he read aloud, "a fine-grained earth . . . composed chiefly of hydrous aluminum silicate materials," produced through the millennia by the breaking down of rocks, mineral, and stone. The soil of the Potomac river valley was a fine reddish clay, a hard combination of sandstone and granite, so pliable and dense it held rainwater like a tub. The photograph showed a pit, a hollow beneath blacktop that held a good six inches of rain and was unable to drain. Scott immediately concluded a refined knowledge was involved in the disposal. The killer had intentionally dug an earthen pool so that the victim's body would be submerged, soaking for years in a vitreous bath. He now understood why the remains appeared to have been interred over a century ago. They were lucky anything was left.

Rage stirring, he grabbed the file marked *Zak* off his desk and slapped the summaries inside. Was it possible that this killer had been operating that far south, and that somehow they had never known? Even after three decades Scott could recite the case from memory. Dobbs had officially ended the pursuit, and his initials were in the upper corner of the file, a faded signatory attesting to failure: *Case Closed, September 14, 1960.*

Scott considered the possibility that he was chasing old ghosts on a futile and endless run backward through his own worst imaginings. This he wanted to believe, that he was simply falling apart with the "agent's disease" and that such delusions were merely a symptom.

But his gut told him differently, registering cold spasms, his heart pounding the human spirit from his body. He leaned forward in his chair, pushing the cone of light against the background on Elmer Janson, and the data forced sweat to pop into beads on his forehead.

The boy's father was dead, his mother had never remarried, and that alone made them the most enticing of prey to Zachariah. His specialty was single mothers; the sex of a child made no difference. Scott's mind drifted as he leaned forward, grabbing the file forcefully.

On the outside of the old jacket he punched downward with a rubber stamp slick with red ink, then routinely initialed the upper-right corner:

CASE ACTIVE.

18

BETHESDA, MARYLAND

"What that woman *really* needs," the manicurist had said under her breath, "is a plastic surgeon." Although it wasn't completely untrue, Irma Kiernan, who knew the remark was directed at her, thought it unfair. Or at least uncalled-for. But that was early on in the day. Throughout the afternoon and well into the evening, she had considered this haunting insult and was starting to agree.

It was now after midnight. Irma sat at her second-story bedroom window combing short-cropped hair, feeling like some old and rejected Cinderella. She studied herself in a hand-held mirror, trying to imagine a young, shapely woman, but with a doctor's effort. A pinch here, a tuck there, a bit of liposuction, maybe an implant. What Irma Kiernan desired was beauty, to be in demand by the best of gentlemen. But plastic surgeon or not, at age fifty-four she knew that no coachman would be bringing a prince to her door.

All through the day, what she had had on her mind was seduction, pure and simple—not an exacting plan, but more of an intensified and concentrated effort. She had spent the entire morning at Jean Claude's Beauty Salon in Bethesda, where she had ordered the works: hair, nails, facial, and wax. Back to the mirror.

The gray was now gone, replaced by a muted brown pageboy, more youthful in appearance, almost perky. Yet without a part, the hair kept curling up at the ends and taking on a life of its own, while the bangs had begun to frizz. Irma tried parting it in the middle, the hair looked like a sick animal was sleeping on her head. No matter how she tried, the image in her hand did not even loosely resemble the slim woman of regal bearing and proud bone structure that had been her mother. Once Irma had been sure that she would grow into such a handsome woman. Her mother's hair had been a sweet golden brown, soft and silky, framing eyes that were a robin's-egg blue, and this was the truth the woman in the mirror faced daily.

"I'm not like her," she said aloud. Irma was short and plain, with a figure more befitting a baker's wife. Daily she fought weight and lost. She peered deeply into the glass, applying a gentle dusting to the lines across her brow. Her skin looked tired, even after a facial, and she imagined the wrinkles that time would soon deliver. That was it, *time,* she thought. Time was running out. Her hands began to tremble as she quickly shoved the glass into a bureau drawer, shutting out the Dorian image that mocked her.

Growing old was Irma's worst fear. But growing old alone was an absolute terror.

Long into the night, she applied two drops of Heavenly Lace behind each ear, and then directly to her pillow, a sweet lilac perfume she had purchased at Jean Claude's that morning. A man would soon be coming for her, and she had prepared well, every detail down to the choice of sheets, which were a pale rose satin. Her mission in life was to retain a vestige of her youth while proving herself fit for marriage.

Her body trembled.

Irma Kiernan saw headlights approaching. He was coming home. The wait was finally over.

* * *

His name was Jeffrey L. Dorn. And the fact that he sometimes stayed out until the early-morning hours while Irma
waited, and the fact that they maintained separate lives, plus
the fact that he would rather sleep alone than with a woman—
all of these things didn't bother Irma so much as the reasons.

Which were not his fault.

Jeff Dorn was in great physical pain, not to mention emotional scars, which Irma knew was not uncommon for such a
decorated hero. In 1951 as a young man serving in the Korean War, he had received a blow to the back that had all but
disabled him. Although it was true that there were no outward
physical signs, at the age fifty-five the old and lasting injuries
prevented Jeff from living any kind of normal existence. Because of severe, chronic pain, he was unable to work. He
could not concentrate more than a few hours at a spell without suffering excruciating muscle spasms along his spine,
spasms severe enough to steal his breath.

Although Irma didn't really understand what triggered
these awful spikes of pain, this price for his heroic service
was something that, over the years, they both had come to accept and share. And that price was high.

As Irma understood the event, Jeff had charged directly
into an enemy bunker in order to save the lives of his men,
who were pinned down in a firefight and running out of ammunition with no hopes for reinforcement. In one decisive
moment, carrying a grenade in each hand, Dorn had flung
himself into the concrete shell. Although he was able to climb
back out before the explosion, avoiding the deadly metal
shrapnel, the resulting blasts were so powerful they caught
him while he was running for his life, blowing him head over
heels, breaking his back in several places, and crushing his
spine in one. Although he was later credited with saving the
lives of many American boys and was honored with an officer's rank, it was clear to Irma that only part of him had survived.

The lack of intimacy between them was the least of it, she
thought. At times Dorn's pain was so excruciating that
he couldn't eat or even walk. And this was just physical. The
woman could only imagine what the psychic trauma was like.

It was the rarest of nights when Jeff was able to sleep without an episode waking him, sending him off into an agonized
world of quiet despair. Some nights he woke in such terror

that from another room she would hear the screams produced by the terrible images that came to him in dreams. Then he would describe these in detail so that Irma might understand. For days after, he would be a changed man.

Cold. Detached. Quiet.

Irma Kiernan feared the nightmares more than he did.

Since Dorn's injuries prevented him from being the family breadwinner, a role Irma knew he craved, she willfully chose to earn the household income, though at times she feared this was depriving him of his self-esteem, a silly sense of manliness she didn't quite understand.

"Life has cheated us for my bravery," Dorn was fond of telling her, while Irma considered quite the opposite to be true. Though not perfect, their lives were rich for having found each other, and they had also been blessed by Irma's profession. She was a nutritionist working for the Montgomery County school system, earning a wage of better than fifty thousand a year, nearly twice the national average for such employment. So her income allowed them a few little extra pleasures that they would have ordinarily been denied. Like visits to Jean Claude's, Irma thought as she watched his headlights flooding into the driveway.

How could the night have been so empty when the day began with such promise? she wondered.

Irma Kiernan's office was located in the administrative wing of the Westwood Elementary School, and although there were no classes or meals to supervise in the county on Friday, April 8, she had stopped by on the way home from Jean Claude's to collect a score of dietary plans, as well as to collect her thoughts. As she strolled the halls, she had received several compliments from her fellow workers over her newly youthful appearance.

Irma was grateful for the admiration and tickled that she had been so daring, placing her sinfully out of character with herself. She spent the entire day pursuing admiring looks. By the time she left school, she felt beautiful and sexy, longing for the man who shared her life and loved her and her alone. As a woman, Irma Kiernan wanted so much to give, but more than that, she wanted to be taken.

It was a short walk home from her office, and she could feel her pageboy haircut tickling the back of her neck as she put a youthful bounce into her step, turning onto the flagstone walkway down into Wooded Acres, an exclusive section of town. It was warm for April, much warmer than previous years, she thought, and she gingerly patted the makeup on her brow with a tissue to keep fresh. Around her, cherry blossoms and dogwood trees were beginning to bloom, and the air carried a fragrant, almost magical scent.

The Kiernan house was a two-story colonial, and as she approached, she noticed that the white exterior was in need of paint. Worse, the red shutters on the upstairs dormer windows were badly peeling, and she mulled over the family budget as she paused at the mailbox out front, seeing that the contents had not been collected. Nimbly she thumbed through a fist of envelopes, noticing mostly bills, when she decided that the front door could also use a fresh coat. She stopped, studying neighboring homes. In comparison, their house was beginning to look like an eyesore. She forced her thoughts back to the mail, heading again for the front stoop.

There was a card in a plain envelope addressed to Jeff, lacking a return address, and she puzzled at this, then placed it on top. There was an overdue notice from EuroCoupe on his automotive service contract; she placed this on the bottom. She was just fumbling in her purse for her house key as the front door swung wide.

"Hi, sweetheart," she said, straightening up and pushing her shoulders back to give her chest a little extra. But there was no answer.

Without a word Jeff Dorn had opened the door, then walked back to his easy chair in the living room and sat down. His eyes were fixed and unfocused, his face seemed flushed and waxen.

"Oh, honey," she cried, dropping her briefcase and purse, propping the mail between them, then running through the hallway to stand by his side. "It's your back, isn't it? Oh, let me help." Gently Irma leaned him forward, propping a pillow low, just above his belt line.

Still no response.

She was reaching to touch his forehead, to check his temperature, when the little man suddenly grabbed her arm forcefully with a twist. "How many times," he mouthed, closing his eyes, "how many times have we decided to leave the air conditioning set at no more than seventy-five degrees?"

The man's teeth seemed clenched with pain.

"Oh, sweetheart," she sighed, "I'm so sorry. I thought you

were going to be out all day, and the electric bills are just killing us. I forgot, I'm sorry . . ."

Dorn looked on vacantly as her voice trailed off. He was pausing for effect. "Irma," he whispered, and his voice became soft like a prayer. His head was stationary, his dull brown eyes glaring in the half-light of closed draperies.

"Yes, hon, I'm here," she comforted, stroking his head as if he were disoriented.

"Irma," he prayed again, "you must remember, it's the pain, I can't stand the heat for very long . . ." His voice tapered off as he twisted in his seat, seemingly fighting a spasm in his back. The woman looked on in helpless desperation and was about to speak when Dorn held a finger up for silence.

"Have you changed your mind about us?" he asked quietly. "I'll understand, but you should be truthful with me, Irma."

For the first time Dorn's eyes suddenly locked onto those of Irma Kiernan, the woman who dreamed of fairy-tale princes who rescued their maidens. She knew better than to ask why he had not simply adjusted the thermostat to a cooler setting. A man like Jeffrey Dorn was too proud to surrender to his own pain.

"He must have thought I purposely wanted the house to get hot, that I was trying to drive him away," she thought sadly, unable to look him in the eye. "It's so hard for him to admit I'm the breadwinner, he doesn't feel in control." Guilt instantly consumed her and her eyes began to well with tears.

"Oh, honey, I do love you!" she cried suddenly. "Nothing will change that!" She started to weep, wrapping her arms around his neck.

He did not respond.

"This flare-up is my fault," she admitted with a shaky voice, and through all of her efforts the retired Army colonel just looked up at her from his chair and blinked feebly.

"Oh, sweetheart, do you want me to get your medication?" she asked nervously.

It was thirty seconds before Dorn broke the silence of suffering. "No, no," he exhaled, "it's passing." Then he stroked her lightly on the thin flesh inside her left arm and said, "I just wasn't sure you wanted me anymore."

The worried dietitian walked over to adjust the thermostat in the hallway, promising herself, punishing herself, that she would never be careless again, when she remembered the compliments at school, when she remembered her womanly role as seductress and lover. Shy usually, Irma summoned her courage and slowly, suggestively unbuttoned her blouse. Removing her bra, she quickly returned to his side, nearly stumbling.

Dorn appeared unable to see as she gently pulled his tortured face between her naked breasts, giving a squeeze, then releasing him.

"Do you notice anything different?" she asked, using her most girlish voice and teasing her hair with one hand.

"Different," echoed Colonel Jeffrey Dorn. "Very nice, you've had your hair done. It's . . . becoming!"

Irma smiled warmly, walking her fingers across his shoulders as he clutched his hands around her waist, delivering a limp embrace. It was a nonresponse. Irma's jaw tightened until her whole face and neck trembled with the fear of rejection.

This was a very minor behavior, what Dorn called a tell. He had planned for it, had waited for it, just hours before, when he had set the thermostat in anticipation of her arrival. As he felt her body quiver, he wondered if she had bothered to plan anything for dinner. A trip to the beauty parlor could mean she was expecting an evening out.

"I missed you, honey," Dorn said, pulling her closer, tightening his grip, and she sighed with relief, feeling at ease for the first time all day. "It was all I could do just to go downtown and get my uniform from the cleaner's."

But the woman heard only a meaningless patter as she reveled in his voice: gentle, loving, and kind. Through his touch Irma had entered the sanctuary of her secret world, where she was beautiful, and filled with life, and married.

"Well, Irma, tell me about school," he demanded for the second time.

And she obeyed.

Earlier in the night, Irma had been thinking a romantic evening on the town was in order. Now she was just thankful to be home with him.

It was clear from his attentiveness that the painful spasms were subsiding. He had taken his pain medication before dinner, ten milligrams of the synthetic morphine Percodan. As Irma scrubbed at the kitchen sink, her mind wandered, and she thought about how his day must have been. Difficult, she decided. Jeff had picked up his uniform from the cleaner's, a uniform that he wore only for special functions. She knew that he missed the routine of being on active duty. For a passing moment she wondered why the Veterans Administration could not do more to help him. "God knows," she said aloud, "it's all I can do to pay the medical bills and coax him into swallowing his medication."

The Percodan was also a problem. According to Dorn, the pills made him feel drowsy, and he did not like the lightheadedness they produced, affecting his ability to concentrate. Irma, who was practical when pushed, knew there was no other choice, and her efforts to force him into swallowing usually prevailed. After seven years she'd lost count of the number of specialists he had been to, and each said nothing else could be done. "The bravest man I'll ever know." She smiled warmly, remembering how she had once demanded to speak directly to his doctors. But Colonel Jeffrey Dorn wouldn't condone interference.

"Irma," he had said, and she could still hear his words, "a soldier's pain is a personal cross, to be borne alone and with pride." Although she admitted she understood very little about men like him, warriors and heroes, it just didn't seem fair. She stood at the sink, hesitating, wondering if she should scrap an entire portion of meat loaf, when she remembered an earlier spat.

Meat loaf dried out quickly, then tasted like sawdust, she recalled, and she scraped the serving plate clean, poking the leftovers into the grinder, then hitting the switch.

"It's the Percodan," she said angrily, "it just wrecks his appetite!" Although Dorn had never admitted this, Irma knew it was true, for all through dinner he had just played with his food to keep her company. It hurt to see him pushing potatoes and meat and carrots around his plate while fighting to keep sitting up straight.

"Pain management, that's what the doctors said," she muttered to herself while her man dozed in the living room. She could hear the canned laughter of a sitcom on TV, but knew he wasn't watching. When Jeff hurt this bad, the set was just a distracting flicker.

Irma's mission in life was to help him find comfort, and she accepted him for who he was, a badly injured hero whose life was lived mostly in the past.

By nine o'clock she had finished the dishes and prepared most of the week's menu. She didn't need her watch, she could tell time by the theme from *MASH,* which Jeff always played at high volume. Even after seasons of reruns it was the one show he would not miss, and Irma knew that making comic theater from a tragic period in his life helped to soothe painful memories. She rose from her place at the dining-room table, turned off the overhead light, and walked toward his chair.

"Can I get you something cold to drink, sweetheart?" she asked from behind, holding the corners of the large buff recliner, peering down to see if he was awake.

The little man, his body stationary, reached with his left hand up over his shoulder to pat her wrist. "No, thank you, honey," he said absently, his eyes intent on the screen. "Grab a seat."

Irma returned to the dining room, fetched a hard wooden chair with a straight back, and dutifully placed it at the colonel's right. As she sat, waiting until a commercial to ask if the medication was working, she studied him.

"Jeff Dorn," she thought, "with the dark and radiant eyes, the strong chin and proud posture, you are my champion. You are not just any man, you are mine, like it or not, for better or for worse . . ." And she began to giggle like a schoolgirl.

"Stop!" Dorn said tonelessly, lifting his right arm. Irma quickly covered her mouth, feeling the laughter bubble through her fingers, as the cool air circulated, while the slapstick surgeons of the Korean War produced comic theater.

That was the best part of the night.

Every few minutes Jeff's eyes would sparkle and he would point with an index finger at the screen. And she thought about asking again if they could sleep in the same bed, just for a night, playing with that thought until the show was over.

She decided not.

The answer was always the same.

Her turning in bed would cause spasms, robbing him of sleep on those rare nights when he fell naturally into a slumber. Most of the time, when he could not sleep, Jeff feared that she would be the one deprived. He was always thinking of her. Jeffrey Dorn had spent his entire life thinking of others first, and as far as Irma knew, in 1951 it had nearly killed him.

She went to bed early, somnolent and tossing. She had wanted to make love, to be fondled, caressed, and held; to mingle and sweat in each other's arms until their bodies and breath and smell were one. Yet she understood the painful limitations that bound him.

In a fit of desire Irma Kiernan woke sometime during the night and heard a brassy chorus playing the national anthem on the television downstairs. The late-late show had ended, and already Jeff wandered through the house alone, staying awake to prevent his nightmares.

A little later she heard the garage door open and his car pull away.

Irma Kiernan feared the dreams more than he did.

At 1:12 A.M., some forty miles to the north, Detective Sergeant Rivers was also considering the unusual heat wave while thinking about sex. He couldn't even remember the last time he had been seriously attracted to a woman, beyond some transient physical need.

But Jessica Janson, he thought, she was a much different item. Her figure was as genuine as her manner, which was warm and maternal in a way he had seldom seen. The job, he reasoned: most of the women he met in the line of duty were hard-bitten characters, even nasty, their demeanor like a cold shower.

For Rivers, matters of the heart produced memories instead of dates, and the warm, humid night quickly brought to mind the lovely vision of a fragrant young woman by the name of Tammy McCain, a highly educated and sensual research scientist whom he had known since her days as a tomboy. He smiled. She looked very much like Jessica Janson, he thought with intimate knowledge; her hair was a shiny dark blond, her eyes a knowing and deadly green, while her figure curved and cushioned in all the right places.

As he remembered, the warming weather had started it all, for the shoes had come off first, after which he removed his shirt. And while he had been thinking of how to delicately romance her, Tammy suddenly appeared with a mischievous giggle in her voice, dragging his twin mattress out into the moonlight.

Once, Frank Rivers thought they would marry, but their careers had interfered and they drifted apart. With a smile on his lips he was sitting outside in the darkness. A small gray tabby strutted and rubbed against his back, and Rivers fluttered his fingers over the soft fur.

A short month ago there had been but two of these little

monsters. Now he counted seven, all lapping away at the little round cans that he had opened. They were feral, ever vigilant, and ever hungry.

His favorite was an old bruiser of an orange tabby who had a notch missing from his right ear, a big old tom of a cat with a heavyweight's constitution. This animal had finished off his last few bites, and the detective sat on his front stoop almost eyeball to eyeball with the distrustful stranger. The cat was watching him lick a cigar, rolling it against his tongue, then taking a clean bite off the end.

"It's like this," he spat, "one more can and you'll own me." He dropped the cigar into his mouth and lit up with a smooth stroke, while the orange tabby sat parked like a battered hydrant, staring up at him with owlish eyes.

Without streetlights and with an overcast sky, the little house sat on a gentle rise in an open field of pitch darkness. After speaking with Jack Scott, Rivers had turned off the lights and taken up a position outside. He liked it dark, darkness helped him think, and except for the contented purring of his companion, it was quiet as death. He could feel his eyeballs swelling to absorb what little line and form were cast from the glow of his cigar.

He had no doubts that this guy Scott had the real juice, of the political kind. One word to Captain Maxwell Drury and the state police had put their best pilot into the air to search for Debra Patterson. That would help a great deal, he thought, and Rivers knew that she would eventually be found, for those were the odds. At the same time, that's what worried him.

As he stroked the gray feline, an old image flashed through the smoke of his cigar. An image of limbo, the nether world produced by sadism and sexual attack. It was different for male survivors, but for women victims of atrocity there was an in-between.

It was not life. And it was not death either. They were like zombies. Their bodies still breathing, still walking, but their minds reduced to lather. In Phu Bai province the first platoon had found a whole village of them, walking aimlessly, bumping into each other, then shrieking, then walking; while their husbands and fathers lay half-buried, rotting away in monsoon-swept rice fields.

He shivered, forcing the image from his mind, placing an aspirin against his rear molars, crushing the pill down into paste. Rivers liked the acid bite. It dulled the throb that emanated from the right hinge of his jaw, and as he was chewing, the bass-heavy speakers suddenly boomed through the little doorway, scoring a direct hit against the orange tabby, who vanished into night.

"This is Eagle One!" the impatient voice repeated.

Rivers leapt inside the house, crossing the room, moving by feel. He grabbed the microphone. "This is Echo-Twenty," he returned flatly, dropping his cigar into an ashtray. The sound of chopper blades tore from speakers, vibrating against the artwork on his wall.

"We've got a Boggie," the voice said sharply. "Mustang, top-down convertible."

"Is it green, is it a new one?" he asked calmly.

"Hard to tell, Franko, late model, over."

"Abandoned?"

"Hard to say. Possible. Do you want units, over . . ."

Steve Adare, the pilot of the Hughes-500 Loach, a jet-powered chopper, was asking if the assignment officer, in this case Frank Rivers, wanted a police car dispatched to the scene.

"Immediately," Rivers said. "Can you put down?"

"Sorry, Frank, I'm regulation poor and running on empty," the voice lamented as Rivers heard the blades begin a hard accelerated *whir,* and Steve Adare peeled Eagle One into the sky.

At exactly 1:48 A.M. Frank Rivers headed out to the location, one click north of the intersect, Foxhall and Wisconsin avenues, directly across the street from a local dive known as Zephyr's Bar and Grill. As he drove, he forgot about Jessica Janson, and his cats, and Jack Scott, and the animal they were chasing.

All he had on his mind was a girl he had never met, and a village in Vietnam, and the man with torture spread across his face.

Jon Patterson.

Jon Patterson loved his daughter more than life.

With her hands trembling ever so slightly, Irma Kiernan closed her mirror into a bureau drawer. Headlights were coming. Jeff was returning home to her.

The wait finally over, she quickly composed herself, strolling-ing seductively down the stairs, then taking a position near the door and waiting as Jeff lingered in the garage.

He reconnected a fuse beneath the dash of his BMW, and with the car door open, the overhead dome light functioned normally. In the white glow that had been absent before, he quickly scanned the expensive red leather upholstery. There were no stains. There were no signs of another occupant, save the lingering of a woman's perfume. Casually he removed a small can of Air Wick from the glove compartment, giving a quick spray, then leaving the windows open.

He came through the back door and braced himself, knowing that Irma would be waiting for him. From the street he had seen her bedroom light go off, and he could imagine her high-pitched whine even before she spoke. He shuddered in anticipation as he placed his car keys on the kitchen counter.

"Is that you, sweetheart?" Irma asked, and Dorn winced visibly.

"No," he hissed quietly, "the tidy bowl man has come to clean up your shit."

She was gliding through the hallway, around the corner and toward him. "What, dear?" she crooned. "I was upstairs, I didn't hear you."

"It's been a hard night, Irma," he said flatly. "I said I'm tired, very tired, I think I should sleep." The man quickly hobbled, as was his way at times, into the family room, where he set himself down in his easy chair. It was not the events of the evening that ran through his mind, but simply the thought of dealing with Irma again. His lifetime with her seemed like a suffering eternity.

"Oh, honey," Irma exclaimed, crooning after him through the small hallway and into the family room, "the nightmares woke you, I heard you leaving. Let me get your medication."

Dorn agreed in an instant. To him Percodan was better than earmuffs or a double whiskey, it helped to make the grating sound of her voice almost tolerable. Like clockwork Irma reappeared with a glass of water and a pill, which Dorn pumped down without delay. "Thank you," he said. "Irma, why don't you go along and get some sleep? I'll be up shortly to say good night."

"Oh, sweetheart, I'll stay with you," she purred. "Does it hurt that badly? It's been a rough night, hasn't it?" Irma sat beside him in silence as the little man blinked, his dark eyes like wet stains against his face.

"Come up to bed, Jeff, let me rub your back for you," she pressed. As she leaned over into his space, he could feel her hot breath and smell the heavy scent of lilacs, and it was hard just to stay in the same room. He couldn't even imagine pinning her to a mattress, and in his mind he had never even touched Irma Kiernan. It took all of his courage just to look at her.

As the drug began to work its effects, fueling his body with a light-headed tingle, his thoughts went adrift, and again he was unwrapping the girl in the bright green convertible. She had cried for her mother, and that had amused him. He had made the woman a statistic in the American war against the sexes, and the numbers didn't lie. In the sports category, he thought, rape, murder, abduction, and mutilation were on the increase anyway. The bitch was at risk the moment she was born.

So in his mind, Dorn reasoned, she could have been anyone's kid, and if her family merely applied a little logic and a few numbers, the loss would not seem so great. "Irma," he said quietly, "I'm bone-tired, run along and get some sleep." His face was a perfect blank. The girl's compact body had been much more generous than he had suspected, and drugged with fifty milligrams of Pow, she had performed like a trained seal, depleting him until nothing was left.

Clank, clank. He could still hear that sound.

"Honey," Irma hushed seductively, "let me make you feel better." She was pressing her body into his, moving to touch his thigh with a nervous hand. But the man she knew as Colonel Jeffrey Dorn suddenly grabbed her wrist and forcefully pulled her face into his.

"Leave me!" was his toneless demand.

At 2:08 A.M. Frank Rivers arrived at the scene on Wisconsin Avenue and spotted a green convertible parked directly under a streetlight. He checked his duty sheet.

That it belonged to Jonathan Patterson was without doubt. The tags were correct, and the parking sticker on the rear bumper was from Debra's high school. Walking from his radio car, he searched the interior with a halogen beam, looking for smears of blood or body fluid, but there were no signs of a struggle, only the usual fouling on the front carpets. There was no evidence to the naked eye that would leave even the slightest clue, save the faint smell of perfume or after-shave.

He opened the passenger door and checked under the seats. It was clean. In the corner of the dash was a lipstick. On the rear seat a Raggedy Ann doll looked up at him with shiny button eyes. He was about to move the front seat when he spotted the keys dangling from the ignition.

He stopped, the chambers of his heart crashing, then beginning to pound. He swallowed hard.

Soundlessly, in one giant stride, he reached his car, grabbing the microphone through the window. "This is Sergeant Rivers." He sneered, leaning halfway into the cruiser.

"Go ahead Echo-Twenty," came the refrain.

"I ordered a backup unit thirty minutes ago, and I'm telling you now they'd better be humping or I'm going to kill something . . ."

There was no response. He took a breath. He drove images from his mind. "Scratch that," he stammered, his voice regaining a calm, deep edge. "Dispatch a crime analysis team, stat, and I mean now," he said. "Notify Captain Drury if necessary, and get those bums out of the sack." Before the confirmation came back, Rivers tossed the mike onto the seat and began to cross the street.

A D.C. cab hurtled in his direction, horn blaring. Rivers gave him his best gob of spit, then waited for a confrontation. A middle finger appeared, but the cab continued as he walked to the front door of the bar, checking through the windows for signs of life. It was empty. Chairs were parked on tabletops.

"The infamous Zephyr," he said to himself. He stood at the door wondering if Debra Patterson had been inside, and if so, why. He checked up and down the street in both directions, but there was nothing else open after eleven o'clock. He then reached up, grabbing the lamp mounted next to the front door. It was warm. It had been turned off only recently, and the bulb was just going wet with condensation.

As he waited, instead of thinking of Debra, he saw only Jon Patterson's spent face in his mind. And then the zombies, walking through the killing fields of his youth.

19

2:33 A.M. NEW YORK CITY

John F. Scott emerged from the Central Records Building facing Lexington Avenue, walking down a long flight of steps, smelling of mildew, the timeworn scent covering his clothes as he stood between marble pillars.

He was a *thief*.

In his mind there was no other word for it.

The black briefcase resting at his side bulged with valuables of which there simply was no higher price: he had paid with his principles. The coin Jennifer Doe had been wearing was a clue without perspective. That's what he was stealing, he told himself, perspective. But there was no excuse. As Matthew Brennon had explained, the exhibit was Dr. Robert Perry's mission in life, his reason for living.

His strides lengthened down the long flights of circular steps. Fleeing beneath two massive stone griffins at street level, he glanced up at the menacing symbols affixed to his memory. The thief paused. A slight rain. His senses were waking.

Across Lexington and down Forty-third Street into the darkness, he walked, looking at his watch. The night was beginning to clear. Thick blankets of steam dissipated into patches that scurried like phantom crabs over pavement. Except for an occasional jogger, a couple strolling, a passing delivery truck, the street was quiet. On any other night he would be going home, leaving the city by way of the Long Island Expressway.

Scott left Forty-third Street, darting left onto the sidewalk, bathed in the halogen glow of low-cost and anticrime lights. There was something wrong, he reasoned, with lights that cast no shadow, and in the wash of manufactured daylight he felt detached, a strange isolation.

Between blocks he ducked into an alley. Empty. A wet chill climbed the back of his neck as the smells of human waste took him by the throat. Two boys, unaware of his presence, peered with a penlight into the dark blue Chrysler parked at the curb. An AM radio, a tattered blanket, good tires with deep treads, but too much work. They wandered on, howling obscenities at the approach of an aging prostitute. Acne-scarred, eyes yellow, she gave a futile kick in their general direction while a middle-aged man tightened his dog's leash, threading a small animal through human barriers.

"Keep moving," the thief whispered.

Headlights approached over wet pavement as a child scampered from a doorway, hurling a brick at a passing car. The projectile shattered on the street, multiplying into smaller weapons as other moppets joined chase. The car rounded the corner and vanished. This was not his business, not his place. The city was closing in on him.

He walked for the car, unloading stolen treasures, placing them securely into the trunk, and positioning ancient charts beneath a blanket. A Cadillac filled with middle-aged men roared by toward Times Square—he recognized them as chicken hawks cruising for boys before Brother Dow opened again—and without thinking he soon followed their headlights through poisoned arteries.

Traffic slowed to a crawl as he turned onto the Deuce in the Square. The city pulsed to its own twisted, paralyzing rhythm. Sex parlors shimmered in neon. Doormen promised to deliver. In the window of a fast-food joint, a large black woman craftily slipped heroin up into a vein. Children peddled drugs, and adults supervised. By day, withdrawal sucked life from the newborn. A city gone mad. His type of guilt had no place here.

Scott pushed the Chrysler hard down the ramp into the Lincoln Tunnel, away from Manhattan. He tried the radio, but music held no meaning. He took a ramp, veering left toward the turnpike, heading steadily south into New Jersey, chasing high beams. Billboards, motels, and parking lots bloomed from darkness, then were gone in a blaze. Images fast appearing, then fading, sixty . . . seventy . . . eighty; the window open, the wind burning at one ear. And he stretched, pushing down hard against his seat with the events of the past twenty-four hours reeling through his mind.

"Something familiar here," he had told Brennon about the Clayton case. "I can taste it." And it seemed like the years were running them all down.

Nicholas Dobbs, Dr. Chet Sanders, and the voice of a young mother who had died of old age, "Just get him, get him for me, get him . . ." Scott's mind skipped, and for a passing moment he regarded the noisy images as ghosts, stages of agent's disease on an endless mental run backward through his own worst nightmare.

The Claytons were merely a coincidence, he told himself. Jennifer Doe was a Civil War child. And for seamless miles he held tight to that belief, simply because he needed to. Zak was dead. But Scott knew better.

Old enemy. Old friend.

How long had it been? Eighty . . . eighty-five . . . ninety— the speedometer soared, the Chrysler lurched on open road toward Washington and his enemy.

For more than three decades helpless mothers and their children were being set upon by the same human predator, an animal without a soul. And at the age of fifty-six, time was running backward and everything that Scott believed in— dignity, hope, humanity—raced beyond him through the night.

DAY TWO:
THE DEVOID

. . . I cut her throat so she could not scream . . .
this went on for a while, but she kept passing out.
—Theodore Bundy, Jr.

Ted, our hearts are with you!
—Protest sign at the execution vigil of Theodore
 Bundy, Jr.

20

The Carefree Diner on Wisconsin Avenue in Bethesda, Maryland, was a landmark of sorts. Once it had been a truck stop, but now it more resembled an upscale imitation of itself, with chrome that was too clean and brightly polished, a menu that was too elaborate and pricey, and coffee that had gone from freshly brewed to electric drip.

When Scott and Rivers arrived, it had been quiet and mostly empty, but with the sunrise locals began lining up at the door, reading their newspapers and being admitted by name. Rivers watched this with some contempt. There was something wrong, he reasoned, with a diner that accepted reservations and prepared eggs Benedict, which was what Jack Scott was eating long after Rivers had polished off two stacks of flapjacks with Polish sausages and eggs over easy.

"So what do you think of the odds?" Rivers asked, having explained the discovery of Debra Patterson's car.

"The odds that she's still alive, or that she was abducted by Zak Dorani?"

"Both."

"On her life I'd guess fifty-fifty, based on personal experience, but on Zak's involvement, I'd rather doubt that. We're only guessing that he's alive, and this is a large metropolitan area. Would you like me to come along when you tell Debra's parents?"

He took a sip of coffee and shrugged. "It's not necessary. Captain Drury volunteered and he's been through that drill before. But what about you, Jack, where will you start?" Rivers had opened a ViCAT folder and was studying the contents. It captured another era, back when individual police files were comprehensive, stuffed with mug shots, measurements, fingerprint records, and lab work depicting detailed analysis.

A black-and-white photo of the man had faded into shades of gray, and the detective could tell that it was taken when law enforcement did not include pampering. "He was cuffed in the nude?" Rivers smiled.

"Strip-searched, a violation of his civil liberties," Scott stated coldly. "We found a woman's engagement ring taped behind his scrotum."

The smile went sour.

"Zak had reasons for everything he did," Scott continued, dipping a piece of muffin into congealed yolk. "My guess is he was about to force some woman to search for it, but we never did find the ring's legal owner." He returned to his eggs, while Rivers concentrated on the photos.

According to measurements against a prison wall, Zak Dorani stood exactly five-foot-five, with a natural posture that curved slightly to the left, and Rivers searched for a physical imbalance. The legs were well-formed, with the knees at a correct angle, which was not overtly bowed or knocked. The stomach was tight, and the torso was well-proportioned to the body. "He's athletic but has a crook in his spine that would get worse with age."

"There's a doctor's report. Zak was under treatment for scoliosis, physical therapy for a rather common condition for lateral curvature. Nothing too serious—about one out of every hundred are born with it—but it can be painful."

Rivers nodded. Because of the smooth complexion, oval face, and brown hair, he thought Zak so plain as to be of almost any descent. The eyes were deeply set like the Dutch, small black mirrors, and the chin was sharp and flat. The nose seemed bobbed, almost too small for his face, and his lips were thin like slivers of veal. "Will you know him on sight?"

Scott took a sip of coffee, pushing his plate off to one side. "Perhaps. Those shots were nearly thirty years ago, though, and there wouldn't be anything that he hasn't changed through cosmetic surgery, hair transplants, face lifts, you name it. We're dealing with someone who is more vain than the most narcissistic female you've ever met, and he's an expert at preventing detection, a real actor.

"Physically, he's small, tough to hide that, and his eyes used to be so brown they appeared black in a poorly lit room. But maybe that's changed as well." Scott shrugged. "Surgery or colored contact lenses, who can say?"

Rivers fumbled in his sweatshirt pocket, found a roll of

small cigars, and continued searching until his hand produced a crumpled pack of Marlboros, which he offered across the table. Scott pulled loose a bent smoke and then lifted Rivers' lighter. Expertly thumbing the wheel, he then examined the battered relic with some interest. On one side was a Pink Panther, on the other a grinning death's-head, images that conflicted sharply with each other.

"A lucky piece?"

"A gift," Rivers responded, remembering back to when the Zippo was America's weapon of choice. He extended his hand across the table, palm up, and Scott placed it back into the man's hand. A waitress appeared with a tray, refilling their mugs, then began clearing the table as Scott produced two black-and-white Wirephotos and laid them down.

"I think this was a lucky piece, or maybe a gift of some type," he suggested. "Have you ever seen one of these before?" They both looked down at copies of the Civil War-era signal token.

"Negative," Rivers said, lighting his smoke. "First and only time I ever saw one was when Elmer Janson gave me this." He reached into his pants pocket and retrieved a glassine evidence pouch containing the small medallion. He dropped the coin on the table.

"Anything else today, Frank?" the waitress interrupted, placing a check and pot of coffee between them.

"No, thanks, Kathy."

She replaced two spoons and moved on as Scott carefully studied the coin, flipping the pouch over from front to back. "Can I keep this?"

"It's on loan."

"And you're sure the boy found this where he said?"

"Absolutely, he's a good little kid."

"What do you make of it, Frank?"

"Hell, I don't know, Commander, it's an old coin. Do you have an artist's rendering of what our *Mook* would look like today?"

Scott smiled. "Mook?"

"Pervert."

"Let's talk about him later," Scott suggested, turning the conversation back to the coin. "Notice at the top that a drill has punched through a word, or possibly a series of words," he pointed out, looking up into tired eyes.

"Yeah," Rivers said, squirming, "I saw that."

"Well, we've established that the coin was made in 1863 at Harpers Ferry, West Virginia."

Rivers leaned back into the bench seat. "So what's that have to do with Zak?"

"Evidence, Frank, and directional forensics."

"What?" He shook his head and then leaned over the table toward the older man. "Look, Jack," he said bitingly, "if it's the same guy, what do we need this for? If you can spot him, it's over. The guy's a grease stain, let's start from there." Rivers coughed, waiting for an angry response. But Scott just smiled, leaning back into the soft leather banquette.

"Humor me?" he asked, holding palms up in supplication.

"Sure," Rivers agreed. But he didn't really. He was thinking that if the killer was territorial like Scott had said, then they already knew he frequented the River Road area, which meant they could flush him out in a sting using a decoy and stakeout. He knew the perfect chick for the job.

Scott cleared his throat. "Age before beauty, detective?"

Rivers chuckled at the old corn. "Haven't heard that since I was a kid." Scott produced a cardboard tube from beneath the bench and started unscrewing the aluminum cap on one end. "What's in that anyway? You've been guarding that real close."

Scott didn't answer but reached inside, producing a scroll of heavy paper, then wiped down the surface of the table with a linen handkerchief. What unfolded was a detailed pen-and-ink chart of the Potomac river valley. The map was painted—Rivers guessed in watercolor—and it looked ancient.

"Damn me for a mutt. Where in hell's creation did you get that?" he asked, leaning across the table excitedly.

"It's on loan," Scott lied. "It's from a series produced by the Confederates before shots were fired at Fort Sumter. This is how the rebs saw this part of Maryland in 1860."

Frank studied the antique closely, sensing the strange odor of parchment mixed with the aroma of coffee and sausages. He could see the Potomac River and Chesapeake and Ohio Canal clearly—these were a tropical blue. But the city of Bethesda was not on the map. "This is great, Jack," he said earnestly.

"Take your time, a quiz will follow."

"Right," and the state trooper moved closely, inhaling through his nose like a bloodhound on the scent.

He loved the names, they were rich and amusing. The river

fell from the map, emptying into Old Georgetown in Washington at a place called Frogland. "Some of the most overpriced property in the nation, Froggyville? Jack, this is . . . fantastic!" he exclaimed, moving closer still. Near Frogland, a tract of property was labeled Conjurers Disappointment.

"Look at this," he laughed, "they probably ate at one of the French restaurants in Georgetown!" And he followed the blue wash of paint as the river curved back up into Maryland.

Two landmarks were clearly marked, an aqueduct known as Widewater and the Great Falls of the Potomac, but surrounding these the famous townships of Cabin John and White's Ferry were strangely omitted. They were gone, or they didn't exist at the time. The detective shook his head. He found River Road, and a little too far north there were two small intersections along the river, one called John's Revenge and White's Crossing, which he had never heard of.

"The devil be damned, but I can't find Bethesda, Cabin John, White's Ferry, and there was no town of Potomac?"

Scott was watching intently.

"Darnestown is here, and so's Rockville," he said, following an index finger, "but they got the river areas all screwed up, Jack, where's Cabin John? My family used to have a house right here," he said pointing to a bluff overlooking the canal.

"You tell me, Frank. I know Bethesda wasn't named yet, but Cabin John and White's Ferry definitely existed as far back as 1839."

"Look," he said with excitement, "they left everything out. They'd be right here," and he jammed a thumb on the chart. Scott cringed. "Sorry."

"Now, let's take a closer look," Scott offered, placing photos of the coin back across the map. And Rivers pushed his fingers over the word "JOIN," which stood out in capital letters.

"What does it mean?" he asked, picking up the real coin and squinting at the little house entwined by a serpent.

"Do you know of any neighborhood with a name that comes close to the word 'join' in configuration, a name having the letters 'j-o-i-n' in that sequence?"

Rivers applied pen to pad, scrawled a moment, and pulled away. "Nothing," he said. "The word is 'join.' I think that's what it means, how about you?"

"Look again," said Scott, pointing to the letters. "The only logical choice is Cabin John, and we know these coins were made bearing the name of other towns. The coin is a patriotic signal token minted by the Union. On the map, White's Ferry is labeled White's Crossing, but there's a similar token that claims another name, which one of my agents tracked down. That coin says White's Ferry just like it is on the Rand McNally today. I think the charts, and hence the modern maps, are in error."

"No shit?"

"It's a theory."

"Was it intentional?"

"My guess is that the mapmakers didn't know any better. These towns were just small communities during the Civil War, and hostile to any outsiders. A rebel spy might have been ignorant enough to ask for help with this chart and was misled, anything's possible. Remember, in the 1860's they didn't plant signs on the road when it came to smaller southern communities, and Maryland was a state divided."

"But how do you get the words Cabin John out of all this? The coin was minted."

"Okay, let's take another look," Scott said, "but remember, this is just speculation."

"Right."

He sketched on a napkin. "Take I-N from the word Cabin. And the J-O from the name John. Now, that won't work in sequence, but it works. And it works in only one way, unless we're dealing with a code, and I doubt that.

"J-o-i-n is a reversal of the first two and last two letters of the name John and the word Cabin, in that order. So if you drilled out the center to make a hole for chain, what would remain is J-O followed by I-N. *JO( )IN,*" he drew on a pad. "John Cabin. And over the years it was forgotten. What do you think?"

"Are you saying that, based on some old coin the name of the town used to be John Cabin?" Rivers asked sarcastically. "I grew up in Cabin John, Maryland. I would have known about something like this."

"It's just an educated guess," Scott concluded. "Take a look at the house on the coin, looks like a cabin?"

"Right."

"In New York, Agent Brennon interviewed an expert on the Underground Railroad, and these tokens were used as a way of warning underground operators that they were being watched, explaining the word 'Beware!' stamped over the cabin," he pointed. "My guess is the town now called Cabin John was an important link for slaves fleeing oppression."

Rivers was excited but confused. He slid back in his seat, wondering. "The killer left the coin on this girl's body some thirty years ago, he must have seen it. No way he didn't."

"He didn't care, Frank."

"Do you think he knew what it meant?"

"That doesn't matter either. Do you think the little girl who was wearing it knew what it meant? She was a black child. Where did she get the token?"

"It must have been a gift. A black couldn't have afforded it back in 1958, so it must have been a family heirloom. If what you're thinking is right, I'll bet she was a local kid. But I checked the records and no black child, boy or girl, was reported missing in this county until 1971. That's a long time, Jack."

"Yes, it is. When did the county start hiring blacks?"

"Oh, hell, when was the Equal Opportunity Act?"

"That would be sixty-nine."

"Well, it wasn't until then for sure. They wouldn't have integrated unless forced to."

"I believe the life of a local child fell through the cracks, unless a black family would have gone to the white police?"

"Not hardly, I see where you're going."

"When we find out more about the coin's history, we'll start to gain hard insight into who this child really was, when the killer first arrived here, maybe what his disguise was at the time, and maybe still is. The list could prove endless, plus it's the best lead we've got. Eventually we'll have photographs of this girl, making it easier to track relatives, and there's a few other tricks we can pull, but that's down the road."

"All right," Rivers conceded, "but what about the killer? You mentioned the Jansons, are they safe?"

"You checked on them?"

"Right until the sun came up, radio reports all clear." He smacked his forehead. "Christ, I feel like I'm talking about a vampire."

"Worse than that. Vampires can't work by day."

"And you think this coin is our best lead?"

"Except for the little girl's body, it's about our only lead. We certainly have damn little from the Clayton murders."

Scott drained his coffee cup, and Rivers saw the blood pumping into his neck and face. The guy looked like a candidate for a stroke. "What is it, Jack? Are you all right?"

Scott cleared his throat. "Sure, getting too old for my job. What I would like to do, Frank, is set up a command post, and I'd like you to be the officer in charge."

"Depends on what value you're willing to assign the Debra Patterson case. They're counting on me."

"Priority one."

Scott watched as Rivers examined the breakfast tab, then dropped a twenty-dollar bill on top.

"Then the next meal will be on me," Scott offered as Rivers suddenly leaned across the table.

"What did Zak do to those children?" he asked coldly.

"Killed them very methodically."

"I read the report at least a dozen times, I couldn't make sense of it. Did he rape those little girls, Jack?" Rivers' blue eyes glinted with a murderous fury, and a vein stood out on his neck.

"No, Frank, he didn't rape them. He did not force them to engage in sexual activities, at least the way you and I think of it."

"Are you being straight with me?"

Scott was watching the man's jaw ticking. "Yes, as honest as I can be. The killer is not capable of having sex, so he finds other means, but we can get into that later. We have to bring ourselves up to speed, and you, my friend, have some catching up to do."

Rivers' eyes narrowed. "I'd like to gut this bastard like a toad," he spat as they both stood, Scott picking up his things.

As they passed through the door, Rivers fought with himself to keep calm, while the cooling air and the coffee had helped Scott. He could feel his senses waking, every nerve suspicious of the new city surrounding him. From the front of the diner he could see traffic starting to swell with a morning rush, backing up at a light on Wisconsin Avenue one block up. Rivers slowed his gait, noticing that the older man had to make an extra effort to keep astride.

"I've read your sheets, Frank, your complete file, but I still don't know much about you," Scott said, his eyes straight ahead as they walked.

Rivers pondered this a moment. "Not much to know," he answered quietly.

"Everyone has a history." Scott paused, making eye contact. "I'm the oldest from a large Catholic family. My father was uniformed NYPD. I had eight brothers and two sisters. One brother was killed in Korea, my twin sister was snatched from a school playground in 1938. A few years later we buried an empty box."

The pent-up breath left Rivers' body in a small moan. "I'm sorry," he said, swallowing. "I suspected something like that. It explains a great deal."

They stopped at a crosswalk, waiting for a light to change, before the sign went to blinking green. "I believe good cops are made, not born, tempered from desire and fashioned from circumstance. So what about you, Frank, why are you a cop?"

Rivers shrugged, looking off into space. "Hell, I'm really not that deep. I'm not even sure I know."

They crossed again at the intersection of Cordell and Wisconsin avenues and into the public parking garage. The blue Chrysler and Crown Victoria were parked side by side in one corner, and Scott stopped between them. "Frank," he asked cautiously, "was your father's last name Rivers? The Social Security number under that name wasn't active until after the fall of Saigon."

The state trooper raised an eyebrow, then gave a knowing nod as he unlocked his car. With his eyes on Scott he reached inside, turned on the radio, and grabbed the mike. "I'm on your side," he stated tonelessly, hitting the indent button with his thumb. "Dispatch, this is One-Echo-Twenty," he piped routinely as the commander checked his watch.

Noticing this, Rivers quickly sought to change the subject. "This job gets old," he offered. And Scott smiled, nodding his agreement.

Old as a lifetime, dark as a childhood scar.

21

The house was red brick, three stories of town house with sidewalks instead of a lawn. Treeless and indifferent, it loosely resembled a colonial, any character derived from paste blue shutters. Looking south from the front stoop, a su-

permarket terminated a patch of green. Across a busy intersection the east side faced a retirement home. One short block
down Ridgefield Drive was the four-lane highway River
Road, where the condemned bowling alley waited.

Scott stood in the harsh sunlight, shielding his brow as he
stared up at the skinny house. "This is to be used as the command post?" he asked.

"Captain Drury's instructions."

"Was he supposed to meet us here?"

Rivers tossed his duty book back into the car and removed
a black gearbag from the trunk. "Last I heard," he said, heading for the front door. Scott tried the latch while Rivers circled the house, checking windows and screens. A minute later
he was back on the front stoop, watching Scott select a pick
from inside a black zipper pouch.

"I can radio for dispatch," he offered. But Scott was already at work, carefully inserting the pick into the lock. His
attempt looked ridiculous. Rivers knew a specialist who could
zap a deadbolt in less than a minute, but Scott was far from
that sort of practice. He was pushing his entire head up to the
keyhole, his face knotted with intense concentration. The
doorknob poked him in the nose.

Then there was the sound of shattering glass, and Scott was
rising, one hand against his back, as the front door opened
and Frank Rivers walked out. His right fist was wrapped in
his T-shirt.

"That's Hollywood shit anyway," he said, and Scott nodded
gratefully as he wiped his brow with a clean handkerchief.

The ceilings were vaulted with recessed lights and the de-
cor was nondescript abstract modern. There was blue carpeting throughout, and bright metal sculptures that resembled
large paper clips. The furniture itself was leather, a sandy
color with overstuffed pillows in shades of neon. All the tables were glass and chrome, lending to the detached and antiseptic feeling of the place. There was no personal warmth,
no hominess, no give, and Scott stood in amazement. Then
seeing Rivers carrying a piece of sculpture to the hall closet,
he chuckled to himself.

"I really can't live with this one," he said, lugging away
what looked like a twisted brass pelvis.

"Don't break anything," Scott suddenly cautioned. "What
do we know about this place?"

"Drury said it belonged to the State Department."

"I was afraid you'd say something like that. Our tax dollars at work." Scott stepped carefully from the foyer, around an enormous brass swan, then down into a sunken room. There was a gilded fireplace decorated with pine cones and plastic logs, and he knew it had never been used. Up through an arched hallway he found a massive kitchen with a floating island and tiled counters, and he strolled to the sinks, which overlooked a rear deck and patio.

To the right a carpeted stairway led down to the garage or up to six bedrooms on two additional floors. It was the type of town house that offered sunken tubs on a postage-stamp lot with a view of your neighbor's bathroom.

"Bet some junior ambassador hired his main squeeze to decorate," Rivers offered from the kitchen, checking the contents of the refrigerator. The unit was built into the wall, something called a Sub-Zero, and it was empty. "If your average wage earner saw this, he'd march on Washington."

"Not a chance," Scott corrected. "We're a nation of sheep with an electronic shepherd."

"Then let's unplug them."

Scott shrugged as he walked for the stairs. "It's a nice thought, but let's just settle for showers and a change of clothes." And he took the entire third floor, which offered a better view of River Road, while Rivers selected the gaming room on the basement level, which offered a Brunswick Slatetop, the kind of expensive pool table that he had always dreamed of owning.

While Scott was changed in scant minutes, Rivers took thirty, steaming himself in a sunken tub that was larger than his living room, twisting a gold-plated gargoyle's head with a ruby eye for hot and an emerald eye for cold.

Though he was slight of build, State Police Captain Maxwell Drury was a formidable man who wore a full uniform and jet-black boots. His olive jacket was accented with gold braid, his white shirt looked starched to excess. From his left shoulder a chestnut bandolier crossed his chest, attaching to an old-fashioned Sam Browne belt at his waistline. In his right hand he carried an officer's campaign hat and a two-way radio, in his left a smallish bundle of cloth sealed in plastic.

He was thin, too thin, worn from worry. As Scott closed the door behind them, he could tell from Drury's expression that his old friend was *cooking* inside with political fallout. "Max," he said warmly, embracing him.

"Sorry I'm late, you're looking well, Jack. Like old times, just like old times." He tried to put a smile in his voice, but it sounded like stones rolling down a sheet of tin. "I stopped off to see the Pattersons, Frank filled you in?"

"Come in and sit down, Max." Scott led him by the arm.

"They're taking the news about their daughter's car being abandoned very hard. If we find a body, I'm not sure they'll be able to live with it. Mr. Patterson told me he'd rather die than entertain the possibility that some bastard has destroyed his daughter. I feel for him. The mind can endure only so much pain—"

"Max," Scott tried to interrupt.

"She's their only child. Maybe some of your psychology would help."

"Anything I can do, you know that, but let's not bury her yet. Frank said the car was clean of assault forensics." Scott led him into a gray kitchen chair, which he pulled from the table. "I'll get something to drink."

From the bottom of the stairs Rivers watched with an uncertain curiosity as the two men talked. He had never seen Drury emotional, it was unlike him, or so he had thought. He pulled a T-shirt over his head, saddled his gun in a high-ride holster at his back, and listened as he combed through a tangle of wet hair.

"Debra Patterson, at least in her pictures, reminds me of my Martha. Maybe it's the hair. I don't know, there's a certain innocence. She's seventeen now, you haven't seen her for ten years, but she's a beautiful young woman, John, you won't even know her." Drury set his hat, parcel, and radio on the table and took a glass of water from Scott.

"Was the information on careers in the social sciences of any help? Has she made a decision about college?" he asked.

"Nothing yet, but I thank you for your trouble. Martha's been chasing some sports-car enthusiast around. The boy will amount to nothing," he growled.

Scott smiled. "As I recall, you were a car enthusiast."

"Humph, so tell me, Jack, what first? How many men for this detail?"

"First would be Patriots Bowl. We excavate the building from the inside, the entire alley if necessary, and then—"

"It will take time for search warrants, and we don't have much of a case, but I have a few favors I can call due."

"If we have to deal with some slack-faced judge over probable cause, we're dead."

"Hail Mary!" Drury breathed hard.

"Max?" he nudged.

The man's voice went to glass. "Don't ask me to condone this. No petition before a judge, no justified cause, it's a gross violation of procedure."

"Max?"

"Oh, God, Jack," he cried, "that same little bit in sixty-eight set my career back ten years."

Scott nodded. "As I remember, you said it was worth a hundred suspensions."

Scott waited as the captain considered the stakes and odds. One thing was certain: it was nonfeasance, and inexcusable, unforgivable. If caught, he would be facing a quiet, political-type retirement, but there would still be a partial pension, he thought. He'd check the book, he was almost certain they couldn't take that away.

"You've got twenty years in, Max. They can't take your pension unless it's a class-B felony, and even then I'm not sure it's indictable."

"You know what you're asking," he said tonelessly, "sweeping uniformed regulations into the can? This may look like Maryland, but it's Washington, Jack, the political theme park, make no mistakes about that."

"I understand."

"And my men? Even if I did commit, I can't expose my men to charges."

"Then offer me something else."

Drury began to ponder, taking a deep breath and a sip of water just as a shadow moved over him. Rivers stepped forward into the kitchen.

"Oh, hello, Frank," Drury said, his brown eyes moving under heavy brows.

"Have a seat," Scott offered, pulling out a chair.

Rivers shook his head. "I'm going to pick up some supplies and fuel the tank. Is that my package?" he asked, lifting the plastic-covered bundle from the table. He examined the contents from the outside, pressing hard with his fingers. There was a gym shirt, socks, and some panties—these were an acid green with large black dots.

"Mr. Patterson was very uncomfortable with the request. Most of Debra's clothes were freshly cleaned, so I urged him to search the laundry facilities. We found the undergarment in the hamper."

"Thanks, Captain," he said. "Is her mother home?"

"Debra's mother?"

Rivers nodded.

"Yes, she's distraught, the family doctor is treating her."

Rivers popped an aspirin into his mouth, opened the back door, and was gone.

"Frank's in some type of physical pain," Scott said, but Drury's attention was elsewhere.

"I have it!" The gravelly voice took on an excited tone. "Let's set up an ambush and drown the bastards in paperwork, they'll never know what hit them. I'll contact the property owner and smack him with a citation, then we'll go directly for the keys and demand their full cooperation!"

Scott was listening intently. "I don't follow."

"I saw the alley on the way in. Technically we're dealing with a condemned structure, so I can employ the guise of inspecting a health hazard. It's not my department—such a case would belong to Health and Welfare—but that should take at least a week for a good attorney to figure out. By then we'll give the place a clean ticket, return the keys and blueprints, and keep sets of our own."

Scott smiled and said, "An excellent plan." He raised his glass of water in salute. "You still have the touch."

"A bit of bureaucratic buggering."

"It should work, but if you can't locate the proprietor or if they are uncooperative, drop the matter and get back to me. I do not want the county notified, and under no circumstances apply for a court order."

"Out of the question, but I'm far more comfortable with this approach. I'll find someone to lodge a complaint this afternoon. Now, tell me about manpower—that could present a problem."

"Frank and I will work the field from this command post. One of my agents should be arriving sometime tomorrow. I have most of the communications gear I need, but in the meantime you can provide two guards for inside the alley, round-the-clock surveillance."

Captain Drury made a notation. "Morning and evening

shifts, split at five P.M. Their movements will be lost in peak activity."

"Old clothes, no police cars. Have them park elsewhere and approach on foot."

"I can't afford senior detectives, Jack. The governor attended the White House conference, and we've had our priorities shuffled to narcotics—"

Scott raised a hand. "I understand. If you can't find a budget, I'll sell some fruit." He pointed to a bowl of sterling-silver apples that sat between them. "Just have the officers dress for the weekend, drive their own cars, and report to Frank. They'll get the short course. Frank has also requested a sound truck in case we need a more sophisticated surveillance, and I agree. I'd like a laser parabolic plus two additional men for that unit, I don't see any other way."

"A laser?" Drury laughed. "Jack, my department can't afford something like that, we still use hard wire for taps. The Secret Service may have one, but you'll have to use your own juice."

"You do have a surveillance truck?"

"Yes," he growled defensively, "and it's complete, a very fine rig. At the moment it's in use. How about late this afternoon or tonight?"

"That would be great. Rivers handpicked several men. What do you think? I can't leave the Janson family unguarded. No second-place winner in this game."

"Human pit bulls, Frank's type of cop. They work on our violent offenders unit."

"Availability?"

"I'll see to it, but haven't we known each other too long, Jack?" His voice raised a notch.

"How's that?"

"ViCAT's always been poor on manpower, so why didn't you just say you need three men for your MAIT team?"

"Because you would have balked and I need seven."

"Wait just a minute"—stress returned the gravel to his voice—"I'm giving you four men plus Rivers."

"I understand that," said Scott. "I'm including Frank, plus my guy makes five."

"And another?"

"To stake out the Claytons', I need a senior man."

"Come off it, Jack. Do you really think this killer will return?" Drury asked sarcastically.

"Can we afford to ignore that possibility? We just had a case in Atlanta where—"

Drury nodded. "I know just the man, but I can't get him until tomorrow."

"And the others?"

"Right now they're on other details, but it will be done."

"Thanks, Max, I know you'll be pitching a lot of excuses on other fronts. You'll keep me appraised of political blow-back?"

"If it threatens to affect your operation."

"And as policy, all communications will run directly from this command post, without crosstown traffic?"

Drury forced a smile. "We'll do our best."

"Good," said Scott. "What else do we have?"

Drury reached into his coat pocket and handed Scott an envelope. "Keys to the CP, the Riser slug is for the Claytons, works both front and back. Now, what about our suspect? Frank mentioned you have some history with him."

"That's what worries me. If it's the same man his behavior has become unpredictable. He's not following the rules—anything goes. As of the Clayton killing, there is no predictive model for him."

"You're holding something back, John, what is it?"

"I'm not holding back," he said, running both hands through his hair. "I just don't have a clear picture, a comprehension of what we're up against. For reasons I can't figure, this killer has become brazen, overt, and defiant, which makes no sense with who he is. At one time he used to make a concentrated effort to hide human remains, and by now he'd be an expert at disposal."

"So why the Claytons, the ghoulish stage setting?"

"In times past that family would have just failed to return home one night, and in time the case would have been dropped, which, as you know, is not uncommon."

"I see what you mean," Drury said. "It's the timing that's bothering you: why now?"

"That's it, something is pushing on him, but I don't have a clue. If I could figure that out, I might be able to anticipate his moves a little better." Scott's voice was tense with frustration. "He's capable of anything. He can't be predicted."

Drury thought for a moment. "Perhaps he's just lost his rational abilities. The years of killing caught up with him, and he's gone insane. Or he's seeking some kind of credit, wanting to punish society with his cruelty."

Scott shook his head. "No, the detail, planning, and skill with which the Claytons were slaughtered could not have been done by a mental case."

Drury sighed. "Then maybe he's just dying, terminal man getting in his last licks?"

Scott winced, and this was followed by a brooding silence.

Finally Drury said, "I'm sorry, but that makes a lot of sense to me, Jack. Try this scenario: the physician has just given you six months. Once you're over the shock, what do you do?"

Scott leaned forward in his chair, tapping the table with a pen. "There would be a lot of loose ends. I'd have to get my sordid little world into order, check with the insurance companies, execute a list of legal forms, and of course I'd say a few good-byes."

"Yes?" Drury pushed "You thought he was dead, and if he's not, and he is dying, how many other cops has he become acquainted with over the years? How many good men spent part of their lives trying to stop him?"

Scott's eyes flared with a strange light as he slowly pushed back his chair. "The big good-bye. The bastard's got nothing to lose this time!"

"It's possible," Drury offered grimly. "Here's hoping I'm wrong."

22

With disgust he jabbed a fork into the hard yellow eye that had been staring at him. The silly bitch couldn't get anything right. Eggs over easy, not poached; toast buttered lightly, not greased; juice instead of frozen concentrate—Jeff Dorn couldn't understand it. Was this a difficult order to fill?

And the phone was ringing. The house phone. Not his private line, and he threw his napkin on the kitchen table with contempt, pushing the plate away from him. "What are you doing that's so damn important you can't get that?" he wanted to scream, but instead he said this under his breath while staring up at the ceiling. It was the fifth ring.

"Sweetheart, would you get the phone?" Irma Kiernan asked from above.

"God," he exclaimed, "how I hate that sound!" Her voice echoed through the ductwork and Dorn knew she was in the bathroom again. Then the seventh ring as a flush of water moaned through the pipes, coming toward him, rumbling by into the basement. Eight rings. He could barely stand her miserable incompetence, and it finally stopped.

"Honey?" Irma cried from upstairs. "Sweetheart, are you there?"

The party dosage of Percodan he had taken the night before had given him a hangover, a slight headache and sour stomach, and Dorn did not feel much like conversation.

"It's for you, sweetheart, do you want me to take a message?" she cried, and he mustered his patience to deal with the inane demands that were crowding his morning.

"No, no, no, thank you, my love, I'll get it," he sang, reaching from his chair and lifting the receiver from the wall. He then listened carefully, not for a greeting, but for background noise that would give the caller away. He groaned. Typewriters and bickering voices, and he knew immediately that it was Marcy Newman, director of preservation for Partners of Living History, the PLH.

"Colonel Dorn," he barked, sounding very much like the professional military man. But what he heard in reply was the reverberation of office clatter from a sparse little hovel where everything echoed.

In the PLH brochures, and in the brochures only, the non-profit foundation was housed in a massive federal office building and maintained a staff of hundreds. In reality, PLH had but two employees, Marcy Newman and a secretary, and as far as Dorn was concerned, the difference between the two was that the secretary got paid for her time.

PLH was a tax-exempt organization that, as Jeff was fond of saying, provided for the future by preserving the past. "Colonel Dorn, will you please hold the phone for Marcy—"

"No, God damn you, I pay your salary!" he snapped.

"J-j-just a moment, please." A confused young woman put the call on hold while Dorn double-checked the contents of his briefcase. He lifted a leather zipper pouch containing a small pistol, and immediately wanted to fire it into Marcy

Newman's substantial gut. But he knew he could not. He needed her, though he loathed that thought.

When Jeff had first met the woman, she was a Senate staffer on an environmental subcommittee, a brassy power-hungry bitch who, over the years, had made him bleed for every little political favor. Now her tenure was over—a failed election had taken her pooh-bah's seat—and she hit the streets peddling her knowledge, which was meager; her contacts, which were questionable; and her looks, which as far as Jeff was concerned could be deployed for the national defense.

The phone was still on hold in a nasty little power game, and he reveled in how Marcy always underestimated people. She was free-lancing the weekend away, using PLH resources to turn a buck. She would be making sure he wasn't coming to the office and crowding her paying clients.

"Hi, Jeff, what a glorious morning. It reminds me of Paris when—"

"Others may fall for that crap, but I happen to know you've never been there. What do you want, Marcy?"

"You should be nice to me, Jeff," she pouted.

"Why, because I'm right about Paris?" he laughed. "Now that I know the truth, I'm going to tell everyone."

"Oh, Jeff," she lamented, "I've been on the phone for an hour with Mrs. Warren. She's pledged four thousand dollars for the bridge project, it's wonderful!" she bubbled with a practiced enthusiasm usually reserved for those in her Washington appointment book who really mattered. Since Dorn had hired her at no cost, he knew, by definition, that he did not.

"Wonderful," Jeff said, "just send her a brochure on Great Falls Park and write a letter for my signature."

"Jeff, are you coming in today?"

"No, I have meetings, and now you have made me late," he said, pausing for effect. "But if I miss my appointment, I could come in . . ." he said suggestively.

"I didn't mean to delay you, I was on another line. There's really nothing you can do here. I've got it well under control!"

He hated the exclamatory suggestion. "Well, thanks to you I don't have time to write a proper note to Irma explaining that I'll be detained until late after dinner." To Marcy

Newman, this was a familiar drill, and after working on the Hill, she played like a pro.

"Let me call her for you later. What time would be good? What time is she expected home?"

Dorn dropped his edge. "She'll be back around five, could you do that?"

"Oh, I'd love to!" she exclaimed contritely.

Dorn quickly terminated with a blind thumb just as Irma came strolling down the stairs and stepped into the kitchen, whirling like a dervish in her new sundress and carrying a picnic basket in her hand. She placed this on the counter, smiling coyly in a manner suggestive of wine, shade trees, and soft blankets. Dorn winced visibly.

"Who was that, sweetheart?" she asked, walking to his side.

"That was Marcy. I'm needed on an emergency, something about a permitting process. They need my testimony ASAP, and I haven't finished writing it yet."

"Oh, dear," Irma said, "I'd thought we'd visit the park together, it's a beautiful day." She saw the breakfast plate he had pushed aside. "Are you in pain, honey?"

"No, I'm feeling quite well, and I was looking forward to spending time with you, but . . ."

"I know, sweetheart," she soothed, "duty calls. Can I help with the report?"

"No, it's a one-man job. Unfortunately, there's nothing you can do."

"Will you miss me?" she sighed, draping her arms over his shoulders.

"More than you'll ever know," he said flatly, stroking the back of her hand as he returned to reading the morning paper.

When he had to, Jeff Dorn could be very agreeable.

Downstairs at the Kiernan home was the pride of Jeffrey Dorn's existence. A windowless, seamless place in the base-ment, just below the family room and kitchen. The room was fifteen by twenty, but it looked deceptively large, the walls finished with soundproof panels, while the floor was covered in outdoor carpeting, a dark leafy green.

In the ceiling, recessed cylinders could be dimmed from a switch at the bottom of the wooden staircase, and he made this adjustment in light levels until a soft romantic glow was achieved. It was clean, spotless, and private. The room had only one door, also painted white, which Jeff kept open most of the time so as not to arouse Irma's suspicion. He had recently read in a woman's magazine how the weaker sex did not understand a man's need for personal space, though he thought that odd for the manner in which silly bitches crowded their kitchens. There had been three in the Clayton house, each one had marked personal space with clothing, notepads, and utensils. It was laughable.

He closed the door, turning to examine himself in the Irma Solution, a full-length wall mirror that looked a tad off-center, for it had been hung low enough to accommodate her stubby body. This security device was silver-edged, tasteful, and it hung just opposite the door. When Irma entered, she would immediately meet her own reflection. Dorn knew she would be unable to stay more than a brief moment with her own face, and he was rather proud of that, the simplicity of it all.

In the room's center there was a glass desk with a typewriter, an organizer, and a tape recorder. He strolled across the carpet, enjoying the feel of the cloth tiles beneath his bare feet, and pressed the play button on the recorder. The basement office snapped to life, filling with the sounds of a writer at work: keys clattering, papers turning, punctuated pauses at just the correct intervals. He listened to the floorboards creak above his head as Irma settled into her routine and trotted up the stairs to her bedroom. Quietly he locked the door and removed the key. He was surrounded by white—cold, disorienting, disarming. The door had vanished into the seamless walls.

The human eye was lost for a focus. Canisters on the ceiling repeated themselves in the mirror, reflecting on the glass table. One spin in place and direction skewed. East became west. Time became trapped. The tape provided a typewriter's march under dim lights, the little room was glowing, and he loved it so—his entrance to a world that nurtured him, seduced him, that gave life meaning.

There was but one picture on the walls, on the far side of the room, nearest the mirror. Just a few moments bathed in white, and the colors nearly screamed from the walls, vibrating, demanding to be recognized. It was an eerie pop-art collage of a sidewalk bistro—part painting, the awnings, people and tables; part photo, the diner glowing under the black flower of a mushroom cloud; part food, rice raining from the sky; and part ink, the faces of patrons sketched with gas masks and helmets. They ate merrily under flamelike letters that said *Welcome to the Atomic Café,* and he lifted the heavy frame, setting it on the green tiles.

Under the metal lip of a forty-five-pound test hook was a hole that on first inspection appeared to be a black smudge. Upon a second look it seemed a shoddy attempt at picture hanging with an oversize nail. From his briefcase he fetched a child's hooded skating key, the antique type once used to adjust viselike binders against leather shoes, and with nimble experience he inserted it, then turned the key while pressing against the wall until a machine bolt spun free, hanging loose from its anchor.

With a two-handed push along the panel's invisible seam, a spring-loaded panel swung loose on hinges, opening slowly like the door to a bank vault, and there was darkness, formless and pure. Jeff Dorn stooped over at the waist, walking crablike, then vanished into the black maw, closing the panel behind him.

The room outside was seamless white, with the sound of a report being hammered into life.

The hallway was a concrete tube, about ten feet long and rounded at the top, some three feet wide and four feet high. It more resembled a miniature train tunnel, the darkness leading to a second door, where an egglike chamber sat at a depth of twenty feet under Irma Kiernan's backyard.

That this structure had once been intended to protect a family from something as remote as a nuclear attack always amused Dorn, who considered it without the perspective of the period in which it was built. Washington in the early sixties was a world that had seen the sole of Khrushchev's shoe as Jack Kennedy ordered the blockade of Cuba, and America waited for a communist promise. In Washington, news pounded at the population, neighbors donned helmets, theaters filled for the movie *Fail-Safe,* and even at public schools children were trained to keep their mouths open to prevent blast damage to eardrums. Wooded Acres, among the better-planned communities, gave homebuyers their choice of luxuries, a swimming pool or a bomb shelter. And so it was that Dorn stood in the coolness of a bunker twelve by twelve, among the smells of liquid Teflon and Hoppes nitrogen solvent. It filled the dead air space, and he threw a light switch, setting the ventilator on low, bringing life into the stuffy relic.

From the backyard, a quarter-acre lot, the only visible sign was a breathing snorkel, which resembled a stovepipe and was about the size of a skinny fire hydrant. This poked up through the ground but had been carefully disguised as a Japanese lantern so that it was functional as well as pleasing. Dorn had constructed the housing device as a filtration system, building elements into the windowlike lantern on three of six sides, then presented this as a gift to Irma, who unknowingly completed the camouflage, planting an elaborate flower garden around the Oriental hydrant; mostly colored perennials in honor of Jeff's comrades who had died on foreign soil.

As far as Irma knew, the shelter was gone, ripped out and filled in, and her Jeff had managed all of this for a tremendous savings, thereby proving that the world is filled with crooks. Most of her neighbors had paid a group rate of upward of five thousand dollars each to have their backyards dismantled, and Irma hadn't minded that it took Jeff nearly a year for the work to be completed, even though a strange and unpleasant thing had happened.

During demolition, Irma was forced to take up residence in a cheap motel, for during the peak of Dorn's efforts, rodents started invading her home. For a short time she had tolerated the field mice.

Soon after, she found two dead rats in her kitchen sink.

It took almost a year for the Atomic Café to take form.

Once clean air was circulating through filters, Dorn began patching the concrete, sealing and painting, building shelves, carpeting the pad on which it was built, then adding two chairs and a love seat. Like the den that preceded it, the walls were painted white, but this carpet was red. The work had been completed in 1981, and since that time he had added little finishing touches—a dehumidifier, a space heater, a magnetic fan in the floor, whatever the family budget would allow.

The ceiling was a small concrete dome with a white pebbled surface, and the door was double reinforced steel, locked from the inside only with a bolt and crossbar. These two features were original, the door forged from high-test steel, then packed with molten lead for weight and protection against nuclear fallout. Over the decades even the hinges had held true, and he guessed that the Atomic salesmen had used these in showrooms as a selling tool because the integrity was beyond question. On the turn-bolt crossbar, the same type used on hatches for large ships, was stamped *W. Charles & Co.*, and he pulled on this, stepping down five wooden steps into the sunken confine.

From the outside, the door appeared to swing shut without a sound. But from within was a deafening thud and a shock of air as the faint hum of the snorkel's magnetic fan began to whirl. He stopped to admire the steps, the original white spruce which he had painstakingly sanded and refinished to its natural condition.

Just inside the chamber to the right was a wall plate with a series of black toggle switches and a captain's chair. To the left of the door, between a taupe love seat and recliner was a large wooden armoire painted flat black. He opened the door to rows of clothes, freshly cleaned, some still hanging in their plastic bags, and counting seven across, he removed a uniform. It was a pale blue jumpsuit with more tool holders than a watchman has keys, and across the breast pocket was the name *Ben Johnson, Supervisor.* On the back it said *C&P Telephone Company,* and on each shoulder an embroidered logo appeared as a bright blue Liberty Bell. He laid this across the love seat, then stripped down to his underwear.

For an hour Dorn sat on the small sofa while running through a checklist of equipment, then pulled a filebox toward him, the ball-casters sliding easily over the outdoor carpeting. He opened a drawer and retrieved a file, removing a news clipping from a New York newspaper. It was a photoless story, less than two column inches, and lacking a byline. Dorn wished the editors of the community page had included more detail.

—LOCAL MAN HONORED BY BROTHERS—
John F. Scott of Greenlawn was honored today with a Lifetime of Service award from Big Brothers of America for his work with children who are lacking male role models.
 Scott, a government analyst, is due to retire from federal service later this year.

He read it again. Then once more. He knew the Clayton package would be sitting on Scott's desk, and that stirred excitement in Jeffrey Dorn.

To this he clipped the small white envelope that Irma had retrieved the night before, and his hand shook uncharacteristically as he held the paper to the light. Earlier in the month he had specifically requested that all such communications be sent without a return address from his doctor on Foxhall Road. It was a dying man's wish. As a patient he could not be denied.

During a routine checkup—Dorn's quarterly trip for pills of various kinds—a blood test had revealed a white cell count over fifteen hundred, indicative of advanced cancer. The shock had crippled him for days as he quickly investigated the possibilities of therapy—chemical, radiation, even transfusion.

Having studied the effects of healing, in many cases worse than simply dying, Dorn held further treatment in abeyance until the specific type and location of the disease could be found. He was scheduled for a battery of tests at the end of the month, and did not want to read more about his fate. When faced with his own mortality, Dorn simply wished to fill his last days with as much living as possible, which meant keeping the secret from Irma, who would fawn over him in such a way that death would be preferable.

Dr. Thomas Landry, whom Dorn considered a basic pill doctor, was lost for words in the first place. That the patient would die was without doubt. The cells and platelet count proved that, however sloppy Dorn considered Landry to be. This was the fourth message from him in a month; it described what to expect, how his body would grow weak, how his strength would ebb. Dorn was tired of dealing with it. Whatever the outcome, he planned on living to the last, pushing his entire life into a remainder of months.

Six of those, or maybe a year, no one knew.

While Dorn considered this, anger stirred him to his feet and he slapped the envelope inside the file. Life was cheating him. He was still young. His prime was not yet over. If he had believed in God, which he did not, then he would have considered this a message.

But Jeff Dorn knew better.

On planet earth there was only mortal man, a being that left messages of reason. No wild dog could ever do the same, no Christ-like figure, no apparitions born from the foolish sands of mankind's collective past. He hated mythology. From the Greeks to the Bible to the gods of Mormon hope to the babbling fools in their sanctimonious stained-glass towers, they spent their lives interpreting messages, reading tea leaves, searching for reason.

Men like Dorn created the lasting messages, and he had left one for Scott, a masterpiece of play, a little retirement package, and their name was Clayton. He knew the case would be sitting on Scott's desk, and it filled a dying man with a wicked delight and special sense of purpose.

That Scott was Catholic only made it better. Guilt ran his soft and shallow life, from the confessional to the squad car to the streets; he couldn't act on a whim without permission from the saints. And Dorn imagined that his enemy had grown complacent over the years, his futile little job failing to provide meaning where the church had promised, but could not deliver.

"Elmer Janson." Dorn spoke aloud, selecting another newspaper and scanning the page. The reporter from *Tempo* was a soulmate to Dorn. Though he did not know the man, they both were itching for details on the boy's slut of a mother.

It delighted him.

A hundred times he had read this thing, and he would read it a hundred more.

In three steps he crossed the bunker to a large metal supply closet against the farthest wall. He opened the double doors, then leaned forward, examining rows of sophisticated weaponry: carbines and assault rifles and machine guns. There was a specialty shelf for knives. On each side of the vault, pistols hung suspended from trigger guards lying three rows across, ten deep, for a total of thirty semiautomatic handguns.

Below, in an enclosed locker, a padlock promised accessories: picks, blades, suppressors, clips and ammunition, pipes, holsters, and cord. He surveyed the inner walls, and from among many gleaming possibilities he selected a .22-caliber Rohm automatic, which he lifted from its hook. For the better part of an hour he stripped, cleaned, assembled, and polished the little weapon, loading the clip with hollow-tipped bullets. Dorn held it to the soft overhead light, releasing the slide, and it snapped shut with a deadly *clap,* feeding a cartridge. Safety activated, he inserted the clip.

Oiled with a liquid Teflon, the flyweight alloy gun, silencer attached, was swift and soundless as a sewing machine. He removed a tool bag from behind the love seat and began to dress.

Within fifteen minutes Ben Johnson emerged from the shelter, a field supervisor from the local telephone company being dispatched on an emergency assignment. This was a role Dorn favored almost as much as Veteran. And he played for the most personal and ultimate stakes. Deception to Jeffrey Dorn was a deeply personal and satisfying amusement, a hobby, a challenge, and a way of life. The role he was now wearing would not fade in the wash of humanity, for he knew it, tried and true, an experienced lineman with the credentials to prove it.

On his way to work he paused, lifting a small but exquisite leather case with a reddish hue that rested on a shelf near the shelter's door. As far as he was concerned, there was nothing finer to be had anywhere in America, at least not as a symbol, and he took it from its case.

The Legion of Merit sprayed a sparkling glint of yellow as he held it in his hand, the light streaming in tiny lines across the shelter, dancing on concrete walls, reflecting on the pebbled ceiling. A blue ribbon lay carefully folded into rows, suspending the heroic shield, and as he touched, caressed, and held it, Dorn felt an excitement that had not waned even after thousands of inspections. There was an enchantment that he could not shake, though he had worn it for years around the collar of his dress uniform, and his breath fogged the shiny medallion, one of America's highest rewards for sacrifice and gallantry.

Before leaving he wrote a note to have Irma apply polish and elbow grease. *White-hot,* he penned, that's the way he liked all of his medals, and he left this upstairs on the kitchen table.

It was true that, under another name, he had served in the Army as a private during the Korean War. But he had been court-martialed for sexual assault, and held a dishonorable discharge to prove it.

During his four-month tour of duty, he had never left the United States.

23

In the northwest section of the Potomac river valley, a gentleman's country estate sat on a piece of land skirting the edge of Great Falls National Historic Park. The vast private property was so close to the highway that during the summer months, tourists often mistook the little farmhouse by the road as a Department of the Interior food concession, and would knock on the front door of the residence expecting menus. The man who answered was James Lee Cooley.

Once, not so far back in time, the Cooley family had maintained a working farm in Cabin John. But with the massive housing development that came to the area during the early seventies, property taxes increased to the point where the only solution to a pending government foreclosure was to sell a tract of land once used for shedding tobacco. And it was thus that the man standing before John Scott and Frank Rivers had became an overnight millionaire.

"Hey, Jim," Rivers said cheerfully as Cooley stepped out onto the front porch. The country gentleman had heard the siren approaching, then the car skidding over gravel and into the long circular driveway.

"Hey back at you, Frank," he said, smiling. "Would you like a menu? Special of the day is lemonade, or beer, if your friend wants one." He extended his hand to Scott, who was standing a little off to one side. Greetings were quickly exchanged, and they found themselves following the lean farmer through the hall, living room, kitchen, and out to an open-air patio.

Frank Rivers had known the entire Cooley clan, and he knew Jim was a compact version of his father, with looks and a manner that were deceiving. Though he was thirty-eight, he could easily pass for fifteen years younger, making him easy to spot by former acquaintances. He was quiet, almost pensive, and his once wild head of reddish hair was a thinning chestnut brown.

"I'll get us some drinks," he said, glancing at Rivers, then at Scott, as the two men settled into lawn chairs. For a moment there was an awkward silence.

"That sounds grand," Scott said.

"Anything's good for me," Rivers returned, and Jim Cooley crossed the gray slate patio, vanishing through the rear door as the two men sat in quiet admiration. From the rear patio they looked out onto meadows and rolling green hills as far as the eye could see, an enormous island of calm in the middle of rampant suburbia. Scott found himself imagining what the Cooley farm must have once looked like, corn rows reaching, golden fields, earthen patches plowed into neat columns. Far off, near the roadway, before a stately oak, he spotted a tractor's rusting hulk, the front blades still attached, locked and frozen above the ground. The open fields, the bright sun, and smells of damp humus stroked the senses, deepening a boiling silence.

On second look, it was a mournful sight, and Scott's brow was heavy with concentration. Clouds moved through sunlight, casting shadows at their feet.

"What happened to him, Frank?" Scott said quietly, pulling his chair closer to the detective.

"In what sense, Jack? Jimmy's good people."

"His parents, you knew them?"

"Died within a year of each other. His mother had a stroke, and Big Jim died from a coronary—they found him sitting at the wheel of his Cat." Rivers pointed to the tractor. "It's a helluva machine, straight eight, don't see many of those anymore."

The commander prodded gently. "In the hallway I saw a picture of you and Jim with another boy on what looked like a camping trip. Who is he?"

Rivers' eyes shifted to Scott, then back out to the fields. "You don't miss much, do you, Jack? That was his older brother, Michael. We were three buttons off the same shirt, couldn't keep us apart. He got wasted, spring of sixty-eight."

Scott could see the man's jaw tighten, a cool breeze soaked the landscape. "The first week in May?" he asked softly, and Rivers stood, fumbling through his pockets for a smoke, then popping an aspirin instead.

"The awards ceremony for Detective of the Year is about the same time. Being with Jim is more important to you. Does he know?"

Rivers' eyes turned to ice. "No, and you aren't going to tell him, and I mean that."

Scott realized that he was digging into a wound, so he quickly dropped the matter as Cooley appeared, tray in hand. He poured three glasses and settled into his seat, watching Scott with a subtle interest, but annoyed by the occasional rumble of cars leaving the national park across the way. Scott took a long swallow from his glass.

"Thank you," he said, as a way of prompting his host to speak, but Cooley said not a word as he quickly stood to freshen the drink. A calico cat appeared, rubbing against Scott's leg, then plopped at his feet. He leaned over and stroked the small animal.

"What's his name?" he inquired.

"Buttercup," said Cooley. "He's a she."

At the sound of voices a basset hound slowly sauntered over, licked the cat, and lay down alongside, vying for attention. "Buttercup's friend?" Scott asked.

"Downboy. Only dog you'll meet scared of his own bark," Cooley offered just as a large black feline leapt up and crawled over his back, draping himself across both shoulders. "Hunley," he smiled as the cat purred loudly, amber eyes glowing in the commander's direction.

"Good name for a cat," Scott remarked. "Wasn't Horace Hunley the inventor of the first American submarine?"

Cooley nodded. "Yes, sir, a Confederate captain, 1864 was the date. The sub went down in battle with all hands."

Rivers was dunking cubes in his glass with a straw.

"So what can we do for you?" Cooley asked, placing the cat in his lap. "Frank made it sound pretty urgent, but he always sounds like that."

"Thanks, Jim," Rivers replied.

Scott put down his glass and removed a notepad from his blazer, which was draped across the chair. "We're trying to understand a relationship between—"

"You have three dead children and one woman, Frank explained all that," Cooley cut him off. "How can I help?"

"The black child," he said gratefully. "I have someone working on an identification, but I need to know: if she still had family or friends, where would they be now?"

"If she was a city kid, Washington. It's a black city, and I don't mean that in an uncharitable way."

"And if she lived around here?" Scott asked.

Cooley looked at Rivers. "She was a local child?" he asked, his voice trembling a bit.

Scott nodded. "We're not certain, but let's presume that she was."

"And she died when?"

"She was killed in 1958."

Cooley stared into the distance and took a sip from his glass. "Then Tobytown would be my guess." He turned partway and pointed. "About ten miles north as you head out to Frederick."

Scott opened his black briefcase, removed an area map, and then handed it to Cooley. "Will you show me?"

"Sure," he said. As he leaned forward, the cat jumped from his lap. "Here's River Road," he said. "A few years ago I sold a tract of bottomland a few miles up—we used it to shed tobacco, that would be a good landmark for you."

Scott circled the spot on the exploded view.

"Look for a housing development right there with a gold sign that says Tara, you'll find Tobytown eight miles up."

Scott chuckled. "From *Gone with the Wind* Tara? That's the best they could do?"

Cooley shrugged, remembering the honey smells of the barn curing tobacco and thinking about the mansions with their purple doors that developers had just seemed to drop there. "Instant identity for thieves," he said. Reaching to the lawn, with the practice of a field hand he pulled a blade of dry grass and dropped it into his mouth.

Scott caught the man's grimace.

"Tobytown," Cooley volunteered, "used to be near where you and Frank are staying, back when I was a kid. It could be she lived there once"—he shrugged—"but her family would have been forced to move north."

A puzzled expression spread across Scott's face. The command post was at least ten miles south, going in the opposite direction, and the only town there was the city of Bethesda. "Jim, do you mean another town used to be near the bowling alley?"

Cooley nodded. "Tobytown," he said again.

"Tell me about that," Scott inquired. "Government records don't reflect what you're saying."

"Jack," Rivers put in defensively while reaching for the pitcher, "if anyone would know, Jimmy would."

"I'm quite sure, thank you, Frank." He turned back to face the lean farmer. "What the devil happened, Jim?"

"Well," he drawled with a slight southern accent, "Tobytown was a mixed village, black and white, poor but proud. My grandfather lived there for a short time when he was down on his luck, so Tobytown was established long before this farm. During the States' War, as people would flee from the Deep South, they followed the river. Once they got to Cabin John, they took River Road toward Washington and just settled there, up by the railroad tracks where the high-rise buildings are. That's the short version. There was an entire town that spread down to Kenwood Forest past the bowling alley."

Drury's office had supplied detailed land records of the area, but there had been no mention of this. "I'm sorry, but I'm confused," Scott said. "You're saying Tobytown is now in the other direction?"

Cooley nodded. "North," he said, "look for the sign that says Tara and just keep going, you'll find it."

"And this town, this Tobytown, used to be near the bowling alley?"

"All true," said Cooley.

"Then why did they relocate?"

"Why?" Cooley repeated the question with a forced laugh, staring at Scott. "Poor people don't have lawyers is why," and there was anger in his voice. "Didn't matter that nobody owned that land, it was sold out from underneath them. Did you notice the small Baptist church between the bank and the gas station?"

"I did see that, yes," Scott answered.

"That's all that's left, the one thing Tobytown residents refused to give up, now it sits in a concrete wasteland. Next to the church there was an adjoining cemetery, but they built right over it. When Frank called, I thought for sure somebody had hit on an old Tobytown grave, but he didn't agree."

Scott winced. What better place to hide murdered women and children? The killer had planned for the future. Just then Scott recalled Elmer Janson's remark about slave burials, perhaps a loose rumor based on historical fact. And the lime to quickly dissolve bone, forcing early decomposition, masking victims among graves of the disenfranchised. Who would have searched there, and if anyone were found, who would have cared?

"And the church is all that's left." Scott's voice sagged. "Do you know what took place there?"

"This isn't ancient history, Jack," Cooley said sarcastically. "I know what happened to Tobytown because the goddamned sky turned red, lighting up the horizon for miles. She burned for three days. Somebody torched them, and the town went to ashes. It was the week of my eighth birthday, I was born July 21."

Scott was taken aback. It sounded like behavior from the turn of the century. "Then that would be around 1957?"

"No, Frank's got a year on me, that was 1958. From my bedroom I could see the flames from Tobytown, and the local men all gathered outside, right here, talking and drinking, but there wasn't anything they could do. Just workingmen, they didn't want trouble not of their making."

Rivers had gulped down his drink and was nervously stabbing ice cubes with a straw for more liquid. Cooley reached over and refilled his glass. "I don't mind," he said to him, though looking in Scott's direction. "So anyway, they were moved way out, we can take you there. You'll see a large sign that says 'Tobytown, Established 1865,' and behind that you'll find some cheap apartments built by the county government. Around here, signs help some people sleep at night. The River Road properties had become too valuable to let the poor keep them."

"There are laws," Scott commented absently.

"No," Cooley frowned, "this is Washington, land of lawyers. Around here the thieves make it up as they go. Some work for the feds, some for the county, some for private companies, but it's all the same, glove-in-hand corruption. Very safe, and very lucrative. Way out here they forced me to sell a field, got better than two million for it, and that's nothing compared to what Tobytown was and where it was located. Difference is, I'm a white boy, they had to pay me."

Scott's lips were pinched tight; he was beginning to understand. "Frank tells me that there's a lot of history around here and that you used to find Civil War artifacts on your farm."

Cooley glanced at Rivers and smiled. "Frank told you that?"

Scott glanced at him. "Was he wrong?"

"No," Cooley laughed, "but to Frank, history was last night's dinner."

"Dogs and beans with slaw," Rivers added.

"Well, I researched Cabin John," Scott pressed on, "and there's very little mentioned, no battles anyway."

"There wouldn't be," Cooley explained. "River Road was an immediate route to and from the major fighting at Antietam, Manassas, Gettysburg, and other battlefields. Federal and Confederate boys would actually pass each other in broad daylight and not fire. A lot of 'em were neighbors."

"Then there was no fighting," Scott concluded.

Cooley leaned forward, straightened the map, and pointed. "You're here directly across from Great Falls National Park, one-quarter of a mile off the main roadway. Anything on either side, including this farm, was a free-for-all. Do you remember seeing the punch-press housing developments on the way in?"

Scott nodded.

"Once they were fields and farms. In those areas, especially down here by the canal or river, it was a no-man's-land. Hundreds of men in blue and gray fought viciously as they were returning from major campaigns, and fighting so close to home, this area saw some of the most desperate hand-to-hand combat of the war, but no historic engagements. Some guy was dying right there one hundred and twenty-five years ago," Cooley said, pointing at the large oak near the roadway.

"Fascinating," Scott said. "Were you hunting for artifacts?"

"No, I don't believe in that," he replied, taking a long sip of lemonade, then locking eyes with Scott. "When I was ten we were tilling near that tree after a storm and the plow blade bit cloth just under the soil. We uncovered a Confederate boy still clutching his cap, so we fetched the pastor and interred him, he's still there. A few weeks later we snagged bone near the park, found a Yankee, and buried him alongside. The Yank faces north, the reb faces south—that was my father's idea. Our guess is that they were on their way home after Antietam in 1862 and killed each other, but who knows? They were young, no wedding bands or filled teeth, but if anyone found out today," the man blinked, "they'd be sold at a flea market."

Scott emitted a sigh and faced Jim Cooley directly. "So we're dealing with a relocated village, a church cemetery, and public records that were destroyed?"

"That would be my guess."

Scott smiled thoughtfully. "That explains a great deal. I've dealt with this type of greed before. You have a beautiful

home, Jim, and I thank you for sharing it with us." He started to rise from his seat, when the man **sudden**ly flared.

"How did it happen?" Cooley blurted, and Frank Rivers stood quickly, seeing anger take hold of his friend.

"What's that?" Scott responded, looking to Rivers for direction.

Cooley seemed confused; his fists were clenched. "One day," his voice quavered, "this was a real nice town. I mean, all places on God's earth have their problems, but it was a real place. Next thing you know, we're overflowing with crooks, everything's bulldozed flat, and it happened so fast no one saw it coming, like we were sleepwalking . . ." His voice trailed into sorrow.

Scott studied the two younger men. "I'm not sure exactly what you're asking, but most places with a cultural legacy would never have allowed this much development this fast. A construction avalanche usually starts when history is forgotten or rewritten. That's obviously what went on here," he said, watching their expressions. His words were having an effect.

"Oh, come on, Jack," Rivers suddenly snapped, "what great fucking history were we known for?"

Scott waved him off with one hand, offering silence.

"Freedom," Cooley stated at Rivers, finding his voice. "Freedom, not the concept but the courage to find it, the strength to allow it. The very name 'Bethesda' means 'House of Mercy,' from the Old Testament."

"But the Urban District, the people who put out that dining guide, said Bethesda took its name from a pool in Israel," Rivers fired back. "They even imported a rock from there, it was in all the papers."

Cooley sat back in his chair shaking his head. "And where do you think they came from, Frank? You should know better!" He turned to Scott. "My father was a boy when Bethesda was named. The town was titled for the courage of a freeman, a former slave."

"John?" Scott asked.

Cooley nodded. "The city was named to honor him. In the Bible it says, 'Go without fear with him whose name is John, for upon his promise they will find Bethesda, house of mercy, of freedom, and of God.' That's where the name came from, Frank. I really can't believe you!"

And Scott knew. He felt it in his gut the way Diana Clayton had felt Zak Dorani enter her house, a shiver, a chill, a heartbeat. He leaned over and handed Jim Cooley a glassine evidence pouch.

The farmer's eyes instantly burned with anguish. "Was this found in the grave?" he asked solemnly.

Scott nodded.

"And Frank told me that this man's been killing for thirty years?"

"Closer to thirty-five," Scott answered. "What is this?"

Cooley closed his fingers around the medallion. "It's a John's Warning."

"The same man Bethesda was named for?"

"John-the-Free. These coins would be put into circulation as a warning that Confederate spies were infiltrating the river area. The only other type was a Scarborough Warning."

"I don't follow," Scott said.

"Southern lynch law. If they caught someone helping slaves or federal prisoners, they'd kill you on the spot, you'd be found swinging from a rope. Only two types of warnings back then, a John's Warning like this coin or a Scarborough Warning, which meant hang them first and they'll get the message."

"First a blow, warning after. The spies were ruthless terrorists, which is why the tokens were so important. Faced with such brutality, no one could be trusted."

Cooley nodded.

"And the house on the coin?"

He shook his head. "It's a symbol of many cabins that were built near here to hide refugees. I'm afraid it would take a long time to explain."

"Maybe not. What type of child would be wearing this?" Scott asked.

"A child who was well-loved," he said, staring at the coin. "A good token is worth several thousand dollars to a collector. My grandfather gave me one so I'd remember what this town is about, I still have it."

"And Frank told me you were born on this property." He paused. "Your birth record doesn't say Cabin John, does it, Jim?"

The intense green eyes sparkled with recognition. Rivers sat mute. Since childhood Jim Cooley had been his closest friend, and they had no secrets, or so he had thought.

Cooley carried his cat into the little house and returned with a bound leather album.

"I was born in a place that no longer exists," he stated, his face a mask of hatred. "A town where it never mattered to anyone what color you were, or religion, or how much you made, or what land you owned. We were hardworking Americans. That used to count for something."

As Scott began to examine the first document, his fingers lightly stroking the words on a Certificate of Live Birth, Cooley handed him a gold wooden frame. It was a country landscape with a village green, a town, a white church steeple, a waterfall, and inset at the bottom was a token in mint condition.

"John's Cabin, Maryland," Scott said defiantly. "I was right, the birth certificate and the coin are the same!"

"Once the greatest town in the Free State," Cooley responded proudly. "The name was changed the year Tobytown burned."

24

He had started to sweat in the hot morning sun, and although he had dressed using the finest of talc, his blue uniform was already clinging. It sagged at the hips, weighed down with tools and equipment, the most awkward of which was a telephone lineman's test set. This was a self-contained telephone with push buttons and a rotary dial built into the handle, and as he climbed the rungs on a pole on Westbard Avenue, it swung from a cord at his waist, slapping against his thigh.

His technique was only fair, not good, and a passing uniformed patrolman guessed immediately that Jeff Dorn, an older man who looked out of practice, was a C&P Telephone Company field supervisor who had been shortchanged over the weekend.

Other tools sprouted from chest, belly, and thighs, and he climbed higher as the police car sped by. He rested at the twelve-foot station where the metal struts began, providing a ladder for authorized workers. He attached a leather safety strap and, holding on tight to the pole, wrapped it around the sticky pylon, clipping the left end first, then the right, to the steel turnbuckle at his waist. Leaning back gently, he felt the support across the small of his back and climbed slowly as he caught his breath.

Now, it was true that on some rare occasions Jeffrey Dorn did have some back pain, for he had inherited a curved spine that could cause muscle spasms when the weather was inclement. And it was also true that the local telephone company issued a quality suit with more holders than a watchman has keys, but the material was still inferior to what he was accustomed to. Cotton would have breathed better and would have been the more logical choice, Dorn thought as he had started to sweat. Then again, he only became a lineman in the best of seasons.

He moved quickly in an upward crawl, using the metal rungs, passing the twenty-five-foot mark, then the fifty, and rested again. Soon he reached the top of the pylon, eyeing a large gray terminal box that connected with power lines and rows of industrial cable.

To repairmen across the land, this type of unit is referred to as a junction box or terminus, but to Dorn it was the hydra, a slang term used in the parlance of clandestine surveillance, which he had picked up from detailed manuals he had discovered years earlier at the annual State Department book sale. Such proceeds always went to charity, which Dorn found ironic, and with a single controlled stroke he slit the back of a cable housing with a straight razor. He then reached inside the hose with a small chrome hook, pulling free a nerve bundle of multicolored wires in every hue of the rainbow.

Methodically he laid these across his palm, searching for one with small white bands. He then denuded a sheath, using a special tool, and attached an alligator clip to the raw copper wire. He leaned back against the belt and studied the massive gray hydra, the black cords playing out to countless rows of houses, and leading to a second box a few hundred yards down River Road.

Throughout his life, Jeffrey Dorn had always depended on the predictability and general competence of other people, and he knew, if the telephone maintenance crew for this block was any good, he could save hours, working by color code and geographic distance. It was a simple affair. The closer the house, the closer the hydra, and inside there were sequentially coded wire leads from near to far. He could count the houses visually against each color lead, but if the maintenance crew was sloppy, it could take all day.

Dorn clutched the tarred, sticky pylon, looking down from the metal struts beneath his boots to the street. The bastards were oblivious, their puny lives looked as dwarfed as their cars two hundred feet below, and he began to work, counting against a notepad. Life itself, he reflected, was an orderly process of elimination, just like working the wires—old against young, sick against strong, mind against will, man over beast, a progression of time and endurance. He counted seven strands and yanked a red wire free. Reaching to a breast pocket for another tool, he stripped that line down to metal. He then searched for yellow, and one green, fourteen wires in, snapping these to bare copper and attaching clips to each. He held the test set to his ear and listened for a dial tone.

Nothing.

Checking for an unstable ground connection, he freed the white ribbed wire, licked the teeth on the clip, and replaced the contact. The headset snapped to life, the connection was true, steady. He dialed, watching his meter, and a phone rang twice.

"Westwood Elementary," a woman's voice answered.

"This is telephone repair," he said in a dry but commanding tone. "We are checking a faulty line, is this Westwood School?" he asked.

"Yes it is . . ." sang a Valium voice.

The woman had to be sixty. "Can you hear me clearly, miss?"

"Yes, I can, I can hear you . . ." she sang for a stranger on a pole.

He glanced at a gauge: the voice registered .9 Biddles, indicating weak resistance on the line for a half-mile span; knowing that this could be improved, he prepared to terminate the call.

"Thank you, I believe we have the trouble corrected," his words firm but routine. "If you have any complaints, please contact your local C&P telephone repair, it's been a pleasure to serve you."

"Oh, thank you," she said as he pulled the plug, made a notation, and secured the book to a belt clip. He replaced the hold on three clips, checking for dust or any fouling, and swabbed these with a premoistened chemical pad. The lines had not been disturbed, for number fourteen yellow-and-green was the switchboard at Irma's school. Thus he had established a baseline he could easily follow. Without further delay he tore into number seven red with tiny metal jaws.

"I don't care, Donna, my father hates him," said the voice of a young woman. "Did you hear that?"

"What?"

"That click on the line, it sounds like someone is on the phone."

Dorn was cleaning his teeth with a thumbnail.

"I didn't hear a thing, Donna, it's not over here. Are you sure you're going through with this, I'm late for school . . ."

He wanted to listen, but didn't have time, and hit blue. ". . . we've got to unload," harped a man's voice, slightly effete. "We've been sitting on it too long, we're not collecting interest on our investment—did you hear that?"

Static boomed, then died.

"What the fuck?" a second man responded.

There was an extended silence, and Dorn shrugged. Making sure his fingers were far from the transmitting bar, he checked a ground lead.

"I don't know what, but I heard it!" whined the effeminate male. "Do you think our phones are tapped? God, maybe it's the DEA, we've got to unload!"

"Shut up, you fucking idiot!" came a sharp retort. "Not on the phone. I'll meet you."

"Where?"

"In the lobby of the Air Rights Building by the photo counter, ten o'clock?"

Dorn pulled the plug and remembered to laugh. He was fascinated by suburban life, the closed doors and private conversations. Residents ran in circles like mice on a wheel, chasing each other, then dropping with exhaustion into twisted nests. The nice young men down the street were really idiot faggots selling dope. Donna worried about Father, who was probably doing Donna anyway—who was he to intrude? He wormed through the coil for a silver line and attached.

"Oh, it's so hard, Beth," she pleaded. "Ever since the children left for college he's been difficult, we just don't talk anymore. Mop the floors, clean the toilets, feed the dog, starch the shirts, do I have ambitions? No, I couldn't have."

The lineman could also hear a television soap in the background.

"When's the last time he told you he loved you, appreciated you, took you to dinner?" asked a sedate woman.

She sighed, "I can't even remember, it's been that long."

Dorn had been on an open line, and since the static interference was weak, the signal clear and steady, he knew he was in close proximity to his target. Since they hadn't commented on the intrusion, he decided to perform a trial run to determine where he was in the neighborhood telephone loop. He smacked the transmitting button on the test set twice, his eyes dropping down a list in his notepad.

"Telephone repair, sorry to bother you, ladies, there seems to be some trouble on the line. Is this 1107 Kenwood Forest Drive?" he asked with authority, charming them with his rounded tones.

"No," said the distressed woman, "this is 1103, you must have the wrong number. Beth, do you have any phone problems?"

"No, Maggie, you know Mark does all of our installation, and we never had a problem. Not one."

"Sorry about the intrusion, ladies, we've crossed a wire," he said, writing in his book. Number 1103 was Maggie Lubbo, at least he was close.

". . . you just don't know how lucky you are, Beth," the conversation resumed before the lineman had disconnected. "He's such a talented and considerate man . . ."

Was it green-on-green or white-on-green? He selected the first.

". . . but we don't know that much about him, honey. I'm sure he's a fine man, a perfect gentleman, but think now. How many times have you met him?" she prodded gently, a creature with an elegant voice. The lineman was enthralled.

"Twice, Mom, two times, why can't I go? You met him."

"Only for a second, just long enough to say good-bye, and that's not good enough."

"But, Mom, please?"

"Well, I'd like to talk to him again before I allow you to go traipsing off into the woods to some fishing hole. Did he leave a number?" she asked gently.

"A con artist fleecing a house of suckers. Snatch the kid for a snuff flick," Dorn said aloud, "it's a dealer's market."

"We can talk about him later. Hon, are you working on your homework? You have two tests on Monday." Her voice was firm but soothing, and Jeff Dorn remembered the first time he had seen *Bambi,* how the little creature loved and obeyed his mother. And he imagined that feeling. It was a good but bitter memory, he could whistle the music to the death scene, the doe had gone down hard.

"Yes, Mother," he sighed, "when are you coming home?"

"Elmer, I've got a meeting in a few minutes, and I'll be home right after. Then we'll go out for some treats. Would you like to see a movie tonight?"

"Yes." His voice perked up, *"Indiana Jones!"*

"You've seen that twice. Pick something else after you've completed your studies, and we'll talk when I get home. And no TV or running around until you've finished everything, or there'll be no movie, understand?"

"Yes," huffed the voice.

"I love you, baby."

"Tripod says hello."

"Hello, Tripod. Now, please get some work done, and if you have any questions, call me."

"Yes, Mom," he said grudgingly.

"And no more sweets until after lunch, it's in the refrig."

"I know."

"Call me?" she tested.

"Yes, Mom."

"I love you."

"Love you too, Mom."

And Dorn mocked their conversation, imitating their voices, listening carefully as Jessica Janson hesitated just a fraction of a second, as if sensing an intrusion, before hanging up the phone.

Jeffrey Dorn worked his face into a cruel knot. If anyone knew about maternal instinct, it was the lineman.

25

The detail moved forward like the hands of a clock, with the two men arriving back at the command post on Ridgefield Drive at 3:10.

To Frank Rivers it felt early, his spirit depressed by his lack of knowledge about the town where he was raised, while Jack Scott was wandering the dark corners of his life, counting faces in a morgue, those bearing the marks of recreational killers. His mind flipped back over thirty-five years as the horrid truth became inescapable. In that period Zak Dorani could have easily claimed scores of lives. By the time the Crown Victoria edged into the driveway, Scott was contemplating the gender ratios of girls to boys to young mothers, considering their fate as his personal failing.

Just then a giant of a man emerged near the garden gate. He stepped from the shadows near the garage, black and looming, in his early forties, and wearing a light blue beret with a purple T-shirt. Quickly the man made his presence known, and just as rapidly he took a step backward into shadow. He was a severe-looking sort with a face that seemed chiseled from a block of wood.

"I do hope he's friendly," Scott said as the engine died.

"I should have known about John's Cabin," Rivers said absently.

"By the time you were old enough to care, the name was long gone, changed when you were a baby living in California, so don't get down on yourself."

Rivers chewed on a bit of flesh inside one cheek as he opened the door and stepped out, waiting for Scott, who drew up alongside.

"How do you want to handle tactics?" Rivers asked.

"You have my every faith. You know what we need to cover our position, and I will leave that in your capable hands." They were heading toward the side lot.

"And if you don't like my techniques?"

"Every faith, Frank. You know your capabilities, men, and resources. If I'm free to concentrate on the hunt while you're minding the store, we'll make better progress. If you hit a wall, let me know, but I'm placing you in charge and I speak for Captain Drury."

Rivers nodded as they approached. Travis Bernard Saul, or Toy as he was known, greeted them both, then slapped Rivers' palms hard enough to sting. He led them between houses and through the garden gate, where three other men in old clothes waited on the patio.

It took five minutes to get acquainted and unload equipment into the house: radios, field parabolic, spotting scopes, cameras, and several banker's boxes filled with files and forms. As Scott looked on, the state policemen hashed over the interior decorations before settling down into the garish leather chairs and sofa.

"Where are you parking?" asked Rivers.

"In the NIH lot on Westbard, two blocks up," Dennis Murphy responded, a large officer with red hair, his fair skin covering a massive skull and bone structure. He was known to Frank Rivers as Mule Murphy, not for his size, but for his tenacity. They had known each other since the Christmas truce of 1968, Da Nang airbase.

"Any problems with the keys to the bowling alley?" Rivers asked a pair of younger men in street clothes.

"No, the captain gave us an extra set," answered Marcus Kocska, the shorter of the two, mirror sunglasses slung over thinning hair. He handed the copies to Rivers.

"The lock's cheap, no alarms or loose windows," said Rudolph Marchette, a slight man with a thick black mustache.

"Ditch the lip, Rudy," Rivers demanded, turning to unroll the blueprints.

"What, Sarge?" the rookie responded assertively.

"The fake brush." He reached over and ripped it loose. "Stick it on your tool, you can play Dick when you get home."

Laughing, Toy slapped him on the back, almost sending the light man tumbling forward.

"Listen up," Rivers demanded. "We're going through this once, no screwups. Marchette, do you know about the fool who went to the Red Cross and gave all his blood?"

"Ah, no, sir," said Rudy the Lip.

"You screw up, you'll wish that was you. Now, listen up!"

Faces became serious as all eyes shifted to the floor, where the blueprint lay weighted down in each corner by Frank's running shoes, gun, and handcuffs. He studied the chart on one knee for a moment, pushing over the blue paper like a bloodhound chasing crickets. He stopped, straightening his back, making eye contact with all four men in the semicircle.

"The detail is physical security and surveillance. There are two teams. There are two targets." He studied expressions; they were on cue.

"Target one is the home of Mrs. Jessica Janson. Their town house borders the parameter here"—he darkened the north side of the bowling alley parking lot with a felt-tipped pen.

"There are two entrances, front door easily seen from the street, back door opens into a small yard connecting to the rear of the alley parking lot. Mule and Toy"—he motioned to the white and black pair—"were working the house last night. They know the property."

"There's a wood basket-weave fence between Jansons' and the parking lot," Toy offered. Rivers drew in a dark slash before reaching into his top pocket to produce a picture. He passed the image around.

"A boy and his dog," he stated. "Child is Elmer Janson, the canine is Tripod."

Toy, who had sides of beef for arms, started to laugh, elbowing his partner with the heavy bones.

"Did I say something funny?" Rivers barked.

"No, Frank, but the dog is missing a—"

"How many legs you got?"

"Three," he smiled, "brothers all got three."

"Dog has four, one up on you." Rivers' eyes were like frozen flames. "Anything happens to that boy, you'll be walking with two of something, and I get to pick."

Toy pulled back instantly. "Hey, Franko, lighten up, I was kidding," he said, instinctively leaning over to protect his crotch.

Rivers continued, "That's the first set: boy, woman, dog—no other players onstage. Understood?"

Four men nodded. "Do we have a picture of Mrs. Janson?" asked Rudy.

"By this time tomorrow. She's a real fox, trust me on that. She's slim and has blond hair, which she parks on top her head in a weird ponytail when she's at home"—he made a cone with both hands—"looks like a straw fountain. Mule and Toy will take the front. Do we have the surveillance van?"

"Affirmative," Mule Murphy responded, "the panel truck. Do you want a sign?"

"We've got Pest Management," Toy added.

"Your cover is congestion monitoring for neighborhood traffic. There's a roll of cable in the rear, just lay it across the street like you're setting up a metered system and park close enough for a clear view of the house. Remember the dog's sound range. Mule, what's the name of that football team you were on?"

"Huskies," he said proudly.

"First team is Huskies," Rivers announced, "responsible for observation of all activities on the street and surrounding the house up to and including the backyard. Rudy"—he looked at the Lip—"your wife gave you a puppy last Christmas, what's its name?"

Bewilderment spread across Rudy Marchette's thin face. "How did you know about that?"

"I'm looking to eliminate provocative words," Rivers said, ignoring him. "There's a chance someone could be using a radio scanner. Give me your dog," he demanded.

"Uh, Pogo, Sarge, her name is Pogo."

"Second team is Pogo," he stated. "Have you been inside the alley?"

"Side door by the gas station," answered Marcus Kocska, "just to look inside."

"Use the rear entrance away from the road, there's a stairwell. Be cautious of observers filling their tanks at the pumps, it's a direct line of sight to an all-night gas station. If you find you are being watched by some pain-in-the-ass civilian, just act like you belong there. Cough, yawn, stretch your legs. If they don't look elsewhere, grab your balls and scratch. Which one of you is working nights?"

"I am, for three running," said Rudy.

"You're first man in. Take the equipment and leave it by the large window in the northeast corner overlooking the Jansons' backyard, that's your position"—he darkened a line with a felt tip on the rendering.

"Rudy, you've been out of the academy for two years?" he asked.

"No, Frank, just one, starting my second."

Rivers turned to Marcus Kocska. "Have you ever worked old clothes before?"

His face begged forgiveness. "No, Sarge, this is my first assignment off patrol."

"You'll do just fine. Now, listen up. I want you two to appreciate distance." He pointed at Rudy and Marcus, then from side to side on the drawing. "I eyeball about ninety, maybe even one hundred feet from each wall, and even deeper heading down the lanes."

They leaned forward on the couch and nodded.

"Now, no one can sneak up on you at that kind of distance, do you understand me?"

They looked at each other.

"Sometimes it gets pretty spooky in a large building at night, you hear things that aren't real. A backfire becomes a gun blast; a falling branch, Ninja assassins; bottles tossed in the parking lot, Molotov cocktails—all you need is a little imagination and you'll think you're under siege, understand?"

"Sure," said Marcus. Rudy nodded.

"You both trained on a twelve-gauge pump, I want you to take my riot gun. Keep the chamber empty, and if you are certain someone has entered—and only if you're certain—pump a round into the breech. Nobody in their right mind would challenge the sound of a riot gun feeding, nobody.

"Commander Scott and I might be checking on you, but we will identify ourselves very clearly. Now, you two like your old sergeant, don't you?" He pulled back and presented a friendly face.

Team Pogo smiled.

"Well, so help me," he said, pointing at them, "if you blow me away I'm going to be disappointed, and then I'm going to regroup in hell with some of my old pals, and then I'm coming back to fuck you over with a fork, do you understand what I'm saying?"

Team Pogo fought confusion, the Huskies wore masks of stone.

"Any questions?" Rivers offered.

"What are we looking for?" Mule asked.

"A killer. Like I said last night, I can't give you details. All we know is he works solo, no team or anything like that, and he's Mr. Slick."

"Is this related to the Clayton homicides?" asked Rudy.

"We're not sure," Rivers responded. "Set your radios to channel fourteen, high frequency."

Both teams adjusted their sets and checked batteries.

"Okay, guys, now, if you see anything—a car pulling into the lot, a flasher in the brush, a dog taking a shit—I want a picture and I want a radio check. Pogo, there's nothing to be ashamed of if you pull a chill, talk to us. There'll be someone on every minute, and you can count on the Huskies. Either way, we hear from you on the half-hour."

Their young faces registered a touch of relief.

"Now, I want you to look at the drawing," Rivers pointed down. "The Janson backyard is blind-side to Huskies. You will be covering their backs, they are covering the family. The world depends on Pogo. You are no longer rookies."

Mule Murphy swung a grinning, massive head, and Rudy the Lip noticed that Mule had no neck. In the meantime Marcus Kocska eyed the giant black man they called Toy.

Even at roll call they used his nickname. Marcus suddenly noticed a pink tattoo, a panther on his right forearm—and the rookie jumped, his pants literally clearing the couch.

Toy was deadlocked on his curious eyes, staring right down into him while digging between his molars with a sharpened ice pick.

"Settle down, Marcus," Rivers demanded. "Toy will be there if you need him."

Mule slapped Toy on the back and grinned. "Give us five minutes, then a radio check," he offered to Rivers, rising from his seat.

At 3:45, teams Pogo and Huskies were deployed.

26

3:12 P.M. WASHINGTON, D.C.

She was there. She was beautiful. She was waiting.

Brought back from the grave, a bust of clay and plaster that stopped just short of breathing, golden eyes that followed Scott's every move around the dimly lit study. He eased closer, placing a hand against her cheek. It was smooth, slightly warm, and he emitted a frustrated sigh.

"It's the light, Jack," comforted a hulking bear of a man in a white gown who was stripping off his lab jacket. Then his powerful hands gently adjusted the desk-lamp beam a fraction. "The eyes are actually a prosthesis used for cosmetic purposes on living patients. They trap low-level ultraviolet emissions, makes her seem alive. I think I'll have a cognac, are you sure all you want is coffee?"

Scott nodded. And Dr. Charles Rand McQuade left him alone with his thoughts, watching as he leaned over the desk, peering intently at the haunting child.

Her face was soft and angelic, the front teeth sparkled between cupid lips. A sweet, sculptured chin with high, subtle cheeks. There was a special innocence that glowed, filling the room; it was not the sunlight dying through the windows. "How could it be?" Scott thought, and he stroked the black hair, silken to the touch. Then he remembered the grave she had been found in, and his shoulders fell slack. For more than three decades she had lain in desolate abandon, a destroyed child, her nameless face a prize from some killer's private burial pit.

Scott grabbed the edge of the mahogany desk, shaking a mane of graying curls, slowly swinging his head back and forth over the edge, his mind leaping, whirring into a smear of thoughts. Good cops are cut from circumstance and experience, he reminded himself, artists like McQuade are born. Because of his skilled hands the child before them was wearing a face of love, artistic license; or it could have really been her face. Scott didn't know, and he had begun to ask just that, holding a finger into the air, then stopped himself. He didn't want to know. It was late, he told himself, he didn't have time to inquire. A coward's invention: time was always the excuse, fools strapped in watches and waiting in crooked lines. Failure was a part of it. The job, he told himself, breathing deeply. What in all of his years had he not seen?

McQuade rested his glass on the desk and handed Scott his cup. "Better than three thousand unidentified youngsters are turned into our office each year and the numbers are growing. You can't save them all, my friend."

The bile had returned to Scott's throat. He took a sip of coffee and swallowed hard.

"The hair is real." McQuade's voice was deep with resolve, echoing into itself like a tunnel through madness. "I selected a wig with very fine husking, not coarse, in keeping with her bone density and structure. A rather attractive little girl."

There was silence. From the window Scott could see the last cars leaving the Armed Forces Institute of Pathology for the day, two young boys in shorts tossing a baseball over the grassy quad, a beagle barking for attention and racing between them. At the far end of the military complex, a uniformed sentry closed a security gate and returned to his booth just as the ball landed beneath their window. A dizzying race between boys and dog ensued as a towheaded girl in blue jeans appeared to tussle for the sphere, the contest taking on a life of its own, carrying them back to the mall.

"She came from attractive parentage. Notice the high forehead, the splendid shaping across the nasal bridge to the eyes, the slight and angular brows," Dr. McQuade said, admiring his own craftsmanship. Scott turned and wondered.

"Yes," he said, studying the child's features, "she is beautiful." A pause. "How did she die?"

"Not sure. There wasn't much left to work with, mostly

bone scatter of a sort, lime mixed with acids, it did the job. The head was easier to reconstruct than the face, but I did find ten complete cranial punctures, one partial, each about twenty-five millimeters in circumference. Any one of them could have been fatal. You knew about them?"

Scott nodded, his eyes focused downward on the child.

"I excised each area"—McQuade pointed at the head ten times—"building duplicate plates, then sent the originals to Mike O'Hare at the FBI, he was waiting for them. He had been alerted by your New York office."

Scott turned away from the child and began to pace. "Tell me about her, Charlie, what do we know?"

"If you don't hold me to it."

"Speculate. I'll wait for absolutes another time."

"Agreed," said the laboratory director. "I believe the blow that killed her was a puncture low on the crown, about half-way to where the spine joins the skull." He gently rotated the bust and pointed. "It was not a gunshot. The wound channel reveals some shatter, very slight, and my guess is the splintering was caused by the surface tension of an object moving with rapidity through bone. O'Hare said he is running a battery of tests on wooden shafts, it's possible they are arrows, but not likely. Too much penetration in curved density, but definitely not a hand-held striking implement. She was hit with something from a distance, perhaps four to six feet, the FBI will be able to tell us more."

"Surface tension? You mean the shaft of the instrument rubbed against the bone hard enough to cause the fracture?"

"Yes, that's close enough, Jack. A smooth object that is moving fast during penetration, let's say a bullet, simply bursts through bone, punching a hole. The heavier the object, at higher velocities, the cleaner the wound. Although a wooden stake may look smooth to the naked eye, friction is created between striking surfaces, in this case bone and wood. A fracture results. I can't tell you much more than that."

Scott's face tightened and he fought to relax, reaching into his coat for a cigarette. Spotting this, McQuade lifted the window open. Boyish voices filled the room, a girl's giggle floated through like a thought balloon, failing in a puff of swirling smoke. He winced.

"Did she suffer?" Scott heard himself asking.

"Impossible to tell, Jack, let's believe she did not."

Scott understood and turned back to the childish form. "She was twelve," he confirmed.

"A positive identification, skull plates and dental evolution matched against carbon dating, buried in 1958. Porous fibers, strands from her clothing, held residue from a yellow weed, almost like a mustard stain. We're waiting on verification from Mike, but our analysis, both chemical and electron microscope, suggests a wildflower is in the culprit, a member of the primrose family."

"What's your source?"

"We ran the molecular structure through the Armed Forces Institute of Pathology's cellular registry, they maintain a computer log of all known plant and animal cells. Sometime before she died, she had come in contact with a flower, leaving us with a reliable indicator for the time of year she was killed." The gentle Goliath strolled over to the liquor cabinet and returned with a bottle and file folders in his hand. Scott smiled. Dr. McQuade had been using personal time if research materials were stored there.

"Notice the tiny flecks of red inside the leaves at the stalk," he motioned with a massive finger, handing him a color print.

"Very unusual," said Scott, "a bundle of yellow flowers with red flaring along the petals."

"Hard to miss in laboratory work. You're looking at yellow loosestrife. The species is one of several local to this area, and this is the rarest of the lot. There's a number on the back, a graduate student at the Smithsonian who is writing his thesis—"

"Thanks, Charlie," he interrupted, tossing the picture on the desk. "I have a local man consulting who will know, but how the hell do you derive any accurate time of year from these?"

"It's only an approximation. We'll keep working, but you said you were rushed."

"I'm sorry, I did sound ungrateful."

The laugh was resonant. "Heavens, Scotty, you an ingrate? I know better. When you catch this man, you'll sleep. Until then, grateful is in your manner, not in your heart."

Scott smiled weakly.

"The flower is a stalk that stands about three feet tall, this child stood six inches higher. The stain was on fabric stuck to her fourth rib—I am presuming her clothes crumbled inward during decomposition. If so, that means she was bending over and examining flowers during the day, or she was buried with one, and I doubt that."

"So she had a soiled blouse?"

"No, she had a specific stain from a rather peculiar species that blooms only in late March and early April, maintaining ribbons of red for just a few weeks. Then the yellow takes over completely. The composite residue was biased with reds. Early April, that's when she died, before the swamp candle loses its fire, about the fifteenth of the month. You might have Mike double-check, but from sample analysis with the scope, I'm certain enough. The stain had never been cleaned, and—"

"What did you say, a swamp candle?"

McQuade nodded, the failing sunlight playing in soft brown eyes that followed Scott in circles around the room. "All in here, Jack," he handed him a folder. "That's the common name. We also included color shots of the child from every angle, and black-and-white in case you need to distribute."

Scott glanced at the girl: the behavior fitted her image. "She was picking flowers," he stated without reservation.

"I didn't say that," the scientist countermanded, "I said I thought she came into contact with one. You're reaching back over three decades with your assumptions."

"You said you trust my instincts?"

"Absolutely, but as a scientist I don't want to force you into conclusions."

"Charlie, if it's called a swamp candle, it must grow near water?" he asked, looking around the room for direction. "It's only the ninth, so they should be in full bloom about now, yellow and red, easy to spot."

Dr. McQuade smiled. "Going to pick flowers? I like that about you, Jack. No chore too great, no challenge too small. Let me freshen your coffee?"

"No, thanks," he said reflexively, "an isolated, quiet community, and the residents bound by a southern tradition of avoiding strangers, minding their own affairs . . ."

"You're running ahead of me, friend."

"Sorry, thinking out loud. In 1958, Good Friday and Easter fell in the first week of April. She could have been preparing a centerpiece for the family table—little girls are brought up to think that way, poor children improvise. As the city of Bethesda started to grow, there were two small towns. Tobytown was for predominantly black families, near where she was

buried. The other town was four miles away down by the
river. The swamp candle grows near water, so she was down
where the flower grows."

"That's the ticket: swampy places, grassy shores, a very
hardy little weed. If you're right, she would have headed for
water."

"John's Cabin."

"If you say so, Jack."

"So let's presume she goes to the river. On foot we're looking at a rough eight miles round trip, but children were more
industrious then. Someone must have seen her, but adults in
that area were leery of strangers, afraid of getting involved.
They would have never challenged a uniform or official-
looking car unless she was in obvious danger, it all makes
sense."

"He uses a uniform?"

"Once he did, and very effectively. The world was less
complex, less populated. It's possible he stalked her, maybe
even her mother or another child, and while they were picking
flowers he appeared in uniform, demanding to take them
home. He drove in the right direction, from John's Cabin toward Tobytown."

"And they never made it." McQuade took a shot of cognac.
"As good a theory as any. How can I help?"

"Well, as a start, I need to find where the flowers grew
back then, and I need to find her mother. I was hoping you'd
ask."

McQuade smiled. "Would it have made a difference?"

"No," Scott said, pursing his lips. There was misery in the
confession, and he stood at the window staring out. "This will
help," he said, turning to face the scientist directly. "And I
have one other minor problem, rather pressing, I'm afraid."

"I'm not avoiding you, Jack."

"The burial site could have been a full-blown cemetery that
was never completely exhumed, and I've got to dig there."

The doctor shrugged. "Of course you do," he responded,
reaching for the rack that held his sports jacket, "and you
need on-site interpretation in your search. I'll also bet you
don't have a search warrant, or even a budget."

"You understand everything."

"Not hardly." McQuade swallowed the last of his drink.
"How much trouble do we risk?"

Scott sighed gently. "Well, even though it's been gutted, we still have a Fourth Amendment, plus the privacy act, in addition to trespass law. Since the site is privately owned, I'd say if we got pinched, the fallout will be substantial."

McQuade nodded. "Then you better have a decent cover, Jack, it's not worth either one of us going to jail. As for funding, I'll cover my equipment, lab costs, and time under another case, but we'd better hit paydirt or they'll be digging up my bones." He turned to his desk and removed another folder, which he handed over. Scott flashed a grateful smile.

"What's this?" he asked, turning the cover.

"That's the jacket you requested on Vietnam, Operation Phoenix to be specific. We pinched a copy from the clubhouse at Langley under the auspices of identifying skulls from Hanoi. We really do have two boxes sitting in the lab."

"Boys from Vietnam?"

"In this case Cambodia, but we'll never be able to give them names, that much I'm fairly sure of."

Scott began to flip through the lengthy treatise.

"It makes for interesting reading. I've seen similar files before, there are dozens of Phoenix operatives still unaccounted for, MIA's, so our office has been involved in identification for quite a while. I might be able to help if you tell me what you're looking for."

Scott sighed, thumbing through the pages. "A young man I happen to be working with has some rather unusual qualities. His last name is Rivers, but I think he had it changed, or someone changed it for him. That smacks of either criminal or governmental behavior, and since he was a marine, I think I'm heading in the right direction."

McQuade raised an eyebrow.

"Explain it to me, Charlie. Operation Phoenix was what exactly?"

"Well, for public consumption it was something called a pacification program, but behind all the cloak-and-dagger stuff it was terrorism of the worst kind, state-sponsored, in this case Uncle Sam. Brought to you by the very incredible CIA. Take a look," he said, reaching over to help turn a page in the report and revealing a summary statement.

" 'The Phoenix mission,' " Scott read aloud, " 'to infiltrate and destroy the Vietcong infrastructure by whatever means possible, specialized units to include assassination, terrorism, and forced interrogation.' "

"A nice word for torture," said McQuade. "It started

around 1967, and in my opinion the entire operation was a crime against humanity, a very dark period in American history." He watched as Scott searched with an index finger. "Looking for something specific?"

"A name," Scott replied bleakly.

"That's what I've been trying to say, Jack, you won't find any. So imagine trying to identify human remains when you only have numbers and codes to work with. That report's no different than others, no photographs, no medical sheets, no physical descriptions, no personal histories, and no names."

"Then how do you get an identification?"

"We don't," McQuade said, shaking his head, "because the record isn't made available, and that's how we know when we're dealing with Phoenix. When Hanoi coughs up a set of bones, and once we have exhausted the standing MIA list, I have to send a complete description of my findings through the State Department, and they take it to the CIA for possible identification of a Phoenix agent. The process always ends there. I'm still waiting for word on four skulls from the 1976 exchange."

"I don't understand," Scott said. "These agents were military men, so why the tight lid after twenty-some years?"

McQuade shrugged. "It's politics, Jack, what is it always? For the most part they were military men, but once recruited, the rules were changed on them. The CIA claims that it is protecting those Phoenix agents who survived, but I rather believe they're just covering their own silly butts."

"Who's to care, Charlie? That's ridiculous."

"Is it?" McQuade responded. "You do know that America is now seeking diplomatic ties with Hanoi and that the United Nations is involved?"

Scott nodded.

"Well, the boys from Phoenix are wanted men, war criminals in the eyes of the government of Hanoi, and more recently the Soviets and East Germans. Behind all of the nice political table talk between these countries, these poor sorry bastards have had the rug pulled out from under them again. You know about the numerous sightings of MIA's, verbal reports, sometimes even photographs?"

Scott nodded, his face intense.

"Well, while they feed the public on a steady diet of 'ain't it awful but it's just not true,' our government has really had the shit laid on their table. Hanoi wants a simple trade, the boys from Phoenix and then a public admission of our actions, and in return we get everything on the MIA's, names, places, real accountability; and it goes even deeper than that—"

Scott held up a hand. "I don't even want to hear it, Charlie. You're saying our potential allies consider them international outlaws?"

"That's correct, Jack. Right or wrong, all that matters in Washington is that these boys are an issue, a diplomatic sticking point. Hanoi wants them for public trial, and we've been saying they don't exist, but more important, that they never did."

"That's nuts," Scott spat.

"Perhaps, but atrocities did occur, documentable crimes, and in some cases there have been international rewards posted for those who were involved. It doesn't matter if you agree or not. For some the war goes on, and the U.S. is taking extreme measures to hide any official government involvement."

Scott nodded thoughtfully. "So these Phoenix agents, their identities are classified, and those among the living have been changed?"

"Yes," said McQuade, "only numbers and general codes, the heat is on and the lid is tight. Do you have anything else that might help? A unit number, perhaps a mascot, they all had those."

Scott remembered the Zippo. "How about a cartoon character, a Pink Panther?"

McQuade frowned. "Nasty group, that would be Marine Phoenix, the Pink Panthers. There were two platoons and four squads. Group One specialized in field terrorism and kidnapping, Two was an ambush team, Three was explosive ordnance, Fourth Squad was a sniper unit. Only a handful survived, and it's little wonder: they did three, sometimes four tours apiece."

"What can you tell me about them?" Scott asked, reading between the deletions made by a heavy-handed censor.

"Panthers were run directly by CIA through a field psychologist by the name of Dunn, Major Bradford E. Dunn, who was killed in action, may the bastard roast in hell. His unit was one of the deadliest legends to come out of the program."

"Dunn was a CIA psychologist?"

"Trained in techniques of terror," McQuade stated coldly, "and he enjoyed his work, hand-selected his men too, except most of them were really boys. My understanding is that he preferred to work with teenagers who had been victims of child abuse, if you get the picture. Rather cunning CIA tradecraft. I really do loathe those maggots."

"And Dunn searched out men according to the depth of their emotional scarring, using his background and access?"

"That was only true of Panthers," McQuade corrected. "The other outfits had their own variations and peculiarities. There were four programs under Phoenix, and the Panthers belonged to Red Rover, kidnapping and terror. Major Dunn gave the orders directly from Washington, playing a child-hood game."

Scott held his hands to the air. And McQuade chanted, "Red Rover, Red Rover, the lawn's gone to clover. Red Rover, Red Rover, send Jackie over."

Scott winced.

"That's the way Dunn declared a state of emergency, then ordered abductions behind enemy lines. If you were Jackie, Panthers would track you down no matter how many they had to kill or torture to find you."

"And the pink mascot?"

"Most of these men were so young when they arrived in Vietnam that their folk heroes were still from cartoons—Pink Panther, Bugs Bunny, Felix the Cat, Tweety Bird, that kind of thing. I suppose it was part of the killing game, since children are more willing to play."

"Not always," Scott corrected. "Is this firsthand, were you stationed overseas?"

"Me?" McQuade smiled. "I was protesting the war on the Berkeley campus, or any other place where there was serious intent. About a decade ago I used my clearances to assuage a guilty conscience. If your request is official, I can give you a name at Langley who will talk off the record."

"No," Scott shook his head while holding up the report. "Burn it for me, Charlie. War's over, these boys have a right to privacy."

McQuade closed the file into a gray safe behind his desk and spun the combination. "I'll give you a lift, Jack, you'll never get a cab at this hour."

Scott stood and worked his features into a smile.

From Georgia Avenue in Washington to Ridgefield Drive in

Bethesda, more than an hour of debate fell by the road, and they covered nearly every subject on which they could disagree. They continued with Vietnam, then world population, moving into abortion versus right to life, then hitting on the cultural effects of rap music. By the time the death penalty popped up, McQuade knew that words would not bridge the chasm between them.

"Have you ever considered gardening, Jack? I find it very rewarding," he said.

Scott lifted an eyebrow; he was thinking about the old-fashioned gallows. With help from a sympathetic hangman, prisoners would last a good minute after their spines splintered into jelly, a technique that allowed a cop to get a word in edgewise. He was staring at his watch and carefully counting sixty seconds' worth of words.

"We'll be there soon," McQuade said, mistaking this behavior, waiting for a light to change on Wisconsin Avenue. And he turned the subject back to starlike yellow flowers.

"Many of the wild loosestrife do well in cultivation," McQuade offered.

The windshield fogged from within.

The street was slick with rain.

27

6:20 P.M. UPSTATE NEW YORK

In police lore they used to say that Old Woodie will swallow no more, by which it was simply meant that the state cemetery at Woodlawn, New York, was full, or had been buried out, depending on your point of view.

It had first opened its gates in 1902, so the only burial room left was in a used grave, on top of someone else's casket, and this was an insignificant thing, or so Matthew Brennon had always thought. But standing in the dying light at a place called Rabbit Run, a hilly drive that was more of a dirt path than a road, the reality was overwhelming.

He had parked his car at the end of the road and stood near the rear of the cemetery where the older graves were, staring out at thousands of headstones. These had been smashed and twisted by vandals, overgrown by weeds, and strewn with litter. As he walked, they seemed to be mourning for his attention, a country mile of graying slabs, and with a sudden gust, yellowed newspapers flitted over them, shifting with the wind, dancing like a parade of lost souls.

Brennon walked casually, briefcase in hand, following an overgrown fence while looking down onto a swell of green. The hills seemed to be rising, then falling, rolling with endless rows of white crosses. These, he knew, were the New York doughboys that the caretaker had mentioned, plowed under in their youth, now standing in waves as far as the eyes could see. Down the path, it was a full five minutes before he had left them behind and approached a valley of travertine crypts and mausoleums that resembled huge marble tanks, tilting toward him in reckless abandon.

For more than eighty years the dead had been coming to rest at Woodlawn, and Brennon was just beginning to fathom the magnitude of lives past as he approached an elaborate ancient gateway that seemed dark and forbidding. He stopped. A huge iron arch had been cast onto circular sandstone pillars, and in the latticework above him, a pair of iron cherubs wept rust on their journey to heaven.

The gate itself was thick wrought iron, sealed by an old chain and padlock, strangled by ivy and crawling brambles. Beyond this a dirt path vanished down into dark, rolling hills, after which he could see nothing. He removed a notepad from inside his windbreaker, checked his notes, and glanced at his watch. Then, cupping his hands to his mouth, with a deep breath he shouted, "Hello!"

His voice went rolling down the hills, echoing through the crypts like a desecrating scream, then filling other tombs in the distance. The silence quickly returned to his ears, not even a bird came to life.

It was Gate Eleven, Woodlawn's northern arch, and at this spot he knew the graves continued for ten square miles into Poughkeepsie, tens of thousands of souls harvested over time and then put to rest by the state. Yet for all the memories among the living, Brennon could not see even a withered flower down the path. The graves were crowded in death as they were in life, close enough to hear your neighbor drip. He cupped his hands around his mouth.

"Hello," he tried again, and his voice blew through the tombs, echoing back at him like a lost twin.

"Hold your water!" a harsh voice suddenly roared.

From behind the gate's thick ivy mane he heard a man cursing. "Goddamned pile of rust," followed by heavy breathing.

"Hello?" Brennon asked.

"Relax, young fella, you're among the living." With that the brambles parted and Brennon was staring directly at gloved hands holding back the vines. A face protruded from shadow.

"Are you Mr. Dudley Hall?" Brennon asked.

"That I am," he chirped. The brambles closed, and he returned to working the thicket, removing a badly overgrown chain, then pumping hinges with an oil can. The man was completely hidden by the dense foliage.

"I'm Matthew Brennon."

"Just a moment," he said, "was doin' just fine a moment ago." The voice sounded like he had swallowed a bird whistle, and Brennon guessed the man was missing some teeth.

"I could just climb over?" he offered.

But there was no response. In several moments Brennon saw the gloves thrashing away at the vines, ripping the brambles, and a beefy plaid shoulder pushed against the iron door, forcing the gate into a painful groan as daylight burst through and onto the path. What emerged from all of this looked like a human fireplug, short with massive shoulders and legs, plus a barrel chest covered by a worn checkered jacket.

"Call me Duddy," the man whistled, removing a glove and extending his hand. They were standing face-to-face as the man released a red stream of tobacco juice from the side of his mouth.

"Yes, sir," Brennon said, "I'm Matt, pleased to meet you." He could see from the smile that Hall's lower front row was missing. His whiskers had gone to gray, not a beard, just a face badly in need of a shave, and it was a worn face, beaten into a patchwork of leathery lines and crevices. Brennon guessed he was in his late sixties, although the man gave him a powerful shake.

"We talked on the phone, didja bring da papers?" Hall asked. "Sure hope ya got copies. I called that judge of yours, gotta have copies."

Brennon sensed the man's uneasiness. "I understand, sir. I brought you a set, all signed and sealed. All you have to do is fill in the details." He popped open the briefcase, reached inside, and handed over a series of documents. The caretaker

began to read, taking his time, and after a
Brennon was concerned that they would soon be
darkness. He needed to be back at the ViCAT slot
night.

"Ain't seen one a these for a time," Hall finally said, ex
ining a writ of exhumation. "Why you folks so anxious
have him back?"

"I wish I knew, I just follow instructions," Brennon lied,
and he did this well, sounding more like a plebe than a senior
federal agent backed by the state's highest court.

The man humphed, then whistled. "Jest like me," he said,
"wassa time a body only got three things at old Woodie—a
plot, a stone, and me. Real personal. Now I'm retired, and
dem still ordering me around like a damn night porter."

"Well, I appreciate all your help, I'm really being hammered," he said. Brennon's call had woken Hall the night before, and it had taken twenty-four hours for a judge to sign for
exhumation.

"Old Duddy understands, son. Higher-ups is always pickin'
and pantin', don't matter none if you're dead." He spat again.
"Sorry to lead ya here, but you'll save an hour gettin' to it."

"How can I help?"

"Just follow me," said Hall, picking up a spade with one
hand and an apple-picking basket with the other. "What dis
man do, anyway?"

"A bad guy," Brennon answered, following him down the
hill and toward the crypts. As they walked, Brennon thought
Duddy's arms looked comic, like small suspended hams, and
his thumbs nearly touched his knees.

They had marched in quick double-step for about ten minutes when Hall spoke up. "So what do you think of 'er,
Matt?" he asked, not turning his head as he talked, trooping
along like a one-man army.

"Woodlawn?"

"Yep," he whistled, waving the spade with his right at the
rolling hills. "I settled 'ere in forty-three, was nothing but a
big pretty forest with lotsa meadows. It's all been buried out,
'tain't no more room."

And Matt Brennon remembered the stories of Old Woodie.
There was a time when he had thought it was poker piss, just
graybeards filling your ears, then telling you that it's raining.
"Have you been the caretaker since then?" he asked, for Hall

walked with unseeing eyes, as if strolling through his own living room.

"Caretaker, hell you say, never heard that doggone word until sixty-four, that's the year we got the backhoe. You musta found my name in the state book, only place I know they call me that."

"Yes I did," he confirmed.

"I'm the diggerman, best thar is, bury 'em by hand," he chirped as he moved effortlessly beyond the graying stones to those of a more modern design, some of them sculptured, praying hands, doves, symbols of eternity.

"Until fifty-eight I'd dig and bury on a first-come basis. Those days was good, the way it oughta be. I'd take my time, dressin' a grave up real nice, then stay for the funeral, I was proud of that. You remember Boltin' Joe Sharkey, the prize-fighter?"

"Well, that was—"

"Right dere." He swung at a headstone that stood higher along the path than the others. "Dug 'im myself. That grave's a seven-footer. Most sevens are for man and wife, used to be we'd place 'em side by side, but we ran out of room. Buried dem on topa each other, real symbolic like, Joe woulda liked that."

"Very interesting," Brennon sighed, keeping the pace, watching the stones as they came and went. "Do you have the plot number that we're—"

Hall spun in his place, walking backward and eyeballing the young agent. "Hell you say, this is my yard, son. Got all the numbers," he put a finger to the side of his temple, "and I got all the plots," he waved the shovel.

Brennon smiled.

"These aren't just sections and graves to me," said the diggerman.

Brennon started to worry, wondering if the batty old man was up for the task.

"See that large marker over dere?" Hall pointed to a large sculptured angel with outstretched wings, never once slowing his pace.

"Yes."

"That's Pancake Louie, just buried his wife this past year. Louie's family spent too much on his stone, and then put him in a cheap box. The weight of the dirt just crushed it, made an awful damn sound, and all at once, *Ka-Boom!*" he yelled, slapping the ground with the shovel's flat side.

Brennon startled. "What did they do?"

"They watched the dust jest belly-up from the pit. A family shouldn't see that, weren't the first time neither. Old Louie's widow never said a word, but we buried her in a Burns casket with a copper lining in it—that's a whole lot of money to be puttin' into a hole. She's ridin' on top of old Pancake Louie in a real money box. Wonder if their marriage was like that?" And he spat, the red stream as true as his step.

As he talked, the diggerman never dropped stride. Soon Pancake Louie was far behind and they were approaching a row of markers that looked like graves in miniature.

"Duddy, what about the state prison system, how do they bury?"

"If dere's family left?"

"Just the state."

"Cremation and a cardboard box, then I'd stuff 'em into a hole anytime I'd git to it. You asking 'bout this Zachariah fella?"

"Yes, I guess—"

"Ashes in a box. Rigby kept the teeth if dere was any gold."

"Who's Rigby?"

"Runs the crematorium in town."

"Works for the state?"

"He's a cooker, burns by the job, he don't care who pays." Abruptly Hall stopped at a small iron fence about a foot high, surrounding a grassy mound. "Here she'll be," he said, advancing into the field and counting rows, measuring by the place markers. The light was starting to gray.

"Three deep, four across," he said, "and three foot deep. Don't take much for a burnt man."

"And you're sure—"

The basket fell and the shovel blade sliced neatly into the dirt, the damp earth giving way as Dudley Hall applied his full weight over the hilt. With his bright chestnut eyes locked onto Brennon's, he began effortlessly rocking the handle back and forth, back and forth, very slow, boring down on the agent.

"So what'd ya say this fella do?" he demanded.

Brennon could feel the diggerman's penetrating stare, and

the eerie quiet of the yard, and the oppressive weight of the stones surrounding him.

"He killed women and children," he said.

Hall nodded thoughtfully, continuing to rock the wooden handle. "Ya know, Matt, in my day I could dig a five-or six-footer in eight, maybe ten minutes."

"Very impressive," Brennon said sincerely, watching the ground quake with each shift on the shovel's handle. They were surrounded by dozens of little white markers, most of them crosses but two of them oval stones.

"Urns jest don't take no time at all," said the diggerman.

"Why is there a difference in these markers?" Brennon asked as Hall pulled a flashlight from his belt, turned on the beam, then laid it on the ground.

"Just like plunking olives from a jar," the man stated, giving the shovel a final push. A bright gold lid slipped to the surface, shining at their feet. They were looking down at an urn, and as Hall twisted the wooden handle, it popped free of the earth in a wad of dirt and turf.

"That really is impressive," Brennon said, bending over and inspecting the burial can.

Hall quickly eased forward onto his knees, brushing the urn with a gloved hand. "No," he said, shaking his head, "something's not right 'ere."

"Wrong grave?"

"Nope, checked the records after you called, this is it, but it's not prison cardboard." Carefully the diggerman lifted the urn, cradling it in both hands. It was about eight inches high, of blue enamel with gold inlay.

"Are you sure this is right?" Brennon asked.

"No, but it's him inside dere," he stated. "Look at the collar." He spat a red stream and the lid dripped. He waited a moment, then brushed it off with his fingers.

Brennon read: " 'Zachariah Leslie Dorani, Born 1/18/33, Died 2/21/66.' That's him, all right, what's the problem?"

"For one thing, it was a prison funeral service, and this is a state plot, so all we should have is a pile of ashes. That's why I bit so far down with the blade and brought the basket, so as to fetch a complete pile. The cardboard pancakes and seepage turns a burnt man to concrete."

"Then how did he get an urn like this?"

"Don't know, but it's a money box—that's real gold. And

here's another thing, your papers list him as an atheist. That's why the stone marker instead of a cross like them others."

Brennon's eyes grew wide as they studied the container. On two sides and on the top, there were gold crosses. "Could it have been a mix-up? Could the prison authorities have made a mistake?"

"Naw, not like that," he said emphatically. "Them's Latin-style crosses, Roman Catholic. Someone bought this urn, paid top dollar too, then had him poured inside."

Brennon leaned over and stroked the thing. "But you're sure he's in there?"

"Oh, he's in dere," Duddy said, shaking the can with both hands, then checking the lead seal at the top. He pointed with a finger. "This ain't been broke neither."

"How can I find out where the urn came from? Would there be any records?"

"Well, not 'ere there wouldn't be, we just put 'em to rest. Wouldn't know who the burnman was neither, but there's a way to tell." His chirp raised a pitch.

"Anything," Brennon said, "it's important."

"It's against the law," he chirped again.

"What is?"

"Gotta check the ashes. I can tell lots from the ashes, but breakin' that seal's against the law."

"Then I'll do it," Brennon offered, but by the time he had reached for the urn, Hall was sitting in the dirt prying at the top with a penknife. There was a scraping sound as his large hands began screwing the top back and forth, back and forth, then a *thump* as the cap came free.

He looked in with his flashlight. Wetting a finger, he dipped it inside. "Got some baby-killer on me," he spat, rubbing his forefinger and thumb together.

"Then it's full? The urn, I mean."

"Oh, yeah, and it was a slow burn," he said, pouring a stream of ash directly onto the lawn until he had a pile the size of a tablespoon. "See here how's it gray and peppered? Should all be a bright white powder. What you gonna do with 'em?"

"Lab tests for blood type and anything else we can get."

"Then you got plenty." He continued to pour, the pile growing like the bottom of an hourglass, when there was a *clink* as a piece of bone fell free.

"What the hell?" asked Brennon, staring at what looked

like a chip of charred wood. "Don't they pulverize the remains?"

"Leon Rigby don't," Hall responded. "Man's got no pride of work, never did, slob of a burnman. Don't bother to do the ashes with a rollin' pin neither. Good houses mash 'em flat, cook 'em twice, nothin' left but powder. He's been cheatin' the state for forty-some years, don't even wait for his fires to go blue."

"Would he know about the urn?"

"No way he'd fill some other burnman's bottle, so it musta been his. You may need that chippy," he offered, picking up the bone and handing it to Brennon.

In the dim light he held it with an uneasy grip, then wrapped it into a clean white handkerchief. "Where would I find Rigby?" he asked.

Hall stood, stretching his back and arms. "In his house or the creamer. I'll take you, you'd never find it."

"I appreciate that," he cautioned, "but I can't ask. Your orders end when you give me the remains."

The gravedigger did not answer. Instead he handed Brennon the elaborate urn and turned his back, then leaned against his shovel. In the darkness that had closed around them, a hollow sound erupted, a soft sound that trilled like the gentle roll of a drum pattering against the turf.

"Baby-killer," Brennon heard the diggerman say under his breath.

Dudley Hall was urinating into the pile of ash.

28

By seven o'clock Rivers had answered Pogo's radio check, returned from Foong Lin's carry-out, and was awash in Szechuan dim sum: spicy san shien Wor-bar, oysters in black bean, hacked Chinese cabbage, and hot Singapore rice. Since he hadn't eaten since dawn, he had also ordered chilled crabmeat-asparagus soup, and had doubled orders of everything. Scott found him on the rear deck hovering over little white boxes.

"What am I eating?" Scott asked, pulling up a seat and grabbing a plate.

"You'll like it. Try the soup, it's terrific," Rivers slurred, pushing a container across the table. Scott poured this into a white plastic bowl, studying the greenish broth as he laid a handkerchief across his lap.

"Is this vegetable soup?" he asked, dipping a plastic spoon. He swallowed and looked up, his eyes instantly welling with tears.

"Hot stuff, Jack, be careful," Rivers said, and Scott could feel the cold brine pumping down hot, the back of his throat tingling. He took a quick sip of water.

"Very good," he said, digging for more.

"It's got everything, white fish, crab, asparagus, seaweed, bean curd, egg white, mushrooms, peas, and rice." Finishing off a dumpling, he lifted another with chopsticks and dropped it into a plate of hot sauce.

"You know that old chart I let Jim Cooley borrow?" Scott asked, giving up on his chopsticks, reaching for the dim sum with a fork.

"Yeah, he was real excited," Rivers said, gathering containers around him and filling his plate. "Try the oysters with black bean, they're terrific." He leaned his head back, dropped a fleshy plum into his mouth, then drained the shell as Scott placed four large mollusks into his dish.

"It's stolen property, felony material."

Rivers looked puzzled, popping another fishy blob into his mouth, moving clockwise around the table, and filling his plate. "How so?"

"I stole it. Breaking and entering, premeditated, first-degree. If it went to trial I'd lose my badge."

Rivers was stunned. He stopped eating and studied him carefully. "You're not kidding, are you, Jack?"

"Not about something like this, no."

The detective grinned, shaking a mane of blond hair. Then he went back to searching through shells for a plump morsel.

"That chart is from a series of three, its insured value is seventy-five thousand," Scott offered, dropping a shell back on his plate. It tasted bitter, and he moved on to hot Wor-bar.

"Seventy-five large?"

Scott nodded, puzzling over the sticky food smothered in black bean.

"Bad oyster?" Frank asked.

"Tart, puckers your lips."

Rivers handed him a cup. "Sweet Hunan fish sauce, try dunking it in this first." Scott followed instructions and the meaty blob mixed in his mouth and slid by his palate.

"Very nice," he said, reaching for another. "Very nice indeed."

The men chewed and passed containers, fueling bodies that had all but forgotten about food.

"Frank," he asked, prying another from its shell, "if we wanted to construct a silencer from parts, where would we go?"

Rivers smiled. "Depends on the caliber. Any good junkyard would have most of the stuff. Are we making a Death Whisper or a Hush Puppy?"

"You tell me, smart guy, what's the difference?"

"Quality is what. If you're disposing of the weapon, we'd just screw an oil filter onto the end—that's good for a few dozen rounds or so. If you want real control, it takes more work. We had a saying, 'one shot one kill, no sound not found.' Anyway, it always comes down to quality."

Scott's teeth dug into his lip and he grimaced. "Let's go first-class."

"How versed are you?"

"Just the basics. You're obviously the expert—Marine Phoenix, wasn't it?"

Rivers shook his head and laughed under his breath. "You obviously know it was, Jack, you must really be tired. I've watched a lot of your starring roles, and dumb's not part of your thespian forte, pal."

"Very good, Frank," Scott said, raising an eyebrow. The man was letting a little of his real self slip through.

"Used 'em and built 'em," Rivers offered. "Our first requirement would be a light metal tube for the suppressor, then a good drill press. We'd also need threading equipment, unless you want to clamp the extension on the gun barrel, that is."

"Go with the best." Scott drained his water glass.

"We start with the tube and drill holes, which would bleed the gases off slowly and deaden the vacuum."

"Vacuum?" Scott inquired.

"Sure." The tall policeman leaned forward. "Most of the noise doesn't come from the charge going off, that's a misconception. When the bullet leaves the muzzle, a tremendous vacuum is created within. Gases are driven out and air rushing back into the barrel makes a loud retort that is confused with an explosion. Once holes are drilled in the extension tube, bleeding the air back in, you've solved sixty percent of the problem. The rest is just padding, what they call buffers, usually a combination of fiberglass with metal retainers."

"And you think that's what our killer used on the Claytons?"

Rivers nodded thoughtfully. "The better suppressors actually catch the gases going out and coming in, dispersing them internally," he remarked, pouring more food on his plate. "But I think he used a combination of techniques."

"And how quiet could you make a twenty-two?"

"What type? You're talking about the most underrated and least appreciated caliber."

Scott leaned back in his chair. "Is this from CIA training?"

"What?" Rivers asked incredulously, letting a laugh slip free. "Silent attack is an art form, Jack. They're just bureaucrats who invent names for what real people do. Are you going to eat that last oyster?" With a shake of Scott's head Rivers' chopsticks reached, plucked, and dropped it home. He then rose, crossed the redwood deck, and quickly returned with a 7-Eleven bag from the kitchen.

"Coffee?" He bowed stiffly, a Manchurian servant.

"Why, yes, Chinese coffee, very thoughtful," Rivers laid large cups on the table, popped the plastic lids, and watched the steam rise.

"You were saying silence is art," Scott pressed.

"Absolutely. I know a man who could land from a swinging rope onto rice paper without tearing it, zap you with a Hush Puppy, catch the shell in his right hand, and vanish before anyone noticed."

"A cop?"

"Hardly, he's a thief, and rather proud of that, a real professional. One of America's best, highly decorated, carried four wounded men out of a hot LZ when their chopper flamed. The CIA wanted to keep him, but he'd rather rob from the rich and give to the poor—himself, an orphanage, and the Catholic church. He's really a pacifist."

"Sounds like it." Scott shook his head at an entire generation of lost boys. "Pick the most high-powered twenty-two you can think of."

"For range or destruction?"

"Destruction."

"If we want to stay with commercially available ammunition, I'd say hypervelocity truncated hollow points, travels better than sixteen hundred feet per second at the muzzle."

If there had ever been any doubt in Scott's mind about wanting to work with Frank Rivers, it had just been vanquished. "Tell me about impact power, what's their capability?"

"Varies with the target. Pick a target."

"Human skull, the cranium."

Rivers thought for a moment. "Hard but thin bone, all mush inside. From a few feet away the bullet is at maximum speed, the soft hollow nose penetrates and expands, then begins to tumble, cutting a path"—he picked a small bit of oyster off a shell with his fingers and chewed. "The shock wave surrounding the projectile burns a channel of its own, rather devastating, burns the brain to jelly, leaving only a small puncture. It's the bullet of choice for professional assassins—you knew that?"

Scott nodded.

"Because skull plates are tough, curved, and the slug is traveling roughly one and one-half times the speed of sound, a glancing blow could actually ricochet. It takes a well-placed direct hit. Is this helping, sir?"

"Yes," Scott answered, "one shot, one kill. Where would you aim?"

Rivers patted the crown of his head. "Shooting from the front or rear, that's the target," he said. "We were taught that anywhere above the spinal cord, in that general area, death is instant or as close as possible. Passing from side to side"—he placed a finger on his right temple—"could leave an enemy disabled."

Scott swallowed as Rivers grabbed a leftover piece of hacked cabbage and crunched. "That helps. I want to think like this killer, and the fascination with an object like that is foreign to me. So how silent can you make this weapon?"

Rivers thought a moment. "From how far away would you be hearing the sound?"

"Like we are now, about six feet."

"Okay, Jack, listen up," he said, wiping his mouth with the back of his hand.

"I didn't hear anything. What are you doing?"

"Sorry," Rivers said, his penetrating blue eyes sparkling

with mischief. "Let's try again, but you have to listen very carefully." He stirred his coffee while lighting a cigarette with his Zippo.

"Okay, smart guy, what's up?"

"You missed the point, Jack." He smiled, and recognition spread across Scott's face.

"That's it?"

"Yep, and I used a staggered clip, ten shots through the mouth. You're rather dead, nothing left but pulp." Rivers flushed down a piece of cabbage with black coffee.

"And how did you catch the brass shells? With a canister made specially for this particular firearm?"

"No," Rivers stated flatly, "a hanging canister's just one more part to foul up, plus adding bulk and weight. Wasn't there a trace of plastic found on a bullet fragment, the one taken from Diana Clayton's brain?"

"FBI suggested it came from a factory bullet coating."

Rivers shrugged, grabbing a white carryout bag off the table and stuck his fist inside, aiming a finger at Scott. "Thump, thump," he spat. "Tell your beloved Bureau to check their evidence against Glad bags. Keeps your kitchen clean without odors."

Scott's eyes narrowed. "You're suggesting he used a trash bag?" he asked incredulously.

Rivers nodded. "Yes, I am. The technique's called bagging, and for stealth, practicality, and maximum control of the weapon it can't be beat by modern technology either. Hell," he crumpled the paper in his hand, "if you really bag a gun properly and use light loads that don't produce a sonic boom, you don't even need a silencer." He smacked his hands together to demonstrate. "Sounds like hands clapping, and not only will you catch the shells, any fouling remains trapped and you're ready for storage, no fuss, no muss."

Scott suddenly looked pensive. "The hot gases would fill it like a balloon, not to mention hiding muzzle flash. It's so . . . simple!"

Rivers smiled. "Glad bags, Jack, aren't you glad?"

"Very funny, Frank. How does it work?"

"Nothing to it. Just stick the gun inside the bag, put rubber bands around your wrist for a seal, make it really tight, and then pull the trigger."

Scott leaned back in his seat. "It's a good thing that's not widely known. We're a real gun-crazy society."

Rivers shrugged, breaking open the lid on a second cup of coffee. And for a few moments the men were silent as their food settled, producing a calming fatigue after so many hours without sustenance. After a time Scott yawned deeply as Rivers leaned forward, propping his elbows against the table.

"I've read everything that's out there on serial killers, fact and fiction, and I still don't get it," he stated.

"Get what?" Scott responded absently.

"Exactly why they kill. If they're not sick and it's not a crime of passion, then what's the motive? All the stuff just dances around the issue, there's got to be something I'm missing."

Scott nodded thoughtfully, reaching across the table for a cigarette. He flicked the tired old Zippo, breathing deeply, and the harsh and familiar smoke drilled his lungs. "It doesn't take a degree in science to comprehend what they are. Shall we take Zak as an example?"

Rivers nodded.

"Zak Dorani is what we call a rake, or recreational killer. On the outside he appears to be perfectly normal, he's unusually bright, educated, and polished. He knows right from wrong. And yet he doesn't feel—there's not a glimmer of emotion left in his soul, if he even has one." Scott thumped his chest while Rivers raised his eyebrows.

"You're suggesting that he has no feelings?" he asked in a startled voice.

"He's what we call devoid, no emotions of any kind, and that's the only thing that makes him different from you or me. Do you understand the principle?"

Rivers thought it over. "Sure, I understand what you're saying, but somehow I can't grasp it. No emotion, so do these rakes know what is missing? I mean, instead of feelings, what do they have?"

Scott smiled, his voice steady as stone. "What is color to a blind man, Frank, to a person who cannot see?"

"Either a memory or a concept."

"Exactly," Scott blinked, "and emotionally Zak is blind."

Rivers cocked his head. "They never felt emotions? That's really weird. If he can't feel, then he's more like an android than a human being."

"Bingo. Emotions *are* what make us human. Now, take the case of innate intelligence, IQ if you will."

Rivers nodded.

"We are all gifted, or cheated, in that department as well. Take Albert Einstein, then compare him with all the poor creatures who are born so deficient in intellect that thinking itself is damn near impossible. In this same manner, some people are born with such a puny emotional base that they are blunted—barely human, as you say."

Rivers sipped at his cup. "So if one of these blunted people had some kind of trauma, like abuse at an early age, they'd have nothing left, it would finish them off?"

"That's it, Frank. Technically we are all born with emotions, but some are born with barely a glimmer. Drive that out, and you produce a devoid. Without emotions there is no regard for the suffering of other living creatures. Anything becomes possible."

As Scott waited, Rivers nibbled a fleshy corner of his mouth, playing with the concept in his mind. "A blank slate . . . so then why do they kill? Without emotions they wouldn't feel anything in return."

Scott leaned forward. "Let's go back to our example. If you were blind, what would you give to experience color and the wonders of sight?"

"Anything, I would imagine."

"And if you were emotionally blind, what would you give to experience a bit of that?"

Rivers breathed deeply, the roots of the idea taking hold. "I think I'm getting the picture. You're saying that killing enables them to feel?"

Scott shook his head. "Get the concept first, it's not that simple. If you didn't have emotions, what would your world be like?"

"Well," Rivers thought aloud, "I'm sure there wouldn't be much excitement. A very boring existence, I'd guess. Could I make love to a woman?"

"Physically you'd be able, but I'm afraid sex won't do much more than raise your blood pressure and respiration rate, so why not swim? It's better for you."

"Then I guess I'd read a lot, and watch sports and movies, but without emotions, would I care?"

Scott smiled. "You're starting to understand them now. Without a vested interest on an emotional level, things would no longer matter. Without feelings"—he unconsciously rubbed his heart—"issues and events and characters, life's comedy and drama, are all meaningless except on a purely intellectual basis. Without emotions, nothing matters, like being stranded for a lifetime in the middle of a big gray desert, no highs or lows, no peaks or valleys, just a torturous monotony."

"So you'd resort to mental pursuit, challenge yourself, break the boredom that way?"

"True enough, the raw intellect takes over without any emotional checks or balances. As they go through life, they are truly unable to comprehend what causes others to smile, laugh, frown, or even cry, and no one could explain that to them, just like describing color to the blind."

Rivers' eyes went wide with excitement. "But they must show something. Otherwise they'd stand out like store mannequins, they'd be easy to spot."

"Correct again, Frank. As children they recognize this glaring deficit that potentially sets them apart, so they learn emotional displays, producing what feelings should look like." Scott parted his lips in a strange grimace. "What's this?" he asked, pointing up at his face.

"Hell if I know, Jack," Rivers chuckled. "You're showing me your teeth?"

"Sure, showing teeth, isn't that what a smile is? Remember, you can't feel it inside, you don't understand joy. When normal people feel emotion, we respond physically—laughter for joy, tears for sadness, violence for hate, that kind of thing— but the important point is that we usually don't notice until we begin to display one of these. It's all second nature, thought simply does not go into it."

Rivers' jaw popped open. "Holy shit, Jack, you're saying they're human parrots?"

"More like accomplished actors, and their performance is very realistic. They teach themselves how to turn their displays on or off like a switch. But surrounded by others for too long a period, it becomes obvious from their miscues that they're acting. They smile at the wrong moment, or even worse, become confused with their displays."

Rivers leaned back, a pensive expression on his face. "I think I understand, but they do feel the killing response?"

"Precisely, the tiny spark of emotion left in them only ignites when they experience the most extreme of human behaviors, such as killing, which carries with it some rather unique physical responses as well. Anyone who has ever killed another person knows this: a change occurs in the body, and it doesn't matter what level of emotions you have. Most combat veterans have felt this sensation, however primitive it might be."

"I remember," Rivers said quietly. "Your body and your mind go berserk all at once, and everything becomes crystal clear in the chaos, you feel like a bottle being filled. God save us, that's what they crave?"

"The killing response and the emotional response are very similar, like identical twins. When our emotions excite us in the extreme, our bodies undergo drastic changes—blood pressure, alterations in blood chemistry, respiration, gastrointestinal activity, erection of hair, pupil size, sweat, almost anything you can name—and that all comes from feeling. Here's an obvious example I use with students: the so-called butterflies in the stomach, you've felt them?"

"Absolutely."

"That comes from emotion, and we take the butterflies for granted unless they become an ulcer. But if you were functionally devoid, you could not experience any such sensations without the administration of drugs—"

"Or killing," Rivers replied bleakly. "You feel very, very different, the body and the senses go wild."

Scott took a deep breath. "Rakes become hooked on this high, these sensations that mime emotional response in the body, and that's as close as they ever come to feeling, to having emotions, to breaking the dull sameness in their sorry lives. Killing is the only thing that excites them, and even then it's brief."

"Holy Christ," Rivers exhaled forcefully. "This Zak really is a cold-blooded monster."

"They don't come any colder. No hesitating on the kill, no repulsion to pain or gore, no remorse. Cold and calculating. When you strip emotion from a human being, all you have left is intellect, the ability to reason without the checks and balances of a conscience. Anything becomes possible, and he feels he is a superior being. We're just fish in his tank."

Rivers was stunned.

"So what do you think?" Scott asked, reaching for Frank's cup of coffee, then taking a sip. "My office is currently tasked with twelve ongoing series, and of these, eight involve men like Zak." He paused and studied Rivers: the man's eyes were slits of concentration.

"So he feels a glimmer of emotion, plus the physical high,

which is sharper than anything else in his existence, like a blind man seeing a flash of color and then darkness again," Rivers concluded.

"Correct. Between episodes they live on fantasy, imagining in their minds what they have done or what they would like to do. Fantasy sustains them at the same time it drives them."

"Do they always rape before killing?"

Scott nodded. "To men like these, people are things to be possessed and then destroyed, and sex is the ultimate control next to execution. Otherwise they wouldn't care, it's just another physical act. They crave power over their victims. To them sex is power, and they confuse that with the feelings we would normally associate with intercourse. Also, their desire to control extends to us, the authorities, it's an element of their possession, another type of rape if you will."

"I don't follow," Rivers queried.

"Domination of the worst kind. Did you notice when the Claytons were discovered, the children slain but dressed for school?"

"Last day in March."

Scott nodded. "In this case a rake crawled out of his stink and challenged me, a feeble cretin he wants to dominate and break. This is all an April fools' joke to him," Scott stated with sorrowful resignation. "It's no deeper than that . . ."

As his voice trailed off, Rivers felt the butterflies. Whatever emotion may have caused them, they were twisting his gut into a tight and sorry knot. Scott remained staring absently into space.

"I once knew a guy who couldn't show any emotions," Rivers offered. "Maybe he didn't have any. When he smiled, it was unreal, like his face was a rubber mask you could just yank off. The bastard loved war. He used to slice men's hearts out and feed them to his dogs."

Scott nodded. "I suspected that. Major Bradford Dunn?"

Rivers immediately tensed at the name, his jaw stiffening as his stare became ice. Scott reached gently across the table, placing a hand on his arm.

"I'm not prying, Frank, just concerned. You don't open up to anyone, you're very quiet, and sometimes that's not healthy. It goes no further than us," he offered gently. "Maybe talking would help some."

Rivers leaned back in his chair, studying the older man who sat before him. "Well," he released a troubled sigh, "I'm not sure what it will help with, Jack, that was a long time ago. I was just a kid, real young and real, real stupid."

Scott smiled. "Young *is* stupid, Frank, we've all been there."

Rivers nodded. "For years I thought the major was my best friend, but he wasn't any friend of mine—" He stopped abruptly. "I'll tell you what. Dunn liked to say that Vietnam was what we were having in place of a happy childhood. That says something."

"Yes," Scott said grimly, "and how did Major Dunn find you?"

At this Rivers smiled, leaning back into his chair. "He was a psychologist, an expert in the polite wars, so it wasn't very hard."

Scott shook his head as Rivers stood. Pushing away from his chair, he slowly bowed at the waist as he parted his hair. On his crown was a large noticeable tear of flesh where the hair would no longer grow. The scar itself looked like a large pale worm. Rivers forced a smile as he sat back down.

"Then that didn't come from Vietnam?"

"Nope, that little tattoo came from my senior prom, Jack. I was dating one of the prettiest girls in school. Anyway, we were all set for that big date, I had rented a suit and was about to pick her up for the reception, when a strange thing happened . . ." Rivers paused and looked skyward.

Scott could tell the man was struggling. "Who hurt you, Frank?" he asked quietly.

"Well," he breathed hard, "I had asked my dad for the keys to his car, and earlier he had agreed, but when I started out the door that night," Rivers shrugged, "my father busted an entire fifth of whiskey over my skull . . ."

Scott cringed.

"The polite wars, Jack, they're the ones you can't win. All very secret, and it's shame and disgrace that make them so hard to fight in the first place. Like I said, it was a long time ago." With that he took a swallow of coffee and lit a cigarette.

"Then what happened to you?"

"In Vietnam?"

Scott shook his head. "That night, what happened to you and your family?"

"Hell, I don't know, it was business as usual, or at least there was nothing my mother could do. I spent prom night with Jimmy Cooley down by the canal where no one could find us. He put seven safety pins through my scalp so that I'd clot by morning . . ."

"Sweet Mother of God," Scott cried, "why didn't you go to a hospital?"

Rivers smiled, genuinely tickled at this. "You still don't understand the town you're in, Jack. You read that *Tempo* article about Elmer, what was their crime? But you saw how they slammed his mother."

"Yes," Scott said, puzzled.

"If there had been a police report, the same little bottom feeders would have tried to destroy my family in public, only they're worse now, a new and improved generation. All you need to become a worthy target is a little social prominence, and my father was well-known, he owned a huge plumbing company. If people knew how he beat his family, we'd have gone broke, then everyone would have starved. So what's the point?

"Anyway, a neighbor who heard what happened had the kind sense to call the Cooleys instead of the police."

"So Major Dunn spotted your scar?" Scott pressed, but it was clear that Rivers would not go much further.

"Sure, Jack, he knew what to look for. You know, it's funny what you remember, but to this day I imagine old man Cooley watching *McHale's Navy* as the call came in. Jimmy was only fifteen, but his dad let him drive the truck rather than miss that show. We still laugh about it, that was a fairly corny show."

"I remember," Scott said, forcing a smile. "And soon after meeting Dunn, you found yourself in a program with others who came from troubled homes?"

Rivers chuckled. "Nothing wrong with the homes, Jack, it was the kids who were abused. Anyway, I can live with it."

Scott nodded bleakly, sipping a cup of cold coffee.

"No, Jack," he shook his head, "what I can't live with is what I read, that victims of abuse lose their emotions over time, or worse yet, revisit the sins onto others. You've probably guessed that I'm not all that great at forming certain relationships?"

"Well, I don't know if that's true, Frank. You may have a hard edge, but you obviously feel things quite deeply. Is that why you're not married?"

Rivers nodded. "She wanted children, but I was afraid of myself, what I might do . . ."

Scott released a stream of smoke. "Sorry," he said, "but you have nothing to worry about, unless you've ever raised your hand to—"

"God, no!" Rivers cut him off with a nasty stare. "That's a hell of a thing to say."

Scott gave a good-natured smile. "You obviously ask it of yourself, so what are you worried about? Trust your feelings and the rest will follow. Frank," he looked at him with dismay, "can't you see how foolish your doubts are when you bond so quickly with a little boy like Elmer?"

"Well," Rivers sighed, "he's a special little kid."

"Sure." Scott dismissed this with a wave of his hand. "I don't think it would matter to you what child was in danger, it cuts deeper than that. You're a good man, Rivers, take it from there and just get on with your life. If you can't trust yourself, then trust me."

"And you're a good judge of character?" Rivers smiled.

"The very best," Scott returned flatly.

And they talked well into the night, fighting to understand what each of them had become in life, and why.

It was a waiting game.

They were killing time by opening wounds.

29

6:20 P.M. THE FLORIDA GULF

Low on the horizon, an angry sun blazed for the last time before falling off the edge of the world. The Gulf of Mexico was unusually calm, so the flames dropped through a placid green mirror, then burst with an eerie afterglow. Overhead, scattered clouds pulsed with incandescent light, casting shadows, and as the light died, the colors changed. As the clouds moved, the dunes were rocked with shadow. Far off to the right, an inlet had become a mystical river of fire that resembled fingers of smoking white lava.

"The beach looks alive," Carol Barth exclaimed, releasing a sigh and pointing toward the coast. To her friend Lacy Wilcott the entire scene was like a huge red planet exploding, for she had been born and raised in a place called Moxie

Pond, just a bump of an agricultural town in western Maine. She had never traveled this far south.

"We're in another world," she answered, her voice filled with soft wonder. "How close are we to the equator?"

"Close enough so that even the palm trees look different," said Carol.

They were first-year students at Loyola University in New Orleans, taking a short vacation before returning home for the summer. Carol was from Newport News, Virginia. They had been on the road for two days, having spent that afternoon touring the Selby Botanical Gardens in Longboat Key.

Lacy Wilcott was a shy and well-developed young woman of nineteen with a light complexion and sandy blond hair, casually dressed in a pink V-neck sweater and white shorts. Carol Barth was the same age, only taller and slim to a fault, with dark hair and violet eyes accentuated by a powder-blue tank-top and matching shorts. These pinched at her waistline, flattering her long legs. Together they leaned against a white Pontiac Firebird, the only car parked at the Coral Cove scenic overlook along the old Coastal Highway. A cooling salt breeze washed over them.

"Whadda ya say?" Carol asked as the day burned into terminal orange. She was bending at the waist and slipping off her blue canvas boat shoes, which she tossed through a window and onto the backseat.

"My tummy's growling," Lacy agreed. "I think we can make Fort Myers by midnight."

"Let's just grab some food on the way, how hungry are you?"

"Snacks will do. The first clean store we see, I also need a bathroom."

"I'm for that," Carol urged sharply as they climbed into the Firebird and closed the doors. It was Lacy Wilcott's turn to drive, so she moved the seat forward and buckled her seat belt while her friend switched on the radio, searching for a weather report.

"It's got to be ninety-five degrees," Carol said. "I'm still sweating."

"That's humidity," Lacy suggested. "We'll be wearing our jackets in another few hours."

And in local news, the search for seven-year-old Lisa Caymann ended in tragedy late last night when her body was discovered along Route 41 in St. Petersburg. In a press con-

ference this morning, State Police Chief Captain Duncan
Powell discussed what he called a mindless atrocity . . .

Carol Barth pushed a tape into the slot with a troubled sigh.
"Who'd do a sick thing like that?"

"Animals," Lacy answered, and she adjusted the volume as
the white Firebird pulled out into traffic.

The sea was unusually calm that night as they drove toward
Venice, discussing their futures in the manner of the young, as
if time were a lasting friend that you courted and fashioned
from leisurely pursuit. And they returned to discussing the
College of Arts and Sciences while listening to rock and roll,
cruising toward a destiny that their young minds could not
possibly have fathomed.

Gregory Corless was seething with anger, and Seymour Blatt
looked startled as the waitress brought a tray and began clearing the table. It was just after sunset and the pair had said
only a few words to each other since breakfast.

"Anything else?" The waitress held a check at the ready.

"No, nothing," Blatt responded flatly. As the woman disappeared, Corless pushed his rotund face across a spot of heavy
syrup that short moments ago had been a large plate of waffles. His face was flushed with hostility, and his voice was
choking with rage.

"How the hell did he know that?" he cursed quietly, his
eyes burning with contempt. "This cop, how did he know
there were two of us?"

Following a commercial-free half-hour of easy listening
music, the evening news had been piped directly into overhead speakers, and the partners had heard the announcement
of Lisa Caymann's death, which registered visibly on other
faces throughout the Wayside Pancake House. Upon hearing
the news, a husky truck driver at the counter had thrown his
napkin onto the floor, stomping it, while another spun on his
bar stool, slapping a fist into his palm. Far off, near the cash
register, an older woman began to weep as a younger teller
spelled her, and she walked past the two men toward the
kitchen.

In the report, a police captain cautioned motorists to be
alert for two men, one heavy, one thin, both late-middle-age,
and traveling together.

"I dunno, Greg," Blatt said nervously. "I dunno where he
got that, but I'm scared." He scratched at the gold vinyl table-

cloth with his fingernails, watching the faces of patrons coming in his direction, toward the men's room in the hallway. Each stranger made him feel threatened.

"Did you catch his name, did you hear this cop's name?" Corless was whispering, shielding his face with one hand.

"Ah, no, no, I didn't."

"You asshole," Corless growled, settling back in his seat and scanning the small dining room. They were silent for a moment, Corless sipping his coffee, the other finishing his milk.

Then Blatt said, "I think we better leave one at a time, Greg."

The fat man's face instantly turned into a mask of red fury. "We leave together. This cop knows nothing, absolutely nothing," he hissed, trying to pin Blatt into silence with his eyes.

"Well, I don't like this," Blatt said anxiously. "How could he have known?"

"Shut up." Corless sneered, again shielding his mouth. At this Blatt's eyes narrowed with hurt. He was incensed by Gregory's disrespectful treatment of him, and they had been quarreling all day.

Just as Jack Scott had suspected in his review of the case from the ViCAT slot, there was a thread of guilt running between the partnership—in the form of Seymour Blatt, who had not wanted Lisa Caymann dead, indeed had even argued for her life, then later covered her naked body with a blanket.

As far as Blatt was concerned, Lisa was an angelic specimen with a serious occlusive overbite, a medical condition, and with treatment he knew she could have grown into a beautiful and pleasing woman. He felt as if his partner had betrayed him. Blatt leaned over the table.

"Lessa," he fired tonelessly, watching Corless squirm in his seat, uneasy with the nonsense word. Blatt waited.

"Lessa," he fired again, and Corless looked away.

Throughout the day Blatt had used a hundred such words, meaningless to anyone else, and he used them as clubs with which to beat the fat man, pressing his buttons at every turn in the road.

"Can't you just let it go?" Corless had begged as they left Sarasota. "You know the rules, and there'll be others that you'll like."

But on April 9, Blatt didn't think so. Lisa Caymann was simply his girl, the child of his dreams, and now he was breaking the rules at every turn. The year before, they had taken a solemn vow that once a game had ended, when it was done, *it* would not be discussed again.

"Rules of the road," he remembered Corless had explained, and once Blatt had agreed, but right now he no longer cared.

"Why did you do that to her?" he had asked Corless over eggs and coffee, but the fat man did not answer. "Why did you want to hurt Lisa so bad?"

"I didn't," he stated calmly, almost absently.

"But there wasn't anything left of her," Blatt cried.

Fat Corless hissed. "I didn't want to hurt her," he explained, speaking very slowly while dunking his Danish. "I wanted to destroy her, there's a difference." Blatt could still hear those words, and it was then, in that mental fog, that he felt his anger starting all over again as he leaned across the table.

"Lessa," he hissed suddenly. "Lessa, Lessa, Lessa!"

Corless recoiled with the sound, forgetting for a moment that no one else in the diner could possibly understand the imitative voice Blatt was using.

Lisa Caymann's deformed bite had produced a lisp.

Lessa was the way the child had said her name.

By eight o'clock the students in the white Firebird and the partners in the Dodge van were both weaving through traffic. This time Blatt was driving, so he refused to allow Corless use of the overheads to look at his scrapbook; Blatt even objected when he wanted the dome light in the van's cargo bay turned on.

At this time Lacy Wilcott was fighting monotony as well as a bit of depression. "I'll be working all summer, but I'd rather be in school," she said, and her voice sounded troubled. "My father wants me to take my degree in agricultural science and then manage the farm, I think landscape design is a coming thing, so we fight . . ."

"Is it bad?" Carol asked with concern.

"No," Lacy shook her head, "we just argue, and I hate that. When my brother declared a major in law, Dad threatened to disown him, but now he calls him every week to see how his studies are coming. There's lots of stress running a farm, I understand all that."

"He wouldn't take you out of school, would he?" Carol asked.

Lacy smiled. "No, once he gets over the shock that his kids have their own plans, he's supportive enough."

"Well, at least you had a brother to pave the way. I'm the oldest and my folks think I'm going into nursing. They're in for a big surprise."

"Then you're going to tell them?"

"What's wrong with teaching? I'd rather treat the ignorant than the sick. Try this," Carol offered, filling her lungs with smoke, then holding her breath. She had fired up a joint she had saved through the semester, and handed it to Lacy.

"What would they be doing in Hog Holler right now?" Carol asked.

"In Moxie Pond?" Lacy smiled. "By ten the town would be gathered at the Stock and Feed, drinking beer and waiting for something to buzz. They slap flies with a wet mop. 'That thar one was a blue-face,' " she said in her most manly voice as she slapped the dash.

Carol shrieked with delight. "You're kidding."

"Oh, maybe a little," said Lacy. "What about the shipyard? Do they have Saturday-night rust patrol?"

"No, they stay up and worry about the Navy, budget cuts, that kind of thing. To hear them tell it, the government never buys enough ships, and when that argument grows old, they'll talk about the ironworkers at Groton, where they build inferior boats."

They had been on the road for an hour when they whisked past a sign that said "Restroom/Groceries/Gas."

"Let's give that a try," Carol suggested. "Somewhere in the next mile, I think it said." Lacy began looking for an exit, steering the car loosely with her left hand.

Soon they were coasting down a wooded ramp toward a smallish street that reminded them both of back roads in the towns where they were raised. At the intersection a stop sign was peppered with buckshot, leaning up from weeds on a greenway.

"Welcome to Butcher Holler," Lacy said. Slowing a bit, she headed toward a two-pump store with a billboard for a sign, spotted by canisters of light.

"Grafton's General," Carol said. "I can almost smell the blue pills in the toilet bowl. Bet it hasn't been cleaned in this decade."

"We can wait," Lacy offered as she braked, inspecting the parking lot and store. It was well-lit and looked clean enough from the outside. Then she noticed Carol dabbing her lips with a stick of gloss.

"What the hell." Carol shrugged as Lacy swung the wheel, creeping toward the top of the small parking lot, toward a bright lamp that reduced shadow.

There were two other cars parked side by side, an old Volkswagen Bug and a new Buick Skylark with New Jersey plates. Next to these were a delivery truck and a battered van, each parked tailfirst against the curb. They were clearly for daytime use.

"So what makes him the 'World's Greatest Grandfather'?" Carol asked as they pulled alongside.

"Don't grow old," Lacy Wilcott suggested.

The cargo bay was a steamy parlor of sorts, and with the heat from the engine compartment stirring up humidity, water was leaching down the walls in small rivulets. Gregory Corless was on his rump, changing his shirt and sweating like a sow, which Seymour Blatt thought he surely did resemble.

The partners were both tired with each other, sitting in the cargo bay arguing. When they talked, their words seemed disconnected, going past each other as if the two had nothing in common. They sensed the partnership crumbling. Each resented that fact, and Blatt was worried by the frequent radio reports.

The van's rear doors were open, facing a thick wall of hedges and allowing privacy, while the cool night air blew through the foul interior.

"I think we should just go home," Blatt whined, and his apple bobbed in his skinny throat. He had removed an expensive dental splint made of gold-filled porcelain, which left his own frail teeth planted in his gums like sharpened gray posts. Without the false choppers, Corless thought he looked like a refugee from a gulag.

"This cop, Duncan Powell, is chasing his own ass," Corless said. The discovery of Lisa Caymann's body was being repeated on the hour, and that was about their only concern. "There are hundreds of men on the road who travel in pairs," he continued, "truckers, tourists, campers, even bikers. He doesn't have a clue, though I'd like to know how he figured out you're a scrawny little wimp."

"What else does he know about us, Greg?"

"Nothing. If they had a description, they would have

broadcast it. No way we were seen. Besides, we've used the backyard snatch before. We're experts, way too good for them."

"I don't know," Blatt was whining. "We shouldn't just sit here, what if a cop pulls in?" The light streaming through a side window made his teeth look like little gray nails, and Corless was about to suggest he rinse his mouth and plug the damn bridge back in, when they heard a car approaching from the roadway.

Corless quickly snapped off the overhead light, and Blatt started to fidget, fetching his teeth from a gearbag.

The car crunched over the gravel, slowing down to inspect the lot. Unnerved by this, Blatt was having dark visions, running for his life through the woods, dogs rending his flesh, a hick of a sheriff watching him bleed to death. "Greg?" he cried.

Corless lifted a lip: he was fantasizing about a girl he had never seen before, ripping off her clothes, making cruel demands on her. An engine died on their left and they felt rock music thump against the van's interior wall. The brassy chorus was quickly followed by silence. And then voices. At least two, maybe more.

"Get the rear door," Corless said quietly, buttoning his shirt, putting his book into a banker's box and closing the lid. "And don't make any noise. We'll leave after they do."

Ignoring him, Blatt rose to his knees and parted the curtains an inch, peering out the window just to make sure they weren't cops. By now he didn't even trust his own senses, and he could just see the driver from the lips down, while the girl in the suicide seat was no more than a torso, one hand pulling a tape from the stereo, the other holding up a marijuana cigarette that was burning to a stub. Blatt breathed a sigh of relief as he twisted around.

"There's two of them," he whispered, "and I think they're getting high."

Corless barked something under his breath, moving slowly on his knees, the van rocking with his bulk as he closed the doors slowly, carefully, quietly as possible, and with a great deal of resentment in his body language. Feeling safe from police dogs, Blatt was enjoying the view, peering down into a white Firebird.

"I like her very much," he said, and on his return trip, Greg Corless smacked him on top of the head.

"You said there's two of them, don't waste your time," he responded. And Blatt smiled, thinking about Lisa, about ways to make the fat man pay. These were attractive girls, and if Corless would only look, he knew that alone would drive him insane.

In combination with the Rule of One, Blatt knew the slob would hyperventilate, maybe even go into cardiac arrest. *Pick more than one and they'll end your fun,* Corless was fond of saying, the premise being that abducting one person was easy. With two or more, the risk of something going wrong outweighed the benefit. Blatt smiled: this time Gregory Corless would face fruit he couldn't pick, and Blatt swam in that joy, digging at him with a vengeance. He studied Lacy Wilcott's mouth as she talked. Her lips were full and wet, her teeth bright and evenly spaced.

"She's still in her teens," Blatt offered after a brief dental review.

Corless hissed, preparing to leave as Blatt made a haunting moan deep in his throat.

"So, what's she look like?" Corless barked, curiosity starting to gnaw at him.

His partner giggled. "I can see the driver pretty good—you'd like this, she has really big tits," he announced with a teasing whisper.

"Well, don't get used to it, too risky. Can you see the other one?"

"Not really."

"And they're smoking pot?"

"Not anymore, they're just talking and . . . Look at that!" Blatt breathed hard. "She's getting out, arranging her shirt. What a show, her sweater's stretching tight, no bra, her shorts are pulling up . . ." Blatt started breathing heavily just to piss the fat man off, and Corless could stand it no more. He pushed hard on his hands and knees, forcing his considerable mass into the small space.

Together they filled the cramped area beneath the window like two evil Kilroys, staring over the edge as Lacy Wilcott and Carol Barth stretched in the shadows, oblivious of the menace above.

"A beautiful night," Carol said with a yawn, looking up at clouds covering a pale moon.

Lacy shivered, crossing her arms against her chest. "Sandwiches and a pit stop, then let's get back on the road. I don't like it here."

"The pot makes you paranoid," Carol offered.

Lacy frowned.

"You mean *women*," Blatt said sarcastically. Corless was going crazy, he really had said mature girls.

"No, women are a pain in the ass. I mean girls whose changes are complete, a woman's body with the mind of a child. Girls. The English language is inexact." Blatt could see Corless was breathing hard over a game that could not be played because of the Rule of One. It was driving him over the edge.

Blatt was rejoicing, watching the girls enter the store, using his voice to drive Corless into a lathered fit. "Big bouncing tits, the girl in pink just loves you. And that one in blue has legs so long she'd make like a river pump and drain your life away!"

Corless huffed quietly.

Blatt was about to continue when he saw the fat man tremble, unable to sit, trying and then losing his balance. His rear slammed onto the deck like two giant hams. "I've got it!" he stated before the floor had stopped shaking.

But Blatt knew he had nothing, except for maybe the cold sweat that was dripping down his fat neck. Gregory Corless was trapped in his own rules like a pig cooking in his own hellish juices.

"Did you hear what I said?" Corless barked.

"Got what, Greg?" Blatt asked aimlessly.

"I've got both of them," he said, grabbing Blatt by the arm. He said this with a resolve that frightened Seymour, with a voice he immediately recognized from other games, and he found himself speechless.

He tried thinking of something to say, of something with which to appease the fat man, of something that would put them back on the road.

"The two-minute drill," Corless ordered, grabbing him by the throat.

By then Blatt was moving too fast to think.

They worked quickly, and with nimble experience.

"The puppy won't work," Blatt cried. "They're going to scream. We're going to get caught!"

"Get the cage," Corless ordered, "and I'm also using the cast."

They thrashed about the steamy cab, pulling the pieces together and setting them down in the middle of the cargo bay. Corless stripped off his pants and then shirt.

"But, Greg," Blatt cried weakly, "the rules. What if one of them gets away?"

Corless shot him an acid glance. "That's your job! Do your job, there's nothing to worry about."

Blatt crawled quickly through the van on his hands and knees, bumping into fat Corless as he dug through a box. In less than a minute they had assembled an odd assortment of trash in the center: coils of rope, rolls of duct tape, handcuffs, an ice pick, a black leather sap, an expensive shirt with a torn sleeve, a pair of navy-blue slacks, a dog's dish, a bag of feed, a can of food, and a small portable kennel with the word "Happy" hanging over the cage door.

"Get it in place," Corless commanded, struggling to pull the designer T-shirt over his head as Blatt arranged the cage just opposite the double loading doors. Covering this with a towel just so, he then placed the dog's dish close to the metal seam that connected to the van's outer stairs. Using a can opener and spoon, he quickly filled the dish with a smelly pile of Kal Kan puppy chow, sprinkling a handful of dry crunchies across the top.

"I don't like this," he whined, grabbing a roll of tape and a pair of scissors. "You're going back on your word. You're breaking the—"

"You fag," Corless cut in, "you said you wanted these two, and we will, clear down to Highland Point. Now, get with it!"

"I never, never said that," Blatt sniffed.

Corless ignored him, unwrapping a large plaster cast that had been covered in bubble wrap and safely tucked into a soft brown leather suitcase he called the Bag. He sat in the center of the van, extending his right arm out toward Blatt like a rotund knight awaiting his armor. "Make sure you only use a small bit at the wrist this time. I need the hand free, and I don't mean for peeling off your screwups."

Blatt covered the arm with a plaster cast that was craftily slit open on the back. With some help, the medical device encased the man's arm and shoulder like a shell, covering the entire appendage, including the wrist, thumb, and fingers. It closed tight and seamless, fitting like a glove.

Corless proudly held his arm from above as Blatt worked, placing a large strip of white tape under the armpit and a tiny one under the elbow and wrist.

"And what if they scream?" Blatt asked again.

"Add a little more under the elbow, I don't want this falling off in the parking lot." Dutifully Blatt thumped the area with his knuckles, and then complied.

"Greg," he tried again, "you just can't walk up to their car! This is a death state! In Florida they have a death penalty and they actually use it!"

Corless smiled where he sat, rotating his entire body, for the cast was now in place and his right side was completely rigid, stiff as a block of wood. His arm was cocked at a forty-five-degree angle from the elbow. In turn, his forearm was positioned high in front, almost touching his double chin.

"Apply the brace," he ordered, and Blatt worked quickly to position a chrome support bar, placing this into a special slot at the elbow, then applying more tape to seal it in. He quickly attached the pillar to the man's belt, and when this was done, he searched through the Bag for a suitable knight's crown. Blatt held a neck brace toward him, a stationary medical support collar made of white plastic.

"Not too tight," Corless cautioned.

"Sit up a little," Blatt returned, and he closed the Velcro strip, adjusting it just so in order to allow for expansion.

Suddenly Corless was struggling to his feet. "We're out of time," he said coldly, having monitored the two-minute drill. And what stood was a pathetic figure of a broken man that would easily spark remorse from any caring human being.

His entire right side looked fractured, possibly crushed, and his neck brace tilted his head back, pushing under the chin so that he had to swing his entire body in order to see. His shirt was torn to accommodate the cast in two places, the shoulder and then the waist, where the metal strut attached to an inside metal cleat that doubled as a gun hook. His shirt remained open at this spot.

"Quickly," he ordered, and with a shaky fist Blatt handed him his gun, frightened of dropping the heavy steel thing. Corless held the large black revolver up to the light where he could see it.

It was no ordinary gun. This .357 Colt Magnum was a weapon designed for psychological intimidation, and had once been commissioned by the U.S. Border Patrol. The short heavy barrel was not tapered like most, but cast into a straight black tube like a stovepipe, as round at the muzzle as it was at the breech.

"Just aim it," Corless hissed, "they just curl up and die. You don't even need a trigger." Without ceremony he pushed this into his pants. After pulling the shirt down, he turned to his partner. "The girl that you'll meet is the only one who can scream. See that she doesn't."

Without another word, he opened the door and was gone.

Lacy Wilcott waited at a glass sandwich bar, comparing the tuna with ham while Carol finished in the bathroom. An older couple were at the cash register, getting directions from a clerk, and she could tell by the nasal accents that they were the ones from New Jersey.

Next to the sandwiches she found a row of drinks. Opening the glass door, she was selecting a carton of chocolate milk as Carol appeared. Lacy could see her smiling as she came skipping down the aisle toward the back of the store.

"Did you see the blue pills in the bowl?" she asked.

"Imported from Newport News. What'd ya get?"

"Ham and cheese with chocolate milk, the tuna looks bad."

Carol examined the shelves. "All they have is white bread?"

"The egg salad is on rye," she motioned to the top row.

"I'll try that."

Corless came through the door, turning sideways with his chin braced back and clutching a piece of paper in his left hand. He was careful not to look directly at the girls, but he saw the blonde's head turn his way. They were aware of his presence. He walked on.

Corless strolled leisurely down the aisle for canned goods while holding the list to his nose. About halfway, just after the tuna and soup, but before the canned peaches and pears, he stopped and listened. The girls were now one aisle over.

"Doughnuts or chocolate chip?"

"You're having that awful milk, sure you want more chocolate?"

"My middle name."

"I was hoping you'd say something like that."

With his left hand and arm he collected six cans of puppy chow to his chest, then brought them to the counter, only to return for three more. Behind the register was a kid, about sixteen Corless guessed, sitting on a stool and entrenched in a comic book.

Corless swung his massive frame, looking for other employees milling about, satisfied that they were alone. He could just see a pink sweater and a blue top reflected in an oval shoplifting mirror above the door.

"How much?" Corless asked the boy, using his mildest voice as he pulled a wad of bills from his pocket.

The clerk got up from his chair. "Dog hungry?"

"Yes."

The kid grabbed a can, turned it upside down, and rang the same number nine times on the register instead of multiplying in his head. Corless sized him up as someone who didn't have the mental capacity to store a man's description longer than a few seconds, and he tried to keep his behavior innocuous.

"That'll be five dollars and eight cents, please."

Then the clerk fumbled in the drawer to make change from a ten.

"Thank you," Corless said. "Would you have a box? An open beverage tray would do nicely."

The clerk glanced at the extensive cast supported by a polished chrome beam. "Wanna bag?"

"I'd prefer a box."

He ducked under the counter and produced an open Dr Pepper box, then stacked the cans into place. "Thanks," Corless said, sliding the crate across the counter to his waist, then lifting with his one good arm.

"Wanna hand?" the clerk offered.

"Ah, no," Corless said. "I have to get used to this thing, seven more months to go."

The kid shrugged and went back to his comics, and on the way out Corless glanced up at the oval mirror above the door. Two girls were headed toward checkout, and he stared at their ample curves, undressing them with his eyes. He felt a fire growing inside him.

He felt the thrill of the hunt.

They paid and left.

The cool night air greeted Lacy Wilcott and Carol Barth as they walked out into the parking lot. The high clouds had been driven by the wind, revealing a sliver of a faint moon, almost a scratch on the night sky. Carol stopped to look up.

"The pollution's gotten so bad in Newport, I almost forget how beautiful the stars can be," she said.

"In Moxie we write songs about them," Lacy said. They strolled away from Grafton's General Store, sipping their drinks on the outskirts of Route 41 near the town of Laurel.

"Did you see that schoolboy looking at you?" Lacy quizzed.

"Very funny, he's younger than my brother."

"He's in love."

"With a comic book."

They were about halfway across the lot to the white Firebird when a can rattled across the parking lot in their direction, and they watched it roll as if this were not a can of dog chow, but a foreign object they had never seen before. When they looked up, an obese invalid locked helplessly into a huge cast was bobbling a box of cans. Two more of them toppled to the ground as the man strained to balance the load.

"Oh, my!" Carol cried as she watched another roll in her direction, nearly bumping into her toes. She bent over and picked it up. "The poor guy," she said, starting toward him.

"Carol?" Lacy cautioned.

Carol kept walking, but turned her head back toward her friend. "He's in a cast, silly, he can't hurt anyone." Just then the cripple near the edge of the parking lot lost his balance completely and the box fell with a crash, cans spinning and Gregory Corless sweeping the air with his stiff appendage.

He smiled good-naturedly as Carol approached, and instead of shaking his head, he shrugged with his entire body. She stood four feet away, looking up into his face, examining his eyes, while Lacy followed after, swinging their dinner in a brown bag and clutching a can of dog food with the other.

"Let me help," Carol offered, picking up two of the cans just as Lacy arrived alongside and tugged her arm.

"I'm sorry," Corless said, releasing a dejected sigh.

"Don't be silly," Carol responded even as her pretty violet eyes darted nervously, reflecting the light. She looked up and saw a wedding band on his good hand and figured it was quite safe.

"Is that your van?" Lacy suddenly asked, and her voice was ripe with concern.

"Lacy?" Carol sounded disapproving as she placed all of the cans into the fallen box, then took the other from her friend. She stood and started to hand these back to the owner, and an awkward shuffle ensued, reminding Carol of crowded encounters—nearly bumping into someone and then waltzing in place.

Corless laughed gently, seemingly embarrassed. The man had only one hand, and it was obvious to Carol that he couldn't carry the whole box, for that's what had gotten him into trouble in the first place.

"He's been parked there a long time," Lacy cautioned.

"Yes, I have, and I appreciate your help, but I can take it from here," he offered.

"Good luck," said Lacy, and started to walk away.

Still holding the box, Carol was looking at the labels for the first time. "Do you have a puppy?" she asked, and Lacy stopped, emitting a frustrated sigh.

Corless turned, his right arm stuck in the air like a frozen crane. "My wife and I are heading south to see my oldest daughter, and we were bringing my grandson a puppy. When we stopped here for a snack late this afternoon, he jumped out of the van. My wife's still looking. You see, we're taking turns."

"Oh, that's terrible," Carol responded.

"Then why all the dog food?" Lacy asked.

"I couldn't think of anything else to do, so I thought I'd buy some extra cans, open them up, then place them around the area in case the little guy gets hungry." He tried to shake his head, but the brace wouldn't budge, so he rubbed the back of his neck with his left hand.

Carol was staring angrily at Lacy.

"I know it's dumb," Corless said, noticing that the brunette was now walking slowly toward the van, carrying the box.

"You the Greatest Grandfather?" Lacy asked as they approached the bumper.

"Not anymore, I'm afraid, not with a missing puppy anyway. We had one for each grandchild, but it looks like we'll arrive with only one dog." And he stopped at the cargo doors, his face sad and strained.

"You have another puppy?" Carol asked, standing by the van. Lacy Wilcott stood just behind her friend, feeling a bit uncomfortable.

"Yes," Corless smiled, "a baby cocker spaniel, cutest thing in the world. They're brother and sister. Well, thank you very much, girls, you've been so very kind." He reached forward with his left hand, awkwardly trying to open the door while his right arm swung, arcing through the air. The door would not budge.

"I'm still not used to this cast," Corless sighed, about to try again.

"Let me," Carol offered, handing the box to her friend.

As Lacy Wilcott took a step back, Corless was standing to her immediate right and slightly behind. The girls took no notice as his arm eased through the splayed bottom of the cast and hung limp at his side while the medical prop stayed in place.

"How do you open this?" Carol asked, having turned the latch.

"Oh, I'm sorry," he said, "it slides. You have to pull."

Carol Barth pulled back the door, and there was darkness.

Lacy Wilcott stood her ground just as Carol stepped forward, first smelling and then seeing a bowl of puppy food inside the steps.

It was reassuring.

Just behind this she saw the little cage draped for the night, and over this, the name Happy. "Is that her name?" Carol asked sweetly, turning to collect the box from Lacy.

"Yes," Corless cooed proudly. "I cover her at night when she's sleeping, but you can talk to her if you like, she's very loving. I don't know how she's reacting to the loss of her litter mate." His voice sagged. "Maybe she doesn't notice. Seems all puppies do is eat, play, and sleep."

Corless took another small, unnoticeable step backward as Carol smiled. "Oh, Happy knows," she confirmed, moving forward and peering into the van, placing the box of cans on the floor. Then she stepped up, leaning over the cage and bending down. She approached with a soothing voice.

"Hi, baby," she cooed, "hi, baby," and she started to lift Happy's curtain.

The horror that struck her came not at once but built slowly, mixing with confusion as she strained to take in what was before her. As it came into focus the world around her whirred into a smear of horrid and confusing images. At the bottom of an empty cage was a photograph of a nude woman being bound into a chair. Terror hit Carol Barth like a bullet in the chest.

Time stopped.

Fear stretched across her face, contorting her features, and she tried to scream and stand at the same time.

"Run!" she started to cry, but the word dropped from her mouth as she fell. A black leather sap had silenced her with a crippling blow.

At the same moment two massive arms had swung around Lacy Wilcott's throat, grabbing her from behind, then lifting her by the chin into the air. Her feet dangled and she kicked frantically, overpowered by fear, struggling for breath and fighting to scream. But her throat was pinched shut and her lungs burned for air as she felt faintness crippling her.

"Go ahead and fight," Corless hissed into her ear.

Seconds crawled by. She felt her strength draining away as Corless slapped the deadly stovepipe revolver across the bridge of her nose, being careful not to draw blood. He then jammed the gun up under her chin.

"Make one sound and you're dead!" he sneered under his breath, and his lips touched her ear.

Still Lacy Wilcott gave a futile last kick as she felt her body being crushed and overpowered, then going limp beneath the attacker's violent hold. There were two of them now. She felt two of them.

Blatt and Corless were dancing together, pressing the girl between them, using their bodies as a human vise with which to force her movements. With expert skill Seymour Blatt slapped Lacy's wrists with handcuffs even as Corless was rolling her onto the floor of the van.

"Tape her," he ordered, lying on top, then smacking her hard across the face, drawing blood at the corners of her mouth. He held her jaw shut with two massive hands as the cargo door slid shut.

Darkness.

It took only seconds, then Lacy was taped and bound. Carol lay unconscious near Happy's cage. The men congratulated each other in the darkness, united again.

"Get the blonde naked. I don't want anything else in my rearview for the next few hours," Corless ordered tonelessly while climbing into his seat and adjusting his mirror.

This done, they headed south.

They were happy now. They were just killing time.

30

Dudley Hall, the diggerman, wound his Chevy four-by-four up into second gear, churning dirt with his tires as he roared down the curving hills on Rabbit Run. As he talked he swerved occasionally to avoid door-size potholes that were puddled with leaves and rain water. To Matthew Brennon, it looked like a miss would spell certain death, and he grappled for his seat belt, snapping it tightly into place.

Observing this behavior, Hall called out, "Ain't been a road crew by since Carter had pills." He spat out the window. "Prison shut down the chain gangs, was violatin' their *serval* rights."

Brennon knew what he meant as he sat clutching the urn with both hands, hoping that the man they called Leon Rigby would be home and that, luckier still, he would have some recollection of the burial jar that held the remains marked Zachariah Dorani.

"Shouldn't we have called?" he yelled back, glancing discreetly at his watch so as not to offend.

"Nope," the diggerman hollered, "where dere's smoke dere's fire." He swerved off onto a circular clearing by the side of the road and stopped. Dust funneled over the cab, and Dudley Hall waited for it to clear.

From this elevation on Woodside Mountain they were looking down a country mile onto a patchwork village of houses, farms, and manufacturing buildings all saddled into a tight valley. Abandoned railroad tracks skirted the edge of the development closest to them, and Brennon noticed a boarded-up train depot and switching yard. There were no cars on the roadways below, and he quickly concluded that Woodside, New York, had been dead for some time.

"What are we looking at?" he asked, setting the urn on the bench seat between his legs.

Hall pointed through a hazed windshield. "See the blinking lights over dere?" In the distance Brennon could just pick out a series of small red beacons flashing from the other side of the depot, and knew he was seeing aviation strobes attached to an aerial obstruction. Something was jutting up into the sky.

"Radio station?" he asked, unable to discern the object's form.

"Chimmy," said Hall, by which he meant "chimney." "That's Rigby's creamer. Gettin' it fired up too. Can just make out the heat plume."

Brennon noticed that a ridge of white clouds slung low on the horizon was being sliced in half right over the obstruction. "Would anyone else be operating it?"

"Justa old fool hisself," answered Hall. Without warning he jammed the pedal to the floor, and the Chevy truck bolted forward over dirt and gravel, slamming Brennon back into his seat. As the truck rumbled along, carrying the men toward a destination Brennon could only imagine, he tried concentrating on other things. The cool air at his sleeve carried a clean, wet smell that reminded him of Vermont, where he had spent part of his childhood, but for reasons he didn't understand, the smell made him think of dust, human dust, and how a real wet season could leach and jell a man down into a concrete shovelful; then centuries worth of people all slipping around under the earth, while others blew on the wind, flitting up some cooker's *chimmy*. And at that moment life seemed a strange and futile thing for Matthew Brennon, his mortal place merely a troubled speck as he clutched the urn and the truck hurtled through time.

Hall fished under his seat with his right hand. Producing a pint bottle of sloe gin, he unscrewed the top with his thumb. He offered this to Brennon.

"I appreciate it, but no," he said as they rounded the bottom of the hill and hit pavement, the truck's tires biting with an angry whine. Hall placed the bottle between his lips and gave a long pull, taking a right onto a side street. Soon they were speeding through the village: houses came and went as the four-by-four clattered along railroad tracks and toward the red beacon.

"Did ya see all the vandalism at Old Woodie?" Hall asked, taking a small sip. Brennon remembered hundreds of overturned stones, it was a dreadful sight. "When I was a kid, we wouldn't dare even raise our voices in a cemetery. It makes you wonder."

"Ain't no kids," Hall said. "It's an unemployed welder, lives right dere." He slowed in front of a small gray house set back from the street. The glow of a television flickered through the window. "Sheriff knows it too, but can't prove a thing. A whole family of shit people live in dat house." Taking a final long pull off the bottle, he rolled down the window and slung it at the litter-strewn yard.

Just then a pungent odor filled the cab, and Brennon covered his face and coughed. "What's that smell?" he sputtered.

"That," the diggerman announced, smiling, "is the creamer."

The truck turned onto a lash of gravel, through a picket fence, and rolled toward a large Victorian house with a blaze of red strobes pulsing from a dark round funnel that towered like a scar against the night sky.

Rigby's crematorium was a concrete room that had been constructed on the back of his residence. Inside, the walls were painted white, and the floor was a slab of finished gray with a fresh coat of shiny sealer. As they walked through the door, a tall figure in blue surgical scrubs turned their way, made eye contact, then went back about his business.

Dudley Hall led them to a spot across the lab near the only window, and Brennon did a quick inventory as they passed. There were wooden cupboards, a glass laboratory case, and large stainless-steel sinks at the end of the room near the oven. In the center of the cubicle was an examination table, the old type once used in city morgues, with chrome drip gutters and drain holes at head and feet. Mercifully, he thought, this was vacant.

From the far end a noise blew through the space, first starting as a whisper, then more like a jet engine firing up. It emanated from a vast chrome tube that resembled a huge septic tank, half-buried in the farthest concrete wall. As Hall moved about, making himself at home, the sound increased to a near-roar, then blasted them with a penetrating whine. They watched as the man Brennon surmised was Leon Rigby peered through a heavy glass porthole at the end of this massive steel chamber, turning a little wheel that sprouted copper tubing from two sides.

Above his head ran a series of analogue gauges with pie zones in the colors yellow, red, and blue. He made an adjustment and the room screamed. As he began turning another knob, this one produced a deep sound like the roar of a boiling ocean. Brennon glanced out the window and could just see a spire of black smoke when he realized he had been holding his breath.

The smell was suffocatingly sweet, like bacon being torched on a bed of apples, and it filled his lungs as he watched a stream of fat flowing down a stainless gutter.

"Why don't you jest let the damn flame go blue?" Hall was shouting above the din, criticizing the red glow that was reflecting against the walls. Rigby waved him off like shooing a fly. He removed the asbestos gloves that had been shielding him up to the elbows, then untied the blue gown. He was tall, thin, and gangly, with a voice that slurped like a bad drain.

"What?" he wheezed, and Brennon guessed the man suffered from advanced emphysema. A husky, wet cough shook his entire body as he moved back to the chrome counters, making adjustments, putting away tools.

"Eight and eight," Rigby yelled, and the two men strolled to the chamber, glancing up at a series of glass-encased gauges on top of the pot. One read eight hundred degrees, and Brennon cringed, thinking the body inside might cook for eight hours. He watched as Rigby spun a little wheel, and the roar suddenly became deafening, like standing at the end of a jet runway on takeoff.

The blue-clad man hit the light switch, transforming the space into a white-hot glow that screamed through the porthole's glass face, washing the cell with fire, making Brennon conjure images of earth's end. Casually Rigby walked by and through a skinny door.

Inside, the Rigby residence was rather shabby: a couch covered with an old afghan, a matching plaid easy chair torn at the seams, and a coffee table that was a slab of raw oak, round with concentric rings. Opposite this, the television set was vintage black-and-white, and somehow Brennon was pleased that creamating bodies wasn't that lucrative. He guessed that Leon Rigby was not a man who parted with money easily.

"This is Special Agent Matthew Brennon. He's on official gov'ment business," Dudley Hall said, using his most authoritative tone. Rigby was studying the lean agent, sizing him up, gauging the importance of the visit. He fought a cough as he extended his hand, which Brennon saw as a thin and fragile cage of bone. "Glad to have the company," Rigby said.

Brennon greeted him warmly.

"Let me wash up. Like a beer?" Rigby wheezed, pulling off his gown and laying it over a wooden chair.

"That would be fine, thank you."

Rigby disappeared across his living room, leaving them in the dingy light cast from an ancient floor lamp with yellowed tassels. Beneath this Brennon spotted a green oxygen bottle with an inhaler attached. The house reeked of smoke, and dampness clung to everything.

Gently the diggerman placed the urn on the coffee table, then sat on the couch while lifting a pillow. "Make sure he don't charge for the beer," he said mockingly.

"How's that?"

"Rigby's so tight, he squeaks. Can't close his eyes, they'd stick shut." Brennon smiled as Rigby returned carrying a wooden tray and placed it alongside the urn.

"So what's this?" he directed to Brennon, handing him a cold bottle of Bud. He then gave Dudley Hall a double shot glass filled with bourbon, and sat down on the couch next to him. The two men had said nothing to each other.

"That was exhumed with a court order, and we were hoping you could tell us something about it," Brennon said, sitting in the tired easy chair. He could feel a spring poking one cheek.

"Cigar?" asked Rigby, lifting a box from an end table and waving this at Brennon.

"No, thanks," he said, then watched as Hall took the box, placed a cigar into his mouth, then dropped another into his top pocket. Meanwhile, Rigby was twisting the urn 360 degrees.

"Oh, for Christ's sake, talk to the man!" Hall suddenly cried. Rigby ignored him.

"Son, do you have a budget?" he asked, lifting his shot glass and taking a generous sip.

Dudley Hall splashed liquid back against his throat. "Dammit, Leon, that's a baby-killer that's bottled up dere, you white-trash rummy nigger!"

Rigby coughed in a convulsive spasm. "Well," he stammered, rattling like a jump-started car, then cleared his throat. "Well, how could I know?" His thin face was flushed as he stood, walking from the couch, then returning with a bottle of Old Crow. He refilled his glass as Hall held his over the urn.

"Seal's been torn," Rigby stated.

"We broke the goddamn seal," said Hall.

"Did you sell this urn?" asked Brennon.

"What are you going to do with him?" Rigby wondered.

"We're sending the remains to the FBI forensics lab in Washington," he explained, "then try for a blood type."

"Don't know his blood type?" asked Rigby.

"That's his business," Hall snapped.

"We just want verification," Brennon offered kindly, "but I'm more interested in the bottle right now."

"Won't get no identification from those ashes," said Rigby, moving the Old Crow to his side of the table as Hall slugged down his drink.

"Why not?"

"Fires burning at over two thousand degrees, nothing left, no cells anyhow. Carbon, that's all you'll get, unless he was burned slow, but in that"—he swung his glass at the expensive blue container—"he would have gotten the best, blue flames. There's nothing in there but dust."

"Show 'im the chippy," Hall suggested, puffing his cigar and standing to reach for the whiskey.

Brennon handed Rigby a white handkerchief, which he carefully unfolded into his lap. The burnman was holding a piece of porous gray bone between his thin fingers and squinting. "*Calcaneum,* tip of the human heel," he said. "That came from the urn?"

Brennon nodded as Hall humphed.

"Let's take a look," Rigby offered, handing Brennon the whiskey bottle, then clearing off the table. He popped the urn's cap, and with both hands began pouring a stream, watching the speed with which the flakes were falling. A pensive expression moved across his face as Brennon watched carefully.

"Ah, you did that, you old cheap screw," Hall cursed as Rigby ran his finger through the pile. Rigby frowned, then shook his head at the urn.

"Are you from the prison authorities?" the thin man asked nervously.

"No," Brennon shook his head, "we're only interested in learning about the deceased, we don't care about anything else."

Rigby rubbed his fingertips together, dipping back into the pile. "That's a discounted job," he said, "a burnt-up yardbird. To torch a body right, it takes nearly fifty cubes of natural gas. Top Fahrenheit costs plenty, and the state has always paid about half the going rate."

"He burns 'em real slow, uses charcoal at the bottom," Hall explained.

"The less gas, the cheaper your cost, and the charcoal continues to burn after the gas is shut off?" Brennon concluded.

"Or I'd never show a profit from the state. But I only do that to penitentiary men, or derelicts, who was this?"

"Career felon, died in prison," said Brennon.

"I think not," Rigby corrected, "at least not in this jug." He lifted the urn. "It's top-of-the-line and spare no expense. If I burned this man, it would háve been fast, all carbonated powder, not gray with chippies. If someone was around to buy a pricey bottle like this, the state wouldn't have carried the cost of cremation."

"You're sure?"

Rigby nodded. "Either the prison pays or the family has to carry all costs. Can't have it both ways."

"What he's saying," the diggerman added, "is that a slow burn is easy to spot. This ash should have been dumped into a cardboard bury box."

Brennon nodded, writing in a black notebook. "What can you tell me about it?" he urged.

"Well, it's definitely my work and my can," Rigby confirmed. "Back when we were fed by the trains, I did a big city business, and I'd sell bottles to funeral homes and private customers." He read the date on the gold ribbon. "By 1964 I had sold most of these because the style was going out, but this," he paused, "doesn't make sense."

"Could bodies have gotten mixed up somehow?" Brennon asked.

Hall laughed as he spoke. "Never," he said. "Leon keeps better track of a corpse than you keep on your dick. A body means money." And Brennon knew there was some truth to this because the burnman had gone stone silent and was shifting uncomfortably on the sofa.

"Sir, is there any way to tell who bought the urn?"

Rigby shot Diggerman Hall a crooked glance as he stood and left the room. Hall quickly grabbed the Old Crow off the table. "He's gone for his records," he said, "hassa mountain of boxes and crates filled with useless shit. Maybe something will happen this time."

"This time?" Brennon repeated. Hall had spoken as if they

were watching a routine, when suddenly the diggerman leaned over and slapped Brennon hard on the knee.

"Lotta old family ties 'ere at Woodie," he said through a cheery alcoholic glow. "In my time I've known most all serious manhunters, least in these parts. Same's true with old Leon."

Brennon smiled weakly and took a sip of beer. That bit of bragging was old as the academy: everybody knew everybody, only they didn't really.

"It's true nuff," said the old man. "Some came lookin' for the diggerman hisself, others jest led by the fate of two million dead. That's a lotta bodies to be telling stories."

"Yes, it is," Brennon agreed, "lots of stories," and his voice sounded worn, even a touch sarcastic.

"Name of Nicholas Dobbs mean anything to a man your age?" Hall asked abruptly, and Brennon nearly inhaled his beer.

"And Tombstone Taylor, Popeye Doyle, the Real McCoy, big Duke Duncan, Mad Max Drury. And that Scotty Dog of yours? Saw him water a few graves in my time."

"Jack Scott?" Brennon inhaled sharply as his jaw sprang open.

But the diggerman fell silent as Leon Rigby walked between them with three file boxes in his hands.

The thin man was proud of his organizational skills, particularly the multicolored rows of plastic file tabs, which arranged hundreds of lined white three-by-five cards.

On the outside of the first box it said *Supplies Wholesale,* and he gave a wet cough as he pulled the floor lamp closer. "You'll have to bear with me," he said as his bony fingers began scratching through the cards. "These are categorized by dates, but that urn could have been a personal sale, wholesale exchange, or even a barter, it could take some time."

"No problem," Brennon said. "Is this cataloging required by code?"

"Hell," the diggerman grinned, "that's jest in case the IRS wants a nickel. He's been preparing for years, ain't that right, Rigby?" The thin man worked unimpaired by the distraction as the diggerman settled back in his seat.

"Is the gold inlay real?" Brennon asked, fingering the urn.

"Eighteen karat, six millimeters deep, roughly one troy ounce." He pulled a card from the box. "In 1960 that metal cost eight dollars wholesale, real money."

"May I see that?" Brennon asked, retrieving the card, then reading meticulous handwritten notes. "The urn was hand-crafted in 1964 at Peterson's Mortuary Services, St. Paul, Minnesota?" he asked.

"A very fine house. In fact, they went belly-up that same year. Always keep your overhead down and the profit up, they did neither. The inside is glass-blown, the outside is leaded copper, and the finish is blue cloisonné enamel with gold inset." He went back to the box.

"Then these bottles would be filled by you and delivered back to a funeral home?"

Rigby shook his head. "If the beloved were to be buried at Woodlawn and the church services were elsewhere, the under-taker would just use a duplicate empty bottle, a dummy. I'd keep the real one here."

"And then these ghouls would charge the family for a phony transport. Priest would be blessin' an empty can." Hall sneered.

Rigby shrugged. "By 1964 I had sold seven as dummy bot-tles to various homes, here's the list," he offered, and Brennon examined the card.

"Then these homes could have been involved in some type of mix-up?"

"No," Hall corrected, "after they milked the bereaved fam-ily for a worthless transport, the funeral home would send the empty can back to Leon as trade for the real one he filled."

"Or they always had the option of keeping the can and splitting all bogus fees," Rigby said, "but this particular urn wasn't involved in any type of wholesale exchange, or it would be in here," he said, scratching the index cards with yellowed fingernails.

"Then it was retail," Brennon pressed.

"It's possible, but I think I'd remember that. Those pur-chases were always bereaved walk-ins. Apparently I had four in stock, I thought it was three." His hand flicked from red to blue tabs, searching out the correct year.

"What was the month he died?" Rigby asked, holding a spot in 1966.

"February," Hall said.

Rigby fished for a card, reading as he went, his eyes dart-ing across the lines. Then he pulled one loose and nodded his head. "Here's the answer," he sighed. "Imagine that, it was a telephone order, fairly rare, I should have remembered." He read aloud, interpreting the note.

"Someone who couldn't attend the services paid for the jar, and he just made it under the wire too. According to this, when the order was placed I had already performed cremation and was about to stick the deceased into a prison box. That's why the slow burn job."

"May I?" asked Brennon, his eyebrows knotted with anticipation.

"February 24, 1966," he read, "Peterson's Eternal Promise ordered by phone for Dorani, Zachariah. Cost of purchase, twelve hundred dollars."

"It was my last one," Rigby shrugged.

"Under method of payment it says 'PPO.' What's that?"

"Personal purchase order. Shorthand of mine, it's the method of payment, which would be cash or certified check before services."

Brennon nodded. "Then under that it says 'Paid in Full,' which means you received the money?"

"Believe it," Hall stated.

"And what's 'Dryer's' mean, for twenty-six dollars?"

Hall spoke first, putting down an empty glass. "That would be Al Dryer, the engraver who did the gold. He's been dead awhile."

"That's all included in the ticket price," Rigby clarified. "Just a personal record if Dryer ever said I didn't pay, which he sometimes did."

"No claim there," Brennon offered, "says 'Paid in Full' on the twenty-fifth. Then under that, the name of the company that bought the urn, DIDS Ltd. of Dallas, Texas, and an old address."

"I wouldn't have settled for that!" Rigby looked insulted, and reaching for the card, he turned it over, and held it under the yellowed lamp. He then leaned toward Brennon, his thin face worked into a broad smile.

"See here," he said proudly, "just ran out of room. I even copied the telephone number. DIDS stands for Dallas Instrument and Dental Supply, and the man I dealt with, Mr. Aaron, was the owner. That's him right there." Rigby pointed, sniffing the air for Hall's benefit, and Brennon quickly scanned the data.

That Zak Dorani was a devoted atheist was well-established, yet the president of DIDS had requested very clearly, and in some detail, that the deceased be buried in a religious bottle, specifically a Christian urn with five gold crosses. "Is there any way Mr. Aaron would not have known about Dorani's religious concerns?" Brennon asked.

"Naw," Hall waved him off, "the prison would've kept it on file, and Aaron would've been told the moment he offered to pay for services."

"And if they didn't, then I certainly would have," Rigby added.

"Then why did you comply with the request?" Brennon asked. "It could have been meant in some mean-spirited way, intentionally failing to honor Dorani's last request to be buried in an unmarked urn."

"Can't make much sellin' a pickle jar," said Hall.

"Oh, what's the harm?" Rigby asked defensively, his wet cough making his body shudder.

"Well, puttin' a man in a jar he don't want is like pissing on a grave, only worse, denying a request that lasts an eternity. You should be ashamed," Hall admonished. Brennon watched as Rigby reached for the oxygen bottle, pulled the mask to his face, and turned on the gas.

Brennon thought back. If what Dudley Hall said was true, then purchase of the Christian urn could have been meant as an act of retribution, an insult of some type, albeit an expensive one. And Brennon wondered about Mr. Aaron's relationship to Zak Dorani, if that's who was even stuck in the jar. It was with this puzzle on his mind that he felt strangely on edge, his instincts warning him into action, and he used Rigby's phone to call the ViCAT slot and order a nationwide computer search on DIDS Ltd.

A half-hour later, 9:45 Saturday night, Special Agent Daniel Flores called back, and Brennon answered on the first ring as Leon Rigby and the diggerman looked on.

"I've found the urn's buyer listed as the CEO of a major dental-supply corporation," Flores announced. "According to Trans-Union's credit sheet, DIDS was a one-man outfit until the seventies. Now they have offices in twenty-three states."

"Big and prosperous," Brennon responded. "So Aaron's still alive?"

"Very much alive, and I just spoke with Commander Scott, he said to tell you this is urgent, so we're pushing the search first-priority. He also said to draft Dudley Hall into service, we need his help."

"I beg your pardon?"

"Jack said ask Mr. Hall to come to Washington, for old times' sake. You are to buy his ticket."

Brennon's head fell on a weakened stalk. "Anything else?" he asked quietly.

"No, but you have a minor slip in your data, a simple inversion. I had to run combinations with Aaron before I got a hit."

"On the name?"

"Yes, sir," Flores stated. "The man's first name is Aaron, you have it reversed."

Brennon scribbled a correction into his notebook. "So it should read Aaron Seymour Blatt?"

"Yes, sir," said Flores, "fifty-one years old, single, and no police record."

31

The phone at the command post had been ringing through the early hours of evening, and Jack Scott terminated a call, his face tired but knowing. It did not matter that he had never heard of Aaron Seymour Blatt. He immediately ordered that all ViCAT stops be pulled out at once, that his New York office concentrate their energies on him, that his history be uncovered and his life laid bare.

Frank Rivers had been testing electronic tracking equipment in the parking lot across the street, and he returned through the rear door to find Scott working on a collage of Diana Clayton's house, scanning her personal appointment calendar as he placed a photo on the table. "Is that necessary?" Rivers commented as he strolled into the kitchen, peering over Scott's shoulder and down into a silver-framed portrait of Kimberly Clayton.

It certainly was a haunting image, and without a clear purpose that furthered the investigation, it seemed a bit macabre. Scott inhaled a puff of smoke, then lifted the glossy of Jennifer Doe, the lifelike clay image staring up with penetratingly human eyes. "Something precipitated the attacks," Scott offered quietly. "I'd like to know what that was, and the answer lies in who they were."

Rivers frowned. "So you're getting to know them?"

"I am, but a bit more. These two families shared something, possibly an activity, I don't know."

"Jack," he said skeptically, "if that child had lived"—he picked up the portrait of Jennifer Doe—"she'd be older than me."

"That's quite true, and the Clayton girls could have been my granddaughters, but age has nothing to do with it. I consider them each as individuals. Their behaviors transcend time."

"Then what do you see?"

Scott smiled. "Nothing so far." Abruptly he changed the subject. "How about the field equipment, is it functional?"

"Sure, but it's primitive stuff. The locator will put us within a mile, not much more." He had planned on dropping a small transmitter behind Jessica Janson's car bumper, but was now wondering if it was really worth the effort. He picked his gearbag off the floor.

"Did Captain Drury call about the Patterson kid?"

"Max said the dogs did find Debra's scent in the women's room, but nothing else. She was there, and that's all they got."

Rivers remembered the acid-green underwear that Mr. Patterson had found in her hamper. They looked ripe for a successful K-9 attempt, and their best team had been assigned to search the Zephyr Bar and Grill earlier in the day. "And the witnesses?"

Scott shook his head. "According to the field interviews, there are none, and the owners were very uncooperative. They immediately threatened legal action for unlawful harassment, and we have no grounds for a search warrant. I'm afraid it's a wash unless we petition a court on Monday, but I think probable cause is going to be a real problem here." He handed over a note. "Those are the owners."

"What the hell," Rivers growled, "it's been going on eight hours since her car was found." He shoved the slip into his pocket just as Mule Murphy's voice crackled through the kitchen radio, reaching their ears like gunshot.

"Base, this is Huskies . . ."

Rivers reached across the table, lifting the microphone, turning the volume down on the receiver. "Go ahead."

"A car's pulling in—white Oldsmobile Cutlass, woman driving. Do you want plates?"

"Negative, Huskies. Is it the mother?"

"Must be, the boy ran out the front door to meet her. He's hugging her back, so yeah, but this lady's nothing like your description. We are exposing film now."

Toy Saul was using a telescopic lens through the van's rear windows, taking pictures on a high-speed emulsion.

"Roger that, Huskies. Are they parked in the garage?"

"No, in the driveway, they're walking for the front door."

Rivers nodded. "Base to Pogo," he said, checking the stakeout position at the bowling alley. "Do you copy?"

"Ah, yes, sir," Rudy Marchette's thin voice responded excitedly, and Rivers quickly made a notation of the time in his duty book. Jessica Collier Janson had arrived home at 6:08 P.M., Saturday, April 9. "Keep us posted," he demanded, then released the toggle with his thumb and began searching through his gearbag.

First he removed a soft leather Galco shoulder rig. Slinging this over his left arm, he pushed an automatic into place, adjusting the holster's tension spring with a small screwdriver he kept on his key case. It was an unusual-looking gun for a state man to carry: the metal was a bright shiny blue and the grips were an inlaid ivory instead of rubber, like most serious combat pistols. Both the front and rear sights had been removed, and Scott recognized the piece as an old Combat Commander. He watched for a few moments as Rivers fidgeted until he was confident with the ease of the gun's release.

"Going hunting?" Scott asked as Rivers grabbed a light gray windbreaker, then placed a small radio receiver on the table.

"Promises to keep," he answered tonelessly, and there was a curious tension in the room that made instant strangers of the two men.

Elmer and Jessica Janson strolled hand in hand up the front walk. The three-legged dog vied for their attention as they climbed flagstone steps, and the boy was talking excitedly as they disappeared through the front door.

Elmer was proud of the way his mother looked, although today she was dressed for work in a navy wool gabardine suit that suggested only sexless and cool decisions. Her matching slacks had creases that could slice, and she removed her jacket, folding this carefully across her briefcase, dropping them both on the tiled counter in the kitchen. As she unbuttoned the choke collar on a white blouse, she dabbed her neck with a wet paper towel. Elmer dutifully poured from a pitcher of iced tea in the refrigerator, then handed her a cold wet glass.

"You're an angel," she sighed, sipping gingerly while removing tight two-tone business pumps with open heels. She bent at the waist and placed these on a sheet of newspaper near the door.

Elmer was fidgeting at her side, Jessica massaging her feet with one hand, when the dog nearly rammed her in the thigh, his ears pulled tight across his head. "Hello, Tripod, have we been ignoring you?" She smiled sympathetically, crouching to stroke the large shepherd, who immediately sat up on his rears, batting his good foot at the air. She gave him a handshake, then sat Indian-style on the white linoleum floor. The dog immediately pushed his muzzle down into her lap, and Elmer drew up alongside, staring up at his mother.

She was tired, that much was easy to see. Her eyes were red and bleary, and her voice was worn. Elmer knew from experience that she was catching her second wind, so he gave her time to relax.

"Mom," he said, working his hands into nervous fists behind his knees, rocking on the floor. Jessica glanced at her boy, and, as often happened, she saw the haunting reflection of his father, the mint-green eyes that were a Janson family trait. She felt a hollow thump inside.

"Yes?" she responded, rubbing Tripod's ear.

The boy hesitated, leaning forward, nibbling his upper lip. "Mom," he said slowly, "do you think I'm a good person?"

"Why do you ask?"

"Dad said the most important thing was that I grow up to be a good person," he explained, and the innocence on the boy's face radiated uncertainty. For whatever misguided reason, he was unsure of himself, and Jessica felt a mournful ache in her heart as her mind drifted, his voice becoming a whisper in the background.

Elmer was remembering words that he couldn't have possibly understood when he had first heard them. He was too young when his father had died, yet now he was playing them back and trying to grasp their meaning. She swallowed hard.

". . . and Dad said that it's not as important what you are as who you are inside."

"Come here, Red," she whispered, and she pulled him close, nuzzling her face into his neck. Then she held the boy at arm's length.

"Daddy would be very proud of you," she said, looking him straight in the eye. Elmer hugged his mother, holding her around the neck. Although they stayed that way for only a few quick moments, to Elmer it seemed forever until she found her reserves, and her lips produced the magic words used in the Janson household every Saturday night since he could remember.

They were joyful words that spelled the end of a working week, that told of only good things to come.

"Pepperoni? Rigatoni! Who's your friend?"

"Mom!"

"At least you're not too old to play." She kissed him lightly on the forehead, then attacked his ribs until Elmer was covering up, no longer able to control the giggles. Beside them the dog barked furiously until their ears hurt.

"Wash up, silly, we'll go to Tony's."

On his way up the stairs, Elmer suddenly stopped in his tracks. "Are you working tomorrow?" he asked.

In the plaintive sound of her son's voice Jessica immediately felt the latch-key guilt of a single parent. "No, Elmer, Sunday is our day." She walked to him, working her features into a smile.

"Can we go to Great Falls Park?"

"Oh, Red, what about tonight? You wanted to see a movie."

"*Platoon*'s at the Circle Uptown!" he beamed.

"No," she said quickly, "you know the rules."

"*Untouchables* is PG-13?"

"And you finished your studies?"

"Not the math."

She nodded thoughtfully. "*The Untouchables* then, and I'll call Gram while you take a bath—now, don't forget to wash up top."

She ran her fingers through his hair.

"That's what bothers me," Jessica said from her bedroom. Changing ears, trapping the blue Princess phone beneath her chin, she removed an earring from her left lobe and slipped this into a lacquered tray on her nightstand. As she shook her head, strawberry-blond hair fell forward across her brow.

"What does, dear?"

"Oh, Mother," she fumed, "you don't listen!" Plopping on the edge of her bed, she unbuttoned her blouse with her right hand, then wriggled away from its cling. "He's lonely."

"Nonsense, Jessie," Martha Collier corrected her daughter. Although she lived in Long Beach, California, like clockwork the two spoke every Saturday evening.

"He has you and his schoolmates and Tripod. Now, stop worrying about his every little mood."

"I'm concerned," she sighed. "I think he'd rather be by himself than with other children, I just don't understand."

"Now, Jessica, just allow him to be a little boy and he'll find himself."

"Well, that's not what he finds, Mother!" Her voice rose sharply with frustration. "Remember his last little stunt?"

"He's adventurous. Just be glad he's not a video-game addict, turns their little minds to mush. Other parents would be extremely jealous."

"Mom, we're talking past each other. I didn't have a clue as to what he was doing at that bowling alley. When I'd ask, he'd just say he was mashing aliens, which means running over weeds with his dirt bike. Next thing I know he's dug up a human skull, the police are asking questions, and when I asked Elmer, he said he was just roaching around. God, it gives me the creeps."

"You forget too easily, dear, you were quite a handful. Remember that time you and Lynne Meade had those little mice?"

"You're a great help, Mother. I call for advice, and you're still grinding your ax. That was an accident!"

"But you did let them escape into the doctor's office. As I recall, Dr. Meade had patients passing out from fright months after you said they were all captured. Weren't you about Elmer's age?"

"Oh, God, Mother, you are such a bitch!"

"Of course I am, dear, it takes years of practice. Just don't be too protective. How're the studies?"

"Fine. His lowest grade this week was a B in math."

"You're the envy of the Long Beach school district."

She sighed. "Mother, maybe I should reconsider work—not

ending my career but cutting back. Maybe I should spend more time with him."

"Nonsense, Jessie, you're doing a perfectly capable job."

Jessica removed her bra and slipped a long-sleeved pink T-shirt over her head and wriggled through.

"Are you there, Jess?"

"Yes, last night, and again this afternoon, Elmer mentioned his father," she said with a questioning sigh. Switching ears, she pulled a pair of light gray slacks over her knees.

"All perfectly normal. A death that early in a child's life is very difficult."

"Mo-ther!" She bit the word in two. "It's the way he asks. 'Mom, do you remember Dad's face, do I look like him?' " she said wistfully. "How can I answer something like that?"

"With honesty. Tell Elmer I'll be visiting in July and bringing something very special for his birthday."

"You're hopeless."

"And you're in fits over nothing. Is the job going well?"

"Yes, just fine. I'm taking Elmer to Tony's for pizza, then we're going to the nine-o'clock show at the cinema. He wants to see *The Untouchables,* but I don't think—"

"Jessie, I've got to go," Martha Collier interrupted, "someone's at the door. I love you, baby. Don't worry so much."

"Love you," Jessica sighed, hesitating only a moment as she hung up the phone.

And in the gathering darkness of a night sky, Jeffrey Dorn felt his blood crawl.

His heart was beating behind each temple as he clutched a steel pylon, staring down from a telephone pole onto the little people who strolled the sidewalk below. He closed his eyes to this inner pulse, having nearly forgotten just how good it felt, eavesdropping on the strange emotional voices, being back in action, back in the hunt.

As he removed his metal clips from the hydra, he felt a thunderous pulse, his stomach stirring, his brain going light. The more he thought about Elmer and Jessica Janson, the faster the blood pounded through the shallow chambers of his heart, racing through his body, ratcheting down into every muscle and fiber and nerve, fueling him with an uncontrollable pleasure.

As he started a downward climb, he felt struck by an urge to laugh, and so he opened and snapped his jaws, wagging his tongue, twisting his face into a hellish obscenity. He was remembering a page from his own childhood, how he had been forced by his mother to stand for so many hours at her bedroom mirror, where she had coached his efforts to produce what feelings should look like.

"Not like that, baby," she would say. "Now, laugh for Mommy! A big laugh for Mommy!"

If he teased her too often, making these hellish little expressions, refusing to perform, a brutal slap would sting his face.

Looking back, Jeffrey Dorn could honestly say that he had grown attached to his mother, a middle-class housewife who knew from the very beginning that something was terribly wrong with her child.

"Zachariah, smile!" she would demand.

And with each stinging backhanded kiss, the boy produced until perfection was achieved.

32

Like most of Washington, D.C., the Zephyr Bar and Grill had two distinct faces, depending upon which personality a customer sought.

One was pleasant enough, that of a neighborhood gathering place in the upper northwest part of the city where the younger crowd could meet on College Night, which always fell on a Friday and was so marked in a front window.

But it was the Zephyr's other face that troubled Frank Rivers, a face of unparalleled depravity for other patrons who knew what specific Saturday nights were reserved for them. He reasoned this by the drawn shades, or perhaps the light that was left burning in the rear alley.

He had been watching from a grassy hill overlooking the back of the building. Finally he got up and started running with powerful leonine strides down the gentle slope, the long muscles of his legs stretching tight, the sculptured arms at his side slick like pistons, hammering him forward through a light mist. Behind this dampness he could feel the building threat of thundershowers, the sky turning black, swallowing shadows.

His effortless glide brought him down onto the broken cobblestones in the alley behind the bar. Swiftly he approached a young woman who was hobbling across the rough patchwork. She turned her head and glanced back. Seeing him, she picked up her pace.

She was tall and fashionably dressed in a tight blue knit suit, a split seam revealing long legs and glitter stockings with stiletto heels. Rivers had been watching her seductive approach with a smile, thinking that with her tight, long waist and swirling hips she resembled an expensive fishing lure, but by this time he was already moving to overtake her.

He checked his watch: 8:17.

Before she had arrived, he had the entire block staked out, watching customers drift through his field of vision and enter the bar from the rear. All of these were men, in their forties and early fifties, well-dressed, carrying briefcases or clutching leather folders, some arriving on foot, others parking on the street with a freehanded ease, then entering and exiting like hungry ants in a food line.

Rivers carried a thick canvas leash in his left hand, complete with a chain choke collar, and since he had dressed casually in jeans and a light gray windbreaker, it seemed natural for him to be searching for his dog in back alleys.

He slowed his pace, and just as he came up behind the woman, she turned around. Her eyes met his, and her hand snapped open the brass catch on her purse, which she clutched to one breast. Her red hair was below the collar, flowing in streams as she moved, too perfect to be real.

"Hi," Rivers offered. Closing the gap with one long stride, he couldn't help but stare. From this angle the woman was all cleavage and legs, her perfume enveloping him like a cloud. He took a position just alongside, trotting in place.

"Get lost, creep," she said, rattled but confidently picking up her pace, the pavement dangerously broken and her heels moving delicately. She stepped lightly, wiggling as she went.

"Looks like rain," he offered.

"My hand is on my gun, my finger's on the trigger," she said coolly, not looking up, her face a pretty slab of stone.

Rivers gave his best smile, raising his hands to the top of his head, then trotting backward with his elbows poking the air. "Where are we going?"

"We?" she mocked with an icy voice. "We are not going anywhere!"

With this she stopped, and a small chrome pistol flashed in the dim light while her heavily painted eyes covered his form, summing him up, seeing him for the first time.

They stood about one hundred feet from the Zephyr's rear door.

"I've already surrendered," he smiled weakly, then quickly shuffled back a few feet as the woman tensed.

"Look, creep," she sneered, and her face became unpleasant. "I can't run in these shoes, so either I pull this trigger or you leave me alone!"

Rivers shook his entire torso, then closed his eyes. "Sorry, you'll have to do it."

"What?" At this her shoulders sagged, and the little gun bobbed nervously.

"I'm really sorry to be a bother. My name's Frank Rivers, it's always good to know the name of a hostage." He pointed down at the gun with a finger and smiled.

"You're crazy!" she fumed, starting to walk again.

"I'm hoping you'll feel you've made a good choice. I'm a very low-maintenance Frank. I only need one walk a day and come with my own leash." He waved the canvas trotter with his left hand, keeping his arms high while walking backward.

Grasping the absurdity of it all, the woman offered a slight smile. Very slight, but a smile all the same. With a tilt of the head, she unexpectedly slid the small weapon back into the purse, stopped, then removed her wallet.

"I need help." His voice was sincere, even a bit nervous. "I'm not used to asking—"

"No," she said, raising her eyebrows, "I can see that." She removed a crisp five-dollar bill and offered this to him. This was done so genuinely that he wanted to accept it, but shook his head.

"No?" Again her hand plunged back into the purse for her gun. "What do you want?" she demanded coldly.

"It's about a missing kid," Rivers said slowly. "Her car was found out front last night," he nodded at the Zephyr.

"And you're a cop," she said coldly. "Now it all makes sense, you lousy bastard!" Her body slumped, the last bit of defensive posturing vanishing as her purse closed tight.

"If I had started with a badge you wouldn't have talked to me."

"You're right, I would have called my lawyer, which is just what I'm going to do. What's your badge number?"

"Look, lady," he lowered his hands, "I'm a human being, and while I'll admit that's hard to believe, at the moment what I do doesn't matter so much as the why of it."

She gave a tight frown, raising one eyebrow.

"Give me a chance, please?"

She watched him closely as he pulled a photo of Debra Patterson from his jacket and held it out. The girl in the picture was standing with both parents, her expression sweet and proud, bedecked in her white confirmation gown. The woman looked closer, studying the face.

"She's very young. Are you related?"

"No, no, I'm not. This was taken two years ago, but you're right. This missing kid could have been anyone, my niece, your sister, the girl next door. All I know is that she's someone's baby, and that should count for something in this world of hurt. She should count for something."

The woman studied this man's eyes: they radiated a kind of deadly blue concern, yet underneath there was pain. She took a step forward and gave a small nod. "Okay, low-maintenance Frank, I'm a player. You have ten minutes from the time you show me a badge, and I can spot a fake."

Rivers flashed his shield, hiding it in his palm as another man walked into the alley clutching a briefcase. There was no doubt that the badge was genuine.

"The only bust on record for these guys is for serving drinks to minors." He nodded at the *Mook* who was now unlocking his car, and they both watched. "There's one hell of a lot of activity in there, and I need to know what it is, gambling, designer drugs, girls, that's all there is to it."

"And why can't you go?"

"My guess is they know all their customers, so they'd make me. Plus we had a K-9 team in there this morning."

"But they'd never suspect a call girl?"

"No," Rivers smiled warmly, "they'd never suspect a lady."

Instead of ten minutes, it took nearly a half-hour. Rivers spotted her immediately as she came through the rear door, her face and posture stern, her eyes cold and sad. He quickly strolled down the grassy hill overlooking the alley as she glanced back over her shoulder, quickening her pace. In double step Rivers drew alongside.

"Come with me," she ordered, taking up his hand and leading him back to the hill. They quickly walked the distance together, then settled down at a curb. The woman—her name was Marcy—tugged at her skirt and stared off into space, her eyes glassy.

"I feel dirty," she said softly, and with that her body shuddered. Again she tugged her skirt, sitting tentatively against the gutter staring up at the sky, but clouds had now blocked the stars. "Do you smoke?" she asked, rattled.

Rivers started to rise, the lean muscles along his jaw pulling tight, when her hand reached up, grabbing his arm. "Squares, dummy, cigarettes. I don't do drugs, although you should try a Valium."

"Sorry." He rolled his eyes, then reached for a smoke, lit it, and handed it over. They made eye contact. Rivers noticed that her eyes were a pretty hazel, almost green, and he guessed her real hair was a soft, shiny brown.

"I've seen some bad shit," she offered, inhaling deeply, "but that's a real nasty freak show you've got in there."

Rivers nodded. "How so?"

"The place is full of little men, and they're buying pop, and there's even two teenagers minding their beer who have no idea what's going on!"

"Neither do I, Marcy. What are little men?"

She looked at him with wide eyes. "Child pornographers, Frank. Freaks, perverts, sadists, call them what you like—"

"And what's pop?"

"You're a detective?" She shook her head. "Pop, candy, lickers, that's kiddy porn and real deviant shit. I told them I had a client with special interests, and they showed me some really rotten things: men, women, bestiality, bondage, children, real kinky." She made a funny clicking sound with her teeth.

Rivers touched her lightly on the knee.

"This is some very sick shit," she cried, "and they enjoyed showing it to me!"

Rivers nodded sympathetically. "What did they have?"

"Books, films, magazines, tapes, everything, they were very proud of themselves." She looked at him. "They said they fill orders you can't get elsewhere. They should be shot, and I could do it too . . ."

Rivers swallowed hard. "And they keep this stuff where exactly?"

"I'm not sure, they were real crafty about that. In the kitchen, I think, but they had photographs under the bar. They had one shot of a little boy and girl . . ." Her voice trailed off and Rivers could see she was fighting back tears. "It was inhuman."

"How old?"

"Eight maybe ten, I don't know. And they have film of teenagers, they couldn't be of age."

Placing a hand on her shoulder, Rivers handed over a slip of paper. "Take this," he said, and she glanced at it with questioning eyes, there was only a number.

"Call me if you ever just need a friend."

"And what about you?" she sighed.

Rivers stood and watched a middle-aged man stroll out the Zephyr's door. The bag in his hand had taken on a whole new meaning. "What about me?"

"What are you going to do?"

Rivers nodded at the bar. "I have to know if they've seen my girl."

He started to leave as Marcy jumped to her feet, cutting him off as Rivers had done with her, holding her hands in the air. "I'll call for you and get some backup. These are very cruel men," she cautioned.

He shook his head, staring past her into an outer darkness, then moving there—so quiet, so easy, it was hard to appreciate that he had even gone.

They were twins.

Kenneth and Bart Dix, two late-middle-aged men with sagging guts, both hard-looking characters, were tending bar, filling and washing glasses. As Marcy had suggested, they were ugly little men, both slightly better than six feet tall with pan-flat faces and unruly, thinning brown hair. Their dull-looking eyes resembled dirty marbles, bulging fishlike from thick skulls, and they followed Rivers as he came through the front door.

The twin on the right spoke to the other, removing a white apron and tossing it onto the bar. As Rivers walked by, selecting a corner table, he heard the word "cop," though he didn't respond as he counted heads.

There were four men seated at the bar, in addition to the twins, two larger men playing cards at a rear table, and only six drinking customers, mostly girls, one looked underage. He considered his options. A nickel bust for serving a juvenile wouldn't slow them down for an hour—the twins would be out before the paperwork was cut—and he pulled out a wooden chair and settled in with his back to a corner.

Over the bar he could just see a blur of faces reflected by a mirror that advertised Bud Light in gold metallic letters. A burly twin approached, leaning over the table and slapping once with a wet dish towel, his shoulders looking as wide as the table.

"What's your drink?"

"Slice."

The twin shook his head. "We've got beer, wine, or whiskey, no mixed drinks. There's a café down the street, try there."

Lighting a cigarette with his Zippo, Rivers looked over this and studied the dull eyes, the turn of his mouth, the double chin. He released a stream of smoke in the man's face. "Which twin are you?"

"They call me Snake, what's it gonna be?"

"And him?" He pointed to the bar with his cigarette.

"That's Younger, he came out second. What's this about?"

Rivers shrugged. "I've got some special interests, thought you might be able to help."

Snake turned, and Younger snapped into eye contact with his brother, an invisible form of communication dating back to the womb. The man came forward from behind the bar.

"Didn't catch your name," Snake hissed from a massive face.

"Francis."

"Well, sweetheart," he mouthed, "let's see the color of your money, then I'll see what we can do for a cop's pay."

Rivers nodded, digging for his wallet, laying some green on the table as the other twin approached, standing a few feet back, watching intently.

"That's twelve bucks," Rivers offered as Younger came forward, his face a hard and heavy mask. Rivers noticed that a scar ran along his chin.

"What's that for?" he asked in a menacing voice.

Rivers was silent.

The twins looked at each other. "Don't even play with him," Younger suggested. "Do you have a warrant?"

Snake placed his hands on the table and leaned toward Rivers. "Let's play trick or treat," he hissed.

Younger grabbed his brother's arm. "I'm calling my attorney. She's gonna bust your silly ass down to humping meters, so I suggest you leave."

Rivers nodded thoughtfully.

Just then another customer strolled through. Spotting him, Snake returned quickly to the bar. Rivers watched carefully: the man was well-dressed, short, in his early forties. When he handed a satchel across the counter, Snake's whole head vanished from sight.

If he was counting cash, Rivers figured it could be a few thousand dollars if the bills were small. What then emerged reflected off the bar's countertop, staining it with bright fleshy tones, filling empty beer mugs with pink.

Rivers stood and in three long strides was at the bar. As he approached, he could just discern a color glossy, not the magazine type, but an expensive color print. Snake skillfully slipped it beneath the counter and flashed his empty palms.

"Lose something?" he said, grinning.

By way of reply, Rivers silently took a stool. Momentarily the front door opened, and another man walked in. Mid-to late forties, six-two and thin, black hair, and Rivers observed that his gray Italian suit was in need of pressing. The man nodded as Younger returned behind the bar and poured a draft. This he pushed directly in front of the customer as he was settling into a chair.

"I just heard you've got fresh poppers." The man smiled, and Younger moved forward, leaning down with a whisper and nodding at the detective.

Rivers reached into his jacket, then held the photograph of Debra Patterson out in front of him, slowly turning in a circle on the bar stool, watching faces, then dropping this directly between the older twin and his customer. Snake's eyes darted nervously in their sockets as Younger rushed forward.

"So what's it gonna be, pal? Isn't it past your bedtime?" he asked, but his voice lost its edge.

Rivers' eyes were like hot pokers. "I'm not your pal," he returned flatly.

Without concern, Younger shrugged with massive shoulders. Picking up the phone beneath the counter, he walked over to a row of bottles in the corner, where he soon stood in conversation with his back turned. The men seated at the bar were avoiding eye contact, so Rivers tapped the tall newcomer on the shoulder. Leaning over, he pointed at the man's gold wedding band.

"Does she wipe your pictures when you're through?"

The thin man twisted uncomfortably on his stool, then stood and quickly fled out the back door.

Younger was holding the phone against his chest, staring at Rivers. "Hey, buddy," he said in a loud voice, "legal counsel says if you don't leave, we are well within our rights to protect our customers, and to use bodily force if necessary."

"That a fact," Rivers returned without tone.

Suddenly Snake was leaning up into his face, poking him once on the left shoulder with a fat thumb. "You should find another line of work. You're not very good at this one."

Rivers glared. "That's *my* finger."

"What the fuck?" Snake hissed. "I'm going to break your head!" Turning, he lifted a heavy black sap from behind the bar and slapped his left palm.

Rivers ignored him.

The bartender hung up the phone as two shadows approached from the rear. Younger stepped out from behind the bar with an insolent grin, a towel draped over his right hand. He stopped within a few feet, studying him closely. Rivers kept his eyes on the mirror as he rolled up the picture and placed it inside his jacket as Younger sniffed, mocking at his airspace.

Customers scurried off to the corners as two large men in soiled T-shirts flanked Rivers on either side. The smaller of the two had the battered face of a former boxer, which resembled a block of clay awaiting features.

"Does your dog bite?" Rivers asked without looking up.

"That's it, you crazy scrot. You know we can't swing first, so why don't you stop running your fucking mouth and do something?" Younger cried.

Rivers propped his elbows on the counter and eyed the three men reflected in the mirror. They were the types that would sport with a cripple. Younger dropped the towel without further ceremony, resting a broad-blade meat cleaver against his shoulder just as Snake leaned forward across the bar.

"You're gonna hurt bad," he whispered with delight. "My brother will split your fucking skull, you weird asshole!"

"Oh, you silly queen," Rivers lisped.

Younger suddenly bolted forward to protect his brother's honor, and the two men grabbed him, then restrained him as he struggled for freedom. Rivers turned casually and stood directly up into the threat.

"You got something to say to me?" Younger screamed indignantly. "You want to threaten me?"

Frank Rivers turned away slowly, easily, effortlessly.

Without another word he was gone.

33

"Wow!" Elmer Janson exclaimed, and the mask of freckles across his face drew tight. He placed an empty box of popcorn on the seat and turned to his mother.

"That *was* a good show," Jessica said. "Please throw that away."

"It was wicked!" Elmer sighed. "The way Eliot Ness saved that baby from falling down the stairs!"

"Good old Eliot." She smiled and rubbed the boy's hair. They strolled after the crowd, up through the theater doors and out into the lobby. Elmer placed his litter into the can and followed her to the windows.

Outside the tall glass entry of Bethesda Square Mall, a solid sheet of rain drove patrons back inside in a mad dash for cover as the wind howled through doors, the water spraying in machine-gun bursts, flowing through the underground parking garage. There were about a hundred people milling into a crowd, more coming in, and the giant slabs of glass started to fog from so much breathing. Elmer rubbed a circle with the flat of his hand, watching a river flow down and over a concrete gutter as Jessica turned to face the shopping mall.

In the background was the eerie calliope sound of a carousel firing up. The music started as a brassy moan, then ground into a loud symphony. Elmer's attention was focused on the stream of children headed in that direction as his mother stared back out onto the streets, knotting her brow. "We shouldn't drive in this," she said as the wind rattled against the panes.

"Svensk's Ice Cream is open," Elmer offered. "It's just past the merry-go-round."

She shook her head. "I know where it is, silly. You've already had pizza, popcorn, and soda, you'll get sick."

"No, I won't." He rolled his eyes as she stepped back from the crowd, starting to mill about anxiously as more patrons dashed through the door for the next showing. She checked her watch: 10:33.

"Come on, Red," she smiled, "are you too old to ride the carousel?"

Elmer's green eyes sparkled. "How 'bout you, Mom?"

She grabbed him by the hand and followed the music.

It was a winding concrete path with high railings, solid pastel walls in a rainbow of colors, and store windows boarded shut with plywood. They moved hand in hand, following a crush of patrons, slowly being swept up by the flow. As they approached the lobby, the music grew louder, wailing, deafening.

The hallway teemed with people, filling from the rear of the cramped corridor like a bottle. Loud voices tried to communicate above the din, and wet blasts of cold air created a wind-tunnel effect as the doors at either end opened and closed. Jessica held tightly to her son's hand, looking down into his eyes, moving in small steps, unable to see over the crush of humanity.

Without warning, the marching line came to a halt.

"Now what?" she asked, and there were shouts from the rear that carried on another cold blast of air.

"What?" Elmer cried, and she shrugged, shaking her head.

After a minute Jessica felt her legs starting to cramp at the knees. It seemed as if they had been standing forever among the teeming crowd, the combined body heat, smell and voices created an overwhelming sensory explosion that was battering to the brain. Suddenly they felt a tremor in the human wall, and then the sounds of shattering glass as the wave rocked forward with an angry power.

Two hands pushed Jessica violently in the small of her back, whipping her spine. She started to turn in confrontational fury as a heavyset man stumbled backward, crushing her left toe, and the crowd pushed forward as her hand slipped free.

"Elmer!" she cried, seeing him vanish into the crush of adults. Jessica saw his face only for a moment, growing smaller and smaller, carried down the corridor, away in the writhing madness and looking for all the world like a drowning child waving a small arm in the air.

"This is nuts!" she cried, her lungs aching from the stale air as her body was pushed again. She followed helplessly, her feet working in small steps careful not to trip. Mustering her reserves, she pressed defiantly, then winced as she took another hard punch from behind. Finally she shoved several people aside and emerged near the front of the room like a battered diver. A distressed man shook a finger into her face, but she ignored him. Grabbing the wooden railing as the carousel spun at her feet, she gulped the fresh air, searching the crowds.

Short moments later, Elmer came unseen from behind and unthinkingly slipped his hand inside hers.

Jessica jumped, crossing a hand over her heart.

"Mom, are you okay? I saved us a place."

She reached out, holding the boy's head tightly to her waist. "What happened?" she breathed.

"Someone made a mistake. All the theaters let out at the same time, and the storm brought more than they expected."

"Oh," she nodded, "it's hard to manage schedules for six whole theaters, very complicated." Elmer, in an attempt to protect his mother from the crowds, pulled her gently forward against the carousel railing. Before them, the ocean-blue carousel tent was spinning in a patterned swirl, fiery painted constellations that seemed to flame like shooting stars as lightning crackled outside and pulsed through the tall windows.

At that moment a strange thing happened to Jessica Janson. When she looked up, she did not see a childlike playfulness in the wooden menagerie, but rather a menacing parade of trapped animals that filled her with horror. The lightning fired like strobes; with every burst creatures were frozen in silent agony, their painted eyes stretched with terror, muzzles carved into a white lather, their witless strides futile against spines impaled on shiny brass poles. She shuddered as they twisted without mercy at her feet, the tearing painted eyes begging her for help.

"Fatigue?" she thought to herself. "A touch of claustrophobia?" She touched her brow lightly for the fever she suspected, but found none.

"Good lion," Elmer smiled.

The machinery rattled and slowed, the race grinding to a

tilted rumble. As the calliope released a mournful, sleepy sound, a man in a red barker's suit quickly moved the line forward, holding back the overeager, placing his arm at chest level, counting saddles, lifting his arm again.

Elmer scrambled forward, and his mother strolled to a giant rabbit, grabbed him by the ears, and swung herself into position. The uniformed man circled the platform, threw a lever, and the music started up.

Once, twice, again the carousel spun, gaining speed. Jessica whirled with painted constellations, feeling her world spinning through time until the faces around her became a blur and the frozen kingdom snapped into a sharp focus.

Just then she felt a hundred adult eyes.

With everything that was woman, Jessica Janson sensed these eyes undressing her, slithering across her flesh. She felt naked, cold to the bone, and she leaned forward onto the cottontail's ears to partially conceal her splendid shape.

"What's wrong with me?" she thought as the giant rabbits went leaping, as the wolves snapped in pursuit, as the sound of a child crying in the distance tugged at her heart, then turned into a vicious snarl that chilled her blood to ice.

"I'm cracking up. . . ."

"Boy, that woman over there is a fox!"

"Ooo, would I love to make it with her!"

Two young men followed the rabbit with admiring eyes before remembering their roles and waving cheerily to their wives and children. Their exchange had been overheard, though, by an older woman who stood rooted behind, her presence noticed by none. She was alone, but more than that, she was lonely.

She pushed back into the thinning crowd, unwittingly shielding her face with one hand, as if the sun were bright and her skin flawed. Having studied Jessica Janson's graceful and ample form, her long legs straddling the bobbing creature, chest tauntingly thrust forward, blond hair falling downward like a shiny cascade, the woman had become self-conscious beyond fault.

She was seething with envy, nearly nauseous with self-pity, and was wandering aimlessly through the mall when she was grabbed forcefully by the arm.

"Oh, my!" she said.

"Oh, my, yourself, Irma, let's go."

"Jeff, do you think she's pretty?" she tried to whisper, following his anxious pace, her face tied into a knot.

Dorn's voice held an edge that could cut. "That will make your job a whole lot easier," he said. "I saw the way you pushed her, Irma, hitting her like that in the spine."

He imitated her aggressive display by ramming the glass doors with the heel of his palm; they shook violently as the couple walked out into the underground parking garage.

Dorn shook his head. "That all looked very personal to me," he criticized.

"Oh, sweetheart," she said, wrapping an arm around his waist, "you said you like it when I'm spunky!"

34

Three hours earlier Jeffrey Dorn had arrived home, having spent his day on the line. He loved the intimate voices, the emotional twitterings, the graphic displays of human behavior in all of its forms, and he almost hated to leave the unanswered riddles behind. The sorry truth was that he had to, forcing himself, for the conversation between Jessica and Elmer Janson disturbed him, the way they toyed and teased each other, flooding him with memories, filling him with regret.

He knew that his own childhood had deadened his core to wood. Zak Dorani was not a stupid man. Once he had known human warmth, and it frustrated him when he tried to remember that.

"Laugh for Mommy?" he huffed aimlessly, sitting in his car inside the garage. Never, he recalled, could he feel that natural joy swelling inside him, as it once had, he was sure it was so.

It was time that beat him. Time. Beating him down into a mannequin man, his face moving with conscious efforts only, muscles tugging into an alien mask.

I cannot feel, you cannot feel . . .

Large woman, tall woman, hands like a club.

Red teeth in a shattered mirror.

You will laugh for Mommy now that Daddy is gone.

"Jeff, sweetheart, is that you?"

Dorn winced at the sound as images collided. Back to the business at hand. The blonde was a slut, he hated the boy, the dog must be killed.

Crying is a waste of water.

He made a mental note to look up Tony's Pizza in the Yellow Pages, not that it mattered, but it would be nice knowing where the Jansons ate regularly, since from the tone of conversation, he knew it was a routine. Jeffrey Dorn thrived on routine. It was the stuff of life. He preyed on predictability.

Jessica Janson spoke with her mother every Saturday night, just like clockwork, and Dorn had been enjoying that. He was planning on using little snippets of their most personal conversations on her, but that would come later in the evening. As he strolled across the bare concrete floor toward the kitchen, he stopped to eye a thin metal rod leaning in the corner. He used it for various purposes, like killing spiders on the ceiling.

Then he heard her coming, for certain this time, and he lifted the metal shaft, fingering it thoughtfully, examining its hard straight edge, wanting to bring it inside and beat her without mercy until nothing was left. A fleshy, broken, silent sack.

"Oh, honey," Irma cried, opening the door, and Dorn winced visibly at the sound.

"Is that you?" he replied mockingly. Who else would come for her? Not even a traveling freak show.

"Hi, sweetheart," she mewed, and he dropped the shaft and his equipment bag, which landed with a sharp knock. Dorn was stone to the form that had appeared, mousy hair combed back and tied with red silk, gray eyes thick with makeup, rouge slapped across thin cheeks: a walking corpse. She hovered in a transparent negligee, edging closer as he came into the kitchen, the folds from her midsection crazed for a belt to lean against.

He swallowed hard. "Leave me alone, Irma," he snapped as he turned to the sink and began washing his hands. He wanted to turn off the lights, avoid the sickening sight of the woman's aging body.

"Oh, sweetheart." She pressed closer, the harsh light revealing a flat plate of skin where cleavage should be. Dorn quickly glanced into the sink as Irma embraced him from behind with pale arms and the heavy smell of lilac perfume.

"Your office called, Marcy Newman has explained everything. I'm so sorry, Jeff. It's been a bad day, hasn't it?"

Dorn quickly tried to figure out what lies the lobbyist bitch had contrived, overstepping her bounds. What could Irma possibly be sorry about? Perish the thought.

"Come, come sit down," she sighed, taking him by the arm and leading him into the living room, where he plopped into his chair, unable to talk, unable to think, still clutching a dish towel and drying his face. The woman was about to flap at him again, when Dorn could stand it no longer. Reaching up, he grabbed Irma by the arm and twisted it.

"Water!" he cried, pulling her face down to his, then pushing her away forcefully. He wasn't sure why, he needed time to think, and water was the first thing that came to mind. With a nervous blink Irma raced for the kitchen, feeling alive, excited by the manly order that Dorn had just issued, excited further by her own desires and the demands she knew he was capable of making.

Masculine demands. Ordering a woman to use her charms for a purely selfish and uncontrollable end, and as she poured a cold glass, she steadied herself, preparing to do her duty. But when she returned, he was staring off into space, his teeth set with pain, his eyes unfocused.

She lifted his right hand by the wrist and delivered the glass. Watching his fingers close around it, she cooed, "Oh, honey, it really has been a bad one, hasn't it? Does your back hurt?"

She was breathing hard, pressing her stubby body closer against the padded arm. "I've held your dinner, ground veal just the way you like it. Let me heat it for you?"

Dorn imagined the slop, like a road kill thrashed in a blender. The woman's cooking was like her appearance, heavy, comic, and tasteless. He was about to politely decline the invitation when he felt fingers walking across his neck.

"Let me rub your back for you?"

Instantly Dorn heard his own voice blow through the room as if another had spoken: "Why don't you just die, you miserable cunt?"

The words hit Irma like a club.

"Oh, my!" she exclaimed pensively. "That's not good, is it?"

"What?" Dorn's head twisted on its stalk, the dark eyes glinted slyly.

"Jeff, why are you upset with me?"

The pupils glared with a cruel intelligence shining in the half-light. "Will you be a good wife to me, Irma?" he said, carefully snipping off each word with his teeth as he watched the woman's knees tremble into a kind of putty.

She couldn't believe her ears, was he proposing?

"Oh, Jeff!" she swooned, the breath driven from her body. She locked her arms around his head, pulling his face to her chest.

"Answer the question!" he demanded, pushing her back, then reaching out with both hands and pinching the nipples on each small breast with his thumb. The woman's body quivered.

"Oh, yes, yes, yes," she mewed. "I will, Jeff, I promise, I will be the best wife—"

He pinched harder. "Did you get my note?" he hissed.

She nodded, a nervous smile twitching at the corners of her mouth.

"Well?"

Irma Kiernan all but flew to her bedroom. Thumping back down the stairs again, she rushed to his side and offered up a small red velvet pillow with both hands.

Dorn refused to look. "Put it on!" he demanded.

With reverence Irma lifted the multicolor ribbon, tossing the pillow aside, then carefully draped it around his neck as Dorn tilted his head back proudly.

Just below his throat, the Legion of Merit shone in glory, polished white, gleaming with distinction. The woman stood back, anxiously awaiting his approval.

"It's a beautiful job," he said finally, fingering the medallion and forcing a smile. He opened his arms, offering an embrace, and she rushed forward, burying her face in his chest, feeling the coolness of the metal against her cheek.

"Irma," he said quietly, closing his eyes, hugging her, "there's something you must do for me."

He made his demands, holding back nothing, just shading the truth the way he liked it.

To Jeffrey Dorn, truth was a simple thing. There was reality, of course, but above all, there was what he wanted to believe, what he wanted to make true.

"And you must help me attend to her," he said, finishing. He held the woman at arm's length, feeling her body shake, watching her gray eyes glaze over.

She was breathing hard, struggling with his hold. "But, Jeff," she cried, "the last time, they were all found dead!" And she began to sob.

"That was not my fault!" he screamed with indignant rage.

Irma dropped to her knees in tears, crying quietly. Eyeing her neutrally, Dorn recalled the expression on Diana Clayton's face as her bathroom door swung open. What was it, a startled, waking expression? Certainly not surprise, more like shock, and her face changed again and again, recognition or realization, and at the end . . . He shrugged, he couldn't be sure really.

"Jeff," Irma sighed, "you're sure someone killed them after you left?"

Dorn grabbed two fistfuls of her hair and pulled. "What? I told you! Clayton killed her own children, then shot herself while relaxing in her tub. You don't listen to me, Irma. I've changed my mind about us!"

With that he stood and stormed away down the stairs, leaving behind a pathetic puddle of humanity that sobbed into the empty chair. "But what about being married?" she cried after him.

Dorn gave her time.

Right to the minute, time was something that he knew how to give.

By 7:29 P.M. on that Saturday night, there were no more tears left in the Kiernan household. Jeffrey Dorn would not speak with Irma other than to say he was packing. In truth, he was preparing to receive guests. And planning. And reflecting.

This widowed blonde was trash, he could see that, even her voice was cold and harsh. Since her telephone calls were an open book, he knew this to be true, and he found everything about her too assertive, too demanding.

If there was one thing he couldn't tolerate about career women, it was their sense of self-importance, their egocentric appraisal of self-worth. Marcy Newman came quickly to mind, she was classic, overstepping at any little opportunity, a simple call to appease Irma became complicated. Dorn wanted all of the working bitches to be where they belonged, serving a daddy or walking the goddamned streets looking for one.

"Jeff, sweetheart, are you there?" A voice floated down the stairs, and Dorn casually sealed the shelter. Checking his watch, he laid out a change of clothes, which he planned on returning for. A heavy rain was predicted, so he made a note to place his umbrella in the car.

"Honey," she cried. "Oh, sweetheart, please answer me . . ."

With his head hung, working his features into what he knew as sadness, Dorn walked slowly up the stairs. He embraced the woman, then caressed her gently.

She started to speak, but Dorn held a finger to her lips. In silence he kneaded her back with both hands, her neck and breasts, then began on the inside of her thighs until her body shuddered and her legs seemed no longer able to support her weight.

"You're beautiful," he said, smiling.

"Can we sit?"

With a clinical eye Dorn watched her pass into another world with her excitement. Walking her back to the chair, he sat first, then grabbed Irma around the waist and pulled her to him. She was so willing, her entire face seemed to be coming unstuck, and he looked away.

"You will please me, Irma," he said in a husky, demanding voice. "You will be a good wife!"

She nodded bashfully as Dorn dropped the garment from her torso. She quickly stepped out and kicked it aside. He brought Irma to her knees, directly between his legs. "Pull your hair back," he demanded, and she did just that, holding it with her left hand as Dorn opened his trousers.

"Listen to me," he said quietly, and he could hear her heavy, labored breathing.

"Today I was on a mission of mercy. You saw my telephone gear in the kitchen, yet you said nothing."

"Yes," she breathed, "yes, I did."

"Well," he cleared his throat, "the woman I'm speaking of is evil. I've heard her telephone calls, she is selling her child for immoral purposes. I am the only one who knows this, hence the only one who can save them. Would you have me just turn my back? Is that the kind of husband you want?"

Champion was the word on her lips, yet before she could answer, Dorn grabbed hold and was pulling her forward as Irma lost control. It was only then that he began to really work on her, caressing her, manipulating every inch of her frame, leaning over, then finally placing his hands beneath her bare buttocks. He helped to lift her as she gave a breathless little hop, her fingers reaching down and guiding him into herself.

As Dorn gave a wild thrust, Irma felt fire pass between her thighs. She gasped. She shut her eyes and whined gently, closing arms and legs around him, lost in rapture. Every thrust brought with it unbelievable pleasure until she fairly screamed and collapsed forward into his arms.

It was over that quickly, so he did it again, wondering why people didn't jog and produce an honest sweat. He felt sticky and didn't care for it.

"You will be a good and lasting wife," he commanded as the woman caught her breath, gasping for air. He lit a cigarette. "Gain their trust. Once this is done, you are free to leave. It shouldn't take long . . ."

Although what he was saying was clear enough, there was no verbal response, and if Dorn had not made a study of this particular woman, he would have sworn that she was stone deaf.

"Just love me," she breathed, sweat dripping from her chin. "I couldn't bear to lose you." She started to sob again as Dorn lifted her chin with two fingers.

"Tears of joy, I hope?"

"Oh, Jeff," she cried, "I do love you!"

Before going off to take a shower, preparing for the show, Jeffrey Dorn drew more promises than he needed, all the while giving Irma several good rides on his chair.

He used mirrors to finally ejaculate.

He made passionate love to his own image.

By 10:48, as was the plan, they were working on the ground level of the mall's covered parking garage, in a premier spot near the stairs. Irma's job was to wave off troublemaking motorists who mistook their very presence as potentially available space to horn in on.

"Irma Dorn," she cooed, "it has a nice ring."

Her statement did not break Jeff's concentration as he opened the passenger door of what he called the Irmamobile, a 1978 Ford Maverick that was simply the zenith of automotive ugly. The color was a nondescript pale green, a hatchback with black vinyl interior, two doors, and plain bench seats. The heavy body was badly chipped and bruised, with dark horizontal streaks where the side molding had been torn away. Dorn also liked to say that it was a "previously owned" vehicle, having bought the car at government auction, but the truth was that neither one of them liked to park it in their driveway for very long. It was an eyesore. Irma had been saving her kitchen money to have it painted, but Dorn insisted it wasn't worth the effort.

"After this, can we trade it in?" she asked, standing in the open door.

"Beauty's in the eye of the beholder," he said, trying to be amiable as he lifted a socket wrench from his toolbox. This in hand, he swung his small body into the passenger seat and proceeded to pull at the seat belt's anchoring plate, which was mounted against the transmission hump.

"Well, I know that, honey, but it's an embarrassment for me to drive to work. I'll buy us a car as a wedding gift."

Dorn ignored the comment as a middle-aged couple wandered out from the mall and into the garage, glancing at their position near the stairwell, summing them up. The structure was a covered five stories, two down, three up, and by early evening it was already full. The man seemed to be having some difficulty remembering the color code for his garage level, and was now moving away, following his wife in the other direction.

It took Dorn but a minute, the ratchet spinning at the single bolt head, and the entire seat-belt assembly came free in his hand. He removed a replacement from a cardboard packing box, then tightened this down into place.

"We can't afford it," he said tonelessly, rising to his feet and pulling the passenger seat forward. With his left hand he felt along the back, along the outside seam, searching for a chrome release plate and latch whose only purpose was to allow the seat to come forward, enabling riders to duck into the rear.

"I've saved some money, Jeff."

It was attached by two machine screws, and without ceremony he quickly removed it, leaving an empty hole in the black vinyl. With a few turns of a wrench, the Maverick was transformed into a rolling house of horrors for anyone who stepped inside the pale green trap.

Anyone, that is, except Jeff Dorn or Irma Kiernan.

"Oh, honey," she asked nervously, standing over him, "are you sure this will work? It just seems so easy."

Dorn was lifting his tools from the pavement and carrying them to the trunk. "Always keep it simple," he mumbled, "life's complicated enough." He lifted a roll of duct tape, snipped off a large piece, then made a sticky loop.

"It's just that—"

"Irma!"

"But last time they were teenagers, this one thinks she's awful damn smart." She was about to speak again when Dorn's hostile glare held her off.

With practiced skill he slithered onto the rear seat, grabbing this at the bottom, then slapping once with his palm. He lifted it off its mount, and the trunk immediately filled with a wash of bright fluorescent light from overhead; the cardboard partition between the trunk and cabin had been sliced in half and discarded, leaving a hole about the size of a window.

Dorn poked his head up through the trunk and watched as a family of four trotted from the sidewalk into the underground parking area, their clothes soaked and their faces dripping. They passed the Maverick without noticing it.

"The goddamn tape?"

Irma spotted the loop attached to the paint over the door. She quickly complied, then watched with admiring eyes as Dorn applied this to the top of the back rest. Pushing down gently, he dropped the seat back into place.

Dorn wiggled out of the car, a strange light dancing in his eyes. "You have a friend in Pennsylvania," he said.

"I know, sweetheart."

She watched as he covered the Maryland license plates with dark blue replacements from the Keystone State. The backs had flexible magnetic strips that allowed them to just slap into place.

"Are you sure their car will stop?" she asked quietly.

Ignoring her, Dorn strolled past the rear bumper and closed the trunk with a *thud*. "Get in," he said.

Jessica and Elmer Janson were finishing double scoops of ice cream, sitting in a window booth at Svensk's Parlor on the other side of the mall.

"You certainly went quiet all of a sudden," she said, watching the ice cream disappear.

"Sorry, Mom, how's your fudge?"

"Great, and your butterscotch?"

"Fine."

"Elmer, you don't have to talk if you don't want to."

"I'm okay."

"I'll give you a penny?"

Elmer sat back in his seat, digging into the last scoop in his bowl, watching other families waiting in line to be seated.

Jessica saw this and leaned back over. "So what do you think?"

"Mom," he asked quietly, "did you and Dad ever go looking for buried treasure?"

"Why do you ask?"

"Well, his metal detector and all. It had been used, there was dirt all over it when I found it in the basement. When I was little, Dad said he was going to take me exploring . . ." His voice trailed off sadly.

"Oh, Red," she sighed, "is that why you went to play at the bowling alley?"

The boy hung his head.

"Elmer, your daddy wasn't looking for anything in particular. He was just interested in the past, he was a history buff." She leaned forward across the table and touched him lightly on the arm. "Most writers are, that was just a hobby of his." She forced a smile as she stroked his hair. "Let's talk about something else, something happy. I don't want you playing with that thing anymore."

He nodded, staring down into his bowl.

"Elmer, would you like it if Gram stayed with us for your birthday? She could come for a week."

"Sure," the boy shrugged, "but I'm not taking music lessons."

She smiled, growing a bit annoyed. "Oh, you're not, huh? And what makes you think Gram's planning something like that?"

Elmer's eyes danced lightly over her and returned to his bowl.

"You mean we're that transparent?"

He shook his head. "You two talk about it all the time."

"Oh, but you have no interest in music?"

"I want to be like Dad."

"Elmer, your daddy played the guitar. Wouldn't you like to learn something like that? A well-rounded person should be able to appreciate music and play an instrument."

He shrugged.

"You're not crazy about it, be honest?"

"When I'm not at school, I'd rather just be roaching around with Tripod."

Jessica cringed and leaned forward. "Stop using that term, it's very unpleasant."

"Sorry." He stirred the last bit at the bottom of the bowl into a cold soup. "Mom, did Dad leave me anything—I mean adult things that I can have?"

"Yes," she said confidently, "yes, he did, I'll give you something when we get home."

"I mean grown-up things," he said in a frustrated tone. "Chet Morgan's father has a gun!"

Jessica closed her eyes with a frown and thought it over. "Finish your ice cream. Guns are *not* toys, and you aren't going to play with them."

"Did he?"

She nodded, holding up her right hand. "Truth?" she said. Elmer's eyes grew wide. "Truth!" he agreed.

"Your daddy had several guns, including a pistol your grandfather got in Germany, and these are yours." She swallowed hard, not knowing why she had said it, why this was important, truly unable to understand the male fascination with instruments of destruction. To her the world, though not without its troubles, did not need any more weapons or wars or killing, and she felt like shouting with frustration as Elmer's voice flowed with a newfound joy.

"Can I see them?"

"Someday, they're locked away at the bank. But, Elmer"— the boy had forgotten about ice cream and she quickly reached across the table, pinching his arm—"you don't get one until you're eighteen. That's the way he would have wanted it." She quickly made a mental note to call Chet Morgan's father as the pent-up breath spilled from Elmer's lungs.

"Thanks, Mom," he sighed, and the wind drove a spatter of rain hammering against the window. They could clearly see the street outside: it was a glassy ribbon of flooded blacktop, cars were creeping through the downpour, although the lightning had stopped.

"It doesn't seem to be letting up," she said, checking the bill and pulling her wallet from her purse. She counted out the exact change, right to the dime, laying this beneath the napkin holder.

"Drink some water," she suggested. "And for Pete's sake, Elmer, wipe your mouth."

Elmer smiled broadly. "Who was Pete? First Pete that comes to mind," he cautioned.

The two launched into a trivia contest of free association they had played since the boy could remember. Anyone dropping an unexplained name or place had but one chance to explain, then face a new challenge.

Jessica frowned, straightening her shirt as she stood, then extending her hand. "Pan," she nodded proudly. "I meant good old Peter Pan."

"Then what did he use to stick his shadow back on?"

The young mother feigned deep thought, leading him slowly from the booth, then out into the mall.

"Just a moment," she begged, "I'm still working on it!" And she gave him a quick little tickle in the ribs.

Irma smiled. It was an answer she liked very much. The blonde's car would stop on command in the pouring rain, and she imagined her drenched like a sorry beggar, asking kindness of any passing stranger.

Dorn's eyes rolled as he talked. "They really have no choice, it will be over in fifteen minutes, and when their car heats up, the antifreeze will blow like Mount St. Helens. It will be spraying directly into the fan, so it should be quite a show."

Jessica Janson drove a 1986 white Oldsmobile Cutlass powered by a six-cylinder 3.8-liter engine with a two-gallon cooling system, and Dorn had made a precision hole in her lower radiator hose, boring through the top so that fluid would not leak out and stain the pavement which would attract attention. Having practiced on trial cars and then followed them during the daytime, he knew with some certainty the maximum distance her car would be able to travel. To Irma it was mysteriously complicated and wonderful, a quick jab with what looked like a sharpened ice pick.

"And they'll be where?"

"Stuck near that salt lick on Little Falls Parkway."

"You mean that storage area where the mounds of sand are?"

He was staring out his rear mirror, watching people leaving the mall for their cars. "It's for snow emergency, absolutely the darkest spot along the parkway, and the county reduces patrols to the hour on weekends."

Irma smiled. "And she thinks *she's* so smart . . ."

Dorn watched pedestrians passing by.

". . . she just doesn't know us!"

Swinging his head, he noticed Irma's heavily made-up eyelids. The humid air had produced blue cracks under each eye, and the rouge looked like dollops of meat. "She'll know both of us soon enough," he said flatly. "Just get it right."

Irma was about to speak, cheer building in her voice, when he grabbed her by the arm, shutting down her response.

Son in tow, Jessica Janson was strolling toward them, walking with an athletic grace, speaking to Elmer as she passed through the stairwell's open door. "Gram means well," her voice echoed.

"I know, Mom. If it's that important to her, you know I'll do it."

35

It was nearing eleven o'clock when, because the pounding rain had choked back customers, the brothers Dix decided to lock up early. They turned off lights, closed the Zephyr's blinds. They were talking as they came down the hallway toward the kitchen, passing the bathroom where the dogs had located Debra Patterson's scent. "I still think we should stay open," Snake complained. "Having only one long night a week is starting to cost us."

"Most of our regulars are family types, home by ten, look at the weather. Besides, we're rich."

"Well, extend the hours, we can get richer."

They passed into the kitchen, pushing the spring-loaded door open, not looking back as they talked, too absorbed with each other to notice the figure sitting in the corner. He held the door to the wall and was now blocking any retreat.

"Damn," said Younger, "did you get the front light?"

"Is the pope Catholic?"

"Pour me a drink, I'll count up."

Snake nodded. "I should have busted his nuts."

Younger was half-attentive as he removed a gray metal box from beneath a floating-island chopping block. "If you mean that retarded cop, it would of kept us in court for a week. That's down time, and no one to pay for our trouble."

"What's wrong with America?" Snake agreed.

"People don't know their place, harassing a family-run business. If we sued him we'd end up with some shitty little house on the tracks and a used car. You know, the score looks very good tonight."

The pornography business was translating into thick stacks as Snake looked on, not bothering to count, for twins have an understanding of trust that's tied in the womb. "Seven thousand so far, and I'm still going." Smiling, Younger took a shot of bourbon. He then made notations on a sheet of paper as Snake placed another pile of dirty bills onto the table.

Younger lifted his glass in salute. "To the new supply," he said. "Quality is our middle name."

Snake beamed and was about to toast when a soft cry blew through the room, sounding like an alley cat complaining into a gust of wind.

They looked at each other, then leapt into action. Snake grabbed a meat cleaver as Younger leaned over and lifted a large automatic pistol that lay under the island. He immediately steadied his aim at the hallway, ducking behind the wooden block.

The door slowly shut, revealing a human figure seated in the darkness of the farthest corner. The two men shielded their bodies, staring slack-jawed at the figure holding white-gloved hands into the air in a sign of absolute surrender.

"I'm going to cut you good!" Snake cried, turning to his brother. "Shoot him!" he ordered Younger. "Shoot the sonofabitch!"

But Younger was too confused by what he saw.

It was a scarecrow. A human scarecrow. His head was a square burlap sack with a triangle cut where a nose protruded, and the bulbous flesh stuck out a bright and seamy lipstick red. The eyes were long horizontal slits that resembled black slashes. The sack itself had once been splattered with house paints, green, red, blue, and gathered at the throat with a silk tie was an ugly orange burst with a pattern of gold metallic swirls. In spite of the knot around his throat, the scarecrow had no chin, but a neck that looked like a rotting tree stump.

Snake noticed a small rectangle at the mouth, and behind this opening were inky black lips. The image was slow to register.

"Hey," he screamed suddenly, pointing his blade. "That's my best tie!"

Gun in hand, Younger was finding his nerve. "He must be a goddamned psycho!"

The scarecrow smiled, the seams of his burlap sack suddenly pulling tight around his grinning head, when it occurred to the twins that he had yet to speak.

"Hey!" Snake took a small step forward, slamming the heavy blade into the hardwood with a deadly thump. "We're talking to you, asshole!"

The scarecrow scratched the back of his head, then peeled a piece of paint off a burlap cheek and dropped it onto the floor.

"He's wearing gloves," Younger said quietly. "Is he surrendering? What's he up to?"

Snake tapped his temple. "The asshole thought he was gonna rob us!" he laughed as Younger smiled sarcastically.

"Is this a stickup, do you have a gun?" He aimed his weapon casually into the corner. "Bang! Bang!" he cried, then turned to his brother with a grin of achievement.

Gently, hands in the air, Frank Rivers stood, his eyes darting between the two men, little blue flashes, the gaiety quickly dying. In that moment Younger wondered if his single-action .45 had a bullet in the chamber, and he tipped off this worry by looking down. Still he kept the gun aimed with deadly precision.

No one moved.

Younger was watching in disbelief just as Rivers came forward and placed himself close enough to smell their sweat. Biting off each word distinctly so there would be no room for further doubt in their filthy little minds, he said:

"Fuck you."

Snake started forward as in one clean movement Younger cocked his gun and went to pull the trigger.

Time stopped.

With an incredible swiftness, form became fluid as Rivers' entire body flew through air, a jagged flash roaring from the gun in his right hand, his left hand breaking his fall—the room filled with the deafening crack of this blast.

Snake caught only a glimpse as his brother's head seemed to explode in a thick red mist; his forehead burst like a bad sprinkler, releasing a bloody spray, turning his face into a horrid red mask as the gun flew from his hand.

Younger's lips parted and moved as his legs buckled, his body dropping backward through space, and before it had hit,

Snake caught a flash of movement: coming down through the air with lightning speed, a solid white streak sliced through spaces above and delivered a thump against wood that felt hot against his hand, painful as the blue lick of a cutting torch.

Younger was just hitting the floor as Snake screamed with agony. Frozen with fear, Snake was; frozen with pain.

As the room went still he looked down in disbelief at a human thumb twitching hideously on the block, kicking like a frog's severed leg. Snake stared at it, eyes wide, as if this slug of human flesh were someone else's thumb, and not his, as if his hand were not the screaming bundle of severed nerves that burned murderous fury as it pumped slick juices onto the floor.

The man screamed again.

The human Snake bellowed like a wild boar, cursing through a face that seethed and foamed with hurt and venom. "You killed my brother!" he cried, staring in disbelief at a kitchen that resembled a dirty slaughterhouse.

"You killed my brother . . ." and his voice trailed into witless agony as he slumped to his knees, only to find himself staring up into the portrait of Debra Patterson.

His body shook like a wet dog.

"It will go numb," the voice said flatly. "Show some dignity, for Christ's sake."

Snake was no longer a twin.

This realization forced him to vomit until he could no longer respond physically. According to his account, Debra Patterson had been at the bar, on the previous night. She had left the Zephyr alive. Her car had been parked when the brothers locked up and left for home.

The reason Snake remembered all this was that the top was down and the night was warm, so they had checked to see if sexual acts were being performed in the backseat, but it was empty.

Rivers wanted to be sure. He lifted the meat cleaver from the block and cleaned the edge on the man's shirt.

"God, no!" he moaned. "I didn't do anything to her, I swear. I was just serving her drinks!"

"And you're sure she walked out of here of her own free will?"

"I swear it!" he cried. "She left with those two other girls!"

Rivers nodded thoughtfully. "And where does the kiddy porn come from?"

"We're only distributors, we don't make it, I swear we don't do the work!"

"Names, give me names and addresses."

And Rivers observed that Snake was nothing like his reputation. Once befriended, he was an agreeable sort. "Eager to please" was the best way to describe him.

Just as Snake had exhausted his knowledge, a horrible moan filled the kitchen. "Ooo . . ." the sound echoed. "Ooo . . ."

As the groan registered in Snake's mind, his marble eyes bulged from their sockets. Rivers strode across the room.

"Maa . . ."

Snake stared up at his attacker, then stared at the body scurrying over. His stump released a trickle of fluid which he smeared with his knees.

"Rigor's setting in," Rivers explained, "the body grows stiff, driving air from the lungs."

"Ooo . . ." came the sound as Younger's lungs filled and emptied.

"Ooo . . ."

"Damn me for a mutt," Rivers said, scratching his face, for the burlap was starting to itch.

"He's breathing!" Snake rattled excitedly. "Do something! Quick, do something!"

"Me?" Rivers chuckled, pointing a finger at his own chest. "No, I don't think I will."

"But he's not dead."

Bending at the waist, Rivers reached down to Younger's forehead, down to where the darkest splotch of blood revealed a wound channel about three inches wide, splitting flesh and showing a splinter of bone. The gloved fingers did some digging and scratching before he plucked out a bloody slug and stood. He dropped the crimson wad at Snake, who caught it with his good hand.

"What is it?" he asked with confused horror.

"Paraffin."

Snake was trembling again. "But you shot . . ."

Rivers shook his head slowly. "You said you wanted to play trick or treat, and that's the best I could do on short notice. Next time I'll do some planning."

"A game?" Snake hissed. "This is a game to you?"

"No, I've seen people die from a wax bullet. Looks like

this one snipped an artery, maybe even busted his skull. Must really hurt."

"But he could have shot you."

"I looked down the muzzle: nothing but air in an empty pipe." He leaned over and picked up the .45, then confidently pulled back the slide. A menacing lead cartridge flipped out, spinning to the floor and coming to rest against the body. Both men felt the shock.

Rivers shrugged at the loaded gun. "I would have dropped him anyway."

"Moo . . . Maa . . ." the moaning returned, and Snake's face went to paste as he watched the scarecrow stroll back to the block and pick up a slug of flesh. Twirling the severed thumb, Rivers tossed it into the air, caught it, tossed some more.

"Call 911, they'll save your brother."

"But a surgeon could also save my thumb!" Snake cried after him as Rivers walked through the door, the moaning twin's mouth popping open like a landed fish.

"Ooo . . . than . . . Maa . . ." like a braying lamb.

Rivers left with that pitiful sound on his mind. "Maa . . . ma?" he repeated, shaking his head in disbelief, wondering if he could believe his own ears. He was quite sure the human sleaze was calling for his mother.

As he stepped into his cruiser, he tossed a human finger into the brush, dropping his stained gloves where they could easily be seen by customers. He settled into his seat, turning the radio to the established frequency, wondering if he should call Jon Patterson about his daughter. The news was promising. Rivers now suspected that they were dealing with a runaway, for according to Snake, there were three girls together that evening, and they had been discussing pregnancy.

As he held the portrait in hand, his mind leapt forward to balance other responsibilities, organizing tomorrow's MAIT team, yet finding time to work with this family. He was starting to pull through the alley as Mule Murphy's voice tore from the radio car, cracking against his soul like an icy whip.

"Base, this is Huskies," he said flatly. "The situation here is Red. Repeat. Code Red."

He had been the officer to establish the scale of colors.

Red was an abduction in progress.

Even with a fireball and siren he was forty minutes away.

36

Afraid of being seen, Scott stepped up from the curb and stood in shadow, motionless, unaffected by the downpour. He blinked once against the water rolling down his cheeks as he studied the red brick house. Finally he pulled his collar up against the wind.

A car approached, speeding down the glassy street, high beams glancing off his worn raincoat, then vanishing into a bland suburban maze. He walked on, pulling a felt fedora low to shield his eyes.

With the streetlight glowing at his back, he walked up the flagstone walk until darkness absorbed him. Rain streamed from his chin, and he stopped to listen, closing his eyes, but there was only the night coming to greet him: rain gutters beating like hollow, rolling drums, the wind rattling against wooden shutters. Abruptly his shoulders fell slack, rounding into age and tiredness.

Scott was hesitant. It had now been nine days since they were killed. He eyed the tall oaks ascending with their branches, green leaves licking toward the windows on the second floor. On the front lawn leaves once raked into neat piles were being pushed by stroking swirls of wind, catching in hedges once squared with perfection. Reaching the front stoop, he peered down into the driveway to where branches were felled among soggy newspapers.

These were rolled and banded, their headlines crumbling pronouncements important to none, and his eyes fell farther, picking up an approaching car on the street below. There was a thunderous hiss as the treads pushed through rain, the headlights sweeping into the neighborhood as if nothing but the present mattered. He started forward in the doorway as a cold wind rapped his teeth.

He stopped.

He stooped low onto one knee, inspecting an empty terracotta bowl filled with rich black soil. Alongside it, in the shadows, he found a small trowel and glove.

Carefully he picked this up, admiring the slender green-

and-white fingers. Although he knew better, in his heart he felt like a stranger violating Diana Clayton's world, disturbing the recumbent solitudes of her former life, peering into private corners meant only for her.

Scott was testing the door when he noticed a dried crust of mud gleaming against the stoop's concrete seam. He picked this up and examined it. A sliver of earth, round like a toe, curved with tiny indentations, it came from the shoe of a girl he remembered with some clarity, though he had never known her: the impish grin, the wide eyes, standing in the doorway with her mother.

"Kimberly," Scott said aloud, rubbing the dirt into dust between his fingers.

He released a long, troubled sigh. Then, peering down, he took up this glove like a child's hand and applied the key.

He removed a penlight from his pocket and flicked it on, the tiny beam surveying the hallway and living room. He took a step forward and the foundation groaned as the walls closed around the house like an old blanket, still soaked with the smells of the living, casting out messages from every corner.

Scott paused, lowering his head. That was the truth about a dead house, he thought.

The living, breathing truth that you did not find in books or carry away from darkened theaters that popularize homes of atrocity. Such places live with a silent language that begins at the moment of death, and the horror kisses your heart with its hooks, and once it does, it never lets you go.

"I am the killer," he closed his eyes to say. "His skin is my body."

Old enemy. Old friend.

He glanced up at the ceiling, imagining faces relaxed into sleep, chasing childish dreams. A smile. A half-closed fist. A sigh as the room again filled with light, dancing across walls, as a car went passing into shadow.

As he neared the kitchen, the sharp odor of cedar chips reached him. "What do you know?" Scott asked. "Killing time? Am I waiting, or have I planned all of this?" And he stopped, breathing deeply, wetting his lips with his tongue. "Tofu," he said softly, "thousands of warm, wet kisses."

He swept the kitchen table with his beam. A round water stain glinted where wax had been applied. He stroked this with a gloved hand. Toasted bread crumbs mounted like a thin line of ash, small chips of bacon clung like grains of sand.

Something else, what was it?

The beam worked into corners, turning up a bead of jewelry, a penny, a small strip of blue satin ribbon. Scott sat down on the linoleum floor, looking up and under the table. Tofu's blood had puddled, smearing a wooden leg.

Standing, he moved toward the sink as an image flashed into his mind: trusting eyes and a brooding *drip, drip, drip.* Suddenly a telephone was ringing, clanging, crying, the chambers of Scott's heart nearly bursting.

He staggered forward, bracing himself on the counter where a red light suddenly snapped on beneath a white telephone with its message pad and pen at the ready.

"Hi . . . this is Diana. . . . I'm Kimberly. . . . This is Leslie."

He held his breath as the adult voice returned.

". . . the girls and I are unable to answer at this time, but we thank you for calling, please leave a message." It ended with an electronic beep, followed by a blasting dial tone.

Sharp. Biting. Endless.

Scott's lids fell shut, tightly. Shut. And he wished that he had not heard the voices, though his eyes popped open all the same as he turned toward the bedrooms.

He swallowed hard as his bladder tightened.

A shot of urine spat free.

Seeking in shadow.

With catlike feet he climbed steps, one at a time, the blood roaring in his left temple. As he walked he imagined the chills that had driven Diana to soak in a hot tub as her children tossed in their sleep.

He stopped, turning on the top landing. It was a narrow hallway. At one end was a small table on an Oriental runner leading into the master bedroom. At the other, open doors and uncertain darkness.

He moved forward, first inspecting the table, a small lamp, an arrangement of dried flowers, and above this a family portrait. There was a timer against the wall controlling light, and he checked carefully, fingering the tiny buttons. The switch was set for dusk to dawn.

"Afraid of shadows, perhaps, little Kimberly?" he said.

Scott moved on, passing the table, creeping through the door to confront Diana.

Sitting down on her bed.

The turned-down sheets released the smells of a fresh machine wash as the swollen mattress gave under his weight. Still waiting. The accent pillows all in place, all in a row, then Scott rose to the mirror above her desk.

"You would have liked this," he grimaced, a flash of teeth, and then the bathroom door swung wide.

I am the killer.

She is waking into a nightmare bursting through her head. "Who's there?"

Only now she sees my full form slowly coming forward, blackness covering my face, my hands, my head; a drum banging through her mind, thrashing her heart as she realizes terror and her eyes explode from a sleepy state, her body still cloaked in a cloud of steam.

Do I know about the children? Thought number one. Has he seen the children, but they could not scream?

She is trying to stand, the water ripples against naked legs, shaking into a trembling form that reaches forward but grabs only air.

"I came for you." A comforting lie. The process. He is after the process.

She agrees, nodding. She dares not scream, for waking the children. Thinking. All the time, thinking: What can I do?

As the gun appears, coming out from behind my back, more like a plastic bag than a gun, and she stares with questioning horror, feeling a piercing blow smash in an instant through her teeth.

Her body jerks. I must break her fall . . .

. . . so quietly.

She cannot think, she cannot see.

Stiff and contorting beneath my hold. Her instincts take over, but it is too late.

The children are sleeping as five minutes pass.

She dies there.

Scott swallowed hard.

He stood at the door of the children's room, asking why. "What did you feel?" he said aloud. "What did you see?" His eyes casting about, he walked slowly, directly toward the dresser and stopped in front of the mirror.

It had been shattered with controlled skill, not a shred of glass missing, long cracks snaking through the center, moving up, coming down. He was about to force a smile for his reflection, to look at this thing, when suddenly he recoiled with horror.

Scott closed his eyes and swallowed. The sudden silences were buzzing like hornets, then screaming through his head.

Broken with perfection.

In the wash from streetlights, puddles appeared like magic in the mirror, stains not visible to the eye directly—glistening, shining beneath two wicker chairs. The girls are parked together at the window.

Their dead eyes are looking out.

They are carefully displayed for anyone on the street looking in.

Scott could see with a clarity that forced air from his lungs, the scale of the atrocity dwarfed by the little room. The images burst in his mind as he quickly fled.

Standing outside the door, he breathed hard, regaining his senses. He fought to prevent losing control. "Keep it clinical," the voice inside slipped out to warn him.

Scott quickly fumbled in his coat for a cigarette. Finding one, he struck a match. Through the tiny blue flame he saw images of pictures and flowers, ribbons and wax, water and crumbs and beads.

And Scott knew.

Instinct or guesswork, it did not matter.

He knew with his gut the way he had always known: "Oh, Mommy, just one more night?"

He closed his eyes and they were standing in the kitchen, the words echoing through the recesses of his skull. The playful, life-loving voice: *Just one more night. . . .*

Scott could see Diana Clayton reacting with guilt, a sheepish smile spreading across her face as she stood over the garbage pail, her younger daughter having walked through unexpectedly. Diana was faced with a heartrending protest over losing something new, the words unfettered by the logic of an adult world.

She had already applied a coating of wax to the kitchen table in an effort to remove the troubling water stains, but she had never returned to wipe it clean. Someone had interrupted her.

All the while a predator had been stalking. For about eight days, Scott was guessing now, that's what he would find. He was sure of it, because he knew.

Lifting the Oriental vase with both hands, he held it above

his head and looked up at the bottom. There was a yellow skin of wax along the pale outer edge.

"Kimberly," he said aloud, his heart pounding. He fingered the dried arrangement, then turned it upside down onto the floor.

Water fell. It splashed into a puddle. He swallowed.

The flowers weren't dried at all, but yellow petals going gray, splashes of red fading to pink, and their stems drooped toward a brittle death.

His throat choked tight. With hurried steps Scott returned to the kitchen.

For perhaps a week, Kimberly's flowers had spread their colors on the kitchen table, where she could tend to them in a carefree manner: a little spill, a little slop, a little love, and who's to care? But on the night of March 31 Diana had cleared and waxed the kitchen table, and was about to throw them away, when she was caught in the act. The flowers had then been brought upstairs to be nearby.

Scott tipped the ash off his cigarette and into the sink. Bending at the waist, he opened a door beneath the counter and removed a plastic trashcan, peeling away darkness with his light.

There they were. Stuck to a wad of pink chewing gum, along with the blue ribbon once used for tying them, directly under an empty packet of florist's preservative.

Carefully he collected all seven dried stalks. Flowers once picked by children, then thinned from an aging bouquet, night after night, saving only the best, the best for last. *Mommy, just one more night?*

Yellow loosestrife, the swamp candle.

37

"Oh, come on," Jessica Janson fumed, "we're just sitting!"

The white Oldsmobile Cutlass edged out into traffic, the windshield wipers slapping at high speed as the rains came pelting down. The pavement was littered with fallen branches and debris, and she avoided this, merging into a line many cars deep at the intersection of Arlington and Old Georgetown roads.

Her left-hand-turn signal had been pinging, pulsing from the dash as the traffic light went to green, but the line remained motionless.

"Tomorrow, if it's not raining, can we go to the river?" Elmer asked.

From far in back came a belting *honk*. The line slid forward a single car length.

"I'm sorry, dear, what was the question?" She wiped her side window with a thin tissue, only to see flashing red lights beating from a block away down Arlington Road.

"About Sunday. After church, can we go to the park?"

"We'll see, Elmer. I think we better find another route, there's an accident down there."

She shifted to a right-turn signal, trying to ease back into the traffic, alternating her brakes with the gas, the car bucking. Behind her, headlights flashed once, signaling as a space appeared. She returned a wave of thanks without looking back.

"I'm cutting down onto Glenmoor and taking the parkway," she said, switching the windshield defogger up a notch. "It's a no-left-turn, but we won't tell?"

She glanced over at her boy, he was smiling.

"Crack your window, hon, I can barely see."

They edged forward by inches, waiting for their turn.

"I wouldn't have done that," said Irma Kiernan, batting at the fogged windshield with a tissue.

"Her car's heating up. Would you like it to die in the middle of Bethesda?" Dorn was switching the windshield wipers to a higher speed just as he caught movement from the corner of his eye.

"Irma, no!" he cried.

She stopped dead. She was holding the seat belt's chrome tongue with her right hand, inches away from inserting it.

"Sorry," she said, "I forgot."

"You're sorry?" he sneered. "No, Irma, you're just plain lucky."

The button release on the attachment Dorn had screwed into place had been welded shut from the inside. Although it looked perfectly normal, once the seat belt was snapped, the entire system had to be unbolted from the floor to free a passenger. The harness was an active restraint system, not much kinder to its wearer than a straitjacket.

Feeling vulnerable, she pulled her knees away from the dash and locked her door. After another few moments, though, her attention drifted. Through the clouded windshield she began considering a choice of colors and textures, a flowing white gown complete with a veil. Having never been wedded, she was truly entitled. Though at her age peach or pink might show more class.

"Jeff," she said, "what's your favorite color?"

"Leave me alone," he muttered, watching the Oldsmobile pull away.

So she considered dates, thinking ahead to the fall, pondering over the ceremony, the brilliant leaves, the harvest moon, the weather still warm enough for an outdoor reception.

Blue! she decided suddenly, though keeping this to herself. A glamorous color, touching on sexy, which brought her to cuts of satin.

"Whew!" Jessica sighed once as she crossed Old Georgetown Road in an illegal left. Passing stately homes through a darkly lit residential area, they left the heavy traffic mostly behind, winding their way west, toward the parkway and home to River Road.

It had taken fifteen long minutes, and as Elmer spoke, she did not notice the temperature gauge on her dash as it flickered a red warning and then vanished again.

"Mom, do you want to play a game?"

"No, Elmer, I'm too tired, haven't we done enough tonight?" She tousled his hair as he sidled up to her.

From Glenmoor Drive to Little Falls Parkway was a few minutes, leading through the intersection at Bradley Lane and into a wooded stretch of highway named for the nearby Potomac River. It looked empty but for the occasional car, tall oaks by the side branching in a dark canopy as they cruised toward a destination they could not have imagined.

She felt a chill. "It's not that I don't love you, but you should have your seat belt fastened," she said. Elmer, having grown sleepy, dragged himself away as a familiar blinking yellow light at Arlington Road passed behind them. They were bumping over railroad tracks, nearly home, when suddenly the car bucked and kicked.

"What the hell?" Jessica cried just as a clattering filled the hood and a strange odor filled the cabin.

"Something's burning," Elmer stated nervously.

"I smell it too!"

She glanced down at her dash: the lights were glowing a bright and steady red.

"We're overheating!" she shouted, the trees spinning past, starting to slow just as a blinding cloud of gray exploded in front of them, covering the windshield like a blanket and enveloping the car.

The road vanished from view.

In that deadly instant she hit her brakes, spinning the wheel as they hurtled blindly, aimed for a black ravine.

It was there that Dorn was waiting.

He and Irma were parked on a side street two hundred yards away on a hill, just across from this gully and through some woodland.

"Right on ... schedule!" he said, and his voice sounded queer, almost emotional.

"I feel old," Irma responded.

"What?"

"I just hate my hair like this," she pouted, referring to the netted bun that hung against the back of her head.

Although he agreed, he demanded, "Let's see your eye makeup."

She turned toward the backseat, batting her lids like a sorry Madam Butterfly. The blue mascara was gone now, as well as the black streaks and fake lashes. To Dorn she looked for all the world like a stout schoolmarm in an ugly green tank. On all windows were membership stickers for the AAA road service, it seemed more like a religion than a motoring club.

"Can we go now?" she whined, taking a more direct posture behind the wheel.

Dorn carefully scanned the parkway through high-powered lenses. A car was approaching from the east, the headlights hogging the road, then slowing as it neared the Oldsmobile, which was sitting in a cloud of steam, its right side in the ditch. The interior light was on, and he could see the woman clutching her child with both arms.

"Let her wait," he said tonelessly.

"But, Jeff, someone might help them."

Dorn shook his head. "This is Bethesda, Irma," he said with confident knowledge.

"Oh, Elmer, you're sure you're not hurt?"

He looked up, more concerned over the way she was holding him, rocking him so hard like a baby. "Mom, it's only a bump on the head, but you look white . . ."

"We were lucky. God, that was awful!" She pounded the wheel. "And I just had this stupid thing serviced! I can't believe it! Maybe they did something to the car?"

"Did you tip them?"

"Yes, Elmer," she sighed, letting him go. "You're too young to be concerned about things like that." She watched his eyes, they were filling with hurt.

"Oh, Red." She quickly pulled him back, hugging the boy all over again as the steam continued rising, obscuring their vision. A car slowly came alongside, and a horn sounded. Jessica quickly rolled her window down just as a young man stuck his head out from a faded gray Cadillac and into the pouring rain.

"Can you call . . ." she started to say as she saw water rolling off a naked torso. A menacing drunken face was leering at her, a beer bottle clutched in his hand. He was leaning out the window to his waist.

"Hey, baby!" he yelled as the car came to a stop. "Are you a par-ty ani mal?"

She quickly rolled the window back up. "Lock your door," she said coolly.

"Hey, baby!" the voice came again. "Fix me, I'll fix your wheels!" They could both hear the sounds of men laughing, their drunken hoots and broken words growing more brazen.

"Mom?"

"Ignore them," Jessica cautioned, noticing a wildness burning in Elmer's eyes.

"Don't do that to your face," she corrected.

"Mom, I think . . ."

"Hey, sugar, come on out, we're having a wet T-shirt contest!"

With this, lewd laughter all but exploded. A soaked shirt landed on the hood with a heavy *whack,* followed by smacking noises and jeers. Jessica Janson fired the only weapon at her disposal. She leaned into the horn button.

The sound was deafening, but she would not let go.

* * *

Dorn was delighted, having heard snatches of their remarks, to watch the Cadillac coast away and gain speed again.

"You see, Irma, there is a God."

"And I want—"

"Yes," he cut her off, "you *want* to hit the red light at the next intersection, so pace yourself accordingly. I need thirty seconds to climb in and close back up."

Placing a hairbrush in her purse, she arranged this on the floor behind her seat, then turned the ignition key. The green Maverick started on the third hit, the rough idle growing steady as she rolled away with her lights off. A tree loomed from shadow and she hit her brakes. Because of this Dorn lost his balance, almost spilling onto the floor.

"Damn you!" he cried. "What the hell are you doing?"

"Moving my seat forward. You have it too far back."

She did this with her left hand, her whole body bobbing like a hinged puppet as she drove the car back into the proper lane. The street was deserted. The houses that lined it were dark as a pagan ritual.

"What if she screams?"

"Hey, that's a new one, Irma," Dorn said with disgust. He just wanted to rescue the Jansons before the punks started to reminisce over what they had left. He leaned over the seat, his breath closing hotly on her ear.

"Are you getting cold feet?"

"No, but something could go wrong."

"You worthless sow," he barked suddenly, "I could have been home relaxing . . ."

"Oh, sweetheart," she said, patting him on the hand, "I just get hesitant. You know I'll be fine once we get started."

As the car moved forward, the old oaks passed on the right like a wall of ancient sentries. She could just see the traffic light in the distance as they started down a steep hill approaching Little Falls Parkway.

"You know what to say, then?"

Irma nodded. "Before I get out I make sure the overhead light is left on so that they see an empty car. I walk slowly to her window, knock if it's not open, then stand back so that they get a good look at me."

Dorn shook his head. "That's obvious. One more time, Irma, do you know what to say?"

"Yes," she nodded, "the only thing I'm unclear about—"

"From the top," Dorn ordered, cutting her off. "We'll go through it one last time."

She slouched forward, adjusting her bun while steering, and Dorn quickly corrected this behavior with a backhanded slap, stinging her head with his fingertips. "I'm Mrs. Janson, you're standing at my window. 'My car's broken down,' I say, or words to that effect," Dorn recounted.

"Oh, my," Irma answered, "it is a bad night for that. Could I make a phone call for you?"

"Right, make sure you don't blow it and just offer a ride, she'd get suspicious. 'Oh, that would be very kind!' Now what?"

"Well, I'm from Allentown, PA, I'm just visiting family, so I don't know the area. What service stations are open this time of night?"

"The Shell station, it's on River Road," he prompted in his own voice.

"Oh, is that far?"

"Make sure you sound concerned, Irma. That was a joke," Dorn said bitingly. "She has to feel you slipping away from her, use some subtle pressure or it won't work."

She nodded. "Oh, my," she exclaimed, "I don't know that street, is it far?"

"Good, and then?"

"She tells me it's close, but I let her come to a conclusion on her own. I act confused, fumble with my hands, very uncertain about the whole business."

"That part will come easy."

"Jeff!" She pursed her lips. "I'm not stupid. I have feelings too."

The car inched forward, the headlights still dark, the intersection coming closer. Dorn couldn't believe what he was hearing, but he continued all the same.

"Now, at this point she'll be reaching a decision over what to do. Should I ask for a ride or give this woman directions and hope? That will be going through her head, so give her time to think. Timing, Irma, everything comes down to timing."

"Then I cut her off when she pauses to think. Go straight for the kid?"

"Exactly, let's hear it."

"Well, he's adorable and I'm a third-grade teacher."

"Yes, but say it like you mean that—just between us girls, he's a nice one."

Irma smiled. "Sweetheart, you make him sound like a piece of fruit—he's a beautiful little boy, so it won't be hard. Besides, we're doing this for him . . ." Her voice trailed off, Dorn closing quickly on her comment.

"That's right Irma, now—"

"Jeff," she barked, jumping back in. Dorn's teeth clenched.

"I bet you were too—I mean, a gorgeous little boy. Just think what would happen if we—"

"Later," he corrected firmly. Then, placing his hands against invisible bosoms and mustering up an effete voice: " 'Oh, really!' " he swooned. " 'So you noticed how terrific my kid is! Well, he's a very good student, the brightest and most talented kid there ever was,' or whatever drivel spills off her idiot tongue. She won't be able to stop talking, trust me."

"So I act pleasantly surprised, like we're all one happy family, when I just happen to mention how silly it is to be standing here in the pouring rain, just talking away, especially with no man around, and it's a dangerous world—"

"No!" Dorn yelled. "No, no, no! If you even say the word *man,* that will give her mind something to bite down on. Just say, 'I'm not very comfortable and it's silly to be standing in the rain.' "

"Sorry," she said.

"She'll ask for a ride at that point, so make sure you're uncertain about that."

"Is it too terribly far?" she cooed in response.

"And since the light in the car is still on, she'll think it's empty, nothing to fear unless you—"

"I won't," Irma put in, "you're forgetting."

Dorn nodded. "Now, you understand that all of this may not be necessary. She could just short-circuit the whole rap, come right out asking for a ride."

"Of course, silly, the important thing is to make sure the boy gets in back."

"That's critical, Irma. Once I pop out from the cell and grab him, we control her easy. So what's the control?"

"I get in first. Then, as I unlock their door, I look right at the boy . . ."

"Yes, make sure he see your eyes, he's very obedient."

". . . and I say, that seat's broken, it doesn't come forward. It's a bit of a tight fit, I'm afraid."

"Right, and raise your eyebrows, challenge him, he'll jump right through the hoop. And if the blonde says anything?"

"Can you believe I've had it fixed twice? Nothing gets done right anymore."

"Very good, Irma, real casual. Little details like that can be important. Then what?"

"As I'm pulling away, I make sure she buckles up, and if she doesn't, I ask her very quietly because of my car-insurance policy. It won't cover anyone if we don't wear our belts."

"Right," his eyes rolled. "When we hear that *snap,* she's ours, she belongs to us. I punch out from the back and hold a gun to the kid's temple, she'll be unable to breathe."

"Well, Mr. Perfect, don't you forget!"

Flicking on her headlights, Irma slowed at the bottom of the hill, then stopped with precision for the light. She was preparing to take a right onto Little Falls Parkway when she glanced into her rearview mirror.

"Jeff?" she said.

The vacant backseat thrilled her in a way she did not understand.

A troubled sigh fell from Jessica's lips. "No," she said, "we stay with the car."

"But, Mom, it's only a couple of miles. That's better than just sitting here."

"Someone will come, Elmer. The police will be along, or a tow truck, you'll see."

She noticed how dim the headlights were getting. The windows were thick with fog, it was like staring out from an eggshell, and she disguised her fears, feeling terribly cold and lost. "Are you warm enough, Red?"

"Sure, I guess so."

It was then that the car's interior bloomed with light, the gravel churning, crunching up slowly behind them.

"Mom, somebody's stopped," Elmer said nervously, and she quickly started to wipe her side window, but the car was directly in back, the motor still running, and she could not see a thing.

"Dear God," was her only thought. "Those men have returned, they've been drinking for the last half-hour."

Suddenly Elmer climbed into her arms to protect her as she shut her eyes, placing her hand against the horn.

* * *

Irma Kiernan felt a wicked delight.

Life was catching up with the Jessica Jansons of the world, she thought, and she planned on discussing some beauty tips with the woman who had been flaunting her body on the merry-go-round, offending any sensible adult, showcasing herself at a time that should have been for the children.

"Cheap trick," she said aloud under her breath.

As she approached, she was Mrs. Irma Dorn, a proud woman of regal stature, moving under the admiring watch of her man, a war hero and mythic champion.

"Mom, someone's coming," Elmer cried nervously.

Jessica furiously tried wiping the window with the flat of her hand, but as quickly as it cleared, it filled with fog.

She was hopelessly locked into blindness.

"Quick, Elmer, into the backseat. Lie down on the floor."

"No, Mom! No . . ." he exclaimed, and fear choked his voice as he struggled with her effort. "I won't leave you, I won't ever leave you." Then someone rapped sharply against the window.

Three times.

Jessica closed her eyes tightly while leaning into the horn. The sound wavered from a weak charge.

His words were running through her mind.

"Little details are important, Irma. Stand away from the car, let them see your body."

Jessica Janson rolled the window down a fraction of an inch.

She was not sure how, but she was preparing to protect her child, wondering if Elmer would be able to sneak off into the woods, but more important, would he go if she ordered? She shook visibly at the thought, barely able to discern a shadow looming over her, and it seemed small.

And a face.

Coming down from above as Jessica pushed herself backward along the seat, the horn still weakly sounding, and her eyes transformed into slits as the dark features started taking form.

"What do you want?" she cried, her voice filled with panic and fear. Elmer quickly came to her side.

When suddenly. Without a word. She felt warm.

Her body and her breath relaxed in a sudden and unexplainable manner that she would take to her grave, never able to cast into words, her heart backing off from a destructive tempo, her fists becoming hands again.

"Mom, who is he?" came Elmer's voice.

But there was only the sound of the rain beating against the shadowy brim of an old fedora. It was an older man. While this face was kind, it was somehow punishing and worn, and in a painted bar of light cast from an oncoming car, the eyes radiated a concern that Jessica had never seen before.

"Mrs. Janson?" he asked quietly.

While she was thinking: *Do I know you? Should I know you?*, she suddenly unlocked and opened the door. Her hands and legs shaking, she stepped out into a horrid rain.

He was dressed in a battered gray raincoat, the hat shapeless and pulled low, the slacks worn and baggy. He was holding a notebook in his hands, following a green car with his eyes as it passed close by, slowing down, then gaining speed again.

A tear rolled from Jessica's cheek, and she quickly brushed it away as Elmer took up her hand.

"Mrs. Janson, my name is Scott," he said carefully, extending a badge that gleamed in the darkness.

While a thousand questions raced through her mind, they would not connect or form into words. In the uncertain strangeness of that night, the three stood on the roadway, locked in time suspended, as if they were not really strangers but rather old friends at last reunited by fate.

"Our car has overheated," she said, and the words seemed to drift with the rain.

Scott nodded. "I know," he concluded softly.

Elmer tugged her hand.

"It's all right," she whispered, and raised a troubled brow. "Why do you know my name?" she pressed quietly, hesitant, almost backing away from the response. "Please tell me . . ." Her voice trembled. "This was no accident, was it?"

Scott studied her eyes, brimming with tears, the young mother fighting with enormous courage. "It could have been, but I wouldn't take that chance. I'm sorry. There's a small tracking device under your car, so I knew you needed my help."

"Oh, God!" she exclaimed instantly, biting down onto her fist. "What have we done?"

Scott looked thoughtfully at her, his eyes warm and knowing. "Well, that's a difficult question, Mrs. Janson. Although you've done nothing to deserve this directly—as I'm sure you've already guessed—an explanation might take some time."

Taking a step past them, he removed the keys from her car and turned off the lights. "There's nothing to fear. Let's have a cup of hot coffee, and I'll do my best."

As his mother was about to respond, Elmer took a cautious step forward. Images and ideas had been popping off in his head like flashbulbs. "Do you know Detective Rivers?" he asked.

Scott leaned over, and water streamed down from the soaked brim of his hat. "Elmer, I hear you have the spirit of a crusader and a lion's heart. You know, that's very high praise coming from a man like Frank Rivers."

At the sound of his own name, an explosion went off in the boy's head, so powerful that his heart began beating double and his eyes grew wide.

Jessica's tears fell freely, the rain beating her hair flat across her brow. "It's that goddamned bowling alley!" she cried, looking up to Scott. "That's the only trouble we've ever had!" She started to speak again, but just shook her head with confusion, looking down at her child, wanting to be angry at him, yet feeling only love.

"No trouble at all, Mrs. Janson, I assure you. Let's just say that Elmer here opened a door to the past, and we were the ones who happened to walk through."

Although this didn't make much sense to Jessica, the expression on Elmer's face said there was no misunderstanding. The stranger and her son seemed to grasp something, on a deeper and invisible level, that was totally lost on her.

"Are you him?" Elmer asked shyly. "Did they give it to you?"

Fumbling in his pocket, Scott nodded. His fist slowly emerged, and then his fingers opened as if he had captured a moth and did not want it harmed. And it was there.

Elmer's coin.

A speck, a promise, a joy. Shining like a star through the red beginnings of time.

DAY THREE: THE VILLAGE

The worth of mankind will be measured by only those things that he was able to leave alone.
— William Oscar Swensk

Evil is the nature of mankind.
Welcome, again, my children,
to the communion of your race.
— Nathanial Hawthorne,
Young Goodman Brown

38

SUNDAY, APRIL 10, 5:56 A.M.

She came like the gray promise of dawn, a shadow passing through the sleepy suburb, moving over the sidewalks with bandaged legs, her frail hands clutching a worn Bible. The day was not yet warm to arthritic bones, so she wore a loose purple shawl across her shoulders, a cobweb clinging to another time.

Her name was Halford, from the English, a title meaning she was born among the privileged, that her family had been allowed into the great manor house of a Richmond dynasty. And she was Victoria. Born in 1892. The last of her clan.

She stood at an intersection while waiting to cross, shielding her face from a slight rain. When the traffic light turned, she carried herself past waiting motorists; eyes would seem to cast a stare upon her but fail to see; the snow white hair in thinning patches, the stooped back curved like some old walking cane, bent with the unseen weight of a mighty hand.

She did not look back as she entered the parking lot, a shadow among shadows, barely moving, hardly there. It took long moments for her to catch her breath, standing in her dress shoes among the foul weeds of Patriots Bowl, beneath a huge section of pink aluminum, large as a billboard, that had once advertised in tall white letters.

Slowly she edged across the wet and broken pavement, coming to the wooden basket-weave fence at the rear of the lot. This was her destination. With spindly hands she opened to a marked passage in the Good Book. With her head held high, her thin lips went trembling over words that had carried her through a lifetime of toil. A threatening rain dampened pages as she lifted her face to the sky, remembering her singing voice, and this was something only she could hear, for the years had laid virtue to ruin. She hummed with a gentle dryness of breath under the secret gaze of a small boy who had come to share the final moments of her world.

Victoria Halford had stopped visiting when the lanes were operating, her time for remembrances lost to drunken gamesmen. But at ninety-six years, Patriot Bowl's brief tenure over the land blew through her mind like candles on a cake, and she smiled, a dark line curving proud and contemptuous. Her position in the thick weeds offered a crooked line of sight to the Jansons' compact town house, and she heard voices from this direction while adjusting her shawl.

"Hi, Mom!"

"Oh, Elmer!" a woman scolded, "don't you *Hi Mom* me. Your hands are like ice, this isn't summer."

"But she's there," he said shyly, and Victoria heard this; as somewhere deep inside the boy a shadow shifted mournfully.

The window closed with a sharp *knock*.

Victoria Halford lifted her head in hymn.

Jack Scott set the high-powered glasses on the Chrysler's dashboard, his face puzzled, yet filled with wonder.

"That's really incredible," Rivers offered quietly.

"Yes, yes, it is."

"If we hadn't been looking for her, I'm not sure we would have seen this."

"I saw." Scott pondered. "Where did she come from?"

From their position in the 7-Eleven parking lot on River Road, they had an unobstructed view of three long suburban blocks, which included the bowling alley some two hundred yards to the left, and on the right, the intersection of Little Falls Parkway. Almost directly across the street, the small white church Jim Cooley had mentioned as the last tangible remains of Tobytown, was sandwiched between a twenty-six-story high-rise apartment and a modern office building. The latter had been designed by a Frank Lloyd Wright enthusiast who had failed lamentably in his basic understanding, which was rather typical of Bethesda.

Before she left the alley, Victoria Halford removed a small package from her purse, leaning it with care against the wooden fence, closing her hands in prayer.

"Pogo to base," Rudy Marchette chirped through the radio, and while Scott heard only the words, Rivers heard serious fatigue. The rookie was badly in need of sleep.

"Go ahead," he responded, having grabbed the microphone.

"She's left something behind, a small package. Do you want recovery?"

Rivers looked toward Scott for direction. He was dressed in his best charcoal-gray suit, all three pieces, with a conservative silver-and-blue tie. He was continuing surveillance through a windshield so heavy with mist it looked like a coating of wax. Around them the pavement and buildings all but sparkled.

"Pogo, what's your rotation time?" Rivers asked.

"Uh, any moment, I hope."

"Then make that a negative, the package can wait."

"Roger, she should be on you about now."

Victoria Halford came steady as time, pushing herself gently down the sidewalk toward the open doors of the Shiloh Baptist Church. The sun was just beginning to cast shadows as the streetlights snapped off.

"That's affirmative," Rivers spoke into the microphone. "Check back at your shift change."

"Roger that."

Scott put the glasses back on the dash. "What did Jim Cooley find out?"

"If it's the same woman," he said, reaching for a notebook, "she's from a family of masons and stonecutters. They used to work on the memorials—Lincoln, Jefferson, that kind of thing. Many of the foundations were laid with the rock and stone of Cabin John and other Maryland towns. Victoria Halford, that's what some deacon told him from the description. She's the daughter of slaves who were freed toward the end of the war."

"She is truly astonishing," Scott puzzled aloud.

Rivers shook his head. "You want to talk amazing, Jack, how about a little ten-year-old boy and this ancient woman somehow hooking up and befriending each other, and no one even knew about it? That blows my mind. Elmer told me they share *his* secret place, but I'll bet Victoria Halford was visiting before I was even born."

Scott chuckled. "And Victoria leaves little gifts for him?"

"Well, one time she left him a hand-carved wooden boat, it's gotta be older than dirt. And then last year Elmer made her a bird feeder at school, then left it by the fence on Christmas Eve."

Scott turned toward him. "So where from here? Cooley suggested what kind of approach?"

"Neighbor to neighbor," he said, "showing a badge in church is like taking a shit in bed. It might help if you were black, you're gonna stand out like a sore thumb." Rivers was silent as the lyric sounds of a choir came drifting from across the street, a hundred human voices like canting ghosts, marching distantly at first, then dancing closely with some clarity and rhythm.

"Gives me shivers," said Frank.

"Gospel, moves the soul," Scott returned. "They must be practicing. According to the sign, services don't start for an hour."

The sound was swelling, beginning to echo gently against the high-rise apartments. Glancing up, Rivers could see balcony doors sliding shut. "So how do you assess our risk at this point?" he asked. "You've got a make on Zak's car. An ugly duck like that's an easy target for an air search."

"No," Scott shook his head, "that car will be well-hidden, believe me, it's a waste of time."

"But you're sure it was him?"

"It was him, the hole in the Jansons' radiator was way too precise. I'm sure he had a detailed abduction plan or he wouldn't have approached. At least we know he's working with a woman."

"That part really turns my guts. How about with the Claytons, was she involved?"

"That's my best guess, so it's starting to make sense. At any rate I should formally thank you for placing a transmitter on the Jansons' car," Scott said, watching Victoria finish her climb up some steps and into the small church. "The ones we ordered from Captain Drury just came in an hour ago."

Rivers nodded.

"I checked on the Pennsylvania license tags they were using last night. Reported stolen six months ago, and came from an identical car, an early-model Ford Maverick. Zak Dorani is the only one who would care about those little details."

"What shape are Elmer and his mother in?"

"Fine, considering what I told her, that Elmer's interest may have attracted a stalker, but she doesn't know what kind, just that we've been watching them and there's some danger. She's pretty well shook, but if you want to know the truth, I think she's been sensing something all along. This is a very bright young lady."

"I already know that," Rivers stated with concern. "I want

them out of town, Jack. I won't allow you to use this woman as some sort of decoy."

Scott turned, looking at Rivers. "It wouldn't make any difference, Frank." He rubbed a fist into eyes that had gone red from lack of sleep. "Zak will just hunt other victims until she returns, then he'll take her and the boy when I'm no longer around. He doesn't give up. In fact, this miss of his will be perceived as a challenge, very enticing, just adds to the thrill. No," he paused, "we've only got one chance at this."

Rivers was draining the last from his first cup of coffee. "Jack, I'm not doubting you, but about that car?"

Scott smiled. "It was a woman driver, it was pouring rain, and where was Zak?"

Rivers nodded.

"It was a female pilot. And even if I hadn't seen her, the approach was way too tentative, just too cautious. In a hunter-prey situation like that, a man's body dumps a chemical high-ball of adrenaline and testosterone, the system goes wild. So the closing attack would have been more dramatic and less controlled."

"Then where was Zak? You said the car looked empty."

"I've thought about that quite a bit. The floor would have been too obvious." He removed his glasses from his top pocket. "My guess would be in the trunk, with some type of false access panel in the back. One of the things he craves is shock value, the pleasure of a quick and merciless attack."

"Jesus, what evil—"

"Right," he agreed, "and just like all the other pilots we've discussed, which are almost invariably men, he's outdone himself this time. He'll be manipulating her like a robot. Zak understands the psychology of this type of relationship better than we do." Scott's voice sounded distant.

"What's upsetting you, Jack, the Clayton house? You saw something?"

"Yes," he nodded. "Zak and this woman are the perfect hunter-killer team." Just then a car roared into the parking lot, heading directly for them and pulling alongside. A pleasant-looking man got out and strolled for the store.

"So what did I miss?" Rivers asked apologetically.

"You missed nothing, Frank, and I have no tangible proof in terms of direct physical evidence for what I think." With those words Scott's voice dropped, his face registered fatigue.

"Something's bugging you?"

Scott was again rubbing his fists into bloodshot eyes. "This is hard for me to explain, but what I saw was a rather withdrawn and shy little girl, very passive and unsure, hardly able to speak above a whisper, which is nothing at all like I had expected."

Rivers raised an eyebrow, uncomfortable with what he was hearing. "You're a strange man. How the hell is it possible to tell any of that? No one I canvassed knew her that well, at least . . ."

Scott swallowed, holding up one hand.

"Hey, wait a minute!" Rivers caught up suddenly. "That's what I didn't understand about you! I get it," he said excitedly, "you use your feelings to interpret a crime scene!"

"Very good, Frank," Scott smiled, "it's called emotional reading, the use of feelings, perception, and imagination, the same type a writer or a painter uses. I've learned to refine mine into somewhat of an art, that's not an exaggeration."

"No, I believe it."

Scott nodded. "Then you *do* understand the principles of the devoid, like androids, robots of pure intellect?"

Rivers was smiling at himself.

"So my single most powerful weapon is precisely what they lack, the human substance. You could learn to do the same."

"So you're telling me you felt them, the Claytons, I mean?"

"Last night I spent a good deal of time employing all the detail I memorized about their lives, envisioning each of them as individuals, and how they lived together as a family."

"So what was different than you thought?"

"Everything," he concluded. "For instance, when I first saw Kimberly's photograph, I was sure I was dealing with a mischievous little monkey who couldn't be controlled. She had this slight turn to her mouth"—he rubbed the corners of his lips with a finger—"impish, almost teasing, a smirk if you will. Yet inside," Scott thumped his chest, "she was grinning, even laughing, but she was just too timid to display that. Everyone else in the family smiled with a natural ease, but Kimberly was shy, even a bit withdrawn."

"Go on, I'm following this."

"So her mother was working to compensate. On Diana's nightstand I found *Small Wonder,* a classic text on childhood shyness. Based on this advice, she had established little spaces throughout the child's territory, like small comforting islands. A shy child engages in quieter activities, so Diana was allowing Kimberly to plant flowers by the front door. I found only her shoeprints there. That space was Kim's because she arrived home from school first. She would play near the front door because it gave her an open feeling, not quite as vulnerable, waiting for the rest of her family."

"You're freaking me out, Jack," Rivers sighed. "I'm not sure I could get to know them that well."

"We'll talk about it," Scott concluded. "How about a cup of coffee? I'm dragging like an old whore."

"It's on me," Rivers quickly returned, and Scott leaned back into his seat, checking his watch, closing his eyes as Rivers climbed out and a black Porsche pulled in, snout-first, parking alongside the little blue Chrysler.

Scott turned his head away as a middle-aged man popped out, swinging his legs onto the pavement, then straightening his light blue sport coat, tugging at the bottom seams. He spotted Scott's relaxed elbow poking in his direction and came around.

"Hi, neighbor!" he said. "Where are you from in Maine?"

Scott drew a blank. He had forgotten his car had Maine license plates, and this was of no significance to him. He had merely grabbed the first set from his trunk when he left New York two days before, an entirely random selection from a dozen choices.

"A small town, you wouldn't know it," Scott returned absently. But the man shuffled closer, leaning down with some enthusiasm.

"Well, I might. I'm from a small town myself, Kennebunkport. Small's nothing to be ashamed of!"

Scott smiled weakly.

"So what town?" he beamed.

Scott blinked, still fighting to find himself after three hours' sleep, so he fired off the first name that came to mind. "Moxie Pond," he offered tonelessly.

"Hummm," the man was surely humming with joy. "That's not a seaport, all the same I should know it."

"No," he replied, still staring into space. "It's an agricultural village in western Maine, population 628." That's really about all he knew, except that a young woman by the name of Lacy Wilcott had come from there, that her life had been destroyed, and that her ravaged body had been dumped like so much garbage onto a trash pile off Florida's Coastal Highway. It had been discovered by a midnight hauler, and at 4:46 A.M. Scott had been notified by the ViCAT slot as Captain Duncan Powell of the Florida state police was pressing for his personal and immediate interdiction. ViCAT was dispatching Agent Matthew Brennon as Lacy's parents were just being notified.

Meanwhile, Scott's new neighbor had not stopped talking for one bleary second. "... and so I think we are becoming known as the Family State, you'll see that I'm right."

Scott looked up, tired and impatient. Rivers was coming up behind the man while sucking red currant jelly through a doughnut hole. Reaching beyond the stranger, he handed Scott a large cup of coffee.

"So I overheard," Rivers said. "You're a political speech writer?"

"Why, yes." The man looked puzzled. "How did you know?"

"Your bumper sticker."

The man nodded. "Are you also from Maine?"

"Nope." Rivers lifted a lip, exposing front teeth, pointing to his face with a torpedo cream puff. "What's this?" he hissed.

"I don't know."

"That means I'm from the nut factory up the road. Dad here just paid to have my screws rethreaded so I don't hurt people anymore."

Scott spat black juice into his cup. "Frank?" he frowned.

"Yes, Dad, can we go to the pet store? I'm still hungry."

The man chuckled. "You fellas are having some fun with me, good chatting with you."

"And with you," Scott returned.

As the man walked off, the commander gave Sergeant Rivers a cold stare. "Was that really necessary?"

But the resulting silence validated a mutual understanding that went far deeper than words. It was several moments before they spoke again.

"Hey, Jack, what was all that shit about a *kinder* and *gentler* nation?"

Scott held up his hands in surrender. "Hell if I know, but the American people will never buy it."

39

Dudley Wren Hall had arrived alone.

He stood in the doorway of the command post, clutching a paper bag that contained a blue enamel urn. A yellow cab waited at his back as he looked for a doorbell. If this was hidden, the diggerman from Woodlawn had faith he could find it somewhere on the molding of the funny tower of a house, not wanting to tarnish the shiny brass knocker with an uncaring and sweaty palm. He had been raised better than that.

He was dressed in his Sunday best, a light brown suit, faded blue shirt, and red tie—this was extra wide at the bottom, but since he kept his jacket buttoned, it didn't matter. He had rested a large, heavy travel case in the corner and begun to look in earnest for the bell when the door swung wide. He was bent at the waist, searching for wires along the baseboard as Frank Rivers spoke. "Mr. Hall?" he asked, raising his eyebrows.

"That I am," he chirped through a missing front row. "Call me Duddy. Note said to ring the doorbell, ain't no doorbell."

"Yes, sir," said Rivers, "it's connected to the knocker. Pull it back and the chime rings. Pretty foolish, wouldn't you say?"

"That I would, son," he said, straightening up. "Cabbie wants a tip, they didn't give me no tip." And he was either annoyed or disoriented, Rivers couldn't tell which.

"Come on in, I'll take care of it," he said as a large man came forward across the blue carpet to greet him. He was wide, with massive features, and had the air of New England aristocracy.

"Hello. Charles McQuade," he offered the diggerman, "I've heard a lot about you."

"And I you," Hall said, taking his hand firmly, then handing him the urn. "Burnt man, they said it was important."

McQuade examined the burial can, noting that the seal had been broken, and he turned to set it on the coffee table in the kitchen. "Thank you," he said. "Can I—?"

"You FBI?" he asked, cutting him off. "Only lab that kin handle burnt man is the FBI."

McQuade smiled. "I'm from the Armed Forces Institute. Can I fix you a drink?"

"Flew in first class, filled me right up. Is that young fella in charge?" he asked, removing his brown jacket and wandering toward the living room. He slung his coat over a sculpture that resembled a large paper clip melting. "That get caught in a fire?"

"It does look like it," McQuade agreed.

Hall was unbuttoning and removing his shirt as Rivers closed the door. From the rear, the diggerman looked like a human refrigerator: his large corded arms failing to hang limp, his shoulders and back massive for a little man, his neck like a block of wood. When he spoke, his voice sounded funny, high-pitched, as if he had swallowed a bird whistle.

"Mr. Hall, we've made up a room for you," Rivers offered.

"That's very kind, young fella, I won't be staying long. Are there any archaeologists on your team?"

"No," he shook his head. "Dr. McQuade does have some background."

"I'm a forensic pathologist, I only dabble."

"Whelp," Hall announced, "we'll be working too fast to dabble. Archaeologists bitch we're destroying things, and I ain't got no time for bitchin'."

As Rivers and McQuade looked on inquisitively, Hall quickly pulled his work boots from a zipper bag, dropped his drawers, then slung these over the artwork. "Wonder what that was," said the diggerman, staring down at the sculpture. "If it was bought by Department of State, could very well be their view of the world, you know, all twisted up and filled with shine like that."

Rivers smiled incredulously. "Scott told you about this place?"

"Known Jackie mosta my years. Said this place would charge my battery, renew the old vinegar."

"How's that?" asked McQuade.

Hall was stepping into his work clothes, a baggy suit of khaki overalls with a zipper from crotch to neck. "This house was built by the federals, and I've been fighting a personal war with the IRS ever since Korea. Fools don't know the difference 'tween a knocker and a doorbell, but they're sure willing to spend my money to get it. I'll be writing my congressman."

There was no disagreement as Dudley Hall reached inside his pants and adjusted his plaid boxer shorts. "Where's dis place?" he asked.

"Across the street," Rivers said.

"And there's no warrant? Jackie said we're trespassing."

"No paperwork at all."

"Good," Hall chirped. "We're here to catch a baby-killer, ain't that right?"

"That's right."

Hall nodded as he took a bottle of talc and shook this into his boots. As he slipped these over his bare feet, his gaze wandered to the center of the room, finding a leather couch with a chrome-and-glass coffee table. He was sitting to tie his laces when his eye was caught by the bust of Jennifer Doe. It was so lifelike he startled. Then he stood back up and pondered the clay-and-plaster bust, reaching to touch a cheek with a weathered palm.

Around the little girl's neck hung a shiny new silver chain, and Diggerman Hall held this in his palm, looking up at McQuade with a severe expression.

"You make this child?" he asked quietly.

McQuade nodded, looking down at the haunting face. There was a special innocence that radiated from her smile and the high, subtle cheekbones. Dudley Hall quickly glanced away, over to the empty corner of the room, and Rivers could see the man's jaw muscles ticking.

"Do you have any whiskey?" Hall asked.

"Black Jack," Rivers stated.

"One shot," said the diggerman, "helps fight the dew."

As Rivers strolled for the kitchen, Hall returned to lacing his boots. "When was she killed?" he asked McQuade without looking up.

"Thirty years ago, in April, we believe. Cause of death—"

Hall had raised a massive silencing hand. "That little boy found her, yes? She was buried under the asphalt?"

"Correct," said Rivers, handing him a shot glass. Dudley Hall splashed the liquid into his throat and handed back the glass.

"Does she have any kin?"

"No, not that we can find," Rivers said sadly.

Diggerman Hall came abruptly to his feet, lightly stroking her head. The hair was fine and silken to the touch.

"She does now," he chirped with conviction. "That I'd truly have to say."

"Aliens," Elmer repeated under his breath, and he was embarrassed by the confession. That's what they had been to the imagination of a ten-year-old child, these weeds that didn't belong, weeds that were somehow different from all the rest.

The boy stood nervously in the bright morning light, his reddish hair freshly washed and shimmering, his mint-green eyes looking up at Detective Rivers as his mother watched, growing increasingly uneasy.

"It will only take a moment," he comforted, holding Elmer's treasure guide in his hand. Jessica nodded agreement as Rivers began to read.

"Study plant growth, previous disturbances often result in a noticeable change in vegetation."

"I was just playing," Elmer said. "I didn't know I'd find a body."

Nodding, Rivers scanned the parking lot behind the old alley. To him, and to Charles McQuade and to Dudley Hall, it was very easy to understand what had attracted a curious little boy. The bowling alley was set on nearly an acre of littered ground. There was a rusted fence that was overgrown with weeds, split and broken asphalt, a roof collapsing in sections, and paint peeling from holes and windows. It was gloomy, dank, and forbidding.

More important, it was boarded shut.

"And you had been watching where the plum-headed aliens were growing?" Rivers asked, looking down at the child. Elmer nodded.

From inside the alley Team Pogo watched with interest as three men and a woman marched into the lot, being led by a little boy.

In the rear of the alley, the blacktop was sinking in more than a dozen sections, more than twenty fountains of weeds, plum-heads, towered over outcroppings of green grass and wild straw. Some sprouted just ten feet from where Elmer Janson had found the remains, and Dudley Hall hovered, holding a thin metal rod in his hand, a device Scott had procured especially for him.

Hall tamped the asphalt with his toe, then grabbed a clump

of wet weeds and tore them from the ground. Already Jessica was alarmed, checking Rivers, who nodded in reassurance. Hall fell forward onto his knees and proceeded to insert the rod into a crack in the pavement.

He worked this carefully, turning the rod between heavy padded work gloves, able to look directly eye to eye with Elmer. "Sooo . . ." His mouth went round with the sound, and the boy backed up a few inches, standing before Frank Rivers.

To a child's eyes, Dudley Hall was a hard-looking old man, his face was worn, the leathery skin beaten into a patchwork of lines and crevices. As he rubbed the rod back and forth between his palms, he didn't look where he was working, but Elmer saw the metal probe mysteriously sinking into the wet pavement.

"Young fella, hear you got a special friend, helluva good hound by the name of Dipper."

Elmer looked up at his mother, and with a flitting breeze Jessica smelled whiskey on the man's breath. Not caring for this, she patted the boy's shoulder and brought him to her side.

"His name's Tripod," Elmer said shyly, "he's part wolf."

"Elmer," she corrected softly, and Hall smiled.

"Every boy should have a dog," he said. "Your friend Jack Scott told me about him. Missing a front leg, he said, he's missing a paw?"

Elmer was immediately defensive. "He's still good as any dog," he said under his breath.

As Hall worked the thin rod, he smiled thoughtfully. "Whelp," said the diggerman, "there's something in that bag for him." He tilted his head, nodding at a brown paper sack. "I brought it special from New York City jest for him."

The probe stopped moving some three feet down into the wet clay beneath the asphalt. Hall pinched it between his forefingers and pulled it back like the string of a bow, giving it a snap. It sang for one strong second, two feet of hard metal poking up from the ground and humming.

Elmer's eyes were bright and wide as he stared down at the bag, and Dudley Hall came to his feet, lifting it and placing it at the boy's dress shoes.

"That's for him," Dudley offered the mother.

She released her hold as Elmer's eyes danced. He was leaning over the bag, peering in with curiosity. Finally he reached in with confusion and lifted an object he had never seen before. It was made of a heavy white nylon with bright chrome buttons, all connected to metal beams with three soft leather belts. The mask of freckles pulled tight across the boy's face as he examined it.

"What is it?" he asked excitedly.

Dr. McQuade stepped forward, smiling broadly. "You're very kind," he said to the old diggerman. Anxious to inspect the device, he leaned over and took it from the boy. It was very professional, very precise.

"Elmer," McQuade offered, "this is a prosthesis. Do you know what that is?"

The boy shook his head.

"It's a false leg. I've seen them on police dogs who were hurt, it's very rare."

His green eyes widened, brimming with joy. "A false leg!" he cried, beaming. "Mom, it's a leg for Tripod!"

Dudley Hall looked up at Frank Rivers. "Young fella," he said, "you work with the K-9 corps?"

"Sure do."

"Get one of them boys to help with this." Turning to Elmer, he placed his hands on his knees and bent down. "Seen these work, son. That hound of yours will be running like he was born with it. A little patience, a little love, he'll never know he was hobbled." And with that the diggerman held three coarse fingers out, then added a fourth.

"What do you say, Elmer?" Jessica quickly nudged.

"Thanks, Mr. Hall," he said excitedly. "Thanks an awful lot!"

"You're very welcome. That was made for a famous police dog up north, an extra." He straightened back up, his eyes leveled at Rivers. The detective gave a nod, turning to the young mother.

"Time to go?" he asked.

Jessica Janson stepped forward. "Thank you so much, for Elmer and Tripod," she said, smiling warmly at the old diggerman. Then reaching up, she kissed him lightly on the cheek. "Bless you."

"Sure nuff, sweet lady," he answered through a broken row.

Rivers was tugging his tie, making sure it was straight, when he felt a soft hand against his forearm. With a slight smile Jessica moved to face him, gently pulling his tie, rearranging his collar, then pushing the knot into place. "When's the last time you went to church?" she whispered.

"Mom," Elmer said suddenly, slipping his hand up into hers, "why do we have to go? We can make it up next Sunday."

Jessica Janson had started to speak as Rivers turned quickly, grabbing the boy under his arms, lifting him through air and onto his shoulder.

"Time for church," he said, his eyes locked on Jessica Janson.

"Pliers," Hall demanded.

Once McQuade had pulled them from a toolbox, the diggerman pinched the rod in a vise grip and spun the metal 360 degrees, twisting and twisting, like unscrewing a long bolt.

"It's dere," he whistled. His face stern with concentration, he grabbed a wooden slab from his bag and threaded this onto the rod through a hole. The block of wood dropped, slapping the ground, and he located a machine nut in a zipper pocket and tightened this into place on top.

"Are you locked tight?" asked McQuade.

Hall stopped for a second to shake the stiffness from his arms. Placing both boots on either side of the rod, he nodded at his toe. "Hold that ground." McQuade stood closer, placing his feet together directly over the spot.

Spreading his legs, Hall leaned over and slid the block up to the top of the rod, where it formed a T-bar handle. The device was an old-fashioned retrieving iron known as a dirt cannon, the bane of professional archaeologists, for it always destroyed what scientists thought of as context, or the three-dimensional placement of an object in space.

There were other names for the weird tool—fouling gun, looter's spade, digger's sword—and it had been used since the time of Dickens to discover and rob from the dead.

The diggerman lowered his torso at the knees like a sumo wrestler, grabbing the beam with leather work gloves, looking up at the gentle scientist. And with all the strength that was the diggerman, he pulled and strained until his face looked like a ripe tomato, gas discharging in a flatulent tear as he moaned. The ground rose into a hillock, McQuade's considerable mass rocking as if on the deck of a small boat.

Hall relaxed his grip and the wave of earth settled again. Shaking the cramps from both arms, he spat fiercely.

"Is it?" asked McQuade.

"It is," Hall said grimly.

Once again he pulled with all his might. The steel rod bent and tilted. Through the hole between his boots the red dirt fizzed, spilling up onto his toes. The shaft seemed to grow by inches, and the ground strained upward in a small swell.

With a sudden tearing of asphalt, the rod snapped free. Dudley Hall stumbled backward with a wad of red dirt attached to the end of the tool. His barrel chest was heaving, his face a patchwork of blue veins as he held the instrument out to Dr. Charles McQuade.

"Snagged cloth," he panted.

McQuade carefully leaned the sword onto a sheet of clear plastic and scraped the tip clean. When the diggerman turned, ready to insert it back into the fractured ground, McQuade cautioned, "Hold on a minute. We're directly over a skull."

"How's that?" he wheezed.

"It's not cloth," he said, "it's hair."

He and Hall quickly dropped to their knees to work the wet wad with a small pick. McQuade's massive fingers separating the sections of dirt until a chunk of bone glistened in the light, holding the empty sockets of two teeth. Their eyes met: Hall's face was transformed into a mask of seething anger.

"How old, Doc?"

McQuade held a sliver of jaw and tooth fragment between his fingers. "Second-year molar, no surface wear, no tartar stains . . . late teens or early twenties. Female, from the looks of the hair."

"One thing's for sure," the diggerman said, "that was not an embalmed body. The ground was turned fertile with flesh, I know the difference."

McQuade rose to his full height and pointed at the next clump of aliens just beyond the "NO DUMPING" sign. "Let's move on," he suggested. "This was a young Caucasian. Her hair was blond."

Hall's shovel bit with dark precision, slicing through blacktop, lifting pieces away and placing them into a neat stack while clearing ground.

The fouling gun had struck three times, and McQuade was examining slivers of clothing, marking each find against a blueprint of the site. They were still outside of the building envelope, working their way toward the wall at the rear of the alley.

Dudley Hall took a long pull from a water jug and doused his head before edging a square into the ground to mark off a section. The spade struck dead center, slowly slicing down at an angle. As he worked the handle back and forth repeatedly, he caught the eye of Dr. McQuade.

"We've got something 'ere, dirt's froze," he whistled, wiggling the blade.

"Compacted?"

"Real tight." Hall stopped and withdrew the blade. Moving it over a foot, he reinserted it with some precision and worked it flat beneath the ground like a giant spoon. After he had lifted and discarded a slab of red clay, he grabbed the jug and sprinkled water into the pit. He knelt over the hole, wiping with a gloved hand. "Look here," he whispered as McQuade came over.

They stared down at a naturally flat stone that had been shallowly inscribed. With two massive arms Dudley Hall heaved the object from its resting place, exposing a brass circular ring. Picking this up, he handed it to McQuade.

"What is it?"

"Casket handle, pre-Civil War, I'd guess." Hall poured more water over the stone, the engraved letters showing in red where the clay had leached through the years. "Cornelius T. Mott," he read, "died 1860. That's quite a marker for the time. Well-respected gent would be my guess."

"God, what is wrong with people?" McQuade sighed as Hall picked up his tools and moved on. "This was a cemetery, they put a bowling alley right over it."

"Yep, look around, dead been comin' to rest 'ere since long before we was born."

"My guess is that they chose to build a bowling alley because it was simple slab construction, wouldn't require anything but a few inches of dirt beneath the building."

"No cellar anyhow."

"Duddy, from the lot size, what would you guess the population would be?"

"Better than six hundred souls resting 'ere, plus what the killer added over the years."

They moved past the rusted engine block to a gold fountain of weeds that all but swirled with strange growth. "Here's the way we think it happened," McQuade offered, flipping through a bound report, the records of the River Road properties. "They knew there was a cemetery, but the original building permit says it was a vacant lot as of 1957 when the property was seized from the Shiloh Baptist Church."

"Back taxes?"

"Right, claimed by the county government, then sold to the highest bidder."

"You can't legislate decency," Hall spat, clearing his mouth, then dropping in a fresh chaw of tobacco. "Who bought it?"

"January of 1958, two thousand dollars and change, the new owner was"—he shuffled pages—"was recorded as a Dr. R. Jaffe."

McQuade, reviewing the file, did not notice that the ground next to him had been broken and that Hall was emptying a shovelful of clay.

"Well, he should be ashamed," Hall said, working the spade. "And it also explains why this old building has never been torn down. If you dig this deep," he said, pointing at the blade, "you'll be swimming with caskets and headstones. Hey, do you think our girl had a sister?" he asked in a somber whistle.

McQuade sprang to his feet as, with a gentleness one would not expect from a gravedigger, Dudley Hall swung the shovel up with his right, cradling the blade with his left. At the end of the outstretched spade was a small human skull, stained red from years at rest in the clay, long black hair carefully woven into braids that had endured. There was a finger's worth of this fine hair neatly preserved between the jaws and teeth. A Latin-style cross swung before them, measuring time, dangling from a rotted silver chain.

Dr. McQuade did not require a close inspection: the high brow, gentle and sculptured cheeks, large sockets to accommodate golden lenses.

This was family.

It had taken him twenty hours to build her sister, and he knew this child with his heart.

Dudley Hall had nothing to say, but silently counted off the other spots where outcroppings of lush weeds sprouted through spongy asphalt. The vegetation was growing thick from human nutrients in a sun that was hot and bright.

They removed their shirts.
They worked in silence.

40

The Shiloh Baptist Church was a small hallway of brick and
beam, built on a gentle rise and painted white inside and out.
The roof was simple gray shingles with a plain wooden cross.
The windows were thick leaded glass.

As Scott climbed the whitewashed steps, he heard a deep
bass voice reciting a passage from Luke. In another moment
he saw a gathering of bowed heads, all nodded forward in
prayer. At the front of the assembly, the choir, in bright blue
robes, hummed quietly, kneeling in a semicircle around the altar and orator.

There were twenty-five pews on either side of the aisle, and
these were all filled with the faithful. As he stood in the doorway, a small black man came forward quietly, Scott guessing
his age at seventy or better. He wore a tie that matched his
red suspenders, his hair a powdery white fringe, his eyes like
troubled pools. As he extended his hand in greeting, Scott noticed his knuckles were swollen with arthritis.

"Thank you for coming," he said. "I am the Deacon
Atticus Cory."

"John Scott," he returned, peering over his shoulder and
through the doorway for Victoria Halford.

"Mr. Cooley expressed your interest in speaking with Mrs.
Halford, and I have mentioned this to her. He told you that
her memory seems to come and go?"

"I understand," Scott nodded. "I wish there were some
other way."

As the services continued, Scott keenly watched a large
woman stand, leave the rest of the choir behind, and come
forward to the small white altar.

"We'll wait until prayers are completed, then we'll go in
before the offering."

"That would be fine, thank you. Does Mrs. Halford live
nearby? She walks to church, I am told."

The deacon's eyes pinched ever so slightly at the corners.

"No," he said, "Victoria has her own pilgrimage every Sunday, and that worries us, her bones are very brittle. She lives in Tobytown, that's about twenty miles north."

Scott nodded. "And how does she get here?"

"Taxi to River Road, then she lets herself out at different spots along the way so that she can walk to church. That's very important to her."

"Then she's alone," he heard himself saying.

"No, Mr. Scott, she is not alone," the deacon corrected sharply. He turned back toward the congregation as the organ music swelled and a soloist's alto voice bloomed, a sweet and graceful sound that filled the little sanctuary and spilled blissfully through the open doors. Taking Scott by the arm, the deacon led him over thick gold carpet, moving slowly down the aisle of rows. Scott felt as if every eye turned on him with consternation as they came to the first pew, and a young woman looked up and scooted over, making room. Next to her sat Victoria Halford, her eyes closed in silent prayer, her white-gloved hands clutched to her chest with ever a slight tremble.

Before he sat, Scott looked up toward the altar, seeing the blue-robed choir at the ready, the candles burning in white fury before the saints, a carved crucifix suspended from above. He genuflected, crossing himself before taking the last seat on the row, and the reverend, seeing this, lowered his head, though he did not smile.

As Scott positioned himself against the hard rosewood bench, he suddenly felt very relaxed. The firm support against the sore muscles at his back eased a tired ache. He felt cool, and pleasantly so, from an overhead fan pulsing gently from the ceiling beams. He closed his eyes, feeling the fatigue of the last seventy-two hours dragging him down, and he found himself thinking back instead of forward, hearing Matthew Brennon's voice on the phone only two days earlier as he was just finishing lamb chops with jelly.

"Sweet Jesus, you've made a cross," he had said, and Scott opened his eyes, fighting to remain alert. Brennon had been studying the Clayton photographic crime scene on his office wall, and the choir was now humming a song that Scott did not know, though it touched him, just so, slowing the beat of his heart and making him feel light-headed. And he heard the questioning voice of Frank Rivers in his mind.

"What did you see in there, Jack, something's upsetting you?"

"My single most powerful weapon is precisely the substance which recreational killers lack. They are devoid, they cannot feel. Without feelings, anything becomes possible. . . ."

"Are you sure it was him?"

"I was in that house and I know it is so." But did he really? Scott was asking himself, and it had been then, there in the gray dawn, that they saw the old woman appear, coming out from the shadows.

Scott watched as a tall young man came forward to the altar, thinking he looked like a law student, maybe a doctor, and he started a sermon, falling into a monotone as the rustle of voices and pages around him became silent. Somewhere past the opening statement, Scott's chin fell gently against his chest.

He did not remember falling asleep.

The young woman was nudging him gently with her elbow.

The commander started, hearing gentle laughter, the voices of children floating overhead like thought balloons, the sound of the organ pipes playing an interlude as he was opening eyes filled with embarrassment, staring down into a worn wooden bowl, a church heirloom used as a collection plate. It was filled with small white envelopes.

"Sorry," he said, smiling weakly to her, then at the well-dressed man on the aisle who was holding the tray at the ready. He fumbled into a coat pocket and removed a twenty-dollar bill, which he laid on top. It looked crude in its naked form, a vulgar green among the carefully sealed givings, and he felt eyes examining him again. He was carefully passing the plate to his left when he caught Victoria Halford regarding him intently. She was a kind but fragile-looking thing, her hands peaceful in her lap, her shoulders stooped and uncertain.

Scott gave a gentlemanly nod, then quietly reached back into a deep pocket as she studied him. His hand emerged slowly and extended toward her in the tight space of the pew. Victoria saw his fist hovering over the plate just next to her, and so he gave *it* there, carefully placing it on the top of the collection.

Sealed in plastic and surrounded by white, the copper coin gleamed in the candlelight. Victoria's eyes grew wide with a certain recognition, and she blinked as the plate moved closer, then swallowed, her thin neck trembling as she nodded. Her frail hands, gloved in church white, reached past the plate and toward Scott as a hushed murmur began to fill the hall.

The young woman's smooth face went blank as she dropped her envelope into the dish, then passed the offering toward Victoria. She helped to support the bowl's weight as the old woman took the platter into her lap and closed her eyes; closed her arms around the thing as though cradling newborn life. Alarmed, Deacon Cory arrived at the pew as her gloved fingertips carefully lifted the John's Warning from its place. Her thin lips parted as she inspected this, and then her mouth produced a pleasing, almost infantile sound as she rocked herself in her pew.

The deacon rushed down the row behind them, his eyes locking onto her as Victoria Halford began to rise from her seat, the wooden bowl still clutched to her chest.

"What's wrong?" a child's voice could be heard, and Victoria smiled a thin, sad line, her head held high, her posture slowly unfolding with the weight of decades. She turned to face the full congregation as concerned whispers erupted and the deacon gently took the heavy bowl from her hands.

"Victoria," he hushed, "would you . . . ?"

But the will that was Victoria Halford, the invisible old woman from Tobytown, held up a silencing hand as she swallowed, fighting for strength, her eyes welling. She was lifting her chin further still, turning directly toward Scott, and then, to the amazement of all, she reached out with both of her hands.

"A pleasure," he said in greeting as she cradled Scott's fingers into the hands of joined prayer. And he moved toward her, his arms closing at the elbows as she held his hands to her breast. He could feel the rapid pulse of her heart, and he felt his own trembling in desperate coils as he peered deeply into her soft brown eyes. The congregation released a troubled gasp.

"Mrs. Halford," the deacon hushed, staring at Scott, eyes like hot pokers. "Victoria—"

Her voice moved in a dry whisper. "Many dangers, toils, snares . . . "

Scott leaned even closer, not sure he was understanding clearly, his police mind working its tight logic.

". . . we have, already, come."

And the sound she made was primal, almost eternal, something he could not understand. "I'm sorry," he said as a large black woman robed in a white satin gown appeared at the aisle. Seeing the confusion on Scott's face, she edged past him to Victoria's side.

Placing a comforting arm around her, this woman looked back toward Scott, if only because Victoria was staring at Scott. It was hard not to see his exhaustion and anguish, so she too placed her hands over theirs. She then raised her head and added her voice to Victoria's. It was then that something moved deep inside of Scott, something that was lifting as Victoria tightened her grip, sure that the stranger would now understand, comforting him, as she gave comfort to herself.

Through many dangers, toils, and snares.
I have, already, come.
'Tis Grace that brought me safe so far,
And Grace will lead me Home.

And at that moment Scott felt quite certain that upon seeing the medallion, Victoria had understood, and all of this on some deeper level that he could not put into words, nor would he ever try. And the thought occurred to him that, somehow, though he could not be certain, it had been the old woman's interests that had captured those of Elmer Janson, and that she was the true reason he was here.

And at that moment in song, there seemed to be some sanity in the crush of madness, something decent left on earth, as the entire congregation was beginning to stand for her, coming to its feet in a spontaneous and joyful rising, Scott looking deep into wells of warmth that were her eyes.

When we've been there ten thousand years,
Bright shining as the sun.
In Grace our souls will journey on.
In Grace our work is done.

And with this hymn, with this spiritual giving he had forgotten, he found life reaching up from his own childhood with a song he somehow *knew* in his heart; yet he did not know it, he told himself. Fighting for the words so that he would understand. And it spoke directly to him, just as she knew it would. For all the chorus, one hundred strong, and for all of the congregated voices surrounding him, the only sound was the whisper of Victoria Halford.

Amazing Grace, how sweet the sound,
That saved a wretch like me.
I once was lost, but now I'm found.
Was blind, but now can see.

41

The beast was incredibly beautiful, graceful as any bird, soaring in endless circles through a void of blue. The large gray underbelly was gliding overhead, blocking the light, the scars of a lifetime like white needlepoint etched upon leathery flesh. The eyes were cold black hollows. The mouth sliding open with white flashes, closing again, the pectoral fins like two stiff wings.

Frank Rivers watched with fascination as it surfaced, the large triangular dorsal fin slicing with hardly a ripple, and he felt the tiny hairs on his neck prickle as the woman beside him was bound with rapture.

"How can you love this thing?" he asked in disbelief.

"They're not like the creatures you hunt," she said proudly. "That's the most perfect predator of all."

Her name was Tammy McCain, marine biologist, and she was the keeper of the shark. She was slim with fine blond hair and dressed in a stylish gray jumpsuit. The tight fitted velvet sheathed and revealed a figure that curved in all the right dimensions, and Rivers turned to her, instantly lost in her glowing green eyes.

"So where's this little boy?" she said. "His name's Elmer?"

Rivers nodded. "You won't believe it, but I took him to church this morning. We're really two of a kind."

"Can't sit still?"

He shrugged. "It's an effort. I don't like being preached at, I don't think he does either, but it's what Jessica wants."

"And you're in love with the mom," she said, chuckling, just as the shark made another pass. Rivers grimaced, conjuring human screams as it slid from some primitive depth to crush hapless victims into jelly, like sucking snails off a platter. Tammy caught the seriousness of his intent, so took him by the arm, walking him even closer. As they moved, the softness of her breasts caressed his arm, and he felt his pulse quicken.

"You wanted to know, so let's start at the top," she offered, but Rivers heard only the gentle lilt of her voice, and not her words, as the shark came directly for them. Subconsciously he ticked the hammer of his automatic with a thumb, wanting to drive holes into its huge blank head, wanting to turn the requiem display at the National Aquarium into a certain still-life portrait of a fish.

". . . and should they bite bone and lose teeth"—she nudged him—"new ones just pop from the gums, sharp as razors. Can cut an entire horse down to pabulum in a few seconds."

"Swell," he responded tonelessly, turning to look at her. He knew Tammy liked swimming with sharks, even diving into caves where they slept, and that had always troubled him.

"How much does he weigh?"

"Nearly two tons, but it's a she."

"That's a girl shark?" he repeated with amazement. "It has to be twelve feet. I didn't know they got that big."

But there was no time, as a huge fur-covered flank suddenly splashed into the water as the fin broke the surface, gaining speed, the mouth hanging open like a snare of knives. Rivers watched in wonder as half a torso, complete with hoof, spun toward bottom and the large torpedo fish bolted into circular orbit, gaining speed, passing them as the eyes went to white, preparing to hit.

"What happened to its sockets?"

"Nictitating membrane. Like a lizard or frog, it closes for protection just before striking. Like I said," she shrugged, "the most perfect predator."

The shark sliced through the water and struck with one enormous bite. The entire blank head took it all at once, as its body gave one massive twist and the water exploded around them. From either side of its head, enormous gill plates released a foul white cloud. Smaller fish began darting, pumping this micro-slime down into their gullets, following the trail the shark left as it slid back to the depths.

"My God," Rivers breathed, "that was awesome."

Tammy smiled. "Fifty pounds of buffalo leg, rounds out her diet. The National Zoo sends it over—death from disease or old age, so don't get humane on me."

Rivers nodded, thankful he hadn't brought Elmer. "And this flounder you said you'd show me?"

"Patience, Franky, that's next." She pressed the button. "Okay, Mike, try the Red Hot. And tickle the water first, don't just drop it."

From their position, looking up to a silver ceiling of water, they could see a live fish at the end of a blue net. As this was eased into the drink, its pale oval form was slapping, breaking the surface, and the shark felt the vibration.

Instantly it zoomed upward, coming toward Rivers, eyes white, the death's-head of a blind torpedo.

"It's flatfish from the Red Sea that has some rather miraculous properties. Watch how it releases a milk when it senses danger. The fluid discharge comes from a spray behind the dorsal fin."

The small flatfish peeled off, swimming for its life, aiming toward the bottom just as the shark's black maw swung wide. As the shadow came over it, a white film was spewed into the water.

Instantly the tank boiled with anguish as the shark leapt violently, breaking the surface, its body twisting out of control, jaws locked open.

"Watch the jaws," Tammy whispered.

Rivers felt his heart pound as the giant killer went mad, flipping and twisting and spinning, haplessly, the head frozen into attack as the little Red Sea sole fluttered away safely to the bottom.

The shark was raging now, gaining speed, circling and circling the tank, the teeth locked tight into an open position, fighting itself, confusion battering at the formidable killer. All at once the great fish shot forward through the void, the jaw sprung, ramming into the thick plate with a tremendous thud that shook the heavy glass.

Rivers pulled back as the shark seemed to fall, drifting through the water, the eyes locked open, the face paralyzed.

"What in hell?" he exclaimed.

"Wasn't that incredible? Watch what happens next."

"Is it dying?"

The shark was veering over the sandy bottom, the entire torso trembling, shaking, convulsing, its compass broken as the belly turned up, then down again, drifting off into space.

"What the living hell is happening?"

"Just watch," she whispered sharply. The shark's face began to close, the teeth coming together, the jaws moving slowly, as if old and brittle—the fish was coming out of a tremendous seizure. Then it started swimming freely, though very slowly, twisting its head and body in confusion as it returned to cruising speed.

"It's clearing itself of toxin, flushing water over the gill plates," she explained. "In a minute everything will return to normal."

"Tammy, that is really incredible. What is that juice?"

She smiled coyly. "That juice is my research. We've collected thousands of those little fishies. They produce naturally occurring nerve toxin. We believe it's a protein, but we're still working on it."

"And it hits instantly?"

"One part per million in the water, it slams into the central nervous system like a Mack truck, producing an instant ministroke, paralyzing the jaws in mid-strike. The Office of Naval Research is carrying all my costs."

"To come up with a liquid shark repellent?"

"Exciting, yes?"

"Very."

She reached up for the intercom, pressing the button. "Thanks, Mike," she said. Then, turning back to Rivers, "So how's that for Show and Tell? Next time bring Elmer and Jessica."

Rivers nodded, then shook his head in disbelief. For all their years, she never failed to amaze him with what she would find to challenge in life, or what she was capable of accepting. He had stood her up for their senior prom, yet even that she had taken in stride.

"What?" Tammy questioned his stare, slipping her arm up through his.

"Wait until you meet them," he smiled. "Jessica looks so much like you, I couldn't believe it. And her kid," he chuckled, "this boy is bright and creative like you've never seen." He quickly fumbled in his coat and then offered her a photograph, which she studied intently.

"She's prettier than I am," she pouted, "and her boy has beautiful eyes," she added dreamily. "He reminds me of you, Franky. Even as a kid you could melt snow with those baby blues."

"Tammy," he protested, "Elmer has green eyes."

She nodded, handing back the picture. "You better go,

Frank," she said, pointing to her watch, "I'll walk you to your car."

42

Jack Scott stood on the slate patio as Deacon Atticus Cory helped Victoria Halford ease herself down into a straight-back chair that they had carried from inside the farmhouse. He viewed Jim Cooley with a new perspective, the lean young man toting a small pillow for her, adjusting this behind her back. Jim had never met Victoria, nor did he know of her; that's what he had said. Her existence had been news to him as the events began to unravel.

Late last night Elmer had told Scott of her visits to Bowl America and in turn Rivers had imposed upon his friend to make a few inquiries. Cooley had put his heart into the effort, and Scott had spent nearly an hour with him alone, waiting for Victoria to come from church, listening to Jim and learning, making notes, moving backward in time.

As recently as 1960, John's Cabin, Maryland, had been a relatively unmolested village, the people who lived there as enduring as the river along which it had formed, changing course very little over the centuries. The Potomac itself started as a brook in West Virginia, then after hundreds of miles roared into the mighty cascades known as the Great and Little Falls, spilling nutrients onto farmers' fields, once promising a lifetime of rich harvests. It had been a plowboy's paradise. Though there had been twists and turns throughout its history, life in John's Cabin never offered much to outsiders. It was too far from the city to support much of a life-style. Even the state highway system had passed it by, though through the years men of ambition had tried to bring the outside world to its door.

During the early 1800's engineers had made a foolish effort to tame the river, building the Chesapeake and Ohio Canal. This ran parallel to the Potomac, but after a brief decade of construction, they called it quits, having carved an elaborate trench that stretched 296 kilometers through some of the most rugged terrain to be found east of the Mississippi. Almost two hundred years later, tourists flocked to think about that, the dam makers having left behind real and lasting beauty by engineering reflective lakes and huge aqueducts to lift and float barges. But as Jim had explained, the rapid transit of the train killed the canal even before it was done, and shortly after, the Civil War killed the train.

While slaves escaping from the South were using the waterway as a lifeline, the Union Army of the Potomac employed the steam engine as a supply route into Washington. So while rebel raiding parties found it difficult to destroy the canal, they did the next best thing. By 1865 the remains of a trellis and rails served witness to another doomed effort to connect John's Cabin with the world. The tracks were never rebuilt.

Jim Cooley was not a historian; he had corrected Jack Scott on that. He was simply the son of a John's Cabin farmer, born on the land, the younger of two boys. So it was quite natural that they used to play among the historic ruins: cabins and lockhouses, man-made lakes and railroad structures. As with other families in small-town America, the Cooleys had been well-known, and since Jim had been named for an uncle who was killed in the invasion of Normandy, his name had recognition before he was even born.

James L. Cooley, he had explained, was a proud family name that had shone from a gold inscription on a monumental obelisk in the village common, a tribute to the lost sons of John's Cabin, just one little slice of America's heart. But in 1958, without permission from the local residents, strangers came to John's Cabin to change the name of the town. Just like that. They said it had been mismarked all along.

Soon after came another sour jolt. Protected by a court order, outsiders removed the John's Cabin War Memorial from the town center—just toted it off to some orphan field so that a shopping mall could be built on the spot. As Jim remembered, an old man by the name of Richard Duffy, a merchant who lived closest to the town center, unloaded an entire box of twelve-gauge birdshot into the moving van, blowing out their radiator, windows, and tires. That was the high point of the protest, since most farm families could not afford to risk violent confrontation. Going to jail could mean losing crops, even losing a farm. By then, as Jim remembered, the fight was already over.

At the age of fourteen, he entered tenth grade a quiet, distrustful boy who took life seriously and had every right. He had worked tending crops since the age of seven, and his first adult memory was of attending Walt Whitman High and finding himself a second-class citizen. The ill-fitting hand-me-down clothes, a bicycle instead of a sportscar, a thermos instead of milk money, the cruelties.

In 1968, Jim's older brother was killed in the Tet offensive. Old man Duffy, he remembered, had put Michael's picture in the window of his hardware store, since there was no longer a village green where his name could shine.

Since there was no longer a John's Cabin, Maryland, where it would have mattered in the first place.

Victoria Halford sat comfortably, sipping lemonade, her head held high as she looked out over rolling hills rimmed with giant pines. And it all seemed very strange to an outsider like Scott, the vast open spaces in subjective error against the landscape, the old farm tractor like some giant insect spit through a time warp and into a crowded suburb.

A bright sun was casting shadows from behind, creating a dark hollow where the slate patio met an endless wash of severe green. The sky had cleared. Now there was gray-blue overhead and everything sparkled with a wet shimmer.

Hearing the soft patter of songbirds nesting from the tree line, Scott eased a lawn chair next to the old woman as she closed her eyes. "Victoria," he said, and the woman turned toward him. The eyes opening slowly, brown pools drifted over his form and stopped at Jim Cooley, who was standing just before her and opening a drinking straw.

"Sorry," Cooley interrupted, leaning past Scott and placing this into the old woman's glass. The ice cubes tinkled, and she thanked him with a tight smile as she clutched the lemonade with both hands, raising this to lips that produced a pleasing, almost infantile sound as she sipped. Her gaze had not wandered from Jim Cooley for a moment.

"Child," she said to him, returning the glass to her lap.

"Yes, Mrs. Halford."

"Child, I know you," she said. Her eyes closed again, blinking away dryness, and the corners of her mouth turned up. "You are the image of Joseph."

"Yes, ma'am," he responded to this reference to his paternal grandfather. There was genuine surprise in his voice as he strained to remember if he had ever seen this woman before—he did not think so, but maybe as a child. He spent a few moments trying to guess what she might have looked like.

"Your mother, bless her soul, was a good Christian woman, though I don't recall her name."

Cooley swallowed. "Marie Catherine."

The old woman nodded. "And should you still be wondering, Jim, my father used to crop and shed on one of your outbacks, tobacco and strawberries . . ." She paused, taking a small sip as a cool breeze swept the landscape. Her tone was weathered like her skin, which was a parched and wrinkled mocha brown.

Cooley smiled, fighting for clear images in what seemed slow and thin as a dreamscape. "That was before I was born."

"Always treated us fairly, honest and proud tillermen, and with you here working the land, why, that's just fittin'."

Jim Cooley glanced at Scott, thinking about the woman's age, considering this time and place, what she was truly capable of understanding. He shook his head. "No, ma'am," he corrected, and there was a note of sadness in his voice. "Times are much different now, but I do grow vegetables for the farmer's market, mostly for others in need."

He turned sideways, pointing across the field in which furrows were spaced neatly, squared into columns, plowed from the soil. "That's eight corn lines. If I grow too much, the county will send inspectors, and then I'll need a special license. I'm a residence here, instead of a farm, technically—I mean, to the law I am."

Scott was watching all of this with intense interest. The little woman's lips pursed tight; she had understood. "Come the judgment!" she leaned forward to say, her voice turning sour with the sound.

"Yes, ma'am," he offered in return, "come the judgment."

"Jim," she said, and again she smiled, as if she liked to make that sound but was not really addressing him.

"Yes, ma'am," he said, bringing his chair closer.

"Jim, do you remember the dogwood petals on your brother's picture?" she asked.

Cooley's eyes grew wide as he unintentionally gasped and his heart began to pound. When his older brother had been killed and his photograph placed in the window at Duffy Hardware, someone, though they never knew who, kept leaving flowers there beneath the frame. By the time mourning was over, if it ever really was, a basketful of white petals had been accumulated. Jim had sprinkled them over his brother's grave.

"That was you?" he asked in disbelief, almost coming out of his chair.

She gave a slight nod. "That was I," she whispered, the corners of her mouth turning up. She returned to sipping lemonade, her lips producing a baby's suckle as she steadied the glass.

"Victoria," Jim asked quietly, swallowing the ache in his throat, "I'm sorry if I've missed something, but how do you know me, through my parents?"

She was rocking in her chair. "Do you 'member that day when the signs came down?"

"Yes, very clearly," he said, raising an eyebrow. "I was eight years old."

"Your father told us how that made his babies cry."

Jim looked at Scott in disbelief. "That was 1958," he reminded him, "the year Tobytown burned and they changed our name to Cabin John." Scott wrote this down, placing a small tape recorder on the table next to Victoria to preserve critical detail.

"We were upset," Jim said, "we were very, very young."

"The worth and soul of a place is as fragile as newborn life," she said, "take care and it will grow." She looked away as tears welled in her eyes. "They was jest killing time, Jim. Your father was gonna fight, needed all us colored to testify. But it didn't do no good, things was changing too fast."

"He never told me that."

Victoria smiled. "You *are* the image," she said proudly, then turned to Scott. "Your friend has questions for me."

"No, no, please go ahead," Scott urged, "it can wait."

Jim looked at Victoria, remembering the flowers that a stranger had left behind in his brother's memory. "Why dogwoods?" he asked. "I never could figure that one out, and my mother didn't know either."

"Bless her soul," she said, "don't you like the flowering tree?"

"Yes, it is very pretty."

Scott found himself leaning forward too rapidly, staring down at the *Kern's Wildflower Guide* sticking out from his jacket. Trying to appear casual, he picked this up and turned to the index. He searched for a page, then read aloud. "The eastern Dogwood produces flowers each spring, composed of four spreading white petals with red tips on each end."

Victoria turned her stiff torso toward him. "It is the resurrection flower," she corrected as Scott held the book in front of her. The four white petals leapt from the colored page, resembling a Maltese cross, and Deacon Cory studied this carefully.

"The petals form the suffering of Christ," she said, pointing with a frail finger to what looked like four bloodstained tips. "From his image on the cross of Calvary, as his mortal life flowed, a branch fell at his feet, and to this day we are blessed with the dogwood to remind us." She turned back to Jim. "That is why I left them for your brother," she said.

As she spoke, Scott noted an intensity in her voice that had not been present before. "Victoria," he said, "can you tell me about the yellow loosestrife, the swamp candle?" He had quickly turned to a dog-eared page and held this picture up, but her eyes failed to see; they did not need to.

"Sweet primrose," she whispered, "the life eternal."

"The swamp candle is a symbol of life everlasting?"

"It is the Easter flower," she stated without hesitation. "We used to collect them for services on Good Friday and Easter Sunday. In parts of the South it is the traditional offering of the children."

Her voice seemed to float beyond him as Scott was filled with a release of tensions, like a coiled spring unwinding for the first time. His body trembled as he emitted a heavy sigh that made both of them pause.

"I'm sorry," Scott said, clearing his mind. It was as he had suspected: there was a tangible link connecting each victim backward in time. In 1988, Good Friday had come on March 25, six days before the Claytons were killed. He surmised that Jennifer Doe had been collecting candles on or near March 28, the last Friday of March 1958, thirty years before.

Victoria again closed her eyes, and when she opened them, Scott was holding the copper coin in his palm.

"John's Warning," she whispered, and she began rocking herself for comfort.

"Victoria, you were crying when—"

She held up a frail hand, silencing him. Her eyes blinked with heavy lids and she cleared her throat, this sounding more like a long dry cough. "Jim Cooley?" she asked, reaching out for him with a shaky hand.

He quickly rose to her side. "Yes, ma'am," he said, "I'm right here."

"Jim, didn't I hear you and your brother used to play at the Widewater?"

He felt his throat constrict. "Yes, ma'am, we did, we surely did." He noticed there was a pinch of panic in her tone that was pulling down at the corners of her mouth.

"Did you see the remains of two old houses near the poplars, where the dogwood clearing begins?"

Cooley moved a chair to sit next to her, never once dropping his hold. "Yes," he said, "we imagined those ruins belonged to John-the-Free, that he would hide there from the rebs and make his war plans."

"That's where I grew up, Jim Cooley, where you and your brother were playing." As she said this, her eyes locked onto him. "Our house was the one with the large stone chimney," she said proudly, and again she went silent. Every spring since Jim could remember he had gone there to see the forest colors.

"The foundations are still there," he said, forcing a smile, "and one fireplace of smooth-cut quarry stone."

"Are there sweet bluebells, are the bushes there?"

"Yes, Victoria, enough for the largest blueberry pie in the state. The entire overlook is just thick with them." He glanced up at Scott for direction; the policeman nodded for him to go on.

"Daniel Stoner is the name you want. Daniel, myself, and my mother planted those," she stated, and suddenly her face contorted as water welled in her eyes. "We were gone many years before you were born, but I knew 'bout you, Jim. From time to time we'd see your parents in Bethesda, so I know about you . . ." And she started to weep.

"Yes, ma'am," he said, stroking the back of her hand. It trembled, but not from fear.

The deacon was on his feet, standing over them. "Is this really necessary?" he asked sternly.

"Please," Scott said, "I know of no other way."

At that moment Victoria Halford patted the back of his hand in a comforting motion, her head high, first looking at Cooley, then at Scott.

"That Warning," she said, "that Warning belonged to Daniel Stoner." She closed her lids unbearably tight. "I know because I helped him drill that coin when we were still children. We made a new word from John's Cabin—"

"Join," Scott stated softly, "the word is *join.*"

Victoria nodded. "The chain Danny wore it on was mine, from my mother. He lived next to us in John's Cabin. I had given him the chain for his tenth birthday—he could not afford to buy one."

"And the token was then passed down to his daughter?" Scott asked.

"Samantha."

He swallowed, leaning forward. "And how old was she?"

Victoria's gaze came to rest on him. "Twelve," she remembered with certainty. "She was twelve the year she vanished."

"And that was about the time Tobytown burned?"

"Only months before. She was gone, her sister and mother too."

Scott could see she was fighting her emotions, so he changed the subject as Cooley reached back over. Thin fingers closed around his as Scott unrolled an ancient river chart borrowed from Dr. Robert Perry's "Prizes of the Civil War." He held the map in front of her.

"Victoria," he asked, "can you show me where your family first lived, and where you were resettled to?"

The old woman was breathing deeply. "We settled in John's Cabin," she pointed. "My father built our house in 1863, before I was born. Nathan Stoner, Daniel's grandfather, already lived there. He was a Union freeman during the States' War, and Daniel was an only child. We lived there until 1954."

"And you were farm families?"

"No, the Halfords, Motts, and Stoners were quarrymen and brick millers, mostly shaving and cleaning lodestone for the government pit bosses fashioning L'Enfant's city. Our men laid cornerstones for Lincoln in 1914, then Jefferson . . ." Her voice went dry and she sipped her drink.

"And you owned that land," he stated.

"Yes." She pointed with a fragile finger that shook against the parchment. "We were moved up to River Road, where we built the church, named our new village Tobytown after the cemetery. The county said they wanted us to have that land instead."

"The cemetery was Tobytown." Scott shook his head. "Can you show me where that was?"

She looked at him with a dark smile. "I think you know," she whispered. And Scott nodded.

"From Bowl America to where?" he asked. "As far as the gas station?"

"They came at night, moving the dead, hauling them away, a week or more."

Scott breathed deeply, his anger growing. "The boundary was Little Falls Road, wasn't it?"

"A country mile."

"And that's why you visit the alley. Your—"

"That part was never cleared. My parents and my husband rest there—"

"Near the fence by Elmer Janson's house. You do know—"

Turning, she stared at him and tapped her chest. "A fine boy, he has a poet's heart. We share, that is his secret place."

Scott was amazed. "And why were you forced from John's Cabin to Tobytown?"

She smiled, a dark and contemptuous line. "The river land had become more valuable, and the county welfare people came with papers. We didn't have sewers, we was living under unsanitary conditions."

"Most families still have septic," said Jim.

"And did Daniel Stoner move his family there at that time?"

"Yes"—she was rocking—"built a nice house where the TV station is."

Jim leaned forward. "That tower is the tallest broadcast antenna on the coast."

"And by this time he had two children?"

"Victoria, born 1943. Samantha, born in the winter of 1946."

Scott sighed. "The oldest named for you?"

She did not answer, but closed her eyes, forcing tears into streams. "When he moved his family, Daniel was a brick cutter for the Smithsonian Castle."

"He would have done most of his work on Brickyard Road in Cabin John," Jim said.

"Did Daniel have any troubles that you know of, was anyone upset with him?"

"In 1956 we heard that private houses was to be built on our river land. Danny hired an attorney from Baltimore to fight them. It was going to court, and everyone said he stood a good chance."

"But then Tobytown burned and his family was reported missing?"

"She was set to blaze and went in a single night." She turned, facing Scott directly. "The smoke was so heavy you could taste it in the water weeks after. It wasn't fit for drinking."

"So you were asked to move again?"

At this question her face became a cold mask. "We were told. Somebody else needed our land, so the welfare folks came again with their papers, gave us a new Tobytown halfway to Baltimore, with new houses donated as charity. Never," she hissed through pursed lips, "never did we need charity!"

"And where was Daniel in all of this? What happened to his wife and children?"

"No one knows," she sighed. "During the ruckus, they disappeared. Some said his Emma ran away and took the little ones, but they were planning on having another child."

Scott took a deep breath. "Daniel looked for them?"

"Yes." Her eyes were again filling with tears. "He searched without sleep, even started doubting hisself. Some said they had gone to swim in the river and drowned, but Emma Dysan grew up on the bayou, so he went to Louisiana, but they weren't there."

"Victoria," Scott guessed quietly, "Daniel is dead?"

She nodded. "His heart died."

"When?"

"That same year, on a tree by the river," she closed her eyes, "hung by his own hand."

Jim Cooley shuddered as Scott rose from his seat. Removing a color photograph from his briefcase, he watched carefully as he moved the portrait of Jennifer Doe closer to Victoria. The image was coming into a slow focus when she turned abruptly, pushing at the picture with outstretched hands. She uttered a small gasp. Jim placed a protective arm around her, and the deacon stiffened in angry confusion.

"I'm sorry," Scott pressed, "but is this child Samantha Stoner?"

Victoria Halford clutched her shawl, wrapping her hands around the Holy Bible, remembering her singing voice, and she raised her head at them in a harsh whisper.

"Samantha," she said, "my heart . . ." And her voice erupted into harsh song. "Oh, way down South in Dixie, with my body hung in the air, I was asking the white Lord Jesus, what is the use of prayer . . ."

"She's been through enough!" the deacon cursed suddenly.

". . . I was asking the white Lord Jesus, what road should we travel on? And he answered with a freeman, and we came to the House of John."

Jim closed his eyes, holding the frail woman's head to his chest.

"And we lived by the word of John," she whispered, "on the banks of the River Peace. And we sought God in Bethesda, for Christ had slain the beast."

43

6:40 A.M.

To Matthew Brennon both the air flight and the day seemed nonstop. He had been up all night collecting materials concerning Aaron Seymour Blatt and making a study of the company known as DIDS, Dallas Instrument and Dental Supply. The corporation was the parent of a national chain of franchised dental clinics, and in his mind Brennon saw these as the fast food of medical dentistry, the Burger King of toothpickers. According to the ViCAT data search, from Maine to Florida to California, consumers routinely had their teeth drilled, their gums sliced, their crowns fashioned, and their dentures refitted by DIDS, yet the odds of a patient's having ever heard that name were exceedingly rare.

Brennon was sitting with his table folded down, the roar of a jet engine at his left ear, his the only overhead light as he skimmed a recruitment blurb in the *Journal of Medical Dentistry* aimed at students. As a dentist starting out in the world, a graduate could work long hours to make someone else rich, then hope for a partnership, or there was DIDS. They advertised the start-up costs for private practice at $650,000 to purchase basic equipment: drills, sinks, X-ray machines, chairs, and work-stations, funds that few graduates could hope to borrow, except from DIDS. Once placed in this context, it seemed a viable option. With an accredited degree in dentistry, a DIDS partnership provided everything required for a student to start grinding teeth into paste, every tool, every die, every bit of equipment, and then, just when you thought it could get no better, turn a profit in two years and DIDs paid for your full education. After that, they owned thirty-one percent of your silly butt for life.

"Did you want sugar with that?" asked an attractive redhead standing at his side with a hot cup.

"Just one, thanks," Brennon replied, and she placed a small envelope on his tray.

"Cream?"

He shook his head. "No, thanks." He lifted a photograph taken from a medical journal that was critical of the concept, while wondering if his own dentist were not a franchise. The thought made his gums itch.

"Sir, did you want the scrambled eggs or the waffles?"

"I think I'll skip breakfast." He frowned, holding a photograph of the first DIDS, sandwiched between a pet store and a dry cleaner's, circa 1960. Beneath a sign which proclaimed "DENTAL OFFICE" was the proprietor's name, Dr. Aaron S. Blatt, then with large lettering "DAYTIME, NIGHTTIME, HOLIDAYS TOO!"

"How very convenient," Brennon murmured.

"Sorry?" responded the stewardess, having arrived to refill his cup.

He smiled. "Talking to myself."

She moved closer. "Doctor, do you have a moment?" she said, and he looked up, seeing her for the first time. Bright blue eyes twinkled in the early glow that had begun to stream through half-closed windows. Most of the other passengers were in that half-sleep state of red-eyed jet travel, having eaten their heavy microwave meals.

"I have this tooth," she whispered, leaning against his chair, her long legs bumping his arm as a bit of turbulence stroked the plane.

"Sorry," Brennon said, lifting the stack of papers. "I'm not a dentist, but I sure wish I was."

She smiled coyly at him.

"This is just research for an interview I'm conducting," he continued. "I'm a journalist, *Life-style* magazine, it comes out on Sunday."

"Oh," she said, disappointed, "my fiancé reads that all the time."

*   *   *

In Fort Worth, Texas, there are some stately homes, and if the length of a driveway is a measurement of substance, then the Blatts had more than most, complete with a yield sign after about a minute. Just in case he was being watched, Matthew Brennon slowed carefully before pulling his rental car through the private intersection, creeping around a greenway circle with a sculptured bronze of galloping horses, then onto expensive-looking brick, coming to a stop under a massive white-columned overhang.

Such was the stately manor of Myra Isadora Blatt. It looked to Brennon like the White House, particularly from where he stood in the portico beneath a lofty chandelier, between rows of blooming roses. He was about to ring the doorbell when the huge wooden door swung wide on polished brass hinges, and he was looking into the face of a middle-aged manservant dressed in starched black, an aging uncle type with a neatly trimmed goatee and slicked-back salt-and-pepper hair.

"Good morning, sir," he said.

"Hello," Brennon offered.

"Are you Mr. Brent Masters?" the man inquired, and his accent was a thick manor-house English accompanied by a slight lisp that sounded phony. Brennon responded by handing him a business card; the gold lettering had cost him twenty bucks extra.

"Please enter, sir," he said, his thin face like boiled chicken. "I am Sydney Oliver, at your service."

"Pleased to meet you," Brennon responded, though the servant had not offered his hand.

"Miss Blatt is expecting you, follow me." With that Brennon found himself inside, strolling over expensive Italian marble beneath vaulted ceilings. It was a long, expensive walk, past a sitting area with velvet high-back chairs, a gaming room with felt-covered tables, a darkly lit den with safari animals mounted on the wall. They came through another portico of domed and gilded ceilings, then rounded into a red-carpeted hallway that resembled an art gallery. Oils and watercolors, some of these portraits, faces glowing from recessed lights.

Sydney turned back, finding him studying an oil of a man-child dressed in a tailored suit, a bright red flower popping from a lapel, a wry smile from lips that seemed too moist and too thin. His face had an unnatural glow of rouge, his hair jet black, a silk white yarmulke covering the back of his head.

"Master Aaron," Sydney offered, "his bar mitzvah."

Brennon nodded. "Very nice," he responded. "Where is Aaron these days? My secretary said he would not be available."

"Miss Blatt is in the atrium."

From the rear of the great manor house spread a vast manicured lawn, every angle correct to the eye, squared hedgerows, circular fountains, a covered tennis court, a kidney-shaped swimming pool with a smaller mansion that, Brennon guessed, was the bathhouse. As they came to a break in a wall of ceiling-high glass, Sydney turned abruptly. "Careful, sir," and he stepped down over glazed tiles with gold and purple edging, entering the atrium.

It was a hothouse of sorts, with rows of planters and flowers in every color imaginable, the lofty ceiling of frosted glass, giving Brennon the feel of moving inside a light bulb. At the far end of this humid room he immediately saw the figure of an elderly woman among the greenery, standing over what appeared to be yellow orchids. She was carefully snipping with tiny pruning shears, removing one leaf at a time. She was dressed in a white blouse and slacks, with a gold braided chain on the outside of a high-necked collar. She looked to be eighty, Brennon guessed, her color a subtle but powdery rouge, her gray hair pulled back into a bun.

Brennon noticed that her sleeves were rolled up, revealing a dark blue tattoo along the inside of her left forearm. He felt his stomach knot as she self-consciously tugged her sleeve, covering the horrid markings. She did not look up, though she was aware of their presence as Sydney came alongside. Brennon heard a fluttering of birds somewhere, but could not tell if they were inside the glass walls or out.

"Mr. Brent Masters." He bowed slightly, handing her the card; then she quickly surveyed the stranger, a smile appearing on a kindly face.

"A pleasure," she said, offering her hand. "I spoke with Mr. Flores on the phone last night. A story on Aaron could not have been better timed."

"Yes, ma'am," Brennon gave a courteous nod, "why is that?"

"The DIDS Center for Research. You'll have the details before anyone else, but I thought you knew?"

"No, ma'am, but I'd like to. Depending upon what I learn,

Aaron could very well lead our list of *Life-style* entrepreneurs."

She smiled. "Then we will get better acquainted and I shall tell you all about it," she said proudly. "It will put a positive spin on your story."

Brennon smiled.

"Sydney," she ordered, "iced tea, and . . ." she turned.

"That sounds very good, thank you."

". . . and also bring some snacks. Mr. Masters looks hungry to me." She addressed him with a raised eyebrow. "Are you eating well, young man? You should not skip meals."

"Right away, Miss Blatt," Sydney responded, and was gone.

"Well," Brennon found himself confessing, "it's a busy world out there."

She emitted a sigh and shook her head at him, her voice carrying a slight European accent that Brennon could not place. "It hurts me you are so thin, a nice-looking young man like yourself."

"Yes, ma'am," Brennon said, feeling awkward to be left alone with the unsuspecting mother of the man who had paid for Zachariah Dorani's burial urn back in 1966. He could not help but feel as deceptive as the devoid he was hunting. Typically they came stalking the innocent from behind the camouflage of their manipulative lies: that was a behavioral hallmark—men sleeping beside wives who never know of their husbands' little whims, mothers embracing sons who belied their secret hobbies. If this mother knew who he really was, or why he had come, her life would end in a tick. Matthew Brennon swallowed his own spit. He hated it when they were so nice, the mothers and fathers; why did they always have to be so nice?

Without hesitation the small woman gently pushed her arm up through his. "We'll sit on the porch, it's more comfortable," she said, gazing up into his eyes as she led him closely down an aisle toward the rear of the greenhouse. "My Aaron gave all of this to me," she said. "I am very lucky."

"Yes, ma'am, I can see that."

"Oh, please," she cried, "call me Myra. Your parents must be very proud, so tall and well-cultured."

"Cultured?" Brennon chuckled.

"A writer," she blinked, "but you're not married!" She

reached, taking up his left hand, examining where a ring should be.

"No," Brennon shrugged. "Not as of yet. Almost, once, that . . ."

"Don't tell me you don't have time," she chastised.

"Well, I . . ."

"You'll find her when you least expect it, and you'll know, there's still time, you're very young."

"Yes, Myra," Brennon agreed as they walked onto a cool deck through an open door. The level of personal disclosure the woman had reached so quickly amazed him.

"I do *not* believe that my Aaron will ever settle down, he's in love with his business."

"My staff told me he could not be reached. Do you know where he is?"

A slight smile crossed her lips as they came to an intimate oasis overlooking a reflecting pool. An elaborate fountain of bronze dolphins spouted streams of water under which a school of koi swam merrily in circles. "Neat," Brennon said, "these are really big guys."

"Aaron had this built for my eightieth birthday—that was some time ago."

Sydney came from between hedges sporting two silver trays. Laying these down carefully on a table, he unrolled a cloth, and carefully lifted the food onto the fine woven linen.

"Thank you, that will be all," she instructed, and he bowed slightly. Placing a silver bell near her plate, he pulled a chair out for her and helped her to settle in.

"I'm sorry," she said, "what were we saying?"

"That Aaron's not available."

"Yes, he's in Florida on business. But he calls home every three days, we'll be speaking Tuesday night. Please try the lox, it's Danish and very high in protein."

"Yes, ma'am." He started reaching for the tray, but instead of thinking of Florida, his thoughts wandered to a small agricultural village in western Maine. Scott's theory had placed Brennon in the position of deceiving some poor old woman over slices of pink seafood cut thin as wafers, and he found himself picking at these, careful not to tip the pile. She leaned over and grabbed the plate out of his hand.

"You eat like a bird," she fluttered with her fingers across the lox. Ignoring the silver serving fork, she pinched a healthy pile, then dropped this onto Brennon's open-faced roll. She continued in a methodical circle, stacking deli delights, then placed a heaped plate in front of him. She picked up the silver bell, ringing once.

"Thank you, you're very kind," he responded.

"Eat, Brent Masters," she demanded. "It hurts me, the way you're so thin!"

The truth was, Matthew Brennon was hurting a whole lot more.

"Yes, Miss Blatt?"

Brennon dropped his eyes as he took another healthy bite.

"A large glass of cold milk."

"Yes, ma'am," he nodded.

"I believe Aaron's been setting up two new DIDS offices in the gulf area, but I don't meddle," she commented, taking a sip of tea. "Is something troubling you?"

"No," Brennon breathed, "this is wonderful food."

"You are familiar with how DIDS works, funding other doctors who would not be able to open practices on their own?"

"Yes," he said, moving quickly to capture control of the conversation. "Aaron is an only child?" he asked.

"No," she said, growing suddenly somber, "he had two older brothers killed during the war."

"I'm sorry."

Sydney was back, placing a large glass in front of Brennon.

"Aaron makes up for a lifetime." She smiled at him, and Brennon glanced into light brown irises that shielded a painful reality that was almost palpable. He took a sip of cool milk.

"You are writing a personality piece?"

"Yes," he lied, "a profile."

"Then you should begin at the beginning," she said. "It is a miracle that he's alive. He was a Holocaust child, born in Poland in 1937, did you know?"

Brennon swallowed. "No, I did not." He removed a small tape recorder from his coat pocket, bumping the grip on his service automatic in the process, and placed the electronic device on the table.

"Then you are from Poland?" he asked.

"No, our families originate from Hungary. Our name was Himmelblatt—that was shortened in America. Aaron's father was a research doctor, and in 1932 he had taken a position at the Polish Medical Institute, so you see, medicine runs in our family. I was a nurse when we first met. Aaron was two when the Nazis came."

Brennon swallowed hard, suddenly thinking of the chrome gutters of Rigby's creamer. He could only imagine the horrors of that dark period.

"Every day since the Einsatzgruppen, I see Aaron as a gift of life—"

"I'm sorry," he interrupted, "I don't know that term."

"The SS," she responded, "very special units. On September 27, 1939, they began roaming the village streets throughout Poland, going from house to house, dragging away men who might oppose the New Order. They were after intellectuals, lawyers, teachers, government officials, anyone who could speak out and become a leader. Aaron's father," she sighed, "he was well-known by our non-Jewish neighbors, so he was taken on the first day."

"To the camps," he concluded sadly.

"No, no, that came much later. They were murdering in the woods then, about two hundred a day. The rest of us were left alone until November, then Aaron's brothers were taken to Treblinka. But the SS left me with my baby, they did not take Aaron. Too much work," she shrugged, "or perhaps pity."

Brennon had stopped eating.

"In June 1942 Aaron and I were taken to Auschwitz. Since I was a nurse, I was able to survive by working in the medical laboratories. And I was able to keep my baby."

"God, that's awful," Brennon declared.

She nodded thoughtfully. "After the war, I came to America with a nickel in my pocket and a hole"—she pointed at her chest—"a hole through my heart. Put that in your story," she said. "Aaron survived and was able to achieve beyond measure!"

Brennon waited a moment, finishing his milk, eyeing the take-up spool through a plastic window. "Mrs. Blatt," he said, lowering his head, "Myra. That picture of Aaron in the hallway. If he was born in 1937 and he had his bar mitzvah at age twelve or so, then that painting was commissioned around 1950?"

"Yes," she agreed, "that's about right."

"That type of artwork is very expensive for someone who came to America with a nickel."

She smiled at this. "A probing question. You have an insightful mind, Brent Masters. The early portraits were paid for by a friend of Aaron's father, a doctor who was with me in the camps. In fact, he helped Aaron to make his start in the world, so if you have time, he'd be a good man to interview."

"Yes," he agreed.

"Dr. Rubin Jaffe. He helped with the expense of Aaron's education, then later in starting the DIDS corporation. Aaron paid him back, right to the penny."

"Is Dr. Jaffe in Dallas?"

"No, he resides in the Maryland countryside. The important point for your article is that although Dr. Jaffe has been a great benefactor to many children who survived the camps, my Aaron would still be a self-made millionaire. It's a question of drive, Rubin will tell you it is so."

"Yes, ma'am, a point well taken. Do you recall another friend by the name of Zachariah Dorani?"

"No," she shook her head, "a friend of Aaron's?"

"I guess not."

He watched as Myra Blatt rose from her chair. "We'll take a peek at Aaron's bedroom," she whispered. "I'll show you something very special."

In a manor large enough to be a grand European hotel, the bedroom of Aaron Seymour Blatt was amazingly small, on the fourth floor and just below the attic stairwell.

It took two elevators and a long walk to get there, but finally they stood in front of a crudely finished wooden door that had been painted green. Myra caught the questioning expression on Brennon's face. "Brent," she soothed, "this is off the record?"

He agreed.

"Aaron had all of this, including the door, dismantled from the house where he grew up on Mission Lane in Dallas, exactly as it was. He does have another bedroom, more adult, it overlooks the pool."

Brennon nodded.

"He saved everything so that he would never forget where he came from, poor but proud." She stopped to insert the key as behind them the wooden attic stairs creaked and Sydney appeared, his face stern, his chin thrust forward.

"Yes?" she questioned.

"Only checking on Madam," the servant said as she turned a worn lock that could have come from a scrapyard.

"We're fine, thank you." She waved him away, then whispered to Brennon, "This is supposed to be Aaron's secret. Sydney's too protective."

Brennon had to lower his head to step beneath the ceiling beam.

The little room was a fresh sky blue, the walls completely bare. A twin mattress lay on a circular rug in the center, the white bedding made to perfection, not a wrinkle to be found. Across from the foot was a highly polished wooden bureau with a dozen small dishes, neatly holding a man's dressing accessories beneath a spotless mirror.

Brennon's gaze roved quickly.

Beneath a small window sill was a workbench constructed of raw two-by-fours, though these had been sanded smooth, and he followed as Myra made her way there. The surface was neat as a pin, not a tool in sight, only an electric vacuum cleaner and brush lying next to an architect's model. This sat beneath an adjustable spring-loaded light, and she reached past him, to turn on the beam. "DIDS Center for Research," she said proudly.

Brennon looked at an expansive structure complete with tiny cars parked in front of the main entrance, which resembled a neomodern recreational center. Brennon thought it antiseptically strange, and was surreptitiously peering beyond the white and silver-sided model when he spotted a perfume bottle in the corner of the bench.

At first he thought it contained seashells, dozens of tiny shells soaking in a blue solution. Finding this strange, he knelt, pretending to study the building's entrance.

"It's his dream come true," she said.

Brennon cringed, fighting the upswell of his breakfast. The bottle was filled to the crystal lid with human ivory.

"The design was his idea. He went through several qualified architects."

Brennon swallowed hard. There were teeth of every size and shape, molars, incisors, eyeteeth, the gum lines showing as a darker shade of white. He hunted for a hint of gold or silver in the collection, but there was none. These were young teeth, a good hundred of them, bright, shining, soaking in a wash of blue.

"Ever since I can remember, he's been interested in premature decay and gum disease. The center will address both, a place for serious research."

"That's wonderful," he answered tonelessly, coming to his

feet. Quickly he scanned the room for a file or bookshelf, pleased that there were none. He turned to face the proud mother, the man who would make sure her son was executed.

"I've read that Aaron's not a serious researcher, which is why he has never published," he said in an accusatory voice.

"Oh, but he has!" she snapped, a hurt expression on her face. "I will show you!"

With that she turned and walked briskly toward the door. "It will take only a second."

While she was gone, Brennon worked quickly.

Removing a pair of white gloves from a jacket pocket, he pulled these on while studying the bottle of teeth. Then he took a black zipper kit from his jacket and laid it alongside. From inside it he removed a small aerosol can. Spraying the entire glass, he wrapped it in a solid sheet of sticky tape, rubbing it into place with his fingertips, then lifting, peeling away. Yellow fingerprints and smudges came free.

He rubbed the jar with his gloves to remove the fine forensic pollen, and set it back on the table. Adjusting the desk beam, he twisted the lid open. Molars, incisors, wisdom teeth, and eyeteeth all glimmered at him. The room filled with a medicinal odor as the top came free.

He spread his fingers, seeking to steady his hands.

First he sucked juices up into a syringe and sealed the needle. Then he laid five small evidence pouches in a row on the bench. Carefully working the zippered seams, he reached down to a gangly wisdom tooth with four long roots. The fluid stirred to his touch, swelling into a blue stain on his gloved fingertips as he removed the human ivory. Holding it to the light, he grimaced. The roots curled inward like the tentacles of cancer, a bit of graying flesh still clinging between them.

He swallowed, his hand steadied by hate.

If Scott was correct, then Lacy Wilcott's teeth would come next, carried like so many pearls in the hands of a killer. Her only sin was leaving the protection of Moxie Pond.

He quickly returned the jar to where he had found it as Myra Blatt came through the door.

Brennon turned to face her, but could not.

He could no longer look into the eyes of this mother.

* * *

At 10:58 A.M., Brennon stood at a phone booth at the Rise and Shine, an open-air bar at Dallas International Airport, waiting for his connection. Although he and Scott had been reviewing their mutual progress, they were both silently scanning notes and documents, double-checking against the record.

As Brennon turned to another page in his notebook, seeking out the date that Aaron Seymour Blatt had enrolled at Georgetown Dental School, he was confronted by a man who demanded five dollars. "To help the children," the stranger told his captive audience, and a collection can came forward as Brennon fumbled through his papers.

"I already gave," he muttered, but the man stood firm, bedecked in black, suggestive of a priest, which he was not.

"For the poor and the crippled," he insisted, "the aged and the ill." At last Brennon fumbled through his pockets and found a crumpled dollar. Handing this over, he looked the other way as a voice spoke into his ear.

"Matt," Scott said, "I'm looking at the deed to County Plat 178, the River Road properties that include the bowling alley. Is the name of Blatt's mentor Rubin Jaffe?" he asked with a nasty bite.

Brennon closed his eyes with a nod. "One and the same, Jack. I don't know what that means, but we've got a hit."

"And what did Mrs. Blatt say about this man, other than the fact he was a victim of the Nazis?"

"She couldn't stop talking about him, a self-made millionaire, very religious, generous to a fault, and a real silent power in Washington. He's known the Blatts since Aaron was a baby, his mother worked with Rubin Jaffe until 1945 when the camps were liberated. I have a feeling Jaffe paid for most of Blatt's education, so it's safe to assume they are still very, very close."

Scott nodded. "When we checked on the land, we discovered that Jaffe owns most of the River Road properties, and damn near half of Washington and Bethesda. I'll start on him from here. What else do we have, did Mrs. Blatt say how long her son lived in this area?"

Brennon checked his notebook. "Five years total, starting in 1955, then he moved back to Texas in June 1960 and founded DIDS. My understanding is that Jaffe also helped to bankroll his business. I'm having numbers run on their mutual financial status, so maybe we'll get another hit, or at least something else we can hook into."

"No," Scott corrected course, "that's not as important as linking Blatt directly into the Florida spree. His mother confirmed he has business there?"

"Blatt calls her like clockwork every week, so she would know."

"And you're meeting with Duncan today?"

"That's affirmative, Jack, in about two hours. Any special instructions?"

"Are you carrying your tape recorder?"

Brennon grinned. "Let's go," he challenged. Reaching into a pocket, he removed a small black rubber suction cup and wet this with his tongue. "How much tape do you want to roll?" He quickly stuck this into place on the back of the telephone receiver.

"Thirty seconds, three . . . two . . . one . . ."

Upon hearing Scott's command, Brennon checked his watch, hitting the button and letting the spool roll forward on record, counting, then snapping the machine off.

"What else do we have?" Scott returned.

"Teeth," Brennon stated grimly.

"And Mrs. Blatt knew they were there?"

"Hell, Jack, she's a very fine old lady. If we're right, this is going to kill her. And besides, what's a bottle of teeth when your only boy is a millionaire dentist?"

Scott nodded. "And you got prints off this collection?"

"A good dirty dozen. If they're on record we'll be able to get a background sheet, provided you make the—"

"It's done," he cut him off. "I told FBI that if they scratch and deliver the wrong files like the last two cases, I'm holding a press conference on their front porch. We don't have time to kill on this one."

Brennon laughed. "Duncan Powell told me that their database budget is being increased another five times this term. Maybe they'll start hiring from McDonald's—"

"Matt," Scott interrupted, "what about this servant, Sydney? Let's run him down just to be on the safe side."

"All right, Jack, but I'm betting he's not a player, he sticks too close to the old woman, but consider it done. But be careful with the alley. I've been thinking about that, and I really don't like it."

Scott nodded. "I understand, but imagine what would happen if we went for a search warrant. Considering Jaffe's budget and political weight, it would take many weeks even if we were successful, which I rather doubt."

"If we get caught, it blows the case."

"I've worked that out with Dudley Hall, he understands the problem, and I've known him since 1953. He's the fastest digger alive—get in quick, get out quick. And if anyone raises the issue, then he found the graves working as a free-lance looter of Civil War sites."

"You're kidding. You think that will wash?"

"Yes, I do. Dudley's brother lives in Wheeling, West Virginia, and that's his line of work, Civil and pre-Civil War antiquities. Dudley will say he was on his way there, having just robbed from the dead. Anyway, he's prepared to take the fall."

"Jesus, Jack, he'd lose his pension!"

There was no answer, for Scott was already moving toward another destination in his mind, planning his approach, working through the details. "We'll talk again from Duncan's radio car," he said.

As Brennon grabbed his bag and headed for the gate, he suddenly feared that the covert nature of this particular investigation had gone too far.

He had plenty of time to think about that. The plane to St. Petersburg boarded a half-hour late, at 11:18 A.M. It then sat on the runway for nearly an hour.

44

10:53 A.M. THE EVERGLADES, FLORIDA

Aaron Seymour Blatt diverted his eyes, holding a collection of human ivory in a tin box, rattling these, looking out from a dirt road into a thickly grown patch of woods.

The young woman in blue was struggling, suspended in the air, kicking backward with naked heels and fighting for her life against the hold of an angry fat man. Gregory Corless had wanted her for intercourse—not sex but pure physical domination. Seymour Blatt had wanted her as a toy, a human living mouth that he could fondle and pick, study and probe. This fascination was no deeper than most other men's lust for a woman's softer parts—breasts, buttocks, legs, hands—and he was merely absorbed in what he required for excitation, while thinking other men equally abnormal for not sharing his concern.

He heard the last breath leaving Carol Barth's body. He knew that sound with his gut, and so turned back to face the end of a macabre dance as the fat man's belly jiggled and the young woman's battered body slipped toward his boots. He removed a cord from her throat. The warm torso leaned against his feet.

"Well, well," Corless said tonelessly, his upper lip twitching with sweat. The lifeless form slid limply off his boots, and he turned, walking toward his partner. They were standing at the edge of a remote wooded lot, thirty short miles from the city of Fort Myers, an hour from the Florida Keys.

What had started as a game of Happy Puppy ended here, with a brief three minutes' worth of actual killing, with their hearts pumping, filled with excitement. Corless seemed more relaxed, more pleased with himself than he had all morning, while Blatt felt a tranquillity that could not be touched.

They wanted to stand there forever, just like this, no sound, no sweeter moment, no interruptions.

The simple act of killing for them was better than fine and blissful dreaming, better than pools of money, better than owning the planet.

Killing made them feel alive, and yet it made them feel boundless, like they were travelers through time. The present lost meaning until it held no significance, nor did the place where they were now; no Florida, no rules, no cities, no concerns of a modern age. Just the living, raging world of primitive man on ancient safari.

After twenty minutes, when they found themselves talking again, it was in whispers, and they did not want to leave.

"Carol and Lacy were awfully good for us," Blatt noted.

"They had no choice," Corless corrected.

"Bakker One-Seven, this is dispatch."

The desk sergeant's voice boomed through the gray box mounted between the handlebars of a bright blue Electro Glide Harley-Davidson. Glades County Highway Patrolman John Brougham was unit One-Seven, six-feet, five-inches' worth of motorcycle cop who lived in a small house just on the other side of the wooded swamp preserve known as Waltzing Waters.

At 10:30 he was dunking a doughnut in front of Marty's Coffee Shop on Route 78, enjoying the fine weather, preparing to finish his weekend shift at noon. He had been on duty since the previous evening, having faced a rather routine Saturday night. There were the usual DWI and traffic accidents, one drug bust for recreational use in a parking lot, and a domestic altercation in a seedy motel near the town of Alva on Highway 80. That had been the high point.

At three A.M. he had been the first officer to respond after a woman busted a gin bottle over her sleeping husband's skull, an unemployed trucker who had, earlier in the night, blackened both her eyes and broken her arm. So in his mind John Brougham was editing his incident report down to a 413, wounding in self-defense, even though she had been feigning sleep for hours before she got the chance to clobber him.

"Dispatch, this is One-Seven," he said between bites of a red-currant-jelly doughnut.

"John, your wife just called, she says to plant more often. You'll know what that means?"

"Roger," he gulped, and the radio cackled with laughter. The code wasn't all that difficult to figure out, and he immediately regretted not helping to devise something just a bit more clandestine. Mr. and Mrs. John Brougham were having difficulty in conceiving their first child, and having ruled out her infertility, his seed was the only possible culprit. They had been waiting a week for lab tests to be returned, and the family doctor had obviously called at dawn on Sunday, knowing how concerned the couple was. The thought occurred to Brougham that all available units had just been informed.

"John, that's good news," the sergeant offered through the box. "A below-normal count isn't unusual, just keep trying."

"Thanks," he sputtered back, knowing the man was being genuine, a real paternal type, just a bit out of touch, enough to have forgotten the pitch and jive of uniformed units. Brougham knew he would be facing locker-room harassment in the days to come.

"Bakker One-Twelve, what's your two-eleven?" the sergeant was asking another unit.

The radio hissed, sparking with laughter. "Speed-trap mile marker five. We can cover for One-Seven . . ."

"Roger that, One-Twelve, take his position intersect I-17 and Gables, traffic monitoring."

"Roger."

"Bakker One-Seven, shave the clock, Johnny," the sergeant offered. "It's a slow shift."

"Roger" is all John Brougham said. He dropped the silver-blue visor on his helmet and fired the powerful machine into thunder. As he sped into the wind, approaching third gear, he picked the microphone back up.

"One-Seven to dispatch," he called.

"Go ahead."

"Thanks," he said, and he meant that. Inside he was a big enough man so that a good laugh, even at his expense, didn't trouble him.

"Are you going to leave her like that?" Blatt said.

Corless shrugged, flipping him a careless bird. Now that the physical high they had felt was over, he really didn't care. Their existence had been transformed back into a bland world where everything seemed gray, endlessly the same. No highs, no lows. They had been to the mountain and returned to a desert wasteland.

"That's not what I meant, Greg, we're only a mile from the main road." Blatt's head spun nervously on a long stalk of neck, straining to find an intrusion, but there were only the sounds of twittering birds coming from behind them.

Corless turned back toward Carol's body, trying to regain his sense of thrill, but staring down and finding none. In life she had been graceful and slim. Now her violet eyes stared aimlessly upward, her mouth a dark red hollow that lacked the sparkle of teeth.

The powder-blue tank-top was torn open, although she had been allowed to dress, and Corless pushed with his right boot, lifting the light torso and heaving it with ease over the edge of the embankment. The body slid limply into a ravine, dark hair streaming behind, and came to rest against a rotting tree stump. The partners waited for a few moments in this peaceful solitude, feeling calm in the still quiet of early morning while gray squirrels fluttered about the body, expecting a treat.

"Where is Newport News?" asked Blatt.

"How the hell would I know?" Corless returned. "In Virginia somewhere, who cares?"

"I liked her accent," Blatt said.

"I'm glad, Seymour. If you bought that jet, we could spend

more time up there." Corless turned back toward the van. "Let's grab some food on the way."

"Greg, we can be at Page Field in a half-hour, it's only eleven-ten."

"Poor pitiful Seymour," Corless hissed, "this safari's still a day ahead of schedule and you're ready to leave? How about one more, we haven't used half our trick bag."

"Greg," he said quite honestly, "I wish you'd stop saying we're on safari, that bothers me."

"Sure, whatever makes you happy." Abruptly he climbed into the cab, waiting for his partner.

"What would make me happy is an early lunch in North Carolina. We could still be in Washington in time for dinner."

"If you let me fly. I gotta fly, Seymour, you know I gotta fly."

Blatt knew this was important to Corless. Like so many middle-aged men who flew small private planes, his manhood was somehow inexorably tied into the cockpit and controls. To Blatt it was absurd, but Corless was set on it.

"I've been thinking—"

"No," Blatt cut him off, "I am *not* buying you a jet." He knew that courteous voice of Greg's, so unlike him to begin with.

Corless was cursing mad at the response. "Seymour," he said, "you're rich as a damn sultan. What's the harm? Buy it as a tax write-off, it would cost nothing."

"Hardly," Blatt puffed.

"If we had a jet, just think of the ground we could cover. An air van, Seymour, a goddamn air van. Able to go anywhere, anytime, and supersonic too. West Coast for blondes. Northwest for pasty skin. Southwest for tanned girls. And the East for society types. We could even bang 'em down in Mexico. Real diversity!" His face wore a manic intensity.

"Twin props are good enough. We already have a Beechcraft, so don't push," he sniped, his thin body plugged firmly in his seat.

"Fuck you!" Corless spat. "You greasy little Jew—" He was about to continue, but Blatt froze, his eyes locked wide with fright like a rabbit too scared to run from a predator. A sound was approaching from beyond the tree line, like an engine without a muffler, or an all-terrain vehicle, coming directly at them.

"Oh, my God, Greg, it could be the police!" Blatt cried, quivering, barely able to control himself.

"Well, then, it's just time to pay for the party." Corless shrugged, his voice dripping with blackmail. "Every man for himself."

"Greg, don't say that!" he whined with fear.

The sound was growing louder, coming from a thicket on the dirt drive they had found off the interstate. The location was so remote, Corless was guessing it was maybe a teen on a go-cart of some type. He was even wondering how old the kid might be. "We wait until they go by, then pull away," said Corless.

"It's a death state!" Blatt cried, gulping for air.

"Cool it." Corless shook his head and casually grabbed the binoculars from behind his seat. Adjusting these and staring through the windshield, he could see a form coming down the soggy roadway just beyond the tree line, moving very slowly over the dirt, the bright blue metallic paint gleaming as he came. He said not a word to Blatt as his hand reached down and wrapped around the grip of the stovepipe revolver. Slowly he lifted the heavy black Magnum into his lap.

Blatt's eyes grew wide, his face frozen in horror with the sound of an engine coming for them, ever steady, coming down on them from the roadway.

"Oh, God, Greg, what is it?" he cried.

"A cop," said Corless, and his face was calm and cruel.

Trooper John Brougham was on his way home through the backwoods, cutting off twenty minutes by using the state land. He crept along the path in an effort to keep dirt off his bike, his visor pulled up, mostly watching for larger stones that could chip paint.

As he reached the clearing he saw a van, but he didn't take much notice of this, since fishing season was upon them and there were two males. But these men were studying a road map.

It was this stall, the use of a map, that caused him to stop.

If Greg Corless hadn't felt they needed to look busy, John Brougham would have just kept going; he would have never stopped to help with directions.

"Oh, God, he's coming straight at us!" Blatt whined.

Corless produced his best grin, lifting a lip and showing teeth because that's what a smile is.

Isn't it?

The bright blue machine pulled next to them. "How you folks today?" Brougham offered to Corless, resting comfortably on his bike, the engine still running, waiting to be asked directions.

"Just fine," Corless responded, "how are you?"

"Good," Brougham nodded, and he straightened up, looking beyond to the other middle-aged male, who seemed a bit fidgety, his eyes blinking too rapidly, his neck bobbing with a nervous tic.

"How's he?" Brougham asked, growing concerned.

Blatt tried not to squeak, fighting to control his bladder. "Just fine, offi-cer," he gulped heavily.

"So where are you headed?" Brougham asked. "Here for the crappies?"

Corless responded thoughtfully. "Heading north, St. Pete, just taking a little rest."

Brougham removed his helmet, looking up at him with penetrating green eyes. The back roads of the Everglades lowlands called Waltzing Waters seemed a strange place for a rest stop, and though it could have been innocent enough, he remembered an APB from the state police. Two men, middleaged, van or station wagon, one thin and neat, the other fat. He turned off his engine and knocked the kickstand forward into place, trying to remember the rest. Something about a decal, that was the best he could do, though he was certainly trying.

"Oh, God," Blatt muttered under his breath, "he's staying."

Dismounting, the policeman maintained eye contact with Corless, then stepped back from the van to what he had been taught in the academy was a safe distance. About six feet, close enough for observation, yet far enough to prevent physical contact. His black boots covered this area in one stride as he smoothly unsnapped his holster and whipped his .9mm to chest level with both hands on a steady regulation aim.

"Step out of the car!" Brougham shouted, studying Corless. "Put both your hands on the wheel, and I want to see fingers—"

An explosion boomed, leaving deafening stillness. The jagged flash from the stovepipe blew through the van's thin door, shredding glass and metal like paper, and hit the policeman squarely in the chest. His body was lifted backward into air as it tumbled onto the bike.

The muzzle's flash was still brilliant in their eyes after the thunderous roar had died.

Corless had kept the .357 in his lap, bringing the gun to rest, muzzle-first, two inches from the door. The heavy bullet had slammed through the trooper's chest, and he lay on his side, a lobe of his heart poking out through his back, still beating as Corless raced toward him, with Blatt scurrying out the driver's door in an effort to catch up.

"I'll be damned," said Corless, staring down.

"Greg, I beg you, I'll buy the jet, let's go, please . . . I'm really scared . . ."

"Of course you are, little buddy," he said, wrapping his arm around him, walking closer to the wounded officer until they were directly over what had been John Brougham.

There's no way to tell, but the odds were that the officer could not see or feel anything, not even the presence of his attackers as they hovered above. His eyes were locked open, but these were dark pools, for shock must have taken over, his life just a biological fact and nothing more, no human element remaining.

And so he very likely did not feel or even know that two more violent charges slammed into his side in one burning instant, though one arm seemed to come alive with the impact, flapping upward twice. The road became visible through a body cavity as the blow-back dust and gunsmoke cleared.

Then silence.

Without hesitation Corless put on gloves and dragged the bike and the body off into the ditch, kicking these downward, where they came to rest next to Carol Barth. They listened for sirens, standing there together, but there were none.

"I want to go, I want to get out of here!" Blatt screamed, near hysteria.

"Yes," agreed the man who would pilot the plane. "We can be ready for takeoff in fifteen minutes."

As he walked, Corless found himself thinking about the protest signs he had seen on television the day they burned Ted Bundy. Now he wasn't sure, exactly, why he had thought of this; maybe because they were in Florida, or maybe he felt that he had beaten the Reaper that took Ted. But there was something deeper, something more.

"God I love this country," he breathed hard as he climbed into the van.

Blatt was his partner, what could he say?

45

NOON POTOMAC, MARYLAND

The Blatt investigation, and the discovery of Samantha Stoner's identity, brought Scott to a country estate called Kilimanjaro, thrusting him into the middle of Washington's powerful high society. Or at least that's what he had been thinking when he arrived, but now he knew better.

There was really nothing sophisticated about what he saw before him, which was money talking in a loud and predictable manner. Kilimanjaro was a huge white mansion in a world of other huge white mansions, row upon row, all gated, all with plaques on paved driveways declaring pretentious-sounding names. Tara had become Scott's favorite, Southland was another, and Wild Mountain still another. To make matters worse, there were no mountains at all in Potomac, Maryland, and certainly no Mount Kilimanjaro, only a silly little green hill.

Scott was sitting in his Chrysler, watching the estate through high-powered lenses. Kilimanjaro was a modern fortress. Staring down from a meadow onto a front yard of perfect green, the house was surrounded by heavy steel Cyclone fence topped with razor wire. A roadway lay between him and the private drive that ran through the menacing wire, and he could see a dark-blue-uniformed guard smoking a cigarette, cap tilted back, his arm wrapped around a middle-aged blonde in gray servant's dress. They were close to the main house.

Immediately to the right was an equestrian center, including a series of barns and what looked like a riding stable with eight stalls. To the left, in a picket-fence exercise ring, a stately gray Arabian trotted over yellow straw as a handler held a restraint, turning in lazy circles.

There were a guest house and indoor swimming pool. A tennis court in one side yard. In the other, a detached garage large enough to enclose a half-dozen cars.

The front gate was deceptive, for there were two back to back. The first was ornate iron, a white latticework to match the house, and the second was about ten feet behind this, composed of chain links and mounted on small rubber wheels to enable a guard to push it aside. There was a guardhouse, again painted white, where a uniformed sentry appeared to be watching television as another approached, walking a black Doberman pinscher on a short leather crop. They were moving together as a tight team, coming down a gentle rise in the bright sun, and Scott could not bring himself to believe that what he was viewing stood in the most affluent suburb of Washington, D.C.

Here, in Potomac, Maryland, just one short mile from the private residences of two Supreme Court Justices, the Secretary of State, and the Attorney General of the United States.

The dog snarled and lurched against his lead as a car filled with church worshipers slowed near the fence to admire the spread. The K-9 was instantly released and the handler grinned as the dog viciously charged the fence. The car sped off.

Witnessing this viciousness, Scott found himself remembering a rumor he had heard one April, scuttlebutt between boys playing kickball on the streets of New York.

As quickly as it had come, this ugly rumor had been dismissed as just that, rumor. But by September 1946 a series of pictures appeared in national magazines, and Scott's father had called him in early in order to take his entire family to Mass. On the way to church, his parents gave one big sorry effort to explain, but they never could, Scott remembered.

Could anyone?

The twisted bodies lying for miles in bright sun. Iron doors caked with ash, their hinges dark and gray. Piles of human hair, pigtails tied with ribbon. And the gallows, strung with wire and the death they made there, of every size and shape, of every sex and age. Private rooms of horror. Meat hooks. Stained floors.

Dachau. Buchenwald. Treblinka.

These were the first images broadcast to the world, and the names that Scott remembered best—names that begged for mercy when said aloud, but names that did not belong to the factory where human beings suffered in the corruptible name of science. News of that came later. Men of medicine inflicting wound channels for study, mothers forced to watch their daughters being sexually destroyed.

Auschwitz.

Backed by a figure of six million souls, John F. Scott had

made a lifetime of study: *The Devoid, the Psychopathology of Recreational Killers.*

If a former victim of Auschwitz was living here, behind the snarling dogs and black uniforms and razor wire, and if this compound did *not* speak directly to that man's memory, filling him with terror—then either he was no victim or Scott was no psychologist.

Walking briskly, with a slick military precision, the K-9 sentry advanced toward Scott, who quickly started his engine as the team crossed the roadway. Upon hearing the ignition, the man immediately released the dog's crop. The jaws quivered and snapped as the K-9 awaited instructions.

Slowly Scott coasted across the street past them, heading up the driveway and toward the gate. Holding up a palm, a tall young man stepped from the booth, approaching in a uniform that was expensively complete with a black tie and matching cuffs. The car came to a stop, and the man leaned toward Scott's open window. From his rearview he could see the K-9 patrolman trotting into position from the rear. Near the guest house on his left, a young woman was sitting on a white stallion.

"May I help you?" the guard asked politely.

"Yes," said Scott, and he held up his badge. The man read the identification card and gave a precise nod.

"Commander Scott," he said with ease, "you do not have the right address."

Scott nodded. "Dr. Rubin Jalle?"

The guard glanced over the car at the K-9 unit, then back at Scott, establishing eye contact. "Sir, do you have an appointment?" he asked in a hard voice.

Scott yawned. "Didn't know one was required."

The woman on horseback was coming forward, riding an English mount, her equestrian dress a bright scarlet, her boots and hat a black inky pitch. She slowed her gait to a walk as she approached. A child, Scott thought, sixteen at best, with dark brown eyes and pale skin.

"We have strict orders"—the guard glanced at a clipboard for effect—"no one is allowed on the estate without an appointment. I do not see your name, so I'm sorry, Commander, I will have to ask you to leave."

Scott nodded thoughtfully. "Son," he said in a condescending voice, "do you know what a warrant is?"

"Yes, sir." The man's face was stone.

"Then pick up the phone," Scott instructed, nodding at the booth, "and tell Dr. Jaffe that I'm here for a friendly visit and that you are making that unfriendly. I do not take rejection well, I'm afraid, and I do have considerable grounds."

"Yes, sir, but—"

"And tell him that I can be a very unpleasant man, in fact, a real sonofabitch when I get cooking. With a search warrant I'll bring in a backhoe and dig up his entire lawn, and I mean that." Scott glanced at his watch. "And the stables too, plus drain the swimming pool and drill for evidence."

"Sir, I—"

"Do it!" Scott raised his voice in a nasty roar, something he rarely did.

The guard looked at the handler, then walked directly to the booth and picked up a red phone. Words were exchanged, Scott seeing only his back; then he quickly returned.

"Sir," he said nervously, "there are no firearms allowed in the residence."

"Open the gate!" Scott ordered.

His face was cold and gaunt, withered as if by harsh desert winds, his eyes a colorless gray. These were watching Scott with graven intensity, set deeply in a freshly barbered face, his jowls sagging with the translucence of age.

His belly protruded, but this was all but concealed by an exquisitely tailored suit, a tasteful gunmetal blue with pleats to cut a figure where there was little. Dr. Rubin Jaffe was standing impatiently in a marbled foyer where water splashed in a stone fountain.

They made eye contact as Scott came through the door, and he noticed that Jaffe was a tall man and that he used a walker, a cage with silver and black ebony struts, the curved handles like two polished baby elephant tusks. The doctor eyed him with contempt, receiving him without a word, observing Scott's every move as he strolled through a high vaulted room with a servant on either side. The commander was sure they doubled as bodyguards for the aging Holocaust victim.

Upon request, with his eyes locked on Jaffe's, Scott removed his service automatic, snapped out the clip, then laid this on the tray held toward him. As the old man started forward, it was at once obvious that the walker was no prop. His torso turned awkwardly, his legs were working stiffly, the thing was gliding toward Scott on small soundless wheels.

"What is this about?" he demanded, and his face and tone were cruel.

Scott came straight to the point. "Serial murder, a criminal investigation." Tersely he explained how the remains of Samantha Stoner had been found beneath Bowl America, a property that Jaffe had purchased directly from the county in 1958, the year she was killed. The doctor did not respond in any manner, no words, no expression, but simply turned his walker away. He was hobbling down the hallway, the thing gliding, when a childish giggle sounded behind them.

Scott turned and caught a glimpse of what looked like a girl, but one wearing bizarre makeup. He guessed eight or nine, with harlot red lips and thick mascara. He was about to inquire when the doctor, never looking back, interrupted his thoughts.

"My nephew," Jaffe said flatly.

Scott felt a twang of nausea as he followed the caged man down a drafty corridor. "I bet you have a number of them," he stated sarcastically.

The doctor did not answer.

There were towering double doors of inlaid oak on two sides of the study. It was dark, the walls paneled in wormwood, with one picture window looking out onto a bright green yard and swimming pool. The tall wire fence was hidden from this view by a thicket and as they entered the room, the doctor, with a slight gesture of one hand, motioned Scott toward a red leather couch while moving to sit at a huge mahogany desk.

Jaffe was adjusting himself in a high-back executive chair as a waiter appeared through a side door. He stood patiently awaiting his master's wish.

"Tea," Jaffe said flatly without looking up.

"And you?" the servant asked without tone.

"Coffee," Scott ordered, "black."

As the waiter vanished, Scott surveyed the walls. It was an old collection of primitive artifacts, including an array of menacing spears with bright knifelike tips. He recognized these as a Moro warrior's from the Philippine Islands, and above, a series of hand-fashioned helmets made from reeds. Six enormous swords were mounted in a huge star, the thick blades reflecting afternoon light, and Scott felt the penetrating stare of Dr. Jaffe, who was inspecting him with some curiosity, perhaps disdain, summing him up.

"Moro Indian?" Scott asked.

Jaffe's brow raised slightly, and he nodded. "You know your weapons, Mr. Scott. Those were a gift from a tribesman. I visited the Moros in the late 1950's."

Next Scott's eyes came to rest on a large wildcat springing from the wall with half a torso. In the corner of the room was a leopard standing on its hind legs like a trained bear, holding an arrow in its teeth.

"Ituri Forest, the Congo," Jaffe offered. "Two hundred pounds, took him with one shot."

Across the great wall to his left were hundreds of artifacts, made from reed and wood, cloth from hammered bark, bows and spears, small drums and musical instruments fashioned from monkey skins, and one sporting the head of a howling red monkey beneath what looked like a thick buggy whip.

"Do they beat their food before eating?" Scott suggested.

Jaffe turned his head but did not smile. "That is a *fita,* a whip used for sacred ceremonies by the forest people of BaLese."

"Stanley's dark continent."

"Yes, the very heart."

"You traveled there extensively?"

Jaffe leaned forward in his chair. "You are a cultured man, Mr. Scott, what is it you want of me?" He said this almost absently, a man who ruled his universe with absolute power. The waiter appeared, serving his master first, then quietly placing a small silver coffeepot and cup before Scott on a three-legged table. The men waited for the servant to disappear.

"So, Jack Scott, tell me about yourself. An Irish cop, what will they think of next?"

The commander smiled. "Tell me about Tobytown," he said neutrally, dropping a sugar cube into his cup before pouring.

"I'm afraid I don't know it."

Scott's eyes locked Jaffe's in a head-on stare as he confidently poured the hot black liquid, then began stirring with his spoon. "Make that the River Road properties, both sides of the street. You own the entire block as well as fourteen buildings, a gas station, a television station, and two banks. The only thing you don't own is the Shiloh Baptist Church."

The old man smiled as if tasting sweets for the first time. "Yes, that is very true, and years ago I also tried to buy that church. Offered quite a lot of money for the silly thing, but the fools turned me down. Even so"—he flitted with both his hands—"I have no knowledge of this Tobytown, other than the housing development that I donated from the goodness of my heart to some displaced persons."

Scott smiled at the sarcasm. Rubin Jaffe was toying with him. "So, you are a charitable guy, a real fine fellow?"

Jaffe nodded without expression. "Ask anyone, Earth First, B'nai B'rith, Center for Creative Nonviolence, Save the Bay, Earth Watch, numerous fine arts, the list is endless."

Scott sipped his coffee. "The village of Tobytown existed until July 1958, then burned to the ground. Arson would be my guess. The following September you bought the entire block, lock, stock, and barrel of ash."

Jaffe exhaled with pleasure. "Yes, that was years ago, these properties are parts of cities now. We house and employ the masses, Mr. Scott. Are you sure that's what they called it?"

"Tobytown, named for the cemetery that was destroyed to make way for development."

"Well, it's a pity. Good thing I was around to help." He smiled, sipping his tea.

"And how much weight did you gain at Auschwitz?" Scott asked flatly.

Jaffe's eyes narrowed but didn't flinch. His mouth turned upward with amusement as he steadily refilled his cup from a copper kettle. "Well, you're a slick sonofabitch," he said. "What do you really want?"

"Who struck the match?"

Jaffe chuckled. "Statutes, you should know better. The limitations are long expired if, as you are suggesting, there was some type of crime involved."

Scott did not respond.

"You *do* know who I am, Mr. John Scott. You do know whom you are talking with?"

He shook his head. "Why don't you tell me?"

Jaffe leaned into his high-back leather chair with a knowing smile. "Read *Forbes,* you will find I'm wealthier than a king, the top ten billionaires. And I do have friends, powerful and worthy ones. While I won't bother you with my net worth," he paused for effect, "you should know where it all came from."

Scott smiled. "Well, we surely can't venture a wrong guess on anything this important."

"Good," he agreed, "because I was thinking you might have to move at the end of the year when your lease expires."

Scott did not take this bait.

"Tell me, Jack, you are a federal employee, so what building do you work in?"

"World Trade in New York or the Federal Headquarters Center in Washington."

"Well, well," Jaffe clicked, "in both instances that means I am your landlord." Scott cocked his head. "You see, Commander, I am landlord to most of the United States government, since they are prohibited from owning too many buildings, I own for them, then lease back. I own nearly every building that houses federal employees by day, plus many they live in by night. Some of the most powerful men on this planet call me just to get a bit nicer office. So you see, I am an unheard-of industry, and I've been able to corner that market by following political corruption. Greed, Mr. Scott. When the government sells out, they sell out to Rubin Jaffe."

Scott nodded, thinking this over. "That's quite an angle. There's a code putting a cap on federal ownership of real estate?"

"Only buildings, I'm afraid," Jaffe noted. "That code has made me rich on your taxes, so I do hope you're current. You should know right now that your little theory about Toady Town, while it amuses me, I find no threat there, anywhere."

Scott nodded. "I'm glad," he stated flatly. "Fear is a wasted emotion."

Dr. Rubin Jaffe smiled darkly, watching with amusement. "I find you to be very perceptive. That alone is of interest. So entertain me, Jack Scott."

Scott considered this offer. He could not tell if it was genuine, so he fashioned a question to test the waters. "Tobytown, do you believe it was torched?"

"Yes," he said without equivocation, "land is money. Where should I have banked it, where do you put yours?"

"In your pocket," Scott said. "I thought we established all of that, though I do find great reward in what I've chosen to do for a living."

"And you do what, exactly? I wasn't clear on that."

"I'm a manhunter, Dr. Jaffe. I remove killers from society."

Jaffe nodded thoughtfully. "But you seem so small and meek to me, Mr. Scott. Do you really have the stomach for it?"

"I do, and I find a great wealth in saving lives, and in the characters I am able to meet, the people I deal with. You'll find no luggage rack on my hearse, I'm afraid. Did you pay to destroy Tobytown?"

"Well, I like that!" Jaffe chuckled suddenly as his eyes danced. "A man with a philosophy—that *is* rare in this age, very entertaining. Rich with the lives of others, and yes, while I'll give no confessions, who else could it have been?"

Scott nodded gratefully. "And the man who lit that fire—"

"Only one?" Jaffe cut him off with a sarcastic smile. "That was over thirty years ago. Is that the best you can offer?"

"Correct me."

"I cannot. You know the law, Jack, skirting the edge of incrimination."

"I've assumed the job was to drive people from Tobytown in any manner possible?"

Jaffe nodded. "They were trying to pay their back taxes, if there was such a place, and they came close, that was my understanding."

"Then does the name Samantha Stoner mean anything to you?"

"I'm sorry, it does not."

Scott reached into his briefcase for a color picture of the clay bust, then walked this to the large mahogany desk and laid it in front of the older man.

He merely glanced at it and shook his head. "Nothing," Jaffe said, "although I do remember a Negro accusing me of kidnapping his family, so maybe . . ."

Scott nodded gratefully. "Do you remember anything about him?"

"A stonecutter, I believe. We bought and sold his business, nothing more than that."

Scott felt sick: the Auschwitz victim was talking about Samantha's father. "This child was killed in April, three months before the fire was set."

"Is that what you're after, some crime from our ancient past? Oh, come, Mr. Scott, relevance, please. I demand relevance." Rubin Jaffe's face grew huge with disbelief. "You disappoint me. You seemed such a bright and cultured man."

"Did you pay the fire-starter?"

Jaffe shook his head. "That is very unprofessional, rather accusatory."

"Then he wasn't a local man?"

"I hired no one, but the towns of Cabin John and Bethesda were rife with inbreeding, tight, and very, very small. We changed all of that, built the cities, and people did the rest."

"The rest?" Scott puzzled.

Jaffe tilted back in his chair, clasping his fingers together. "They breed, Jack, ergo they did the rest. It is mankind's only true and predictable behavior: if you put people together, they *will* fuck. Any man that accepts that can make a fortune. Humans breed like space is not a finite thing, and it is this behavior," he paused to smile, "that makes men like me wealthy beyond reason."

Scott removed a photograph of Zak Dorani from his file and approached the desk slowly. He held this in front of the doctor and watched his eyes carefully. There was no change, no expression at all.

"Then I thank you for your time," Scott said, returning to close his briefcase, his posture curled into intentional defeat, sagging shoulders, chin turned down slightly as he was preparing to leave.

"You are a very cunning man," Jaffe said darkly. "Your body language is a skilled performance, you are very good, really."

"No," Scott stated, "I've taken enough of your time."

"I think not." His eyes smiled with amusement. "Your mind is bursting with questions, yet this, for whatever reason, is the most important to you?"

"Perhaps," Scott stated.

Jaffe leaned forward on his desk. "I never saw his face, and I never knew his name. Tell me his name."

"Zak Dorani."

The doctor gave a knowing nod. "Quite possible. From that old photo I can tell you that he *would* have been my choice, but I leave those things to others so that I have no immediate knowledge."

"Fascinating, but why would he be a candidate? How would you know?"

Jaffe sighed with annoyance. "Oh, please, better than that, I grow weary."

Scott's mind flipped instantly back to the camps, to the pictures and films he remembered as a child. "The eyes," he concluded. If Jaffe had really been there, he'd know, and he obviously did, for he was nodding thoughtfully.

Slowly Dr. Jaffe placed a finger under each lid, and then

pointed directly at Scott's heart. "No one home," he spat, "emotionless. And, yes, I truly have seen it before."

"Then would it trouble you to know that women and children were disappearing at his hand because he enjoyed his assignment so much?"

"That is unfortunate," Jaffe stated coldly. "I am not a killer, and that was not part of the request."

"And your involvement ended there?"

"What involvement?" He held up his hands. "The darkies have always been good for me, Jack, they rent my slums, they give me properties to develop."

Scott stood slowly, wanting to vomit into the man's face. Instead he walked toward the monkey head on the wall, then admired a row of sticks set into a design that resembled the spokes of a wheel. "May I?"

Jaffe nodded, watching with great curiosity as Scott stood on his toes to finger them. They were black, darkened from fire, sharp as needles to the touch.

These, in turn, were surrounded by shiny steel rods of half the length and thickness. Scott tried not to choke while fighting the sickening tide that was now pulsing, coursing through his body as he stared into the open maw of a red monkey, the thin white teeth glistening like angry needles.

"And these?" Scott asked.

"The metal ones are fléchettes, the wooden ones are *njobo*. They are really one and the same. One modern, one ancient, death's most perfect instrument."

"Very interesting," Scott responded, and his voice sagged. "These are hand-held instruments?"

"No, no, again you disappoint me, such limited knowledge. The wooden shafts are from the lost tribe of Ituri, proving that peoples of the Congo are not so primitive as the Western world would like to think."

Scott shrugged, raising a questioning hand, and though this trembled slightly, he did not believe the aging doctor saw it.

"They are used in various forms to kill and control *nyama,* or the devil spirit of the forest. They had a saying for it, *evil controlling evil,* that's the rough translation. The shaft is actually the weapon, the delivery differs according to purpose. The steel fléchette was developed by the U.S. Army's Armed Forces Special Weapons Project in 1956 and is based entirely on the primitive system."

"I don't understand."

Looking at him with puzzlement, Jaffe rose from his desk, pushing the walker before him. Tall enough to reach the display easily, he removed a wooden shaft and handed this to Scott.

"Feel how light it is, the balance and strength, the metal toughness, cuts through air like a deadly spirit. Certain tribes thought it was spirit, made from a living thing. Every speck of the forest is thought to have a soul, even trees and fire, so they were used in combination."

Scott did not have to examine too closely. He had held this a thousand times before, and was fighting with those images now.

"During a hunt," Jaffe continued, "a BaMbuti warrior could place several of these into his prey from a great distance, depending upon his skill. While it would slow a being down, it was not uncommon to see the head of an adversary filled like a pincushion."

Scott swallowed. "So death was not instantaneous?"

"Hardly. Those are special bolts used for shooting the red monkey you see grinning at you. He took ten, the precise number to steal evil and transfer it to the warrior. This makes him stronger, increasing his powers."

"And the method of delivery?"

"A blowgun, very accurate, very effective for stunning prey. They whistle through the air like deadly insects, impaling the victim's head. And it's impossible to know the direction of attack."

"And the fléchette?"

"Potentially the deadliest small-arms projectile ever designed, but it was dropped by the armed forces as inhumane. They were also used as small arrows, what we would call bolts or quarrels. My fascination was with the surgical precision of both the ancient and the modern version. It is because they are so thin and sharp that their velocity is so great."

Scott had seen footage of blowguns at work. They were silent and capable of delivering a projectile with incredible violence.

"When it comes to the fléchette, nearly every country on earth has experimented with them. As for the ancient version, more than a hundred living tribes around the world still use them. But these"—he held the black wood in his hand— "would be known only to the most serious of hunters. The study of them is an art by itself."

Jaffe was pointing Scott toward the door, the wheels on his cage gliding across a Persian carpet.

"Then that technique you explained," Scott followed, "ten nails or better—in the ancient beliefs of the Congo, that was considered killing deeper than life?"

Jaffe nodded. "You are a well-educated man. A pity we will not speak again."

"And my question?"

Jaffe smiled darkly as his manservant moved before them, opening the giant wooden door to the world outside and offering Scott his gun.

"The ancient fléchette is used to extract power from death and suffering. It kills the body, but more important, it kills the soul."

Scott stood on the front steps, gazing deeply into the doctor's eyes. "Did you explain all this to Aaron Seymour Blatt before or after he hired you an arsonist?"

The man's dark pupils instantly constricted into pinpoints, though his expression never changed. "Good day," Jaffe said as he turned away.

"Indeed," Scott added as the door closed tight.

46

Jack Scott strolled down from the gas station on River Road, having parked his car in the rear of the church. "Entertaining," he repeated aloud, his voice filled with disgust. That's how Dr. Rubin Jaffe had explained the ancient blowgun and its fléchette, the use far more satisfying to a killer than a firearm or bow.

A swift, fatal, and silent weapon, that in turn offered the user myth, magic, and perfect control for either slow or instant destruction of life. Since the shaft was shaped for balance, there had been no markings to tell of its origin, only the slight spittle from the attacker, lost to forensics after only a few days. As he walked, he remembered the hands of a victim batting at her face, having to be restrained as she fought off invisible hornets, batting at the air without being able to explain. And there had been others, the shafts removed after death, even before Scott had arrived on the scene.

Why, he thought back, had they not known? Even if the police sciences were in their infancy, that was his job; looking into his mind and watching women and children batting away deadly insects, it was obvious. Suddenly the image of Dr. Chet Sanders appeared to tell him otherwise. "There is nothing you can do, save yourself," Dr. Sanders said, and Scott could hear that old man's voice, soft but clear, tired but never despairing.

"There's still hope," Scott remembered he had responded, and he couldn't believe that now, how hard he had tried to cling to hope, to his own failings, to not being able to fail. A part of the job, he told himself, and he carried his mental baggage down one short flight of crumbling concrete stairs to a damp hole in the ground that was a metal door. This had once been red, but the paint was badly faded into a tomato-soup pink and covered with dirt.

Scott knocked softly with the flat of his palm, hearing Sanders' voice in his mind, a towering man with dark brown hair and warm brown eyes. "She's too badly beaten, Jack, the meninges, the protective membranes enveloping the brain. I'm sorry . . ." Scott heard footsteps. Mercifully. Footsteps were coming.

"Hi, Jack," Rivers offered, "any luck?"

Gazing up into the hard-looking face of a friend he had met only forty-eight hours ago, Scott felt an abiding sorrow for the young detective. He felt like warning him of what his life could become if he stayed in the game, in the manhunt, a haunted old fool with festering memories, it was on the tip of his tongue.

"Jack?" Rivers repeated, and Scott shook himself.

"Sorry, how are we making out?" His gray eyes appeared bloodshot and worn.

"That depends on your point of view, come on in. Dudley Hall is really something, never seen anything like it."

"Good," Scott said, crossing the threshold. He stepped inside an enormous ghost, the ruins of what had been a gaming theater for fun and recreation. The once-polished wooden lanes had been torn apart, revealing strips of concrete with scattered boards where the glue had resisted. The ball-return gutters had been removed, leaving metal support rods poking up from the floor like strange sculpture. At the end of the

lanes, where family and team members once cheered for
strikes, a series of plastic lights dangled from rotted wire.
And an entire third of the building was a still, festering pond
where insects and rodents traded places in the food chain.

It was a breathing darkness.

Only around the splintered plywood by the main door did
light stream through, and as his eyes adjusted, Scott glanced
across the wide expansiveness of Patriots Bowl to where a
snack bar must have stood. The counter was still in place, the
wall behind it destroyed in the removal of sinks, stoves, and
fountains.

Dudley Hall turned toward him, a smile spreading across a
toothless jaw as he watched them approach, his arms swinging at his sides with excitement.

"Scotty dog!" he whistled, advancing in quick steps. Embracing Scott like a small bear, he unintentionally lifted his
feet from the floor.

Scott chuckled loudly. "Hey, great to see you, Duddy," he
gasped as the air was crushed from his lungs.

"Well, let me look!" Hall commanded in an excited chirp,
"a sight for sore eyes!" He held him back by the shoulders,
shaking his head. "Ah, Jackie," he sighed, "your hair's gray."

Scott smiled. "Put on some weight too, can't stop the
years."

"Old, you say!" he cried sharply. "Born at the step of the
grave, why, we jest getting younger!"

Looking over his shoulder, Scott nodded. "Hello, Charlie,"
he said, and Dr. McQuade came forward from the shadows.
"So how do you like working with a real diggerman?" Scott
asked, patting Hall on one massive shoulder.

"I can't keep up," McQuade said. "A truly remarkable tal-
ent."

Hall led Scott by the arm toward the battered counter.
"We've got eleven." He paused. "You do want to work,
Jackie?"

"Yes," Scott said.

"Then eleven it is," Hall affirmed. "Thought we'd make
twelve, but the yard's clean, jest one final check."

As he spoke, he pointed to a series of human skulls, all
washed and lined into a neat row with numbers scrawled on
their foreheads in black marker. The shades ran pinkish to
burnt red, the product of years beneath Maryland clay,
twenty-two dark sockets staring back at Scott, filling him with

blame. He released a heavy sigh and fumbled in his pocket for a cigarette.

Rivers reached over to give him a light, and the familiar gases drilled his lungs. "God save us," Scott mumbled, reaching toward a skull with seven black fléchettes protruding in a sharp circle. The largest skull was an adult, the smallest the size of a large grapefruit.

"Do you know what these are?" Hall asked, holding a stick.

"Yes," Scott said grimly, and it was clear from the hard expression on his face that he would not be pushed further. The men watched as he walked back and forth along the snack bar, moving like a military commander inspecting troops, nodding thoughtfully at each one. Scott turned. "What about Samantha's family?"

McQuade pointed with a heavy finger. "Her sister, Victoria," he offered, then counted eight down. "And Emma."

This skull was of an adult, and Scott swallowed, his eyes narrowing. "You're sure?"

"I can't be certain of the mother, but there's no mistake about this child." McQuade lifted the skull of Victoria Stoner, cradling it in one massive hand like a small globe, the teeth grinning at them.

"Note the nasal bridge, similar to Samantha's, the high cheekbones, the splendid curving of the forehead," he offered. "They were a pretty people, Jack. Even in the bone structure there's a great deal of similarity."

"Yes," Scott said, "a pretty people. I see no darts, Charlie, so how did they die?"

"Impossible to tell for sure, but I believe a sharp blow to the cranium on Victoria. Notice the hole, the splintering . . ."

Scott saw and quickly turned away. "And the lethal instrument?"

"My guess would be a small hammer, that kind of thing, not a bullet punch. Death was instantaneous."

Perhaps the killer had slipped, Scott thought, delivering a harder blow than what was really necessary. "And the mother?" he asked, holding up a hand. "The short version, please."

"Strangulation, a broken neck."

Scott nodded. "And you believe the property to be clean at this point. Was there a graveyard?"

McQuade raised the skull toward Dudley Hall. "Yep," he

said, "damn near buried out. Whoever discarded them"—he pointed at the red skulls—"he sure knew what he was doing. Jackie, we think the reason this property hasn't been resold is that folks who own it know there's a graveyard."

"Can't miss it?"

"Ain't no place a blade can hit that won't produce dead."

"Duddy, how old is it, when did it start?"

"Can't tell for sure, most country yards jest start as a family plot, then develop over generations. First real busy period was around 1840, lots of stones from then, Civil War was mighty active, right up to after World War I."

"And they're mostly black?"

"The graves or the modern victims?" McQuade asked.

"Sorry, graves first."

"Whelp, there's some white folk, not many," said Hall.

"As for the victims, six black, the rest white," said McQuade.

Scott nodded. "What now, Charlie?"

"We were just taking a break when you arrived. We have a few holes to cover, and a few spots to recheck."

Scott smiled thoughtfully. "Thanks," he said quietly. "I really appreciate it." And he wandered away, making eye contact with Frank Rivers as they moved for the door.

47

1:05 P.M. SAINT PETERSBURG, FLORIDA

Matthew Brennon laid a tape recorder on a pine coffee table as Captain Duncan Powell motioned with his hand for his driver to leave the room. A younger officer nodded, then quickly dismissed himself as the captain turned to Brennon.

"I have a working relationship with the family," he said calmly, his bass voice filling the small room. "I will tell you when time is needed for composure, and I will ask the questions."

"Yes, sir," Brennon said with clipped precision.

Captain Powell was a natural leader who was known for having never raised his voice in anger, yet when he controlled a situation it was with absolute authority. His demeanor was sobering yet kind, a professional from the old school of police brass.

Brennon saw that clearly in the polished stance, barrel chest thrust out, feet parted one length, hands placed behind his back and holding a gold-braided officer's hat by the shiny black brim. This revealed a full head of silver hair as he nodded slightly downward. The young federal agent felt relieved for the overwhelming presence of Captain Powell, for this large man in full dress, his face like chiseled granite, was preparing to shoulder the tremendous burden that would surely come, and then carry the responsibility on his wide and rigid back.

Brennon took a deep breath as he watched Phillip Caymann stroll into the room, a minister at his side, though Powell did not look up until spoken to directly.

"We have told her what is required," Caymann said softly, "she is preparing herself."

He was a small man, made smaller by the captain's presence, and his face was the color of his suit, pale gray. On March 27 their eight-year-old daughter, Lisa, had been playing in their backyard. As Dorothy Caymann recalled, she had left her daughter for only a minute to answer the phone, and shortly thereafter the state police were called in on suspected abduction. It was a clean and professional job. No witness. No evidence. Only a vague recollection of a telephone conversation with an insurance agent and some material evaluations from Lisa's body, which was found in a gravel pit covered by a blanket. The Caymanns had been mourning for only two days when ViCAT dispatched Brennon from Fort Worth.

Duncan's bass voice filled the small room. "I apologize, but it is a necessary intrusion," he said to Caymann. Extending his hand to the pastor, he went on, "Hello, Father, I'd like you to meet Special Agent Matthew Brennon, who has been working with me."

"A pleasure. Thomas O'Brian," he said.

As the men shook hands, Brennon felt a light-headedness from lack of sleep. It wasn't a far enough trip for jet lag, he thought, though something had caused his stomach to sour, and he was sipping a cup of hot tea, his tape player at the ready, waiting for Lisa's mother.

She had not been up from her bed since the news of her daughter's death, and Brennon thought back to his side trip where he had seen the remains of a girl from Moxie Pond, the pathologists hovering under hot surgical lamps, the chrome gutters, the sound of high-speed instruments.

"Well, someone will have to identify the body," said Dr. Cyril Kline, the Jacksonville coroner. Brennon had turned his back as Captain Powell stood fast at the dead woman's feet.

"I've spoken to the father, but I will not allow him to see this," the captain replied. "We've located a friend of the family who is willing to take the trip." He handed a slip of paper to the rubber-gloved pathologist, who laid it off to one side without looking.

"You better be damn certain, Duncan. We have no dental forensics to work with on this one."

"How's that?"

The white-coated assistant was now mowing across Lacy Wilcott's blond head with a barber's shaver, sweeping hair into a bag as Kline lifted her jaw with one hand.

"If you don't use family, I'll need a signed affidavit of the relationship for my files."

"I understand," Powell said grimly.

Brennon stepped forward. "Cause of death was strangulation from behind?"

"Yes and no," Kline muttered. "She would have died anyway." He turned and lifted the sheet. "Any of these wounds could have been fatal, but technically . . ."

Instantaneously Brennon blanched, and he stumbled into a drip gutter, fighting a fluttering in his stomach and a weakness at his knees, remembering the pink lox that Myra Blatt had served him for breakfast.

"Matthew?" Powell cried with concern, but that came too late.

Brennon shuddered in one wild hot instant as the pit in his gut became a fast-rising ball and vertigo took him violently by the throat.

"Cover her back up," Kline quickly ordered, then snapped off the overhead lamps.

Brennon had remained silent for most of the day, and his stomach was just beginning to settle.

A ghost of a woman entered the room, her black hair combed with nervous abandon, her face drawn and pale. She was small, wearing a pink bathrobe tied at a thin waist. A nurse moved slowly at her side.

There was no worse illness, Brennon reminded himself as she came to her husband's side, greeting Captain Powell, then the preacher, looking straight at Brennon. He could see from the dilation of her pupils that Dorothy Caymann was heavily sedated, and though he knew her to be but forty-three, she looked much older.

They all remained standing as she took a chair by the table. Her gaze shifted from the nurse, down to the tape recorder, then up to Captain Powell. He nodded at her, and following his lead, everyone sat but Father O'Brian, who came to the woman's side, standing just behind her chair.

"Have you found them?" she asked flatly, without looking up.

"Perhaps," Powell said. "As I explained earlier, it will take some time, and we require help." He introduced Brennon, who stood to take her hand—it felt cold as death.

"Phillip said you wanted me to hear?"

"Yes," Powell said grimly, "tell us if it is the voice you heard, and please, take your time." Without further delay he nodded at Brennon, who pressed the button.

The tape spun onto its take-up spool as a stranger's voice popped from the small speaker:

"Hello, this is Jack Scott. I'm not available to answer your call, but if you leave a message, I'll get back to you when I return."

Brennon quickly stopped the machine and leaned slightly forward on the couch, carefully gauging the expression on the woman's face. Her eyes were dark and deep, lacking sparkle, her lips pulled tight.

The silence was like a cold blanket as he pressed the button on a second time:

"Hey, now, this is Duddy Hall," the voice chirped. "I'm not available, but if you leave a name, I'll call back."

Sighing, the woman looked up at her husband, shaking her head. The captain nodded.

"Hello . . ."

Dorothy Caymann responded as if to a gunshot, flying to her feet, her body shaking toward convulsions as Father O'Brian and the nurse quickly held her, keeping her in place as her torso was growing menacingly stiff, her eyes burning with a murderous rage.

"Kill him!" she screamed. "Kill him for me . . ." and she released a horrid cry that sent a corkscrew of ice through Brennon's spine, that caused Captain Powell to bite into his cheek, that forced tears to roll from the face of a father.

They were all on their feet, instinctively trying to help as Phillip Caymann quickly grabbed his wife and locked the struggling woman in his arms.

"Play it!" she shrieked, and Brennon looked at Powell. Then the voice filled the room.

". . . this is Aaron Blatt. I'm not available to answer your call in person, but if you leave a message I'll get back to you when I return."

The woman released a tortured cry. "Kill him!" she screamed again through clenched teeth, her fists pounding against her husband's frail chest.

Lisa Caymann was buried that week, one short mile from her home.

48

On the way back to the command post, Frank Rivers cruised down the George Washington Memorial Parkway, then north toward Potomac and the home of Mr. and Mrs. Jonathan Patterson. As he drove, he radioed for messages.

Rudy Marchette was having troubles at home and would be late for his return detail as Team Pogo, covering the alley. Toy Saul and Mule Murphy had taken an early dinner break and were proceeding directly to the Jansons' home.

Rivers was considering breaking Team Huskies into two, perhaps putting Mule inside the condemned structure, but decided against that. Scott did not believe the next twenty-four hours was that pressing, so Rivers' mind flowed back over MPR 780, Debra Ralson Patterson.

What Rivers had determined with the kind assistance of the brothers Dix was that Debra had been drinking with two other girls on the previous night. And while Debra had left with one, the third girl, described to him as a blond in her twenties, had stayed a bit longer.

Just a short week ago, that news alone—that Debra frequented bars—would have horrified the Pattersons, but it was joyful, trivial to them now. Life-and-death pressures have strange effects on normal people, Rivers reflected. Things turn upside down faster than a snake can spit.

There was a dark side to Jonathan Patterson's daughter that her parents had never known existed, and this, he thought, was one hell of a way to find out. Even if she turned out to be a runaway, the FBI stats claimed better than twenty percent of all missing teens were abused or exploited before they were found. Certainly no man felt the clock ticking more than Jonathan Patterson, who dashed out the door as Rivers pulled into the driveway, coming under the circular overhang.

Running forward to greet him, the man was still carrying a telephone book in one hand and clutching a paper bag in the other. His thin face was pale, with dark circles under his eyes, but although he looked drained, this time there was some life and excitement to his voice.

"Frank!" he cried. "Thanks for coming, I have something to show you."

"Good to see you, sir. You managed to get some sleep?"

"Yes, first time last night." He held out a bag and pulled it open. "Look," he said, "we found it in her room!"

"A pregnancy test," Rivers concluded.

"Yes, and we've tracked it to the pharmacy up the street. We think she was going there for another kit when she left to get milk. The instructions say to test two times if the first one is positive!"

"Well, that would be good news," Rivers said. "Did anyone recognize her photo?"

"The druggist, though he couldn't remember which night she came in. A nice chap, he says these things are very popular with the high-school kids."

"I'm sure. How's Mrs. Patterson holding up?"

"Better," he sighed. "Your information lifted her spirits like I cannot tell you, thanks so very much."

"No sweat, Mr. Patterson, I have a feeling that if we keep pushing, something will break." He forced a smile. "Do we have any idea as to who the other two women are that Debra was with?"

"No," he shook his head, "not so far, but we're calling everyone back. That's our best hope right now, don't you agree?"

Rivers nodded, looking away. Jonathan Patterson was a

man obsessed. By five o'clock that afternoon he had already distributed photographs of his daughter to every abortion and pregnancy clinic in the immediate area, and his wife continued to man the phones. For extra measure Patterson had distributed fliers to other teenagers, visiting haunts and hangouts that young adults Debra's age were known to frequent. Yet nothing had been forthcoming.

"Frank," he said, quieting down, "your sources, did they say she was . . . ?" he stammered. "Dee, I mean, did they say she was in good shape when she left the bar?"

"Yes," Rivers comforted, "she wasn't sick or drunk, just unhappy about something. We'll find her if we just keep trying."

Patterson placed an appreciative hand on his shoulder. "Would you thank them for me?" he asked with a desperate sincerity in his voice.

"I'm sorry?"

"Your sources, whoever they are, will you thank them personally for us, Mrs. Patterson included, I can't tell you what a difference they've made. They've given us hope . . ."

As his voice trailed off, Rivers thought about the brothers Dix and of their callous disregard for this man's pain and his daughter's life. "I already mentioned that to them." He smiled warmly. "I'm sure they understand."

At 5:49 Sunday evening, the Montgomery County police officially opened their investigation into the missing-persons case of Debra Patterson, now that their seventy-two-hour rule had been fulfilled. Assigned was Sergeant Tyler Conroy, for he had taken the first essential information that previous Friday.

Officer Conroy arrived at the house at six, very much relieved when he found that the mother had returned home. He had not believed Patterson's mission-of-mercy story about a relative being sick in some other state, and he expected to find Mrs. Patterson cowering in fear, covered with bruises and welts.

Sergeant Conroy took his watch in front of the Pattersons' television, pleasantly surprised but not distracted as he studied quietly for the county's detective exam.

49

In the kitchen of the command post Jack Scott hung up the phone just as Frank Rivers came through the front door. Untying the laces on his running shoes, he kicked these from his feet and pulled off his socks. He was standing in the hallway, massaging his sore feet, as Scott came toward him. "Any luck on the clinics?" he asked in relation to the Patterson case.

"Negative. How about with Brennon, wasn't he finishing up with Lisa Caymann's family?"

"We've got a positive on Aaron S. Blatt," he said tonelessly. "His voice was the one that distracted Lisa's mother when she was abducted."

Rivers shook his head in disgust while lifting off his shoulder harness. Slinging this across his back, he started toward the kitchen, where he could hear Dudley Hall and Dr. Charles McQuade talking. "Do we know where Blatt is? You said he has an appointment to testify before the FDA, what's that about?"

"Blatt's mother told Brennon that he's coming to Washington to announce the opening of some sort of research center—sounds more like a PR push to get the health regulators off his back. At any rate, he's not due for another week, so unless they have some serious change of heart, they'll stay in the field, and that bothers me. We've ordered taps on all Blatt's phones, including his mother's, so maybe something will come in over the transom. They could be anywhere."

"Did Brennon find out who his partner is?"

"No, a complete dead end, but Captain Drury is running data for me on Blatt's private plane. That gives them real mobility, KingAir 300 Beechcraft with a cruising speed of better than 350 miles an hour at 18,000 feet. It cost better than a million bucks."

"Good for him," Rivers snorted.

"Pocket change for the right dentist. The important thing is that Blatt doesn't know we're looking for him, so if he should file with the FAA, and if he lands in a major airport, then we've got him."

Rivers knew the procedure. For a private carrier to fly, an interstate-flight plan had to be registered with an FAA official, containing such relevant information as the plane's identification number, the type and number of passengers, route of flight, time of departure, and true airspeed. "How much damage can they do in a week?"

"A lot," Scott said sadly, and they walked into the kitchen eating area, where McQuade and Hall were staring down into the sockets of yet another skull recovered from Patriots Bowl.

Rivers and Scott stopped in the doorway as McQuade snipped a thin lock of hair the color of red clay, still attached to the brow. It was an adult skull, albeit young, with a neat hole just over the right eye socket. Across the corner, twelve of these were arranged in size from small to large, with packing boxes carefully laid out for each. Scott strolled toward the macabre collection and stopped before Emma Stoner, Samantha's mother. Even reduced to bone, there was a family resemblance.

"And you're sure this is all of it?" Scott asked rather callously.

"Yep," Hall said. "That alley couldn't swallow another victim if it had to. Only thing left are cemetery bones," he chirped, "embalmed, except for the slaves."

Rivers was studying a chart on the wall near the back door. It was now almost entirely filled in, yet still took some puzzling to sort through. To the right was the heading *Clayton Killings,* step by step, every room, every face. On the left was a photograph of Samantha's reconstruction and the words *Stoner Family.* Directly beneath these:

1. Zak & Female Partner
2. Jaffe/Tobytown burning
3. Blatt & Male Devoid Partner

To the right and left of the Claytons and Stoners was the cutout picture of yellow loosestrife, and above this a photograph of Great Falls Park, showing a dramatic scene of waves crashing through a rocky gorge.

"So you believe that the common link between the Claytons and Stoners was this flower?" Rivers asked, pointing at the red-and-yellow trumpets. It seemed incredible to make a connection that stretched so far back in time.

Scott handed him a can of cold Coke from the box and

opened one for himself. "What about it, Charlie, am I chasing smoke?"

McQuade rubbed his eyes. A set of magnifying lenses was strapped to the top of his broad head and they jiggled as he yawned. "Well, let's take a look," he said, coming across the room. He counted out skulls, then picked one up. It was medium in size and behind it was a patch of aged cloth that looked like a pad of bad cheese.

"Notice the colorless nature of this weave," he said, poking at it with long, thin tweezers. "My guess is that this is a blouse, or perhaps a dress, but if you look very closely you will see little red dots and just a smattering of gold or yellow."

The three men all leaned into a semicircle and studied this closely. Intrigued, the diggerman turned the splotch over to review both sides. "It does have red specks dere, Jackie."

"And that," McQuade's voice was deep with resolve, "is precisely the bias of color that we found on Samantha, though in her case it was more pronounced. The stain comes from the swamp candle. And these"—he reached for the counter and into a large evidence bag—"are what Jack found in the Claytons' garbage."

He held up the collection of stems, the petals dried, leaving a network of burnt orange and mustard gold on starlike veins.

"So both families were attacked while pickin'?" Hall questioned.

"Perhaps," Scott said. "I believe so."

"And Jimmy Cooley showed you where these grow?" Rivers questioned.

"Yes, and not surprisingly, it's very close to where Victoria Halford was raised. In 1958, when the Stoners were abducted"—he pointed to a circle on the chart—"that property would have still belonged to them, although they had moved to Tobytown up near the church. Zak watched them pick flowers in the woods at their old home site, and when he grew bored with this, he challenged Samantha and her older sister, Vicky, along with Mrs. Emma Stoner."

"But because of the remains, we know that he killed them elsewhere?" Rivers asked.

"They were abducted down by the river, but I do not believe they felt threatened at this time. Maybe he appeared as a cop, or a security agent of some type, then drove them away. He could have come up with a thousand stories about how they were not safe there and needed to go with him. Each girl was still carrying flowers—that's the key. They were lured into a false state of security. Otherwise they wouldn't have cared about the flowers and would have left them behind."

"Which is why the stems were so routinely dumped with the bodies. He was just cleaning up after the kill," Rivers concluded.

"Yes," Scott agreed, "Zak must have driven them to the Tobytown cemetery, because the alley hadn't been built then, it was just being planned. Perhaps he stopped so they could place flowers on a grave. After all, their grandparents were buried there."

"And this is the only spot where the flowers grow?" Rivers asked, pointing at a circle on the wall chart.

Scott inched closer, then tapped it thoughtfully. "It's hard to know for certain where they grew in 1958, but it's a safe guess it was along the canal somewhere."

"Very likely," McQuade offered quietly, "that descendants from the original plantings are still nearby or within easy reach. The loosestrife are a hardy lot, and the only thing they cannot survive is drought."

"But, Jackie," Hall asked with confusion, "what would the Clayton girls be doing in the same area more than three decades later?"

"In 1971 the canal was named a national park. Think about it. This is a big city, not many places to go if you're looking for nature, or wildflowers, anything like that. Your choices are limited. Also, these flowers, plus the dogwood, are religious offerings and well-known to children, who use them at Eastertime. That's when the killings took place. I will bet that when Charlie gets a time fix on the rest"—his hand swept over the skulls—"he will discover most were slain in early spring."

Hall nodded. "So while children were pickin' flowers, a killer was pickin' dem. Sometimes I think the world's not worth living in."

"I agree with you, Duddy. This wild garden that he's used for abduction over the years is what we call a *site magnet,* a natural attraction for women and children."

"Flowers," McQuade sighed. "Beauty attracts beauty."

"Yes, and he may have worked other site magnets as well, there's just no way to tell."

"Then what about Blatt?" Rivers pushed with his finger on the name. "You're saying that he and Zak were partners?"

"At one time, but that was long ago. Like me, I think Blatt fell for Zak's funeral trick and thought he was dead. Blatt was duped, I was duped—"

"But how'd he do it?" Hall whistled. "A body was cremated."

"That's true, and according to prison records, there was a death, another prisoner. We'll never know, but my guess is that Zak left prison in a pine box after disposing of the real corpse right on the prison grounds somehow—he was working in the infirmary. He had to have come up with another body for a contractor to burn. Maybe it was a hitchhiker, who knows, Duddy?

"The important thing is that rather than attending services for a yardbird, Blatt bought an urn for Zak, and that was their only major blunder. Going back in time, it ties them together very neatly."

"He was 'fraid of the funeral?" Hall asked.

"Not the way you mean it," Scott corrected. "As a graduate of Georgetown, with society types for friends, he wasn't in a position to expose his dirty relationships, or let his hobby spill over into his professional life."

"Then how did they hook up with dis old Jew?" he cried, pointing at the name Jaffe on the display. "He was their leader?"

Scott shook his head. "Yes and no. Jaffe is not a killer, at least not in the strict legal sense. His passion is money, and I believe he recruited Zak to burn Tobytown for him, and Blatt was the middleman who negotiated the deal. At about that time Aaron Blatt was living at Jaffe's house while completing his dental degree. Blatt and Zak met under his roof, finding common interests. They started by employing terrorism in an effort to drive Tobytown residents off their land."

"And the final act was to target the Stoner family, abducting their children," McQuade concluded. "It makes sense. Didn't you say Samantha's father had hired a lawyer to fight them?"

"To fight the county," Scott amended. "Jaffe always works with direct governmental pressure, and the county served a tax notice for him. So, yes, he made this family a target, that's my best guess."

"Yes," McQuade said pensively. "When the abductions

didn't work, maybe even united the people, then they simply torched it."

Scott said, "I'd guess Zak did most of the violence, while Blatt served as businessman and observer, at the same time protecting Jaffe from direct involvement."

"Nonprosecutable?" McQuade questioned.

Scott shrugged. "With Jaffe we'd never be able to prove a thing, except that he's a heartless leech. If we said one unkind word about the man in public, then we'd also have to fight every Jewish defense group in the world. The man was in a concentration camp, and ever since, he has used that as a shield from honest criticism or criminal investigation."

"The Holocaust is the ultimate sacred cow," said McQuade. He was about to go further when Rivers shook his head.

"Sorry, Jack, I don't buy it. You're saying Jaffe has spent his life hurting people, even ordering abductions and executions?"

"I am."

"No," Rivers scoffed. "If he was in a concentration camp, the horror of his memories wouldn't allow him to act that way, I'm sure of it."

Scott's face was a mask of sorrow. "I didn't say he was a victim, Frank, I said he was there. Interestingly enough, Aaron Blatt's mother was with him in Auschwitz, so believe me when I say Jaffe did not spend money spoiling her child from the kindness of his puny black heart."

"Hush money?" Rivers asked incredulously.

"No, not as we think of it. But Myra Blatt does know something that Jaffe doesn't want public. That's a guess, but I think a very good one. Ever heard that old Mafia saying: Keep your friends close, but your enemies closer?"

Rivers nodded as Dudley Hall filled a cheek with Redman chewing tobacco, offering this around as heads began shaking at him.

Scott shrugged. "If you want my humble opinion, I think Washington deserves Jaffe as much as Jaffe deserves the Washington he created. The material fact is that Blatt killed for the first time about thirty-five years ago when he lived under Jaffe's charge, and Blatt's partner was Zak Dorani. Both of them are still alive, both are out there killing, and both are young enough to continue for another ten or fifteen years."

"Jack," Rivers asked, "this guy Zak has been hitting houses

with first-rate locks, yet he gets in with no sign of entry. How does he do that? He has to—"

Suddenly they heard a sharp rap on the front door. A moment later, Rivers was bracing as a man in an expensively tailored uniform entered, his face drawn, his mouth covered with dried antacid paste.

Captain Maxwell Drury looked like stress alone would drop him any moment as he rushed into the kitchen. Alarmed, Scott came forward, and the group broke away from the counter, leaving the skulls staring up at Drury in blank horror.

"Captain." Rivers gave a grim nod.

"Hello, Frank," Drury acknowledged, then turned to Scott with trouble burning in his eyes.

"What is it, Max?"

"A new ball game," he announced in his gravelly voice. "Duncan Powell just called me at home. Rather urgent news, so I came myself."

"Lacy Wilcott's companion?"

Drury nodded a sorry head while removing his cap. "Carol Barth. She was found at a place called Waltzing Waters in the Everglades, but there's something else, John."

The four men in the room could feel the stress. "What happened, is Duncan okay?"

"No, no, he's not." His body stiffened with anger. "They killed a cop," he said flatly, "a highway patrolman. Blew his heart clean out his body with three shots, when one would have been enough."

There was an ugly silence. Rivers' jaw started to tick as he paced past Dudley Hall, who handed Drury a shot of whiskey. The captain tossed this back, swallowing hard, then spoke again.

"In savage mockery they manipulated this policeman's body into a suggestive position with the dead girl. They're worse than animals . . ."

"Jesus," Rivers swallowed, turning sharply where he stood.

". . . and it gets worse. They're heading this way, John," Drury said, his voice wooden. "I need Frank," he concluded. "The vile bastards just filed a flight plan from South Carolina." He handed Scott a slip of paper.

"Columbia to Richmond to Washington," Scott read.

"They're running straight at us."

50

On two Sundays of every month, Great Falls National Park opened its gates to volunteers who provided scenic educational tours to church groups, school classes, and senior citizens. Guided Adventures through history, as they were called, were given by invitation or appointment only.

At a lockhouse overlooking the C & O Canal, the docents had assembled by eleven o'clock and were preparing to educate the classes that were now arriving, elementary students from four nearby public schools. They were dressed in turn-of-the-century clothing, the waterway garb of old, with heavy black work boots, dark dresses, and broad bonnets, some with wire spectacles, others with leather work gloves.

Off near the lock, two men were hitching five mules into a train, preparing to harness them to a wooden barge anchored in front of the visitors' center. Jessica Janson made her way there, holding a tired little boy by the hand.

"Can't I just go on the ride?" Elmer asked, pointing toward the mules.

"You have to take the tour first, the ride is last."

"But, Mom, they—"

"You wanted to come, Elmer. You accepted the invitation," she reminded him.

"But what are you going to do?"

"I'll talk to other parents and have a soda," she said. "Maybe I'll buy some crackers and feed the ducks." Jessica smiled at him, for once they had arrived, she knew why the boy didn't want to go. He was shy in front of classmates, and as they approached, his mother saw a girl staring at him.

"She's cute."

"Yuck."

"Now, you be a gentleman," she commanded as they came to a stop at a throng of parents and children, the crowd still forming. The mother of a little brunette smiled at them.

"Hi," Jessica offered, holding Elmer in place.

"Hello," the woman said warmly, "I'm Janet Lynch, Mrs. Martin's third-grade class."

"Pleased to meet you," she said, shaking hands. "Jessica Janson. That's our class too."

"Then they must know each other," she replied, looking down at the little girl with pretty hazel eyes.

"Hi, Elmer," she mewed, and Jessica was appalled that her son turned rudely away. She squeezed Elmer's hand tight enough to drain color from his cheeks.

"Hi, Beverly," he snipped, then returned to studying the mules. Jessica glanced down at Elmer with daggers.

"He's being a brat," she teased, "today's brat day." Elmer blushed visibly.

Janet Lynch smiled. "I wasn't sure why we were honored with invitations for this event," she said, watching the crowd milling about.

"Oh, they invite a different class every time. It's supposed to be very interesting, supported by the county education board. They take the older children camping." They watched as a matron dressed in a colonial-period dress with wire hoops at the fringe came forward from the house, clutching a stack of papers and a clipboard.

"Attention!" she called out in a high-pitched voice. Children and adults stirred and became quiet as the woman came forward. "Thank you for attending the canal's Sunday retreat, a four-hour Guided Adventure and field study for children. We would like to extend a special warm welcome to Mrs. Martin's third-grade class." The woman paused as the crowd turned inward to survey itself.

"For the children, the trip will begin just on the other side of this bridge." She waved across a lift lock, and a dozen fair maids all waved back. "These docents are volunteers who will be working with small groups so that more can be accomplished in a short time. Please have your invitations ready," she demanded, and as the crowd began to shuffle for papers, Jessica removed one from her purse and handed it to Elmer.

"Can't we just leave?" he said, squirming at her side.

Jessica stroked his hair. "Give them a chance. It's only a few hours, you may like it."

"Children," the matron commanded, "say good-bye to your parents now, and as you start across, a docent will place you into a group. Girls, if you have purses, you should leave them in the lockhouse, you will want both hands free."

The children started forward, Elmer turning to face his

mother. "See ya," he said quietly, and she rubbed his freckled nose with an index finger. As he strolled off, little Beverly Lynch tagged right alongside, watching him with admiring eyes.

From across the waterway two old mule skinners with Dutch-boy hats struck up a banjo chorus of "Erie Canal." The woman continued, "Parents, for those of you who wish to wait, we have refreshments inside the lockhouse. The classes will return at four o'clock, but we ask for your patience should any group be tardy."

Jessica watched as the children formed on the other side of a chained area, handing over their invitations, and in return receiving identification markers. Beverly was having a blue ribbon tied into her hair by an older woman.

"I guess they'll be in the same group," Janet Lynch noted. Jessica smiled, for Elmer was rolling his eyes at her, barely able to stand still as an old mule skinner pinned a green clover to his chest.

"Well, that's that," Jessica said, watching the small crowd being factioned off according to color by characters in period clothes. "I'll buy us a soda."

"Let's all get better acquainted." The docent smiled easily, moving her flock of six children closer to a huge shade tree by the river. The banjo pickers were still singing, and the canal gurgled as water flowed through the gigantic lift lock.

The docent was an older woman with a bluish-gray bonnet fastened beneath her chin, pinching the thin flesh of her neck. Her eyes bulged from behind old-style horn-rimmed spectacles, and around her waist there was a white apron, this covering a light gray dress with a metal hoop for fullness. Completing the picture, her boots were tight black leather with rows of buttons. Elmer thought it strange that grown-ups would go to such lengths at capturing the past, when the woman's bright pink nail polish gave it all away.

"Today I am dressed as a lock keeper's wife," she said. "Does anyone know what year that would be, when the Chesapeake and Ohio Canal was in full operation?"

The children looked at each other but would not venture a guess. The docent leaned forward, placing her hands on her knees, the giant hoop reaching out into the semicircle. She pointed at Elmer Janson.

"I'll bet you know," she said softly. "There's no need to be shy."

Elmer swallowed his spit, fidgeting in a pocket, Beverly Lynch admiring his every move. "Eighteen-sixty?" he asked timidly.

"That's very close," she said. "The correct time period is about thirty years earlier, 1828. Now, let's all pretend that's the age we are living in, and introduce ourselves." Leaning over, she smiled at the boy and extended her right hand.

"My name is Irma Kiernan," she said.

They had been strolling for nearly an hour, stopping to sip drinks and learn about the park, when they came to the end of a harsh gravel path, seeing their images reflected by the still water of the canal. Overhead there was a wooden bridge. Just to their left, a lift lock and small white house. Although this was boarded shut, it was well kept, and before it spread a meadow composed entirely of wildflowers in every shape and color of the rainbow. Holding Beverly Lynch by the hand, Irma stopped here to look out over a splendid view of the raging Potomac River and huge granite cliffs.

"Children," she said, gaining their attention and motioning for them to gather around, "does anyone know where we are?"

"A lift lock," Elmer offered, "near Little Falls." By now he had become comfortable with the group.

"Very good," she said. "This house is where a lock keeper by the name of Horace Marsden lived, and we will be showing you pictures of his family when we take the boat ride. Now, the lock keeper's job was more than waiting for a boat to come. If you look overhead"—she turned and the children eyed the wooden bridge—"you will see a series of rope elevators. These were used for lifting cargo down onto the boats. What do you imagine that cargo was?"

"Food," Beverly said.

"Yes," Irma agreed quickly, "grain and livestock. They'd lower pigs and cattle from these ropes onto the decks, then the boat would proceed into Washington. What else would Mr. Marsden be in charge of?"

"Building supplies," Elmer said.

"Very good," Irma winked at him, "bricks and stone, as well as coal for heating the cities. Other cargoes would include tobacco, furs, iron ore, whiskey, and timber. Now, while

Mr. Marsden looked after the cargoes from Cabin John, what duties did his wife have?"

"Cooking," said Beverly, "she would bake all the bread and clean the house."

"Yes, plus she had to be a teacher, for there were no schools, and she had to be a veterinarian as well, taking care of the mules and other livestock. A boat would only come about once a month, so that's how often they had visitors, and Mr. Marsden would hook up his mule team and continue down toward Washington. Then, when he arrived in George-town, what did he do with his boat?"

"Bring it back," said a tall black girl by the name of Audrey Morris.

"No, they could not go back, so they would dismantle the boat and then sell it for lumber. Many of the early houses built along the river had boat in them!" She smiled, and several children giggled.

"Mr. Marsden and his family lived here from 1836 to 1884, but they were not the only family on the waterway. Who else would have moved here?"

"Slaves," Elmer said softly.

Irma Kiernan was impressed: the child was bright for age ten. "Elmer is correct," she said almost proudly. "In 1860, Negroes began escaping up the river from the South. Now, why would they choose to live here?"

After a few moments of silence, from the back of the group a thin black child with a bright red cap offered his opinion. "Maryland was the Free State, so they came to find freedom."

"Yes," Irma confirmed, "Derrick is correct. But once they arrived, why did they stay? Once they crossed into Maryland, they could go anywhere. So why not take the boat into the city of Washington?"

It was a hard question, and the children were silent. "The answer," she said slowly, "is religion. From out of the cruelty of slavery, the American Negro managed to build a way of life by worshiping what you see around you right here, sym-bols of the freedom God could give. Can anyone pick out such a symbol?"

"The river," Elmer said.

"Flowers," said Beverly.

Irma Kiernan was smiling, for the children had grasped the concept.

"The trees and the forest," said Derrick.

Irma nodded. "That's fine, these are all powerful images of freedom, a piece of heaven right here on earth. Now, who can find where the slaves lived? Who can find the chimney in the woods?"

The children turned excitedly to scan the horizon. Faint as a scar, an object was jutting up from the treeline. Irma saw the boy's eyes grow wide, locking onto this.

"Let's follow Elmer," she said. "I think he's found it."

They came to a small clearing in the center of a wooded grove, standing high overlooking the Great Falls. To their right was an expanse of the canal, an aqueduct known as Wide Water. There were a stone foundation, a fireplace, and a rock chimney, and Elmer's heart quickened when he thought what could be buried beneath this.

Surrounding the house were millions of bright blueberries and scads of wildflowers, and Beverly quickly wandered off to explore the bright colors. All the children were filled with excitement, bounding through the glade and into the old foundation.

"What do you think this was?" Irma asked of them all. "What type of house?" There was no answer. "This was all made by hand from the natural things you see all around you: rocks from the river, limbs from oaks and redwoods, bricks from red clay, slate from the falls." She pointed to a rocky gorge that frothed and churned with a raging, powerful current.

"Runaways settled and made this house," she continued, "in the beginning of the Civil War. As they were escaping, they followed the river and the canal. Notice all of the lush plants and bushes. These were started by them and then used as food and decorations."

"How many were there?" Derrick asked with awe, moving from room to room, looking at where the walls had been.

"No one kept track, but this was a big house, so as many as ten families all slept under this one roof. Notice that there are two fireplaces. Slaves were poor, so there must have been crowds of them in here."

Elmer was crawling into an enormous stone spit, the huge granite rocks still held together by a fine gray mortar, and little Beverly was moving beside him, her index finger following a line of concrete. "Look," she said excitedly, "someone wrote something with a stick."

Elmer edged forward, blowing dust away from the fireplace as Derrick came alongside on his hands and knees. "Can you see what it says?" he asked.

"I dunno," Elmer puzzled. "I think it says *picky*, it's real fancy writing."

Both boys worked the scrawl with their spit before Beverly forced herself between them. "It's a V," she announced with a giggle. "That's not a P, silly."

"Vicky," Derrick stated. "It's a name! And there's a date too!"

"Children," Irma said, coming from the yard, "please come back out of there. It's all spiders and bugs, and we can't have that."

"But there's a date!" Elmer repeated excitedly. "I think it says 1918." His voice filled with bewilderment. "Hey, Miss Kiernan, there weren't any slaves in 1918."

"That must have been when the house was rebuilt by preservationists. Now, I want you to come back out of there," she said firmly, "it's dangerous." And the children complied, although begrudgingly.

"We have ten more minutes to explore the slaves' quarters, so let's split up and have a quick look around. Please be careful not to touch any plants that have three bright green leaves or funny berries. Also, there are some very special flowers that you should look for. They have bright red and yellow petals and were once used by the slaves to celebrate Easter. Who can find such a flower for me?"

She took two sly steps to be closer to Elmer. "Do any of you boys have a pocketknife?" she asked, though she was careful not to make it appear as if she was addressing anyone in particular. Derrick was still fumbling in his pocket as Elmer produced his knife.

"I do," he said proudly, handing her a scouting blade on a key ring.

Irma fought off a smile as she stared at the single key swinging from a brass loop. She took it in her hand and glanced at the knife.

"Thank you," she said. Looking up, she continued, "We are going to pick Easter flowers to take home, so everyone look around and select that group of plantings that looks the prettiest to you."

With that the children scurried off through the damp glade. Beverly and Derrick and Elmer were now somewhat of a team, and together they raced to a bluff that dropped quite steeply to the raging river. Below, the currents were howling, roaring into white waves, and at this spot, in the moist and swampy ground, there were thousands of flowers of every shape and color.

Some had huge white petals, like the Dutchman's breeches, and stood as high as Elmer. Some were blue with what looked like purple fruit, the jack-in-the-pulpit, though the children did not know these names. Others had bright orange blooms, like the sweet clover, and there were tall and furry cattails that resembled large corndogs on a stick. Just at the bank of the river the colors came like explosions, red and yellow, as far as the eye could follow.

"Look at that!" Beverly cried with delight, and all the children seemed drawn by these fragrant, gentle blooms running along a small creek that ran in a furrow down a hill. They gathered here, pinching and touching, stroking and collecting the vibrant trumpets of the swamp candle.

Irma had not counted heads as she briefly watched the children packing flowers into small bouquets. Her heart was fluttering rapidly as she brought herself to the task at hand. Sweat popped to her brow as she carefully reached into her dress and removed a small black tin that said *Hide-A-Key* across the top. Turning her back to the brood, she steadied the box in her left hand, then quickly slid the lid open.

Within lay a gray mixture of plastic clay that resembled a huge flat eraser. Taking Elmer's key from the knife, she laid it flat, then pressed and kneaded with both hands. With expert care she worked the key's toothy edge with her thumb before lifting it out, leaving an impression that was clear and precise. Next she turned the key over. She had just begun the process again as Beverly Lynch bumped into her hoop, rolling it slightly, and tugged on her dress from behind.

Irma jumped, but did not turn around.

"Miss Kiernan?" she said shyly. "Miss Kiernan . . ."

"Just a minute," Irma muttered, pressing with both hands, her heart now beating into her throat.

"Miss Kiernan?" the small, distressed voice asked again as the woman worked the key down into the mix and back up, making certain that the center groove showed clearly. Jeff insisted on that, she knew. When making an impression of a key, shoddy work could mean extra metal that had to be filed away by hand.

"I have something in my eye!" Beverly suddenly cried from behind.

"Yes, honey," Irma murmured without looking, "we'll wash it out when we get back."

"But it hurts . . ." she was crying now.

A one-second mistake, Irma knew, could cost Jeff an hour of extra filing, and as the child sobbed behind her, Irma completed an impression that was clean and nearly exact, then rubbed any fouling away with her apron. She carefully sealed the box and dropped this back into her pocket. When she turned around, Elmer was inspecting Beverly's eye, trying to remove a fleck of dirt, his finger covered with a shirttail.

Derrick came up alongside, placing his flowers on the ground, then peering into her pretty hazel eyes.

"Stop that!" Irma barked at them. "You could make it worse!"

Elmer's mouth dropped open, and his arms fell limply to his sides. Irma quickly took Beverly's chin in her hand and peered into her face.

"Well, you weren't doing anything . . ." Elmer said under his breath.

"I heard that!" Irma fired back, her heart thumping madly.

"Well, it's the truth," he said quietly. "She hurt herself and—"

Irma was on him. "Don't you back talk me," she warned, aiming a finger. "I know what is needed here and you are *not* it!"

The boy backed off quickly as Irma bent at the waist to assess the problem. As she examined Beverly's left eye, Irma found herself wondering why in hell her man wanted to save the Janson kid, who at the age of ten was pushy beyond redemption.

"Men," she muttered to herself.

"But it's all very simple," Dorn had instructed. "Why do women have to make things so complicated?"

Irma could almost hear his voice as she looked down on Beverly Lynch. The tears were drying, but the eye was starting to go puffy, swelling from the bottom and covering up the speck that was buried in the soft tissue of her lid.

"You have the mold, Irma, it's new plastic, and you know how to work it. Now, stop complaining and start practicing."

They had been driving from their house down River Road and toward the canal.

"But he'll be watching me," she had said. "We've never done it this way. All of the others—"

"Dammit, just forget them. Janson's only a little kid, why is this such a problem?"

"Well, last night I thought—"

Dorn cut her off. "An old bum in a trench coat, they got lucky and you just waited too long. If you had made it ten seconds earlier, he would have seen us and just driven away."

"But it's too much of a coincidence that he stopped . . ."

Dorn shook his head, applying the brakes while slowing for the light at River and Falls roads, a half-mile from Great Falls Park. "No, for the love of God, he was from out of town. You said Maine?"

"Yes," she said.

"So he probably came here to feed off the public tit. The president's campaign manager comes from there." The light changed and he pulled the black BMW ahead, slapping in a tape of Chopin's nocturnes.

"Oh, honey," she said, still worried, "he'll be suspicious. Can't we wait for a girl? There's no one around when they put their purses in the lockhouse. I have all the time I need to get their keys. You liked it when—"

"No!" he snapped. "If you can't handle it, I'll do it myself!" His voice was dripping with venom. "You and Jessica Janson are like Beauty and the Beast!"

"Oh, Jeff," she cried, "that's a terrible thing to say to me. You don't mean that . . ." Her voice trailed off weakly as Dorn shook his head apologetically; it had just slipped out.

"So you ask if anyone has a pocketknife, the kid's real proud of it. Jessica talked to his grandmother for hours over the stupid thing, deciding if she should let him have it. The first thing Elmer did was to attach his house key, so it's perfect."

"You're sure this is the right thing to do?"

Dorn's stare was icy. "How long did it take for that bitch to mail in the RSVP for an event as worthy as the Adventure?"

"The Jansons were the very last ones."

"Well, you see, Irma, that's how involved she is with his life. She doesn't give a shit about his education. So just make sure you're standing closest to Elmer when you ask for a knife. All little boys have one, regardless of what Mrs. Janson thinks." And he pressed the stopwatch he was holding with his right hand.

"Two minutes and thirty seconds, you have to do better than that, now try it again."

"Miss Kiernan," Elmer said, looking at Beverly's hurt eye as they walked. It was nearly swollen shut, so he was holding her hand, unintentionally slowing down the flock. They had been walking for nearly ten minutes, Derrick on the other side, telling Beverly when there were larger stones in the towpath.

"Yes?" she crooned absently as his voice registered, for she was dreaming in the golden light filtering through the thick wood. It was late afternoon, soon the sun would set, and she was pondering a wedding in such an ethereal glow. For the correct light, timing was important, and she had almost decided on an early-evening service when the boy again interrupted her thoughts.

"Miss Kiernan, you still have my knife!" Elmer stated loudly, and the woman blushed. She had been holding it tightly in her right fist, and she quickly turned it over to him.

"Elmer?" Beverly cried suddenly in a shy, unhappy voice, and, swallowing, the boy picked up his pace and came back alongside.

And only because she came right out and asked, and for no other reason—and because little Beverly had really hurt herself—Elmer politely took her hand as they walked. Taking notice of this, Derrick gave him the old rolling eyeballs, but he was a pretty decent sort and said nothing.

"What's a guy gonna do?" Elmer shrugged.

"Tell me about it, I got two sisters."

From his fishing spot at Wide Water, Jeff Dorn was watching through powerful field glasses, and he was pleased by what he saw. Whenever Irma had failed at something, her shoulders and face fell like a mud slide.

He saw her now, prancing dreamily down the path, holding flowers beneath her chin.

By the time the Jansons arrived back home, shadows clung, the night had begun to settle.

DAY FOUR:
THE CITIES

I shall tell you a great secret, my friend. Do not wait for the last judgment, it takes place every day.

—Albert Camus

51

It was all one and the same, and Seymour Blatt, who had spent a great deal of time there as a young man, recognized this fact. Bethesda, Cabin John, Potomac, Silver Spring, Falls Church, and countless other once-small villages in adjoining strips of real estate known as Maryland and Virginia had been reduced to being just parts of the same huge, singular and sprawling city.

That city was Washington, D.C., land of monuments and commuters, and from the cockpit of a luxurious KingAir 300, they followed an ugly stretch of highway dubbed the Inner Beltway, which appeared as a crooked river of red lights. It was the first sight that caught their attention as they sliced through the heavy cloud cover that had dogged them from the moment they reached the coast earlier in the day.

Gregory Corless, who did not understand this urban ring, believed that to stay at a hotel in Bethesda was to be away from Washington, and not smack in the middle of its affluent upper core. Although Blatt had tried to explain, Corless thought being near the seat of federal government would somehow place them where the action was.

"Greg, there *isn't* any action," Blatt corrected. "The Bethesda Hyatt is absolutely it, we couldn't do better. In Washington everyone leaves after five o'clock for the suburbs. It's all the same, the city is the suburbs."

"But it's got a view, the room has a view?"

"Yes, I had to use a favor to get the executive suite, and in Washington favors are like toothpaste: when you use them up, they're gone."

"I appreciate that," he said sincerely. "I've never spent any real time here."

"Sure," Blatt said.

"Roger, Nancy-five-one-eight, you're clear for approach, runway six, wind northeast at seven knots, time 8:04:10." The radio was clear as crystal, and Seymour Blatt placed his high-ball glass back into its holder. Grabbing the microphone with his right hand, he pressed the button. They were tired and hungry and anxious to land.

"Tower, Nancy-five-one-eight prepared for landing."

"Come ahead, five-one-eight."

Greg Corless drained the last from his martini glass, licking the lip with his tongue before handing this to his partner, dimming the already soft cabin light.

"I didn't want that interrupt feature," Blatt said, turning up the stereo. When the tower kicked in, it interrupted the music, and the Beach Boys were playing in concert. He loved the Beach Boys. Once he had wanted to be a carefree surfer, but he had decided it just wasn't a very secure life-style.

"There's a place where I can go and tell my troubles to . . ." Blatt was rocking and singing as the tiny blue strobes of National Airport pulsed in near-perfect time, and the Washington Monument came into full view, the powerful white lights streaming upward along the bright marble, then filtering off into low cloud cover.

"Buckle up," the captain ordered smartly, and although Blatt shook his head at the fat man, he did just that. As an experienced pilot, he knew how tricky the wind coming off the Potomac could be, even though the overhead gauges were showing a calm night.

With effortless skill Corless straightened and adjusted his wing tips as the plane soared in, the blue and red lights streaming from blacktop, the wheels hovering scant feet above the ground. There was a gentle swell as they touched down, followed by the engines quickly spinning twin props in reverse, Corless applying a gentle braking motion that could hardly be felt.

"In my room, in my room . . ."

"Hey, Seymour, let's settle in quickly and get some supper. We haven't eaten since morning."

"We had ham on rye, that was pretty good . . . *and leave the world behind . . .*"

"Welcome to Washington National, five-one-eight, hangar deck C-4, take tarmac Alpha-Seven." Corless turned the plane according to alphabet, rolling toward the white temporary housing that was Washington's idea of an airport.

"I don't think they'll ever finish this," Blatt complained, fingering a button. "Roger, tower, five-one-eight proceeding to hangar C-4." He had waited to respond, for "In My Room" was playing, and he loved that song almost as much as "Surfer Girl." He opened a small blue box and slipped a pair of perfect ivory choppers over his gray dental posts, these looking more like flat gray nails than teeth.

"Thank God," Corless spat as he parked at a loading bay. They both felt relaxed, the giant KingAir provided a cockpit with all of the comforts of home. "I'm going to leave the trick bag and the collection here," Corless stated, unbuckling, then stretching to the ceiling.

"Do you think that's a good idea, Greg? This is a public place, even if we do pay for the slip."

He shrugged. "It's always been good enough before. Besides, that alarm system of yours is class, real class."

They performed a ten-minute drill, transforming themselves into expensively tailored conservative executives. Blatt had learned well from Dr. Rubin Jaffe, a Washington power broker he once described as combination rabbi and coach. "Remember," Blatt said as they prepared to debark, "this is a town where attitude and appearances are everything. So please call me Aaron until we leave, it's more formal."

"Who cares," Corless huffed, moving Happy's cage down into the storage bay. It was filled with pictures that had helped to break the monotony of air travel.

"We do," Blatt corrected. "We are representing DIDS, so for the sake of appearances you and I are business associates. Try to remember, in Washington no one has permanent friends, only permanent interests."

Corless grunted.

Through the American terminal, they were entering a city that judges character by the cut of clothes, by what you drive, by how you talk. For these reasons alone, they were immediately men not to be taken lightly. Their clothes were expensive, their manner elite, and they stood patiently waiting for a limousine to take them to their hotel.

Unfortunately, their car was one of many in a solid wall of identical limos, so they had to endure the employee-grade travelers scurrying around them for cabs and buses. A man holding a placard to his chest shuffled by, an older man with baggy slacks, and although Blatt scanned the crowd quickly, he did not see him. The man's open collar spelled *no count being*. His battered old fedora cast a line of shadow across his face, though beneath this his eyes were edged like flame and his mind cut quickly into them.

Five-six, balding, wide eyes, cupid lips, long neck, frail face, expensive dentures. Commander Jack Scott knew Aaron Seymour Blatt on sight—thin, neat, precise. From his dress and demeanor it was clear that Blatt was the type of man who would analyze every little detail down to infinity: how a person dresses, how much he drinks, how often, how he carries himself, where he lives, what he drives, how he speaks. His suit was dark European, his shirt a frosted white, his tie an artsy but smart Armani in shades of purple. This, Scott reasoned, was his little fashion statement.

Six-two, 245, clean-shaven, eyes close-set, pudgy hands and fingers, wide of chest, thick neck and lips, double chin, his hair but a memory: Gregory Corless. Though Scott did not know his name, he had a face so full it resembled a hog's backside with human features.

"So this is Blatt's partner," he muttered to himself, standing off to the right and holding a sign that protested fare hikes. The fat man was clad in the classic uniform of Washington—a blue blazer with tan slacks and Italian tasseled loafers, these extra wide to support the heavy load.

The two men were chatting with each other without a care in the world, while Rivers sat directly across from them in a small ten-minute parking lot. He was watching through high-powered glasses.

"Panther, this is Eagle One." The voice of Steve Adare, the designated MAIT team pilot, blared in the tan Crown Victoria. The Loach jet helicopter was panning high in the air, and the blades sounded thin over the radio, like playing cards on the spokes of a bicycle wheel.

Rivers held the microphone with an easy hand. "Go ahead, Eagle."

"They crossed over to the American terminal on foot. They should be passing to you about now, coming onto the sidewalk. Their hangar is still being sealed off."

"Roger that, we've got them."

"I'm maintaining, do you want me to hold?"

"Affirmative, Steve, they'll be taking a limo. We'll flag it for you, then everyone follows."

"Roger."

Scott had returned and was opening the door, swinging in

as Rivers pulled the fireball off the dash and onto the seat.
"All set?" he asked as Rivers double-checked a .45mm Combat Elite. This he locked into place under his left arm, the tension spring adjusted to mush. In a high-ride holster at his back he inserted a 45 Commander, the hammer locked into the stage-three position.

"Let's do it," Rivers said with unsettling calm. Scott watched as the man popped an aspirin and ground this into paste, his jaw ticking as he stared into space.

"Frank?"

"Yeah, Jack, just thinking about Waltzing Waters. You know, I have no idea where that is. I sit here looking at those two bastards, the way they just stand there without a care in the world, and only this morning they killed some poor kid and then, just for fun, blew away a cop. It's insane. I don't care what you say, it's crazy."

Scott shook his head at Rivers. "We take them as planned, Frank, in their room at the Hyatt. Wouldn't you like a vacation to Florida so you could watch them burn in the chair?"

Rivers nodded, his eyes dancing, jaw ticking, holding his hands in front of him and spreading his fingers: closing, opening, exercising. "They put that officer's tool into her mouth, I can't cope with that. As far as I'm concerned, this is showtime, Jack. The rag is off the bush, and this is what I do best."

Scott was watching Blatt and his partner in a new light as they calmly bought a newspaper from a vendor, then eagerly divided this into sections. His stomach twisted into a knot as he turned back to Rivers. Their eyes locked tight in one sudden, deadly instant, like two bolts of fire striking in midflight.

They held this stare for a long, merciless moment, then Scott looked down calmly at his watch. "They're going to be armed," he cautioned. "If they smell a cop, they will not hesitate . . ."

Rivers nodded. "I'll deal with it. I just don't like being away from the Jansons, this is not good timing."

Scott nodded.

"I'll need the air cover," Rivers said flatly. With that he opened his door and stepped out, his long strides carrying him with almost a lazy certainty. On his back he carried a plastic dry-cleaning bag, slung without purpose, working into darkness, his mind cooking up his own private terror.

By now Scott had come to understand him, not the details, but he knew. It had something to do with a Cambodian village he once thought of as family. Qua, he had called it. As a young man Rivers had been responsible for protecting them, using that village to monitor enemy troop movements. In July 1969 he had been returning from long-range patrol, hoofing it solo across a mountain ridge, when he saw them.

Zombies, he had said, like walking dead. Their eyes filled with shock, women and children savagely tortured, but seeming to work the rice fields. As he entered the village, they greeted him in the silence of atrocity, laying baskets at his feet in offering, for this had been ordered by the V.C. who had spent the night.

"There was nothing I could do," Rivers had explained. "They were like family, so I helped them fish out the limbs, then matched them with bodies. They butchered every male in the village, including children." Scott could still hear his agony.

"Something called a Spider Patrol. It took me months to track them all, but I did, every last one."

Scott watched him blending with shadows, fearless and brave to a fault. As a young man he had given horror a face, and he wore it well, Frank Rivers did.

His armor was a village called Qua.

52

For Aaron Seymour Blatt it was a high-tech world of modern convenience, though at times that world seemed to go very wrong. He looked at his watch: 8:34. They had been waiting forty minutes even though he had called ahead from his KingAir to reserve a limousine. He had specified white, but now he knew that was truly a fool's folly.

"Well, that's it," he stomped suddenly. "I'm not paying!"

"Let's take a cab."

"That's image busting. I've got an image."

"Suit yourself," said Corless as he turned back to eyeing the crowd. As a rental cop strolled behind him, he leaned into Blatt's left ear. "Bang, bang," he whispered.

The dentist cringed physically. "Don't do that."

Corless shrugged. "But it brings luck." He pointed to a white sedan cruising their way around a traffic circle, pulling quickly across the lanes and threading traffic. The large wheels crunched an empty can, and they watched with disdain as a driver climbed hurriedly out, holding up a sign that read *DIDS*.

Blatt was on him in seconds. "You've killed our schedule!" he shouted, grabbing the card from his hand and throwing it on the street.

The driver, dressed in a black coat with white shirt, said slowly, "Sorry, sir. There was a bad accident. Are you with DIDS?"

"Obviously!" Blatt fumed as the driver quickly came around to open the rear door for the two men. Corless was studying a young woman in a tight skirt, Blatt emitting a heavy and troubled sigh.

"The Hyatt Regency, sir," the driver said, checking. "We should be there in twenty minutes."

Blatt huffed as the driver waited for a response. "Well," he barked, glaring at him. "Are you going to get the damn bags?"

Instantly the beleaguered driver hopped into action, popping the trunk, then grabbing two suitcases. Corless leaned toward Blatt. "What's the problem?" he asked.

Blatt's entire body shook. "I hope he's careful with his ancestors," he said, "my luggage is genuine pigskin."

"Then we have to?" she asked.

"No," the man said, "but we really should."

"But why can't it wait until morning?"

"Because," he sighed, "I want them to see the lights."

"They're very tired, Thomas," she said with reserve—she used his full name only when extremely frustrated. On his lap a young boy had fallen asleep.

"Oh, Lindsey," he sighed wistfully, "it's something special, something they'll never forget."

Thomas Alvin Wheeler watched his wife carefully, looking for signs of surrender. Her name was Linda, and in her arms she cradled their daughter, Katie, nearly five years old. She was wearing her good pink dress with white frills on the bottom and shoes to match, and she yawned, looking up at her father with bright blue eyes, her blond hair shining like America's best hope.

Linda and Tom had been up since dawn, starting their day with the Capitol Rotunda, then touring the Smithsonian Institution, the Air and Space Museum, and finally the U.S. Mint. They had just finished supper at Bob's Big Boy in the upper-northwest part of the city. By 8:15 they were done.

They sat in a shiny new Toyota minivan in the parking lot on Wisconsin Avenue. The license plates were Iowa green, and they were from Osceola, just south of Des Moines. Katie started to yawn again.

"Come here, cupcake," he said, scooping her up, then holding her alongside her brother. She grabbed his earlobe and gave a curious pinch.

"They're just too tired, Tom. Michael's sound asleep."

"Oh, Lindsey," he said again, "I can still remember when my father took me, I was even younger than Mikey."

The boy stirred, opening his eyes. "Kennedy?" he asked with a sleepy voice. Michael was seven and starting first grade in the fall.

"No, something better," he whispered, patting his head. Face to face with his father, the resemblance was striking: blue eyes, fair skin, bright teeth, brown hair. They both looked at the young mother.

"Okay," she sighed, "I guess it's important."

They headed south, into the city of monuments.

By the time the passengers in the limo had passed the Fourteenth Street Bridge, they had gone silent, sipping drinks from the bar. For a while Corless had fiddled with the small television, but there was nothing of interest. Blatt scrunched forward and rested his hand on the front seat.

"Take a left," he ordered as they slowed to a stop at the intersection of Constitution Avenue and Twenty-third Street.

The driver laid a lazy arm across the seat. "It's out of our way," he said pleasantly.

Blatt's eyes narrowed. "You!" he cursed. "You just damn well do what I say!"

"Take it easy," said Corless.

"And," Blatt added, "you can start by putting on your cap!"

The driver complied without response, shaking his head as he pulled away with a jolt toward the Lincoln Circle. Within minutes they were cruising slowly behind the enormous white monument. It was lit with huge powdery lights that caused the structure to gleam with an almost ethereal brilliance, as if it were the stone itself that was glowing.

By the southwest corner two young men were huddled together on the lawn, watching the flicker of the Eternal Flame from John Kennedy's grave across the river in Arlington Cemetery. They were unfriendly-looking men, passing an orange flame between them, and this light ballooning with a struck match. They were smoking a Dipper, a liquid narcotic known as PCP that had been soaked into a cigarette, the ether creating a small fireball on ignition. As they stood, they were dancing, skipping in boxerlike steps. They were oblivious of the white limousine that slowly rolled in, circling the building.

"Stop the car!" Blatt ordered sharply as the driver slowed in front of the massive structure, with steps leading under the scornful watch of a stone president.

"Well, I'm not going anywhere," the fat man puffed.

"Greg, there's an elevator, it will only take a moment," Blatt said as he opened his door.

"I'll go with you, sir," the driver offered kindly, stepping out of the car.

"Oh no, you won't," Blatt corrected.

As the two men walked out into the night, the chauffeur closed their doors for them, shaking his head in irritation. He wanted a raise. He didn't get paid enough to put up with this kind of personal abuse, though he understood the harsh restraints that Captain Drury faced daily.

For the past nine years the state police budget had been tighter than teeth, and Frank Rivers knew that was true for all of law enforcement except the FBI and the U.S. Department of Justice.

Scott pushed the fedora back on his head as he approached the white car on foot. He was watching the two partners tackle the monument. Since there were some fifty-five marble steps to be faced, they immediately headed for the handicapped elevator off to the left, moving down a neatly trimmed path lined with greenery.

"We're all set," Scott said, coming into a line of trees next to the limo. "We'll take them in their hotel room when we get to Bethesda. But can you tell me what we're doing here?"

Rivers grimaced, removing his cap. "Blatt saw a movie once and has to talk with Abe. I feel like I'm driving a garbage truck."

Scott nodded. "Did you get the name?"

"On his luggage, Gregory R. Corless. It looks like he has a .357 in his belt, but I can't be certain. What's the deal on the limo?"

"We smash it, we own it."

Rivers watched intently as headlights approached and a car pulled in slowly, a silver Toyota minivan with Iowa plates: father, mother, two children, and a dog, their faces all pressed to the glass as they admired the marble man.

"Oh, just great!" Rivers hissed, his lungs emptying completely. "That stupid sonofabitch thinks it's a goddamned Norman Rockwell canvas!"

As the van eased into the empty parking lot, Rivers noticed the two men on the lawn extinguishing their Dipper. In quick time they hurried toward the darkness of the south wall facing the street, their features vanishing into the shadows.

Scott shielded his brow against the sharp glare of floodlights covering the entrance to the monument, sidewalk, and elevator path. The man and his wife were stepping out of the van, each taking a child by the hand, then hurrying forward.

"I better stop them. We could have a problem here," Scott said with concern.

"Tell me about it," Rivers said flatly.

"Cupcake," Tom Wheeler said sweetly, swooping his girl up into his arms while moving toward the bright building, "do you know who that man is way up there? Do you see that man?"

"Bob?" she squeaked, her eyes bright and wide.

"No, no," he cried, whooshing her quickly forward down the path. His wife was holding Michael by the hand, and the boy was pulling her forward with excitement. Once on the dimly lit path, Tom Wheeler eased his gait.

"Children," he said proudly, "that's Abraham Lincoln, our finest president." Suddenly a form appeared from the shadows and stepped onto the concrete sidewalk directly in front of them. Seeing this, Wheeler stopped.

The stranger was tall, black, and dressed in a dark T-shirt with the sleeves ripped out. He advanced toward them with a purposeful strut, swinging his arms in time to an inner beat.

Instinctively Linda edged closer to her husband and took Katie from him. "Tom," she said, trembling, "he has something in his hand."

Wheeler felt his pulse climb. The man was closing, staring at him. His wife spoke again, quickly grabbing Michael's hand. "There's another one behind us," she said with panic.

"Mommy," a small voice cried, and as Wheeler turned his back to assess the threat, both men rushed the family, not a run, but a strutting sweep. A knife appeared from behind, a gun in front.

"Hey, mudderfucker!" yelled the gunman, not ten feet away, coming directly at them.

The family instantly closed around each other, scared witless.

"My God, Tom!"

"It's going to be all right," he said.

"What will we do?"

"I'll reason with them."

As the black hollow of a gun muzzle approached him, though, he threw his hands into the air. "Don't hurt us!" he yelled with sudden fright. In panic Linda was turning away.

"Don't ja go anywhere, ho'!" the man with the knife yelled.

As the children began crying, grabbing her by the legs, Wheeler cried, "What do you want of us!"

"I wont your life, you white mudderfucker." The gunman quickly laughed in his face. He jammed the gun under his chin, twisted it, then pushed his head up into the air.

"Take my wallet!" he screamed. "Please don't hurt us, please take my wallet . . ." he was reasoning with them.

"Yeah, I'll take your wallet and I'll take your ho'!"

"Mommy . . ." Katie cried.

The man with the knife had started for Linda and her children, grabbing her forcefully by the hair, when something happened.

Something strange.

Though Wheeler could not see, for this took place at his back, a man quickly appeared on the sidewalk in front of the memorial, intentionally walking directly for them. And he did so totally without fright while whistling a tune, which everyone heard echo from the vault where Lincoln sat.

"Whattda fuck?" said the knife man.

A low, mournful series of whistled notes, which sounded

like an old Negro spiritual. Every head turned, including Katie's and Michael's and Linda's, and focused on this apparition. As he stepped into the bright white lights, he smiled easily. Stopping but ten feet away, he casually stuck a cigarette into his mouth.

"Who dat? Who dat?" the knife man asked nervously as he jumped behind the young mother and forced her to face the stranger.

The intruder lit a match, a tiny blue flame glowing under the brim of a battered fedora as he puffed, hiding eyes that never failed to watch them steadily.

"Whattja wont?" the gunman called, his eyes glazed, his thick lips moist and parted. "He's jest an ol' bum, Louis, dat's all he is."

"What's he wont, Roy?"

Just as he said this, Blatt and Corless emerged from the elevator tunnel. Down the neatly manicured path and toward the Wheeler family they strolled, oblivious of the threatening situation.

"Hey, you!" the gunman yelled at Jack Scott. "Whattja wont, you ol' mudder? You wont some snatch, you ol' dawg?"

With careful ease Scott removed his hat and tossed it away. "No, Roy," he said, "I want you and Louis to lay down your weapons very slowly while you still can."

"Say what?" the gunman cried. Enraged, he rammed the pistol hard under Wheeler's throat, enough so that blood trickled from a laceration.

As Corless and Blatt stepped out into the light, they stopped abruptly. The fat man instantly sneaked under the curve of his belly to draw his gun. The gun sight snagged on his ample midsection, then came free at last. He pointed the pistol aimlessly toward the Wheelers, uncertain who was the threat.

"Please put that away," Scott said calmly to Corless.

Seeing the .357, Blatt started shaking. "Greg, let's go. I don't like this."

"Who dat?" the gunman barked, for he was holding Tom Wheeler and was unable to turn around.

"Mudderfuck!" Louis growled, grabbing Linda around the waist.

"Oh, my God," she sobbed, closing her eyes, and her captor reached up and smacked her hard on the chest. Responding, her children clung to her side. Katie was crying now, almost screaming.

"Mommy?" Michael whimpered. "Mommy . . ."

"I'll do him, I'll do him right now!" Roy snarled, his face seething with the drug.

Corless had not moved. He was watching the show with interest, studying Scott especially, sizing him up as if the others simply did not exist. This little gray-headed man in baggy pants was unarmed, yet calm as a duck in water. Something, he knew, was terribly wrong.

"You can walk out of here slowly," Scott offered Corless, pointing toward the street and careful to misdirect him, for Frank Rivers was easing closer from the green hedgerow by the path. He was holding a .45 in each hand. His left was trained on Corless, the other at Linda Wheeler's assailant. Unfortunately, this latter was a bad shot. The angle, Rivers knew, would drive a slug through the knife man and into the woman's back.

"Please," Scott said quietly, "you don't need that. You can put that away and return to your car."

"What?" Corless hesitated, his eyes growing large.

"Whattda fuck?" Roy echoed.

"Oh, please—" Linda began to beg. Rivers moved forward in careful strides, walking on his toes. He stopped on Blatt's left, his gun aimed at the fat man's head.

Suddenly Blatt spun and recoiled in shock, seeing his chauffeur with two guns and a gold star swinging from a chain around his neck. Rivers' eyes narrowed as Blatt's went wide with horror.

"Greg!" he screamed, and Corless turned, swinging his large frame with panic.

"Go ahead!" Rivers spat, snapping both barrels on Corless from scant feet away. The fat man swallowed hard, his face a cold mask.

"We're backing up!" Corless immediately shouted, turning his gun on Rivers. In that instant Scott drew his gun, locking Corless into the sights of his .9mm, slowly kneeling to reduce body mass.

"Say . . . what!" Roy barked nervously, twisting his gun into Wheeler's throat.

In the meantime Rivers was easing, one step at a time, toward the street, going for an angle that would allow a margin of safety for the young mother.

"Dear God!" Linda wept as her attacker tightened his grip.

"Don't mess with me!" Louis screamed at Rivers, who stopped instantly, his right aimed at the black man's head, his left still leveled at Corless. Blatt's hand dug nervously into a pocket, producing a small pistol.

"Whattda fuck?" said Roy.

Louis cursed, staring at Scott. "He ain't no goddamned ol' bum!"

"Jack," Rivers stated calmly, "I'm going to take my left off the fat man. If he shoots, drop him."

"Like a brick," he answered, kneeling with both hands gripped on his gun.

"But we were backing up!" Blatt complained, as if this wasn't fair.

"On three, Jack."

"Right."

With nearly invisible swiftness Rivers snapped his left into position on the knife man's head. Startled, Louis lifted Linda's feet off the ground.

"Mommy!" Katie cried. "Mommy!"

Rivers emptied his lungs. "Three," he breathed.

"Whattda goddamn?" Roy yelled.

"Greg!" Blatt implored.

"Don't you get it?" Corless snapped, staring over his sight, his puffy cheeks raised in quivering jowls. "They know who we are, Seymour. Why do you think that punk was driving?"

Blatt was mute.

"Isn't that true?" Corless stated flatly, aiming his barrel at Scott's chest.

He returned a slight nod. "Lisa Caymann," he said.

Blatt froze, stunned but quivering.

"Her mother sent us." Rivers' voice was ice, but Corless had no real expression for any of this.

"Lacy Wilcott," said Scott, "and Carol Barth."

"Jenna Simpson and Janet Moore," added Rivers.

"Bobby Vought and Susan Cooper."

"Officer John Brougham."

"Whattda fuck?"

Suddenly, without warning, with the bursting howl of a halogen beam, daylight came blasting down from above even before the sound of a jet engine had reached their ears. Night became day in that instant as a terrible roar came thundering down. *Eagle One* dropping like a stone.

The blades were a violent blast as little Katie opened her mouth to scream. In that one terrifying, chaotic moment, time stopped.

The world exploded.

The monument grounds burst in a terrible blaze as deafening blasts roared into the night, echoing against marble like godless cannon fire.

Instantly Linda Wheeler toppled onto both children, a dark gel splattering over them as Rivers' guns kicked. The knife man fell backward, his head exploding off his neck like a split melon.

Scott was rolling onto one hip as a slug slammed the pavement before him, driving concrete across his face, drilling his torso.

Corless fell backward, crying out as a sledgehammer blow tore through his gut. He fought for control, his face a seething mask. He raised his gun at Rivers, but both his hands were releasing red flames, sending precise bolts into the fat man's shoulders, then once to the midsection, and he spun away.

Corless screamed in agony, thrown back with such force that his head cracked the pavement. For his part, Blatt stumbled backward while aiming with both hands, jerking the trigger. Rivers flinched as a bullet caught the bone of his left shoulder. Ignoring it, he leapt into air and slammed Blatt in the middle of the chest, punching the human weasel onto the concrete.

Rivers was all over him.

Grabbing Blatt from the back, he laid a forearm against his throat, then lifted him skyward. Staring into his face, he folded his torso backward.

Blatt screamed with horror as he felt his spine begin to splinter like a hollow stick.

"Lisa," Rivers hissed as Blatt's torso dangled. Then he threw his full weight into him, crushing the dentist's rib cage and snapping his spine in two.

Blatt shrieked in high-pitched agony as he came apart—the sound of ice being crushed. Rivers' face was twisted in vengeance as he folded him backward until Blatt's head thumped against his rear pockets. "John Brougham," he cursed, dropping him. In his fury he delivered a swift kick, aiming for his right temple but missing this, connecting with his mouth.

Blatt's teeth flew out, spinning and clattering over pavement, and landed by Corless in a puddle of human fluids.

"I'm gonna do him!" Roy screamed through a drugged rage, pulling Wheeler from behind as he backed away from Scott, who was now on his feet and moving toward them, his face peppered with stones and blood. His left eye was closing, his pants torn, his belly a dark brown pool.

"God, please . . ." Linda cried, clutching both children, watching her husband being dragged into darkness. At that moment Officer Steven Adare appeared behind them in the grass. Quickly assessing the situation he laid down his assault rifle.

"Quickly!" he said to Linda, grabbing the woman by the arm. "Get them out of here!" The woman covered both children in a huddle and scurried away crablike.

Once they were safe, Adare dropped into a prone position. The laser scope on his .308 HK-91 beaded a bright red dot on Wheeler's face. This he flitted from side to side, trying to draw a good line on the black gunman, but it was no good. Facing Adare, Roy's body and head were shielded, for Wheeler was much taller. Suddenly, without provocation, Roy tore into Wheeler's throat with the front sight, creating a red tear in his skin. "I'm gonna do him! I'm gonna do him now!" he screamed.

"No," Scott said calmly, "you don't want this, Roy. You haven't killed anyone yet, there's still time to save your life—"

"Fuck you!" Roy shrieked, his eyes glazed and rolling with PCP, his teeth bared with instinctual terror.

Scott was peering over his gun sight, seeing Adare's red beam flicking from Tom to Roy to Tom. "We will take your habit into consideration," Scott said to appease him. "The drugs are not your fault."

Roy responded by grabbing Wheeler by the hair and jerking his chin up. He exposed smooth skin as he jammed the muzzle under his victim's jaw.

"Please don't kill me." Wheeler was begging. He knew he was going to die at the hands of this rabid animal. And all of this in sight of the Lincoln Memorial, so clean, so ageless, so American. Like peering through the wrong end of a telescope, he watched Abraham Lincoln growing smaller and smaller as Roy dragged him into darkness. Strangely detached, he looked down the barrel of Scott's gun and discovered a curious peace.

He made this peace with himself very quickly, for he had seen his family moved away, and they seemed unhurt. And though he wasn't sure why, his mind started calculating assets—life insurance, stocks, savings, money market—and he had started to work on how far that would go as the world burst around him in a bright, jagged flash.

Orange and red daylight, that's all Wheeler saw, then he was blind. He felt his body falling through space, his ears roaring, a warm stickiness slapping his face, then pelting down on him in a slippery rain.

Roy was gone.

Roy had backed up into Frank Rivers, who had placed his .45 one foot from his skull, behind his left ear, and fired.

"Oh, Lord," muttered Scott, shaking his head.

"Shit, are you okay, Jack?" Rivers asked. "You look like death—"

"No." Scott was checking himself for the first time. "No, I'm not all right, I hurt all over."

Wheeler lay on his back, digging gel from both eyes. As his vision cleared, he found himself staring up into a man's face, his eyes blue as bottled glass cleaner.

"Your family's doing just fine, you okay, buddy?" Rivers asked.

Wheeler was speechless as sirens screamed through the capital city.

Gregory Corless was sitting upright like a fat Buddha, staring vacantly. As Scott and Rivers approached, he was trying to move, moaning against the stained concrete. Seemingly from nowhere he heard a quiet *splat* of flesh ripping open.

He heard rather than felt this.

Only then did he catch the smell of what was happening to him. Corless had been trying to reach for his gun, twisting his torso slightly right. As his mass shifted downward, it forced his bowels to split open, releasing a foul, sickening odor that even he could not believe.

He squirmed, trying to ease the painful pressure. His liver seemed to moan as it ruptured and started to slip downward.

"Oh, God!" he cried, and with that, he froze.

The pain was growing, expanding in his gut. It had started as a sharp fire just under his ribs where the bullets had slammed into him, but now that fierce agony was blinding, his belly felt like someone had driven a jagged spear clean through and turned the blade inside him like a corkscrew. And he sensed things inside him slithering around, as if his organs were coming alive and starting to crawl.

In his mind he moved his hands over and across the tear in his belly, holding them in place so that his liver would not *slap* free. But bullets had severed the nerves in both his shoulders, and his arms would not obey. In an animal urge, he twisted his torso toward Blatt for help. He was trying to cry out when there was the sudden sound of a *bedsheet* being ripped.

There was no bedsheet.

For all the world, Corless looked like a beached whale, leaning forward, sitting on two giant hams. A brown slipper lay between his legs, and another large piece of him was poking through.

"Help me . . ." he groaned, his eyes fixed, his body slung forward but unable to move as the two policemen stood over him.

"No," said Rivers, "I don't think I will."

"So, Gregory," Scott said, leaning over into his face, "if you're so smart, why are you so dead?"

"Help . . ." His lips moved as his gut discharged a spurt of brown fluids.

Squatting directly in front of the fat man, Scott lifted his head from his chest with one hand and looked him directly in the eye. The pupils were dilating, the lids had stopped blinking. "You know, your life wasn't a total waste," he commented.

"How so?" Rivers asked.

"Think about it, that poor family of civilians. If there had never been a Corless and Blatt, we wouldn't have been here tonight."

"That's true," Rivers replied.

"And I think Roy and Louis would have killed them. At the very least, they would have done real damage."

Rivers nodded thoughtfully as Scott edged even closer to Corless, so that his nose almost touched the fat man's. "Thank you, Gregory, for saving the lives of a nice family. You didn't know you did that, but you did!"

"Help me . . ."

"You're dead, Gregory!" he growled, biting these words off

sharply. "You died in order to save a little girl and boy. *You died* so that a family can live. Just think about that on your way to hell. All because of you and Aaron Blatt, they're going to live happily ever after."

The fat man couldn't move, or Scott was sure he would have. Corless was trying to speak, the heavy layers of skin on his throat quivering as Scott disgustedly shoved Corless onto his back. This movement produced a strange sound.

A sound like a knife ripping through a canvas sail.

The inner mass that was Corless tumbled swiftly downward, his belly emptying into his shirt.

He moaned with agony.

He did that several times before he finally died.

53

Sitting at his kitchen table in Wooded Acres, Jeffrey Dorn slipped a needle into red meat, driving fluid from a syringe with his thumb. Irma was watching, flipping through a catalog of summer fashions while listening to a live performance of classical music broadcast over WETA public radio. Dorn returned the needle to the vial, filling it again, jabbing it violently into a flank steak.

"Oh, sweetheart, please be careful with that."

Dorn shot her a wild look, his dark eyes glinting in the soft light as the music swelled. Unnerved, Irma lifted the small bottle and inspected the clear fluid. "DANGER," the label warned, *"DMNA dimethyl nitrosamine."*

"What is it?" she asked.

"As far as I'm concerned it's heart medication," he said tonelessly, lifting the steak and flopping it over onto a serving dish. "It's actually a corrosion inhibitor for rocket fuels, but it's also used in cancer treatments. When ingested, it causes the heart to explode."

Irma cringed as he took the bottle from her hand and jammed the needle back in.

"Is this for her?" she asked, and her face carried a dizzy expression.

He shook his head.

"Then who's it for?" she pressed, and Dorn reached over and touched her hand.

"Tell me about this Beverly Lynch," he demanded. "You said her father has filed for divorce and left town?"

"Oh, Jeff, she seems happy to me, she doesn't need us."

"Irma, you described her as sullen. That's a symptom of abuse. All those years of specialization and you don't know that? We should rescue her as well."

"Oh, Jeff," she said, rising from her chair and sidling up to him, "let's stay home tonight, just the two of us." She rubbed his ear with her fingertips as he continued to work. "Last night you said it was too early to make another try at the Jansons. You said you needed time to plan—"

"I've planned," he interrupted.

"*MASH* comes on in ten minutes, it's your favorite."

"I have another show in mind. Go polish the key. A little extra steel wool wouldn't hurt."

"Oh, honey, I've worked it to death. Would you like to talk about the wedding?" She flipped to a page in her magazine, to an advertisement for a bridal boutique, while Dorn injected the meat until it glistened with small pools of liquid popping up from the flesh.

"Hand me a paper towel," he demanded. Soon he had covered the platter, patting it down, blotting away surplus. He waited until more fluid had leached through, then patted it again and flipped it over.

"I don't think this is right," Irma said softly.

Dorn lifted his head, his eyes dark and punishing. "Don't start with me," he warned.

"But what will you do with Elmer, honey? How will you save him?"

"It doesn't matter."

"Yes," she pouted, "yes, it does." She looked as if she was about to cry.

"You nitwit," he said absently, "you're a big part of this."

As Irma began to weep, Dorn stopped work with a heavy sigh. "Irma, what the hell is the matter now? You know the plan, why do you do this to me?"

She looked over at him, her eyes pinched and troubled. "Jeff, you're not being honest with me," she said, and sobbed once more.

"What? Irma, why are you doing this?"

"You've been sick," she cried, "and you didn't even tell me . . ."

Dorn rose abruptly from his seat, smacking his forehead and staring up at the ceiling. "God damn you, Irma, you've been reading my mail!"

"Oh, honey," she whined, "are you going to sue Dr. Landry?"

Dorn drew a perfect blank. "What are you rattling on about? Why would I sue him, Irma? Dead men can't sue anyone!"

In response she pulled a plain white envelope free of her dress. It had been torn open by a nervous hand when the stress of so much mysterious correspondence finally broke the woman down. Dorn looked upon this as a vile, alien thing. Quickly he snatched it from her hand and started to read.

When he had finished, his face was contorting without control, his knees were shaking his entire frame, and he felt bile rushing up from his stomach.

"My Lord," Irma cried nervously, "what's wrong? That's good news. Sweetheart, you should be happy."

"I can't believe this . . ." Dorn muttered, swallowing hard.

"Sweetheart, if you're mad at him, then I think you should sue! Mistakes like that don't happen without a price. They either screwed up in his office or at the testing facility. Either way, you should be happy. You're so brave, Jeff, living with something like this all by yourself—"

"Shut up!" he cried, and he read the letter again:

As stated in our previous correspondence, the mix-up between your blood sample and that of a terminal cancer patient was made at the Wyro Technical Center. Frankly, we are concerned, since we have not heard from you as to your course of action in this matter . . .

"I can't believe it. The goddamn insufferable incompetence! Bastards! God, Irma, we have to get busy!" While Dorn's personal message to Scott flashed through his mind, Irma was on her feet, twirling in place.

"What, Jeff?" she said. "I think we should celebrate. A dark cloud has been lifted from this house!"

"Stop it! Irma, you don't understand the trouble we're in!"

"It will pass, Jeff, you were never sick. I know how hard this—"

"No!" he cried, and held up a silencing hand. "What happened to the Claytons could have drawn attention to us. And that kid has found—"

"Jeff, that family wasn't your fault, you were trying to help them."

"If that kid keeps digging, it's over for me, Irma, and over for you. God damn, I cannot believe this has happened to me. . . ."

"I don't understand, Jeff, what are you saying?"

Dorn released a heavy mechanical sigh. "It doesn't matter." He added quickly in a confused and confidential voice, "People are out to get me, you'll just have to accept that. From now on you help without questions, Irma. I don't want to waste any more time answering your—"

She stood suddenly at this, crying with alarm. "Hold me, Jeff, hold me."

54

Jessica Janson was in her bedroom, listening to the rippling of flutes and the lazy depths of cellos as the fourth movement of *Fantasia* played over the radio. As she folded clothes, she was wishing she could have afforded tickets to take Elmer, for hearing the London Philharmonic was an event that he would remember, especially at the Kennedy Center.

Then and there she resolved not to give up on her efforts to instill an appreciation of music in him, though the strings, piped into her bedroom speakers, were sounding a pinch shallow.

As she frowned noticeably, Elmer asked, "What's wrong?"

"Be a doll and go downstairs and adjust the bass to the right setting," she whispered. He had been sitting on the end of her bed, digging through her jewelry box and toying with treasures.

"Mom, what's this?" he asked, holding up what looked like a dozen very thin rings all interlocked with each other into a four-inch chain. She smiled, sitting alongside him on the bed.

"That's a puzzle ring from Egypt. Your daddy gave that to

me in 1979 when he was covering Secretary Vance's trip to the Middle East."

"Why is it apart?"

"Because," she said, poking him in the tummy, "the tape that held it together fell off, and I don't have time to go to Egypt to find a puzzle master to fix it."

"Can I have it?"

"It's very expensive, Red. You can play with it if you like."

He shoved it into a pocket. "What's this?" he asked, opening a long velvet box, which she quickly took away from him.

"That's for another night, you have school tomorrow."

Elmer pushed off the bed as Tripod stood, tail wagging, preceding him out the door. "Mom," he asked shyly, "do you like Mr. Hall?"

"I think he's a very nice man, very special."

"Can we invite him over for dinner?"

"Yes, Elmer, if he hasn't returned to New York, we can ask."

"Mom, are you in love with Detective Rivers?"

At this Jessica shook her head, then reached over to pinch him gently on the ear. "Elmer, why do you ask questions like that?"

"I saw you hugging."

She emitted a heartfelt sigh. "Red," she said softly, "that was just a thank-you hug for helping us. Come on, I think it's getting late. While you're fixing my speaker, will you get me a soda?"

"Orange?"

"Ginger ale. And no ice cream scoops for you, either."

Manufactured by JBL, the expensive intercom had been installed by Elmer's father just to the left of the refrigerator, facing the hallway. Flipping on the light as he came through, Elmer quickly adjusted a knob, then opened the door to the freezer.

Inside he saw a box of chocolate-covered bonbons, and he squinted, flipping the switch to his mother's bedroom.

"Just one," she responded before he had asked, and Elmer smiled.

"Mom, do you want a cookie?"

"No," her detached voice said firmly, "no cookies. You can have a bonbon, or you can have a cookie, not both. And you have to brush your teeth again."

"Okay, Mom."

As he peered back in at the ice cream, Tripod rose on hind legs, pressing against the boy's back and pushing him forward. "Oh, hold your horses," he giggled, pulling at the box, then removing two balls of ice cream with his fingers.

"Sit!" he ordered, and as the dog obeyed, he held an ice cream ball before his nose. Tripod gulped without chewing as Elmer popped his, letting it melt in his mouth. He then grabbed a vase from beneath the sink and began filling this with tap water. Suddenly the dog rammed him from the rear.

"Tripod!" he laughed, poking him gently in the nose, and the dog sat, wagging his broomlike tail. Over the sink and just to the left, Elmer opened a cupboard and removed a box, this with a smiling cartoon puppy on it. He was just reaching inside the flap, grabbing a handful of cookies that he held to the dog's muzzle, when Tripod dropped forward, his jowls quivering.

The skin on his nose was raised into a snarl, exposing teeth, looking eye to eye with the boy. "What's wrong?" Elmer asked, startled. He sniffed the biscuits as the dog hopped away toward the back door.

As Elmer came alongside, the dog released a low, menacing growl.

"Come on, boy," he comforted, stroking the ridge of fur on his neck. But the shepherd would not come. Instead he reared up and rapped at the door with his front foot.

Elmer quickly threw the intercom lever and spoke excitedly into the wall-mounted speaker. "Mom?"

"What is it, Red?"

"Tripod hears something."

"Yes, dear, he always does. Now, only one bonbon apiece, and I've counted them."

"Not like this, Mom. Tripod is really upset."

"Give him a cookie and come upstairs, Elmer. It's way past your bedtime."

Elmer looked at the dog's bared teeth. "What is it, boy?" he leaned over to ask. But the shepherd kept growling, saliva dripping to the floor, his large brown eyes fixed in a menacing stare out the window.

"Come on," the boy urged, tugging his collar, but the dog would not budge. Elmer flicked a wall switch, and as the outside yellow light came on, Tripod reared onto his hind legs, his body stiffening, his massive head tilted slightly down as his fangs glistened.

But there was only the wind.

And a shadow fading into darkness.

Jessica Janson was sipping a ginger ale while putting up her
hair, combing this straight up, then gathering it directly on the
top of her head. With practiced ease she took an elastic tie
from between her lips and secured a tight bundle. Rivers had
been right in his earlier description: the result was a funny little ponytail that resembled a straw fountain. From her scalp it
bloomed in every direction, and she batted this down into
place.

Sitting in bed, she kicked her feet into the air and pulled
her slacks from her hips. Standing, she shook the wrinkles out
and hung them with automatic care. *Fantasia* was still playing, so she glided with the strings toward the closet and back,
retrieving her choice of dress shoes for the morning, parking
these beneath her side window by a nightstand.

It had been a long day, she reflected, and she was alone for
the first time that weekend. Elmer, who had seemed sad on
Friday, had certainly perked up when Rivers was around.
How the boy had tried to mimic the way Detective Rivers
walked, quiet and confident, it was almost comic, though she
had been careful not to snicker. She wondered what it was
like for a boy Elmer's age to be missing a male role model.

"Should have had a brother," she said aloud. At times she
did sense that lack in her struggle to raise someone who
would be worth knowing. That was really her only criterion,
that her son grow into a man that made a contribution to the
world, and not just take from it. Frank Rivers was just such
a man, she thought, strong and caring and dedicated, and yet
somewhat of an enigma, a mystery she wanted to decipher.
"That will take some time," she said aloud, removing a package of stockings and breaking open the plastic seal. Then she
proceeded to lay out a pale gray executive suit.

The week began to form in her mind. Verdone Apparel, she
remembered, her gears shifting quickly. Since 1983 she had
been the commercial account executive, and through no fault
of her own, they were going to run over budget on a television campaign, and she wondered how the agency would absorb that.

Check with accounting, she dashed quickly onto a notepad,
staring down at her briefcase. As she started to pick this up,

she stopped abruptly. She stretched catlike, pushing her arms above her head and releasing a relaxed yawn.

This behavior was contagious.

Irma Kiernan was yawning with her.

Not more than forty feet away, the two women were facing each other through the window, though Jessica was oblivious of this presence. The older woman could barely tolerate the way her man had been staring up at her, breathing heavily as the blond tart really put on an act. As she started slowly unbuttoning a blue silk blouse, Irma wanted to throw stones through the glass.

Irma wanted to resurrect the witch trials of Salem and burn, stone, crush her into nothingness. Even without binoculars it was easy to tell how smooth and taut the woman's skin was, and that made Irma feel old beyond her years: her rounded back, her sagging chin and face falling forward in defeat. She quickly looked away.

From the rear, the light in Elmer's bedroom was casting shadows against the fence near the alley, while Jessica's room was in the front northeast corner. Her side window faced the lot between houses, and Dorn stood here, looking up from a neighbor's wall through binoculars.

Once the wall had been painted white, but Jeff had explained how old the owners were. Although the red brick was showing through in ugly strips, there was no one to maintain the property line. As she steadied herself, flecks of paint stuck to her palms in the humidity. Brushing herself off, she grew quite angry as the woman in the window slipped off her shirt, exposing herself in a peach-colored bra. And just when Irma thought it could get no worse, Jessica unsnapped this in one sweeping motion and let her breasts bounce free.

The woman did have a substantial figure, and seemed to be tracing red lines with her fingers. Unable to stand this anymore, she looked at Dorn, quickly interpreting this display for him. "Nothing special there!" she laughed.

Dorn did not respond. He knew better on two counts. First, it was a rare night when the Janson house wasn't shut like a tomb with the wooden shutters drawn tight, so he reasoned that the boy must have toyed with these. Second, Jessica had curves that could fog a camera lens.

The window was partially open to the cool night air, and the classical music swirled through the yard, reaching them.

To distract herself, Irma tried looking up to a scattering of clouds. The stars came stabbing down like angry needles, and she was thinking of other ways to distract Jeff when they heard voices.

"Mom?"

Jessica quickly threw on a silk bathrobe, then turned for the hallway.

Dorn's face was a perfect blank.

"In for a penny, in for a pound," Irma said, pressing her argument.

"No," Dorn corrected, "I'm going in alone. We go back home, I assemble my gear, then you'll drop me off again."

"But, Jeff, I think—"

Dorn held up a hand. "Irma," he hissed, waving the tainted meat at her, "it will take time for this to work anyhow."

"But isn't the dog in the house? He'd be barking at us."

"Very good, Irma, they always unlock his doggy door just before they go to sleep. He'll come out and have a nice snack, and then," he rapped his chest—"*blam-boom,* he'll blow like a cheap party balloon."

Dorn strolled the short distance of green to the rear fence and, standing on his toes, peered over to study the backyard. Selecting a spot near a small elm tree, he removed the meat from a plastic bag and hurled it with some precision. There was a muted thud.

"But how will I know when you're done?"

Irma was standing behind him, and Dorn shook his head with frustration. "I told you," he whispered wearily, "it will be about four or five hours, so I'll call, just wait by the phone." He turned toward the street and began to walk away.

"But why so long, Jeff? I still don't understand why you will take so—"

"Irma!"

"Oh, honey, that's dangerous. You shouldn't use the phone."

Dorn was almost to the street, turning for their car, which was parked down the road. "Reach out and touch someone, that's why we have phones."

"And you're sure she's guilty? She uses the boy for—"

"Irma, you saw her public striptease. You read that article about her. She's a kinky slut and that kid needs us, he's in for some real trouble."

As they headed down the street toward the car, Irma considered this, though not so carefully, as the next question was more nagging, overpowering. "Jeff," she squeaked, pressing herself against him.

Dorn turned, walking backward. "The answer is no, Irma! I do *not* want to touch her, you are my only bed partner." He paused for effect. "I'm happy the way things are."

She smiled coyly as Dorn laid a hand on her cheek. Her skin felt cool and lifeless as vinyl.

He opened the door.

Irma believed because she wanted to.

55

Scott and Rivers had left their cars, including the limo, and taken *Eagle One* to Suburban Hospital, more than ten minutes away by air. There were many closer choices, including the Washington Hospital's MedStar unit, but they wanted to be near the command post.

Scott was in surgery for nearly an hour, not for the severity of wounds, but for the sheer number of them. Corless had shot the concrete just at Scott's feet, driving debris into his legs, crotch, stomach, and chest. As of 9:52, the commander had taken thirty-nine stitches.

Rivers sat nearby on a table in the gun-wound operating theater. "Then it's not that bad?" he questioned, peering into the warm brown eyes of Dr. Anh-Bich Pham, a Vietnamese American with skin like smooth cream on the face of an angel. Still in her operating blues, she was taking his pulse.

"Mr. Rivers . . ."

"Frank, please, you've inspected my entire body."

She dropped his arm. "You better use that sling. The muscle is badly bruised and torn in two places. I'd suggest lying on your right side when you sleep, and don't plan on working for at least a week."

"I appreciate that, Doc. How long until it closes up?"

"That depends on how you treat yourself, but there's a piece of cartilage that may have to come out, we'll see in a few months. In the meantime I would recommend bed rest, no exercise on this side until you're mended, and I'm also putting you on antibiotics."

"Is that really necessary? They fry your guts to hell."

"Yes," she smiled, "they do. Now, stand up and bend over."

"I beg your pardon?"

"Bend over, Sergeant. I have a little present for you—that is, unless you want lockjaw."

Rivers shrugged and, dropping his pants to his knees, assumed the position. "Is this going to hurt?"

"Fiercely," she winked, "but you're a tough guy, so . . ." And she quickly hit home.

"Eeeeee yow!" he cried. "Damn me for a mutt!"

"Told you, tetanus, it's not a nice shot."

"Terrific," he winced, rubbing one cheek, "just terrific."

"And I'm serious about my instructions, Frank. I can see you don't listen to doctors very well, but this time you'd better."

"How's that?"

She pointed to a scar on his chest and another on his left forearm, the latter like the sealed flap of a small envelope. "Who sutured these?" She gave him a nasty glance as she examined his flesh.

"Oh, those are mine. Safety pins, it's an old trick."

She nodded. "Very macho, Frank, you gave yourself stenosis in the tissue. Come see me in another twenty years when those scars become cysts or tumors."

He smiled. "You've got a deal, but the arm's going to mend okay, just take it easy?"

"That's a nasty little wound channel there. You're lucky it was a twenty-five and not something faster: the bullet was on the surface because it hit the bone and bounced back out. It really is more serious inside than you can tell, so take it easy, you've lost a pint of blood."

"I'll eat some liver."

"I'm sure." She glanced at her watch. "Your friend's going to be another thirty minutes, so you might as well get comfortable."

"He is going to be okay?"

"Mr. Scott has taken nearly forty *real* stitches so far, and they're still picking stones out of him. The bullet carried the full path of debris into his skin. By the way, did you know the slug tore a hole right through his pants?"

"It hit him?"

"No, the bullet sliced neatly through the baggy seam at his crotch. He was very, very lucky."

Rivers swallowed hard. "It musta ricocheted."

"Yes," she said, turning for the door. "I'll be giving you something for the pain. You are going to hurt when the IM wears off."

"Sorry?"

"Intramuscular injection—pain killer. I did quite a bit of digging in there, as well as curettage against the bone, which you couldn't feel, but you will. This will start to hurt, believe me, so I'm going to get you started on something very hippie."

"I'll take it later."

She eyed him steadily. "We'll see. Your captain's waiting for you, if you'd like to see him."

Rivers nodded as he rubbed his wounded shoulder.

"If you need me, you call, that's my beeper," she said, handing him a card.

He slipped this into his pants without looking at it. "Thanks, Doc, I really appreciate it."

She smiled warmly. "Try to duck next time, Frank. You have enough hard miles on that body of yours."

"Tell me about it."

She nodded thoughtfully and edged closer. "Who shot you in the face?" she asked in a concerned whisper. "I didn't see a reference to that in your medical history."

"Oh," he sighed, "it's that obvious?"

"No, no," she said. "But I was a trauma surgeon at Da Nang air field. I know reconstruction when I see it, and you have a replacement cheek." She stroked it lightly. "It's beautiful, no one would ever know."

Rivers grimaced. "Please don't put that in the file."

She shook her head at him. "Our secret, but it was Vietnam?"

"Cambodia."

"That's a very special job they did," she affirmed.

She was slowly opening the door as Captain Maxwell Drury suddenly rushed in. "Sweet Jesus, Frank, I've been worried sick."

"Hiya, Max, I just gotta thump is all."

"Detective Rivers?" Dr. Pham questioned, waiting until she

had his full attention. "Take those pills, you're going to need them, all of them."

Rivers waved. "Thanks."

"My God, Frank," Drury cried with dread, "that lousy bastard almost shot off Jack's goody bag!"

"I know," Rivers grimaced. "What about Jessica, Max? If you're here, I take it you put an extra team on their house?"

"Are you all right, son?"

Rivers stood suddenly, "I'm fine, Max, what about the Jansons? Did you pull Toy and Murphy out of the bowling alley? They can't see the house from their position!" His voice was flushed, his tone accusatory as Drury was breathing deeply, his eyes flinched with anger.

"Don't you start with me, Frank," Drury cautioned suddenly, "I've just been reviewing the contents of Blatt's plane, and I'm damn near fed up. They recovered enough teeth to make three mouths, plus a shitload of the cruelest video your mind can imagine—those bastards were playing a weird sadistic sex game, trading their pleasure for a little relief from torture—"

"Max!" Rivers cut him off, raising a hand. "I don't want to hear it. If Blatt's dead there's no one to prosecute. What about Jessica?"

Drury's eyes flared and then narrowed as Dr. Pham held open the door to the recovery theater. What appeared from the shadows was a patient who bore the look of a man brought back from life. Scott's eyes were swollen and hollow, his face bruised and covered with tracks, and he looked old. Very old. He limped forward with a body that trembled.

Drury stared at the apparition.

"Captain," Dr. Pham said nervously, helping Scott to a chair. "This patient has refused admission, and—"

"Oh, Jack," Drury cried, "you should stay and get some sleep."

Scott slowly shook his head, watching as Rivers laced his jogging shoes. "What about the fat man?" he swallowed, his breathing labored.

"Gregory Richard Corless, superintendent of public schools for Mercer County, Alabama. We don't know his history with Blatt just yet, but he's married and has three children. Two of them are girls."

Scott nodded.

"Blatt all but came apart into two pieces when they cut his

clothes off, I was going to ask Frank about that." And though Scott had started to respond, he knew with a glance that words were not necessary. Rivers was quickly holstering his guns, his shirt still open across his chest, his eyes like stones, his jaw muscles ticking with anger.

"The Jansons, Max," Scott charged quickly. "Who is covering for you?"

Before Drury could answer, Rivers pushed out the door.

56

In the Janson backyard there was undisturbed silence. By the corner of the house, under a small elm, his victim lay lifeless.

Dorn looked skyward as the last shuttle to New York roared overhead, some thirty minutes behind schedule, and was gaining altitude. The Sunday traffic on River Road had slowed to a handful of cars. The air was cool, his black body sock cutting the breeze, so he only felt this on his face. The Dacron hood was tucked back behind his ears, enabling him to discern the direction of any noise.

On his waist he carried a gear pouch of black nylon, and from it he removed a lipstick, applying this to thin lips that were quickly going dark blue. With three more strokes, they were nearly black.

He stood in the very rear of the side lot, looking over the gate and into the backyard. The light in Elmer's window cast a muted glow. Below, Dorn could just see the form of Tripod lying near some bushes, still as a stone. And this delighted him.

All along Jeffrey Dorn had known something about this particular dog that had gone unnoticed by most people. At one time he must have been a trained attack dog from some military or police K-9 corps, though Dorn didn't know which. His educated guess was armed forces, for the shepherd rarely barked, even when there was a threat. The mutt had been trained in stealth, though the boy was starting to ruin the animal's instincts.

Tripod's type of attack, Dorn knew, would be silent, merciless, and without warning, the product of professional conditioning. And it almost seemed a waste to kill such an obedient instrument of destruction. After only one bite of tainted meat, the mutt had crawled into the darkness to die.

Dorn checked his watch: 10:42. Through the upstairs window he could hear the Kennedy Center's final prelude, and he saw Jessica's graceful shadow gliding against the half-drawn shades.

"Good night, Mom," a voice flitted through.

"Night-night, sweetheart. Did you let Tripod out?"

"Yes."

"Elmer, did you say your prayers?"

"Yes, Mom. Tomorrow can we take Tripod to the park?"

"Monday's a workday, Red, you know that. Next weekend, okay, and you have to do well on all your tests. School's almost over, then you'll have all summer to play."

"Mom?" he asked shyly.

"I'm right here, Elmer, aren't you tired?"

"Thanks for everything, I mean the pizza and movies and all."

"You're quite welcome, baby, give us a kiss." There was a pause that caused Dorn's heart to flutter. "Good night," the woman sang, "don't let the bedbugs bite."

Dorn closed his eyes, breathing hard, as Jessica turned out the light in the boy's bedroom. The voices, the stillness of the yard, the key in his hand, all of this was almost more than he could take without screaming.

In Jessica's room the lights stayed on, and he placed his ear to the outside wall. As the music died, the sounds of running water filled in behind. From the street there were only the blinking traffic lights on River Road, and he waited, seeing headlights slow before moving on.

In his younger years, he thought, he would have simply used the dog's plastic door as an entrance, lying on his side and wriggling through with ease. In his later years, though, the scoliosis of his spine and the age in his joints had taken their toll, and he was half the man, forced to live with memories. And in the torn light he remembered dropping right through a chimney on Christmas Eve and into a living room, savoring that, recalling the terrorized expressions that received him.

He crept down along the front of the house, against the hedges, toward the front door. He had considered the rear, but the back light had been left on, casting a glow that could reflect a tall shadow.

A car veered from the intersection toward him, and instantly he pulled back. The headlights streamed through the sleepy suburb, passing the little house before dropping off into distant dark. He stood quickly, removing from his bag a pair of rubber gloves with a soft, subtle cotton lining that felt clean as death on his fingertips.

He held the key up to his face. Irma had polished it until a shine glowed from smooth edges, the teeth like gold. With the practice of a game-show host he inserted this gently, as with his left hand he covered the hardware, muffling the sound of a bolt lifting. It turned freely, and his eyes fairly burned.

Like so many others who had entertained him over the years, the woman had made use of a safety chain, and the rings of tarnished brass dangled against the jamb. In scant seconds he slid the metal tongue from its groove with rubber-coated forceps, the thing slipping with ease through its track. The chain swung once before he skillfully steadied it, his heart now pumping with a mad and merciless pursuit.

And he *felt*. Something, he wasn't sure what.

But it was wonderful, this feeling, causing his skin to crawl, writhe, forcing sweat to the surface as his pulse continued to climb. He felt the blood tingle through his torso, battering at his brain, driving his senses wild. Looking out from the hood, his eyes were like moist coals, wild with delight, and he could now hear his own twisted life tide roar in an angry ocean, rocking him, bursting in his ears as the door swung open.

He walked into darkness.

It was the violated spaces that he craved.

"Jessica," he mumbled, practicing her name, closing the door behind him. "There is nothing, Jessica, that you will not do to please me!"

Her voice drifted down the stairs to him. It was a tired voice, yet filled with hope. "I think he really would love an instrument, Mother, just not this year," she was saying. "Right now he needs boyish things."

Dorn stood in the living room listening to this as his eyes adjusted to the darkness very slowly, feeling his pupils grow as he smelled the domestic wonders around him.

Every house, he knew, was different. Odors came alive,

having soaked into fabric and wood. Some pungent, some sweet, he had smelled them all. Except for the aroma of wet dog food, the Janson house smelled *clean* somehow, and as he strolled for the kitchen, he decided he would change all of that. Change the smell. The dog would help some, so would Jessica, maybe her kid, he wasn't making a detailed plan, just kicking it around a little. And he stopped. A calendar in the breakfast nook caught his eye, then the morning's breakfast placed neatly on the counter. Cereal, bread, jams, and a pan for eggs.

"Mother," Jessica sighed, "that's not at all what I'm saying."

Dorn glided for the sink. The smell of ripe dog chow hung in the air, and he didn't care for this. The refrigerator released a quiet, steady hum, and posted on the door he saw Elmer's report card. While the silly woman had penned a gold star on top, there was a B in math circled in red. He imagined that really chewed on Jessica, the kid wasn't perfect, Dorn guessed her lovemaking was also poor.

As he edged out of the kitchen toward the staircase, he felt like he had known them for years. He was looking forward to meeting them for the first time, face-to-face. His heart pounded with sweet cruelty as he imagined her expression.

He stopped.

In a photograph on the staircase wall he saw his reflection in the glass. And even though this was an image of the entire Janson clan taken when Elmer was born, Dorn saw only himself. And some fish. His features were all but invisible as he lifted his upper lip, then tightened the masking over his head.

The stair creaked.

"Mom, I'd like to talk more, but I left the shower running."

Dorn steadied himself with a gloved hand against the wall.

"Love you too," she said, and there was silence. Formless and pure. Through the thin walls, pipes began to moan gently into a soft bass tone as Jessica added hot water to the flow of her shower.

He moved quickly up the steps, stopping midway and listening intently. A door with a magnetic catch snapped open—the linen closet, he guessed—and he heard the steady shower-head spray being muffled by human mass, the *rapping* echo less prevalent, then a glass door clicking shut.

Toe to heel to toe, step by step he walked, stopping at the

top landing. Before him, on a burnt-orange space rug, lay a large rubber bone that had been chewed to ribbons. Swooping this up, he strolled right for Elmer's bedroom.

The blue door was cracked a foot so that Tripod could nudge by, so Dorn batted at this, his fingertips making a scratching noise as he peeked through.

Sound asleep, Elmer was curled around a stuffed panda. At his feet was a large beanbag doggie bed, the type sold from catalogs, but from the scattered hair on Elmer's sheets, it was clear this wasn't used.

"Bedbugs," Dorn mocked tonelessly under his breath as he reached down into his pouch. He gave the boy a chance to wake: holding a pair of brightly polished handcuffs by the chain, he rattled them at him, then rolled the rubber bone across the carpet.

The boy did not wake.

Turning, Dorn slid the door shut, so silently. And even before he had entered the master bedroom, steam poured out to greet him, making his oval face tingle in the tight mask. Every nerve was now coming alive.

Jessica had let the hot water spray during the length of a phone call, and the steam filled the air, this seeping through the bathroom door. He could clearly hear water thumping against a glass cell, echoing from her bathroom.

He entered with a nod, for the bed was readied, the sheets meant to receive him, turned down with hotel perfection. Interesting, he thought, a glass of water on her nightstand. Dorn quickly placed a gathering of rope on her pillow, the kind bought at the better sporting-goods stores, and with gloved hands he picked up the glass, holding it to his lips to test the temperature with his tongue.

It was cold.

He drank it down in a single shot, moving soundlessly as though for the bathroom door. Dorn knew Jessica would be out quickly, not because of the lateness of the hour but from the way she had tied her hair. She would cover this with a rubber cap instead of washing it, and he knew how the steam would cause fluff if she stayed too long. Jessica had mentioned that to her mother once.

Vanity, he thought, *thy name is vanity.* He imagined how she would be willing to soak it, just to please him, or shave it off completely. With two fingers he pressed against the white wooden door.

It opened by inches.

Peering right, directly into a wall mirror, he saw her blurry form reflected from the shower stall. He decided to watch as she danced about behind the glass, cold and inky black eyes darting over her naked form. She was thin and tall, her hands held in back of her neck, rubbing with a washcloth while both elbows poked out with her breasts saddled between. She turned, facing the far wall, her left foot rubbing the calf of her right, when he heard an audible sigh. Suddenly she tilted her head backward, opened her mouth, and let the water rush over her face.

With his pulse soaring, he eased onto the carpet, closing the door quickly, for he did not want a draft to warn her.

Not this time.

Dorn wanted Jessica to see him pressed against the glass. So what if she screamed? That was fine. The possibility excited him further.

She turned. The water was rolling down her back, and she had one hand on each shoulder, bending slightly forward at the waist.

As Dorn approached, he removed his gloves.

Again she turned, facing the wall as Dorn quickly propelled himself forward, standing just to the right, his heart like a sick animal beating at his ribs. She rubbed her eyes, tilting her head back.

She was closing her eyes, her beautiful eyes, caressing her face with light fingertips, letting the water stream in restful strokes.

Blindness. Dorn saw she was blind. If only for one second, and that's all it took.

With a step he came into position directly in front of the glass panel, a movement that brought him incredible pleasure, a thousand times better than anything else he knew. Standing directly on top of her with certain perfection, man against prey, the little gun steadied in his right hand.

Standing within inches.

He watched her play with ribbons of water, streaming off her chin, tunneling through cleavage, flooding over her belly where her hands were cupped. Collecting a pool of bathwater, she splashed her face. She repeated this several times as Dorn rolled his eyes, the whites popping up.

Mouth open, he thrust his jaw forward. He licked his lips, wetting these until they fairly dripped. Pressing his face against smooth, warm glass, he inched closer still with every tick, edging his entire body, laying his features flat.

Chest, pelvis, knees, and then, as one final touch, he thrust a broad tongue onto the pane and sealed his face with its glue.

As the woman's hands gently crossed her chest, Dorn was contorting every muscle, twitching like a hellish mask of impossible cruelty.

Then, as if sensing something that should not be, that could not be, the woman's eyes suddenly snapped open and she turned, facing him in one wild hot instant: their bodies flat against the glass, his face mocking at her with obscene malevolence.

She opened her mouth to scream.

No sound came forth.

Her jaws yawned with absolute terror, and she reeled backward in terror, fighting for breath, feeling her stomach empty as this nightmare image drilled into her mind.

With a violent shudder she shut her eyes and stumbled backward into the farthest corner, a shaking, vulnerable mass that Dorn was now anxious to see in full view, though he was savoring this moment.

He was making memories.

He was opening the shower door, working his face into a heinous knot as Jessica's voice tore loose, crying with such clear and savage hate that it instantly struck Dorn with confusion—for it was coming from the bedroom outside.

"Zak!" she was screaming for all she was worth.

"Zak Dorani!"

57

Dorn froze with terror.

As he lifted his gun toward the hall, the shower door slammed open and a forceful hand grabbed his wrist. Other human figures pounded toward him through a frantic darkness.

Dorn screamed with rage.

"Freeze!" Frank Rivers yelled, pushing himself out of the

shower. Dorn felt a warm gun under his right eye as men filled the room.

Dorn's eyes stretched wide with horror as he struggled against Rivers' viselike grip.

"Drop the gun!"

Scott suddenly charged forward and rammed a shotgun into Dorn's throat. Someone ripped off his hood and Dorn felt a sharp rap to his head, dropping him like a stone as the lights came on and he gazed up from the carpet. The room was whirling, he was seeing faces of hate surrounding him in a blur: male faces, hard, unforgiving, their voices like spokesmen from hell.

"You are under arrest. The charge is fifteen counts of murder!" cried Rivers. Though Dorn could not see a face, someone else grabbed him, approaching with handcuffs, and he screamed again, fighting to stand, throwing both fists as he felt his body moving under a great human force.

Dorn was spinning through air, slamming down onto the sink with such force that his skull shattered the mirror and he felt something in his spine giving way.

"Shut up!" Rivers cried as Dorn screamed with agony into the night. As he felt his arms being pulled and gathered, caught in a powerful vise by a wall of men, his heart was nearly bursting.

Dorn's body was becoming spastic, shaking, trembling, as suddenly the contents of his stomach flew into the air and emptied out onto the floor. As he felt the cold metal collars pinching shut around his wrists he began to sob at the painful pressure. The human wall suddenly parted as an older man stepped forward until the brim of his hat rested against Dorn's brow.

Scott waited a moment for his image to register. Dorn began shaking his entire body in disbelief. "You have the right to remain silent," he hissed at the killer. "I strongly suggest that you use it!"

Dorn's eyes stretched with terror, his face frozen; then he burst into a quivering slab of absolute agony. His feral cry sent chills through each man, terrifying the woman behind them, who was left cowering in the corner of a running shower.

Frank Rivers, dripping in his soaked Jockey shorts, reached over and smacked Dorn on the top of the head with his open fist. "Search him," he ordered. Then he draped a bath towel over the shower stall and stood on his toes to look inside.

"You okay?" Rivers asked.

The woman was sobbing quietly in the corner.

"Hey, fellas," Rivers yelled above their voices, "she wants to get dressed. Get that maggot outside!"

When the bathroom had cleared, Rivers opened the door and climbed in. Turning off the water, he wrapped the woman in a towel.

"Oh, God," she sobbed. "Franky, that was so awful . . . I didn't even *have* to act, I couldn't even think . . ." And again she broke into tears.

"I know, Tammy," he sighed, holding her tight. "I know, but you did just fine."

Tammy McCain looked up at him, her large green eyes still apprehensive, and she was shaking, whimpering softly. After a career filled with oceanic predators, she had faced a true terrestrial monster in Jessica's shower. Whereas a thousand pounds of requiem shark didn't faze her, the cruel little man had scared her to her bones, and she was sobbing for the horrid reality of what this thing did for kicks.

"He would have killed them . . ." she cried.

"Everything is going to be just fine," he comforted. And Rivers believed this to be true.

58

In the bright wash of kitchen lights, there was nothing particularly special about Jeffrey Dorn. If anything, he was a plain-looking little man with a thin face and thinning hair, his eyes so deeply set that they sparkled through shadow. Of outstanding characteristics, he had none, and what four policemen saw was a cowardly worm of a being that filled them with loathing. They had carried him downstairs. They had plopped him on the floor like an old rug that was rolled and could not be cleaned. It was clear from his rigid posture and glassy stare that he was in shock.

Leaning over, Scott pulled him farther into a corner by the rear door, by Tripod's water bowl.

As Rivers entered, he scoffed. "Don't drink any of that. It would turn the puppy's stomach. Jack, he doesn't look like he knows you."

Scott frowned. "Oh, he knows, but he won't do anything to please us, and that includes recognition. Isn't that right, Zak?"

Dorn's face was stone.

Rivers huffed in dismay, his eyes narrowing as he strolled over to the intercom by the door. "Listen up," he said to Dorn, pressing the rewind button on the cassette player. As the little killer watched with abject disdain, Rivers pressed the play button and switched the speakers to the kitchen. It caught in mid-sentence, and voices filled the room.

"Good night, Mom," Elmer's voice said.

"Night-night, sweetheart. Did you let Tripod out?"

Jeffrey Dorn showed no expression at any of this. Scott looked on as Rivers ejected the tape, then dropped in another. The voice of a small boy filled the room.

"But I don't understand, why does he hate us so bad?" Elmer was asking.

"What about it, Zak?" Rivers said, taking a step forward. His face was the mask of a stone killer.

"Frank?" Scott cautioned.

Dorn's head turned smoothly, his moist lips parting. "This is entrapment," he said coldly. "I want an attorney."

As Scott turned to face Rivers, Mule Murphy came forward. The huge, powerful man stood over the little killer and pointed down at the massive toes of his combat boots. The older man saw this and backed up a step.

"That's what he wants," Scott offered. "In a minute Zak will be begging for bruises, a brutality charge, anything to blow us out in court."

Murphy nodded and backed up again.

"I'm entitled to a phone call," Dorn suggested. "You're violating my rights, Scott, you're depriving me of counsel."

Scott raised an eyebrow at Rivers. "He's a lawyer too." With that he produced a notepad and pen. Leaning down into Zak's face, "Okay," he offered, "give me the number and I'll dial for you. After that you can meet with your attorneys in the state lockup."

There was no answer, no recognition.

"All right," Scott said, turning to the men, "take him out of here while I call to arrange transport to Jessup. I think we'll go for federal maximum security, but I'll need a court order."

"My call!" Dorn barked.

Scott nodded, holding up a hand to stop the men, then picking up the phone. "I'll hold the phone to your ear, but the cuffs stay on," Scott said. "What's the number?"

Dorn's eyes glazed with secret amusement. "555-0817."

Scott punched it in and, holding the phone to Dorn's ear, heard it answered on the first ring.

"Irma, red button!" he yelled.

Scott jerked the phone away violently.

"You bastard!" Dorn cried. "I'll ruin you in court, you old psycho!"

Scott nodded, touching a finger to his temple, listening intently.

"Oh, Jeff! My God! Sweetheart? Are you there—"

Instantly Scott hung up. All he needed was the number; an address was seconds away. "Drury is waiting at the command post," he said to Murphy. "Radio the number and tell him the charges are conspiracy to commit murder and attempted kidnapping. On second thought," he said, "ask Max to throw in murder one, I don't want her making bail."

"Jack," Rivers suddenly protested, "let me work with Drury. I accused him of dropping the entire setup, and—"

"Frank," Scott corrected, taking a step forward. "We both did. I even cursed him out for leaving them alone, when he had already moved the Jansons from the house. Let me talk to him later, I'm hoping this is nothing that can't be healed over." He looked to Murphy, and with a nod of his head, the policeman lifted a radio off his belt and began to speak.

"Let's go, Zak," Rivers snapped, coming forward. "We're moving."

"Go easy, Frank, your shoulder," Scott reminded him. Instantly Toy Saul and Murphy hovered over Jeff Dorn as well, Mule's massive, grinning head looking down at all the smaller detectives.

Rivers nodded.

"Don't touch me!" Dorn hissed.

Reaching down, Murphy jerked him hard into the air, bringing Dorn's face up to his. "Be nice," Mule demanded.

On the way out the door, just out of the commander's sight, Murphy shook him violently, using a third of his strength. Dorn's head slapped like a rag doll coming unstuck.

"Hey, Franko," Toy Saul offered, "should we let Zak see the dog?"

Rivers shrugged.

"Well, I haven't seen it," Mule said, bouncing the killer under one arm. As they approached the elm tree, Rivers blinked with pleasure as Mule held the little man by the waist, his legs and upper torso folding, dangling in air.

"It's really something," Rivers explained. "It took Doc McQuade less than four hours to build and assemble the entire thing, framework and all, a fairly complete dog. He's a serious genius, just look at the eyes." Rivers leaned over, pulling the K-9 mannequin from the shadows. From a short distance it looked very much like the lifeless remains of a Belgian shepherd. In reality it had been Mrs. Drury's lynx coat.

"Hey, that really is remarkable." Mule swung his head at Dorn, showing thick white teeth. "But I wouldn't have fallen for it."

"I want a lawyer!" Dorn demanded with disgust.

Rivers said nothing, but merely stared down at the glistening slab of tainted meat as Murphy carried Dorn through the back gate, placing him on his rump and leaning him against the house. They were well in the shadows, the lights streaming through the windows creating a dull wash of white.

"Mule," Rivers said as the man straightened to his full height and backed away, "can you imagine what those apes will do to a mouse like this in the big house?"

As Toy Saul laughed, Mule grinned. Dorn seemed to be having some kind of fit. His head swiveled back and forth, his tongue wagging as his eyes rolled.

"Bring me Elmer and his crippled dog!" he shrieked, and then his voice broke into a wicked laugh as Rivers' eyes flashed with a menacing clarity.

Dorn laughed. Then smiled. Then suddenly he began to cry, his tears flowing in streams down his face as he sobbed. Then he snapped this display off and laughed again, staring up at them and hissing over his teeth.

"God, that's creepy," said Mule.

"Wonder if that's the last thing his victims saw?" Toy asked incredulously. In response, Dorn's tongue thrust from his face and he rolled his eyes up to show white. Toy moved away, uncomfortable with this performance. "I can't take this," he said softly. "I'll be waiting out front."

"Nigger babies!" Dorn shrieked after him. "Kill the niggers!"

Just then Jack Scott bolted from the house and through the back gate. Coming alongside Toy, he placed a calming hand on his shoulder to restrain him from trying to get at the little man, his eyes wide with rage. "Detective Saul," Scott said in a calm, commanding voice, "he's not worth it. His life is finished."

The prisoner released a savage cry and then started to laugh. "Scott's a fucking loon," he mocked, "the man is crazy as a squirrel." Then Dorn smiled, pursing his lips, cooing like a baby.

"Fuck you." Murphy stepped forward and spat at his feet.

The commander turned to Rivers. "Frank, we've got her name and address, I'm leaving you here with him. It shouldn't take thirty minutes, and a uniformed unit will be taking Tammy home."

"Is she doing okay?"

Scott nodded, looking at his watch. "She's recovering, said to tell you Zipper can't compete with this, whatever that means. I think she's still shook."

Rivers smiled.

"You old burn-out case," Dorn muttered at Scott's back.

Scott turned, his eyes seething, the left nearly swollen shut. "I'm going to watch your brains smoke," he said coldly. He turned toward the troopers and added, "The worst thing we can do to him is just walk away. Without an audience he's nothing."

With that Scott turned and started to stroll toward the street. As the men vanished into the shadows, Rivers pried a cigarette loose and lit up.

"Burn me?" Dorn asked pleasantly.

Rivers ignored him.

Then came a shrieking, hollow cry that touched Rivers right on the spine, and he turned, facing him. Dorn was grinning, eyes going white, flashing his teeth.

"That's not a smile," Rivers growled, leaning over so they were face-to-face. "You don't know who you are dealing with, so I'd suggest you shut up."

"Hit me!" he barked.

Rivers backed up and leaned against the wall, listening to the sounds of distant sirens. His left shoulder was growing stiff, giving him pain.

"I'll be out in five years, and Elmer will be fifteen . . ."

Rivers spun, the bolts of fire in his eyes startling the animal, who broke into a fit of girlish laughter. "Elmer," he whined, "that's it . . ."

In a single stroke, Rivers cut him off. The barrel of a gun materialized, leveled at Dorn's head. Slowly Rivers poked the tube down into the soft tissue under his right eye.

Dorn winced, twisting uncomfortably.

"No," Rivers glared, "this time you're wrong." He grunted as Dorn blinked. It was not a normal-looking gun, but had a long, thick barrel.

"A sexual device?" Dorn suggested calmly.

"No," Rivers shrugged, "it's a prison with a life term,"

Dorn's face was a blank.

"Take a good look, Zak, smile at your chamber. The gun itself is not that big a deal. Hell," he said, taking a puff, "I could deliver my load with damn near anything, a blowgun, a slingshot, a crossbow. But I chose this."

"An air gun?" Dorn asked.

Rivers twisted the barrel a little. "That's close enough. It's a CO_2-powered dart gun. I learned all about it on *Wild Kingdom,* and that's where I'll be sending you."

Dorn's face was stone. "A tranquilizer pistol—so you're going to put me to sleep."

"No." Rivers shook his head while baring his teeth. "I'm going to drill you with a fléchette," he stated flatly, and Dorn froze.

"Only it's much smaller than the type you use. The shaft in here carries a very special type of toxin—they think it's a protein—and I'm going to seal your brain inside a dead body."

Dorn shook, then regained control. "If there was such a thing, I'd know about it."

Rivers took in a puff of smoke, then exhaled slowly. "It stops a one-ton killer shark, one part per million in water." He said this so convincingly that Dorn began to tremble.

"Wait a minute," he panted, "you can't get away with this . . ."

Rivers removed the gun and took a step back. "Sure," he offered, "and I'm going to nail you with plenty of witnesses too. The only thing they'll see is a stroke victim." He tapped Dorn on the head. "Just an ugly little frog doing his last dance."

"But you're a cop!" he protested loudly, as if this wasn't fair.

Rivers nodded. "To serve and protect. I take that very seriously, even when the systems fail. No," he paused, "your mistake was mentioning Elmer. You see, the kid adopted me, I'm his Uncle Frank. And as for his mother," Rivers sighed, "I don't think I'll ever meet a finer, more sensitive woman, or a better mother, for that matter. You know—"

"Kick me!" Dorn cried with sudden panic, cutting him off, struggling to hit Rivers with his right toe.

And while Rivers really did think this over, he just walked away.

"No," he said thoughtfully, "I don't think I will."

59

Irma Kiernan was horrified, her hand shaking as she hung up the kitchen phone. She had heard the panic in Jeff's voice, and that alone filled her with fear.

"Jeff said the code was red," she muttered, fighting to steady herself. "Jeff said to implement the plan . . ." Her voice trailed off as she hung her head, her eyes glazed with a certain shock. Finally she came out of her daze.

With small animated steps she walked toward the living room, one careful foot at a time, then headed slowly down the stairs toward the basement. The hallway was cool and dark. In the soundless passage she heard her own labored breath, her pounding heartbeat falling in small, uncontrolled bursts as she rounded the steps and came to a door. Jeff's door. She stopped for a moment, considering this.

His den was his sanctuary, a private place, but more. Though Irma did not know why, this was the well from which he drew his strength, and although she did not want to intrude, she needed that strength now, she reasoned, they both needed it desperately. Yet her body would not obey as she reached, in her mind, for the latch. For greater than her wish to protect their lives from outsiders was her simple fear of the mirror that waited just inside, plus whatever secret it held.

Jeff had warned her many times.

She stood frozen like a jacklighted deer, conjuring images in her mind that might protect her: dreams of gallant knights and fairy-tale endings. While she prayed for this, she reached with a cautious hand. Her body shuddered as she pulled and the door swung wide with a sharp breath.

It was there to greet her.

Her face twitched as she set eyes on her own full-size image. She recoiled for an instant, then came forward under her own gaze. Irma trembled, for what she saw was another woman staring back at her as she crossed the floor. This other was nothing like Irma had ever imagined—tall and stately, well-curved and feminine—and the truth screamed at her, calling her by name.

She stood at the mirror. It was a brutish sack of a being that moved as she moved, blinking together, studying eyes like dull gray marbles on either side of a bulbous nose. With her lips pursed tight, she reached to pinch a fold of loose skin that sagged below her chin. Then she shook her head, hearing her own heart, forcing her stubby frame into movement.

"Minutes," she remembered, and the words seemed so unreal to her now, Jeff's voice reeling through her mind, coming back from a distant time: "You will have only minutes."

As she considered this, her obsession with the face in the mirror faded, just a troubling witness to her movements as she pushed, toe to heel, confronting her image with an unwonted purpose. Reaching, she grasped the silver frame with both hands. Her arms shook as she began to lift.

The mirror was rising from the wall, coming free, when she felt its weight pushing on her like a slab of lead. She double-stepped, stumbling backward under the enormous weight.

The mirror fell with a crash. The glass shattered, the frame landing on her knees. Irma Kiernan saw blood, fighting to right herself, her pounding heart stealing her breath.

"Oh, dear," she moaned, looking at her cut and bleeding hands. "Oh, my!" As she lay wounded under shards of broken glass, she began to sob, but not for the sharp, silvery needles that had sliced through her fingers. She was sobbing for Jeff. All his life he had worked with a hero's courage to help others, against such great odds, and Irma knew how the world had treated him. Like old tissue, once used, ready for discard.

Lesser men hounded him, persecuted him, unable to face their own inadequacies when placed in his large shadow. She knew such men had come for him now, had taken him captive, and more than ever she was determined not to let that happen without a good fight.

Steeling herself, she was pushing the shattered frame from her body with great resolve, when she saw a thick envelope taped on the back. With some reverence she removed this, opening the flap with care, her heart pounded in her throat as she spilled the contents onto the floor.

A child's hooded skating key fell loose. And a note. In Jeff's handwriting. She smiled, for it was addressed to her. She breathed deeply, closing her eyes. The opening salutation was causing her heart to flutter like an enraptured schoolgirl's.

Darling. Jeff was addressing her as *Darling.*

"My darling Irma," the note read, "if you are reading this, then tragedy's dark shadow has come over our house . . ."

"Oh, my," she pursed her lips, "this is not good." Her hands trembled nervously, she sipped every word like a sacred and aged wine.

". . . only you can save us, it will take great courage!"

Irma closed her eyes, reaching into a pocket, feeling the warm tears rolling off each cheek.

She placed the Legion of Merit around her neck.

Jeff had called it the Atomic Café, and Irma followed his instructions to the letter, inserting a hooded key into a dark little smudge, then pressing with both hands against a panel.

A soft light came on the moment the seal was broken, and a dank little chamber bloomed into life, beckoning her through a tiny hallway.

Though it startled her, this strange entrance to a world she did not know, she thought the mysterious humming of magnetic fans a pleasant sound, filling the buried shelter with swirls of cooling air that came fluttering against the tiny hairs on her face and arms.

She hunched, scurrying forward.

She stood looking down into what she thought had been removed and filled in years before, not really angry with Jeff, for their problems ran much deeper than that. Irma was more curious than angry as she watched her shadow grow tall in the recessed confine, blooming large and stately across the little room. As she entered, it spread like a giant black wing over the white domed ceiling, her eyes immediately spotting an antique lamp made from brass, the muted glow sending a sparkling golden aura, spreading out in every direction, and filling the little chamber with a soft romantic glow. She gently stroked the shade, a lovely tan leather, and quite old, Irma thought, fingering a small pink butterfly that lay suspended in the center of the buttery hide.

"This should be upstairs," she said, turning the shade. It was shaped in a pentagon, and as she rotated this, a small blue flower came into view. To Irma the image seemed a small, distorted painting, the purple stalk and bluish petals looking somehow withered, and she did not care for this. She turned the lamp again, rotating until a splendid bloom came before her, and this was a beautiful and symmetric sight that calmed her pounding heart.

The colorful image glowed from the muted backlight, a blood-red rose with black outlines, the full petals seeming to come alive. Just beneath a green-and-blue stalk the word "Rose" was scrawled in dark blue letters.

Irma smiled for the first time. "Oh, we all know that," she mumbled, thinking that Jeff had crudely drawn the word with a rounded hand. But when she turned to the fourth side, her heart began to pound, for she had seen this image before.

She swallowed hard.

Locked dead center on the buttery hide was a bright red heart with a large blue arrow passing through, and underneath, the name DAVID in capital letters.

Irma Kiernan quickly closed her eyes.

She felt something hot rising fast into her throat, and she fought to swallow with all her strength, then gulped for air as her knees trembled.

She looked down onto the table as her hand twitched, faltering at the wrist, fighting to grasp a large photograph that Jeff kept there. She breathed deeply, her entire body beginning to tremble as she pulled the picture closer to the light.

The image registered.

Vertigo slammed into her like a bullet in the chest as she fell, dropping to her knees, coughing once before spilling down onto her own vomit.

She had been staring at the naked figure of a rough-looking teenager with long dark hair, and above the girl's right breast, just below her shoulder, was a tattoo. A pierced heart. The same heart she had been touching on Jeff's lampshade.

She screamed, fighting for her feet.

Disoriented, she grabbed for the display case, fighting to stand, staring up and into the blank sockets of a dark hanging form. Although it took all her remaining strength, she rose, pulling frantically on the doors while Jeff's letter came burning in her mind with impossibly cruel deception.

Irma nearly tore the doors off their hinges, violently grabbing his albums, one by one, throwing them on the floor. "My darling," the note had instructed, "please do not look at the albums. These scrapbooks are *not* mine. You must ignore these things and quickly press the red button over my display case.

"You must trust me . . ."

But Irma's trust had fully and fatefully expired as she looked down into the face of a mummified head suspended neatly with wire in front of a wanted poster listing a runaway teen from 1979. She had started to read the name, when suddenly she began shaking with uncontrollable violence, her knees folding, then her body dropping like stone as she gave a wild, tortured cry. "My God . . ."

She wept freely, her eyes locked open with shock, the pupils dilating into dark little pools. "No . . ." she moaned, moving her hands in the manner of the blind, her fingers crawling over the carpeted floor for the instrument she had seen there.

She knew.

She knew by the hot flame that licked into her palm, and though this was split open as she grabbed, the warm fluid running down her arm, she did not react. She was holding one of Jeff's many straight razors, and without closing her eyes, she placed this against her right wrist, sucking a deep breath, then drawing a sharp and violent bite across thin flesh.

Both wrists.

It was with a cold, deliberate malice that she used all of her strength to kill Jeff Dorn in the only manner she knew.

"If you don't destroy these things, they will destroy me," the note had said. "You must, darling, you must . . ."

As her world began to vanish, expanding into a soft and blurry focus, Irma Kiernan recited a prayer while hearing voices gathering above her, hushed and kind, and she smiled, imagining that a fairy-tale knight had finally come to save her from the darkness.

Oceans of darkness, coming now.

The waves beating from some distant shore, closing over her as a last breath came seeping from her lungs.

"Jack!" Drury cried again, as Scott's anxious shoulder rammed a second time against the front door, thumping painfully as he cringed.

"Break it down!" he ordered, as Murphy quickly came forward, looking at his captain, who gave a nod.

With one sharp step backward, Mule's right boot slammed against the lock face with such power that the entire jamb crumbled inward, breaking loose in fragments of splintering wood. Before Murphy had even cleared the space, Scott was advancing in against the beam of Drury's flashlight, and a hallway appeared from shadow, lifeless and gloomy with the smell of boiled cabbage.

"Spread out!" Drury ordered, his gun drawn. "Scott has point. If she so much as touches a weapon, do not hesitate!" With that cold caution the men rushed in, guns drawn, filling the little house with sweeping lights. In minutes they had covered the first two floors, and regrouped in the living room near a buff recliner.

It was then that they heard, or thought that they heard, a small moan, like some animal's dying gasp drifting up to them through a kitchen door. Scott sprang instantly into action, peering over his gun sight, moving with clocklike precision. He passed through the hallway and into the kitchen. There he spotted a syringe and bottle on a table, though he did not stop, pressing quickly for the basement door. Though his body was torn and bruised, he traveled down the steps in seconds. In another moment the stairwell behind him teemed with men.

Scott rushed in.

The basement room was a crisp white, nearly barren, and Scott's eyes strained to focus, following a glitter of glass and the wounded spoor of his quarry, which appeared as a drizzle of red across the green carpet. When he saw it, his eyes stretched with hate. The panel removed, the maw of a hidden room screamed at him with murderous secrecy, electric motors filtering air, buzzing at him like angry wasps, buzzing in the recesses of his mind.

"Careful, Jack!" Drury cautioned, as Scott was gone in that instant, racing into the dark corridor as fast as his feet would carry.

Then Drury heard Scott scream with anger and frustration. Following, he dropped into the sunken bomb shelter, where he found Scott banging with both fists at the chest of a fallen woman. Pulling himself back upright, he reached beneath Irma's neck, pinched her nose, then breathing his life into her lungs.

"Tie her wrists!" Scott yelled, gulping air, staring into the dilated eyes, pressing his mouth over hers. As her lungs emptied, he crossed his hands over her chest and began to pump.

Drury laid a stoic palm on the man's shoulder. "It's over, Jack, she's gone."

"One one-thousand, two one-thousand, three one-thousand . . ."

Scott breathed again, forcing air, filling her rib cage.

"Jack, it's a code blue . . ."

Scott shook his head sadly. He hadn't noticed that he had been kneeling in a dark pool, the circumference spreading every time he pressed against her ribs. Without her wrists being tied, each thrust had pumped more blood into a hideous puddle, which Scott now felt being drawn into the coarse fiber of his slacks as he continued to work in the sticky sweetness.

The smells began to choke them both.

"Jack, let her rest," Drury said quietly. Lifting Irma's right hand, he placed this higher over the body to prevent further drainage. He draped the other arm across her chest as Scott pushed himself back, releasing a heavy and mechanical sigh. He was fighting to right himself when Drury took him by the arm.

"Is this a torture chamber?" he asked, pulling Scott to his feet.

Scott shook his head. "More like a trophy room." He leaned over, picking up a scrapbook, placing it beneath an arm. Turning, he saw anger register on Drury's face as he studied the mummified head in Dorn's case, the skin like leather stretched across an obscene grin.

"And official Washington says the threat of serial killers is overrated." He was breathing hard, voice chilled, his face like stone. Scott nodded in understanding, for they both knew what would come next.

In an effort to close the standing case list of 17,435 people who have simply vanished without a trace, investigators and relatives of the missing would soon be flooding Drury's office with requests, calling from every state, then waiting in line for information that could help. Mostly it did not.

Drury pushed past Scott. "It's the calls from parents that hurt the most," he said grimly, moving quickly through his own voice and up into darkness.

Scott nodded, he knew it was so.

60

"I'm entitled to my day in court," Dorn stated coldly, his face etched with outrage. "I have a right to face my accusers!"

Rivers glanced over his shoulder at him. "You bet," he answered without tone, thinking first about the Claytons and the rights he had given to them, then the grisly skulls from the bowling alley, not to mention his cruel designs on the Janson family. He had started to think about the rope Dorn had placed on Jessica's pillow, when he suddenly removed the dart gun from his sweatshirt, jamming this back under Dorn's left eye.

"One more word," he cautioned.

Dorn twisted his head. "But I have something you want," he said. "I have answers!" His dark eyes gleamed with spite.

Rivers dropped a cigarette into his mouth. "Okay," he said, "did Rubin Jaffe hire you to torch Tobytown?"

Dorn grinned, lifting a lip. "It *was* his money, but I was hired by another, a serial killer. I will give him to you if you hit me hard."

Rivers shook his head. "Tell me who Dr. Jaffe is, tell me about him."

At this Dorn's eyes closed and opened, his face twisting into a wicked knot. "*You* are Jaffe," he said flatly. "*We* are Jaffe. He is everyman!" He started to laugh, but with incredible swiftness Rivers delivered a controlled kick to his thigh. Dorn hissed back into silence.

"Do you know anything about Debra Patterson?"

Dorn's lips pursed tight, his eyes laughing at the man. "She begged me!"

Rivers nodded his head with murderous fury in his eyes. His body coiled tight like corded steel as he unbuckled his belt, pulling it free, then wrapping his right hand across the knuckles. He was reaching over with his left, grabbing the man, when a voice broke through the yard.

"Frank!" Scott cried, running with a painful hobble.

"Quick, do it!" Dorn yelled. Instead Mule Murphy grabbed

Rivers around the waist, hauling him backward through the darkness.

"Frank," Scott said, "that's what he wants, don't give in."

Captain Drury and Toy Saul and Rudy Marchette appeared, trotting with three uniformed officers, Toy carrying a canvas straitjacket and video camera. The team was preparing to transport the prisoner according to the strictest provisions of the law, documenting every procedure to counterclaim the inevitable brutality charges.

"Who gave him his rights?" Drury barked as eight men gathered around in a semicircle before the accused.

"I did," Scott answered. "It was clean, Max."

Drury directed a questioning look at Rivers. "Did you hit him?"

Rivers rubbed his wounded shoulder. "No, Captain, I'm barely able to move. But what happened to you guys? You're covered with blood."

Drury answered with a nasty stare, turning to Toy Saul. "Give Frank the camera, I consider this my collar." As the man complied, handing Rivers the equipment, Dorn writhed, fighting for his feet.

"He's going to kill me!" Dorn howled. Rivers took a cautious step backward. "He's going to shoot me!"

Rivers shrugged.

"Stop him!" Dorn screamed. "Stop him . . ."

"Take it easy, Zak," Drury's graveled voice barked as the men moved in and the prisoner released a horrified cry, his eyes wide and glaring at Rivers, who was backing up one foot at a time, bringing a video camera into position.

"He's going to kill me!" Dorn cried with panic. "Don't you understand he's trying to shoot me?"

Drury turned suddenly and glanced at Rivers. "We know," he winked, "I told him to."

While all eyes were on the prisoner, Dorn watched in horror as Rivers, working in shadows, expertly removed the air gun from his shirt and placed this under the camera for support.

"Killer!" Dorn screamed. "Please—"

The outburst caused the policemen to pause, stepping back to examine their approach.

In that moment Dorn suddenly leapt straight at them, up into the air, propelled by a violent and unseen force, his legs and torso thrusting stiffly, as if he had been hit by a massive electric charge. He was shaking, flipping, shuddering in rapid vibrations as if he were holding a raw power line between his teeth.

"God save us!" Drury yelled, backing up.

Dorn's body slapped the ground violently, then raised on his shoulders, bouncing again like a paratrooper slammed to earth without a chute; his entire torso going rigid in that instant, spinning onto his stomach with a powerful thrust, flipping again, shuddering with a tremendous quake.

"Do something!" Drury yelled at the stunned faces. Dorn's mug was frozen, his body convulsing, head, legs, arms, and torso shaking stiffly without control. The captain quickly dropped to his knees, throwing away his cap.

"This man is having trouble breathing!" he yelled. "Frank, you're a trained medic, for crying out loud!"

Shaking his head, Rivers sauntered forward. He laid his camera on the lawn and peered down. Dorn was stretched flat, his face skyward in frozen agony, his maw locked open. He was vibrating with violent inner spasms when suddenly a foul odor was discharged and his body went slack.

"Jesus Christ!" Drury exclaimed, standing quickly as the sickening smell hit him. He started to pace. "I've never seen anything like it," he concluded anxiously. "That was a bizarre fit!"

"A stroke," Scott agreed flatly.

"Sir, it looked to me like he'd been struck by lightning," Saul said excitedly. "Medical assistance will be here in one minute."

Drury was face to face with Scott as the other men had gone silent, Toy working a handheld radio as Rivers was leaning over, and discreetly pinched Dorn's right thigh just above the knee.

Staring into Zak's stony eyes, he whispered, "Told you no one would notice. And now," he added, jerking a small black needle from his flesh, "I need my dart back."

"What's that, Frank. Speak up!" Drury ordered.

"Sorry, Captain, I said it's not a heart attack."

"Oh, for crying out loud, Frank, we already know that!" Drury cried with frustration. "Why do you have to say things like that?"

61

Alsop's House on the Virginia side of the Potomac in the suburb of Falls Church had been named for Isadora Gene Alsop,
a grand old matron from the age of suffragettes, though Jonathan Patterson doubted very much that she had ever fought
for equal rights, or rights of any human kind.

Standing in the tight little lobby, surrounded by young
women, he could discern many things from the matron's
stare, which was cold as a tomb. Her hair was worn in a tight
bun. Her four-cornered nursing cap carried the cross of the
ages. Her white uniform was crisp and precise, and there was
a Bible on her lap. In her right hand she held a large ruby-
studded crucifix, holding this outstretched, readied to ward off
evil. *Alsop the Protector,* the brass legend read beneath the oil
painting.

A round of joyous giggles erupted from the pregnant
women, who were really just girls, as the 11:30 television
broadcast of the *Dating Game* started. There were about a
dozen teens, and though they saw him standing in the stuffy
wood-paneled receiving room, he felt like an invisible man,
waiting there, wondering, his heart pounding into his throat,
his armpits and palms cold and wet.

His journey had started an hour earlier after an unsolicited
phone call. Two of them, in fact. Eventually they had led him
here in clandestine search of his daughter and before the punishing stare of Madam Alsop, where children Debra's age
were preparing to have children. What troubled him was the
thought of the childhood these girls were abandoning so easily, the lives they were giving away instead of bringing new
life into the world. His thoughts wandered back to the way he
had been staring bewildered into the phone, incredulous, fear
and anger coursing through his face as his wife began to
panic by his side.

"Who are you?" he had demanded, quickly summoning Sergeant Tyler Conroy of the county police to his side, expecting
a ransom demand.

The telephone voice dripped with secrecy. "First tell me if the reward is good. I have a poster from the drugstore that offers five thousand dollars for information."

"Only if she is found, if the information leads to her. I need your name and—"

"Oh, no, I've got to go, I'll call you back." With that the voice had terminated, leaving Patterson with a dial tone.

Minutes crawled by in agonizing torment, every sweep of the clock's hand a painful progress to watch, until the phone finally rang again. Patterson answered before the ring had silenced.

"Is the reward still good? I mean, I have expenses, and this is very dangerous for me."

"In what way? Why is it dangerous?" he demanded with fright. "Where is my daughter? Do you have information about—?"

"I work in a halfway house, and if anyone finds out that I've broken the rules of confidence, I'll be fired. I need my job."

Patterson breathed deeply, mustering his reserve. "How old are you, son?" he asked gently.

"Eighteen, and this is the longest I've held a job, I'm the building engineer."

"And how much do you make a year?"

"Eight thousand, plus my meals."

"All right, then," Patterson said calmly, "tell me about this confidentially. If you get fired, I will pay you a year's salary if we find Debra."

"Well," he paused, considering this, "I think it's the same girl, but the flier I got was wet and the image was blurry. Does she have curly hair?"

Patterson's heart crashed. "No," he said weakly. "Does the face look the same as the photograph?"

"I think so, but I'm not sure. But I could sure use the money."

"Where do you work, son, what's your name?"

"Brian Daily, I work at Alsop's House."

Daily, as it turned out, was himself a child.

As Patterson stood beneath the canvas of the patron who had founded the shoddy little house, a young man dressed in jeans and a Madonna T-shirt strolled to the television set in the corner and adjusted the picture contrast, which did not need adjusting. As he did this, he winked at Patterson, the girls seeing this, then turning back around. Daily was lean like an alley cat and his face was scarred with acne. He sauntered across the room as if he often came forward just to study the portrait. As he stared up at it, Patterson asked quietly, "Are you Brian?"

He nodded. "Mrs. Handry is in back with her and another girl, I only got a minute."

Patterson nodded and removed a photograph from his jacket. Fighting his fears with enormous courage, he held this down and Brian Daily positioned his body between the picture and the girls. The man-child studied for a moment, his brows knotting, his lips making a weird clicking sound, and Patterson all but slapped him.

"Well?" he cried, and the girls turned, looking up at them.

Daily waited patiently, rubbing a hand through a black head of hair that needed a shower. He nodded. "She has curly hair now. I wonder when she did that, does she have a sister?"

"No," Patterson shook his head, "is this the girl?"

"That's her, okay, she's in back with Mrs. Handry."

"And you're sure?"

"I dunno, yeah, sort of."

"Why would she be here, is this for runaways?"

The expression that crossed Brian's face was blank with confusion. "You don't know what this is?" he asked, incredulous. "This is a baby farm, a right-to-life house for expecting mothers who can't afford to—"

Patterson held up a hand and gave a precise and sorry nod.

"You have no right to keep my daughter. She is not of legal age," Patterson said the moment the older woman came forward, an official-looking clipbook in her right hand and a Bible in the other.

Mrs. Helena Handry, a wide load of a woman in a white uniform and dripping with crosses, knotted her face at him. "She came of her own accord because she had no one else to turn to."

"She could have come to me and her mother!" Patterson barked. "She is only sixteen, so either you produce her now or I'm calling the police and my attorneys. And then"—he took a deep and satisfying breath—"and then, I will close you down!"

"I will protect her rights to bear children with my last breath!" the woman said, raising her voice and her chin.

"Then you're going to need it," Patterson hissed through his teeth. As he started toward her in the dark hallway, a figure emerged slowly, a small suitcase in her right hand and tears streaming down angelic cheeks.

"Debbie!" Patterson screamed, and instantly the figure ran toward him.

"Oh, Daddy, Daddy," the girl cried. "Daddy . . ."

In that moment of painful reunion Mrs. Helena Handry became their mutual enemy, casting about the room for someone to give instructions to.

"I'm going to have a baby," Debra sobbed against his chest while looking up into her father's eyes.

He sighed, holding her for all his worth. "Why didn't you tell us?" he wept. As she started to answer, he stopped her with a warm kiss. "Never mind, we have time for all of that. Let me look at you!"

And he did. And they cried. And Jonathan Patterson held on to his daughter, determined to never let her go.

"You said if I ever got pregnant, you would disown me," Debra suddenly blurted, and the man's heart crashed to the abyss of parental anguish.

"Oh, Dee, I never said that . . ."

"You did, Daddy, I heard both you and Mother. She said she'd make me have an abortion and then lock me away for the rest of my life."

Patterson winced, thinking back. He vaguely remembered that there had been a documentary on teenage pregnancy a few weeks before, and he had been speaking with his wife—when it hit him. They had been drinking, they had just gotten the news about Debra's grandmother, they were upset.

"But we weren't talking about you!" he said. "We were talking about a girl on the television. You're our baby!"

"Oh, I love you, Daddy . . ."

"Dee, it's your decision, honey, it's your life. Whatever you want to do, we will always support you."

"I don't know . . ." She was crying freely.

As they walked through the door of Alsop's House together, Brian Daily rushed down the front path from the curb. "Psssst, Mr. Patterson," he whispered.

Jonathan Patterson nodded. Holding his daughter with his right hand, he removed a white envelope from his jacket with his left. He was handing this to the young man as a car roared to a stop. A frightened father quickly stepped out with a photograph in his hand. He was haggard and his face showed a tired and aimless strain as he made eye contact with Patterson.

"Mr. Coaler?" Brian Daily hissed quickly as Patterson placed his daughter into their car.

Debra has been missing for just over three days, and on the way home they stopped for a cup of chocolate so that he could call and alert his wife. He told her to leave a message of thanks for Detective Sergeant Rivers.

"Debbie, do you know where your car is?" Patterson asked.

She nodded. "I lent it to Jammie Wolfe."

"Do you know where she is?"

Debra shook her head. "She's run away from her boarding school, she'll bring it back. Oh, I missed you, Daddy." Debra was starting to cry all over again. As she curled into his arms, Patterson closed his eyes tightly, the tears running off his chin, the nightmare finally over.

"Everything's going to be fine," he comforted.

And for the Patterson family, this was true.

62

The Shiloh Baptist Church was gone with a headlight blaze as the tan Crown Victoria hurtled by, red and blue emergency globes pulsing off stained glass windows in a single beat, and nothing more, as Frank Rivers sped toward the city. In short moments he was rounding a corner on Elm into the heart of a seemingly instant modern metropolis. With a glance he caught a shimmer of lights coming off a patch of cobblestone that had once been a village street, laid from ship ballast, then ripped from the ground. For a short moment he was speaking to Elmer Janson in his mind, of tall ships and seafarers, of how they had plied a trade in a wrinkle before the Civil War; but the site was far behind as he was spinning left, speeding down onto Wisconsin Avenue.

The upscale diner came and went. A huge empty pit filled with light, and he remembered how the Deco Theatre had stood there forever; even in haste he could not help but notice these things, for they were the familiar, the pitiless remnants of another age found in a crush of high-rise glitter, glass and chrome; the personality of a temporary city born on the ruins of history and permanence.

"One-Echo-Twenty," the radio crackled, and instinctively he reached forward, but it was too late.

Scott had grabbed the microphone and was opening the line, his mellow voice but a smear against images that carried Rivers through the night. He roared by the stone post office, proud as an old matron, her mica-flecked quarry skin pulsing with red and blue, just an instant of light, and nothing more.

Gone in a blaze.

Forty-fifty-sixty, toward the main intersection at East-West Highway, where he triggered the sirens, forcing by a nest of drivers, applying his foot to the floor.

"Slow it down, they're not going anywhere."

But Rivers heard only the sound of his heart as it beat a strange song, as the road was swallowed by his blaze of lights.

It was over, he was going to them.

Like the men who plied the waterways of old, his journey had been relentless.

Elmer Janson was sick of television.

There was nothing on, and he idly watched a black-and-white image flickering against his dog's fur as they lay side by side on a soiled throw rug that Jessica guessed hadn't been cleaned since the late sixties.

"I wish you'd stay on the bed, Elmer, I don't have the strength to fight with you."

"I'm okay, Mom, Tripod's on the rug."

"I can see that. Can't you try to get some sleep?" She leaned over and tried brushing the bangs off his brow. "Tripod's sleeping, let's both give it a try?"

"I'm not tired," he said, beginning to renew his protest, when the dog raised his massive head. With a healthy growl, he bumped into Elmer as he moved toward the door.

"Mom," Elmer said cautiously, "Tripod hears something . . ." The dog released a growl from deep within, his head lowered, his brown eyes menacing and leveled.

"Elmer, come back here!" Jessica demanded as the boy scampered to the door. The distant sounds of a siren became audible, only weakly at first, like a faraway cry, then demanding like the piercing wail of life hanging in the balance.

"I'll bet it's Frank!" Elmer fidgeted nervously, reaching for the doorknob, his voice filled with excitement.

Jessica grabbed his arm forcefully. "We don't know that," she cautioned, then tested the chain on the door.

The wheels of the tan radio car burned with a fury as the sirens died and Rivers sped into a darkened alleyway, rumbling over a concrete drive that warped and cracked years before. At the very end of a series of driveways he spun the wheel through a chain-link fence.

They headed toward a low-slung building that resembled a series of stalls, an old-fashioned apartment court. As they pulled in, Scott spotted a sign over the only door with glass in its paint-sick face: FURNISHED ROOMS, DAY/WEEK/MONTH.

The building facade was a drab and uniform pea green, which reminded them both of the tasteless surplus-store color. "So why here?" Scott asked as the car slowed, crunching over the broken gravel.

Rivers shrugged. "Tripod and Elmer refused to be parted. Could you see them walking through the door at the Hyatt?"

Scott chuckled. "Yes, I can picture that."

"Anyway, who'd ever guess about this dive? Besides, this is the only lodging Drury could find that wasn't owned by Rubin Jaffe, either outright or indirectly. I wasn't about to trust anyone."

"I'll wait in the car," Scott offered. "I've had enough excitement to last through the night."

But Rivers didn't seem to hear as the red and blue fireball burst against the green shell like raindrops splattering a sponge.

The place swallowed light.

It was dark and seedy.

"Elmer, please stay away from that door."

"But, Mom, a car is pulling up, it has to be them! Look at Tripod, he's wagging his tail."

She opened the door, but only to peek. Oblivious of her caution, the dog bolted out with the boy fast behind.

"Frank!" Elmer cried, his voice bursting with joy as Rivers stepped forward. In another instant the team was on him, Tripod ramming his leg, Elmer tugging at his jeans.

"Did you catch Zak?" he asked, a little breathless. "Mom says I don't have to go to school tomorrow."

Rivers was smiling down at the child when a shadow of movement caught his eye. Standing in a bar of painted light filtering through the doorway, Jessica Janson steadied herself as she watched. She looked tired and worn and beautiful, her hair shining in this half-light, her eyes wet, still fearful, still questioning.

"Come here, Elmer," Rivers said quietly. He reached down, swooped the boy up under both arms, then swung him through the air until a spark of laughter fell free. He carried the child toward his mother, the dog nipping at the boy's running shoes.

"Mom, can we go in Frank's radio car?" he asked.

"We have our own car, Elmer, and we will follow Frank," she responded, and her voice was firm. Disappointed, he turned his face away.

"She's upset," he whispered. "Are we still in trouble, Frank?"

"No trouble at all, rooster," he whispered back, his eyes steady on Jessica. "Let me talk with your mom a minute."

The boy's feet started to move the moment they touched earth, but Rivers held him back with a gentle hand.

"Can I sit in the radio car?"

"Sure, ask Jack if he'll let you have the wheel."

It was a biting, awkward silence.

Jessica's eyes were red, a film of tears covered them, but never once did they fall from Rivers' blue stare. He wanted to comfort her, to say something, not to come across sounding like a hard-bitten man finally with time on his hands. He was thinking of how to do this when he noticed that his heart was oddly fluttering. He had been this way the first time he saw her, his spirit falling inside him like a heavy rain.

"Are we safe?" Jessica suddenly swallowed, and he saw her lower lip tremble.

For reasons he did not understand, this made him feel like he was coming apart inside. He was searching for words in his head, trying to answer, when he saw a tear tumble off one cheek. As though he was watching somebody else, his hand moved slowly forward with an alien gentleness that simply brushed it away, then stroked her cheek.

"You caught him," she had started to say, when her emotions slipped to the surface and her knees buckled. Rivers caught her, and she laid her head against his chest, where his heart beat like a watch wound to destruction.

"Frank?" Scott questioned, appearing at his back. "I'm going to take Elmer home, he wants to ride in a police car. You two can follow."

"Thanks," Rivers agreed, releasing the woman. She quickly brushed the tears from her face as her son came alongside and slipped a hand up into hers.

"Is it okay, Mom, can I go with Jack?"

"Yes, Elmer," she said, her eyes never once leaving Frank Rivers. They listened together as the doors closed, the emergency lights pulsed back into life, and the headlights pulled away into darkness.

In the light cast from the doorway, their eyes met in such a clear and certain way that words became meaningless. Rivers started to speak as Jessica suddenly placed a finger across his lips, and he knew.

This feeling was like no other, far more than sexual, deeper and driving, begging him on, like the flame he found in the solace of her eyes. This feeling was like a great and lasting storm.

For the couple in the green motel, the room was drifting in time, not a shabby cubicle with a small single bed, but a place that held no meaning beyond themselves.

As he closed the flimsy wooden door, Jessica moved toward him, her hands gently stroking his neck where a large white surgical dressing rose from his left shoulder. Frank studied her every curve and movement, the turn of a wrist, her fingertips, the way her eyes seemed to lead or to follow. Her lips pulled tight as together they crossed the small room in a single stride.

Closer still Jessica came. As he leaned over to kiss her neck, the woman pulled her hair from place with a slender hand, then reached up for him, accidentally touching his wound.

Rivers winced.

"Then it does hurt," she whispered, but Frank only gave a slight smile. Pain was reduced to a meaningless concept as he studied the soft curves of her shoulders and arms, the splendid silky skin that ran from her neck where her sweater had parted. With a feminine curiosity she watched his eyes, then she took a last step backward. He tried to reach for her with both hands, an awkward movement, for his body had grown stiff and sore.

Jessica shook her head. Her hair shimmering in the light, her breath falling in small bursts as she reached with her right hand to unbutton her sweater, she wriggled free from it like a teenager. Frank lightly stroked her throat, moving down over the swell of her breasts. He was feeling light-headed as he enveloped her with both arms, locking her tight in an embrace. Her mouth met his, her eyes closed as their bodies suddenly shuttered in unison.

They were closing upon themselves and closed to the world.

Exploring. Touching. Caressing.

They fell onto the bed as their clothes came undone, and Jessica quickly moved under him with a subtle grace, then even closer up into his arms. Covering his mouth with hers to silence him, as Rivers had started to speak, had started to doubt, had started to think.

"Don't," she said, reaching down for him.

At her soft female cry he felt a powerful union. She pulled him from his elbows, buried her face into his neck. They fought with each other to get close. Closer still. Then, impossibly close, moving like skaters in a tight, perfect dance, breathing each other's breath in mutual symphony, their eyes wild and undone with the merciless pursuit of each other's flesh.

They made a kind of mad and reckless love that Jessica had thought could never be again.

A kind of healing and lasting love that Frank Rivers had never known existed.

"I think we're onto something here," Jessica giggled as she lay spent in his arms.

"My entire life," Frank stammered, then cleared his throat. "My entire life I've spent looking for you," he said, or thought he said, and in his mind his voice was sounding like it once had, like it must have once, he told himself, in a time so long ago that happiness was a distant memory.

And he heard this memory now like lost waves rolling on some faraway shore, and he steadied himself, his eyes locking onto hers to see if she had even heard, or if he had even spoken.

Jessica brushed his hair from his brow and snuggled close to him, her lips gently kissing his eyes. "Then I only wish I had known," she said softly, with a sudden sadness in her voice that had not been there before. She pulled away to study the deep blue pools of his eyes. With gentle fingertips she began tracing the jagged scars that edged across his body.

"Frank," she asked, "why don't you have a family?"

At this his body tensed. He started to speak, to explain, to reach out so that explanation was not necessary, but she quickly moved back onto him and delivered a long, wet kiss that saved them both from looking back.

63

MONDAY, APRIL 11, 5:17 P.M.

The kid on the red Schwinn was coasting, aiming down the street in an easy glide, his red hair shining in late-afternoon light, his mint-green eyes sparkling and wide with anticipation. Down in front of his house, Sergeant Rivers held the boy's dog as Tripod whined, struggling for freedom, his large frame wobbling uncomfortably on all fours. His right front leg was a bright and shiny white.

"Okay, Elmer, call him," Rivers said.

"Come on, boy!" Elmer shrieked, the mask of freckles pulling tight across the bridge of his nose as he increased his speed, leaning over the handlebars in a backward glance.

"Come on . . ." he urged. "Come on, Tripod!"

With a tentative bobbing motion, the dog tried to hobble in his old and accustomed way, but could not. He landed stiffly on his left where once there had been only air, and with sad brown eyes he watched his playmate whiz by.

Tripod edged forward, then suddenly stopped to sit, waving the alien leg in front of him. Upon seeing this, Elmer spun in place, kicking hard against the pedals in a power drive, then hopping the curb near Dudley Hall.

"What's wrong?" the boy asked, breathing hard as he dismounted.

"Elmer," Hall chirped, "go git him. Jest show him what he needs to do and he'll follow."

As the boy approached, the dog instantly leapt, punching him in the chest with two front limbs and driving him back.

"Whoa," Elmer laughed as the dog snipped at his clothes with excitement. "Tripod, sit!" he cried.

Hall came over to them. "He jest don't know what it's for yet," the diggerman said. "Git Tripper to walk for a while."

Elmer did just that, rubbing Tripod's chest until a rear leg was thumping, then moved him forward. The dog started walking cautiously on all fours.

"That's good. Now jest put some weight on his shoulders so he knows it's gonna support him, he's gotta know he can trust it. Been a time since he felt dis part."

Elmer complied, hugging his dog around the mane, applying some weight, then rocking him up and down. Tripod was enjoying this action, and his broom tail swung furiously in metered strokes.

Jessica approached, her face tired, eyes slightly puffy from lack of sleep. She carried a tray of drinks, walking airily toward Rivers.

"Where's Jackie?" Hall asked suddenly.

Rivers shrugged. "Making memories would be my guess."

The braying of piston strokes echoed through the halls of Suburban Hospital's emergency critical-care ward, sounding like scuba divers snoring beneath the smells of antiseptics. Scott stood just outside Room 7-B in a corridor of pastel blue with a swarm of medical personnel in green gowns running in every direction.

Medical teams clattered by with crash carts and life-saving equipment, and Scott stepped back, patiently waiting for someone to appear through the closed wooden door behind him. It had been fourteen hours, allowing the MAIT team a chance to shower and sleep, and he shifted his weight, standing in his gray suit, holding a notepad in his hand to jot down details.

The cuts inflicted by Greg Corless's gun now burned with a fierce intensity. Angry flames licked his legs and groin, and though he squirmed over and over again, he could not get comfortable.

He was wondering how Irma Kiernan had handled Kimberly and Leslie Clayton when they came to the park for their educational tour. It must have been easy to demand that they leave their purses inside the lockhouse so that she could make copies of their keys.

The door opened and Dr. Anh-Bich Pham strolled from the room. Seeing him, she removed a blue mask from her face and released a troubled sigh.

"How is he?" Scott asked quickly.

She raised a concerned eyebrow. "You should be resting, Commander," she said in a chilly tone. "You'll be a very unhappy man if those stitches break open."

Scott nodded thoughtfully.

"As for your patient, at this time we've exhausted our treatment, so we'll just have to wait. He has suffered a severe cerebral hemorrhage, a stroke. It seems as if three sections of the brain are involved."

"Then he's paralyzed?"

"Completely," she said, "except for the breathing mechanism. The stroke was about the most massive we've seen. The cerebellum and medulla have been destroyed, and with that"—she raised her hands—"any chance of regaining motor function."

"Will he live?"

"If you want to call it that. Like I said, he's regained his ability to breathe, but he will not recover, no one could. From the tests, I can tell you that his brain looks like it's coated with black ink."

"How long does he have?"

She shrugged. "Six months, maybe more, it's impossible to say. If he could feed orally there would be more of a chance, but I'm afraid he has no movement capability at all. He can't even blink, so we are using drops to keep his eyes moist."

"Can he see, does he have vision?"

"Well, yes, we have him hooked to an EEG, an electroencephalograph, a monitor that reads brain function. According to machine response, he can think and see, so we won't be able to get a court order to justify termination of life support—at least without a great deal of difficulty." She rubbed her eyes. "He'll be dead by the time a court came through anyway."

"But he is capable of understanding?"

"I don't really know. His brain waves respond to conversation, so his hearing is not seriously impaired. Now, how long this will last, I can't say. I can only imagine the terror of complete and total paralysis. Being able to hear and see must only make it worse."

Scott nodded. "Can I visit with him, or is it too early?"

"Two minutes," she said, turning to open the door for him. "Just go easy. We can't predict how his heart will react to much more stress."

It was a cubicle with pale white walls, and at the center of the room a hospital bed was surrounded by machines. Spread-eagled on a flat slab with turned-down sheets lay the animal who had killed Diana Clayton and her family, and Samantha Stoner, her mother, and sister, and Scott could only guess at the rest.

Even locked into a rigid body, his thin and frozen face looked cruel: the pinched cheeks, the lips like cut veal, the black eyes aimed up at the ceiling. His head was shaved and capped with white gauze.

To his left was emergency resuscitation equipment, to his right the scrolling blue EEG machine monitoring his brain waves. From this pale but living corpse, tubes sprouted every-where, through his nose, mouth, between his legs, down into each arm.

"This shows his brain activity," Dr. Pham explained, and as she spoke, a bright little wave of light rolled across a blue screen. "He heard us coming in, watch this."

As the line began to flatten, she leaned over and placed drops of fluid into both eyes. These were fixed and frozen in his skull. "How are you feeling?" she asked softly, and Scott watched with interest as the monitor broke into a wavy blue line. She pulled off the oxygen mask and swabbed his lips and tongue with a moistened pad.

"See, he does hear us." Just as she said this, the page beeper on her belt went off, emitting a piercing series of tones.

"Damn," she sighed, "two minutes, I'll be right back."

Scott stood silently, peering down at the little killer.

Slowly he moved to the right for a clear view of the brain-wave monitor, and as he approached, a flat blue line wavered a tiny bit and went still again. Scott remained just out of sight, waiting until the only sound was that dry sucking action of the patient's lungs, dark and empty like the bray of pistons produced by his victims.

Scott edged nearer the bed. "Hello, Zak," he spat.

The line boomed into a sharp curve and the black eyes rolled toward him with a vibrating fix. Scott removed Samantha's photo from his jacket, holding this just above his face, blocking his sight. The monitor instantly took the appearance of an angry ocean tide with jagged peaks and crests.

"I thought so," Scott concluded softly. "The Stoners send their regards."

He quickly stepped back, waiting until the line approached horizontal again, pulsing down into softer waves. Scott removed the portrait of Kimberly from his briefcase, the silver-encased frame with the almost-perfect-looking little girl. The line was flat as he moved this into position, then suddenly the screen exploded into a mountainous range of wiggling swirls.

Scott's jaw started to tick and bile filled his throat. Swallowing hard, he dropped the photo onto the man's chest and leaned down so that his lips nearly touched him.

He reached behind Dorn's head and snatched away his pillow. "Now, you listen to me, you cruel and evil sonofabitch," Scott heard himself hiss, "at last you are receiving some justice, so let me explain what is happening to you . . ." Scott quickly caught himself as the brain-wave monitor began beeping audibly, the lines hitting the edge of the screen. The black pupils of the killer spread like melting tar.

Scott waited, leaning back toward him. "I've spoken with the doctors and you are *not* going to get well. In fact, you are dying very, very slowly."

Beep, beep, beep, the monitor toned and went silent.

"Your body is drying up like a landed fish. Your feet, your hands, your legs, your arms, these will start to go one at a time, shriveling like salted snails, rotting . . ."

Beeeepppppp . . .

The monitor warned Scott off with a solid crest of waves. He pulled only slightly back to a *beep, beep, beep,* though, lines and shadows of line pitching and falling, before he moved even closer, until his lips blew moist against the killer's face.

"Your eyes will crack like drying grapes," he hissed, "and your lungs will tighten and rip like old paper bags. Eventually," Scott paused, "and no one knows how long, your liver and kidneys will begin to fail, but you will still be alive. You will *not* be dead just yet . . ."

As the monitor beeped again, Scott reached over and lifted

the killer's cool, limp left hand. With frightening malice the tired policeman brought his right palm down hard in a tremendous stinging slap that cracked like a gunshot. The beeping little lines sailed right off the screen.

Scott waited.

"And I'm going to be spending a great deal of time with you, Zak, because you no longer will be able to avoid my questions. Your brain is hooked to a machine that will answer for you—and you have thirty-six years of killing and torture to discuss before you die. I will not allow you an easy death . . ."

Beeeppp! Beeeppp! Beeeeppppp!

The monitor was beeping fast, piercing, merciless, Scott backing away quickly, assuming a look of sad reserve, as Dr. Pham rushed in. Glancing at him, she laid a hand to Dorn's wrist and began counting.

"What happened?" she asked rather flatly.

Scott shrugged. "I told him what happened to his friend Irma, how she failed in her mission to trigger an explosion in their toy room, and then how she slashed her wrists. But you know, Dr. Pham, I don't think he understood what I was saying . . ."

Again the monitor burst into a hot boil, solid, piercing, penetrating.

"Please," the doctor cautioned, "his heart . . ."

"We found her clutching the Legion of Merit. She had pumped her blood all over the damn thing—"

Beeeeppppp . . .

"Let him rest!" Pham ordered, and she then dropped fluid into his eyes. With a tender hand she closed his mouth, replacing the oxygen mask, then turned on the juice.

"Doc," Scott interrupted, "do you think he'll be seeing me in July? I'm coming back for a little boy's birthday party."

"It's a good bet," she said. "He just seems to be reacting to stress, the anguish of paralysis, we should let him sleep. And you, as well, Commander."

"Yes," Scott smiled darkly, "we sleep not, unless we have done mischief."

Dr. Pham cocked her head at him. "That's sounds vaguely familiar," she said. "Is that from the Bible?"

"No, no, child, that's an old proverb," Scott corrected, "a favorite of a very old friend."

"Please?" she asked, smiling.

Scott recited: "And our sleep is taken away unless we cause some to fall. For we eat the bread of wickedness. And we drink the wine of violence."

EPILOGUE

The late-afternoon sunlight filtered through the trees in the Jansons' backyard, where a short night ago a killer had come stalking. Jessica was standing at her kitchen window with Jack Scott, preparing dinner, watching her child at play.

"Frank!" Elmer called gleefully, and his voice burst through the window with sweet and innocent joy. "Frank, Tripod's running!"

As Rivers smiled broadly and waved them on, Jessica pushed her arm up into Scott's. "He's a very special man," she said warmly, leading him to the kitchen table.

"Don't let him get away from you," Scott advised, and she winked as she pulled out a chair. He sat awkwardly, the wounds licking at his torso with a day-old intensity.

Seeing his discomfort, she said with concern, "I don't think you should be out of bed."

Scott grimaced. "I've felt better, but not in my heart." He watched intently as the young mother sat alongside him, sweeping bangs from her brow.

"Then would you please ask your heart something for me?" she said, her eyes puffy, her voice concealing fear with a faint tremble.

Scott smiled warmly. "I think I know what you're feeling," he stated gently, reaching for her hand. As he did, he saw tears welling from under her lids. "You and Elmer are very safe. It's just the horrid reality of what has happened that you are dealing with. That's what troubles you now, the fact that men can be so cruel, and for no reason."

Looking down, she pondered this.

"It's not surprising this experience has left you feeling sad and alarmed. But I can tell you, while Elmer may become more cautious, he has *not* been harmed by this. In fact—"

"He loves the attention," she finished his statement. "But

he's really just a little boy, Mr. Scott. He never understood how grave the situation was. Maybe he never will."

Scott nodded in agreement. For long moments they sat in silence, watching Elmer and Detective Rivers and Tripod. From time to time the old diggerman would offer the boy advice, then spit a stream of red juice onto the lawn as Jessica would quickly divert her gaze. Then suddenly, without saying why, she leaned forward, peering into Scott's eyes. They were deep, sad wells.

"I know," he stated grimly.

"Then you knew that I felt him? And I thought I was cracking up!" She placed a finger to her temple.

Scott nodded. "That's not unusual. Some mistake their feelings for the flu."

"From the beginning," she said slowly, "I knew something wasn't right, but I couldn't put my finger on it. I had a very creepy feeling, a sensation." She touched her heart and leaned closer across the table. "Last night, even before Captain Drury came to get us, every hair on my body was just dancing." She closed her eyes as a tear rolled down her cheek.

"Let me tell you a secret," Scott offered.

Jessica nodded, crossing her heart the way she had seen Elmer do a thousand times, and Scott leaned forward.

"What you have been feeling is instinct, pure and simple, your emotions and soul warning you of danger. You are safe now, but should you ever feel those sensations again, please trust them. They can save you, and rarely will they lie."

Jessica nodded, her pretty green eyes blinking away the wetness.

"It is unfortunate, Mrs. Janson, but in this country of ours, women and children are almost always the potential victims of exploitation and violence. I only wish that other mothers knew what you already do. Maternal instinct is a tremendous weapon, and with that you can feel what others cannot even see."

"Then why doesn't the government tell everyone?"

Scott sighed. "Because you can't lay instinct on the table and poke it with a stick."

She raised a questioning brow.

"Trust your instincts," Scott said sharply. "It's as simple as that. They will warn you better than anyone could, so listen to them. What do they tell you now?"

The woman closed her eyes, then thought for a moment. "I feel depleted," she said, "very low and tired."

Scott nodded. "Then the threat is truly gone." He worked his features into a smile as he stood, looking out the door. "Your boy and his dog," he said, "for whatever reason they brought me here, I am truly grateful."

They watched together as the two shadows came soaring across the lawn, side by side in perfect step, like a broken spirit that was suddenly made whole. Jessica pressed Scott's hand as he opened the door, and they strolled out onto the patio. To the right of the doorway was a line of fragrant roses in bloom, a bright yellow climbing a green trellis.

"Elmer's father planted these," she said, leaning over and snapping a perfect bud. She handed this to Scott as they toured the garden, standing over lilies which bloomed in a shower of colors, followed by tulips in sweeping rows of cultivated brilliance. Yet for all of the beauty of that spring afternoon, Scott felt drawn to a simple cluster of weeds trapped in a plain vase near the door, where Elmer had left them.

He returned to these flowers as he knew he always would, the vibrant blooms glowing in the dying light, their ribbons of red like burning candles. Jessica sighed, touching Scott gently on the arm, seeing the red flame reflected in his eyes, a tired dove gray, his features hard and worn.

And though she did not know why, she suddenly knew that she would always remember him. Not like this, all battered and cut and worn, but standing in a cold, pouring rain on some lost roadway, there to comfort others that he did not know.

A gust of wind suddenly flared through the yard. Treetops sang, felling the white petals from a dogwood tree. As these came flitting through the yard, circling at his feet, Scott instinctively placed his body into a protective posture around the little flowers.

He stood for a long, tender moment in the dying light, imagining Kimberly planting flowers by her door and waiting for her mother to come home. Then Victoria, and not the old woman, but the child once named for her. And then Samantha, hurrying by, chasing her sister through a flowered glade in a time so very long ago.

Her sculptured face and golden eyes were a haunting memory, never once failing to see Scott clearly. And for that fleeting second he saw all of his faces beginning to gather, lost faces asking him why.

It was time to go, Scott told himself.

His promise was to the living.

ACKNOWLEDGMENTS

Without the expert contributions and support of others, this book could not have been written. To John F. Scott, Tuck Woo, Peter F. Thall, Bruce A. Plesser, Robert N. North, Jim Morresette, Gordon Irons, John Barlett; and the many contributions from the U.S. Park Police, Montgomery County Police, Maryland State Police, U.S. Secret Service, National Science Board, the National Center for Missing & Exploited Children, and the U.S. Department of Justice's criminal research divisions—my many thanks for ensuring a high degree of technical accuracy. Any transgressions are mine alone.

To Jonathan Atkin, Sandy Blanton, C. David Chaffee, Alan R. Gartenhaus, Howard and Katie Rosenburg, Jim Slade, Thomas A. Thinnes, Mr. & Mrs. William O'Donnell, my many thanks—your humor kept me laughing.

To Susan E. Wynne, whose thoughts and guidance are reflected on every page, my deepest appreciation for her unflinching creative skills. To my agent, Peter Lampack, who carried this project through a fire storm of protest and controversy, my undying gratitude for ensuring a worthwhile outcome.

To my American publishers, Elaine Koster and Kevin Mulroy; and my British publishers, Clare Bristow and William Massey—my salute for taking a certain bold step where the timid dare not tread. And to Clive Cussler, dean of the American action-adventure novel, my heartfelt gratitude. It is to his instruction and lessons in plot that this book owes its very completion.

Make Room For Great Escapes At Hilton International Hotels

Save the coupons in the backs of these Ⓢ Signet and Ⓞ Onyx books and redeem them for special Hilton International Hotels discounts and services.

June
REVERSIBLE ERROR
Robert K. Tanenbaum

RELATIVE SINS
Cynthia Victor

August
MARILYN: *The Last Take*
Peter Harry Brown &
Patte B. Barham

JUST KILLING TIME
Derek Van Arman

July
GRACE POINT
Anne D. LeClaire

FOREVER
Judith Gould

September
DANGEROUS PRACTICES
Francis Roe

SILENT WITNESS:
*The Karla Brown
Murder Case*
Don W. Weber &
Charles Bosworth, Jr.

2 coupons: Save 25% off regular rates at Hilton International Hotels
4 coupons: Save 25% off regular rates, <u>plus</u> upgrade to Executive Floor
6 coupons: All the above, <u>plus</u> complimentary Fruit Basket
8 coupons: All the above, <u>plus</u> a free bottle of wine

(Check *People* Magazine and Signet and Onyx spring titles for Bonus coupons to be used when redeeming three or more coupons)

Disclaimers: Advance reservations and notification of the offer required. May not be used in conjunction with any other offer. Discount applies to regular rates only. Subject to availability and black out dates. Offer may not be used in conjunction with convention, group or any other special offer. Employees and family members of Penguin USA and Hilton International are not eligible to participate in GREAT ESCAPES.

ONE COUPON

OFFICIAL GREAT ESCAPES COUPON

Send in coupons plus proofs of purchase (register receipt & xerox of UPC code from books) for each certificate requested to:

**Signet/Onyx Special Offer, Hilton International,
P.O. Box 115060, Carrollton, TX 75011-5060**

Name_____

Address_____Apt. #_____

City_____State_____Zip_____

Offer subject to change or withdrawal without notice.
Certificate requests must be postmarked no later than December 31, 1993.
Travel must be completed by March 31, 1994

ONE COUPON